The Enchanting Escapades of Phoebe and Her Unicorn

Complete Your Phoebe and Her Unicorn Collection

Phoebe and Her Unicorn
Dana Simpson

Unicorn on a Roll
Another Phoebe and Her Unicorn Adventure
Dana Simpson

Unicorn vs. Goblins
Another Phoebe and Her Unicorn Adventure
Dana Simpson

Razzle Dazzle Unicorn
Another Phoebe and Her Unicorn Adventure
Dana Simpson

Phoebe and Her Unicorn in
The Magic Storm
Dana Simpson

Phoebe and Her Unicorn in
Unicorn Theater
Dana Simpson

Unicorn Bowling
Another Phoebe and Her Unicorn Adventure
Dana Simpson

The Unicorn Whisperer
Another Phoebe and Her Unicorn Adventure
Dana Simpson

Camping with Unicorns
Another Phoebe and Her Unicorn Adventure
Dana Simpson

Virtual Unicorn Experience
Another Phoebe and Her Unicorn Adventure
Dana Simpson

Unicorn Famous
Another Phoebe and Her Unicorn Adventure
Dana Simpson

Unicorn Playlist
Another Phoebe and Her Unicorn Adventure
Dana Simpson

Unicorn Selfies
Another Phoebe and Her Unicorn Adventure
Dana Simpson

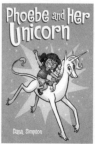

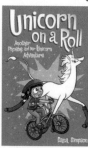

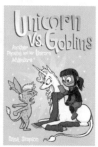

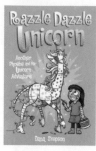

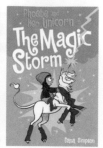

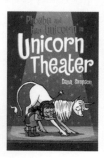

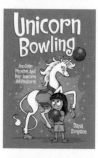

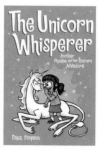

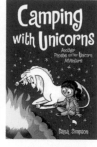

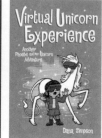

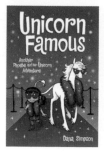

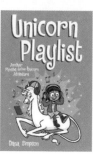

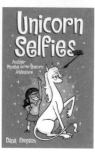

The Enchanting Escapades of Phoebe and Her Unicorn

Dana Simpson

Featuring comics from *Unicorn Crossing*
and *Unicorn of Many Hats*

Andrews McMeel
PUBLISHING®

Phoebe and Her Unicorn is distributed internationally by Andrews McMeel Syndication.

Andrews McMeel Publishing
a division of Andrews McMeel Universal
1130 Walnut Street, Kansas City, Missouri 64106

www.andrewsmcmeel.com

22 23 24 25 26 SDB 10 9 8 7 6 5 4 3 2 1

ISBN: 978-1-5248-7694-4

Made by:
King Yip (Dongguan) Printing & Packaging Factory Ltd.
Address and location of manufacturer:
Daning Administrative District, Humen Town
Dongguan Guangdong, China 523930
1st Printing—5/9/22

Unicorn Crossing

Crossing

Another
Phoebe and Her Unicorn Adventure

Hey, kids!

Check out the glossaries starting on pages 175 and 348 if you come across words you don't know.

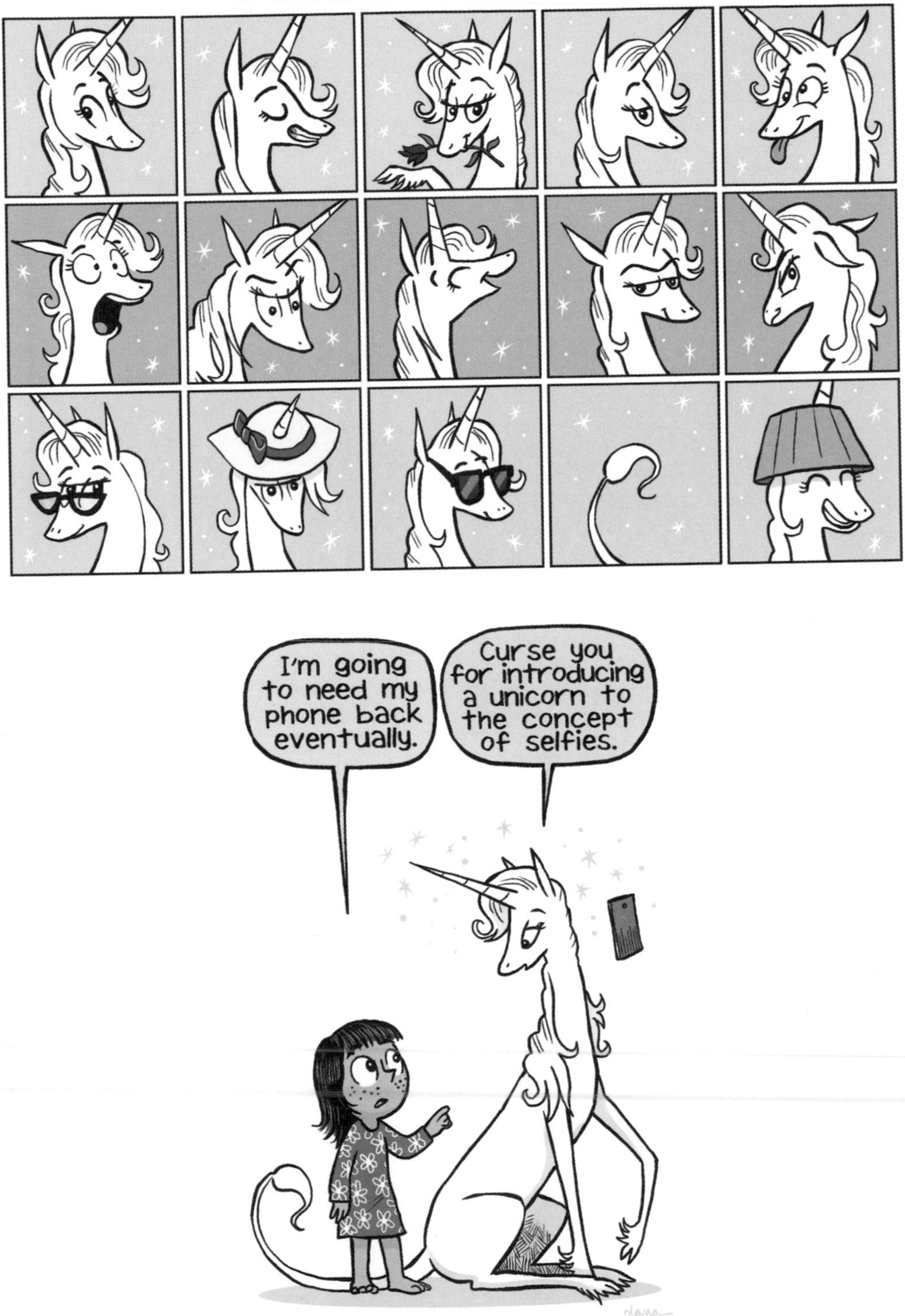
I'm going to need my phone back eventually.
Curse you for introducing a unicorn to the concept of selfies.
dana

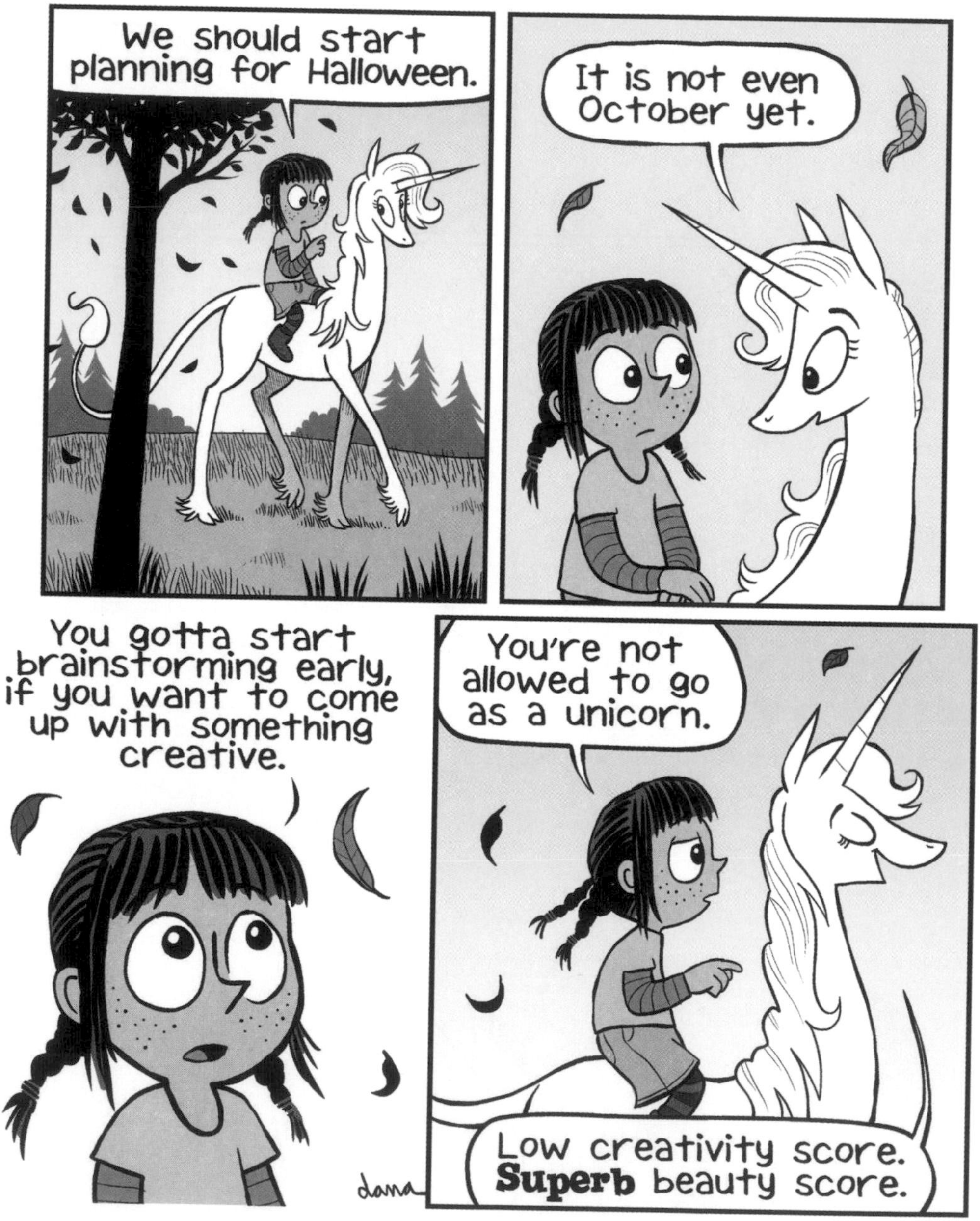
We should start planning for Halloween.
It is not even October yet.
You gotta start brainstorming early, if you want to come up with something creative.
You're not allowed to go as a unicorn.
Low creativity score. **Superb** beauty score.
dana

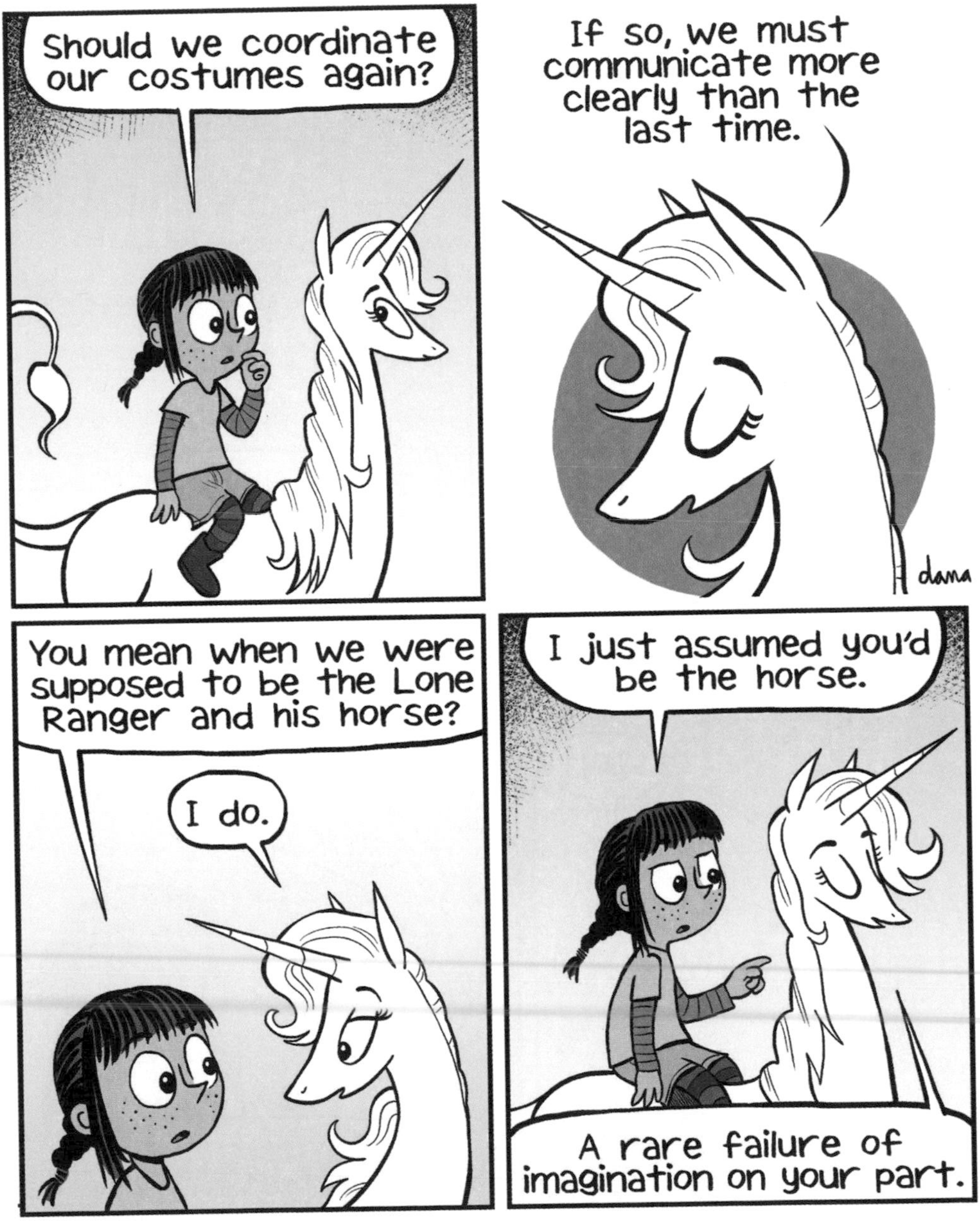
Should we coordinate our costumes again?
If so, we must communicate more clearly than the last time.
dana
You mean when we were supposed to be the Lone Ranger and his horse?
I do.
I just assumed you'd be the horse.
A rare failure of imagination on your part.

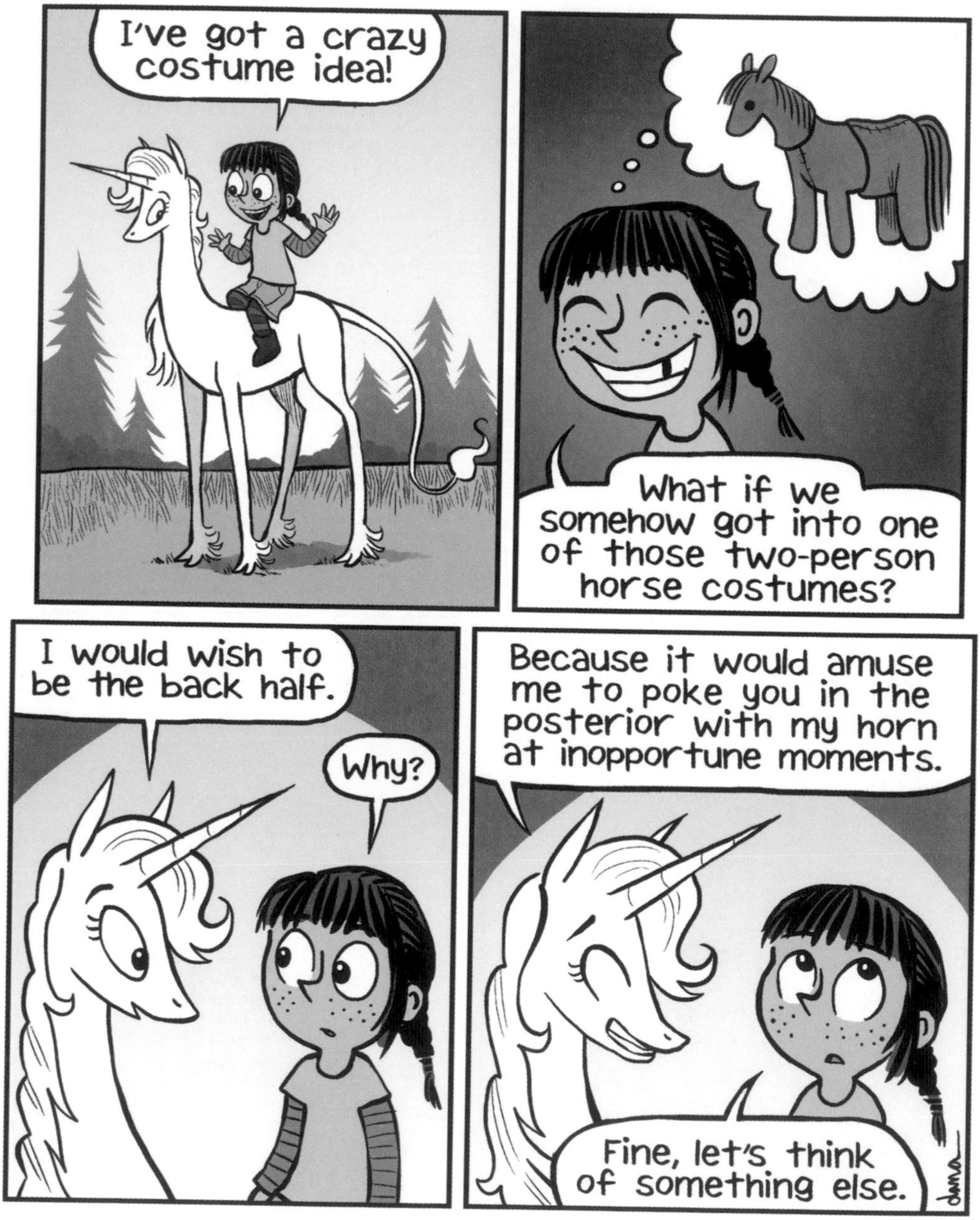
I've got a crazy costume idea!
What if we somehow got into one of those two-person horse costumes?
I would wish to be the back half.
Why?
Because it would amuse me to poke you in the posterior with my horn at inopportune moments.
Fine, let's think of something else.
dana

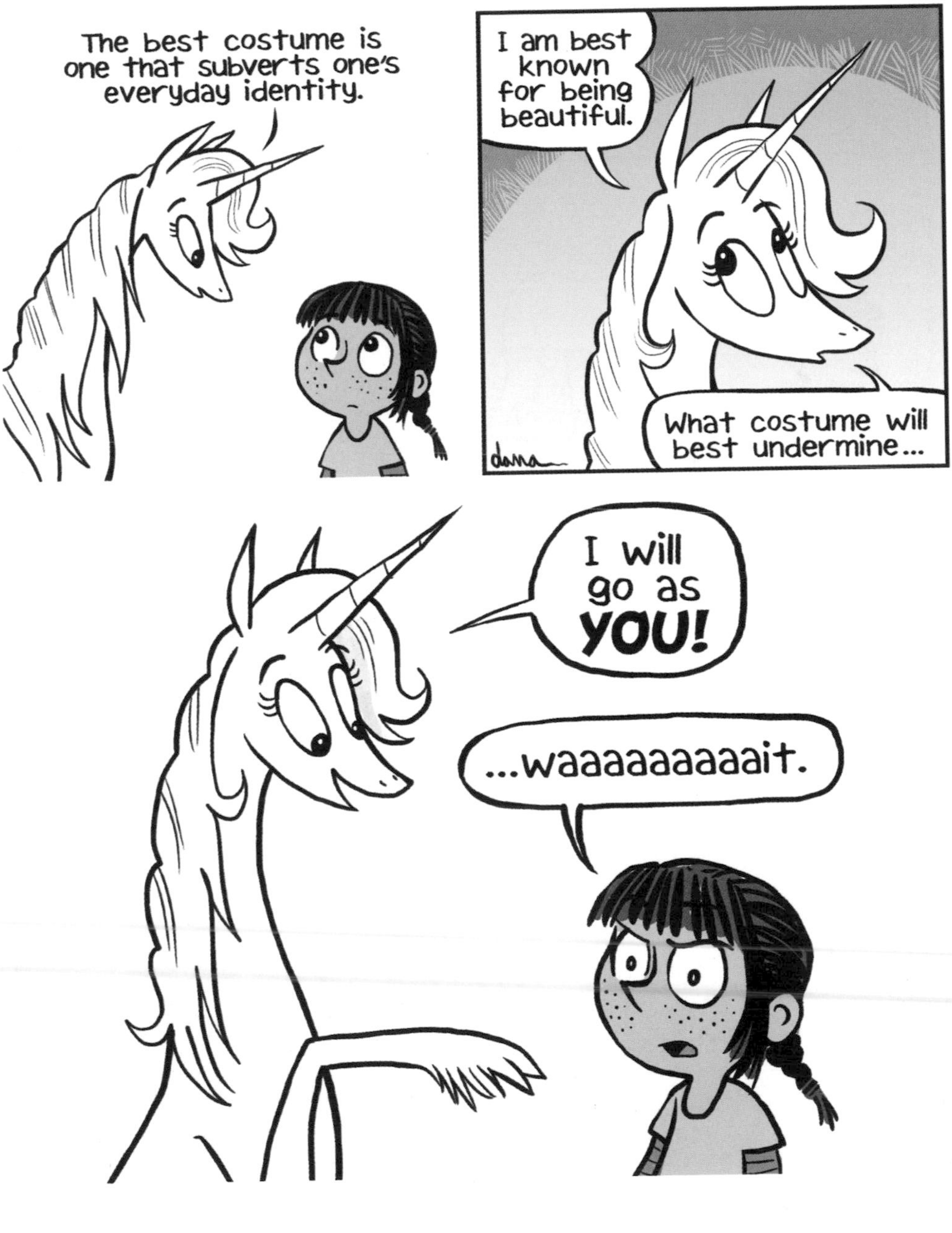
The best costume is one that subverts one's everyday identity.
I am best known for being beautiful.
What costume will best undermine...
dana
I will go as YOU!
...waaaaaaaaait.

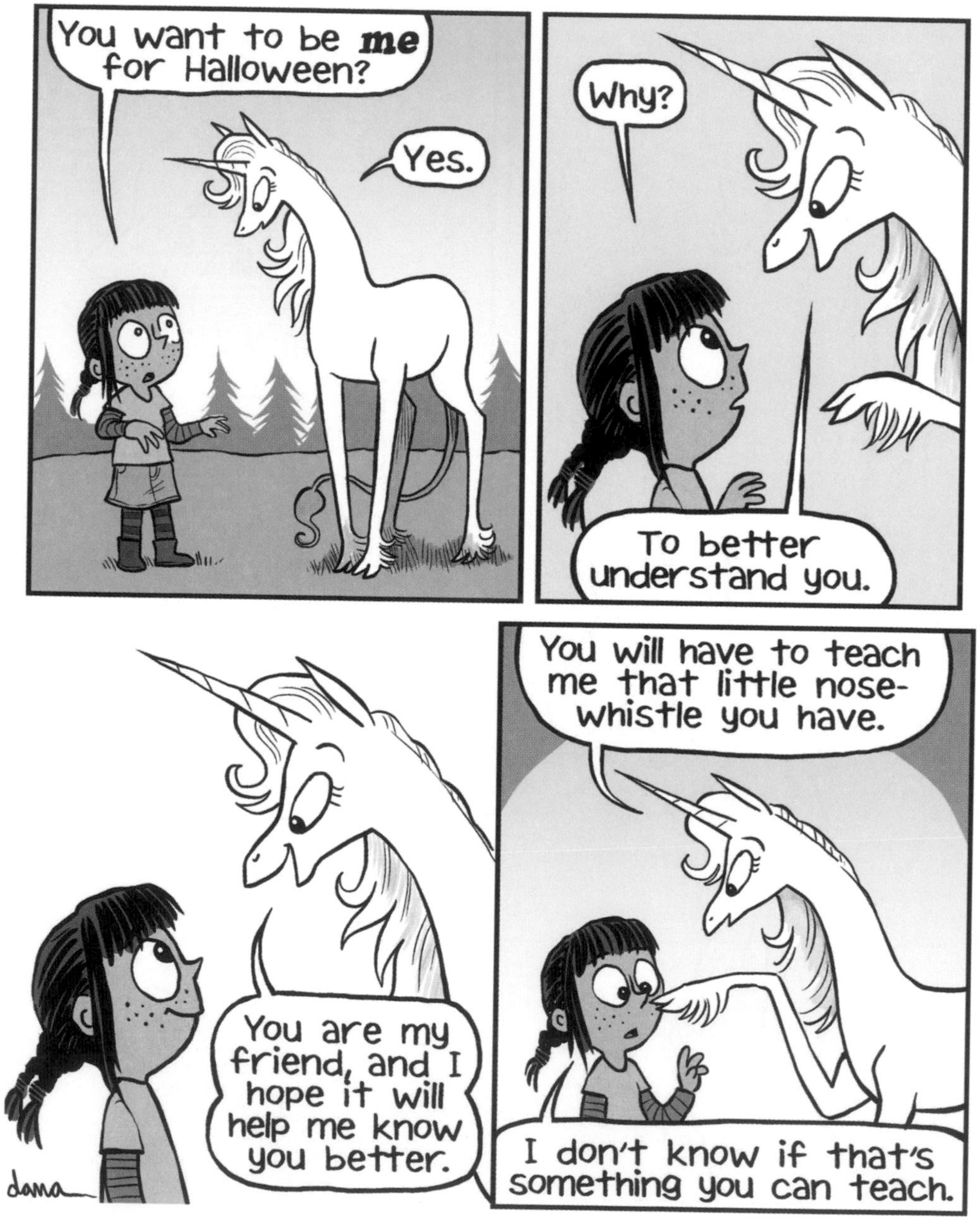
You want to be **me** for Halloween?
Yes.
Why?
To better understand you.
You are my friend, and I hope it will help me know you better.
You will have to teach me that little nose-whistle you have.
I don't know if that's something you can teach.
dana

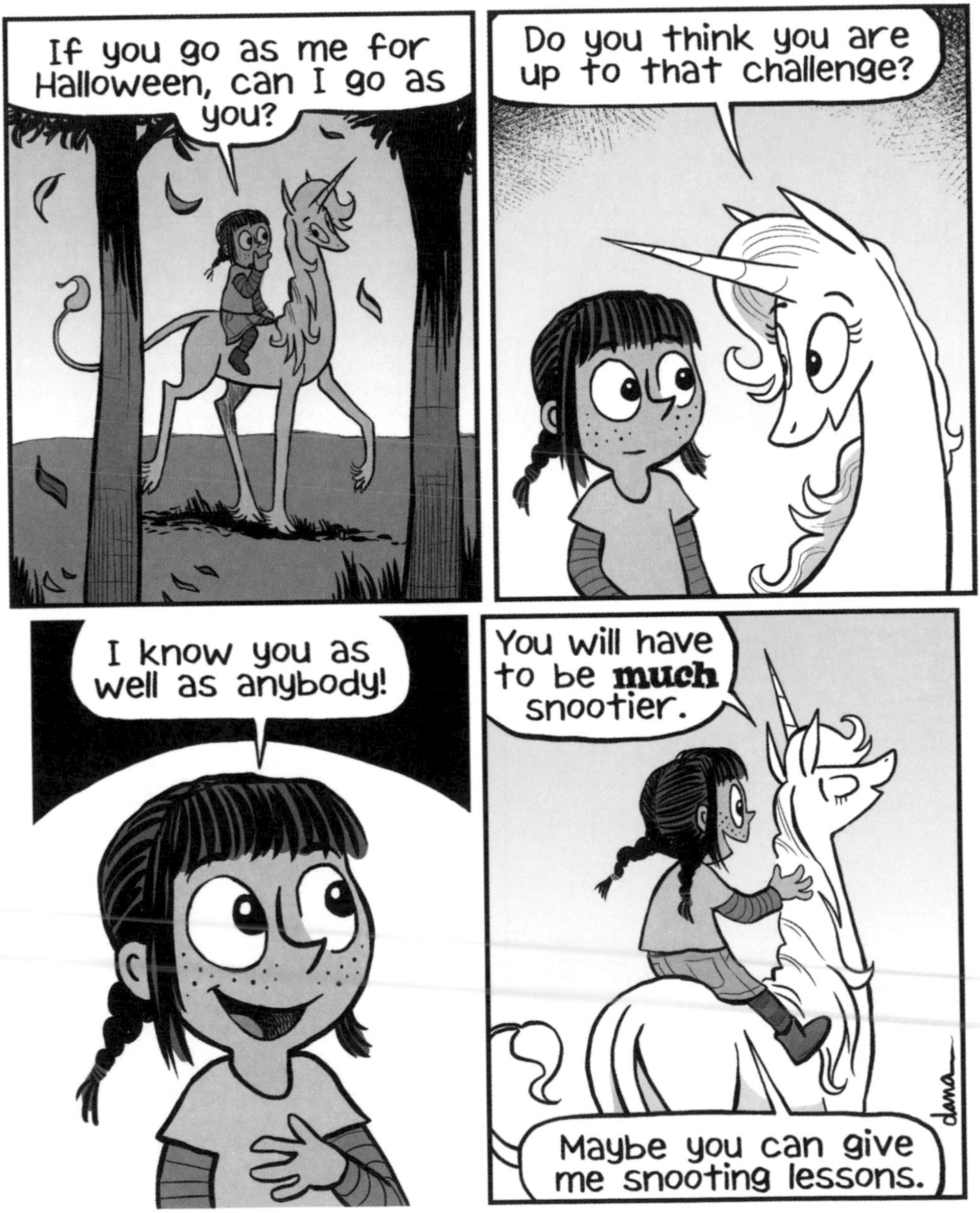
If you go as me for Halloween, can I go as you?
Do you think you are up to that challenge?
I know you as well as anybody!
You will have to be **much** snootier.
Maybe you can give me snooting lessons.
dana

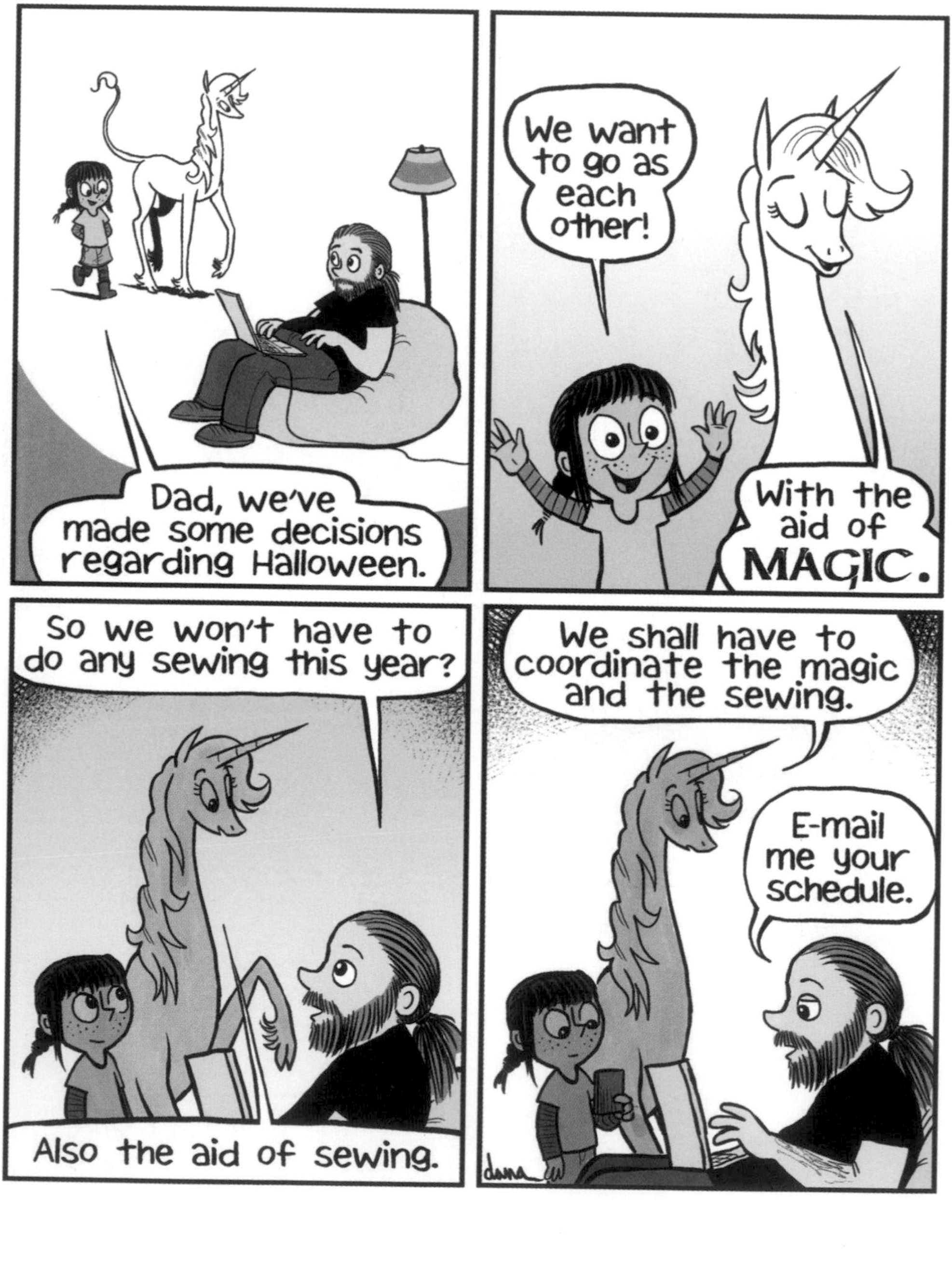
Dad, we've made some decisions regarding Halloween.
We want to go as each other!
With the aid of MAGIC.
So we won't have to do any sewing this year?
Also the aid of sewing.
We shall have to coordinate the magic and the sewing.
E-mail me your schedule.
dana

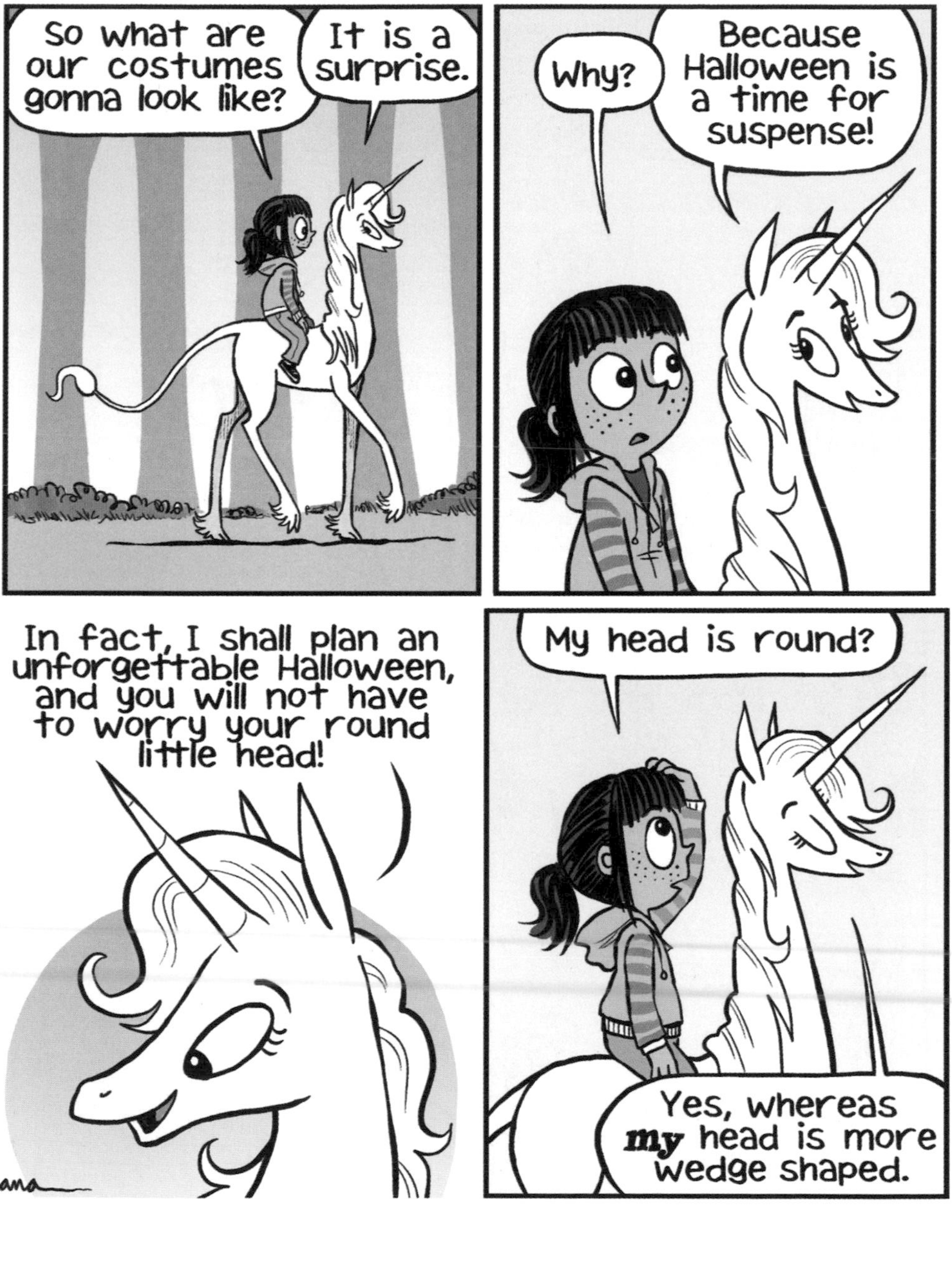

So what are our costumes gonna look like?
It is a surprise.
Why?
Because Halloween is a time for suspense!
In fact, I shall plan an unforgettable Halloween, and you will not have to worry your round little head!
My head is round?
Yes, whereas **my** head is more wedge shaped.
dana

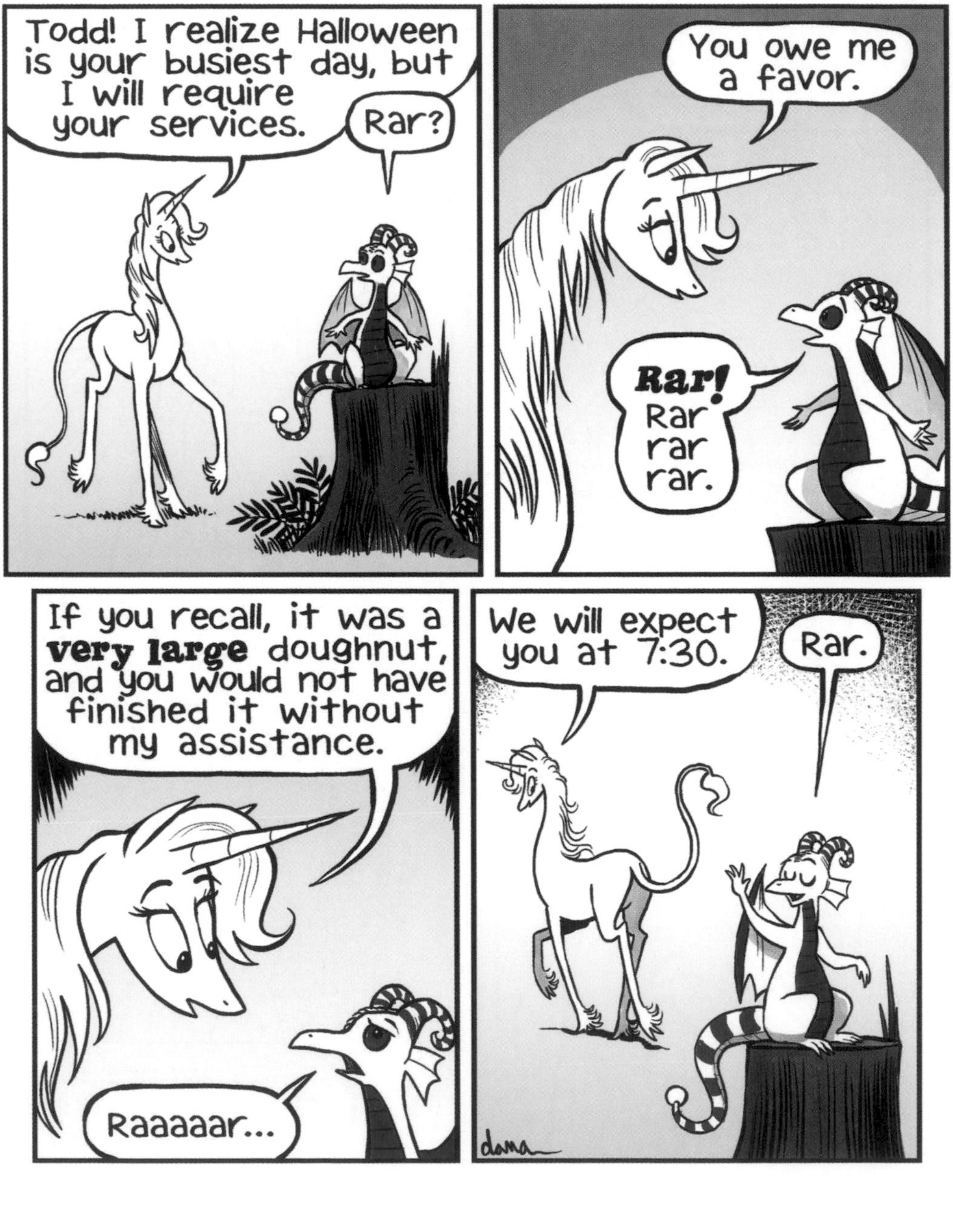
Todd! I realize Halloween is your busiest day, but I will require your services.
Rar?
You owe me a favor.
Rar! Rar rar rar.
If you recall, it was a **very large** doughnut, and you would not have finished it without my assistance.
Raaaaar...
We will expect you at 7:30.
Rar.
dana

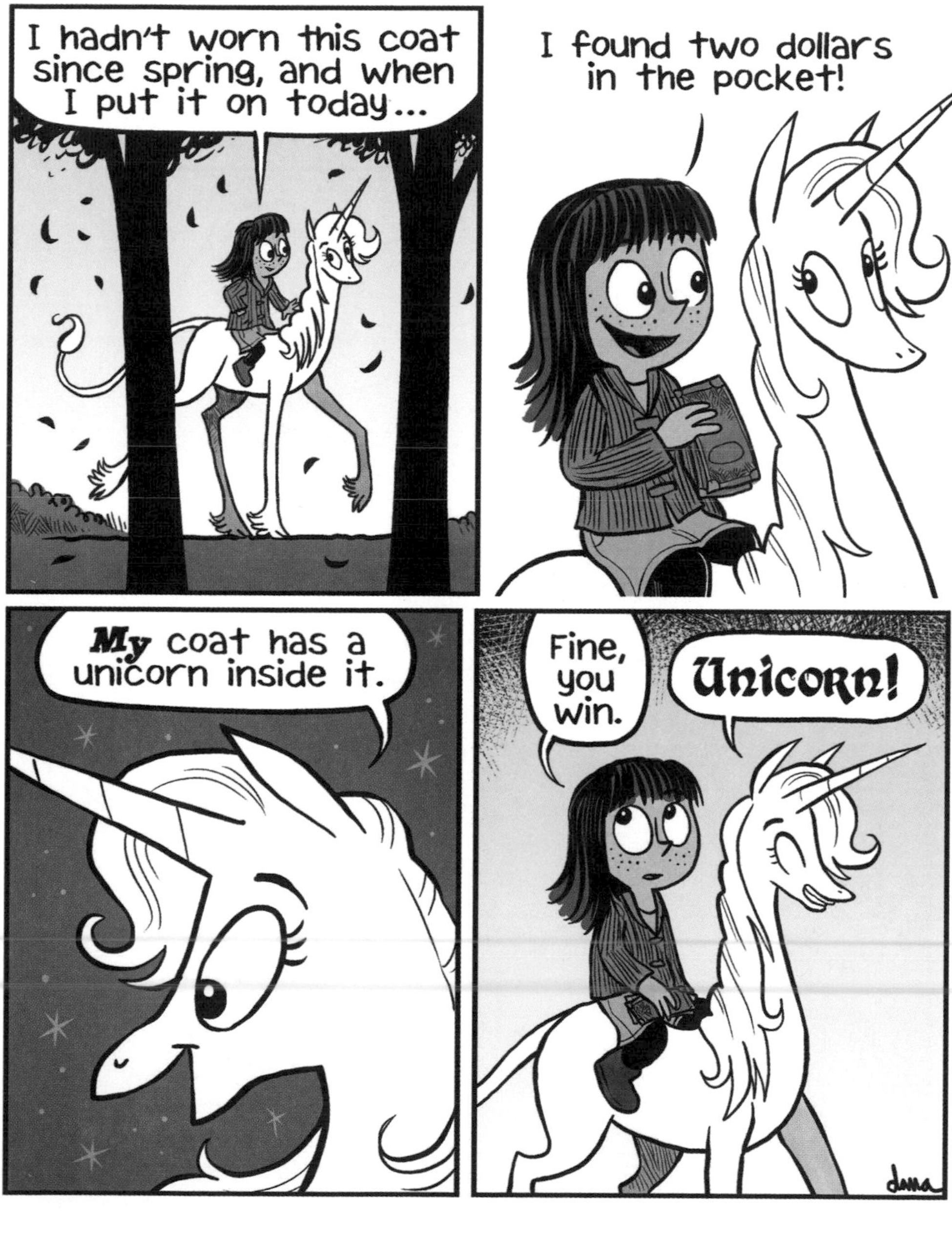
I hadn't worn this coat since spring, and when I put it on today...
I found two dollars in the pocket!
My coat has a unicorn inside it.
Fine, you win.
Unicorn!
dana

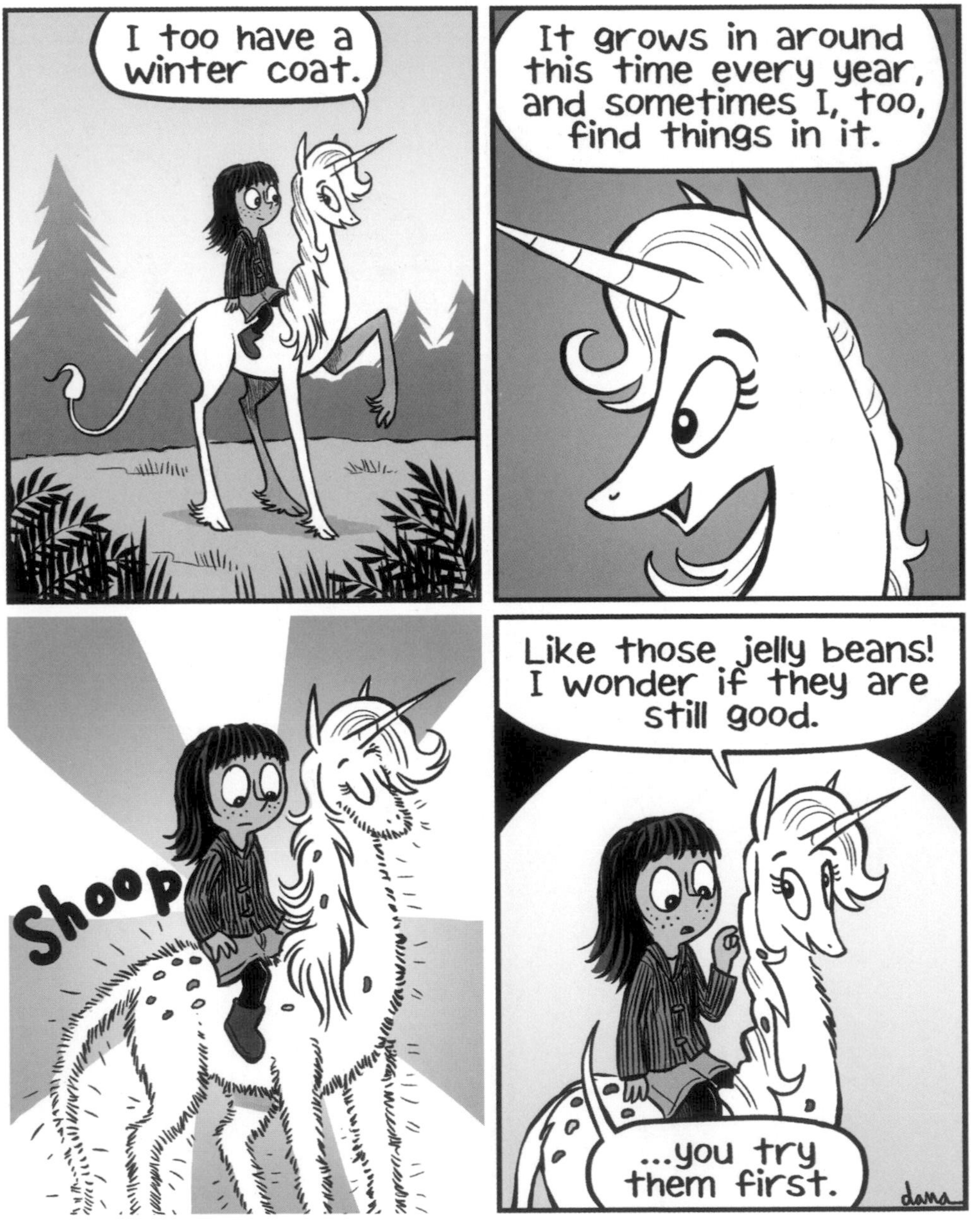

I too have a winter coat.
It grows in around this time every year, and sometimes I, too, find things in it.
Shoop
Like those jelly beans! I wonder if they are still good.
...you try them first.
dana

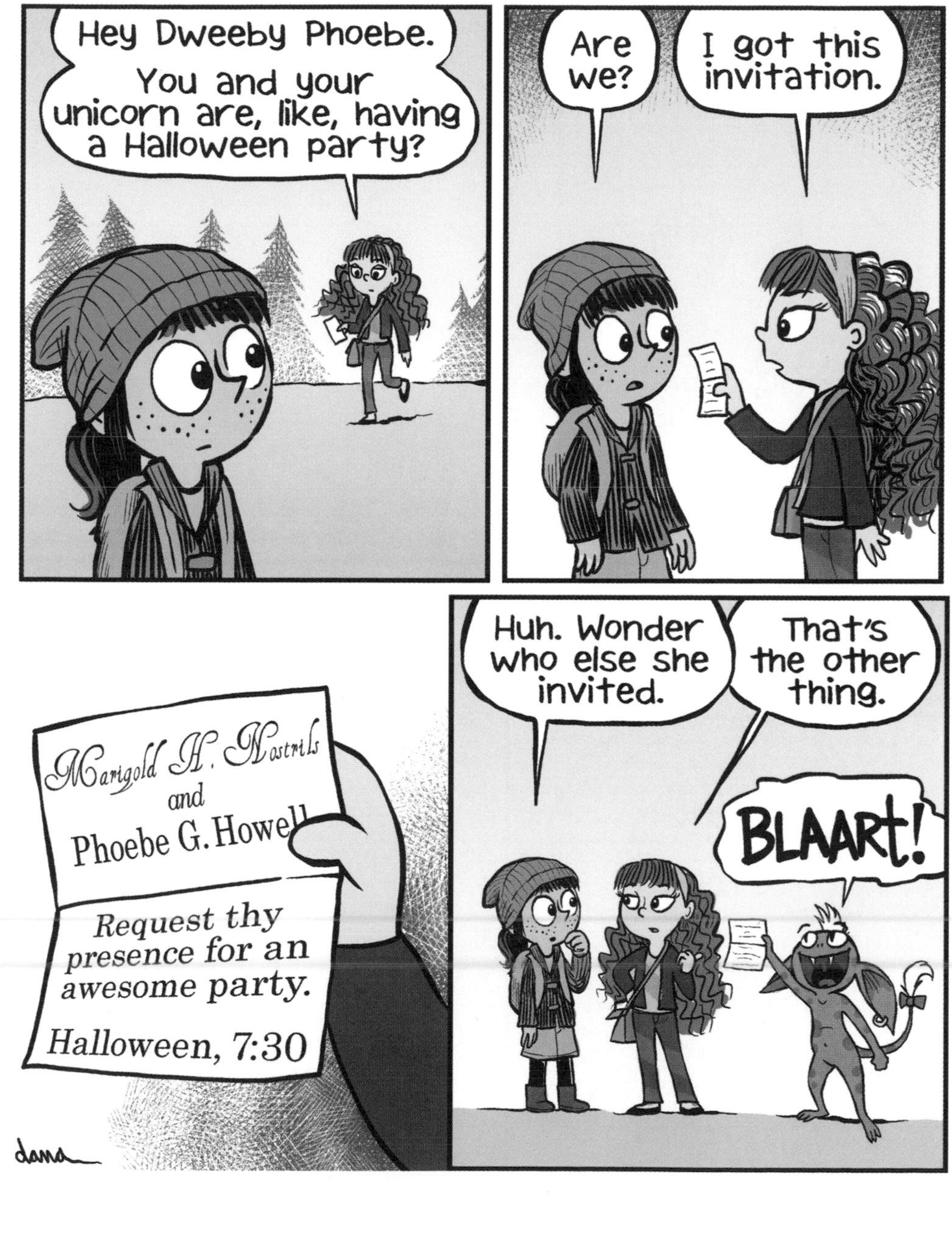
Hey Dweeby Phoebe.
You and your unicorn are, like, having a Halloween party?
Are we?
I got this invitation.
Marigold H. Nostrils and Phoebe G. Howell
Request thy presence for an awesome party.
Halloween, 7:30
Huh. Wonder who else she invited.
That's the other thing.
BLAART!
dana

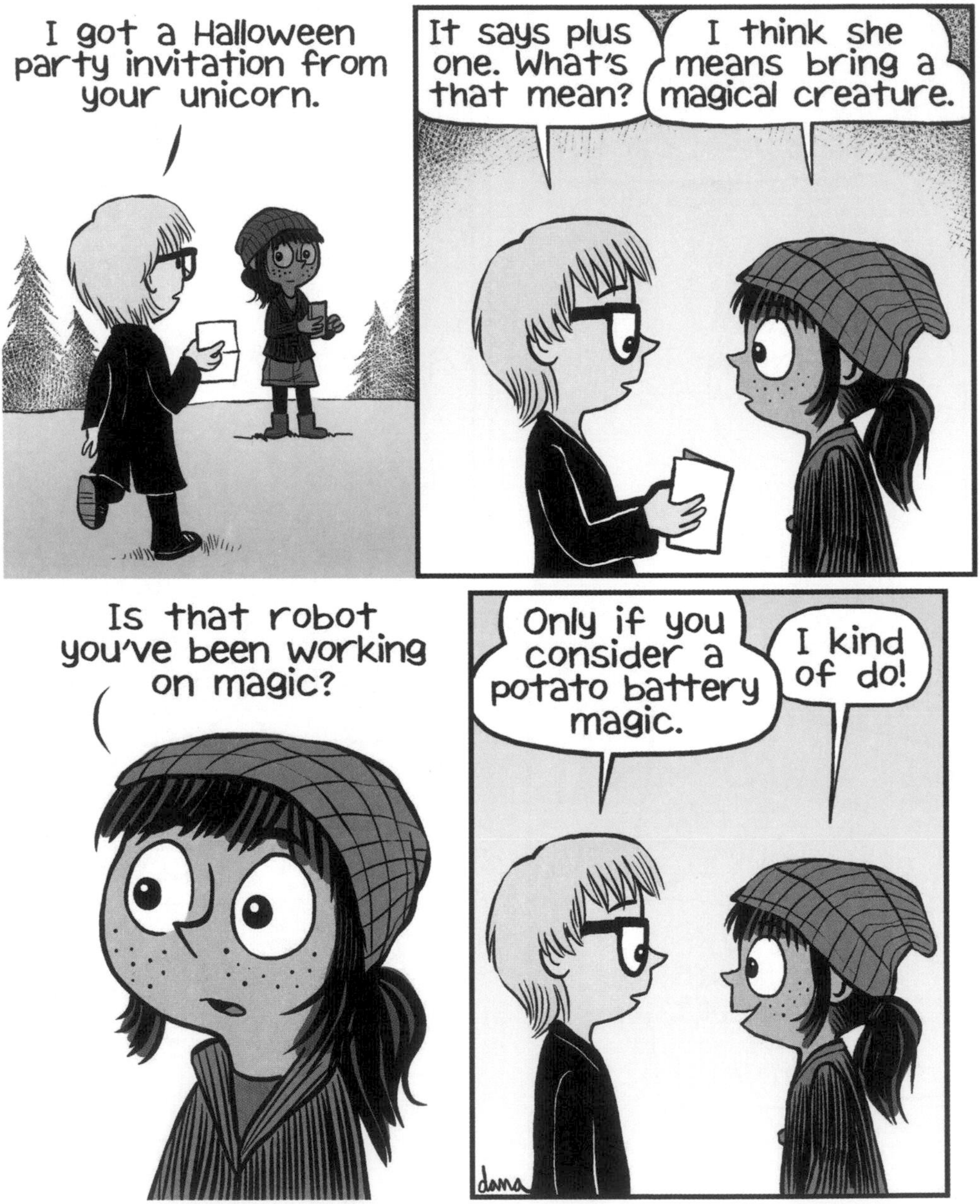
I got a Halloween party invitation from your unicorn.
It says plus one. What's that mean?
I think she means bring a magical creature.
Is that robot you've been working on magic?
Only if you consider a potato battery magic.
I kind of do!
dana

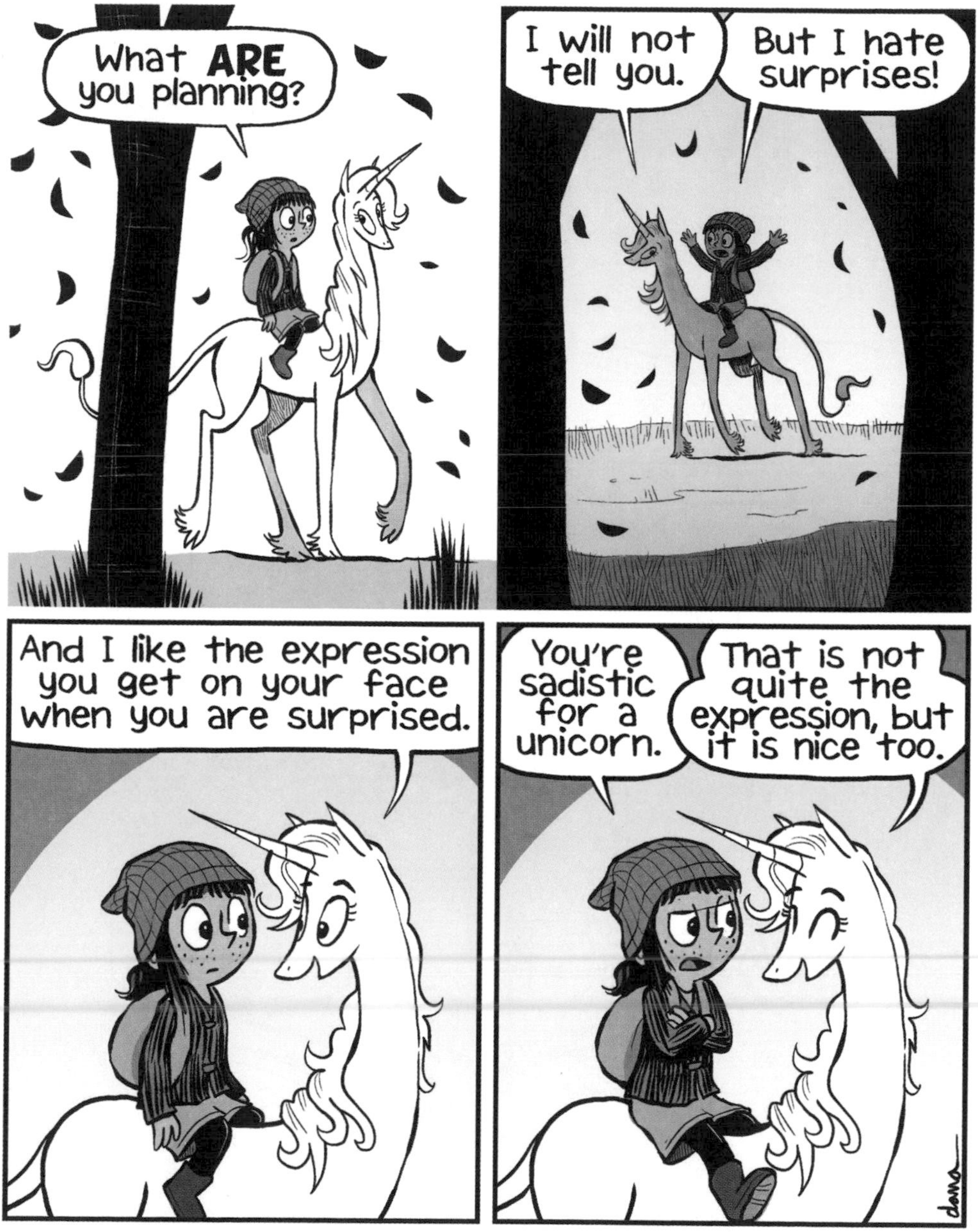
What **ARE** you planning?
I will not tell you.
But I hate surprises!
And I like the expression you get on your face when you are surprised.
You're sadistic for a unicorn.
That is not quite the expression, but it is nice too.
dana

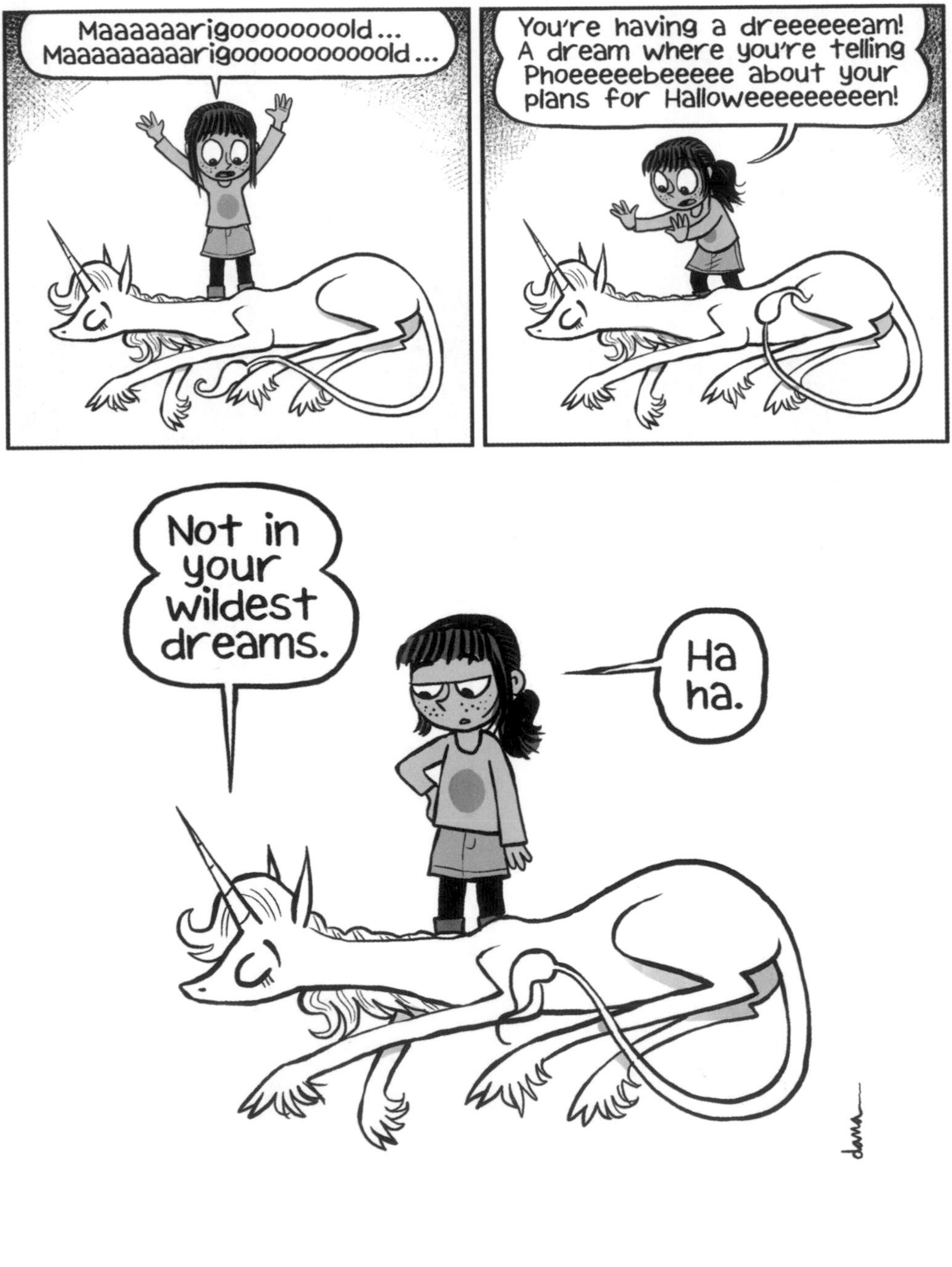
Maaaaaarigoooooooold...
Maaaaaaaaarigooooooooooold...
You're having a dreeeeeeam! A dream where you're telling Phoeeeeebeeeee about your plans for Halloweeeeeeeeen!
Not in your wildest dreams.
Ha ha.
dana

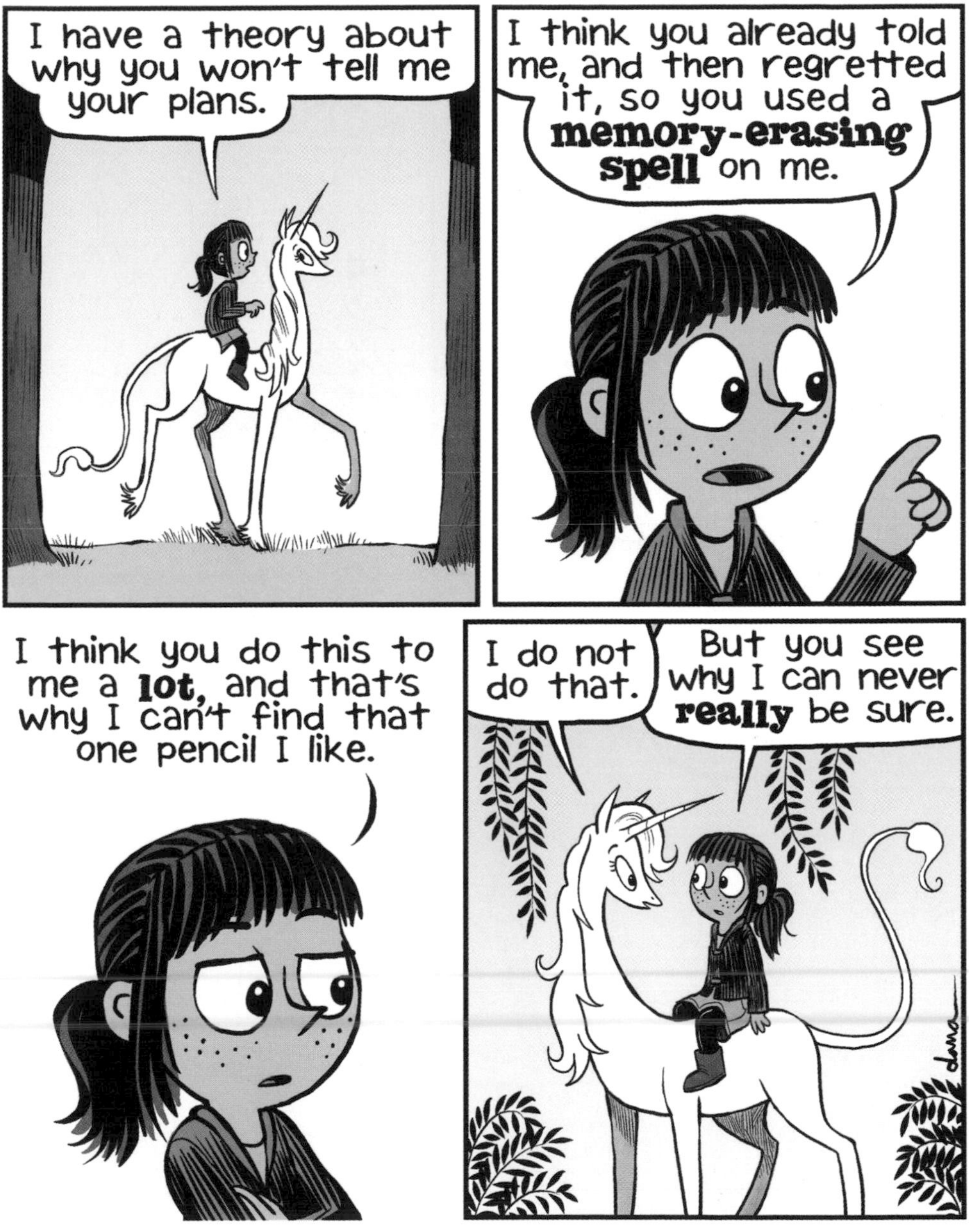

I have a theory about why you won't tell me your plans.
I think you already told me, and then regretted it, so you used a **memory-erasing spell** on me.
I think you do this to me a **lot**, and that's why I can't find that one pencil I like.
I do not do that.
But you see why I can never **really** be sure.

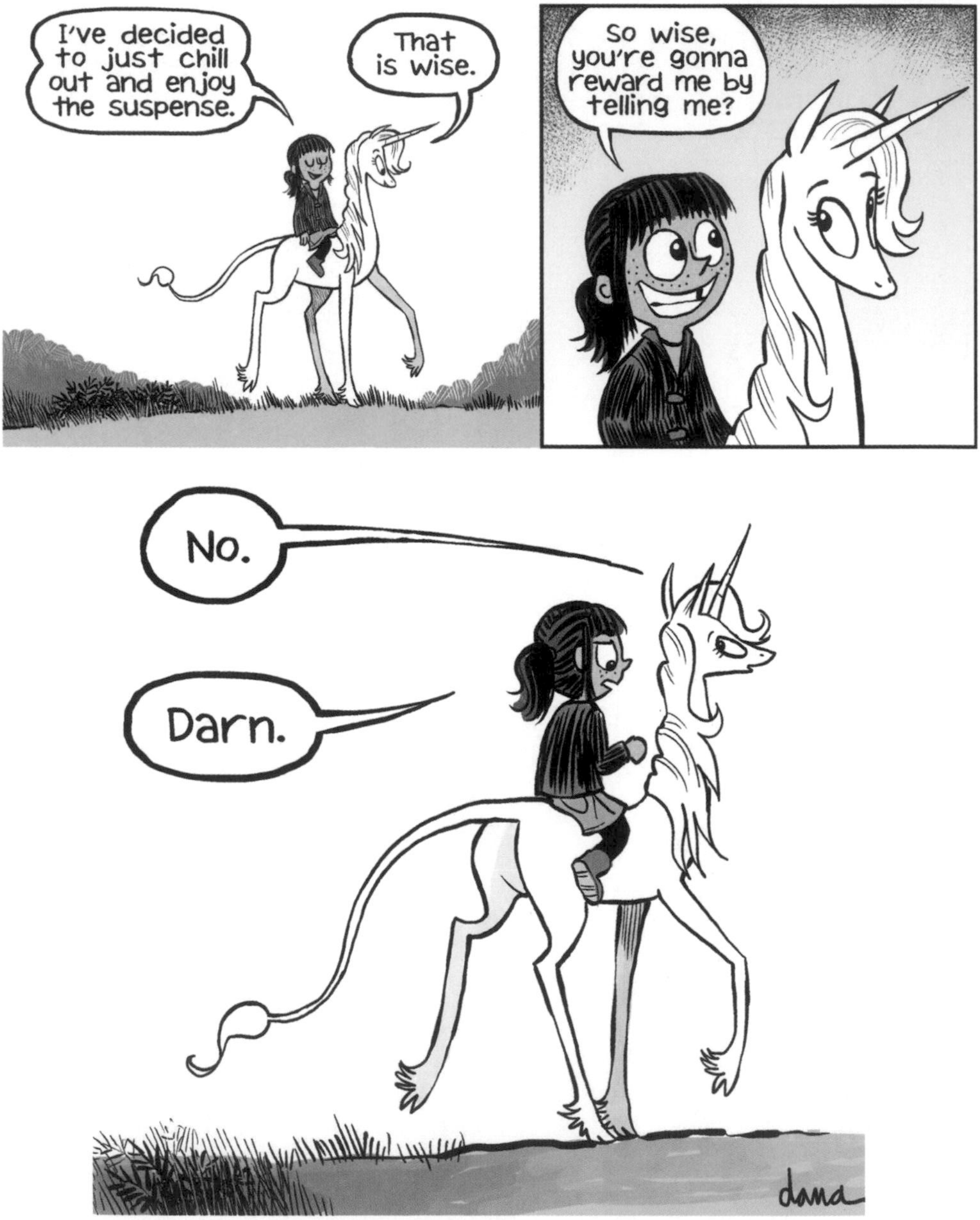
I've decided to just chill out and enjoy the suspense.
That is wise.
So wise, you're gonna reward me by telling me?
No.
Darn.
dana

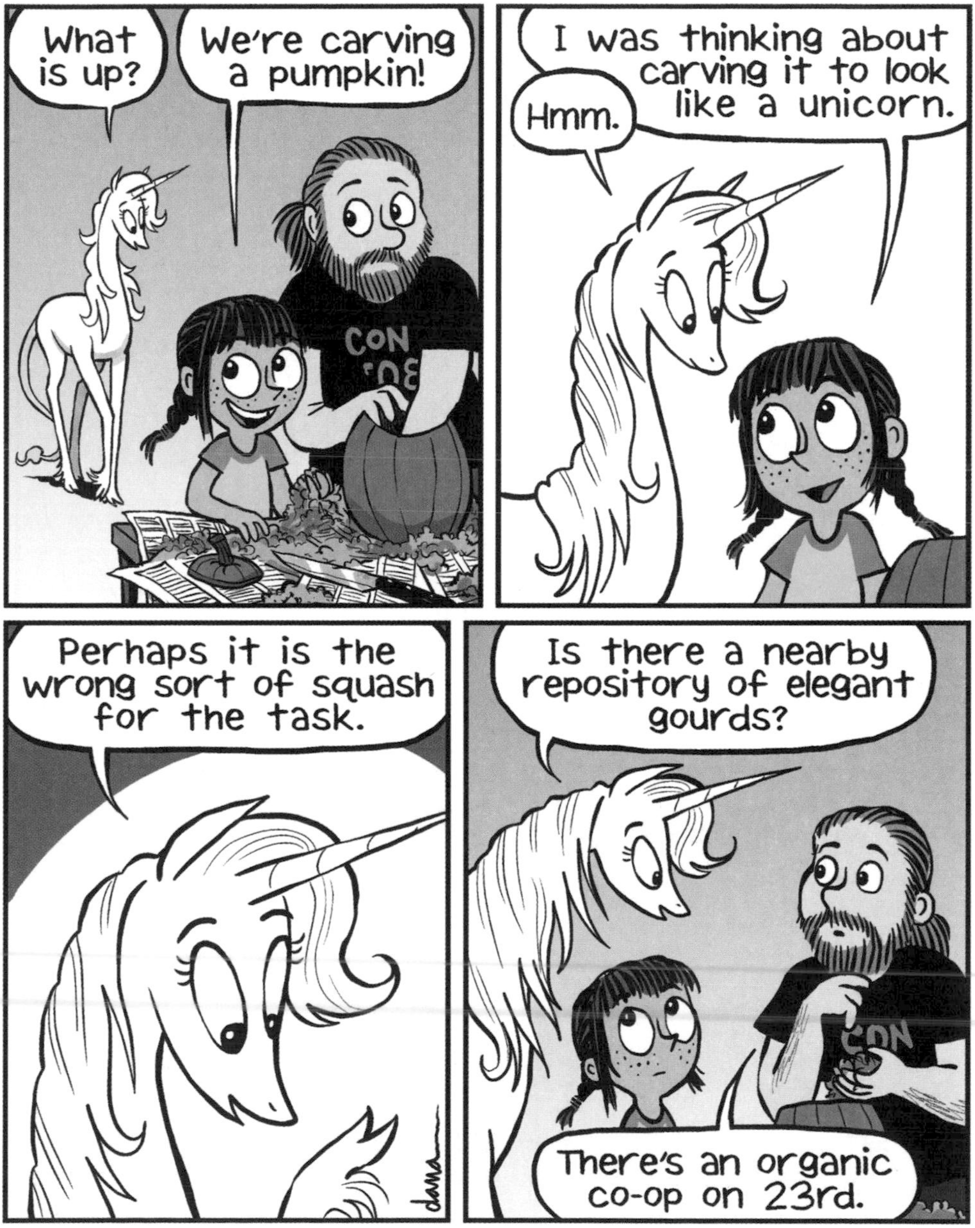
What is up?
We're carving a pumpkin!
CON
I was thinking about carving it to look like a unicorn.
Hmm.
Perhaps it is the wrong sort of squash for the task.
dana
Is there a nearby repository of elegant gourds?
CON
There's an organic co-op on 23rd.

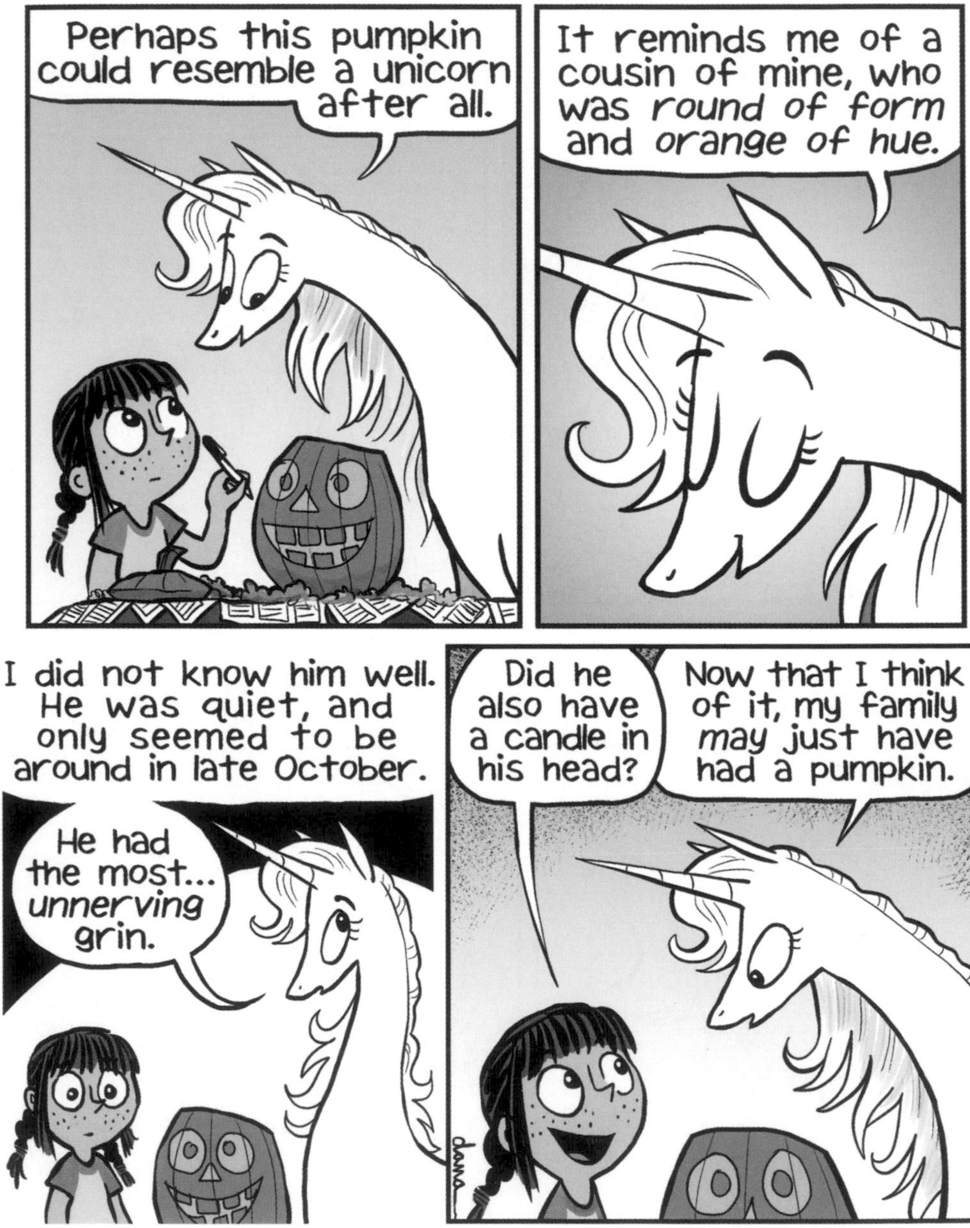
Perhaps this pumpkin could resemble a unicorn after all.
It reminds me of a cousin of mine, who was *round of form* and *orange of hue.*
I did not know him well. He was quiet, and only seemed to be around in late October.
He had the most... *unnerving* grin.
Did he also have a candle in his head?
Now that I think of it, my family *may* just have had a pumpkin.
dana

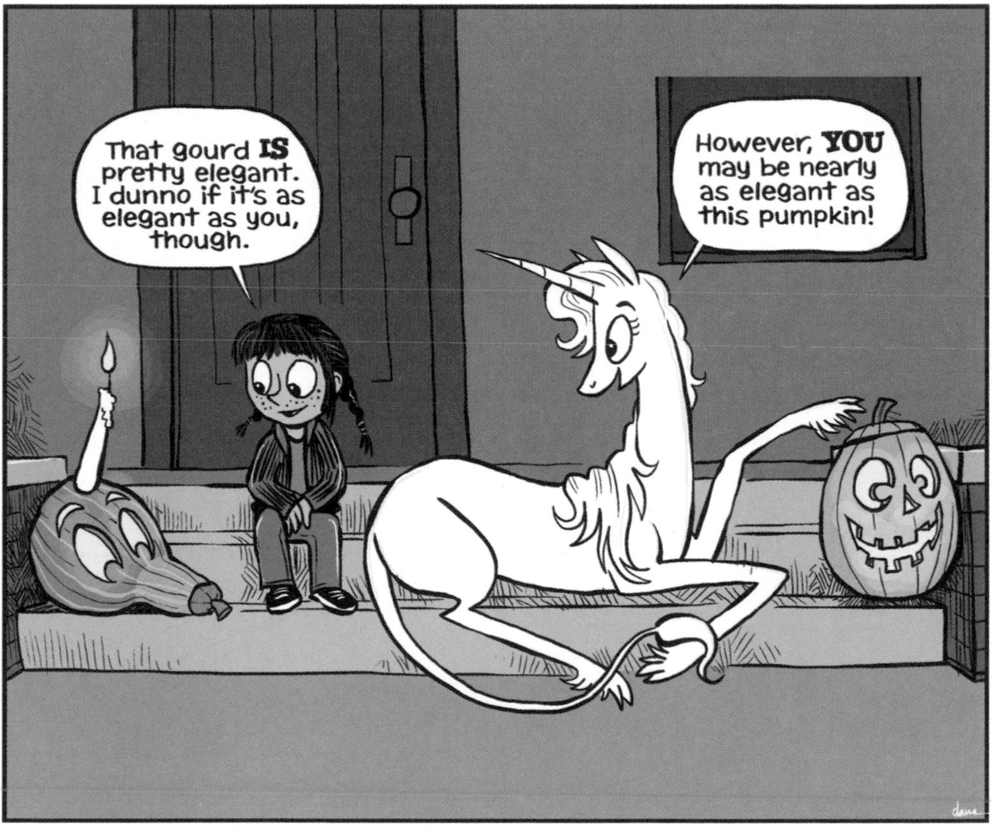
That gourd **IS** pretty elegant. I dunno if it's as elegant as you, though.
However, **YOU** may be nearly as elegant as this pumpkin!

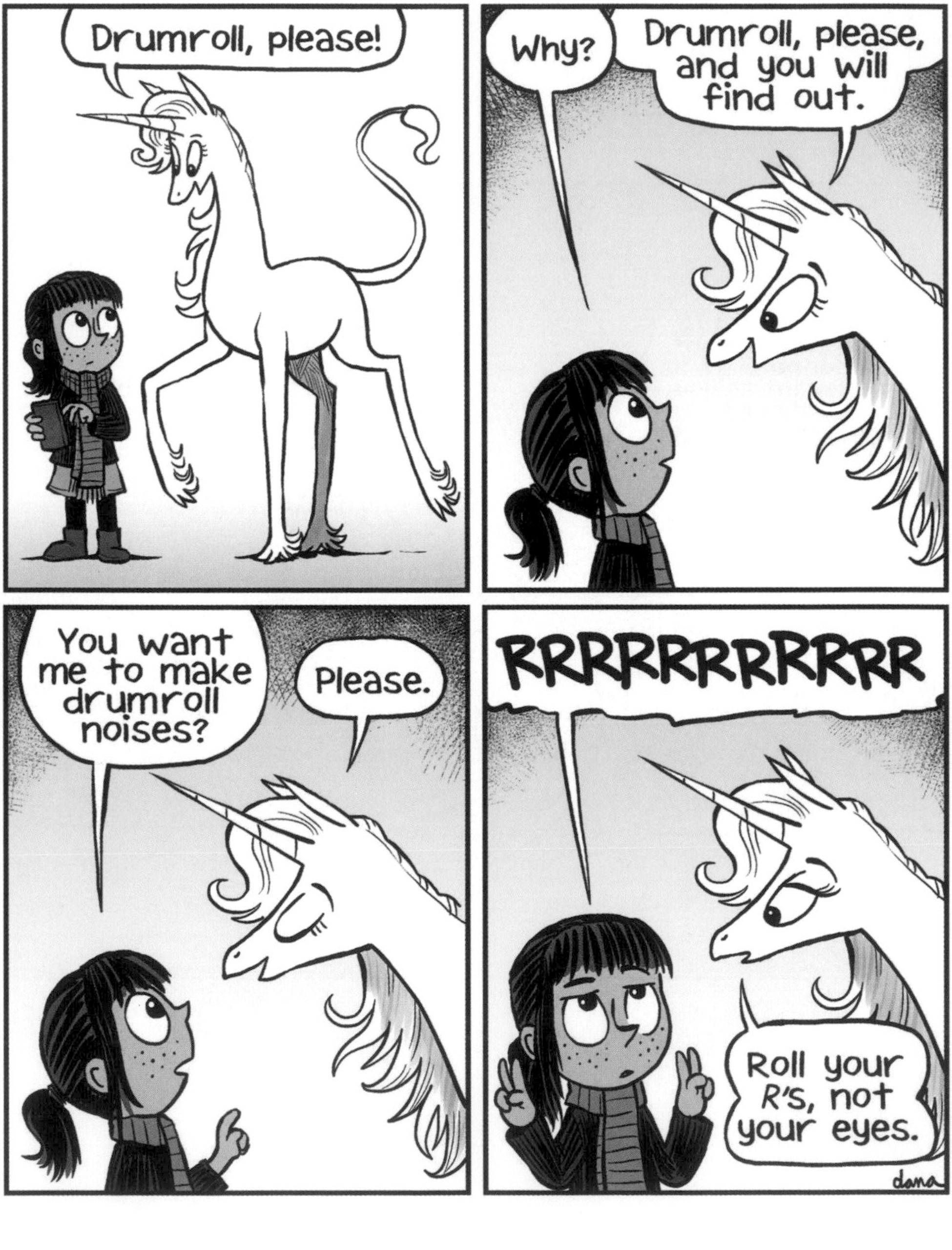
Drumroll, please!
Why?
Drumroll, please, and you will find out.
You want me to make drumroll noises?
Please.
RRRRRRRRRRR
Roll your R's, not your eyes.
dana

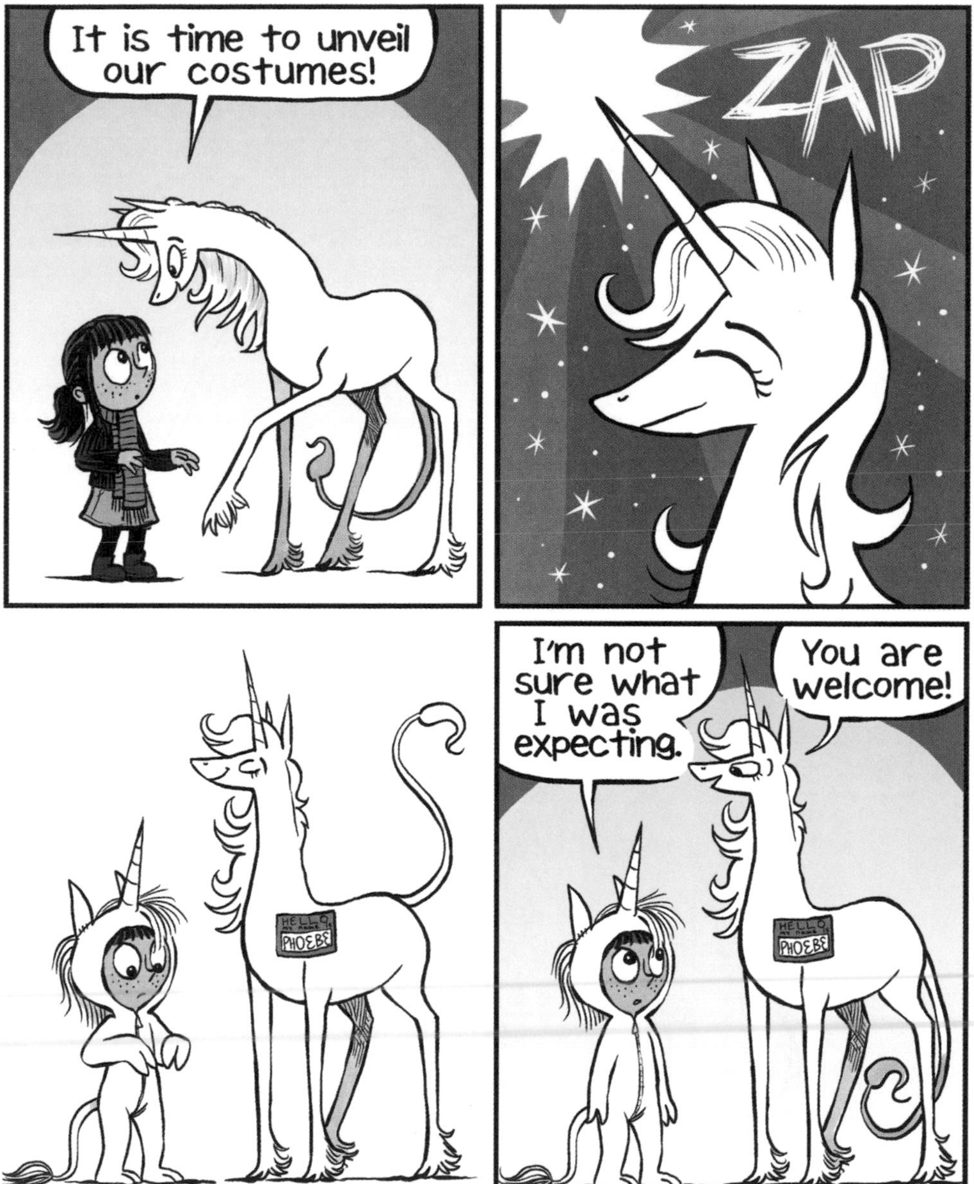
It is time to unveil our costumes!
ZAP
HELLO my name is PHOEBE
I'm not sure what I was expecting.
You are welcome!
HELLO my name is PHOEBE
dana

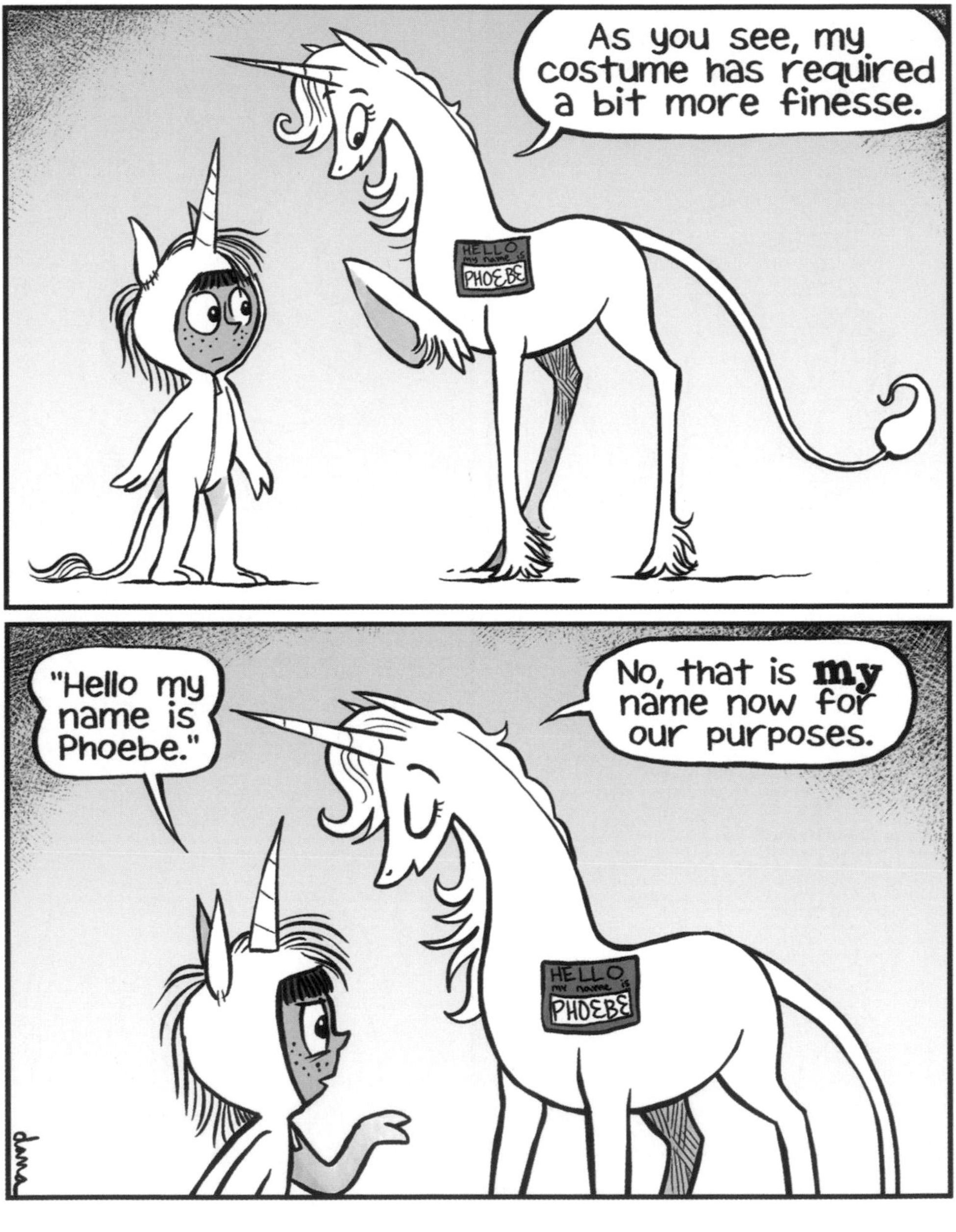
As you see, my costume has required a bit more finesse.
HELLO my name is PHOEBE
"Hello my name is Phoebe."
No, that is **my** name now for our purposes.
HELLO my name is PHOEBE
dana

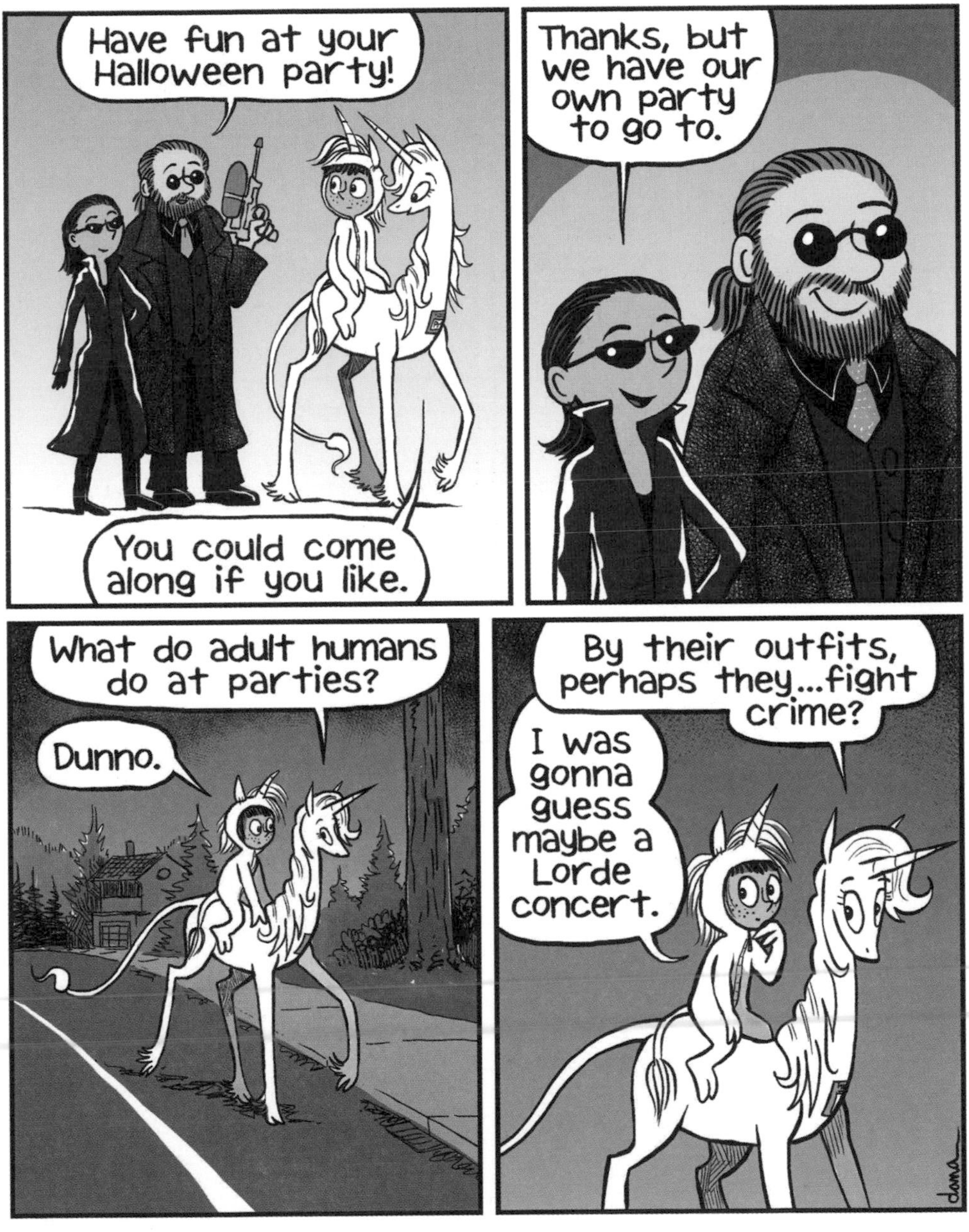
Have fun at your Halloween party!
You could come along if you like.
Thanks, but we have our own party to go to.
What do adult humans do at parties?
Dunno.
By their outfits, perhaps they...fight crime?
I was gonna guess maybe a Lorde concert.
dana

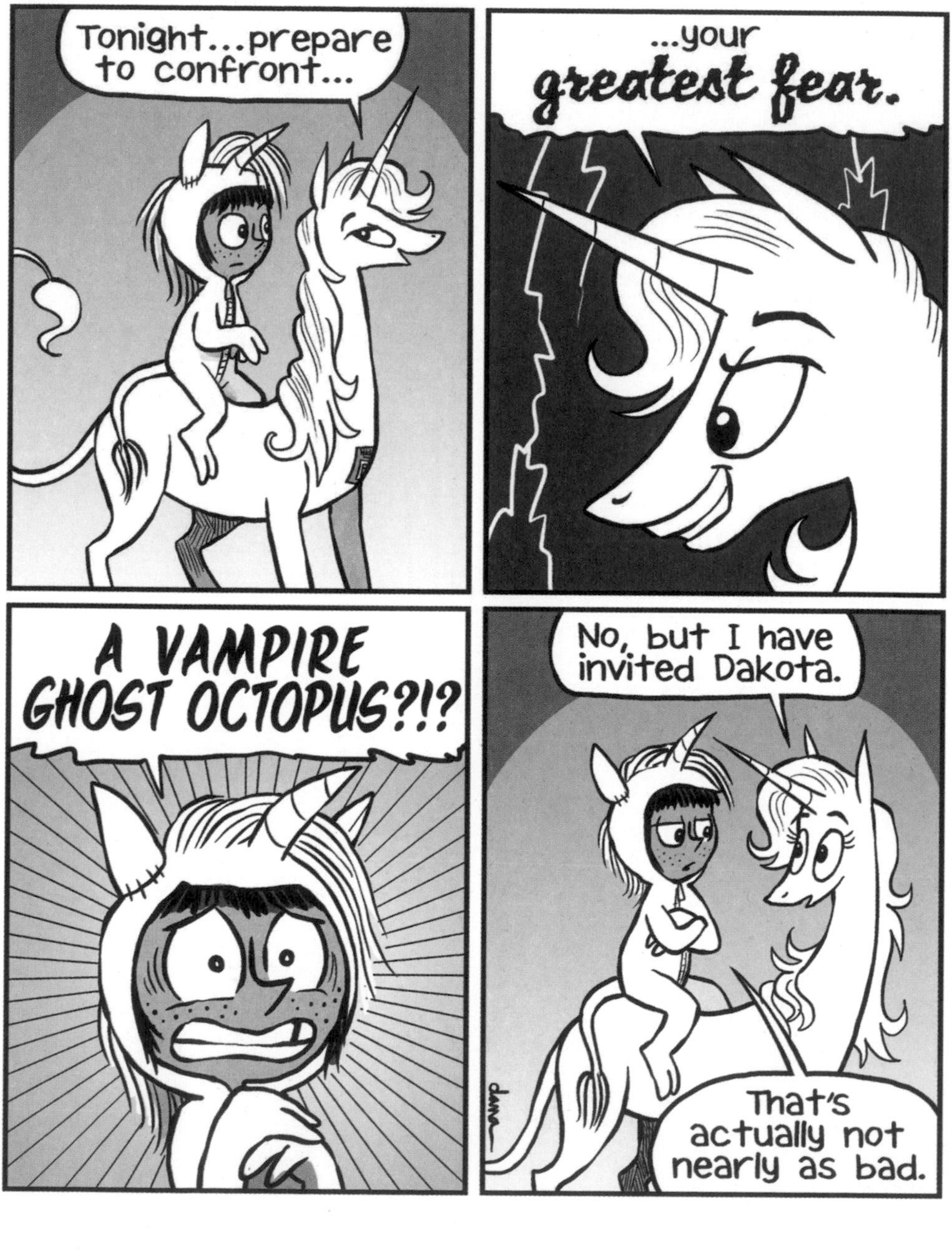
Tonight...prepare to confront...
...your greatest fear.
A VAMPIRE GHOST OCTOPUS?!?
No, but I have invited Dakota.
That's actually not nearly as bad.
dana

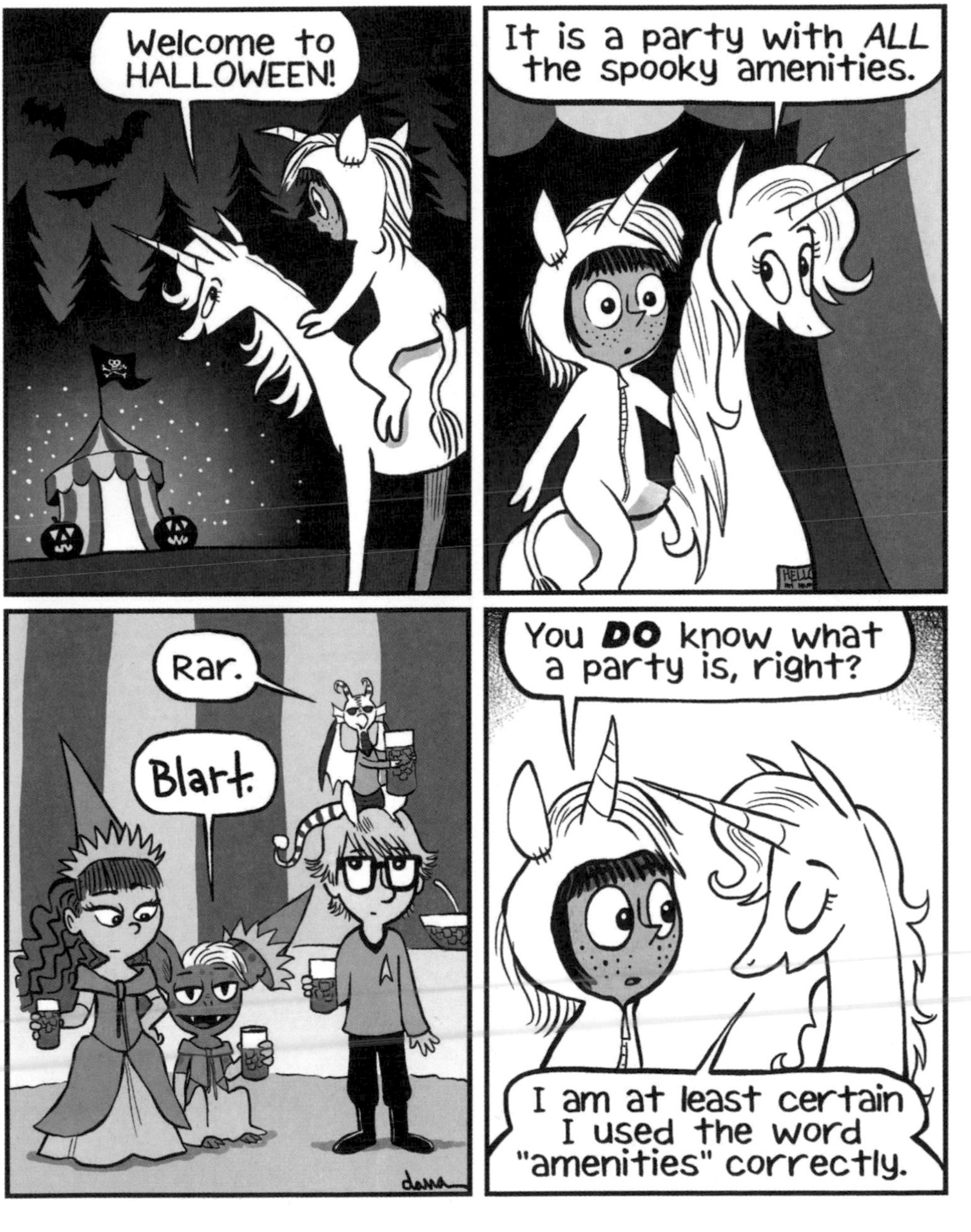
Welcome to HALLOWEEN!
It is a party with ALL the spooky amenities.
Rar.
Blart.
You DO know what a party is, right?
I am at least certain I used the word "amenities" correctly.
dana

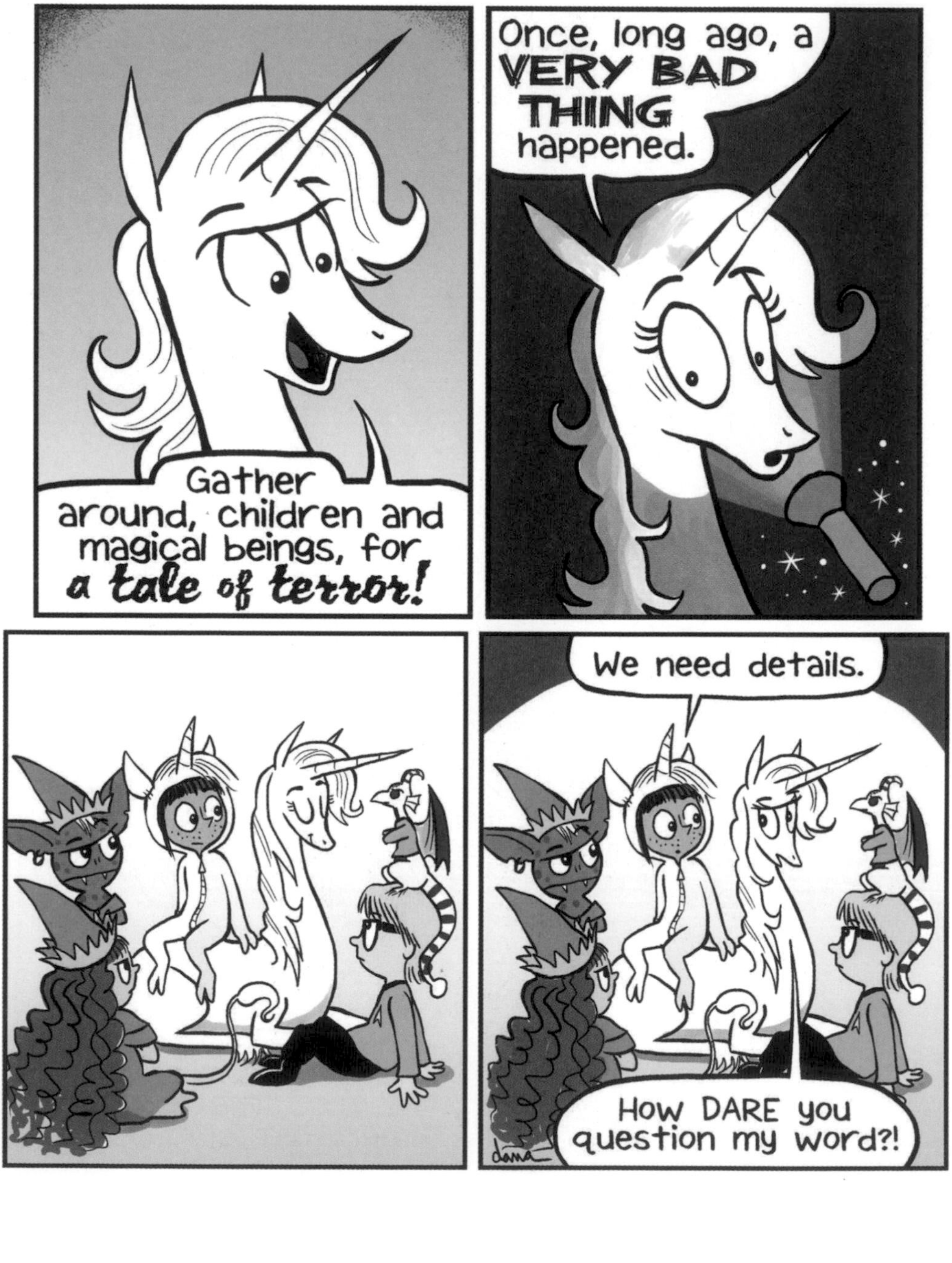

Gather around, children and magical beings, for a tale of terror!
Once, long ago, a VERY BAD THING happened.
We need details.
How DARE you question my word?!
dana

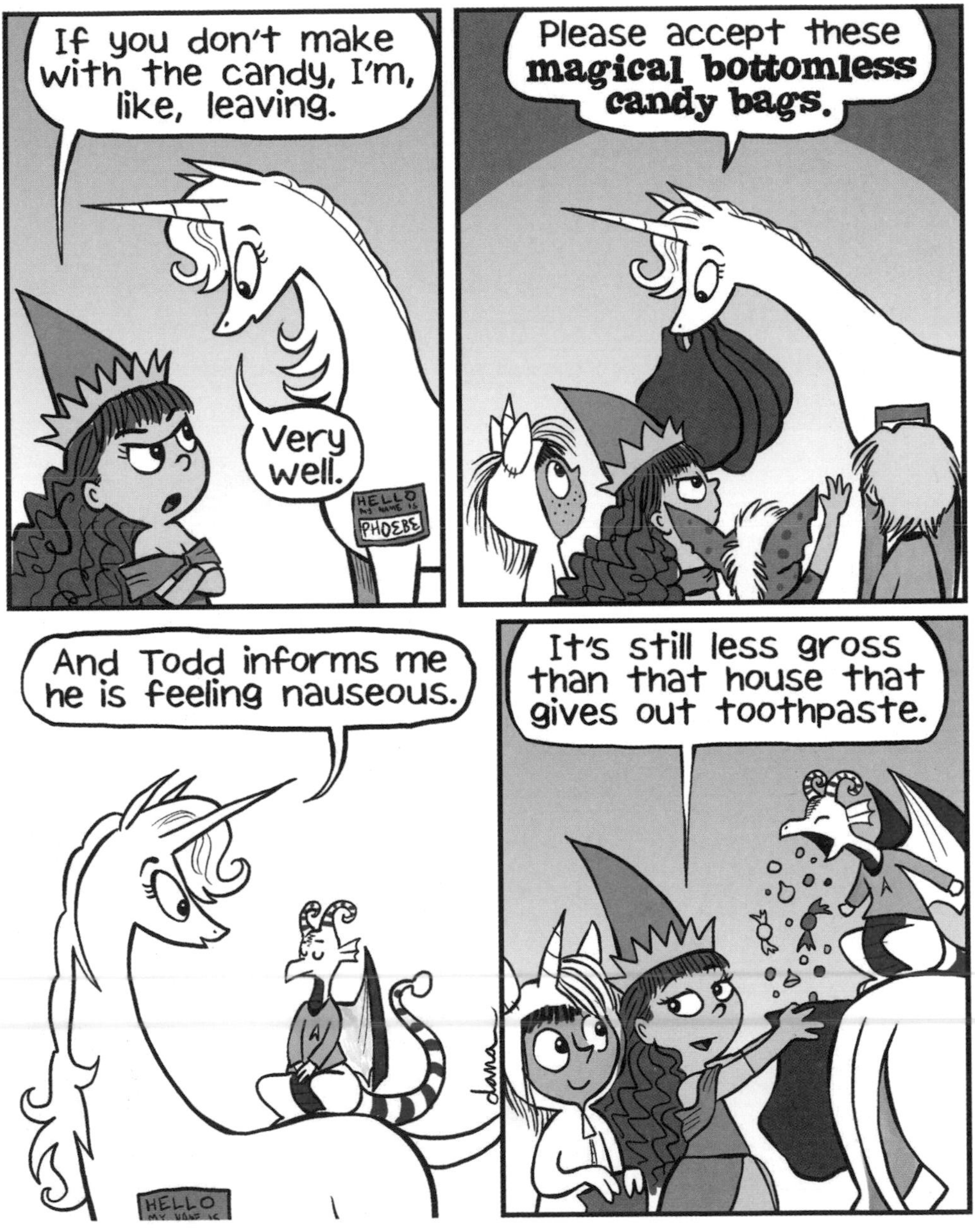
If you don't make with the candy, I'm, like, leaving.
Very well.
HELLO MY NAME IS PHOEBE
Please accept these **magical bottomless candy bags.**
And Todd informs me he is feeling nauseous.
HELLO
It's still less gross than that house that gives out toothpaste.
dana

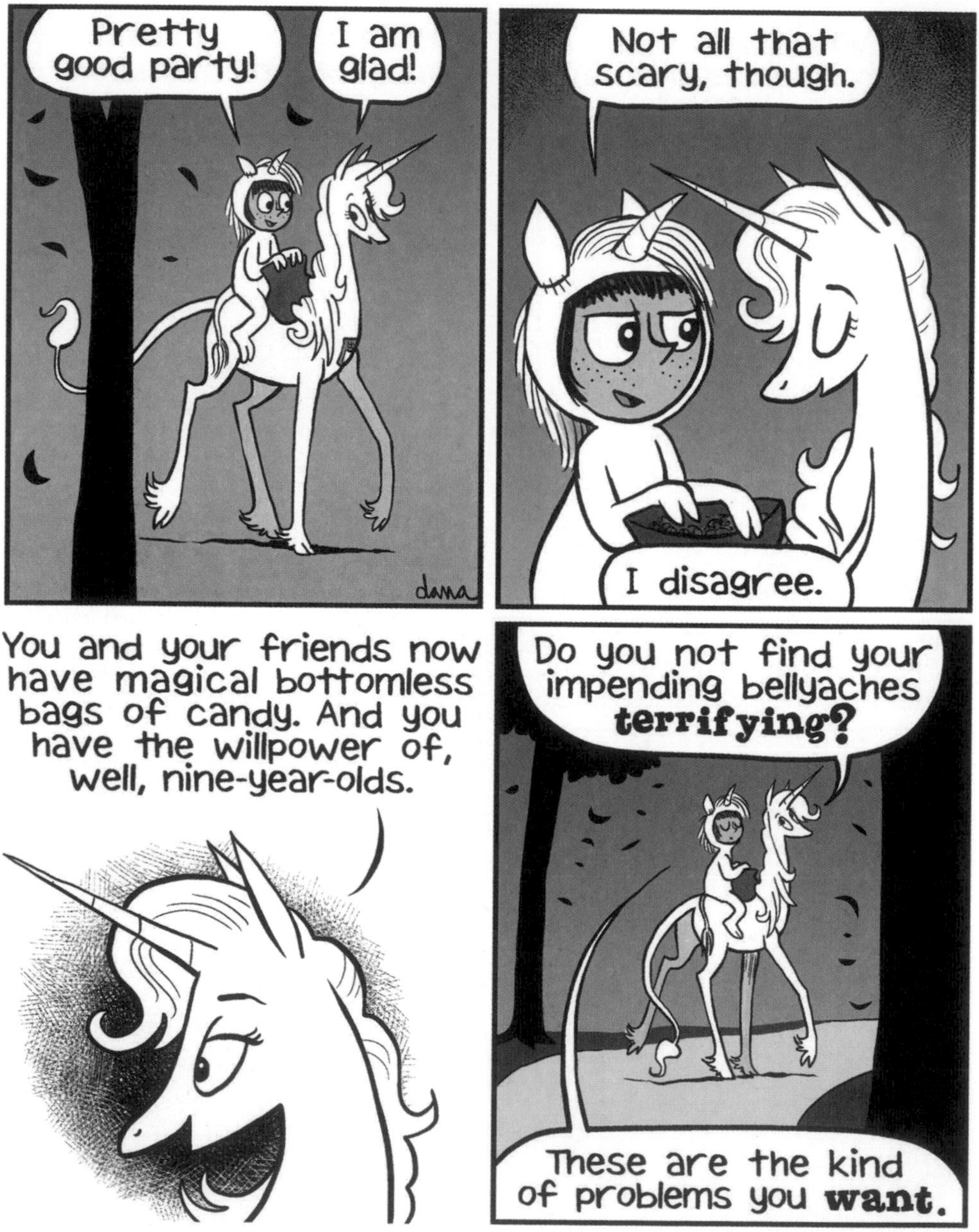
Pretty good party!
I am glad!
dana
Not all that scary, though.
I disagree.
You and your friends now have magical bottomless bags of candy. And you have the willpower of, well, nine-year-olds.
Do you not find your impending bellyaches **terrifying?**
These are the kind of problems you **want**.

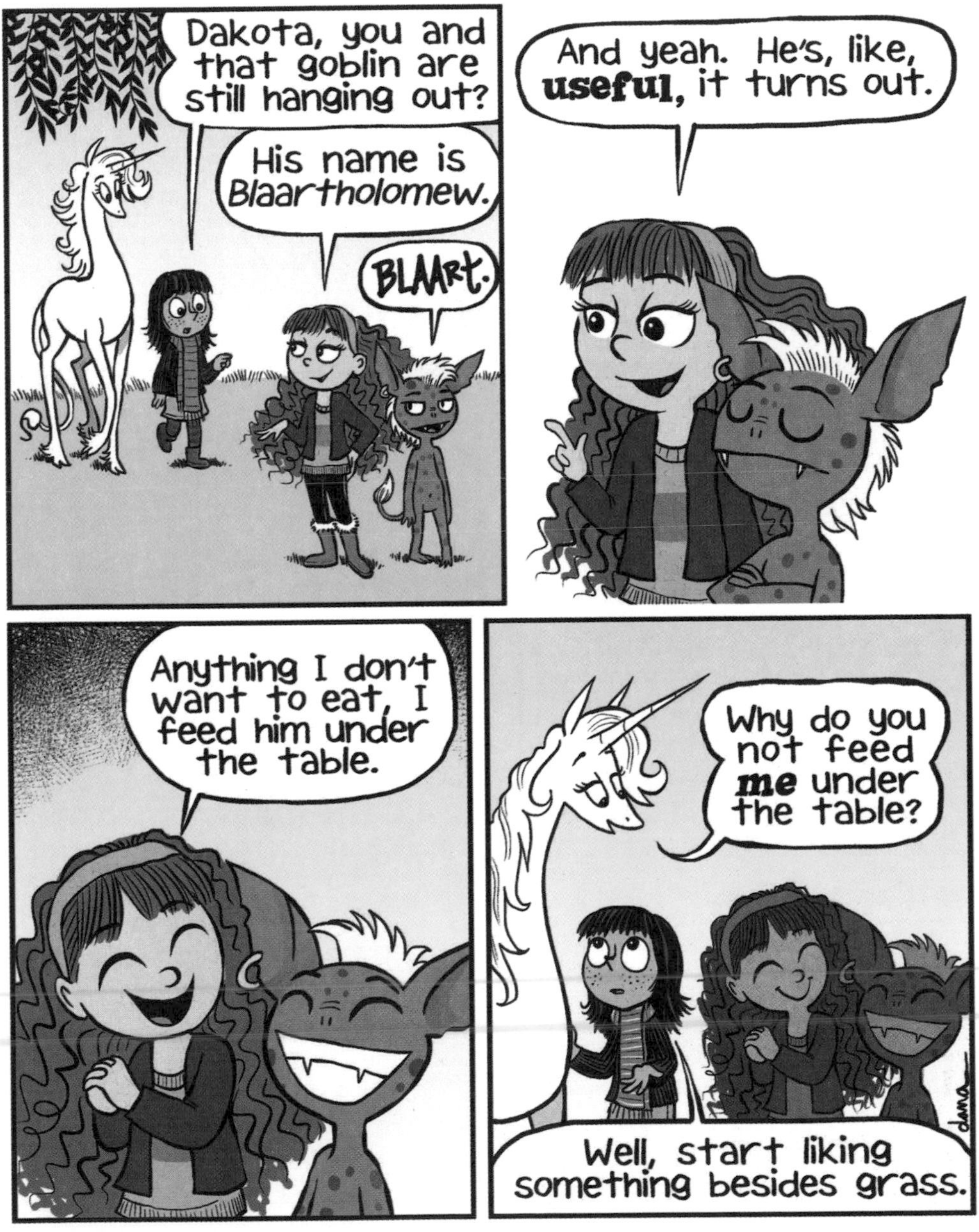
Dakota, you and that goblin are still hanging out?
His name is *Blaartholomew.*
BLAARt.
And yeah. He's, like, **useful**, it turns out.
Anything I don't want to eat, I feed him under the table.
Why do you not feed **me** under the table?
Well, start liking something besides grass.
dana

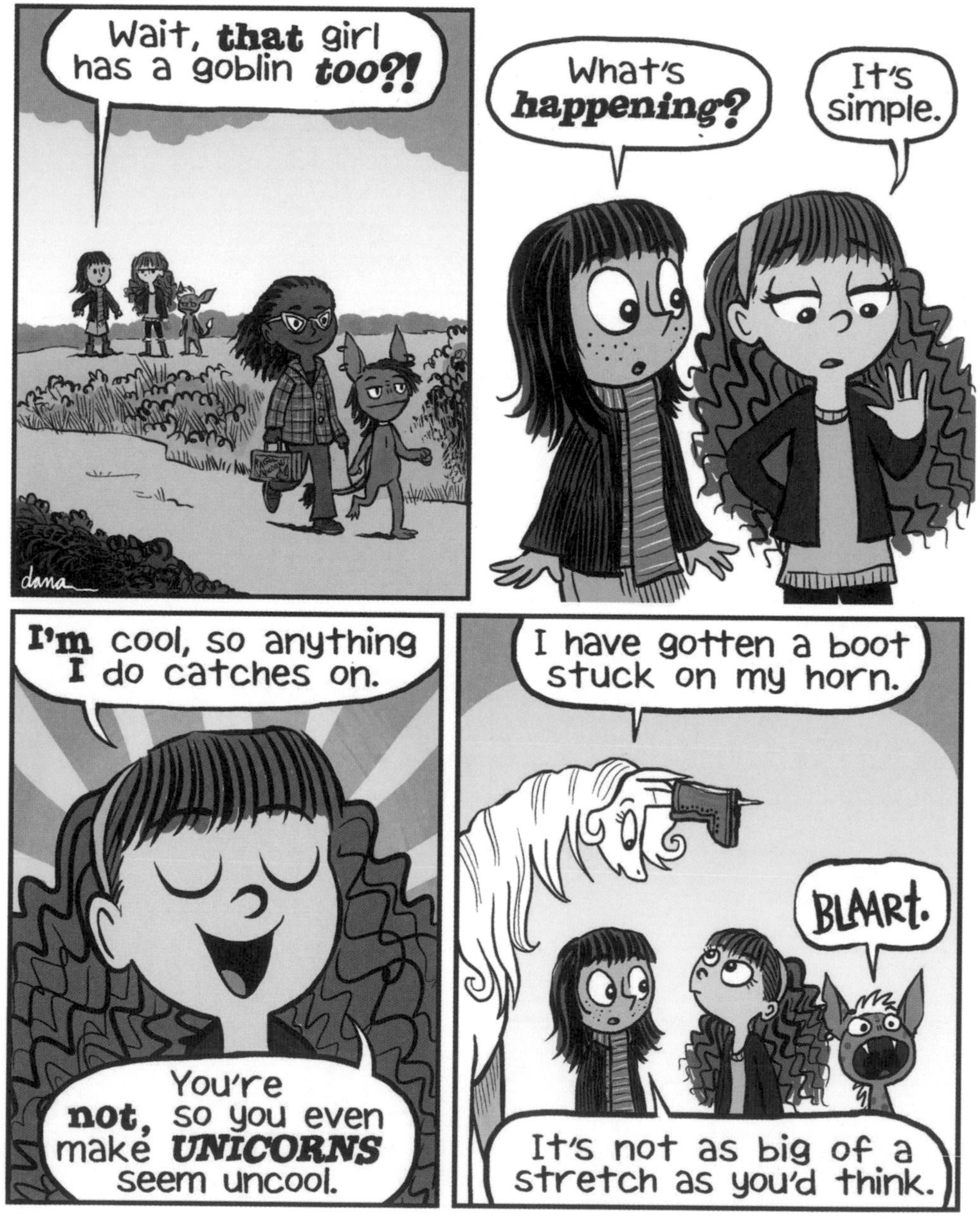
Wait, **that** girl has a goblin ***too?!***
dana
What's ***happening?***
It's simple.
I'm cool, so anything **I** do catches on.
You're **not,** so you even make ***UNICORNS*** seem uncool.
I have gotten a boot stuck on my horn.
BLAART.
It's not as big of a stretch as you'd think.

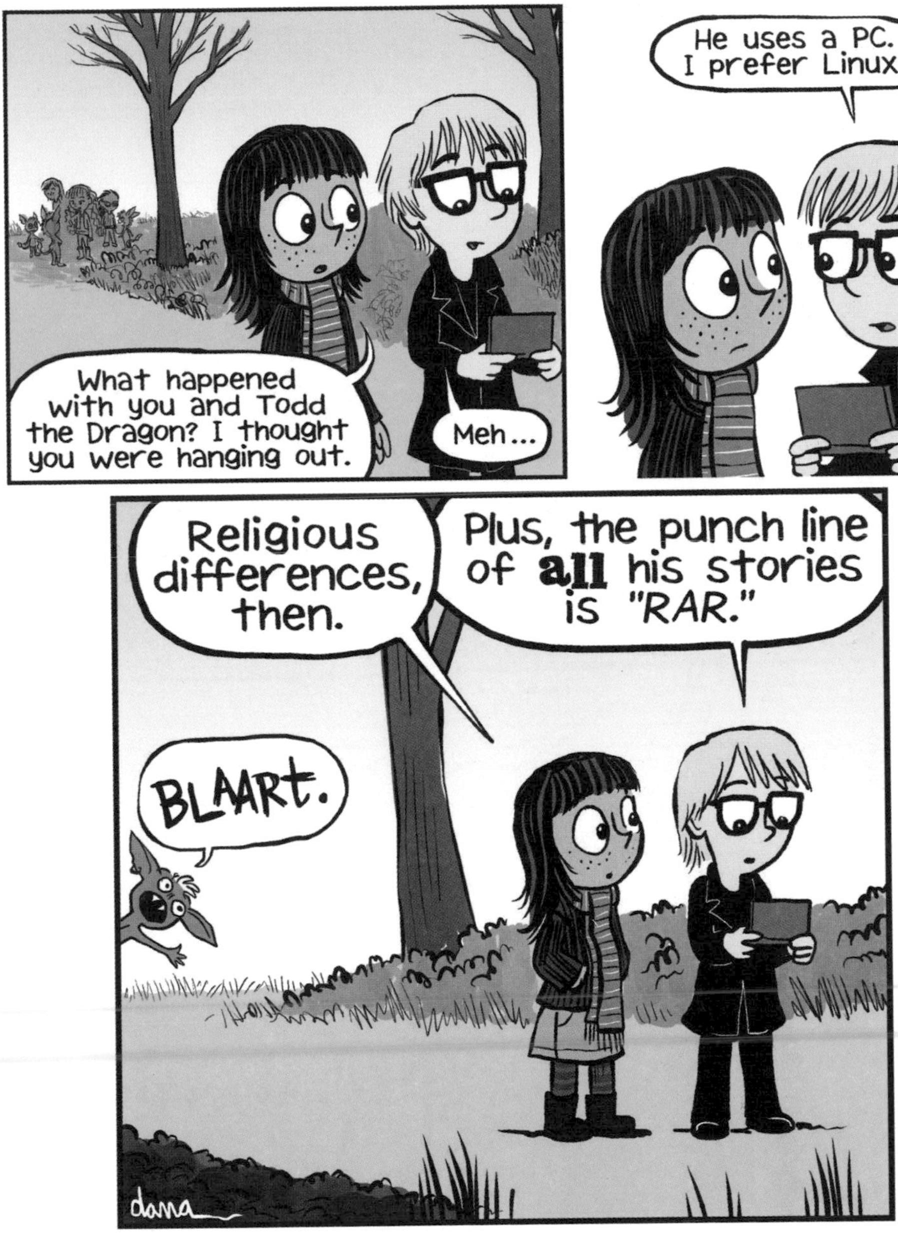
What happened with you and Todd the Dragon? I thought you were hanging out.
Meh...
He uses a PC. I prefer Linux.
Religious differences, then.
Plus, the punch line of **all** his stories is "RAR."
BLAART.
dana

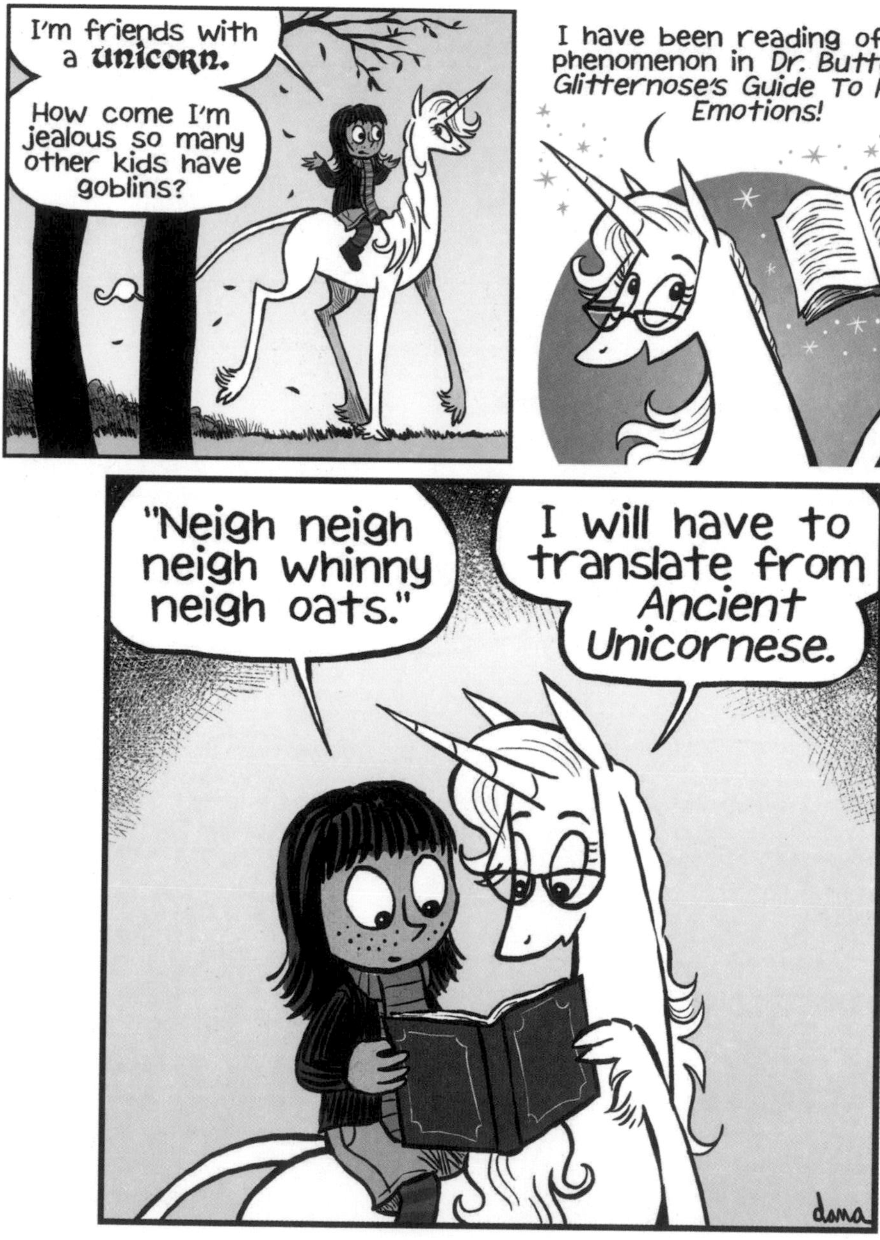
I'm friends with a UNICORN.
How come I'm jealous so many other kids have goblins?
I have been reading of this phenomenon in Dr. Buttercup Glitternose's Guide To Human Emotions!
"Neigh neigh neigh whinny neigh oats."
I will have to translate from Ancient Unicornese.
dana

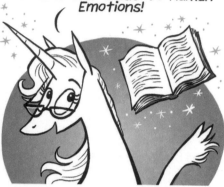

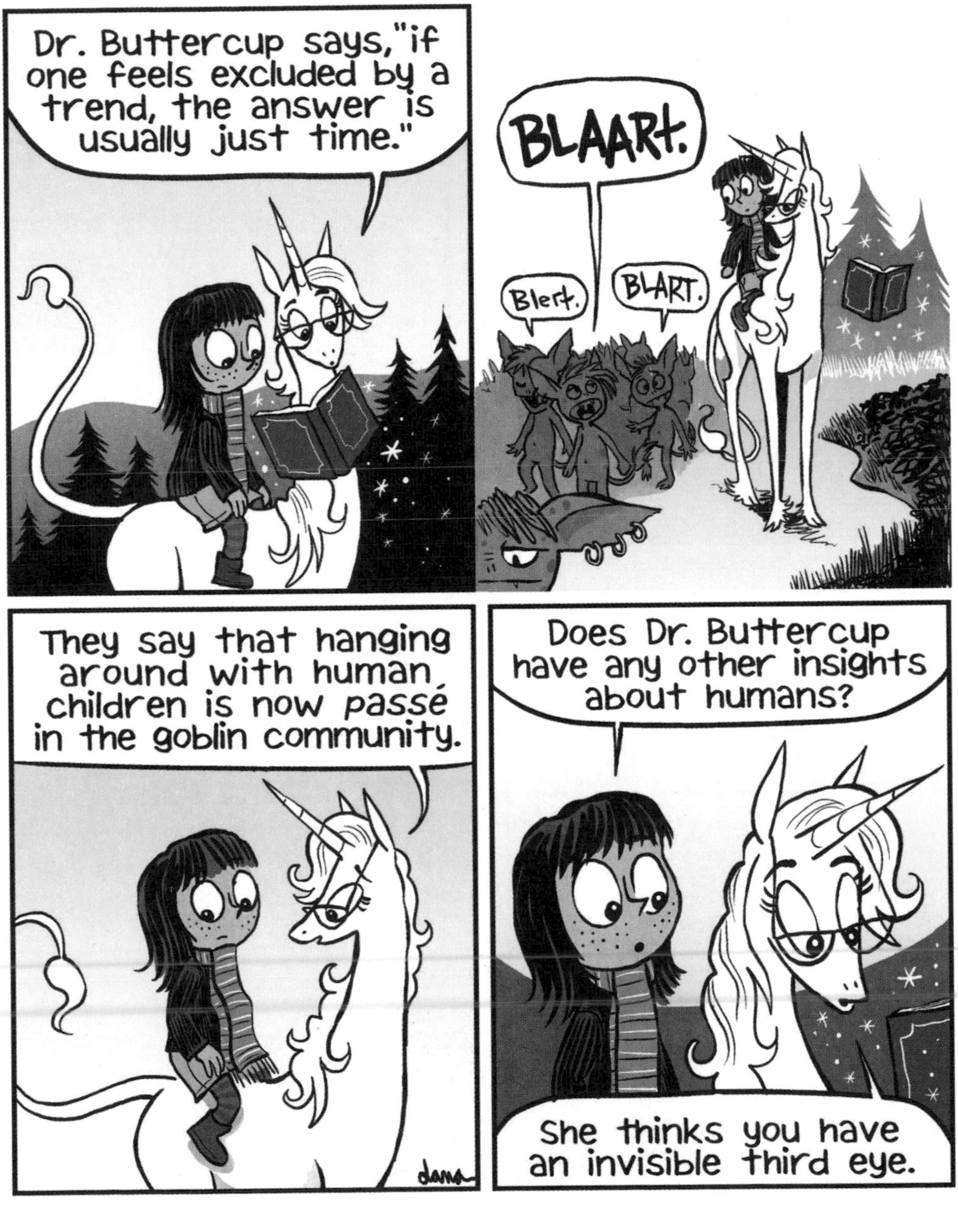
Dr. Buttercup says, "if one feels excluded by a trend, the answer is usually just time."
BLAARt.
Blert.
BLART.
They say that hanging around with human children is now *passé* in the goblin community.
Does Dr. Buttercup have any other insights about humans?
She thinks you have an invisible third eye.
dana

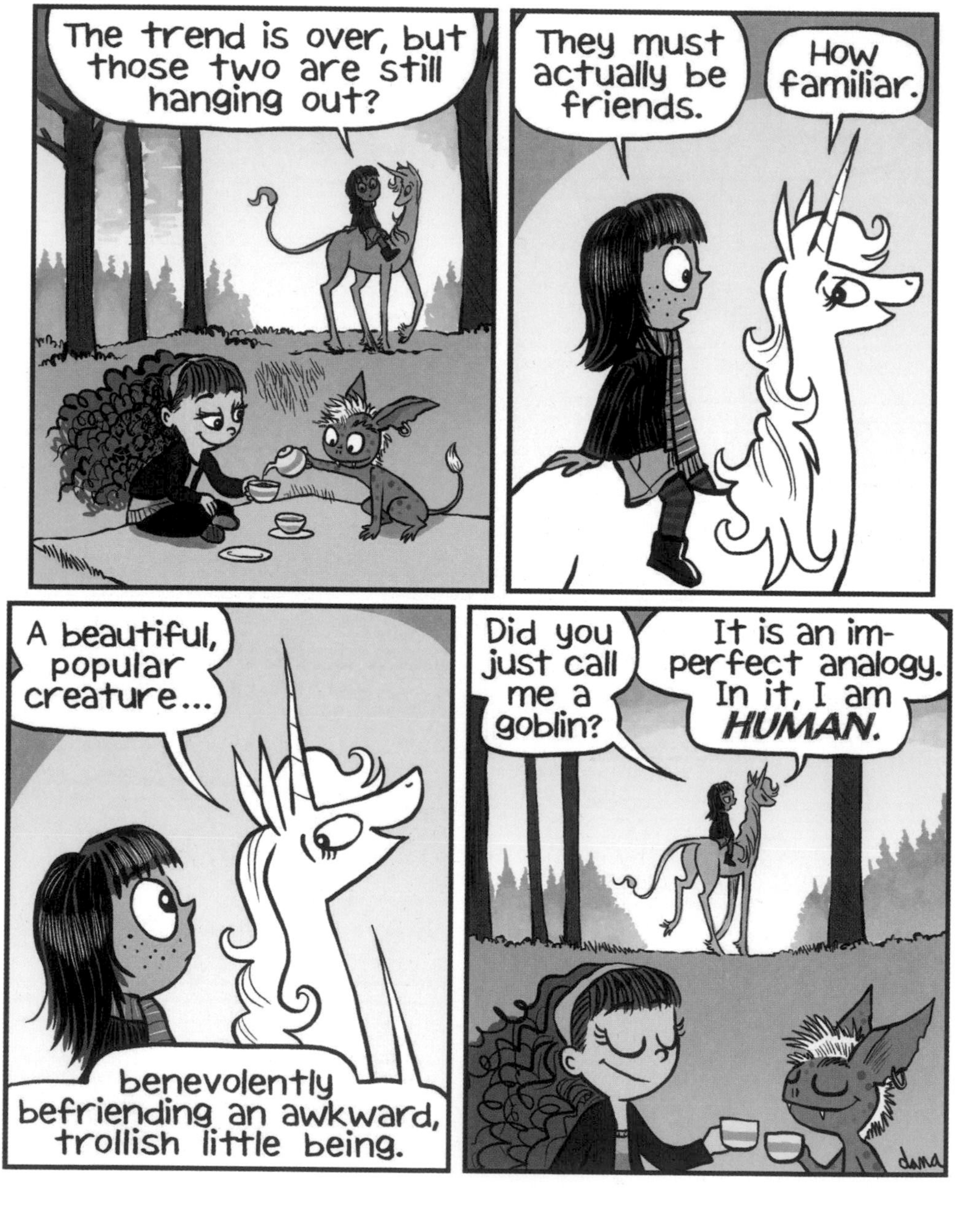

The trend is over, but those two are still hanging out?
They must actually be friends.
How familiar.
A beautiful, popular creature...
benevolently befriending an awkward, trollish little being.
Did you just call me a goblin?
It is an imperfect analogy. In it, I am ***HUMAN.***
dana

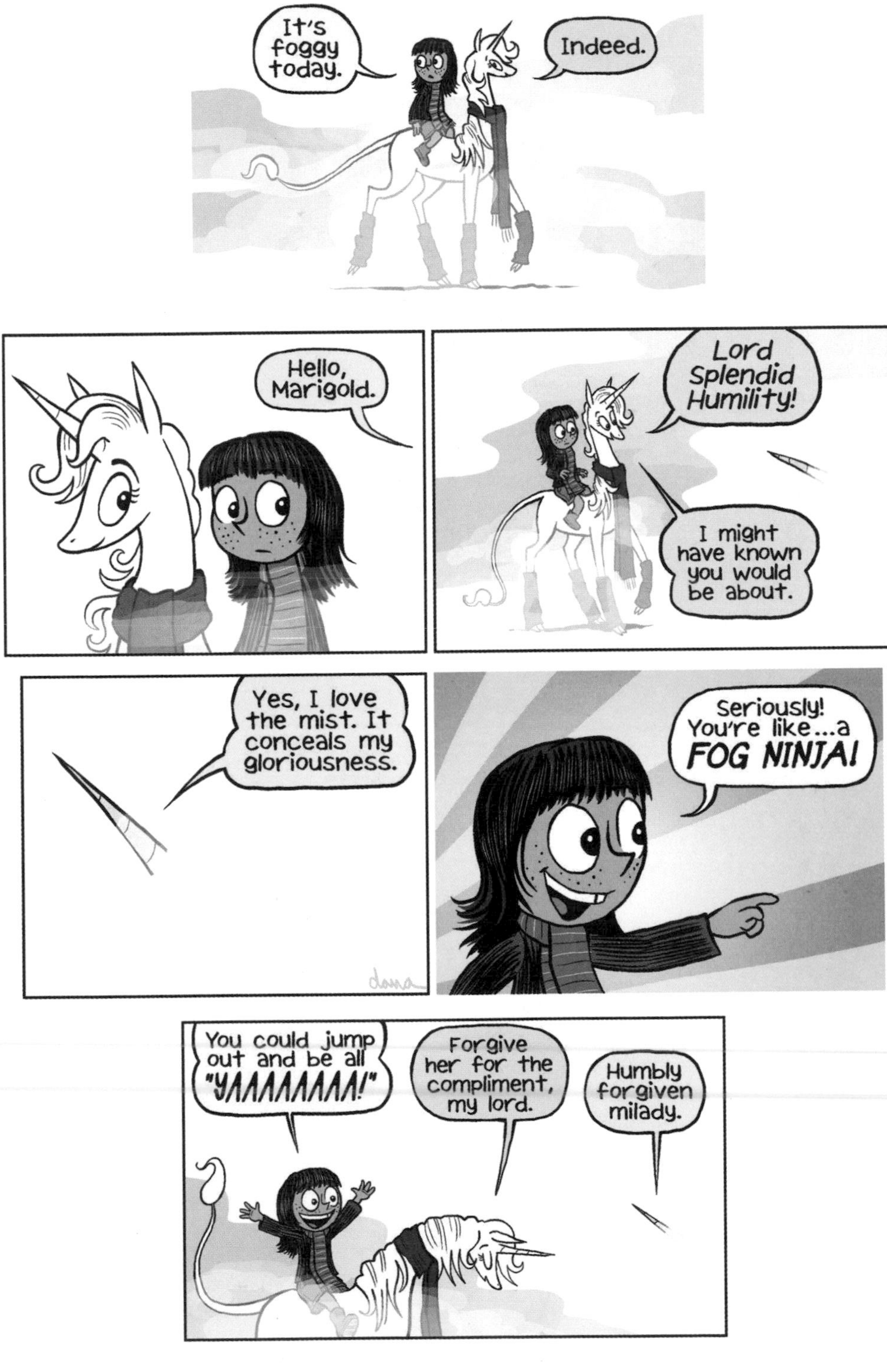
It's foggy today.
Indeed.
Hello, Marigold.
Lord Splendid Humility!
I might have known you would be about.
Yes, I love the mist. It conceals my gloriousness.
Seriously! You're like...a FOG NINJA!
You could jump out and be all "YAAAAAAAA!"
Forgive her for the compliment, my lord.
Humbly forgiven milady.

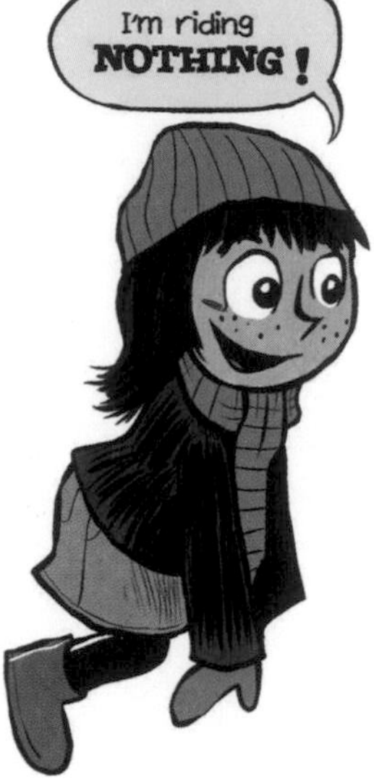
I'm riding NOTHING!

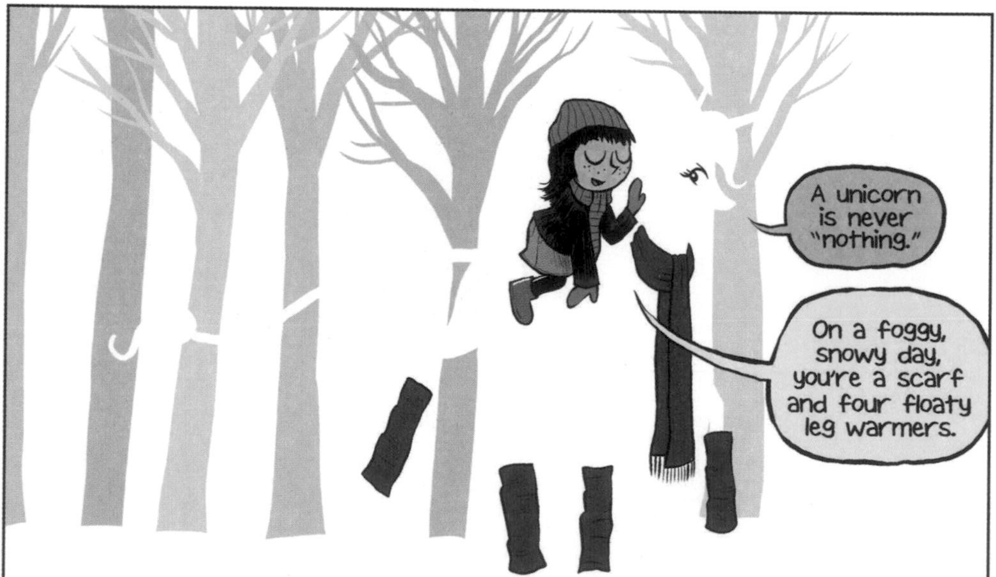
A unicorn is never "nothing."
On a foggy, snowy day, you're a scarf and four floaty leg warmers.
dana

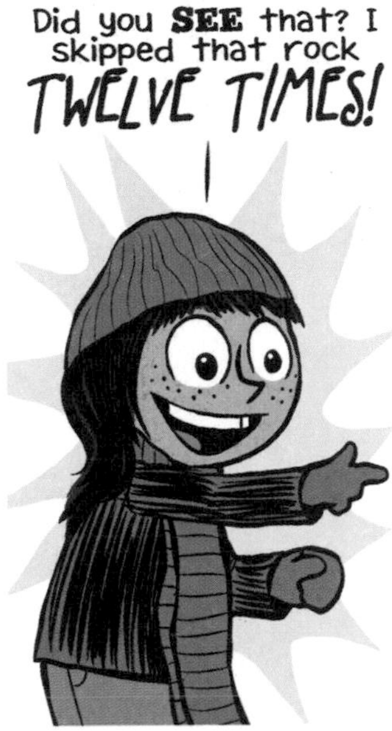
Did you SEE that? I skipped that rock TWELVE TIMES!

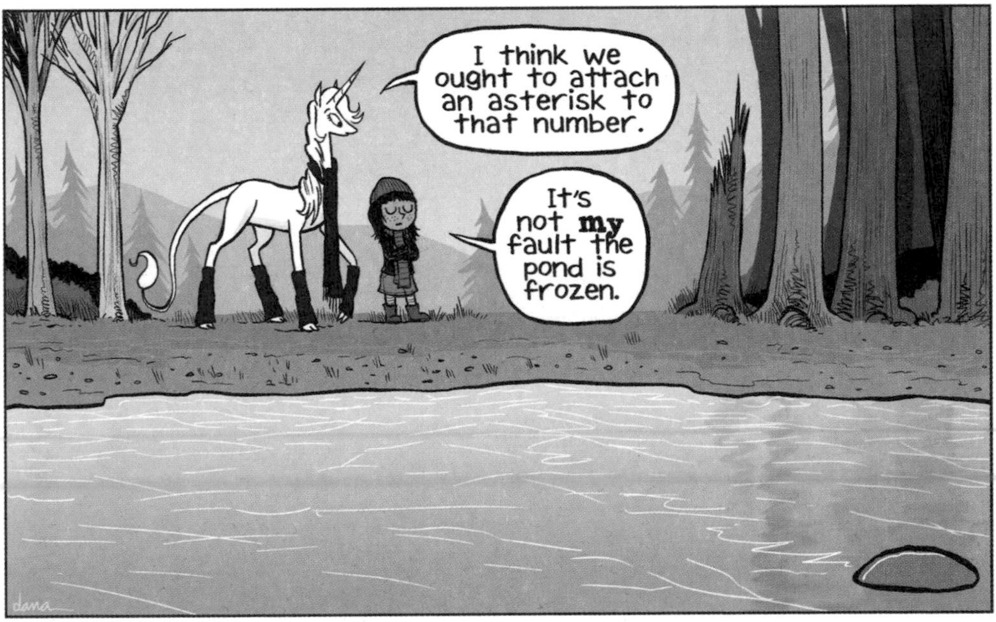
I think we ought to attach an asterisk to that number.
It's not my fault the pond is frozen.
dana

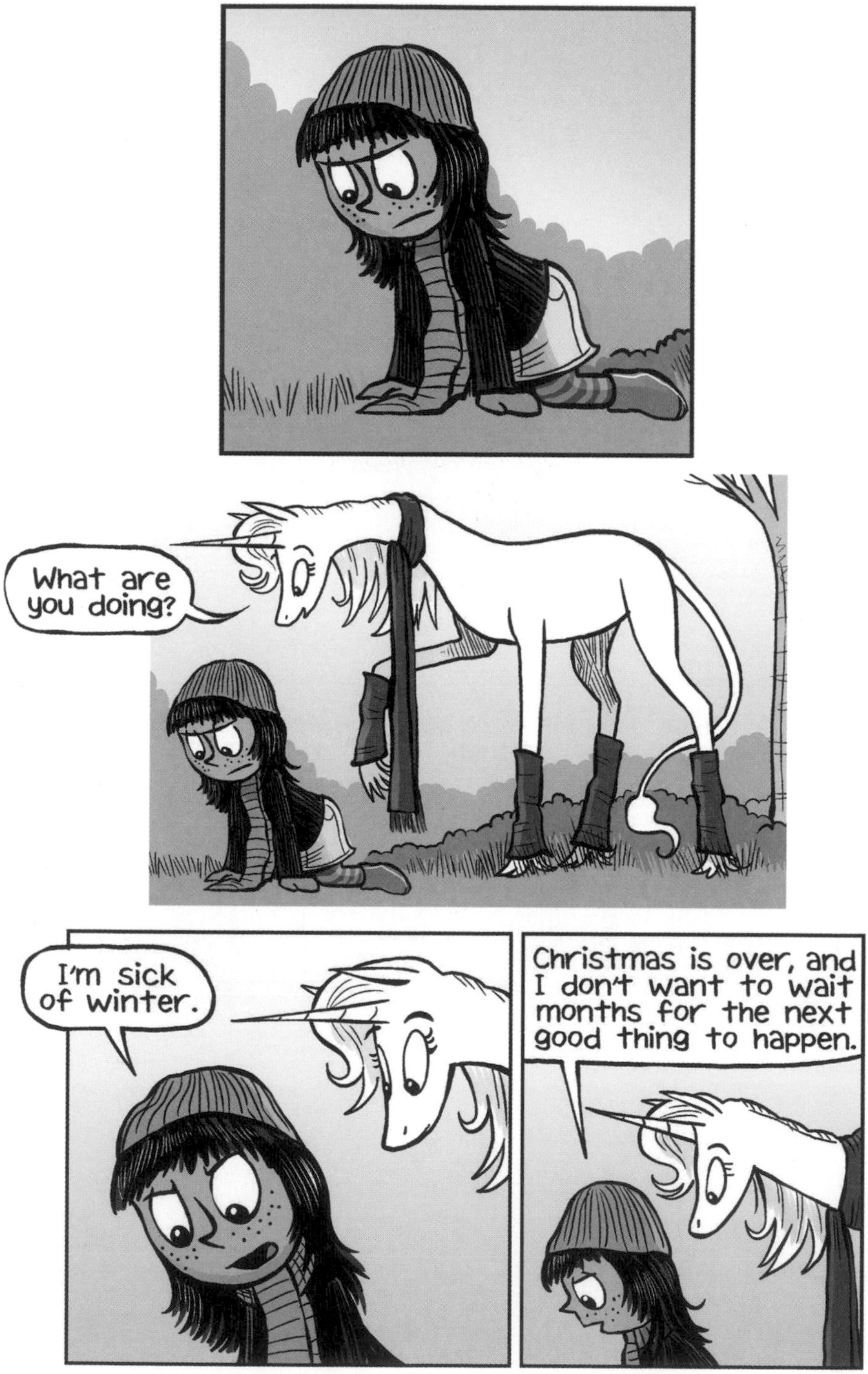
What are you doing?
I'm sick of winter.
Christmas is over, and I don't want to wait months for the next good thing to happen.

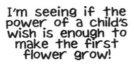

I'm seeing if the power of a child's wish is enough to make the first flower grow!

ZAP

Spring is a state of mind.

Promise me that thing isn't feeding off my brain.

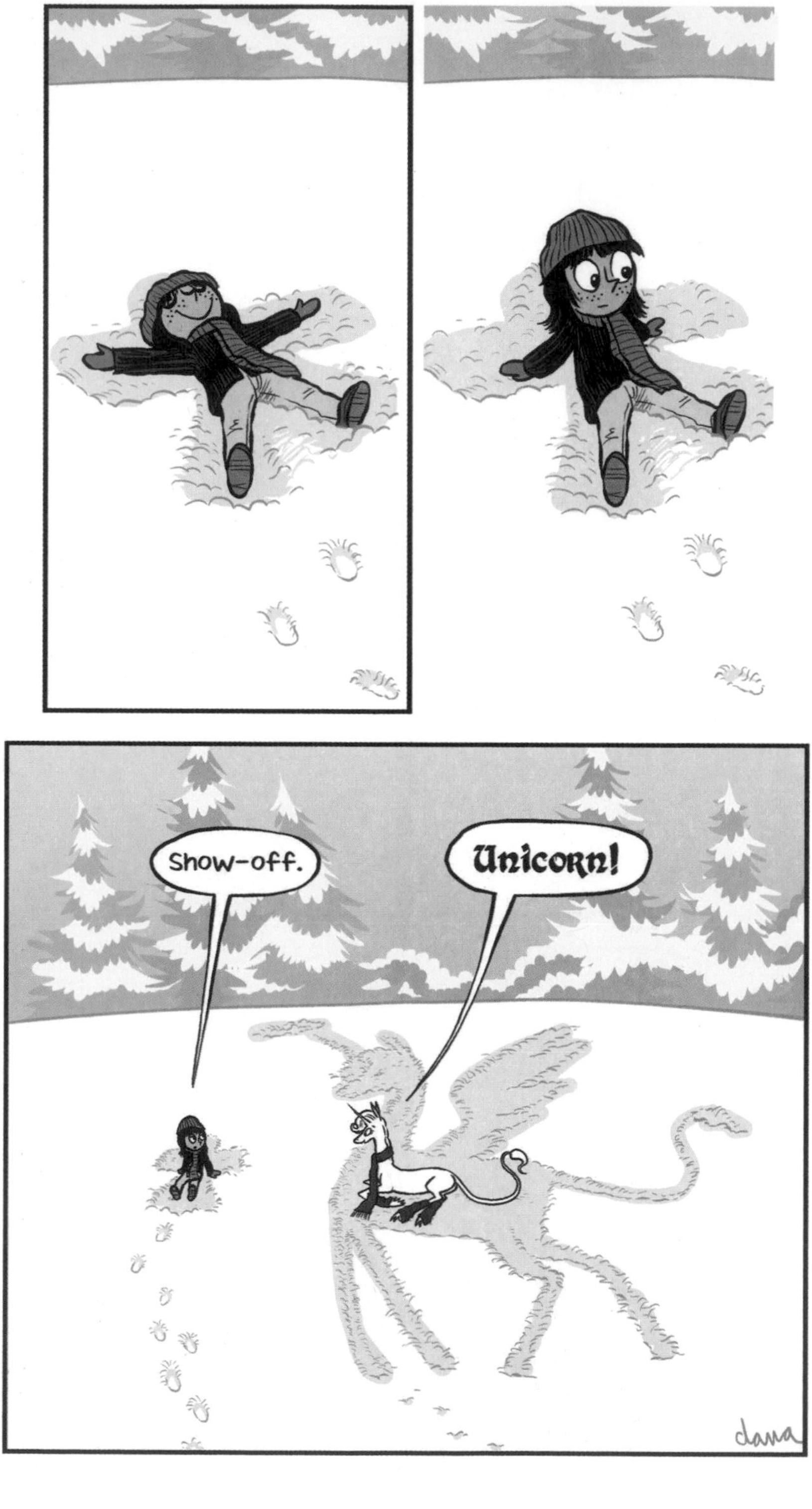
Show-off.
Unicorn!
dana

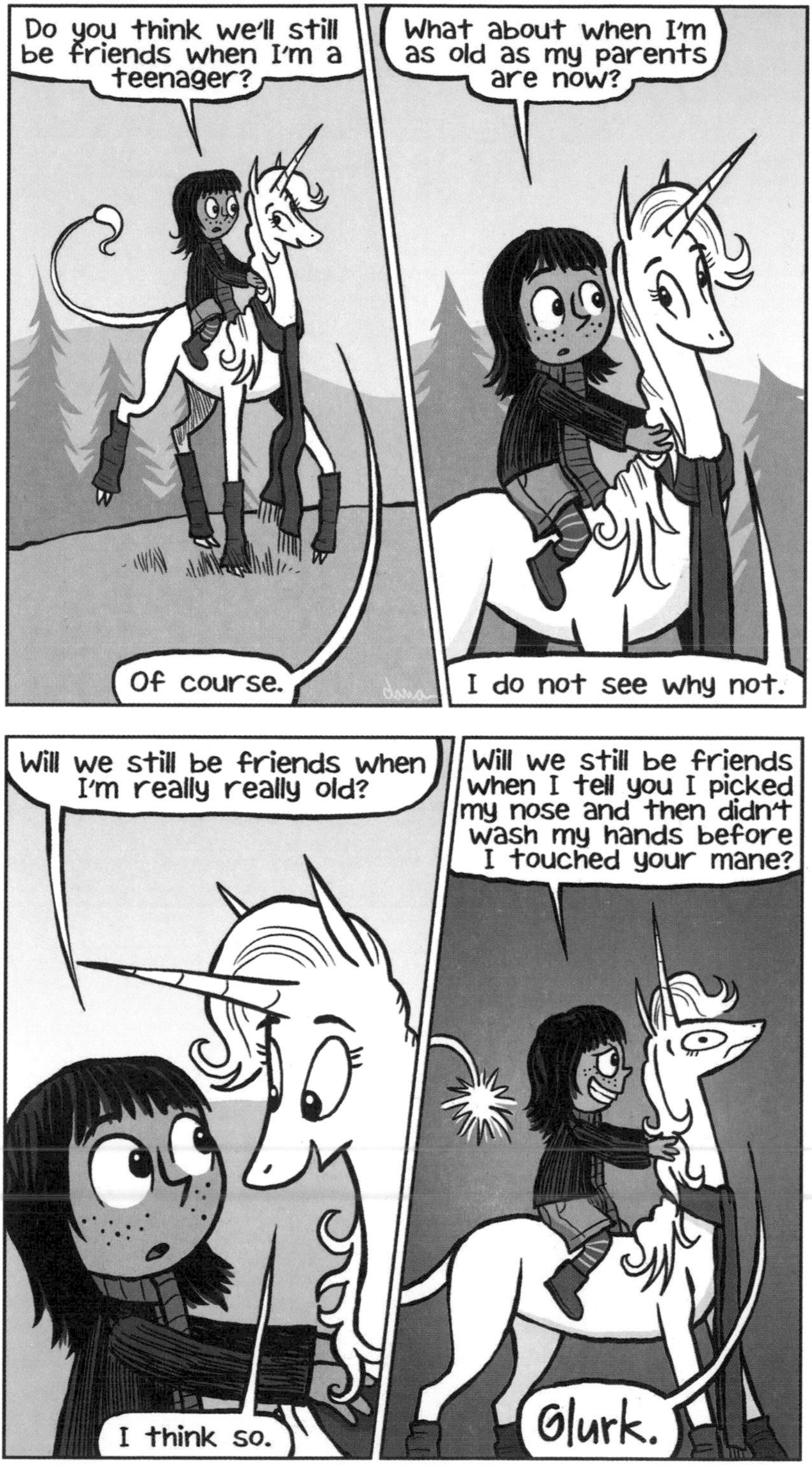
Do you think we'll still be friends when I'm a teenager?
Of course.
What about when I'm as old as my parents are now?
I do not see why not.
Will we still be friends when I'm really really old?
I think so.
Will we still be friends when I tell you I picked my nose and then didn't wash my hands before I touched your mane?
Glurk.

Phoebe?
What?
You should get up.
Why?
Out here there are unicorns!

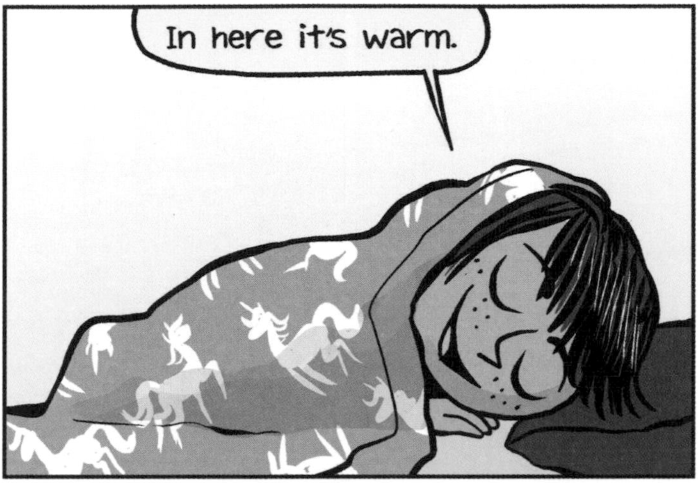
In here it's warm.

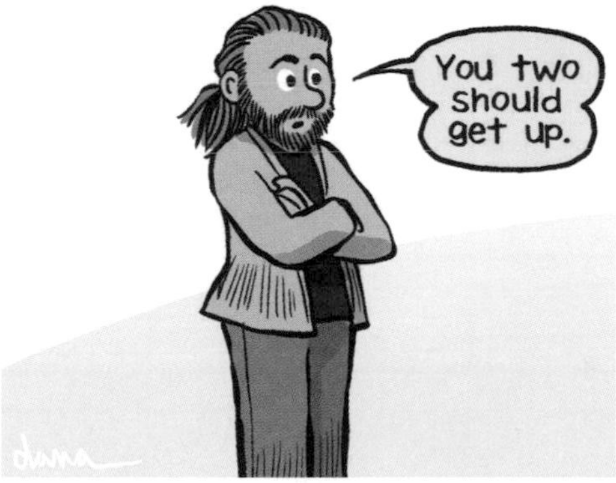
You two should get up.

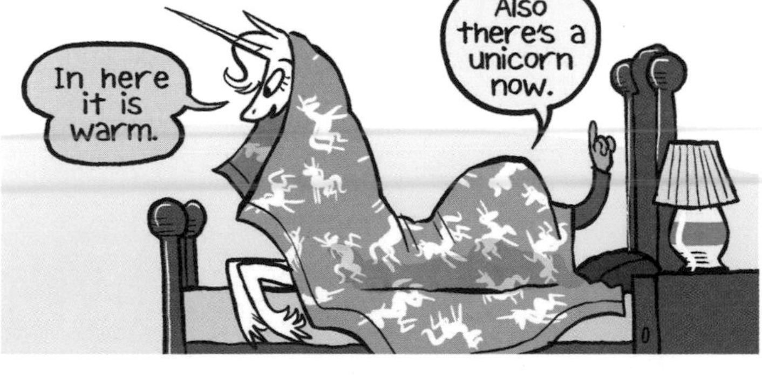
In here it is warm.
Also there's a unicorn now.

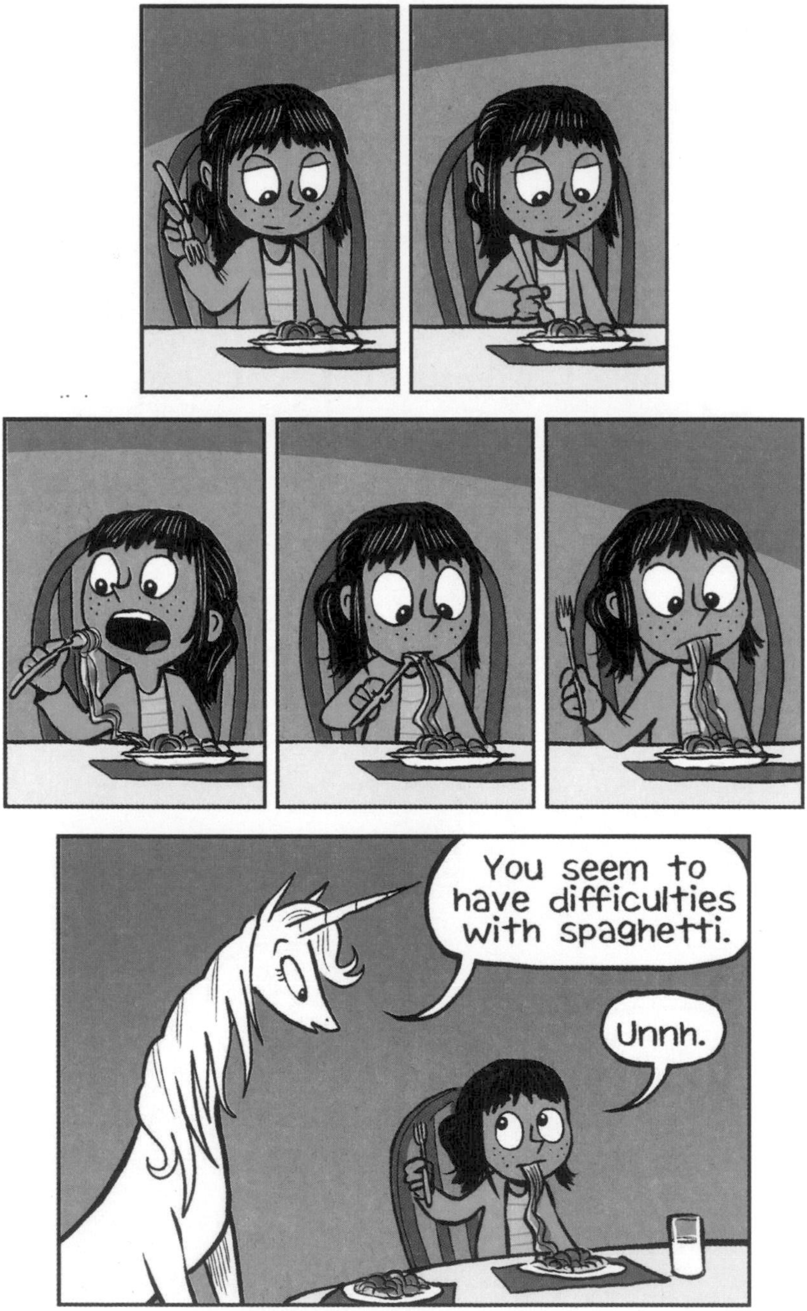
You seem to have difficulties with spaghetti.
Unnh.

I notice **YOU'RE** still sparkling clean.

Thank you for noticing!

Run, Marigold!
RUN!
WHINNY!
We're not gonna make it!!
We must! WE MUST!!
It is right on my tail!
RUN FAST!!

WE HAVE MADE IT!!!
That was close!
You know, though...running from the rain is just as much fun when it **does** catch us.
You are not the one whose tail is wet.

Your book is just ONE book.
Our e-reader thingies have LOTS of books.
I still like how books smell, and I like turning pages.
"Books" indeed. You humans and your newfangled devices.

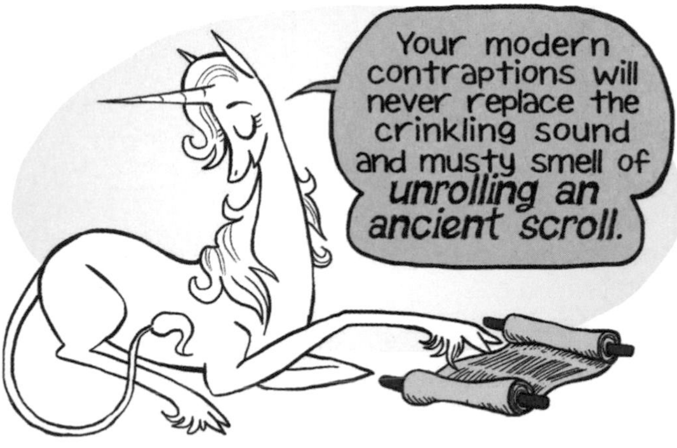
Your modern contraptions will never replace the crinkling sound and musty smell of *unrolling an ancient scroll.*

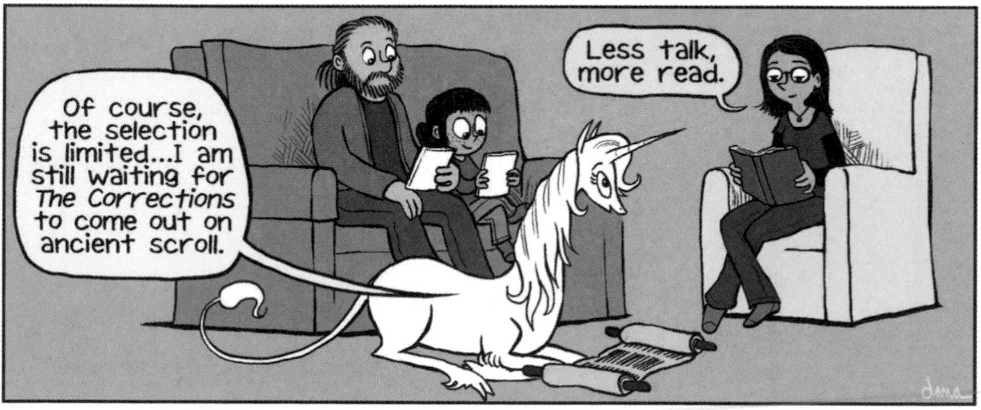
Of course, the selection is limited...I am still waiting for *The Corrections* to come out on ancient scroll.
Less talk, more read.
dana

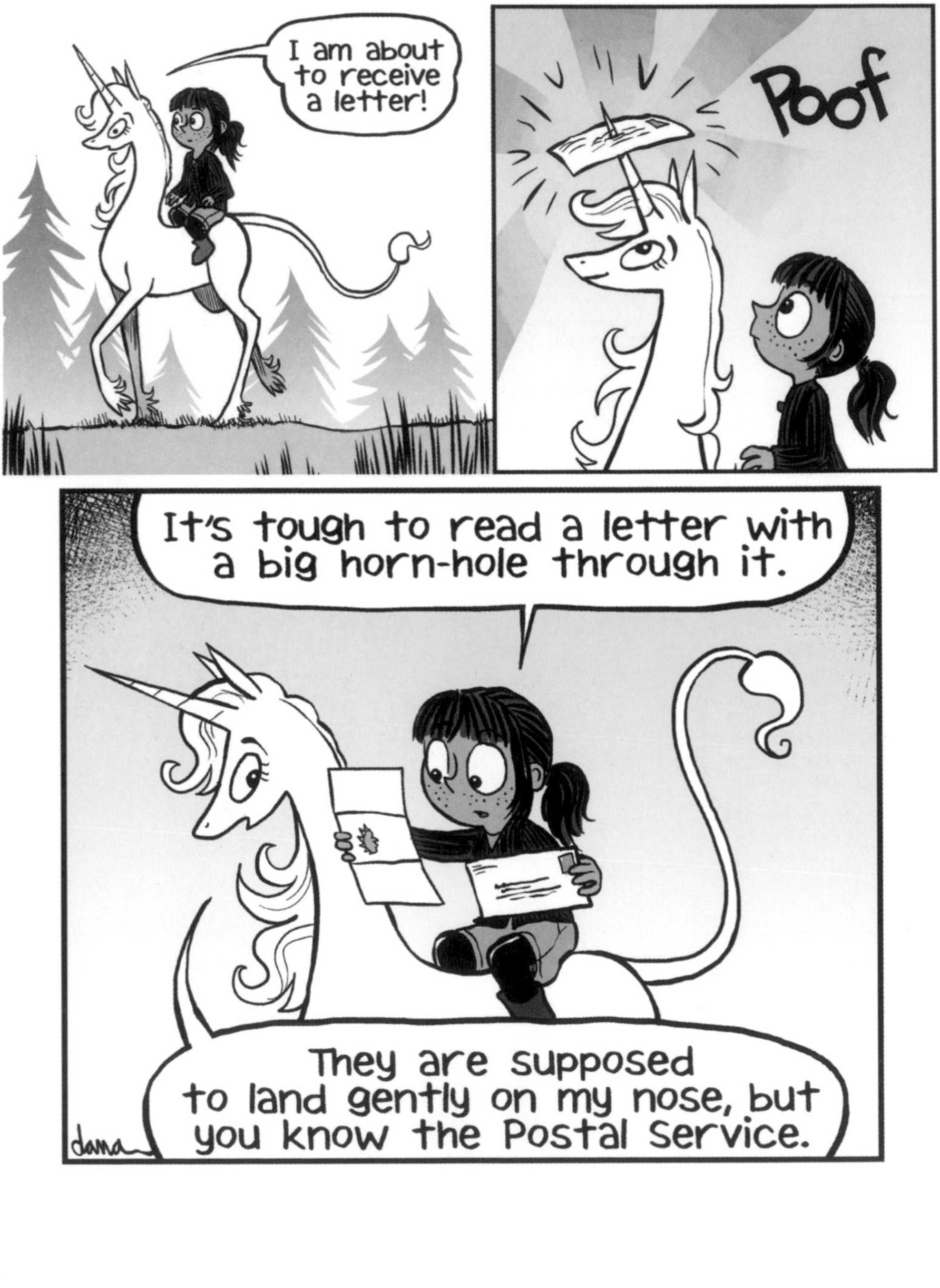
I am about to receive a letter!
Poof
It's tough to read a letter with a big horn-hole through it.
They are supposed to land gently on my nose, but you know the Postal Service.
dana

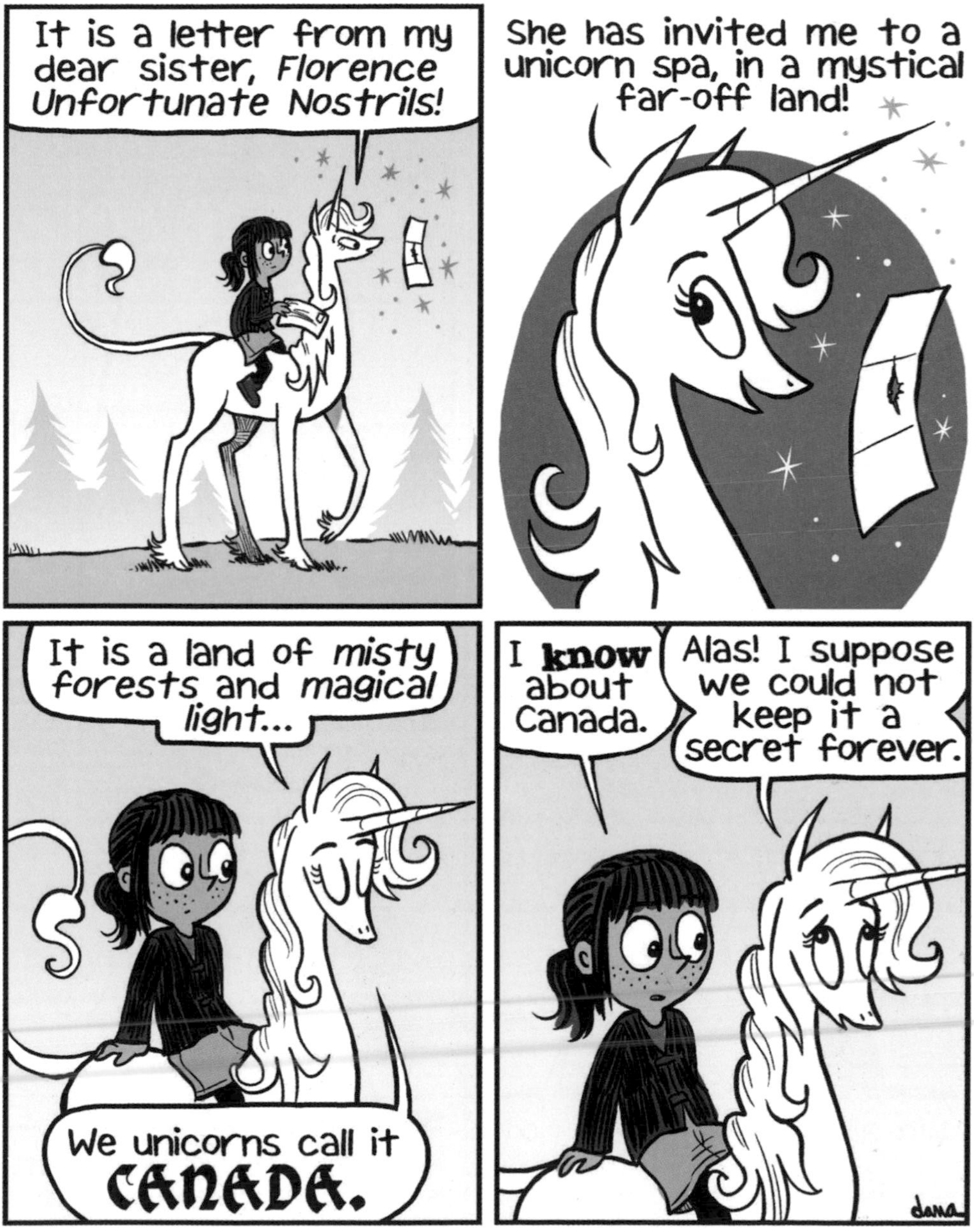
It is a letter from my dear sister, Florence Unfortunate Nostrils!
She has invited me to a unicorn spa, in a mystical far-off land!
It is a land of misty forests and magical light...
We unicorns call it CANADA.
I know about Canada.
Alas! I suppose we could not keep it a secret forever.
dana

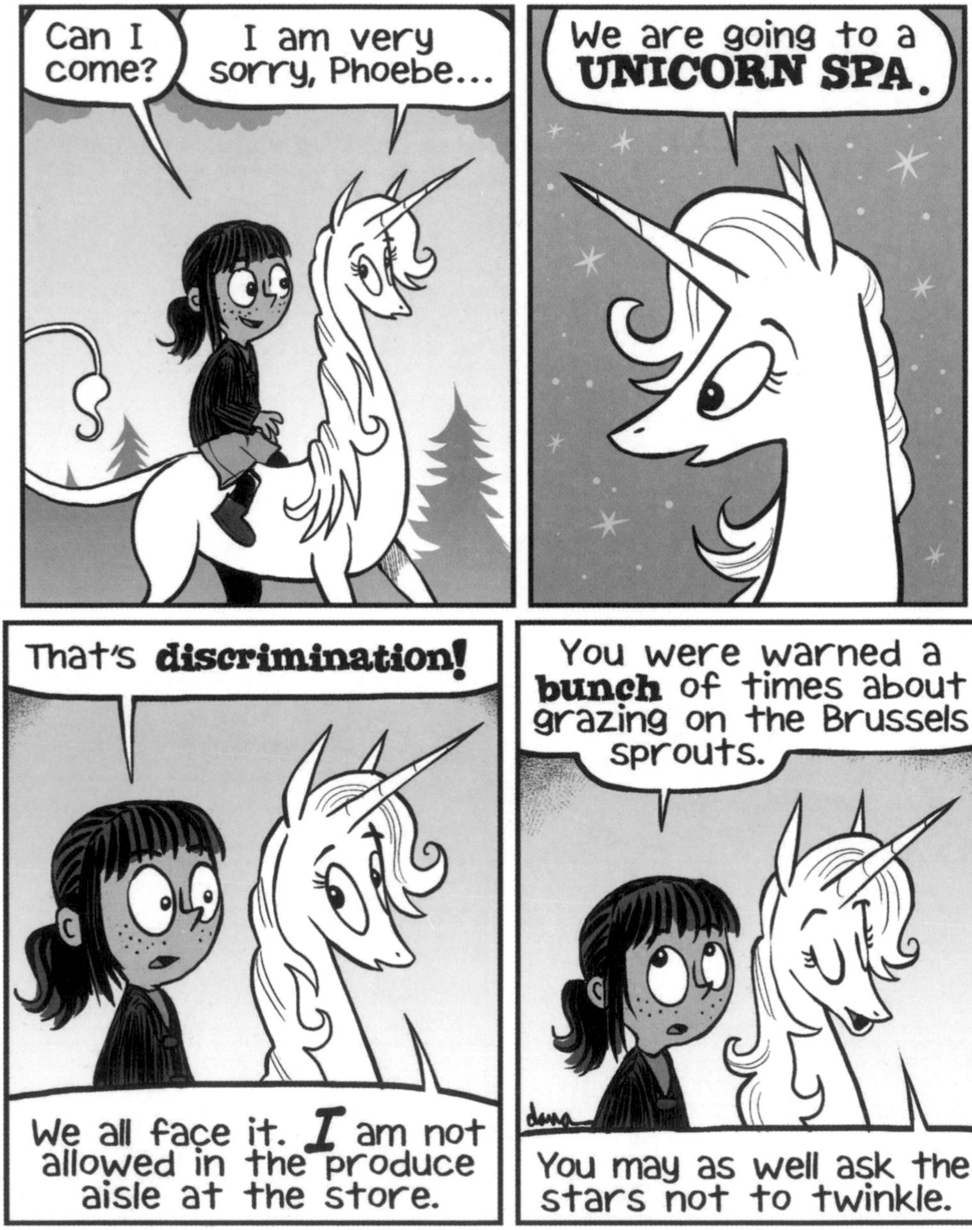
Can I come?
I am very sorry, Phoebe...
We are going to a **UNICORN SPA**.
That's **discrimination!**
We all face it. *I* am not allowed in the produce aisle at the store.
You were warned a **bunch** of times about grazing on the Brussels sprouts.
You may as well ask the stars not to twinkle.

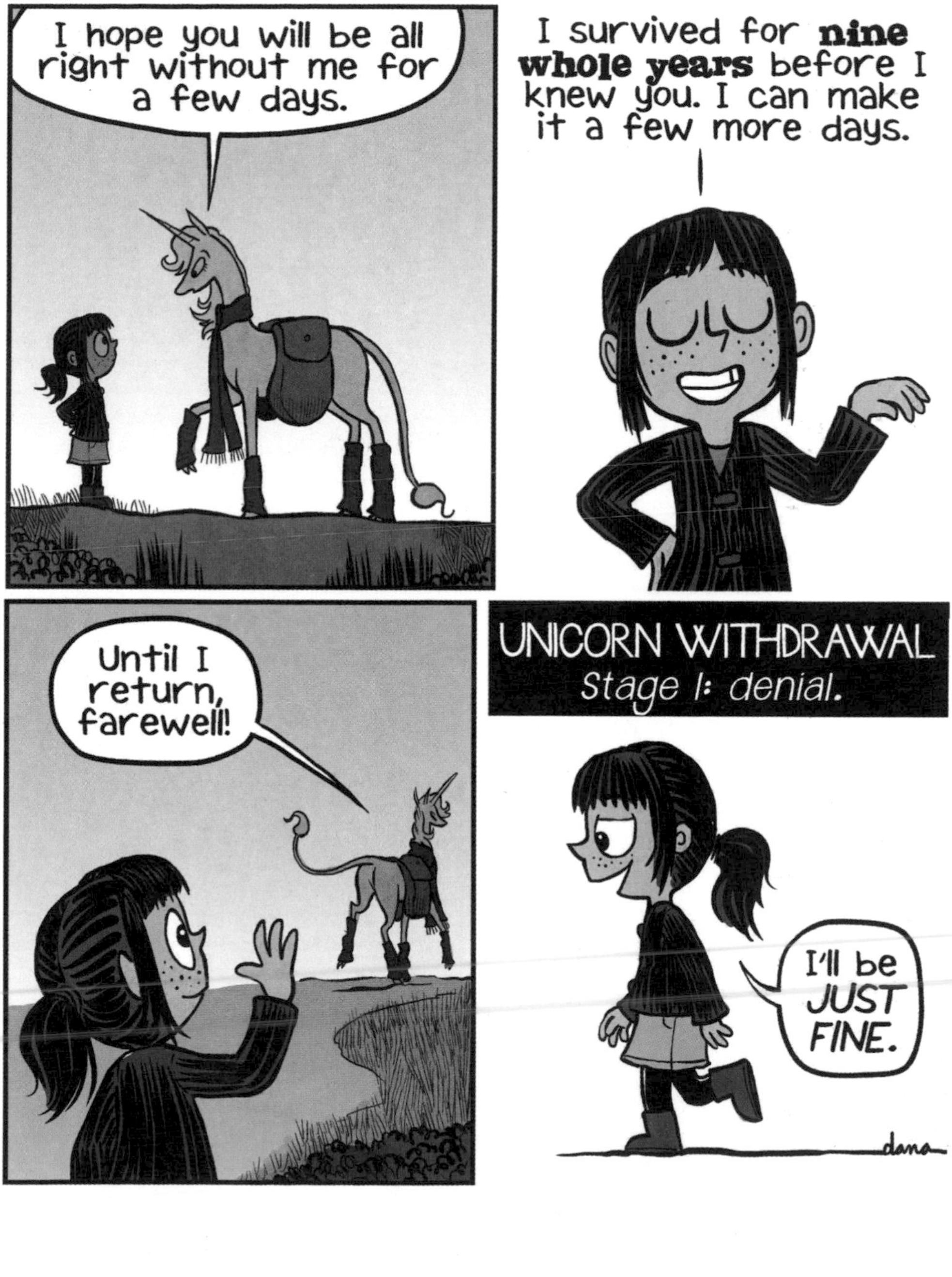
I hope you will be all right without me for a few days.
I survived for **nine whole years** before I knew you. I can make it a few more days.
Until I return, farewell!
UNICORN WITHDRAWAL
Stage 1: denial.
I'll be *JUST FINE.*
dana

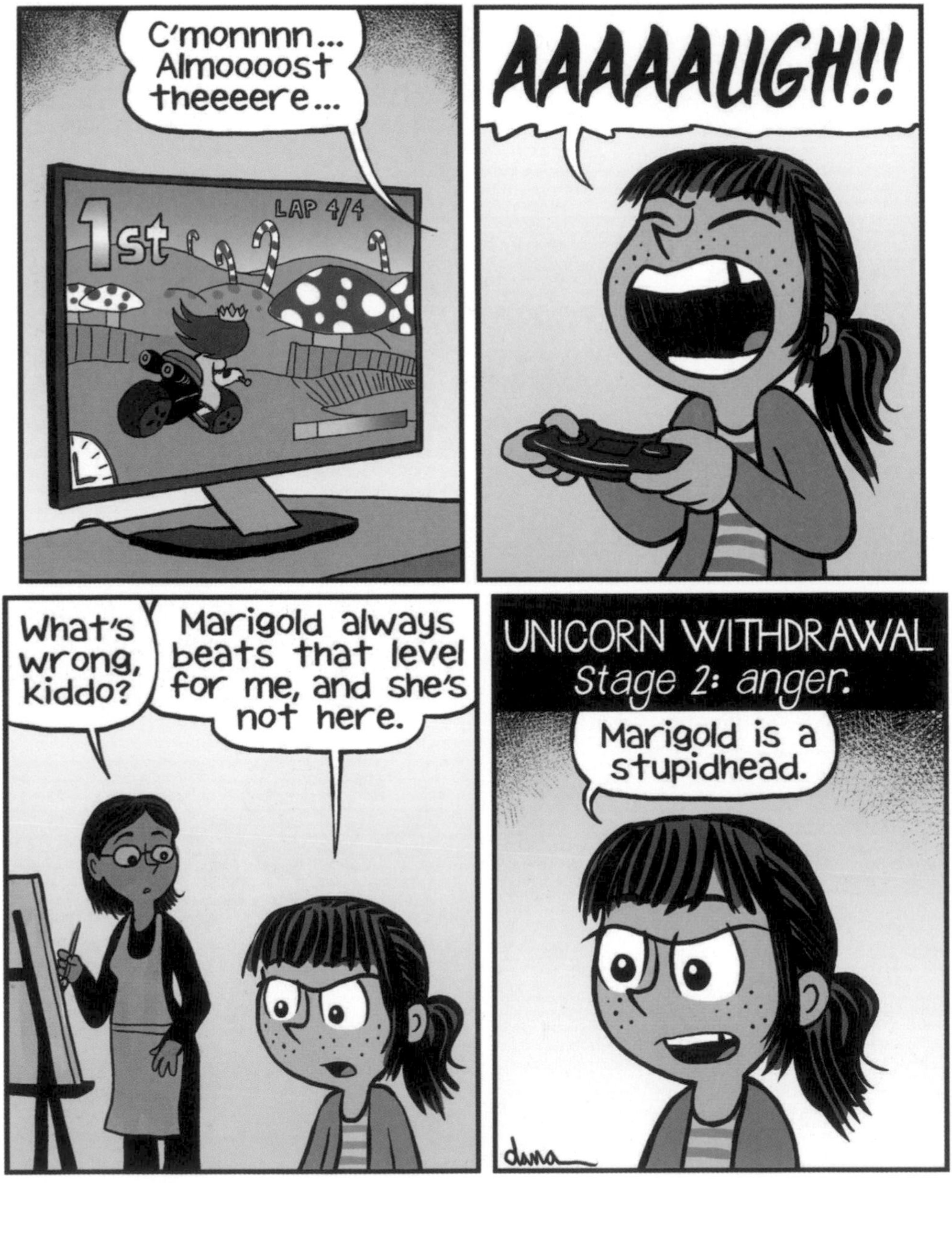
C'monnnn... Almoooost theeeere...
1st
LAP 4/4
AAAAAUGH!!
What's wrong, kiddo?
Marigold always beats that level for me, and she's not here.
UNICORN WITHDRAWAL
Stage 2: anger.
Marigold is a stupidhead.
dana

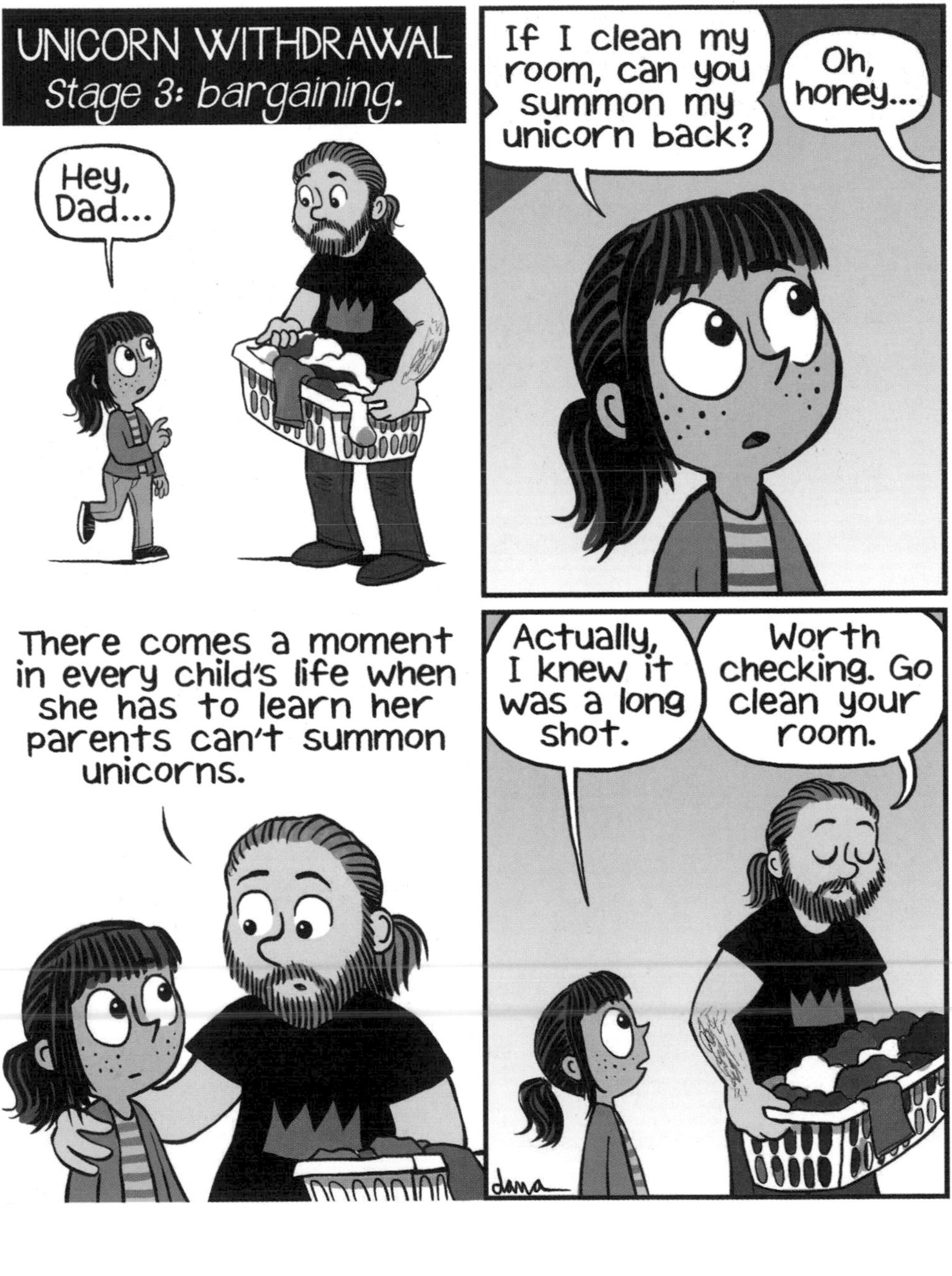
UNICORN WITHDRAWAL
Stage 3: bargaining.
Hey, Dad...
If I clean my room, can you summon my unicorn back?
Oh, honey...
There comes a moment in every child's life when she has to learn her parents can't summon unicorns.
Actually, I knew it was a long shot.
Worth checking. Go clean your room.
dana

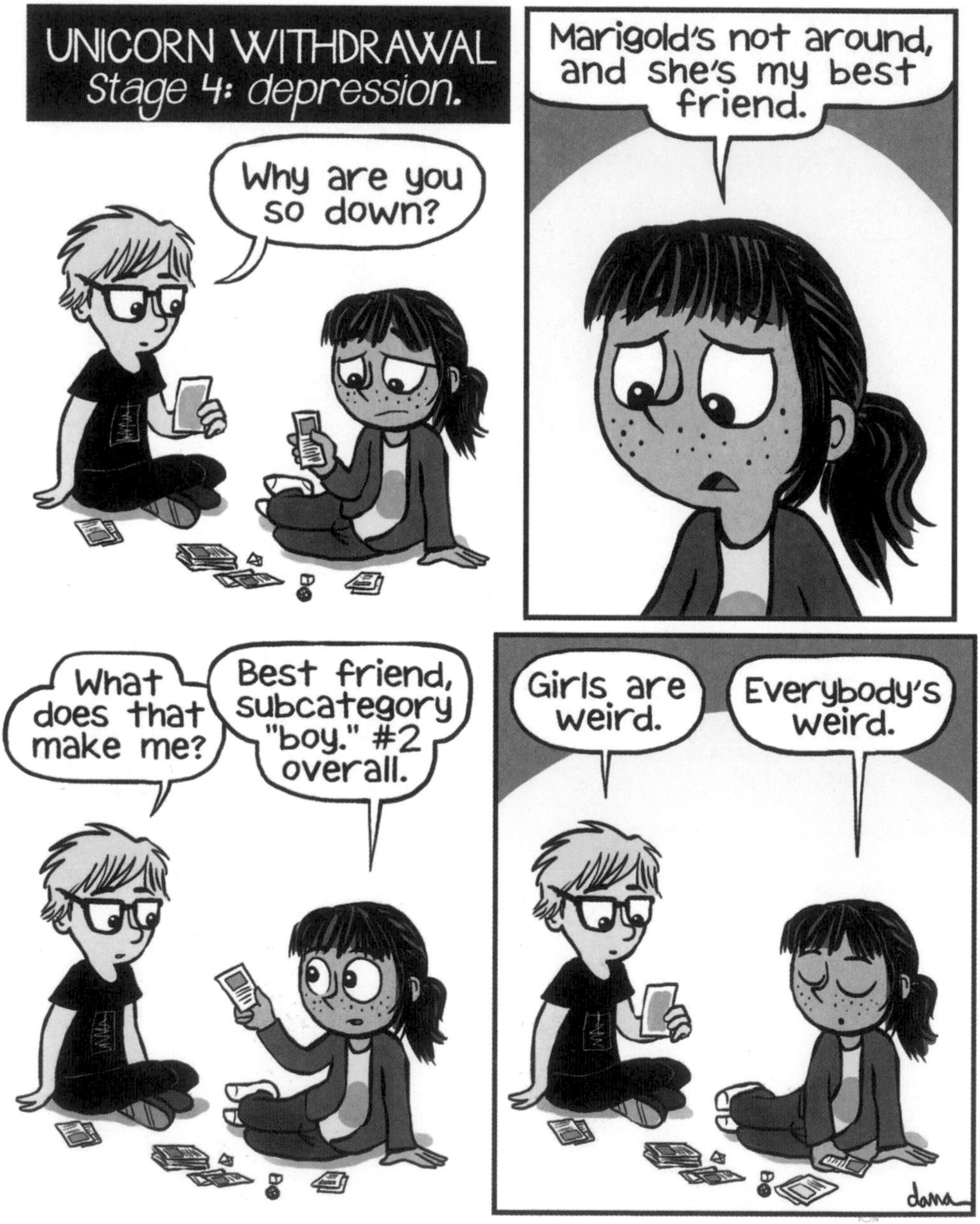
UNICORN WITHDRAWAL
Stage 4: depression.
Why are you so down?
Marigold's not around, and she's my best friend.
What does that make me?
Best friend, subcategory "boy." #2 overall.
Girls are weird.
Everybody's weird.
dana

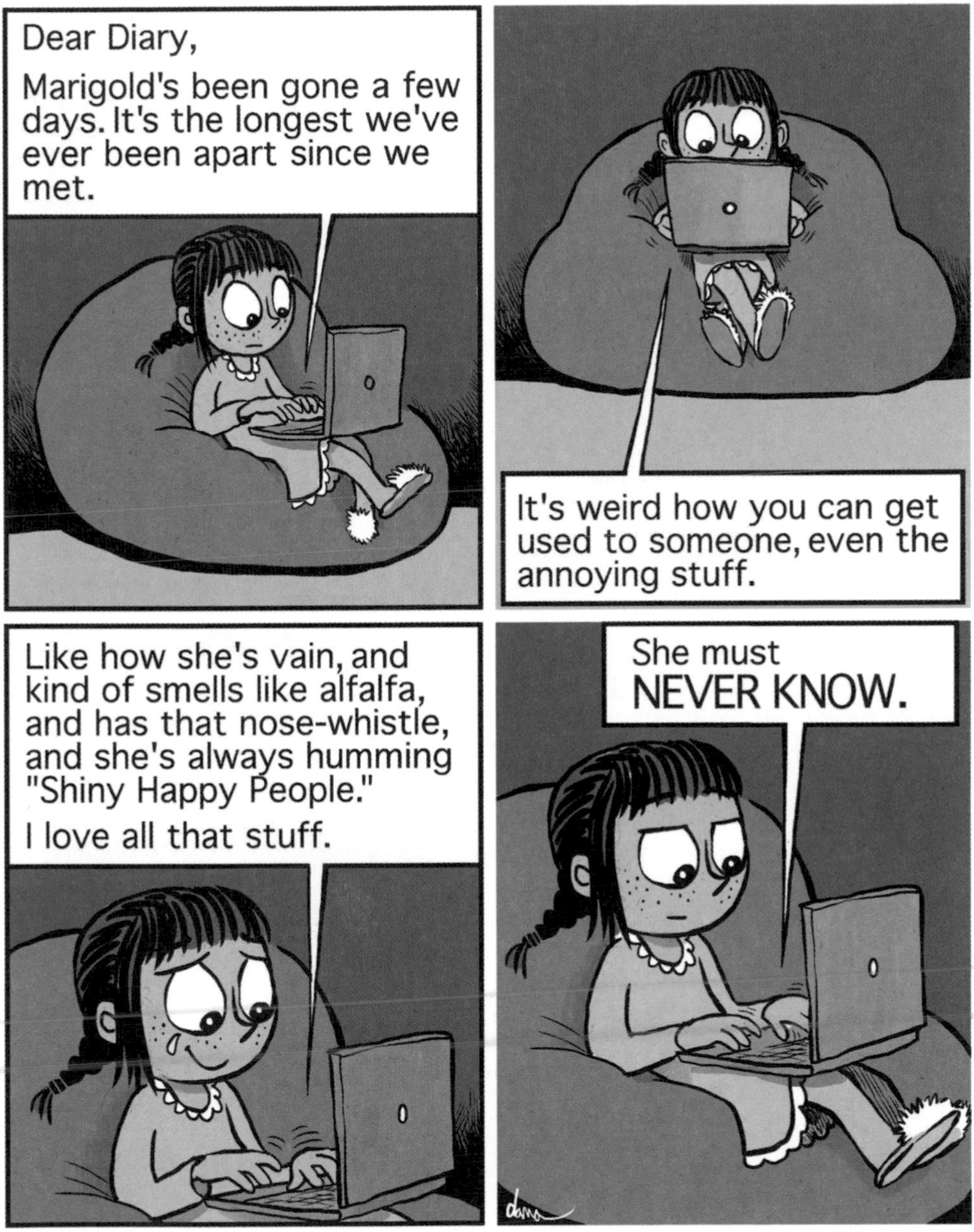
Dear Diary,
Marigold's been gone a few days. It's the longest we've ever been apart since we met.
It's weird how you can get used to someone, even the annoying stuff.
Like how she's vain, and kind of smells like alfalfa, and has that nose-whistle, and she's always humming "Shiny Happy People."
I love all that stuff.
She must NEVER KNOW.

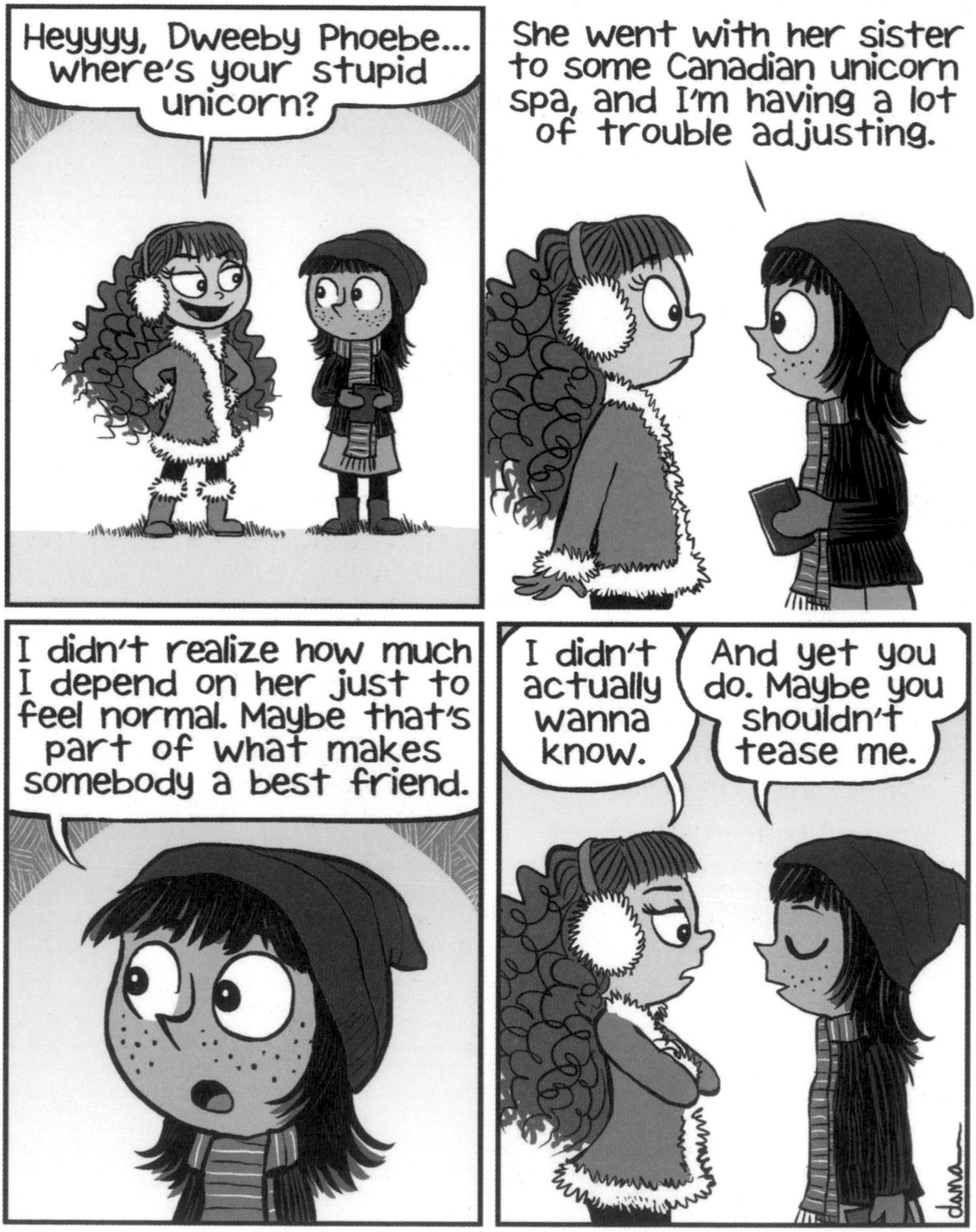
Heyyyy, Dweeby Phoebe... where's your stupid unicorn?
She went with her sister to some Canadian unicorn spa, and I'm having a lot of trouble adjusting.
I didn't realize how much I depend on her just to feel normal. Maybe that's part of what makes somebody a best friend.
I didn't actually wanna know.
And yet you do. Maybe you shouldn't tease me.
dana

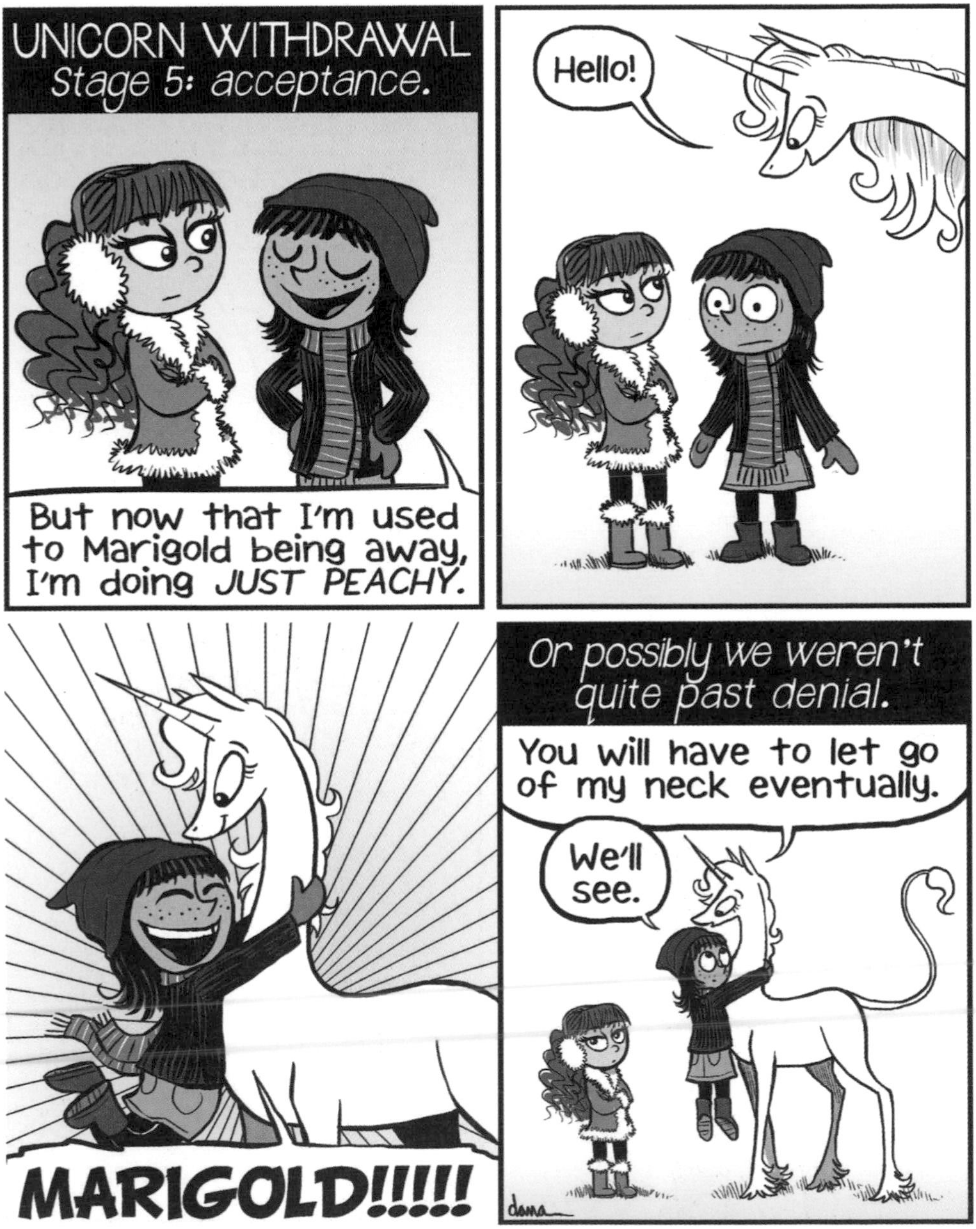
UNICORN WITHDRAWAL
Stage 5: acceptance.
But now that I'm used to Marigold being away, I'm doing JUST PEACHY.
Hello!
MARIGOLD!!!!!
Or possibly we weren't quite past denial.
You will have to let go of my neck eventually.
We'll see.
dana

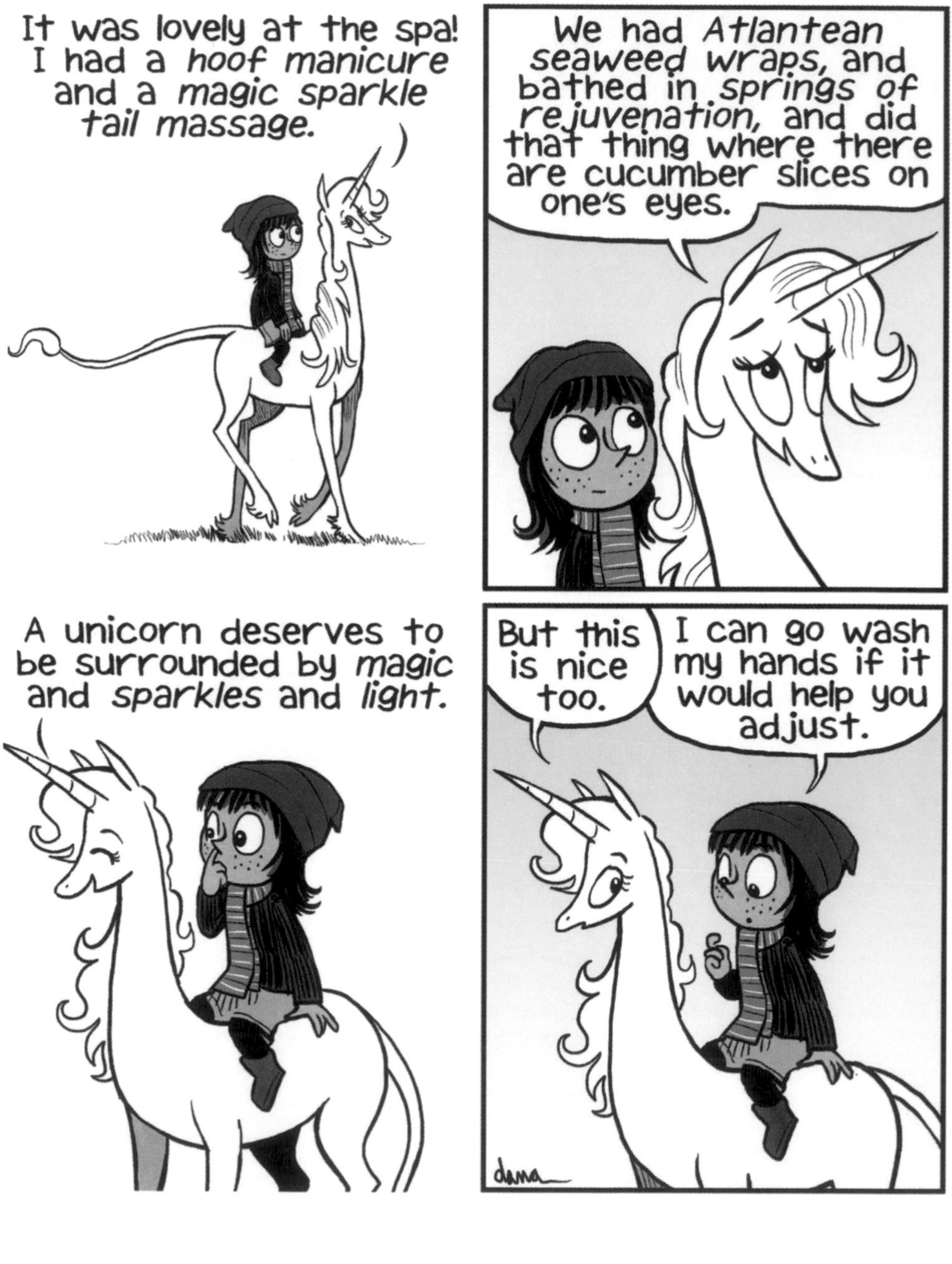

It was lovely at the spa! I had a *hoof manicure* and a *magic sparkle tail massage.*
We had *Atlantean seaweed wraps,* and bathed in *springs of rejuvenation,* and did that thing where there are cucumber slices on one's eyes.
A unicorn deserves to be surrounded by *magic* and *sparkles* and *light.*
But this is nice too.
I can go wash my hands if it would help you adjust.
dana

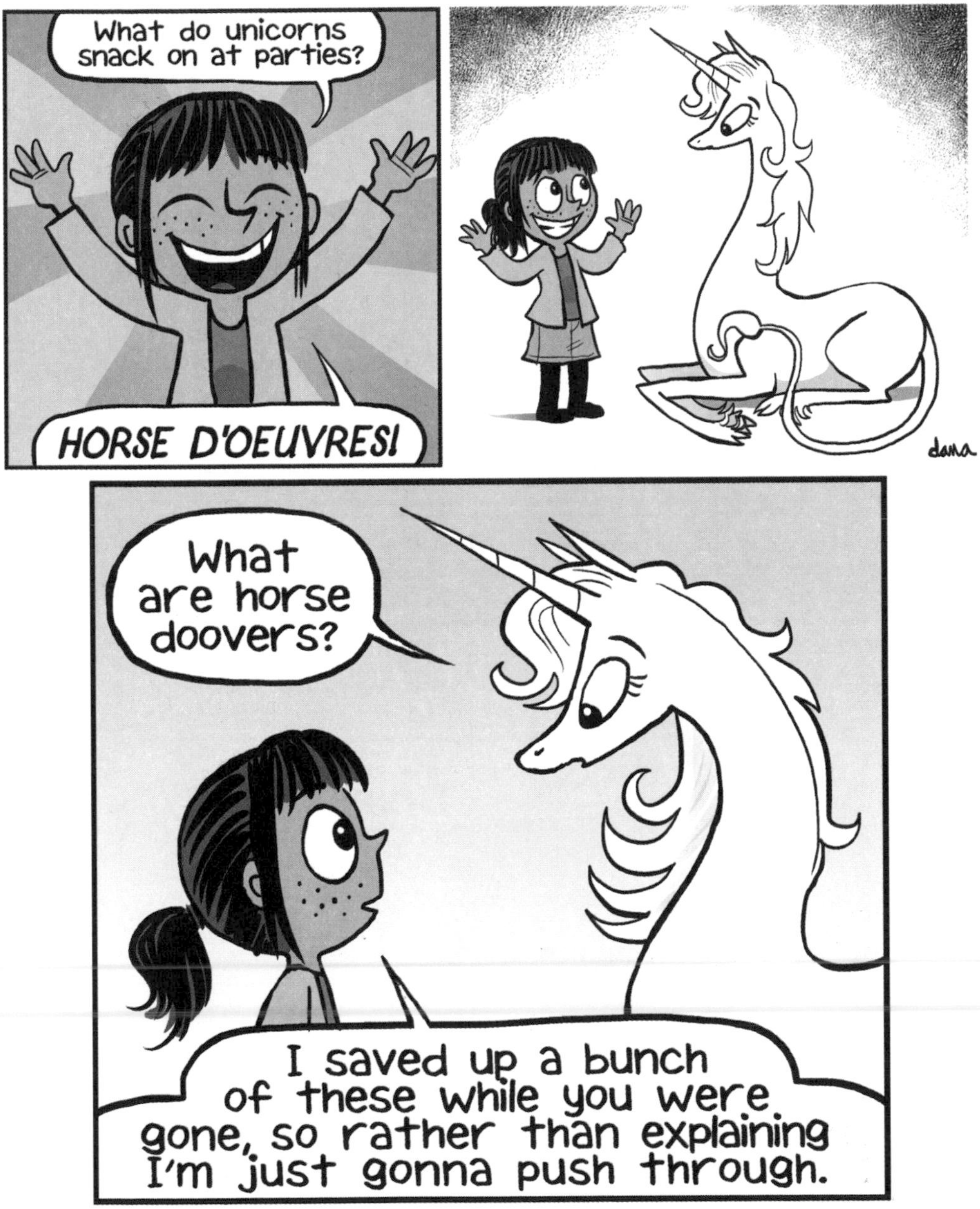
What do unicorns snack on at parties?
HORSE D'OEUVRES!
dana
What are horse doovers?
I saved up a bunch of these while you were gone, so rather than explaining I'm just gonna push through.

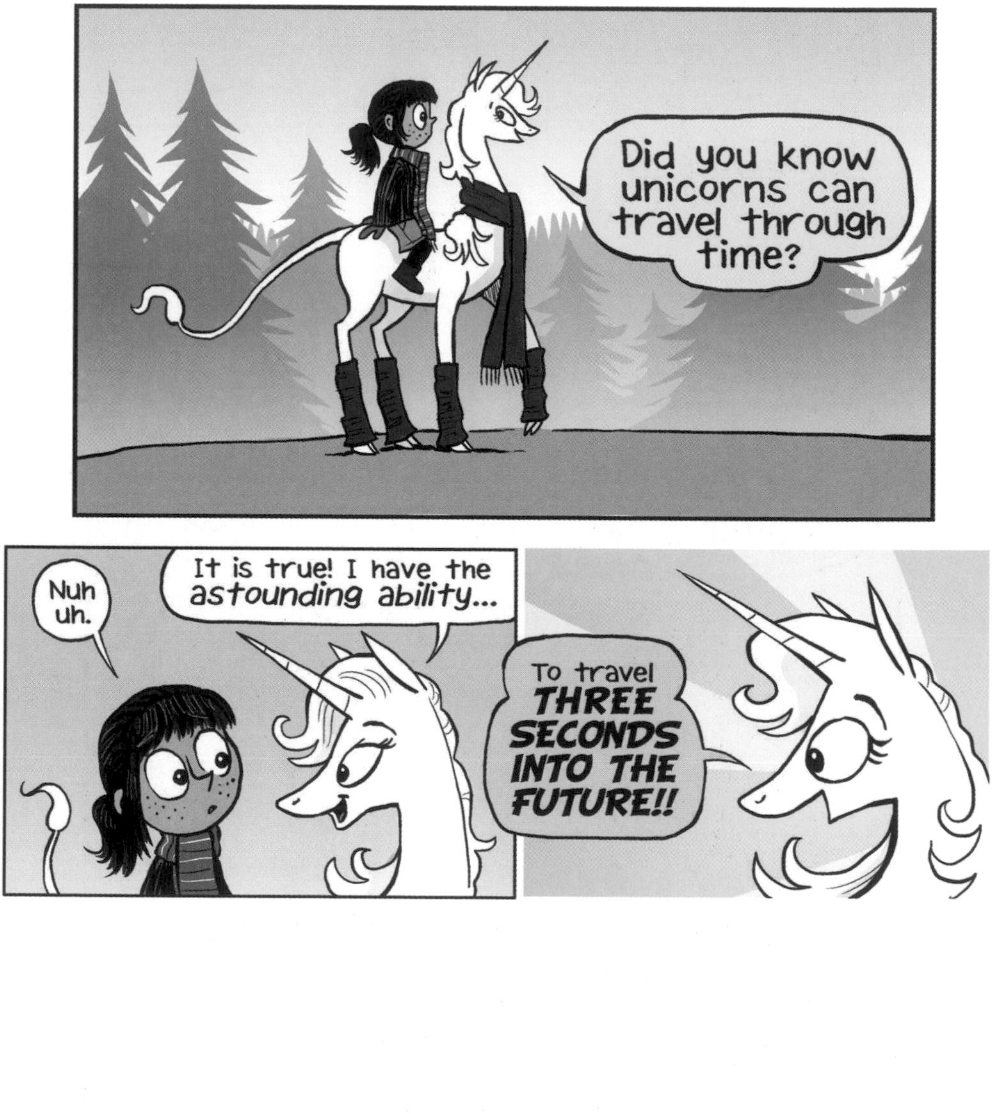
Did you know unicorns can travel through time?
Nuh uh.
It is true! I have the astounding ability...
To travel THREE SECONDS INTO THE FUTURE!!

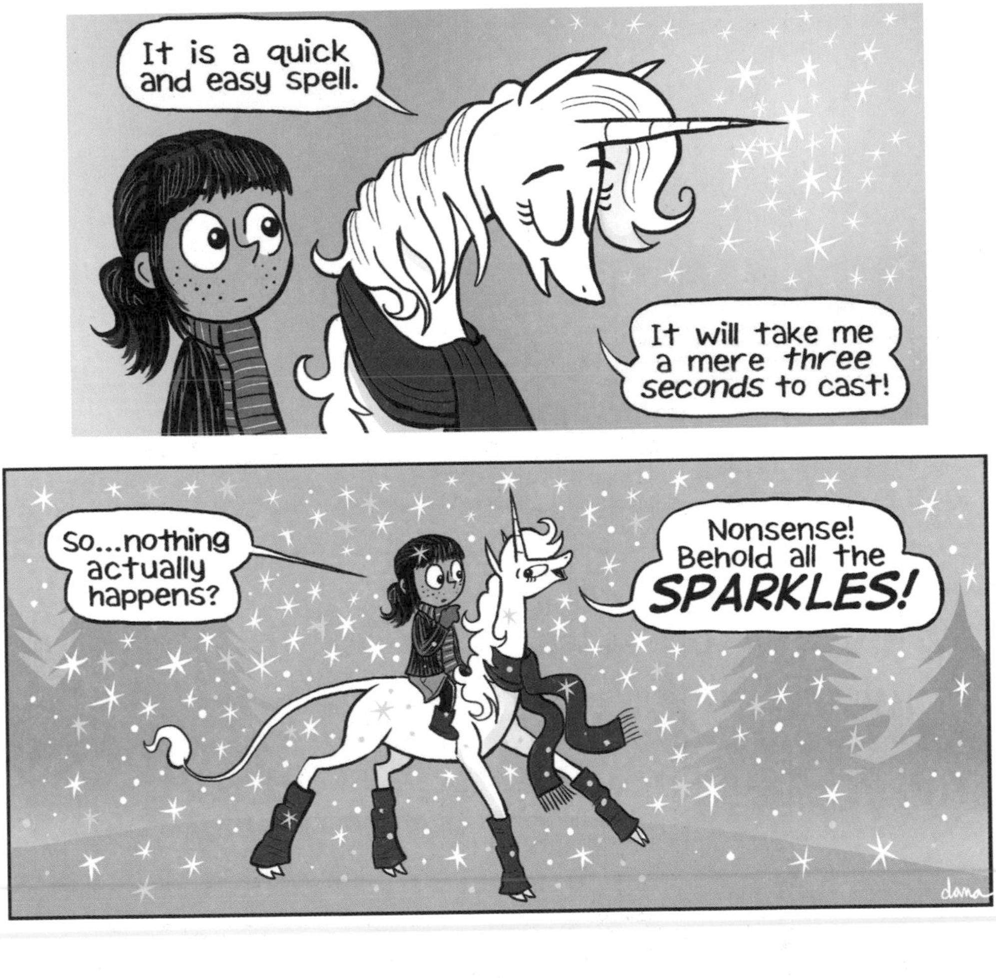
It is a quick and easy spell.
It will take me a mere *three seconds* to cast!
So...nothing actually happens?
Nonsense! Behold all the **SPARKLES!**
dana

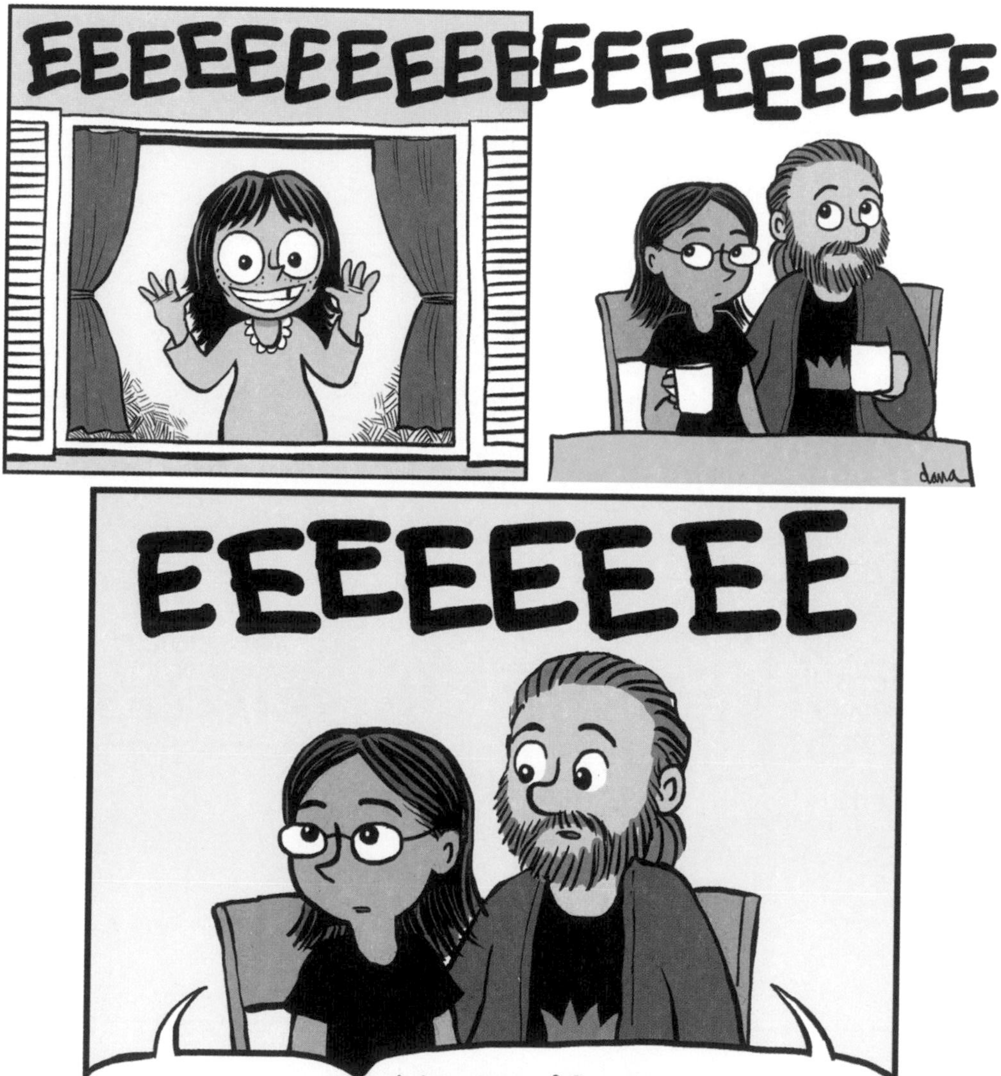
EEEEEEEEEEEEEEEEEEEEE
dana
EEEEEEEEE
I think she noticed it snowed.
Maybe if we put the school closings on the radio, she'll pause and take a breath.

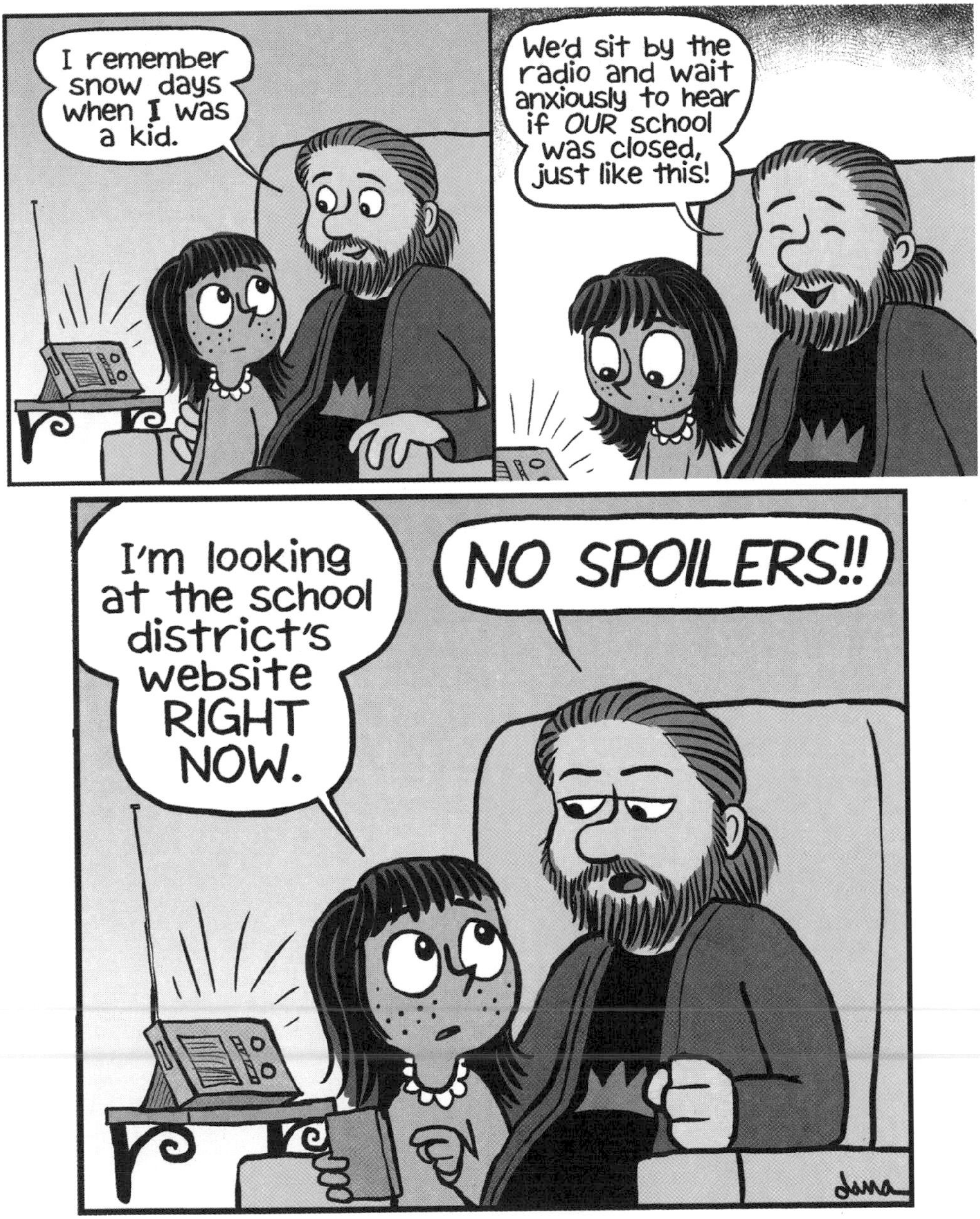
I remember snow days when I was a kid.
We'd sit by the radio and wait anxiously to hear if OUR school was closed, just like this!
I'm looking at the school district's website RIGHT NOW.
NO SPOILERS!!
dana

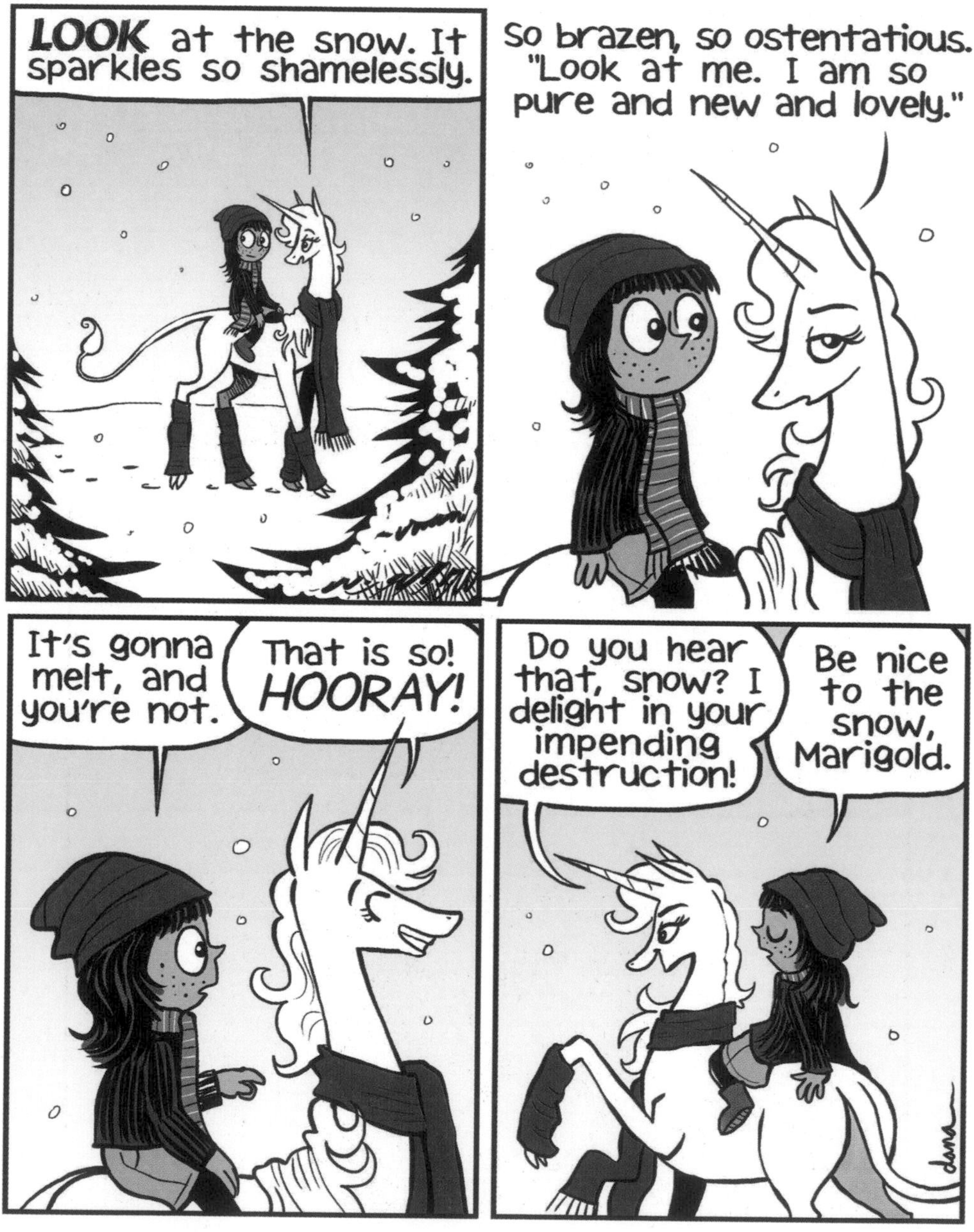
LOOK at the snow. It sparkles so shamelessly.
So brazen, so ostentatious. "Look at me. I am so pure and new and lovely."
It's gonna melt, and you're not.
That is so! HOORAY!
Do you hear that, snow? I delight in your impending destruction!
Be nice to the snow, Marigold.
dana

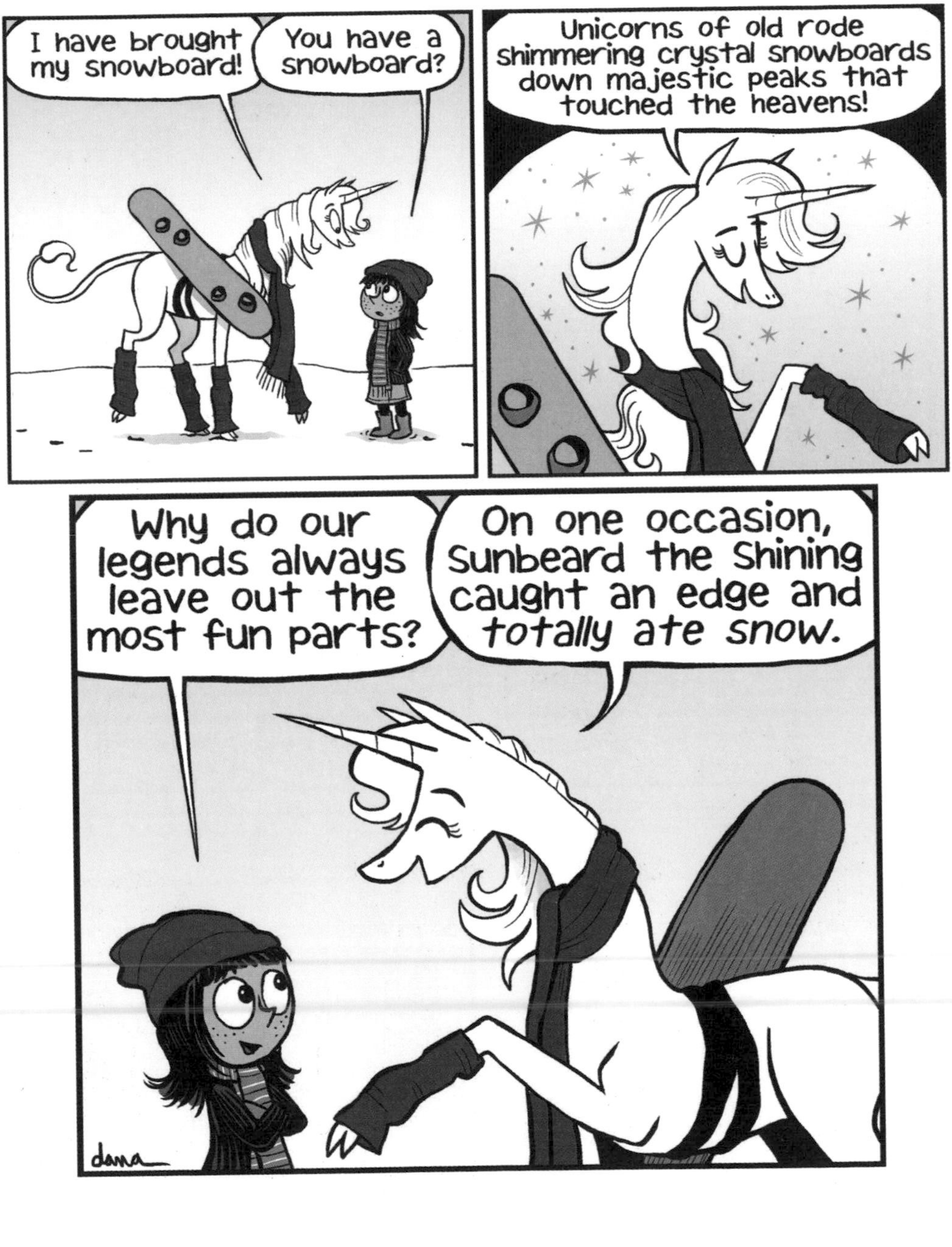
I have brought my snowboard!
You have a snowboard?
Unicorns of old rode shimmering crystal snowboards down majestic peaks that touched the heavens!
Why do our legends always leave out the most fun parts?
On one occasion, Sunbeard the Shining caught an edge and *totally* ate snow.
dana

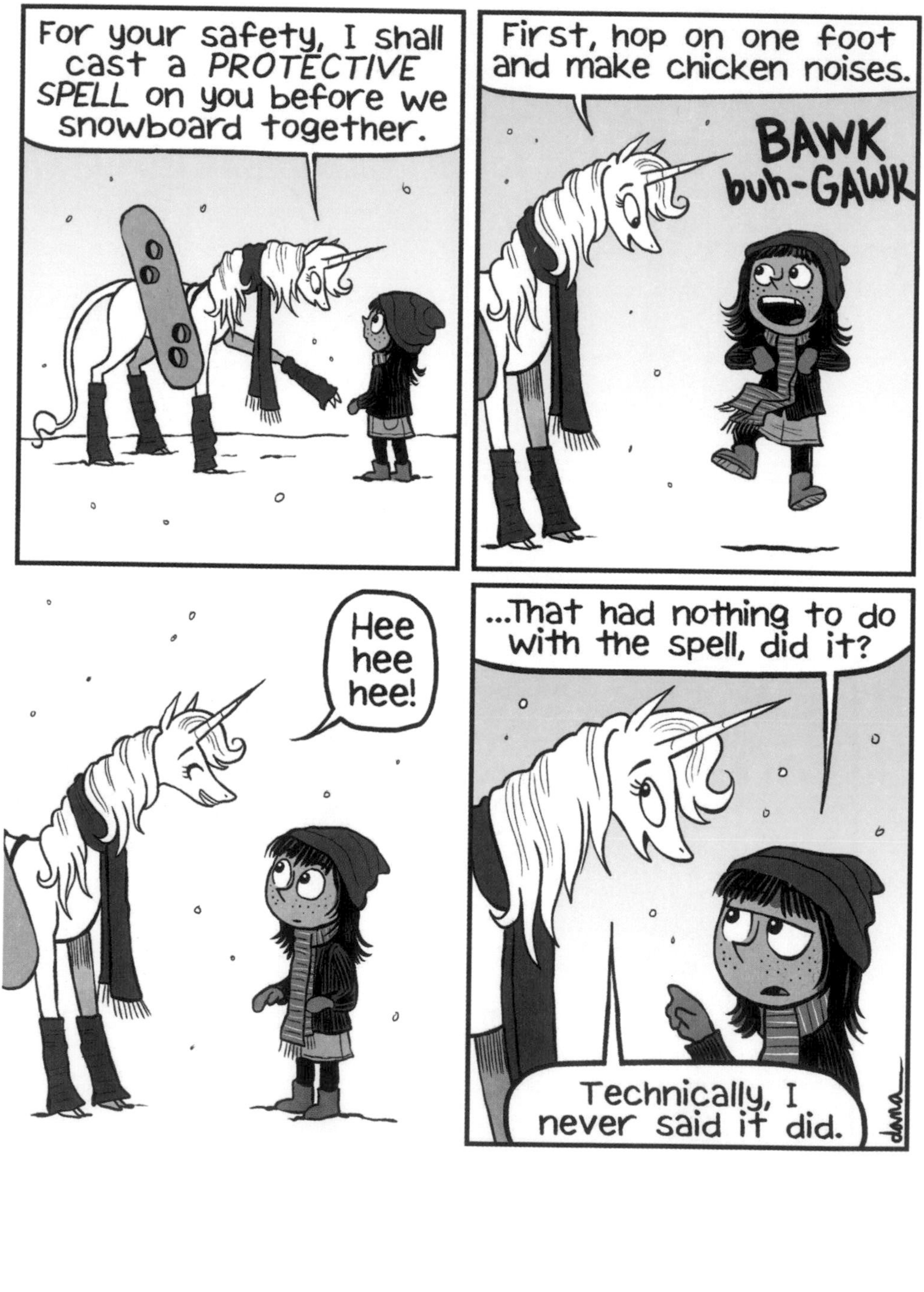
For your safety, I shall cast a *PROTECTIVE SPELL* on you before we snowboard together.
First, hop on one foot and make chicken noises.
BAWK buh-GAWK
Hee hee hee!
...That had nothing to do with the spell, did it?
Technically, I never said it did.
dana

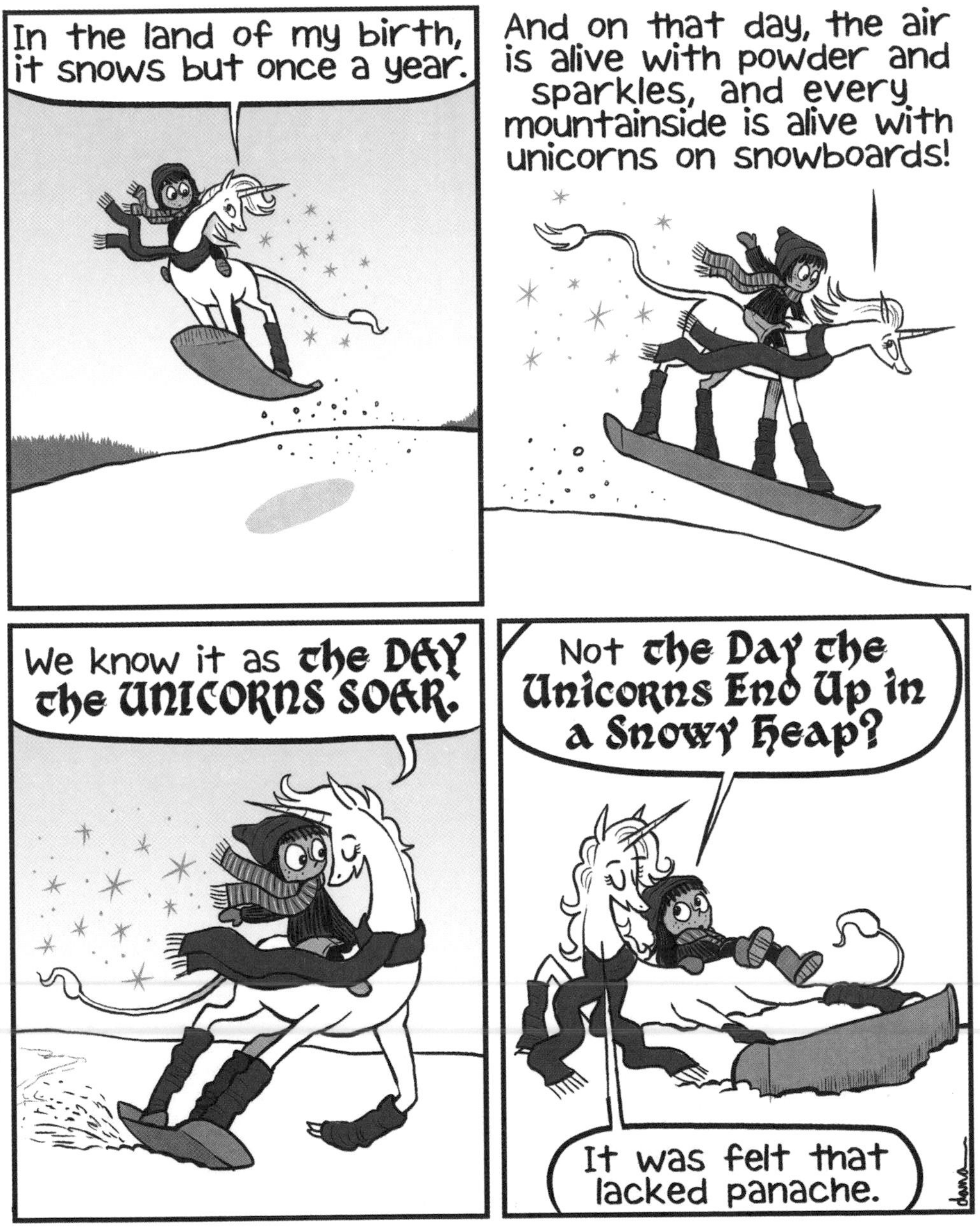
In the land of my birth, it snows but once a year.
And on that day, the air is alive with powder and sparkles, and every mountainside is alive with unicorns on snowboards!
We know it as the DAY the UNICORNS SOAR.
Not the Day the Unicorns End Up in a Snowy Heap?
It was felt that lacked panache.
dana

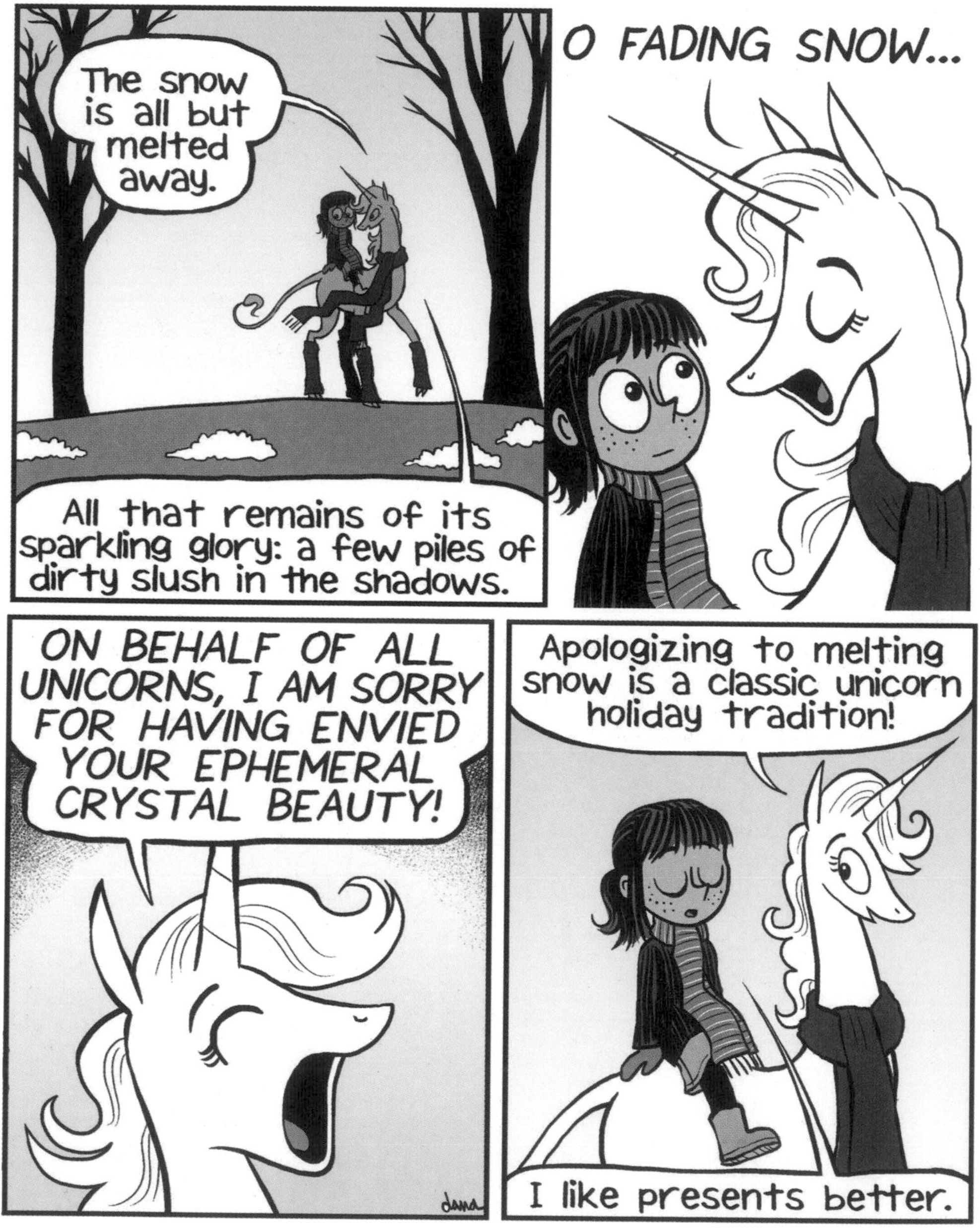

The snow is all but melted away.
All that remains of its sparkling glory: a few piles of dirty slush in the shadows.
O FADING SNOW...
ON BEHALF OF ALL UNICORNS, I AM SORRY FOR HAVING ENVIED YOUR EPHEMERAL CRYSTAL BEAUTY!
Apologizing to melting snow is a classic unicorn holiday tradition!
I like presents better.
dana

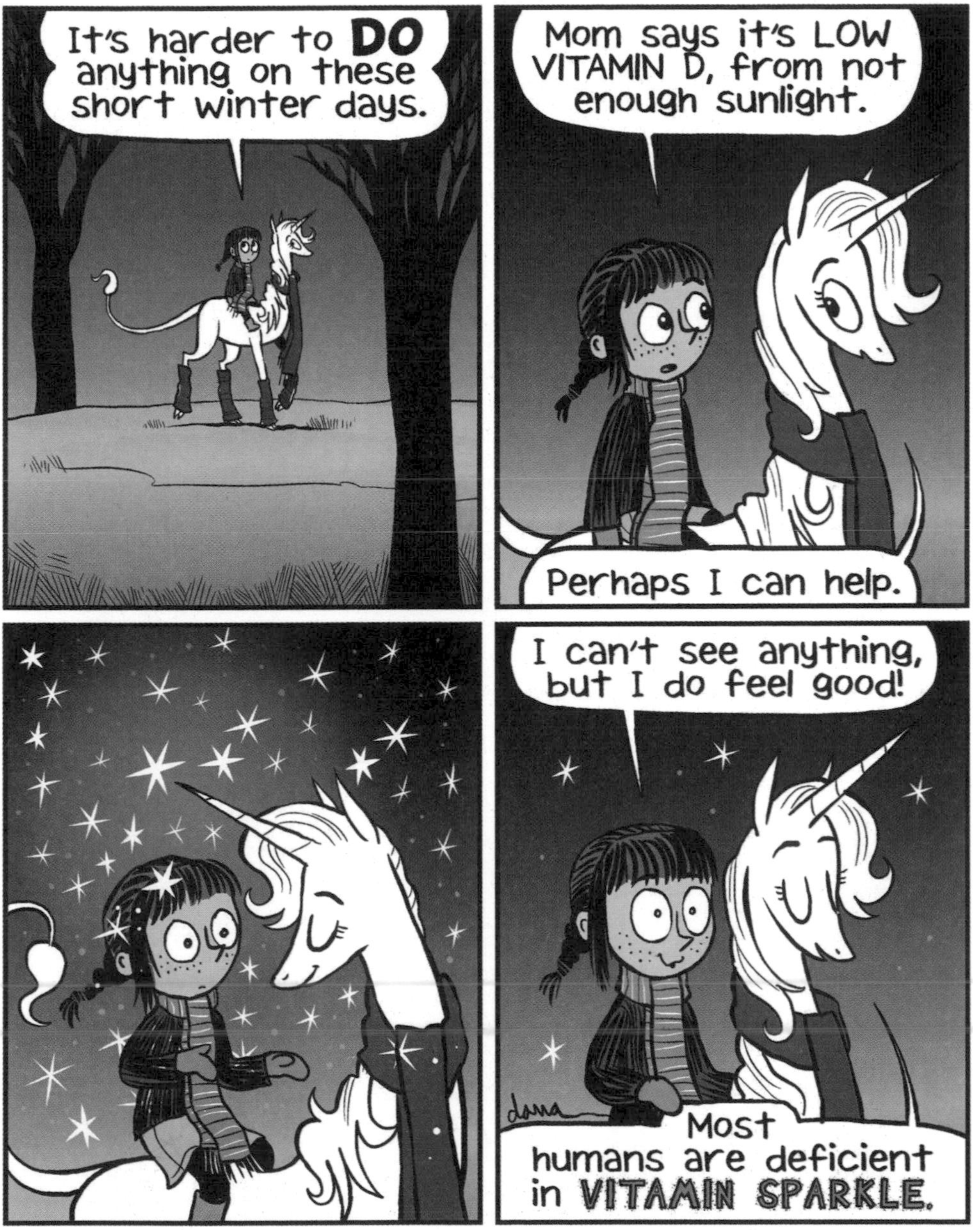
It's harder to DO anything on these short winter days.
Mom says it's LOW VITAMIN D, from not enough sunlight.
Perhaps I can help.
I can't see anything, but I do feel good!
dana
Most humans are deficient in VITAMIN SPARKLE.

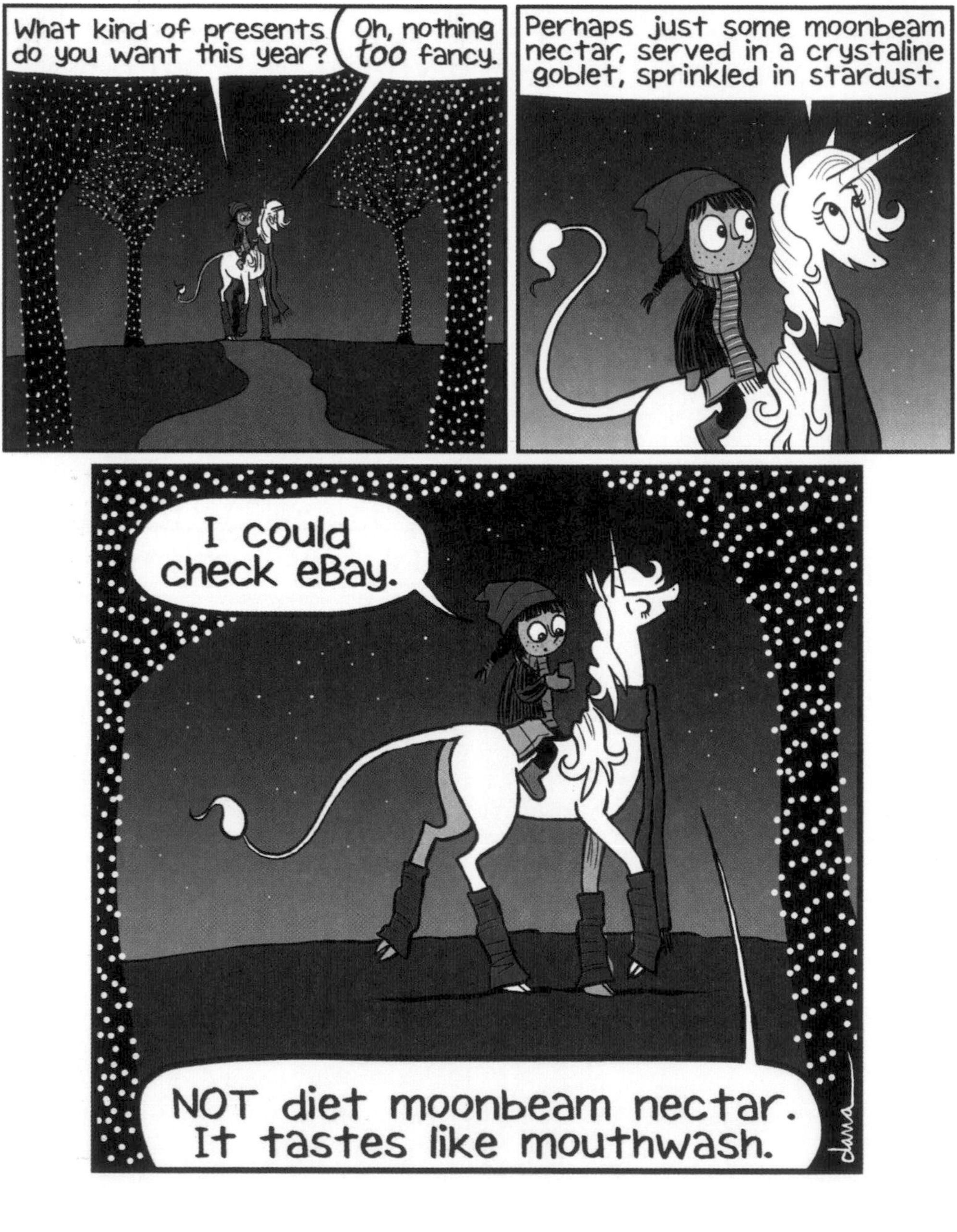
What kind of presents do you want this year?
Oh, nothing too fancy.
Perhaps just some moonbeam nectar, served in a crystaline goblet, sprinkled in stardust.
I could check eBay.
NOT diet moonbeam nectar. It tastes like mouthwash.
dana

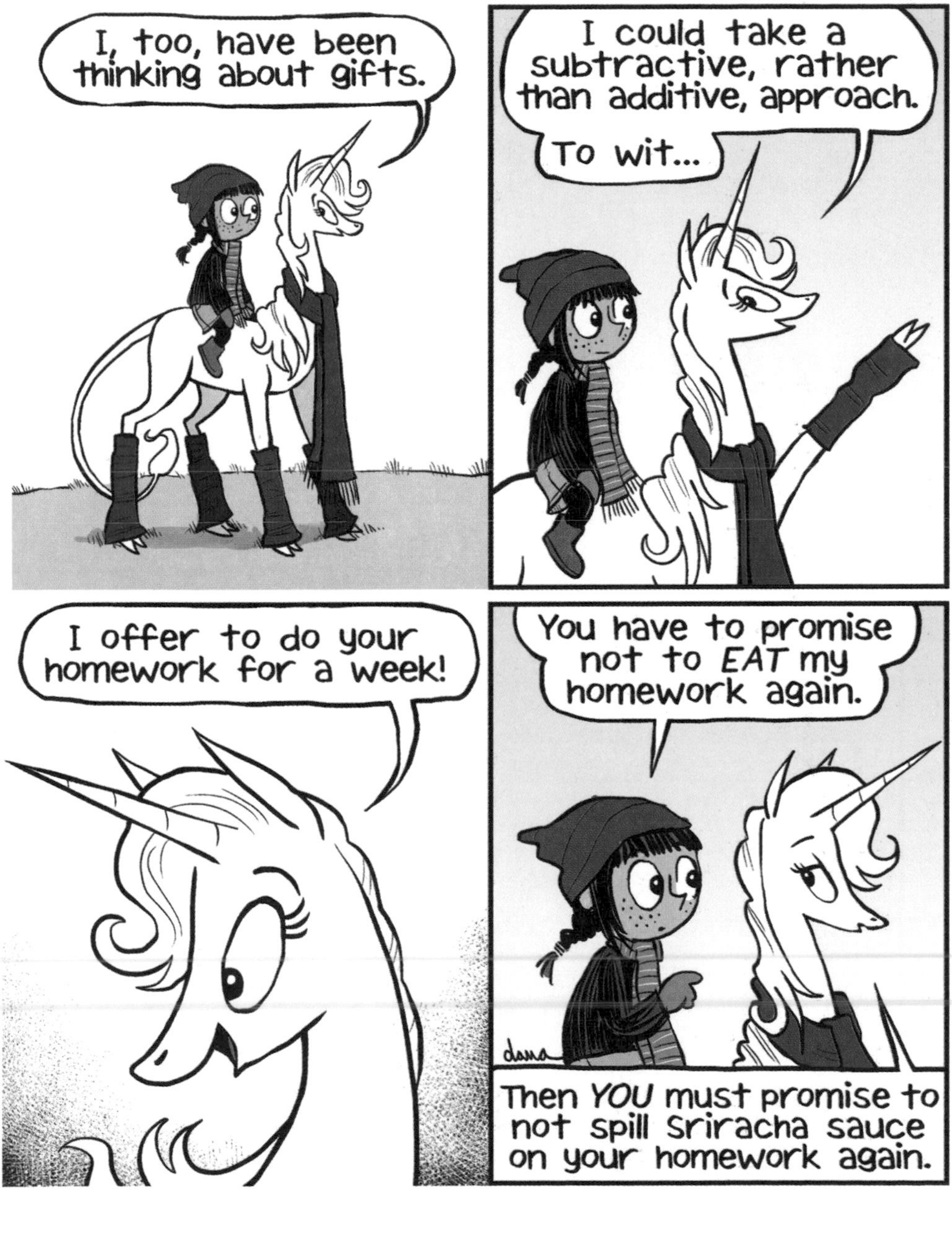
I, too, have been thinking about gifts.
I could take a subtractive, rather than additive, approach.
To wit...
I offer to do your homework for a week!
You have to promise not to *EAT* my homework again.
dana
Then *YOU* must promise to not spill Sriracha sauce on your homework again.

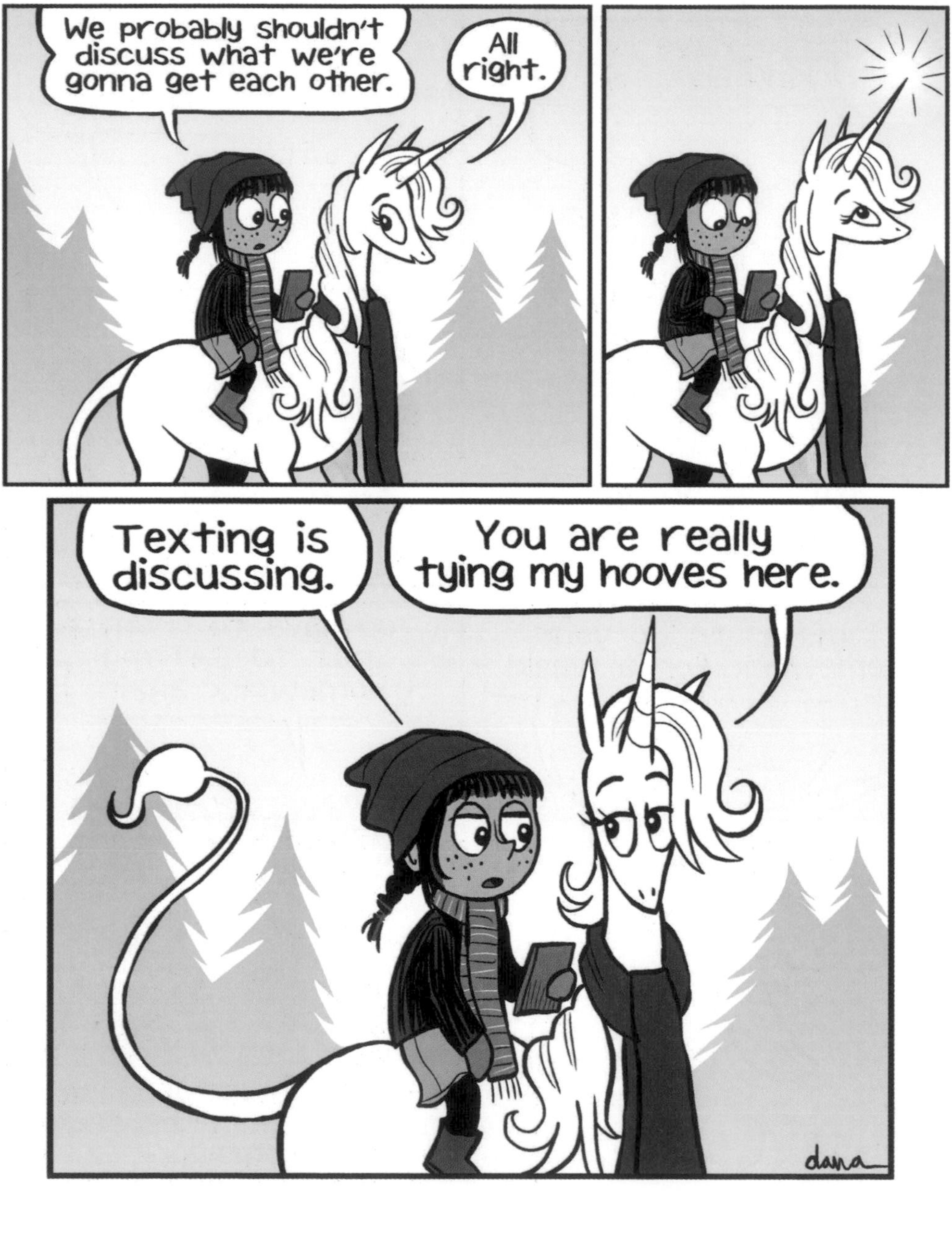
We probably shouldn't discuss what we're gonna get each other.
All right.
Texting is discussing.
You are really tying my hooves here.
dana

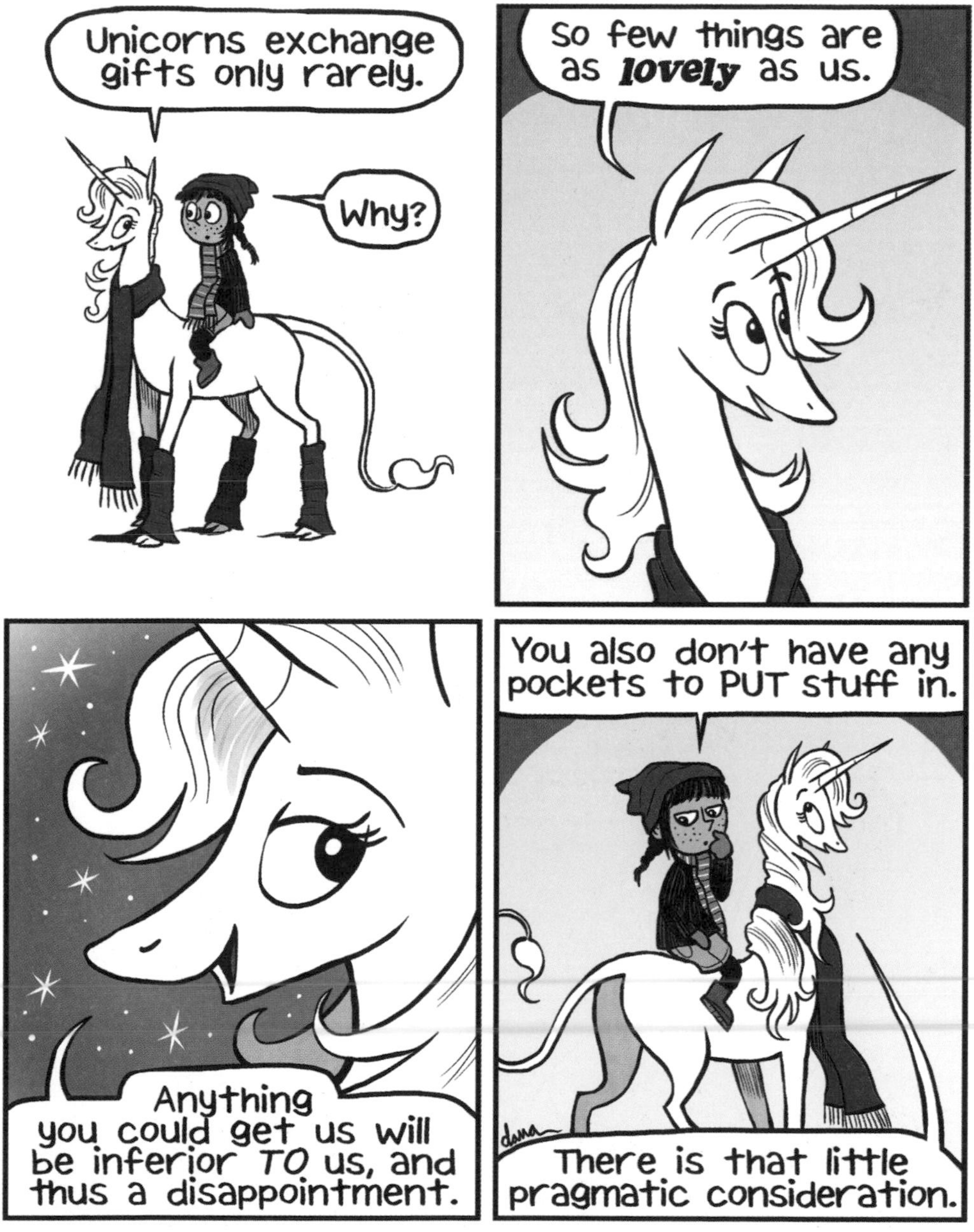

Unicorns exchange gifts only rarely.
Why?
So few things are as **lovely** as us.
Anything you could get us will be inferior *TO* us, and thus a disappointment.
You also don't have any pockets to PUT stuff in.
There is that little pragmatic consideration.

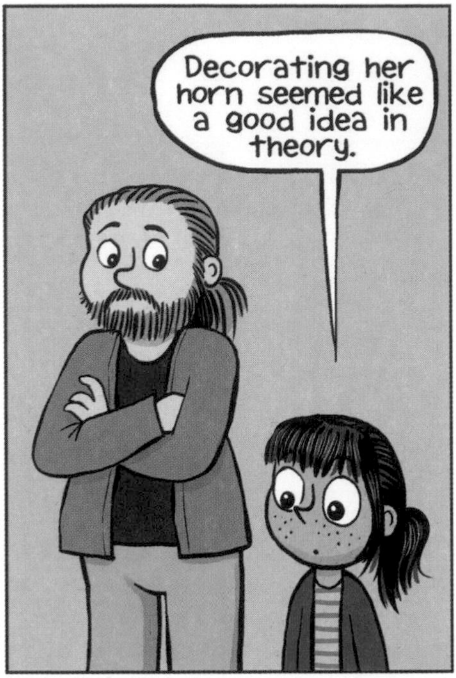
Decorating her horn seemed like a good idea in theory.

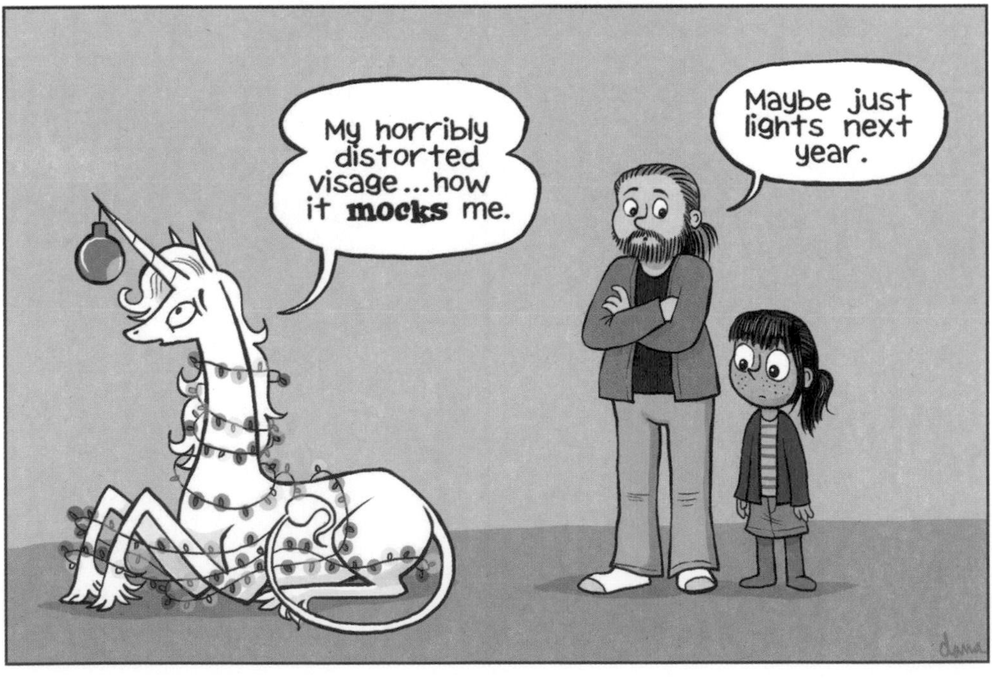
My horribly distorted visage...how it **mocks** me.
Maybe just lights next year.

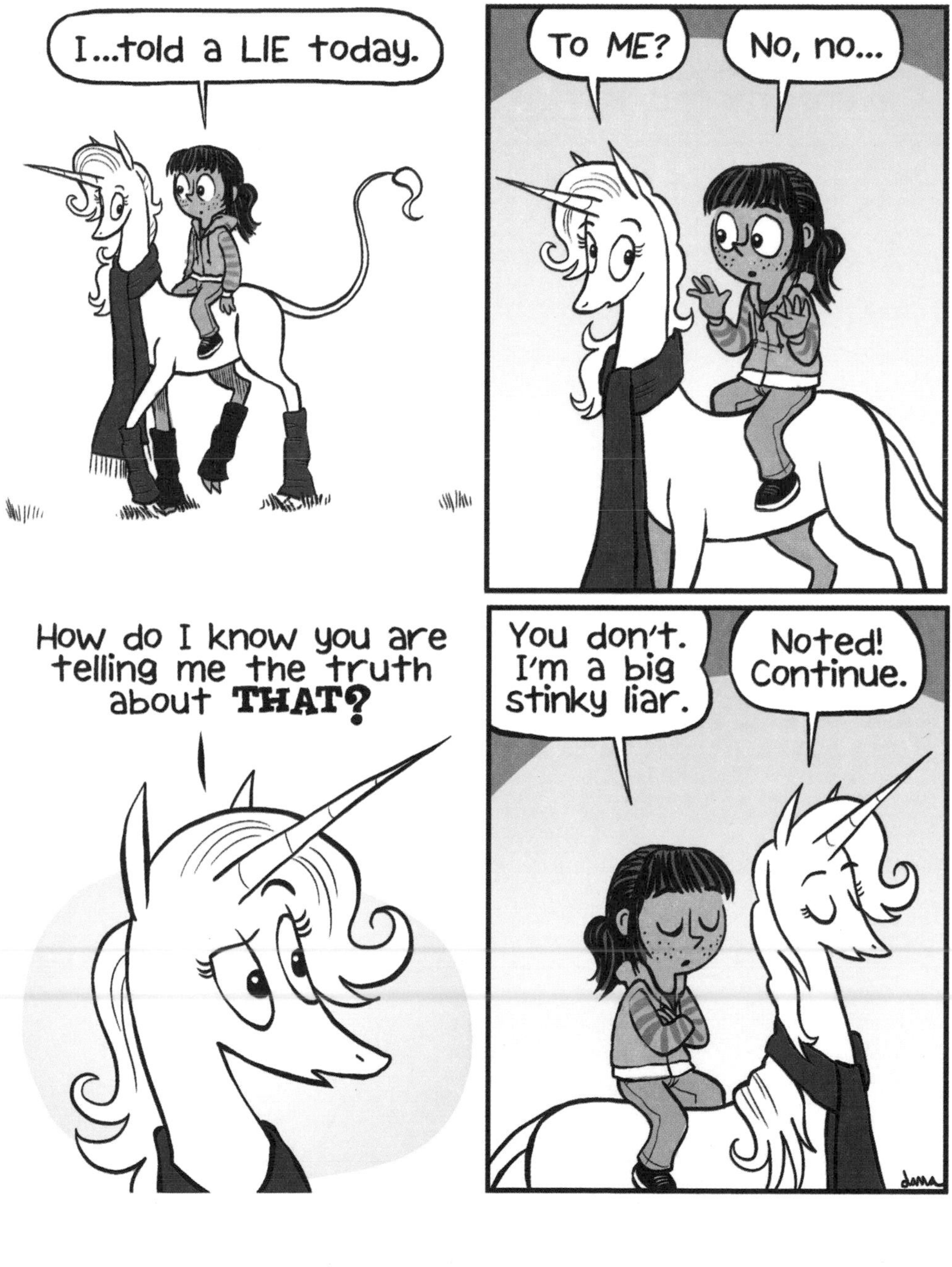
I...told a LIE today.
To ME?
No, no...
How do I know you are telling me the truth about THAT?
You don't. I'm a big stinky liar.
Noted! Continue.

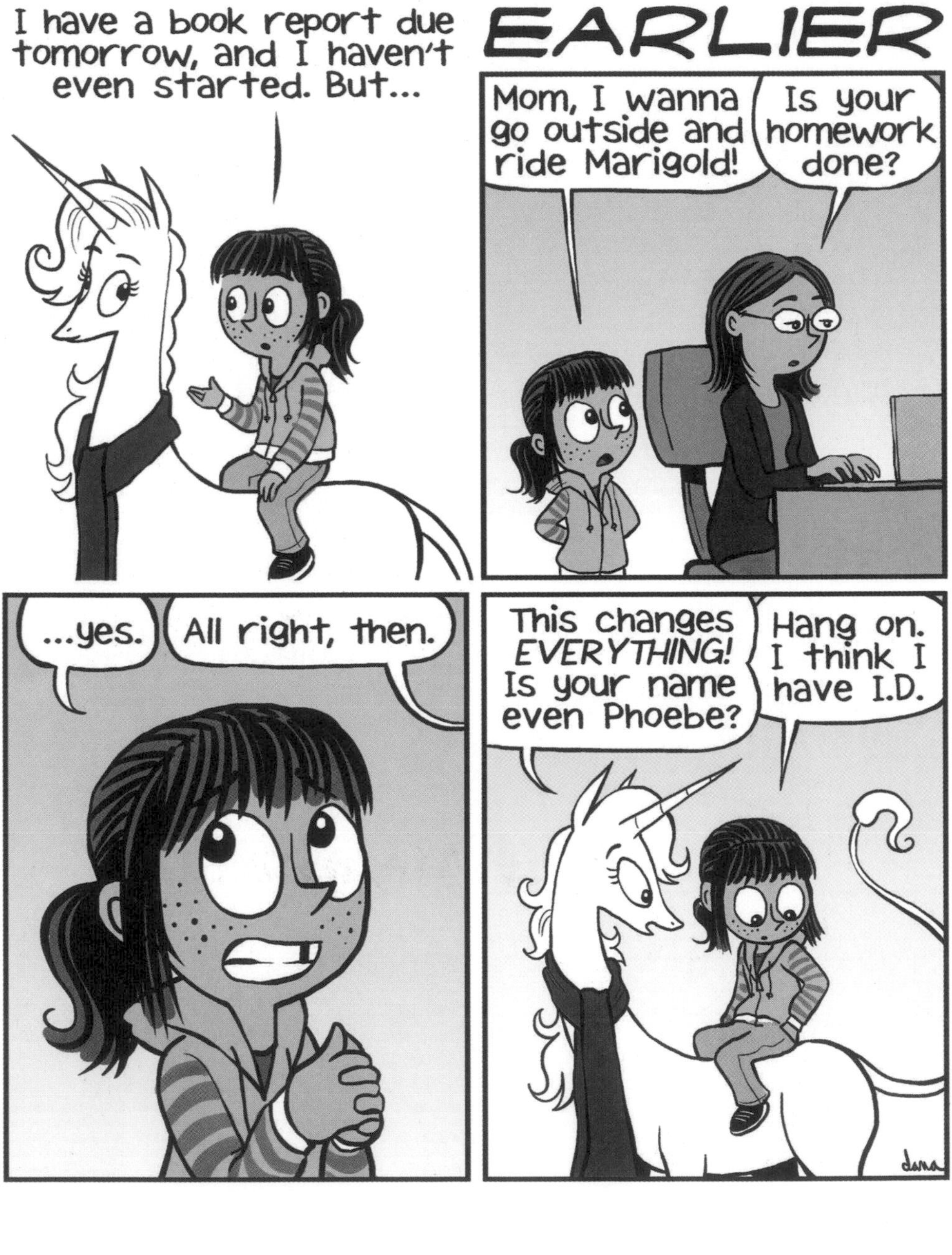

I have a book report due tomorrow, and I haven't even started. But...
EARLIER
Mom, I wanna go outside and ride Marigold!
Is your homework done?
...yes.
All right, then.
This changes *EVERYTHING!* Is your name even Phoebe?
Hang on. I think I have I.D.
dana

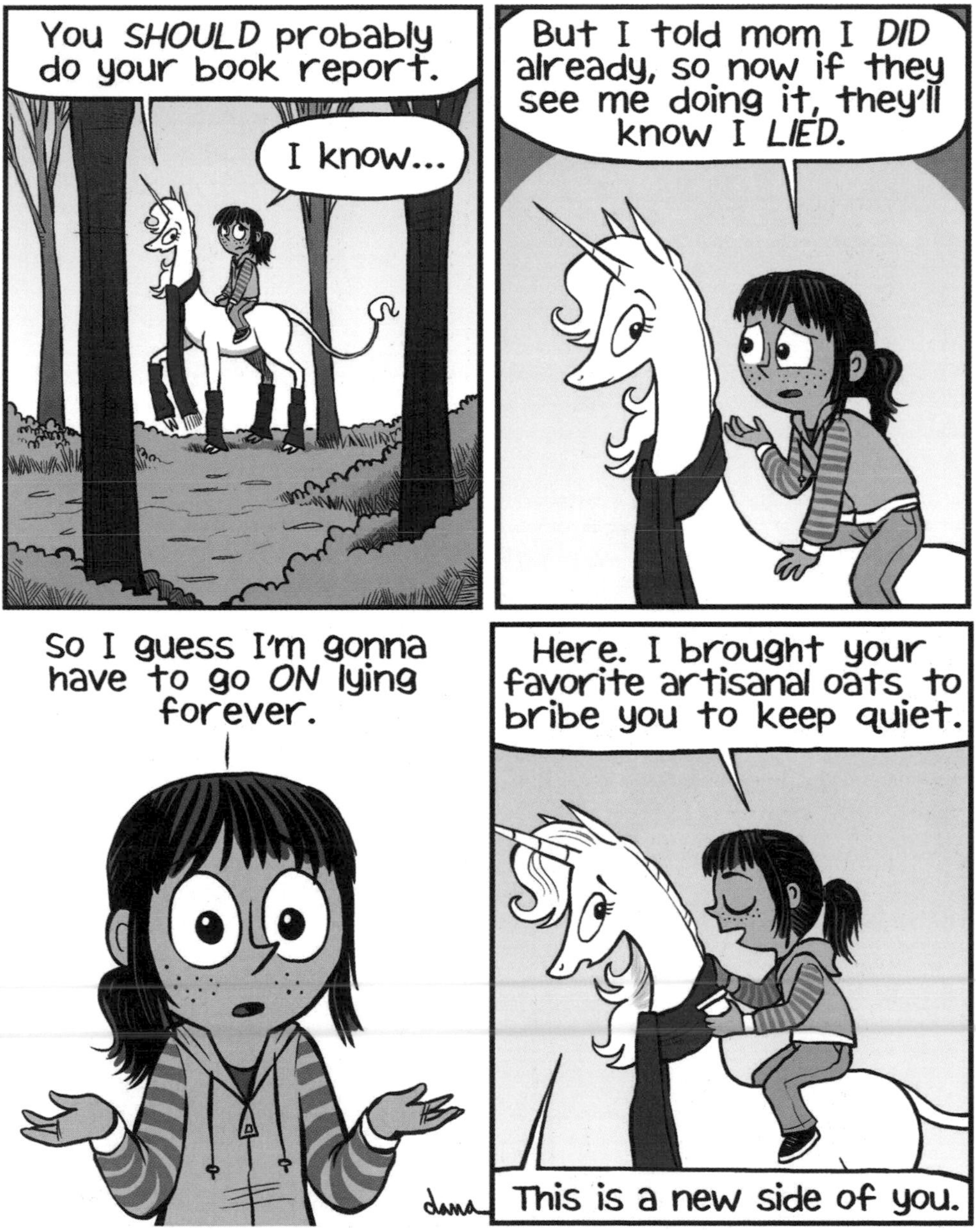
You SHOULD probably do your book report.
I know...
But I told mom I DID already, so now if they see me doing it, they'll know I LIED.
So I guess I'm gonna have to go ON lying forever.
Here. I brought your favorite artisanal oats to bribe you to keep quiet.
This is a new side of you.
dana

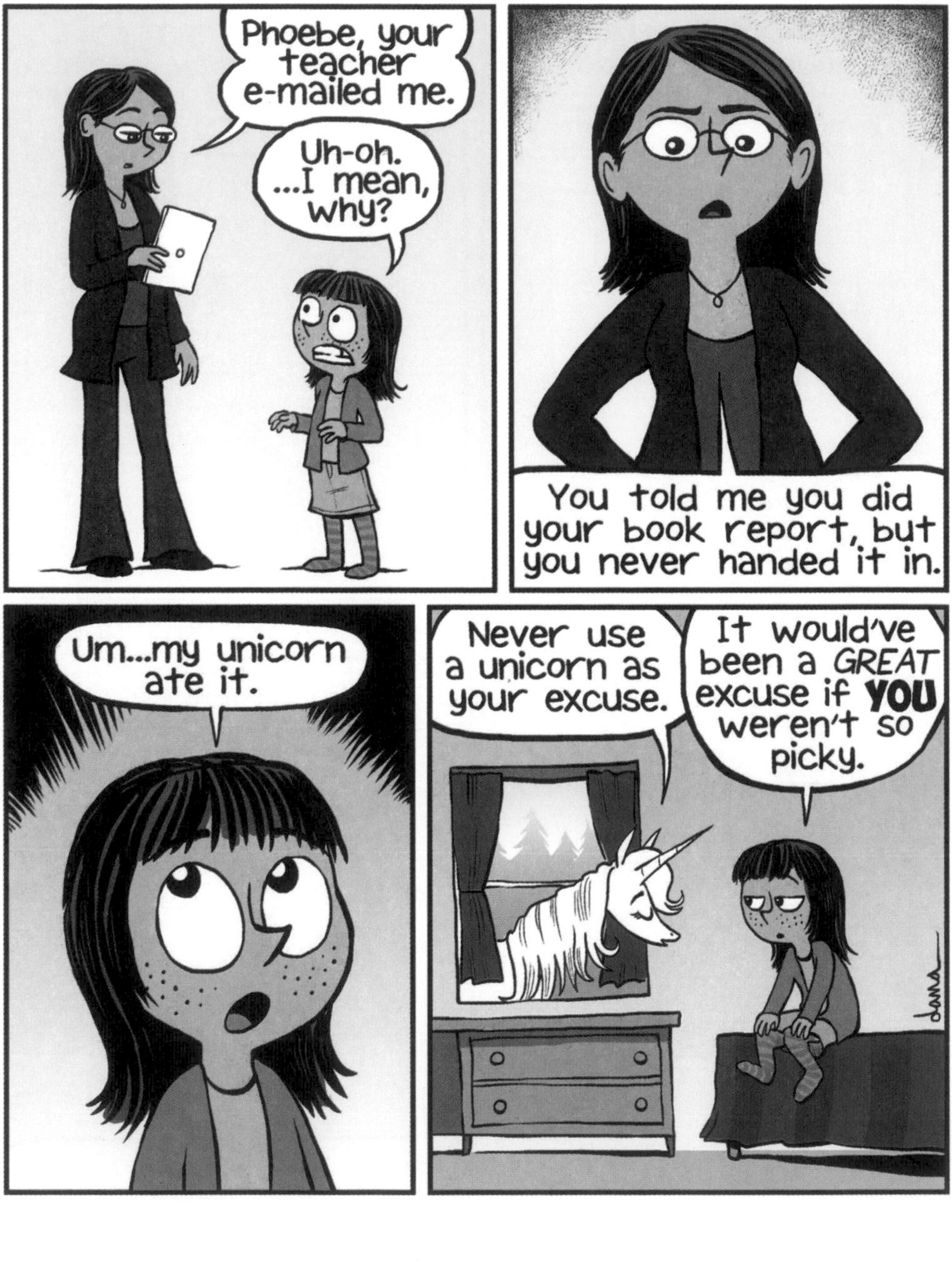
Phoebe, your teacher e-mailed me.
Uh-oh. ...I mean, why?
You told me you did your book report, but you never handed it in.
Um...my unicorn ate it.
Never use a unicorn as your excuse.
It would've been a GREAT excuse if YOU weren't so picky.
dana

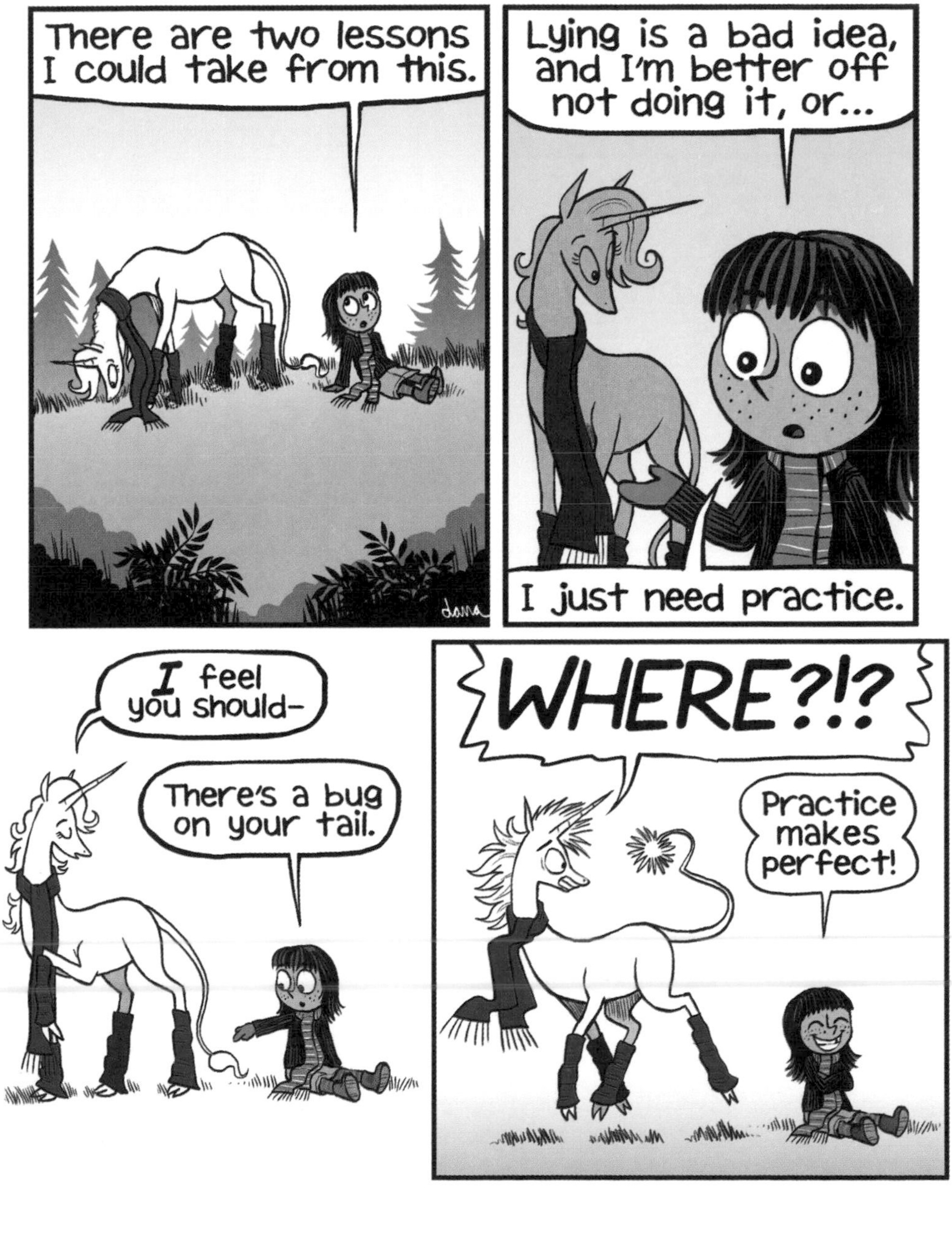

There are two lessons I could take from this.
Lying is a bad idea, and I'm better off not doing it, or...
I just need practice.
dana
I feel you should-
There's a bug on your tail.
WHERE?!?
Practice makes perfect!

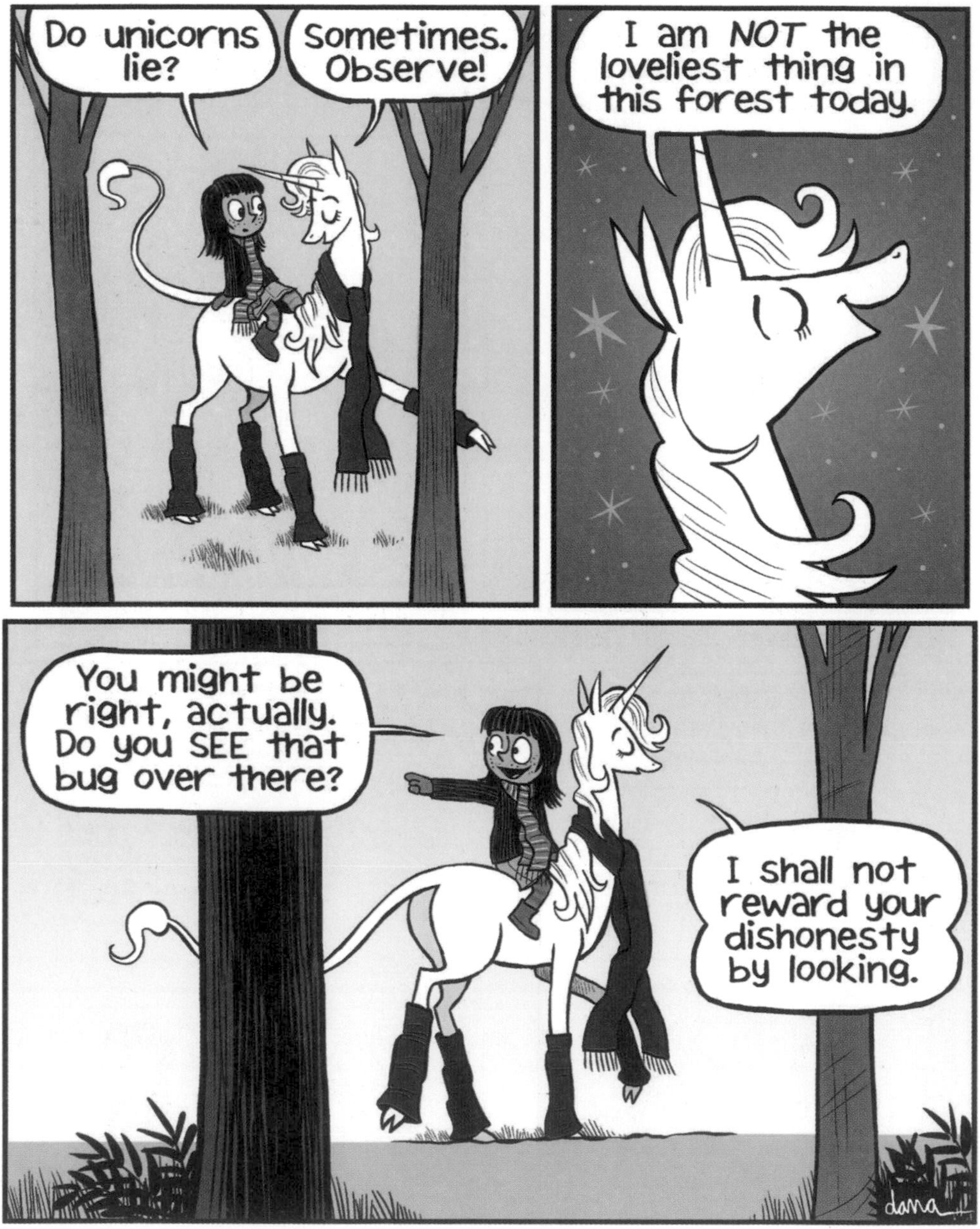
Do unicorns lie?
Sometimes. Observe!
I am *NOT* the loveliest thing in this forest today.
You might be right, actually. Do you SEE that bug over there?
I shall not reward your dishonesty by looking.
dana

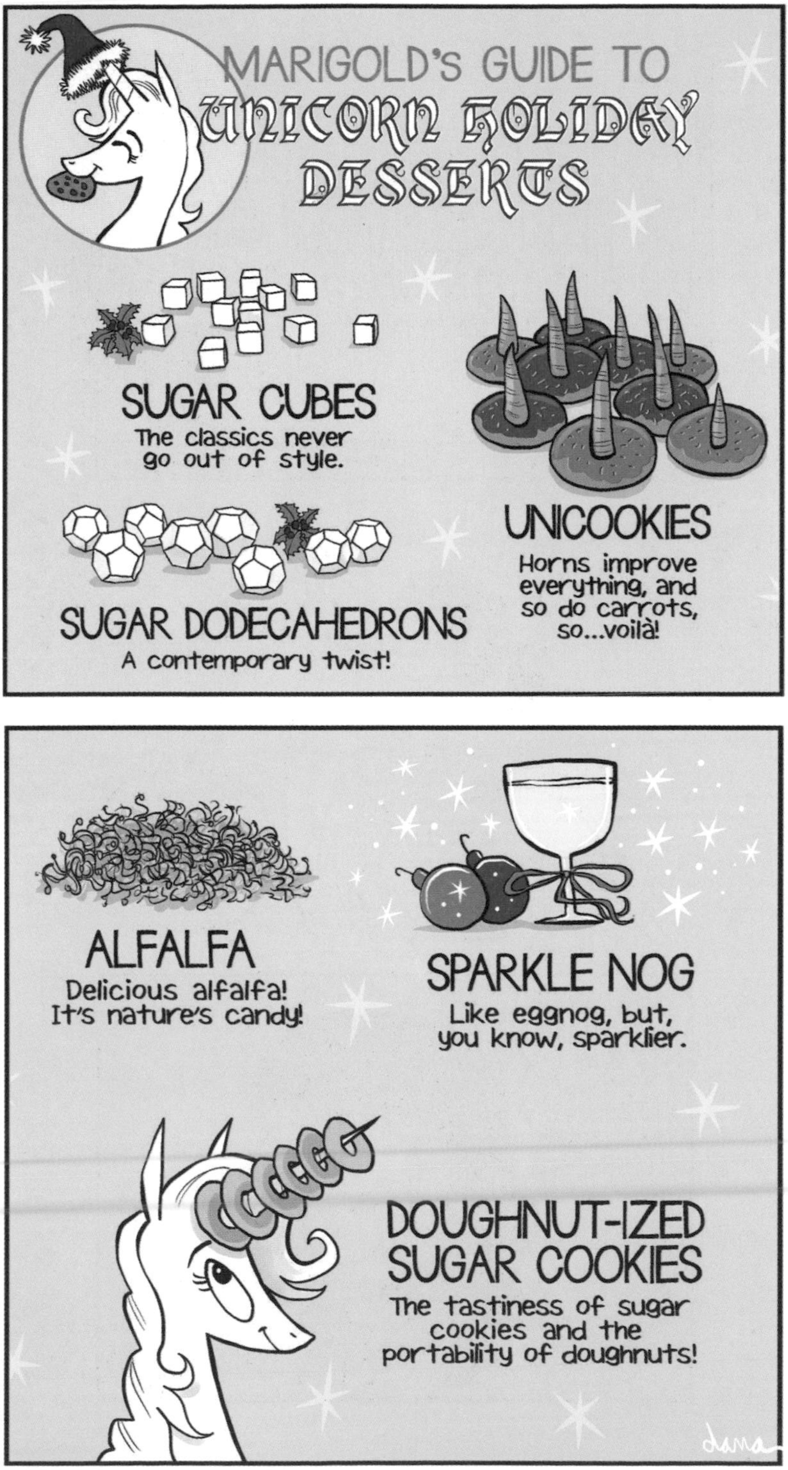
MARIGOLD'S GUIDE TO
UNICORN HOLIDAY DESSERTS
SUGAR CUBES
The classics never go out of style.
UNICOOKIES
Horns improve everything, and so do carrots, so...voilà!
SUGAR DODECAHEDRONS
A contemporary twist!
ALFALFA
Delicious alfalfa! It's nature's candy!
SPARKLE NOG
Like eggnog, but, you know, sparklier.
DOUGHNUT-IZED SUGAR COOKIES
The tastiness of sugar cookies and the portability of doughnuts!
dana

Is that the same game you were playing yesterday?
Yup!
I am surprised you have not won it yet.
You don't actually "win" *Animal Talking.*

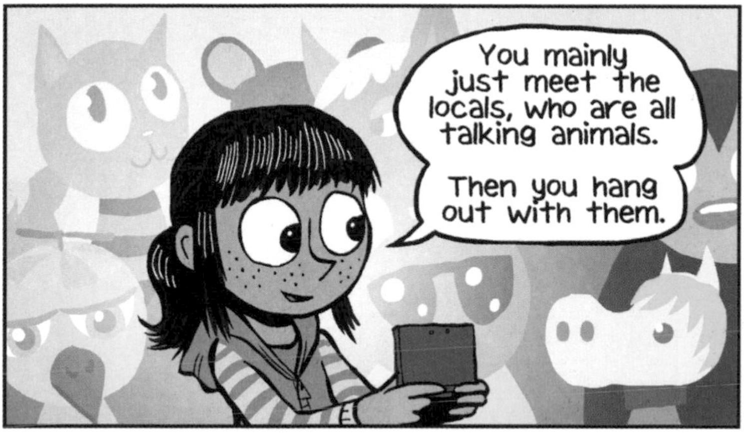
You mainly just meet the locals, who are all talking animals.
Then you hang out with them.

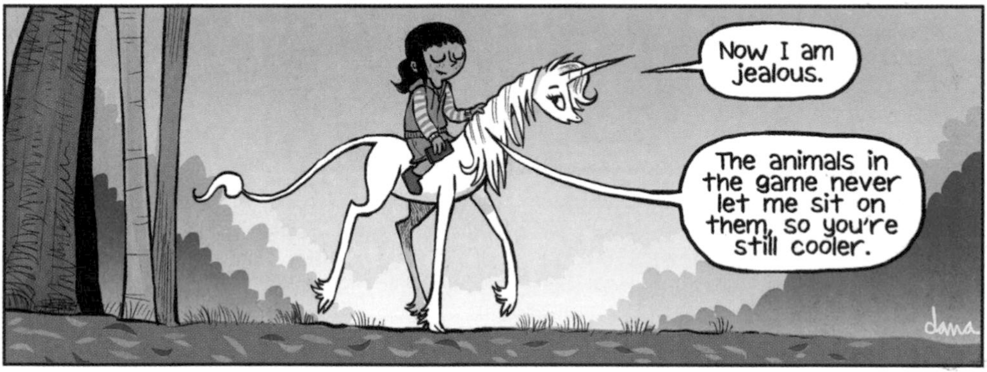
Now I am jealous.
The animals in the game never let me sit on them, so you're still cooler.
dana

Hey, I know. Let's play Thrones of Ermagard!
What is that?
It's a show. It takes place in a realm of fantasy and magic!
I'll be Targarys Denaryen, the Princess of Dragons! She rides a white horse and is awesome.

And you can be my horse!
I am tired of always having to be the horse.
I want to play a game in which I am a majestic unicorn, and you are a little girl I know.
That sounds like reality.
I enjoy reality.
dana

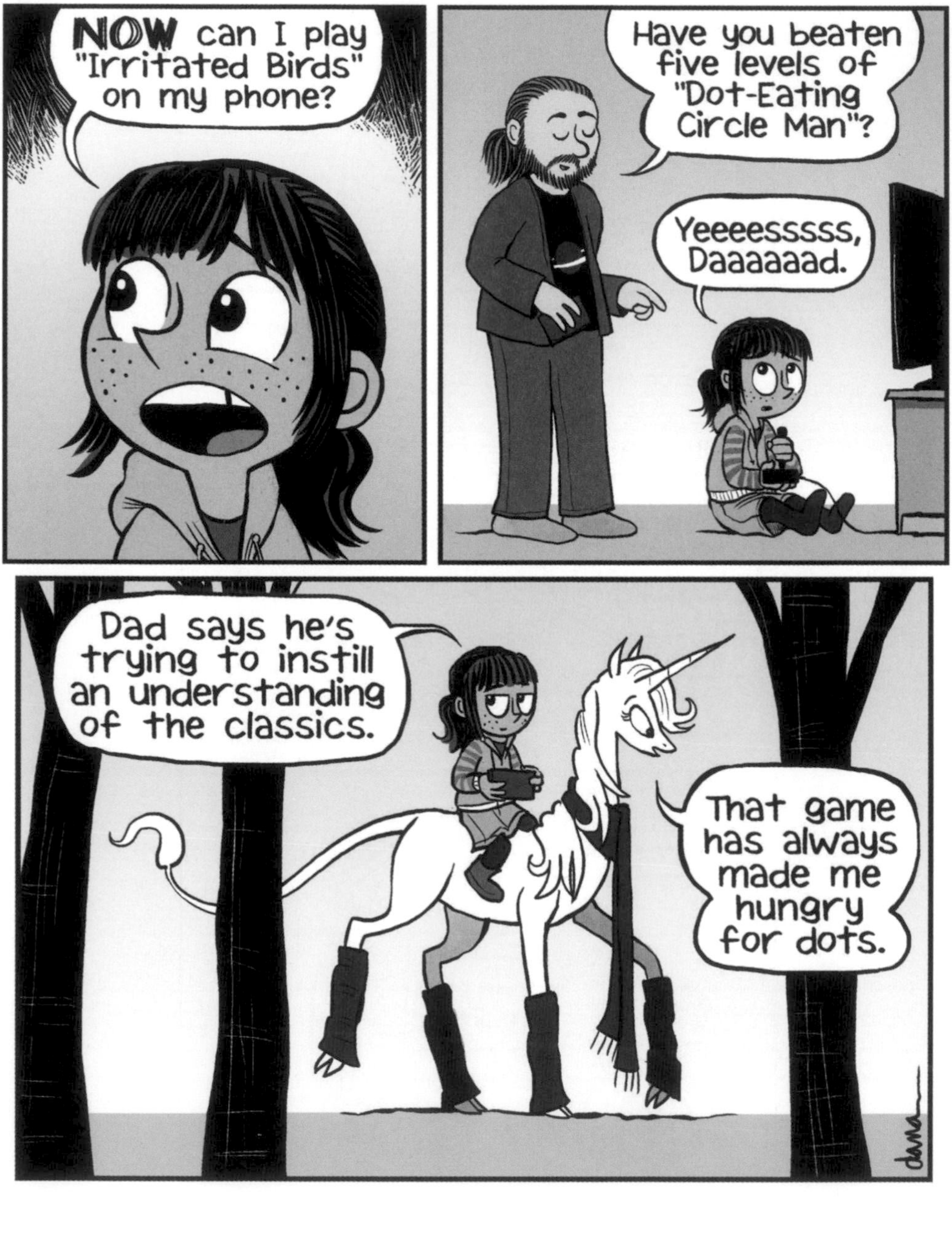
NOW can I play "Irritated Birds" on my phone?
Have you beaten five levels of "Dot-Eating Circle Man"?
Yeeeesssss, Daaaaaad.
Dad says he's trying to instill an understanding of the classics.
That game has always made me hungry for dots.
dana

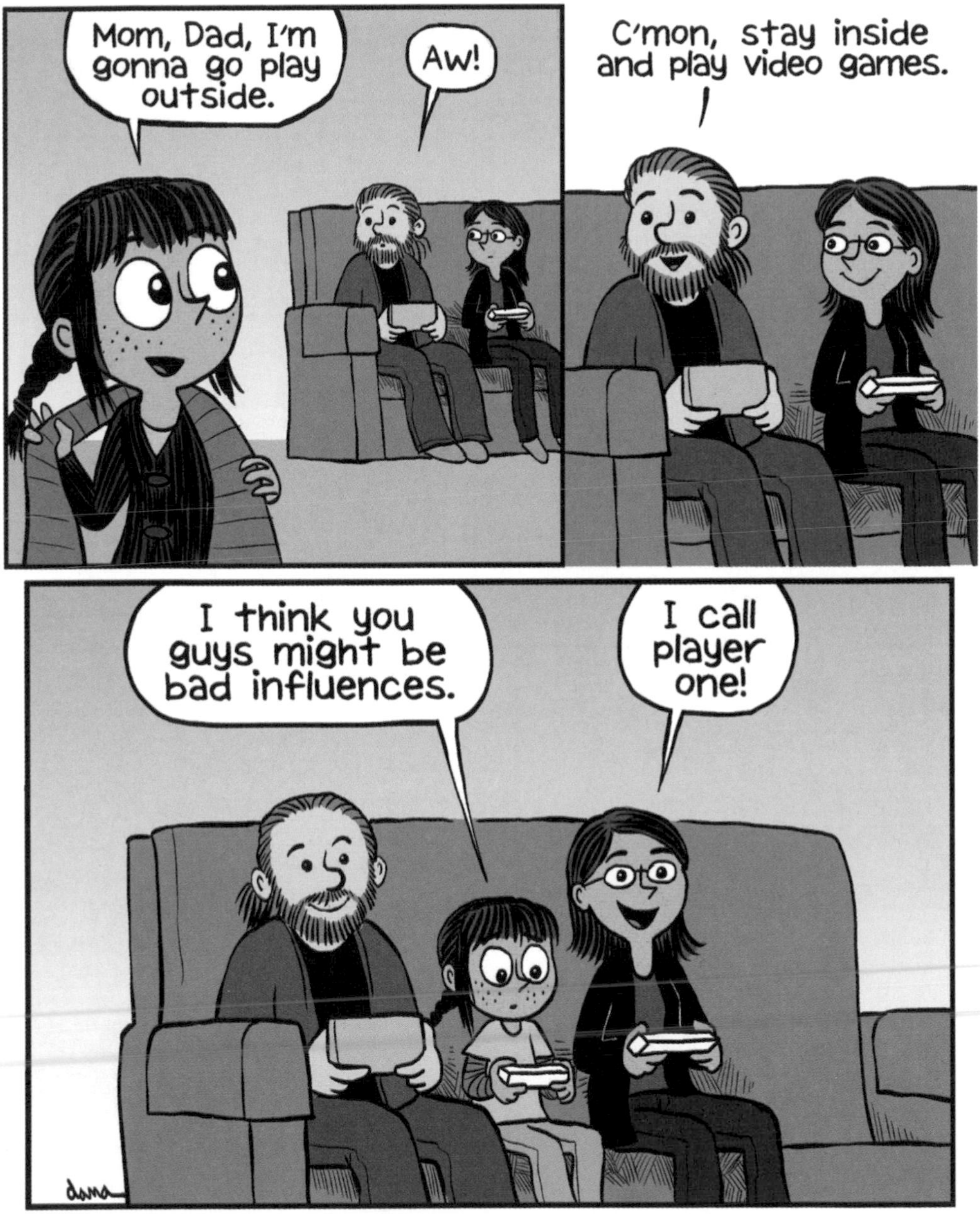
Mom, Dad, I'm gonna go play outside.
Aw!
C'mon, stay inside and play video games.
I think you guys might be bad influences.
I call player one!
dana

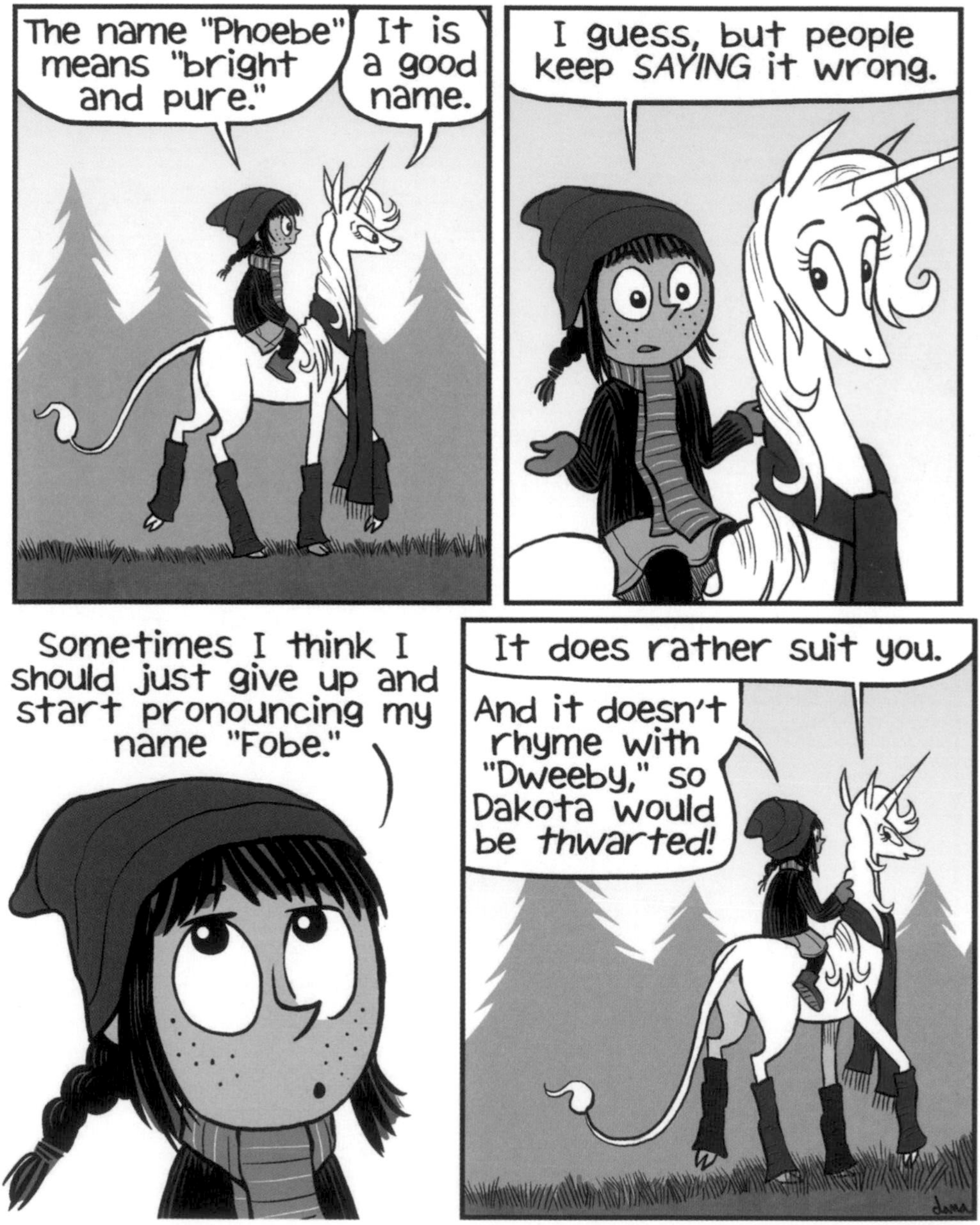
The name "Phoebe" means "bright and pure."
It is a good name.
I guess, but people keep *SAYING* it wrong.
Sometimes I think I should just give up and start pronouncing my name "Fobe."
It does rather suit you.
And it doesn't rhyme with "Dweeby," so Dakota would be *thwarted!*

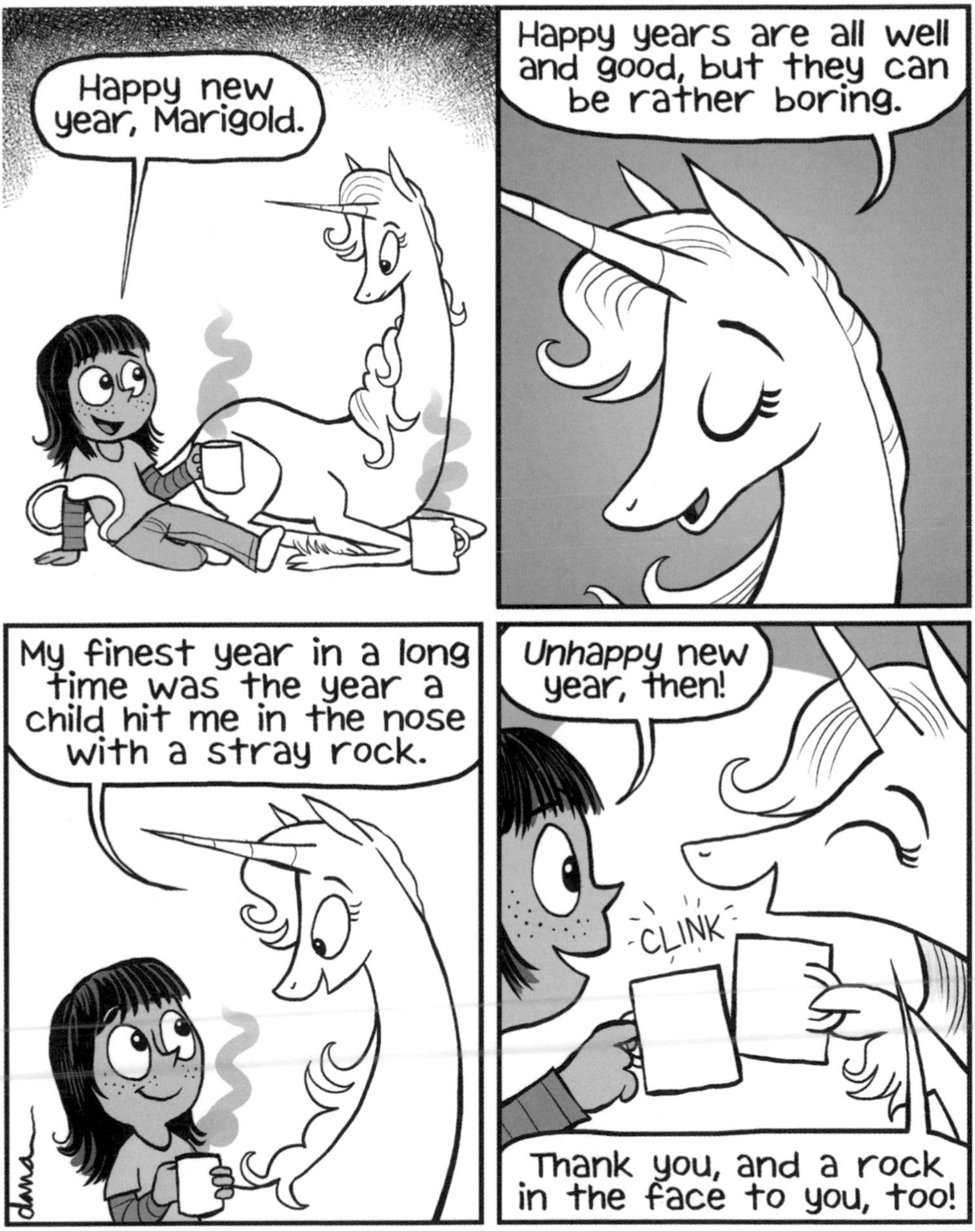
Happy new year, Marigold.
Happy years are all well and good, but they can be rather boring.
My finest year in a long time was the year a child hit me in the nose with a stray rock.
dana
Unhappy new year, then!
CLINK
Thank you, and a rock in the face to you, too!

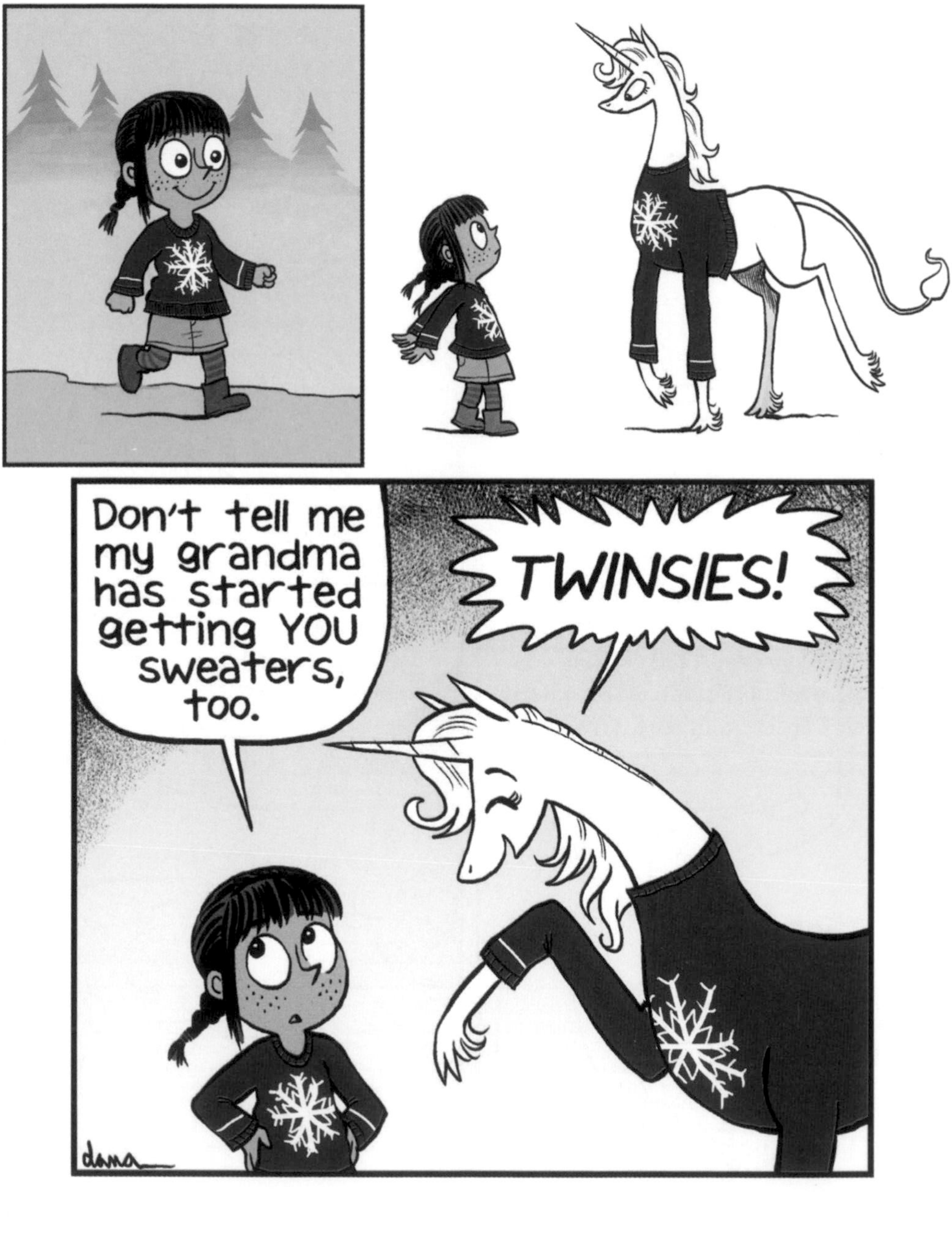
Don't tell me my grandma has started getting YOU sweaters, too.
TWINSIES!
dana

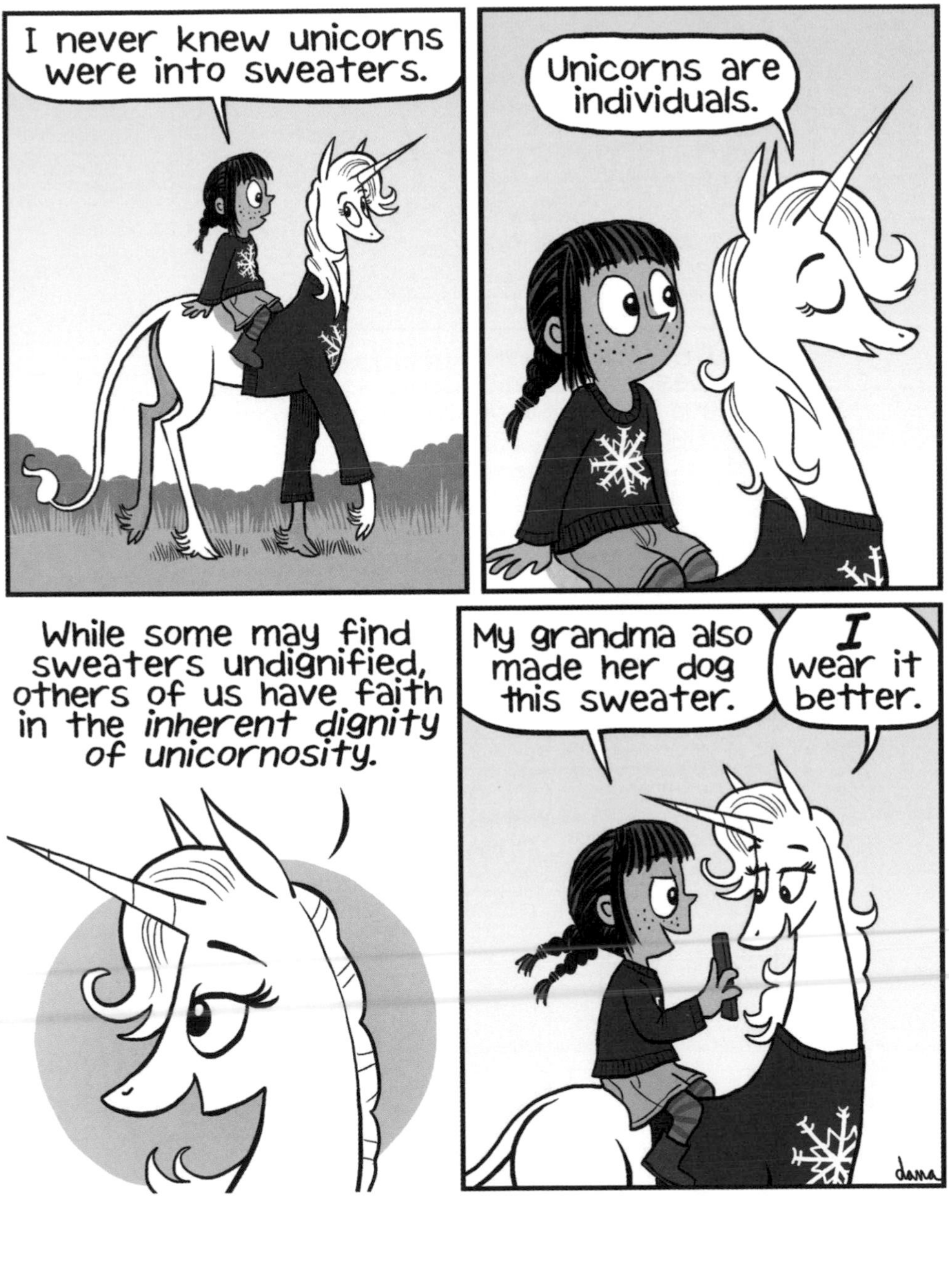
I never knew unicorns were into sweaters.
Unicorns are individuals.
While some may find sweaters undignified, others of us have faith in the *inherent dignity of unicornosity.*
My grandma also made her dog this sweater.
I wear it better.
dana

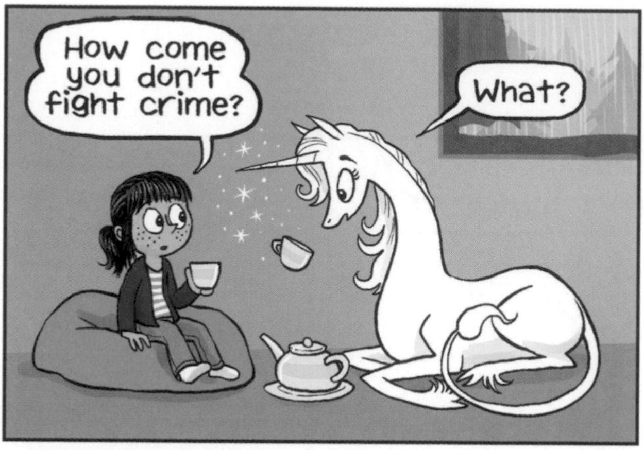
How come you don't fight crime?
What?

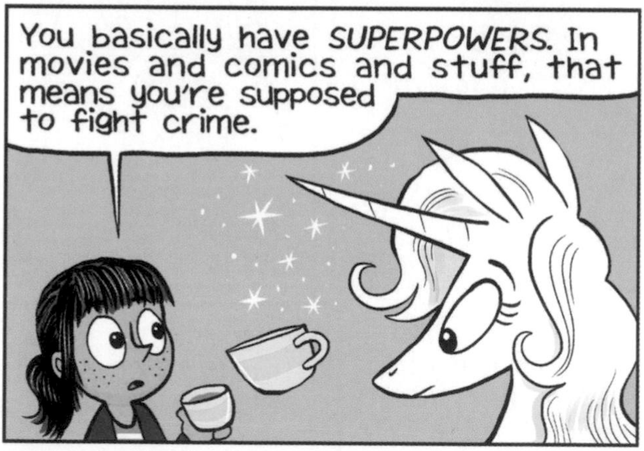
You basically have *SUPERPOWERS*. In movies and comics and stuff, that means you're supposed to fight crime.

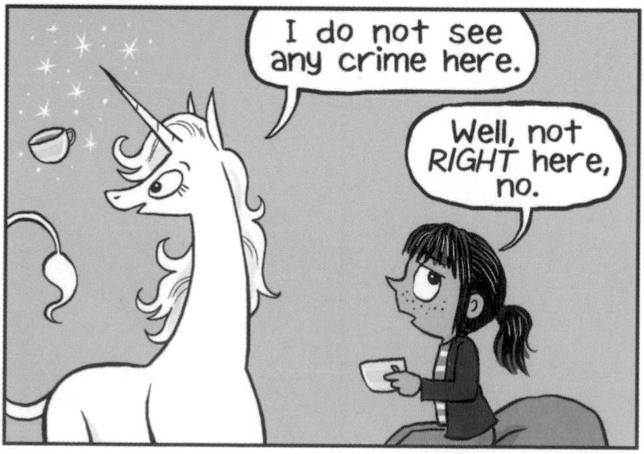
I do not see any crime here.
Well, not *RIGHT* here, no.

Then perhaps I have already FOUGHT all the crime.
I don't remember THAT.
It was when you were not here.
Well, that's just super then.
UNICORN!
dana

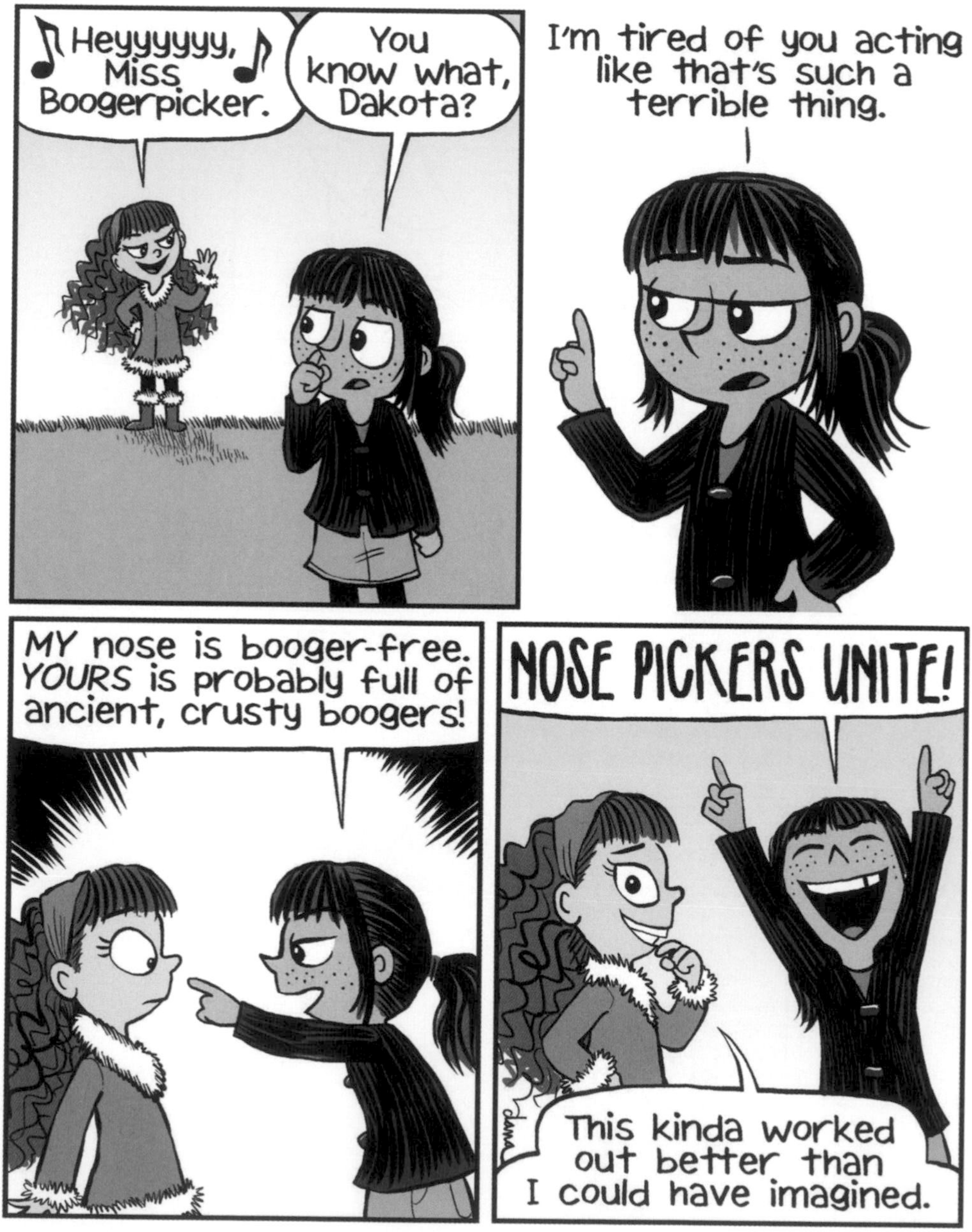
Heyyyyyy, Miss Boogerpicker.
You know what, Dakota?
I'm tired of you acting like that's such a terrible thing.
MY nose is booger-free. YOURS is probably full of ancient, crusty boogers!
NOSE PICKERS UNITE!
This kinda worked out better than I could have imagined.

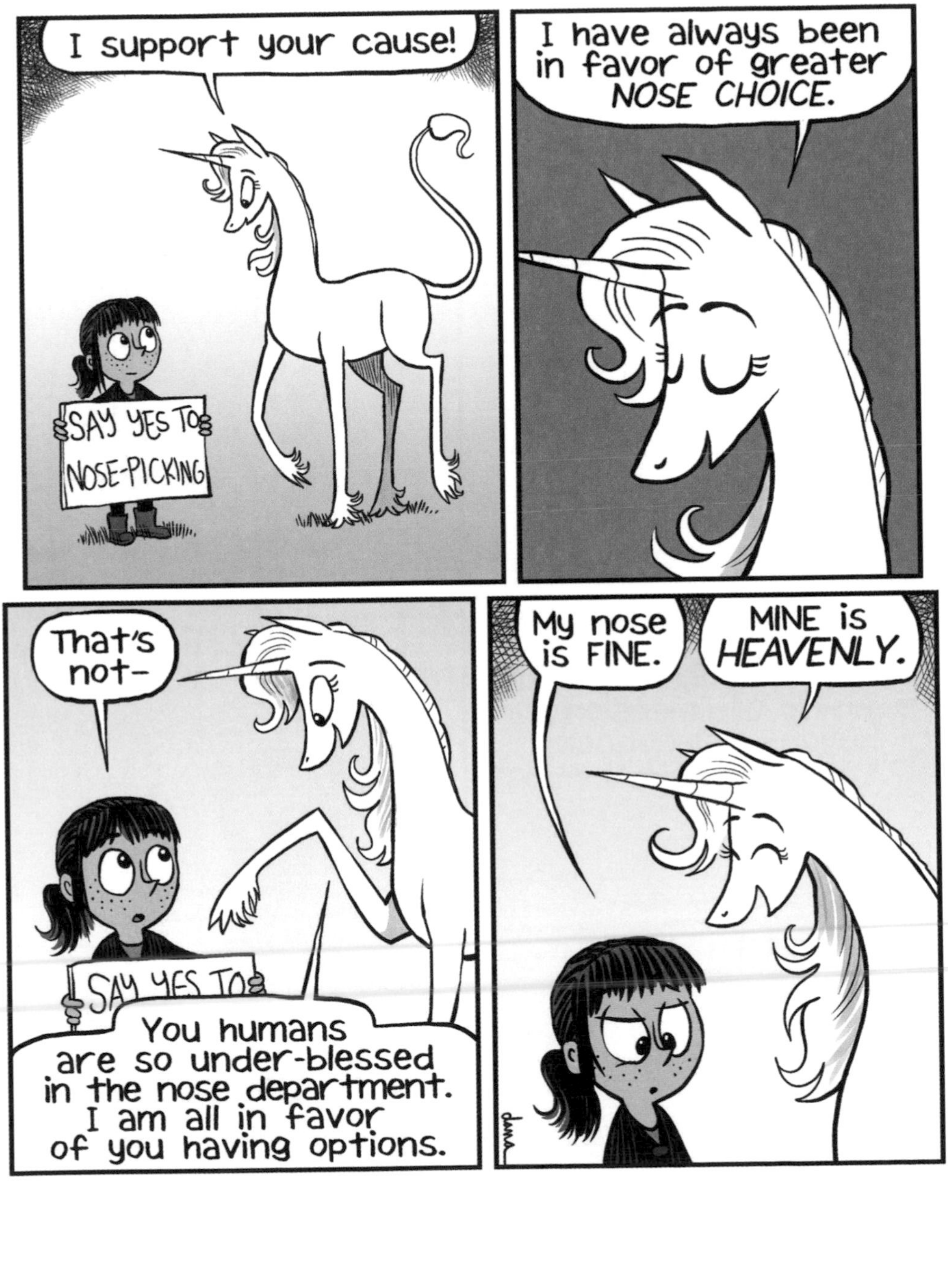
I support your cause!
SAY YES TO NOSE-PICKING
I have always been in favor of greater NOSE CHOICE.
That's not-
SAY YES TO
You humans are so under-blessed in the nose department. I am all in favor of you having options.
My nose is FINE.
MINE is HEAVENLY.

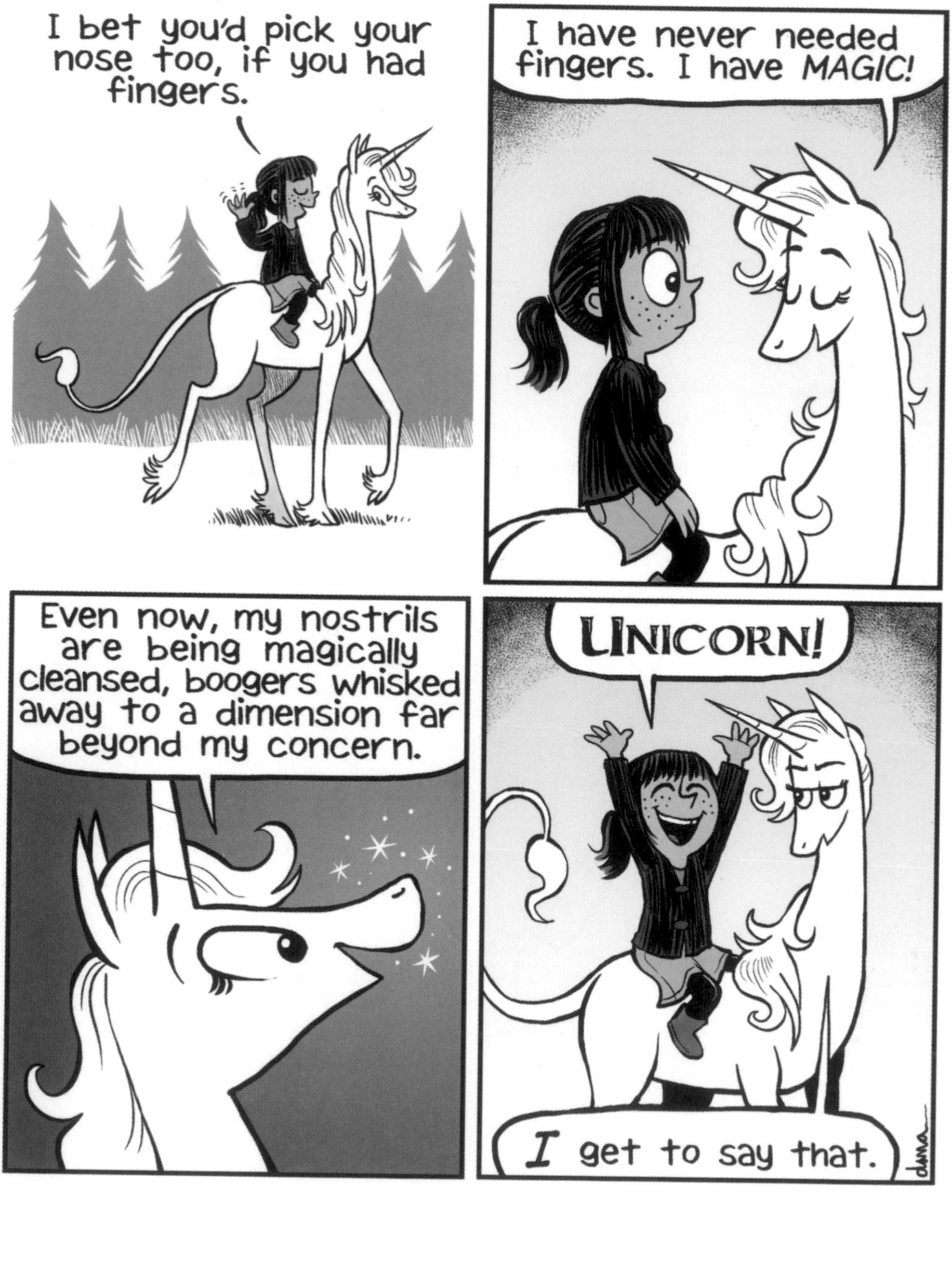
I bet you'd pick your nose too, if you had fingers.
I have never needed fingers. I have *MAGIC!*
Even now, my nostrils are being magically cleansed, boogers whisked away to a dimension far beyond my concern.
UNICORN!
I get to say that.
dana

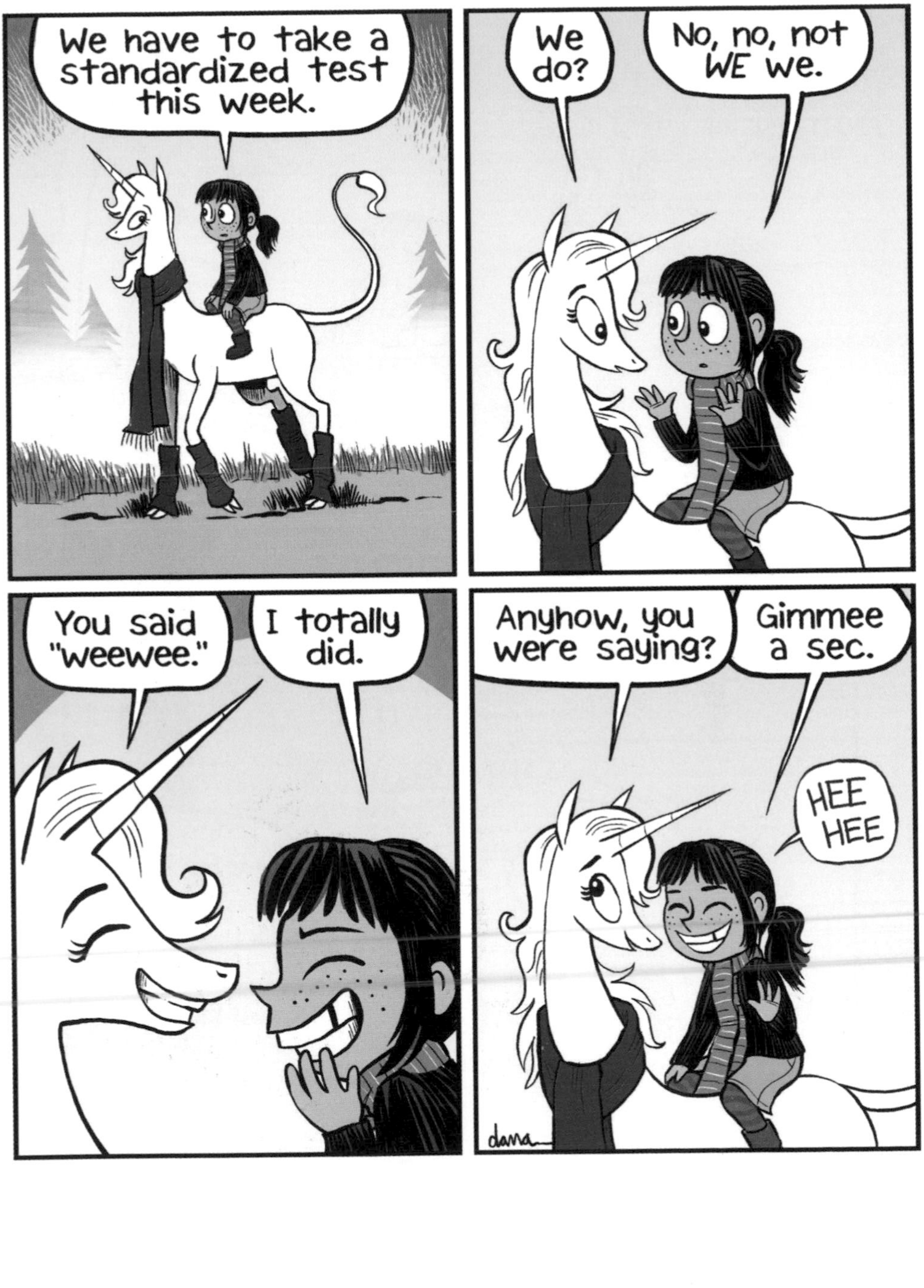
We have to take a standardized test this week.
We do?
No, no, not WE we.
You said "weewee."
I totally did.
Anyhow, you were saying?
Gimmee a sec.
HEE HEE
dana

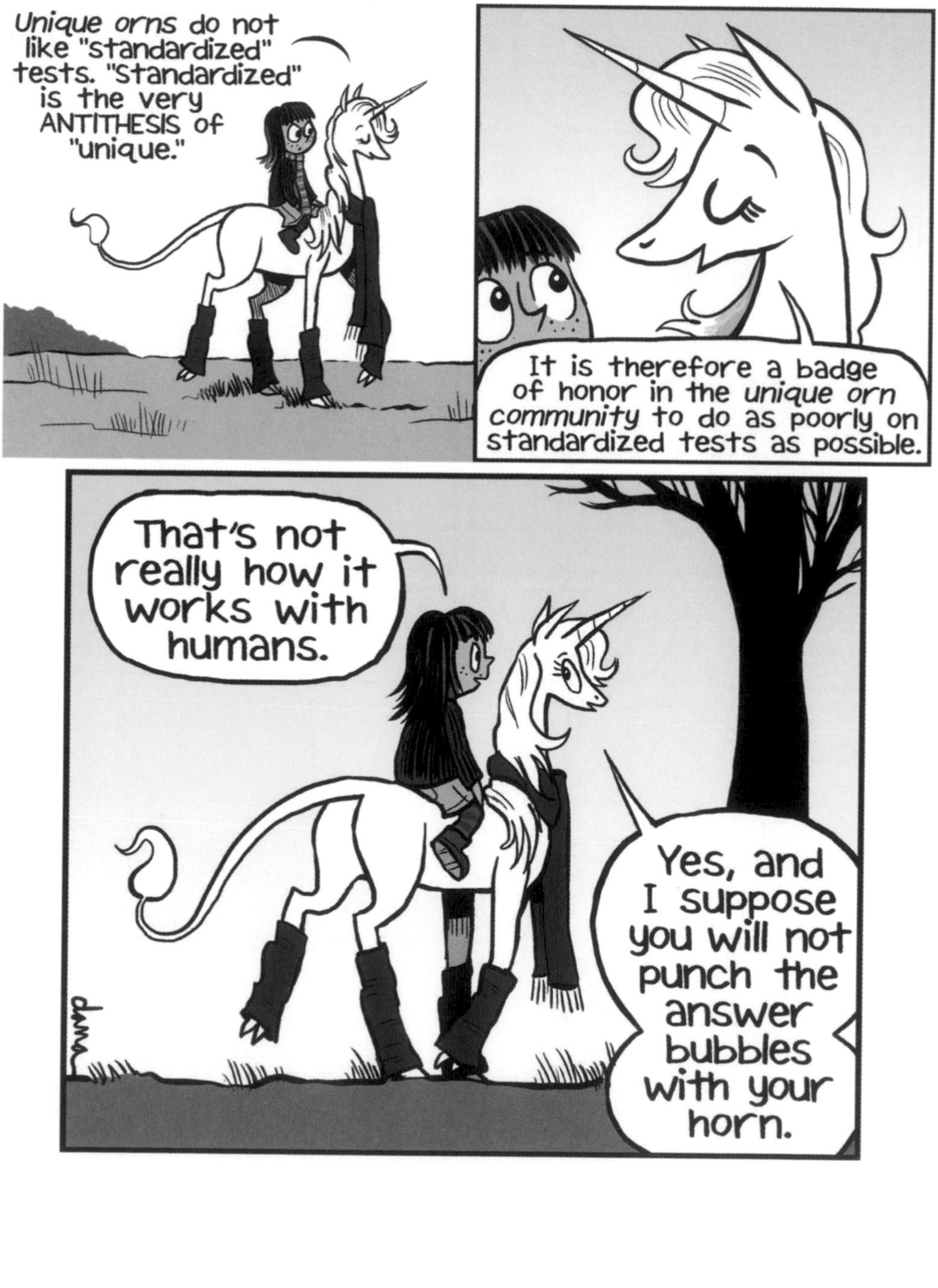
Unique orns do not like "standardized" tests. "Standardized" is the very ANTITHESIS of "unique."
It is therefore a badge of honor in the unique orn community to do as poorly on standardized tests as possible.
That's not really how it works with humans.
Yes, and I suppose you will not punch the answer bubbles with your horn.
dana

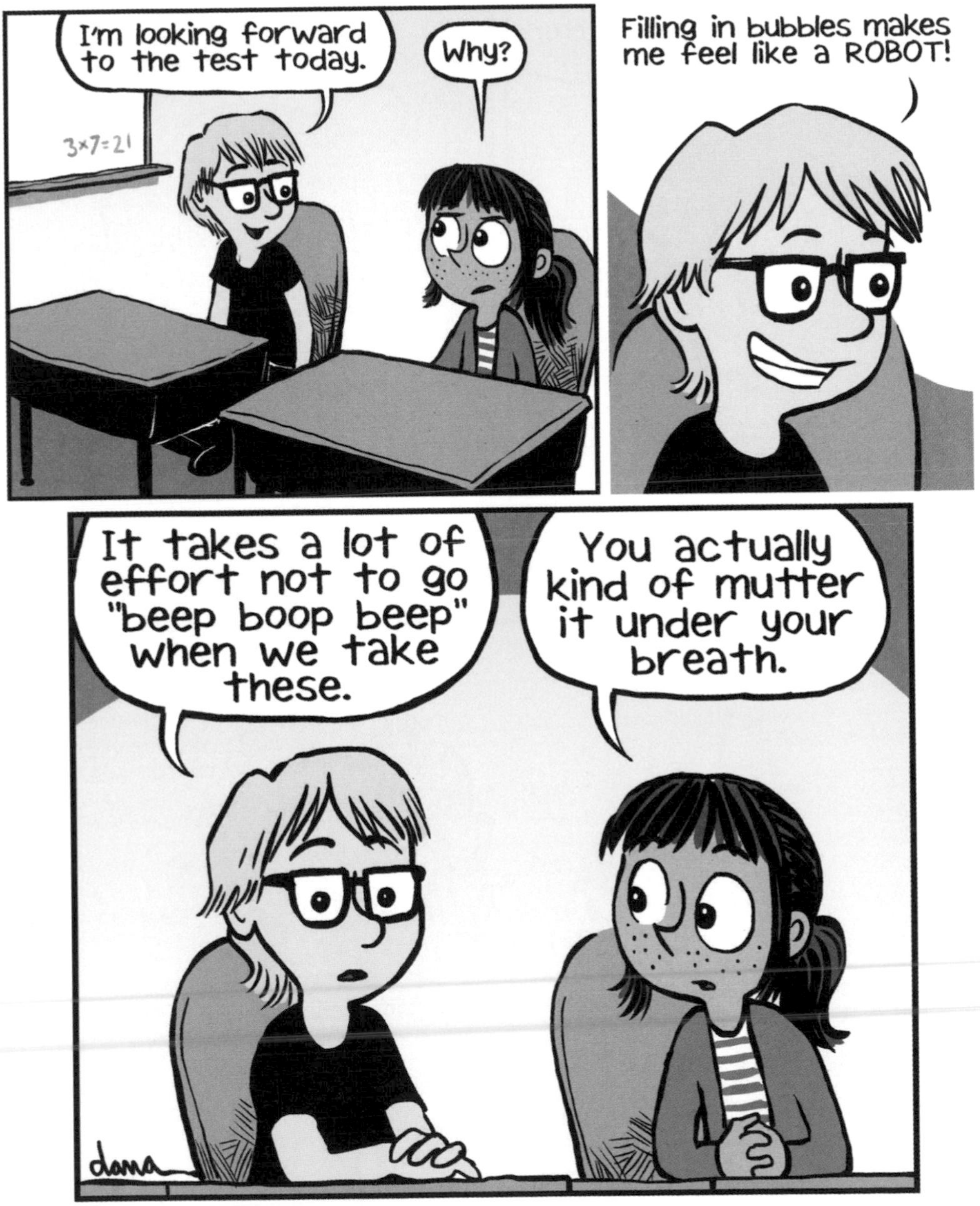
I'm looking forward to the test today.
Why?
3×7=21
Filling in bubbles makes me feel like a ROBOT!
It takes a lot of effort not to go "beep boop beep" when we take these.
You actually kind of mutter it under your breath.
dana

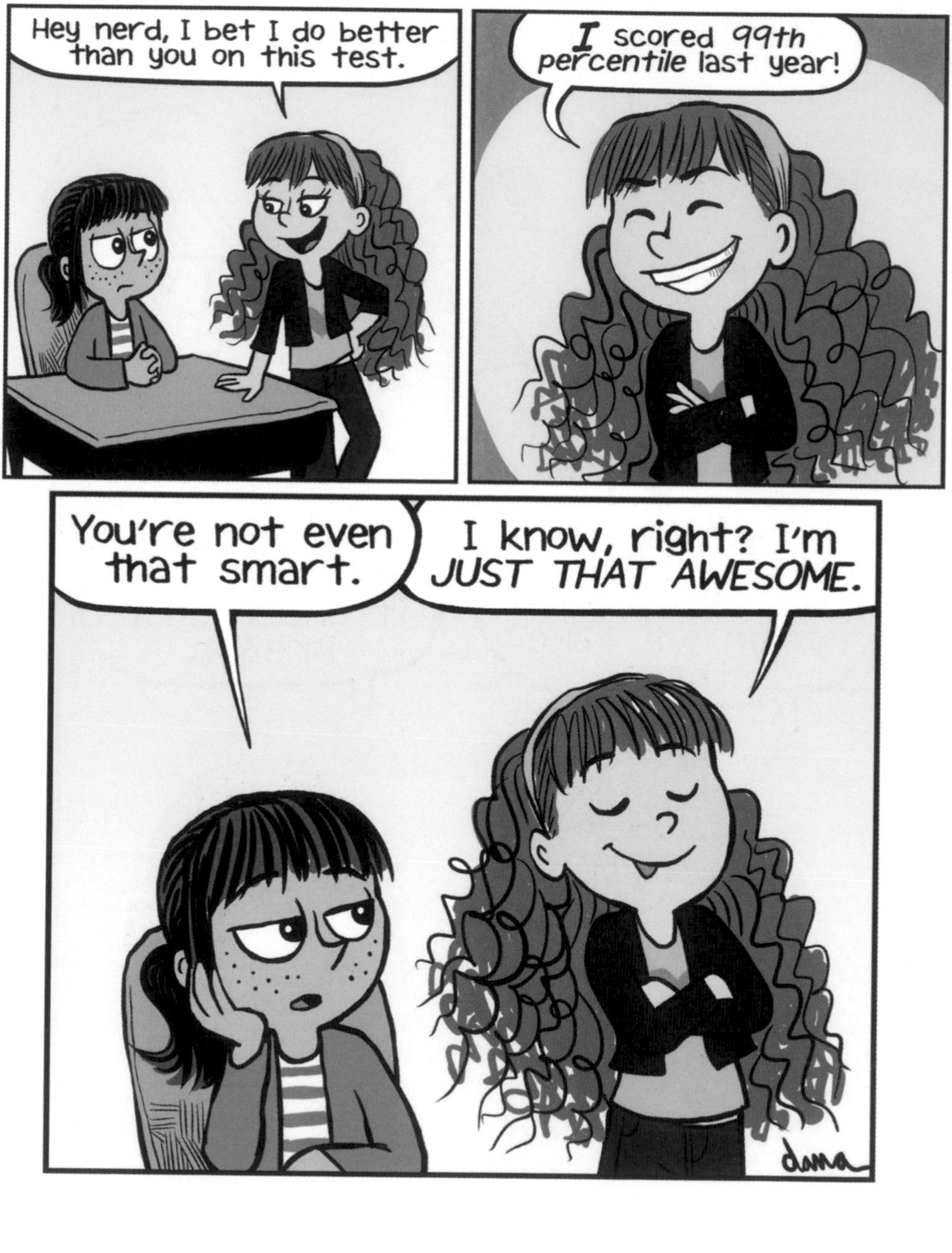
Hey nerd, I bet I do better than you on this test.
I scored 99th percentile last year!
You're not even that smart.
I know, right? I'm JUST THAT AWESOME.
dana

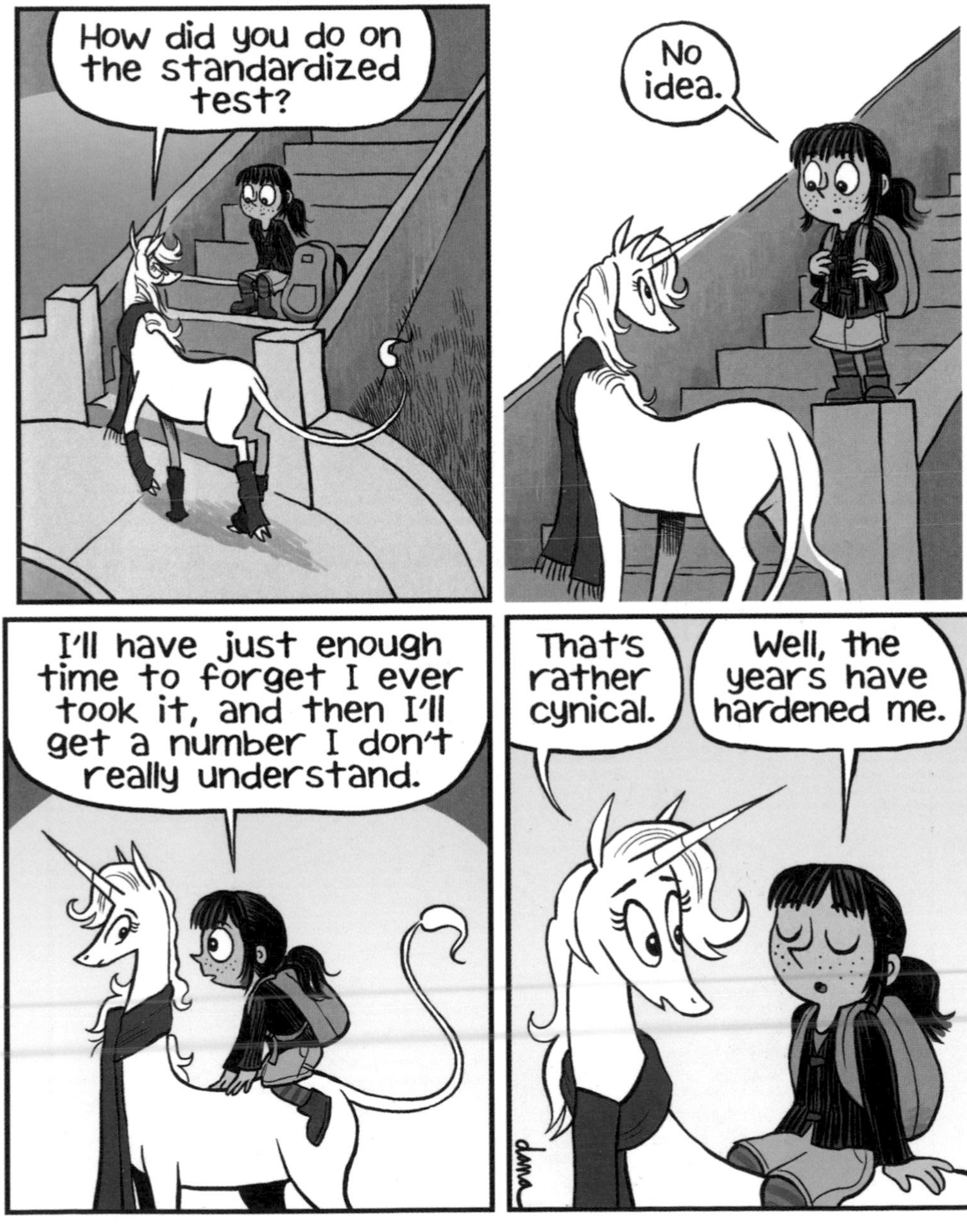
How did you do on the standardized test?
No idea.
I'll have just enough time to forget I ever took it, and then I'll get a number I don't really understand.
That's rather cynical.
Well, the years have hardened me.
dana

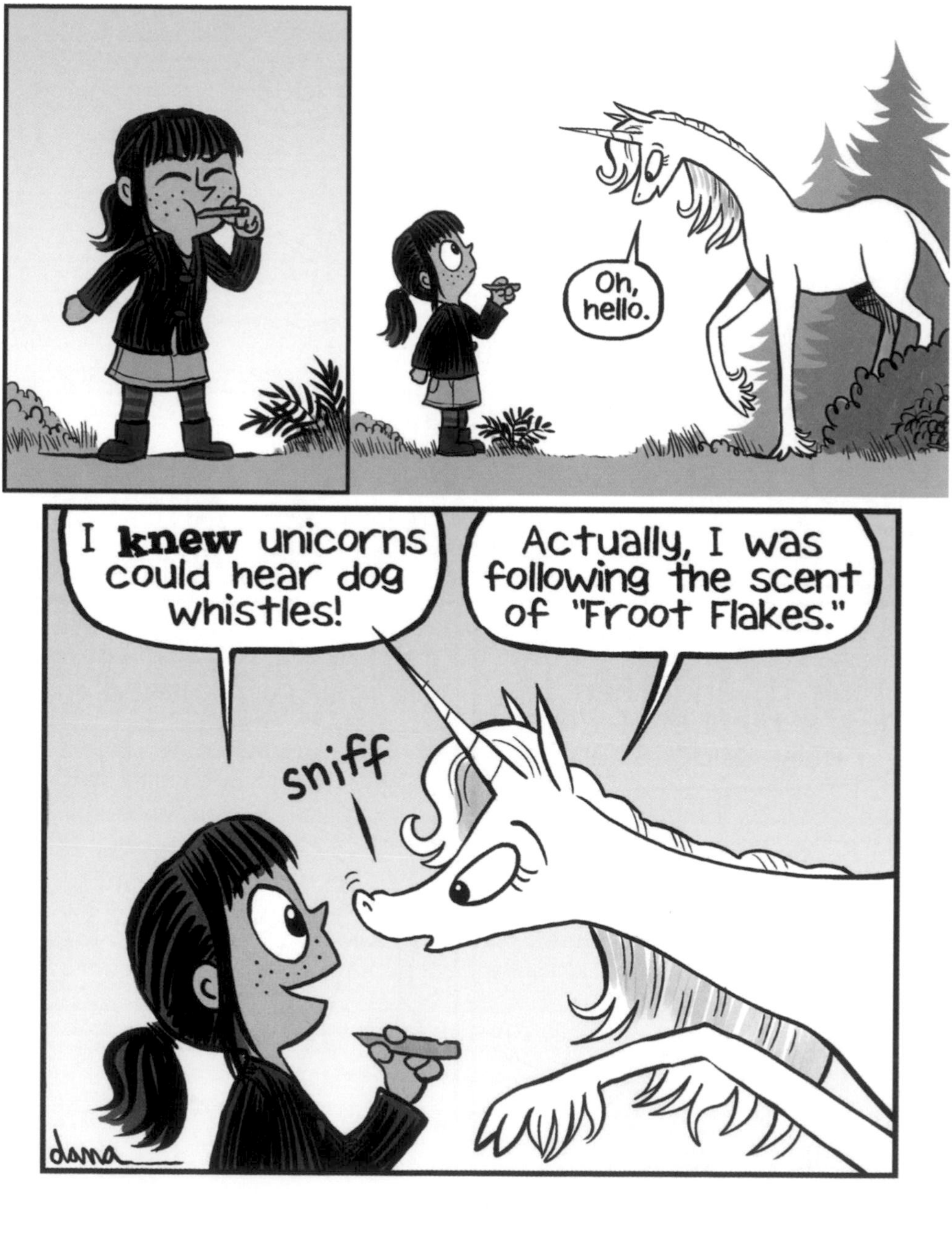
Oh, hello.
I **knew** unicorns could hear dog whistles!
Actually, I was following the scent of "Froot Flakes."
sniff
dana

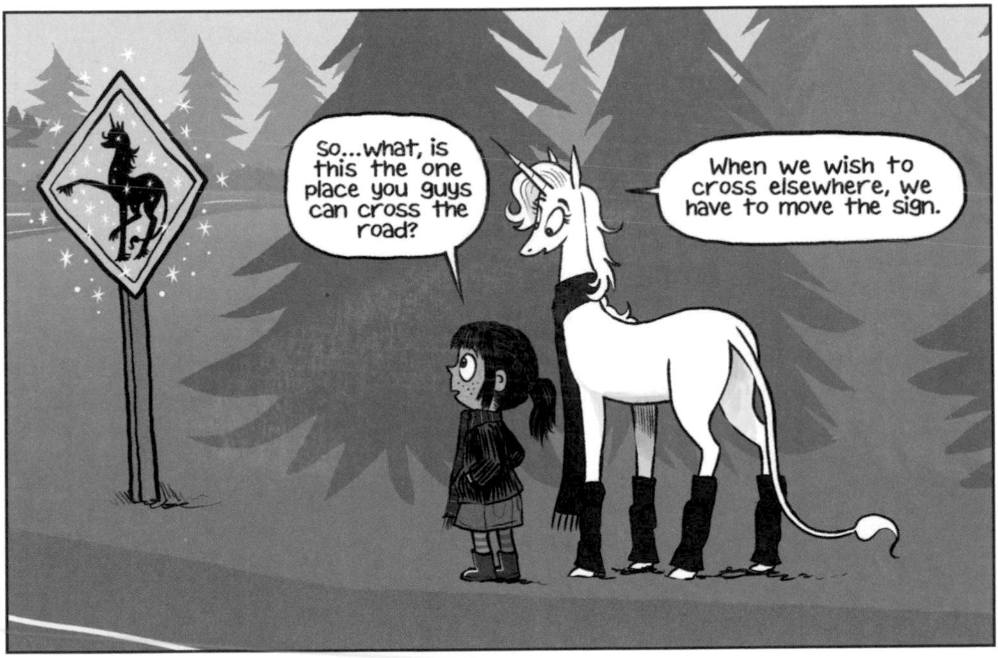
So...what, is this the one place you guys can cross the road?
When we wish to cross elsewhere, we have to move the sign.

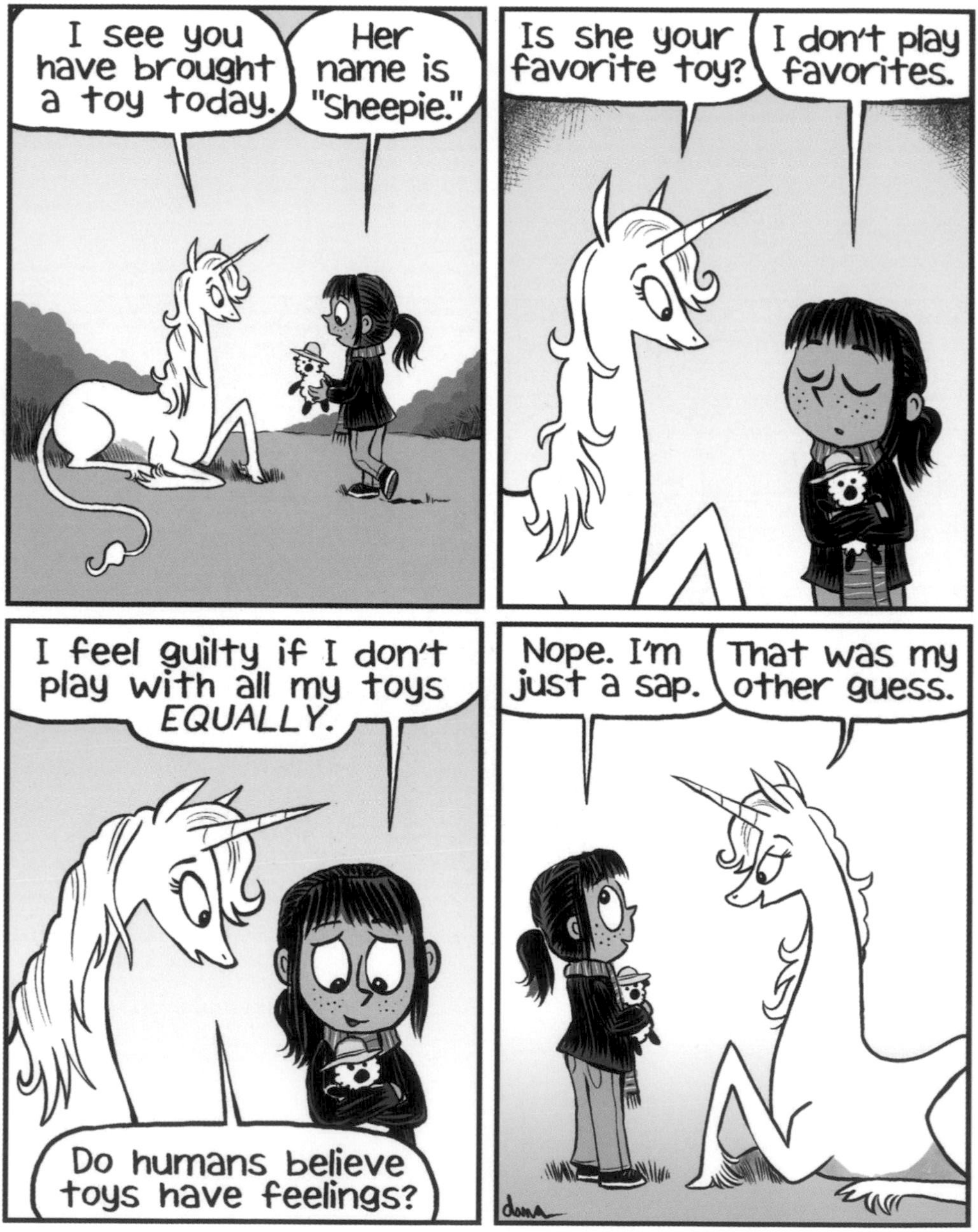
I see you have brought a toy today.
Her name is "Sheepie."
Is she your favorite toy?
I don't play favorites.
I feel guilty if I don't play with all my toys *EQUALLY*.
Do humans believe toys have feelings?
Nope. I'm just a sap.
That was my other guess.
dana

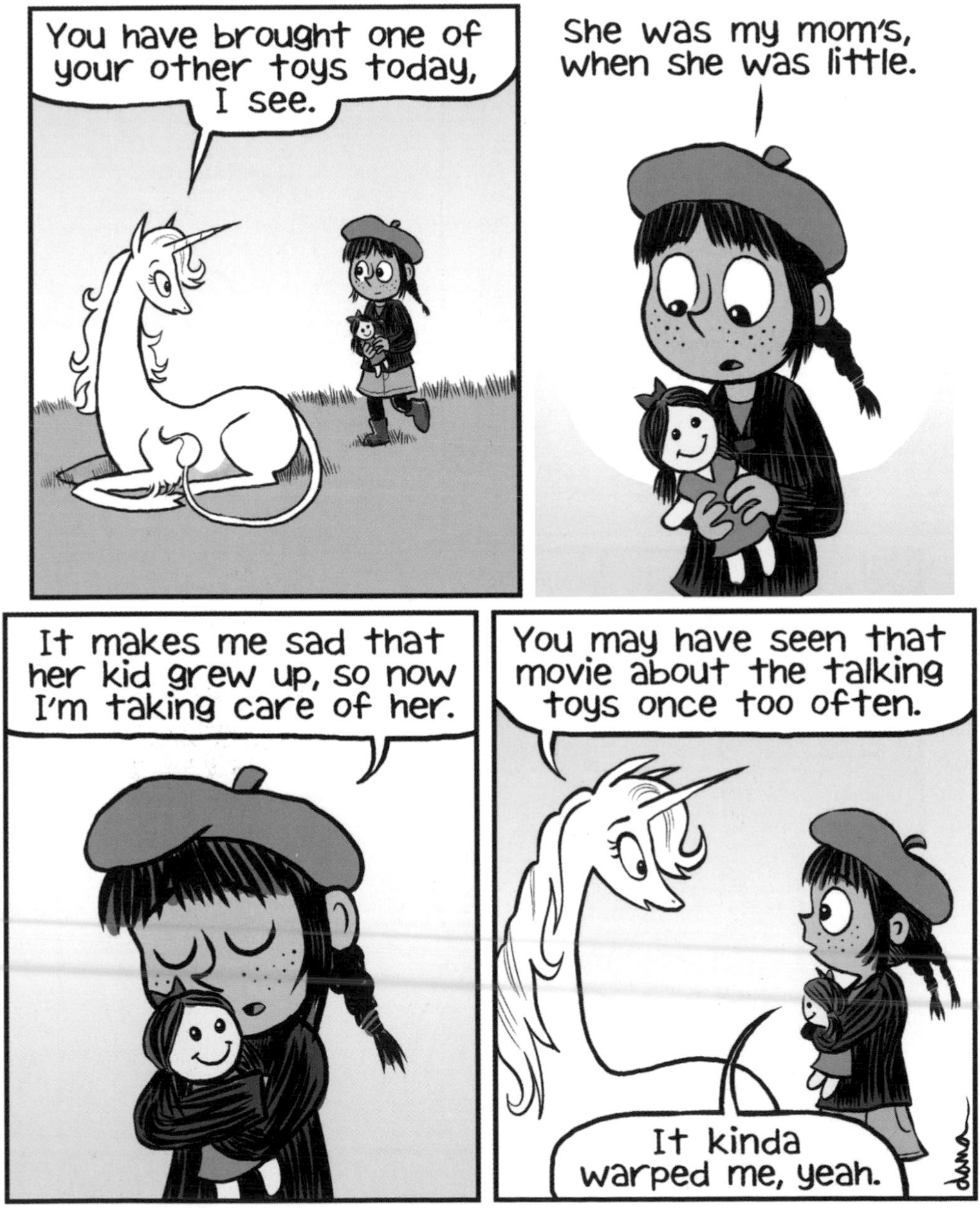
You have brought one of your other toys today, I see.
She was my mom's, when she was little.
It makes me sad that her kid grew up, so now I'm taking care of her.
You may have seen that movie about the talking toys once too often.
It kinda warped me, yeah.
dana

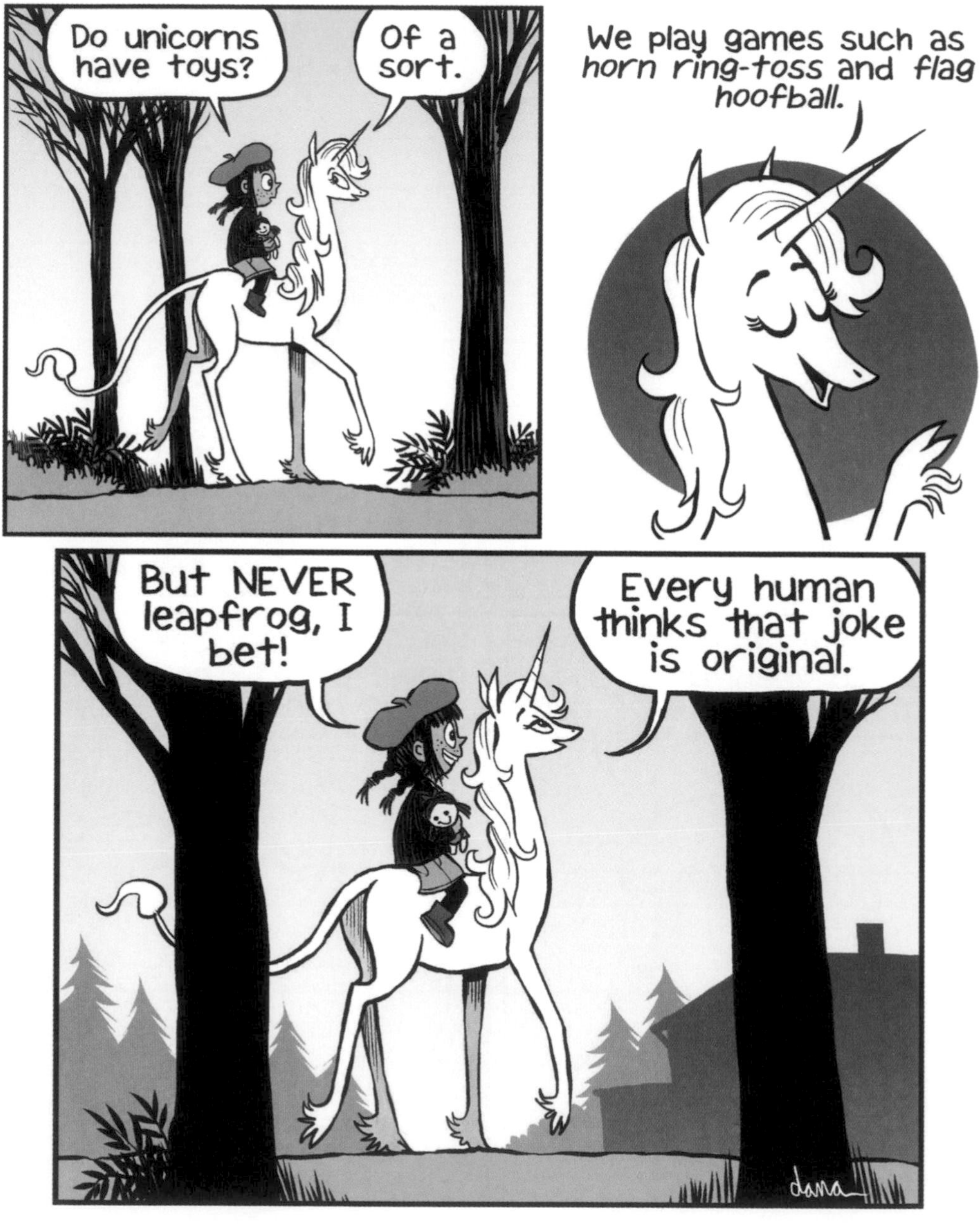
Do unicorns have toys?
Of a sort.
We play games such as *horn ring-toss* and *flag hoofball.*
But NEVER leapfrog, I bet!
Every human thinks that joke is original.
dana

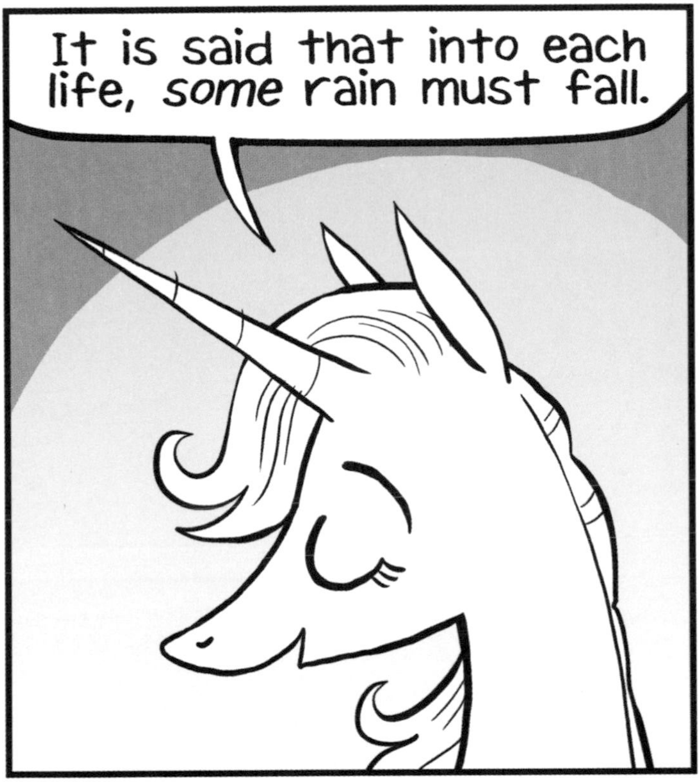
It is said that into each life, *some* rain must fall.

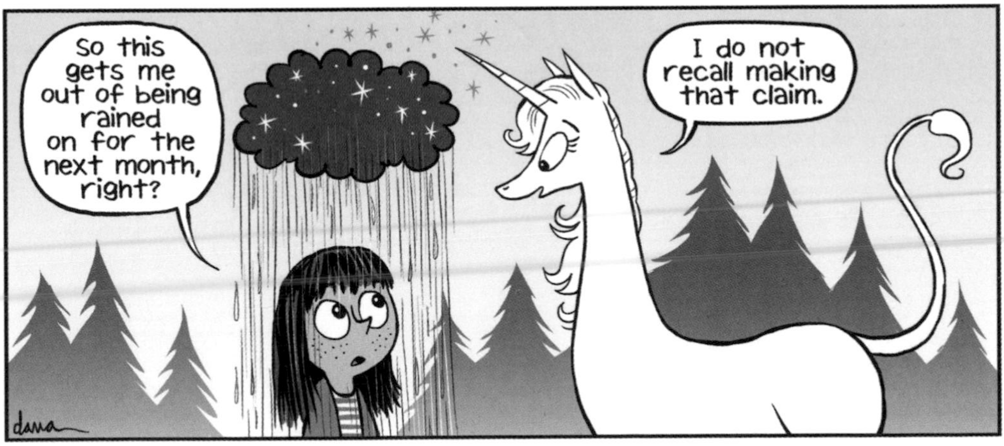
So this gets me out of being rained on for the next month, right?
I do not recall making that claim.
dana

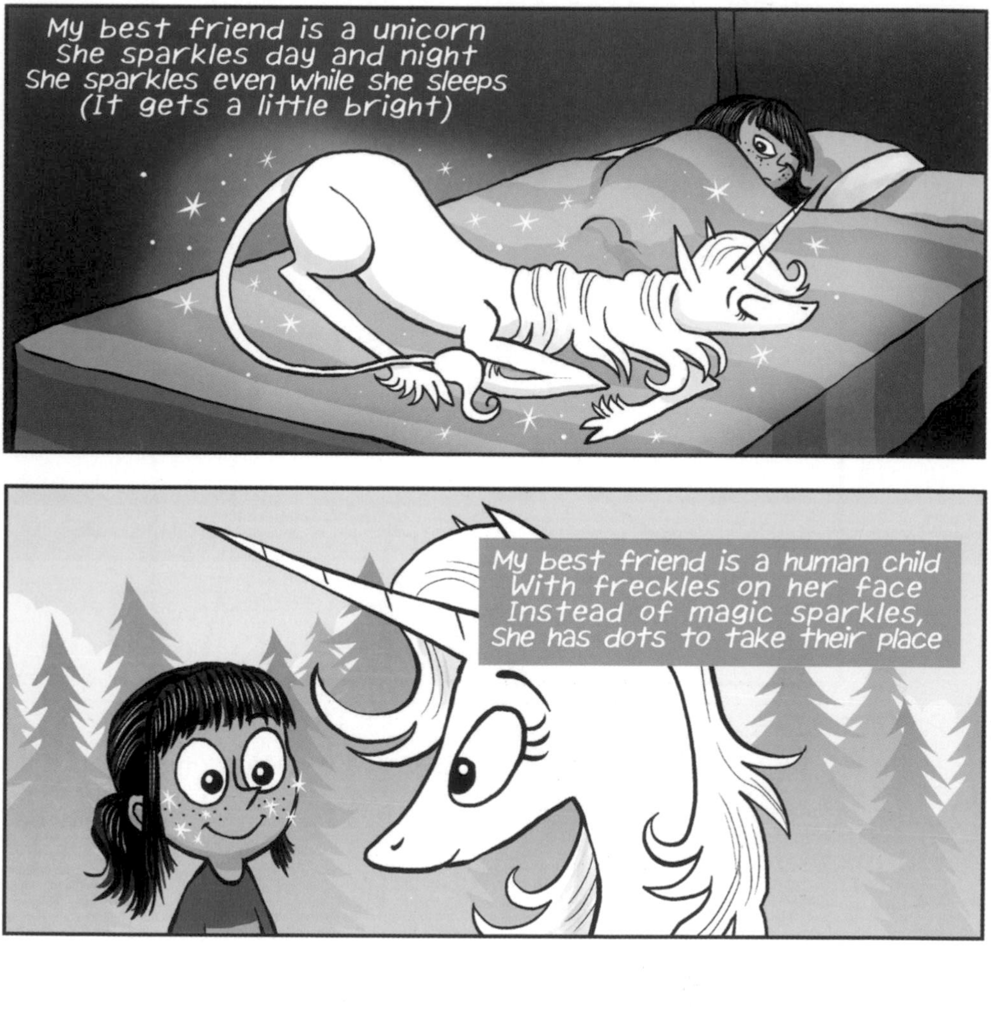
My best friend is a unicorn
She sparkles day and night
She sparkles even while she sleeps
(It gets a little bright)
My best friend is a human child
With freckles on her face
Instead of magic sparkles,
She has dots to take their place

"Enough with all the sparkling,"
I sometimes want to say,
But in the end, as my best friend,
She sparkles up my day.

She may not be a unicorn
But freckles are a start
For when I see her freckled face
It sparkles up my heart.

fwip
fwip
fwipfwipfwip
SPROING
fwip
fwip
fwipfwipfwip
SPROING

I don't understand why your "tail aerobics" take so long.
I take tail fitness very seriously.
dana

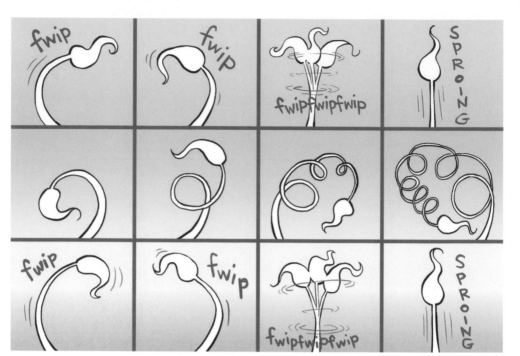

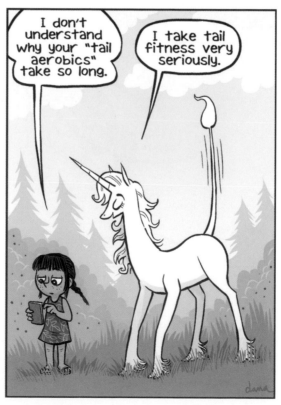

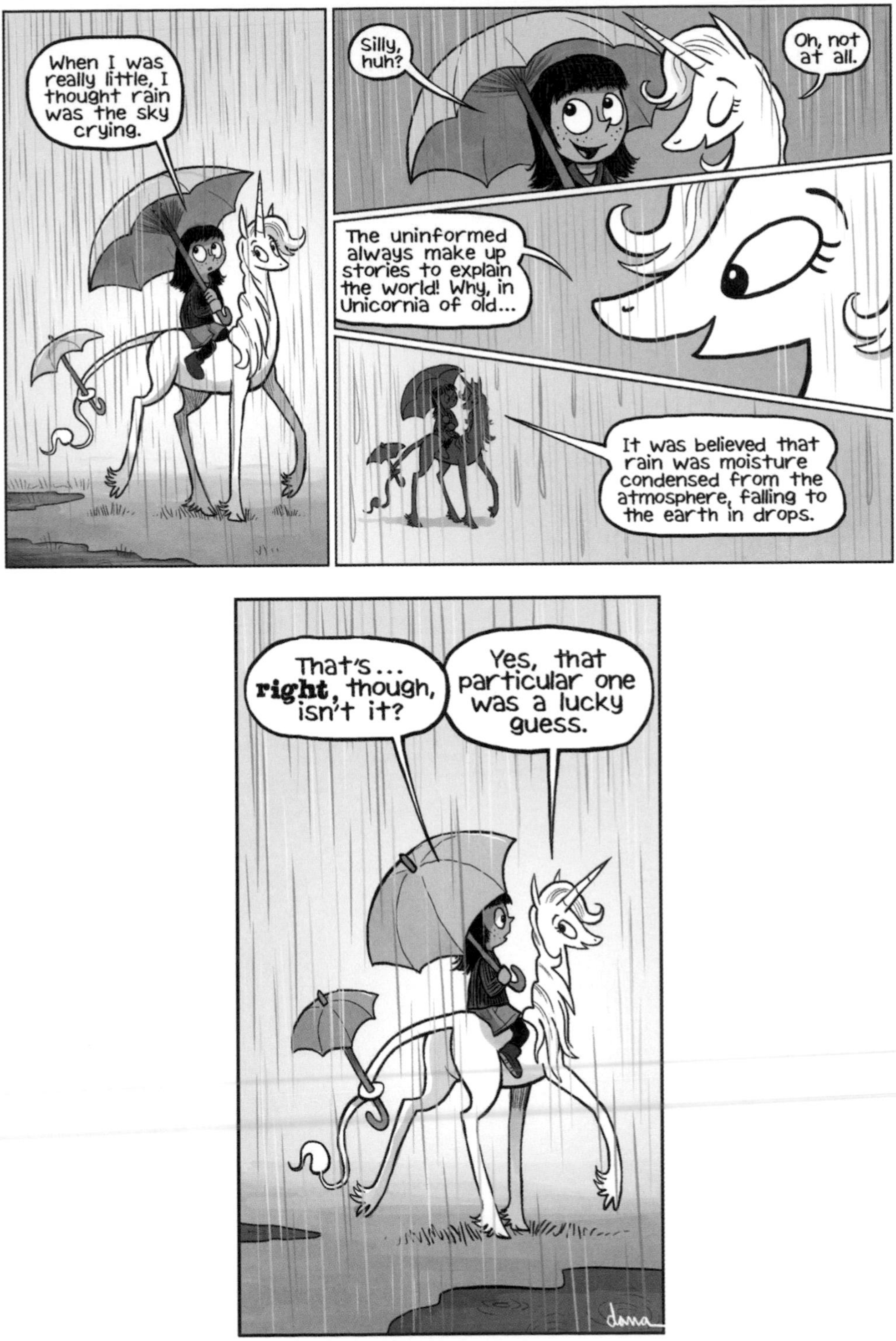
When I was really little, I thought rain was the sky crying.
Silly, huh?
Oh, not at all.
The uninformed always make up stories to explain the world! Why, in Unicornia of old...
It was believed that rain was moisture condensed from the atmosphere, falling to the earth in drops.
That's... **right**, though, isn't it?
Yes, that particular one was a lucky guess.
dana

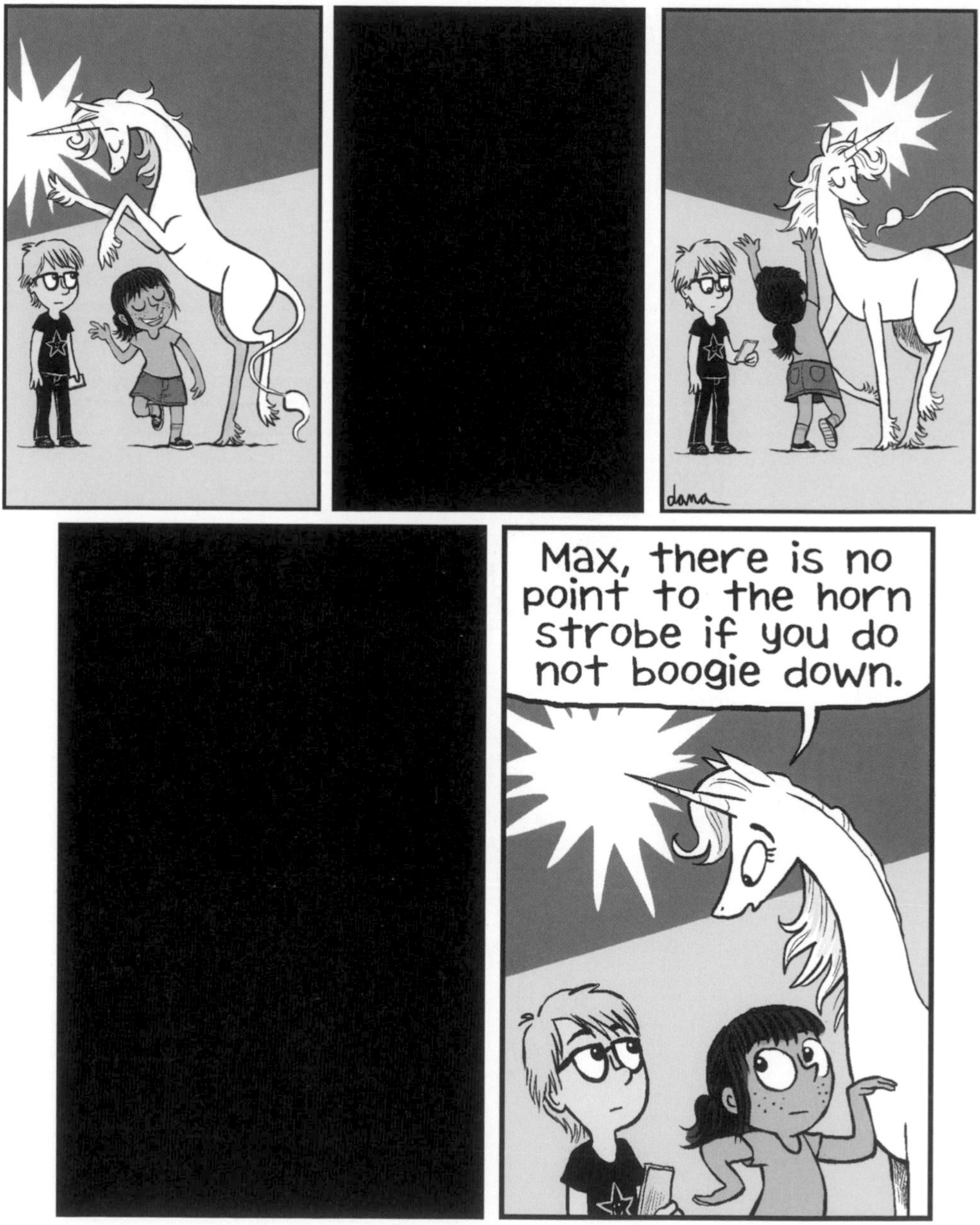
dana
Max, there is no point to the horn strobe if you do not boogie down.

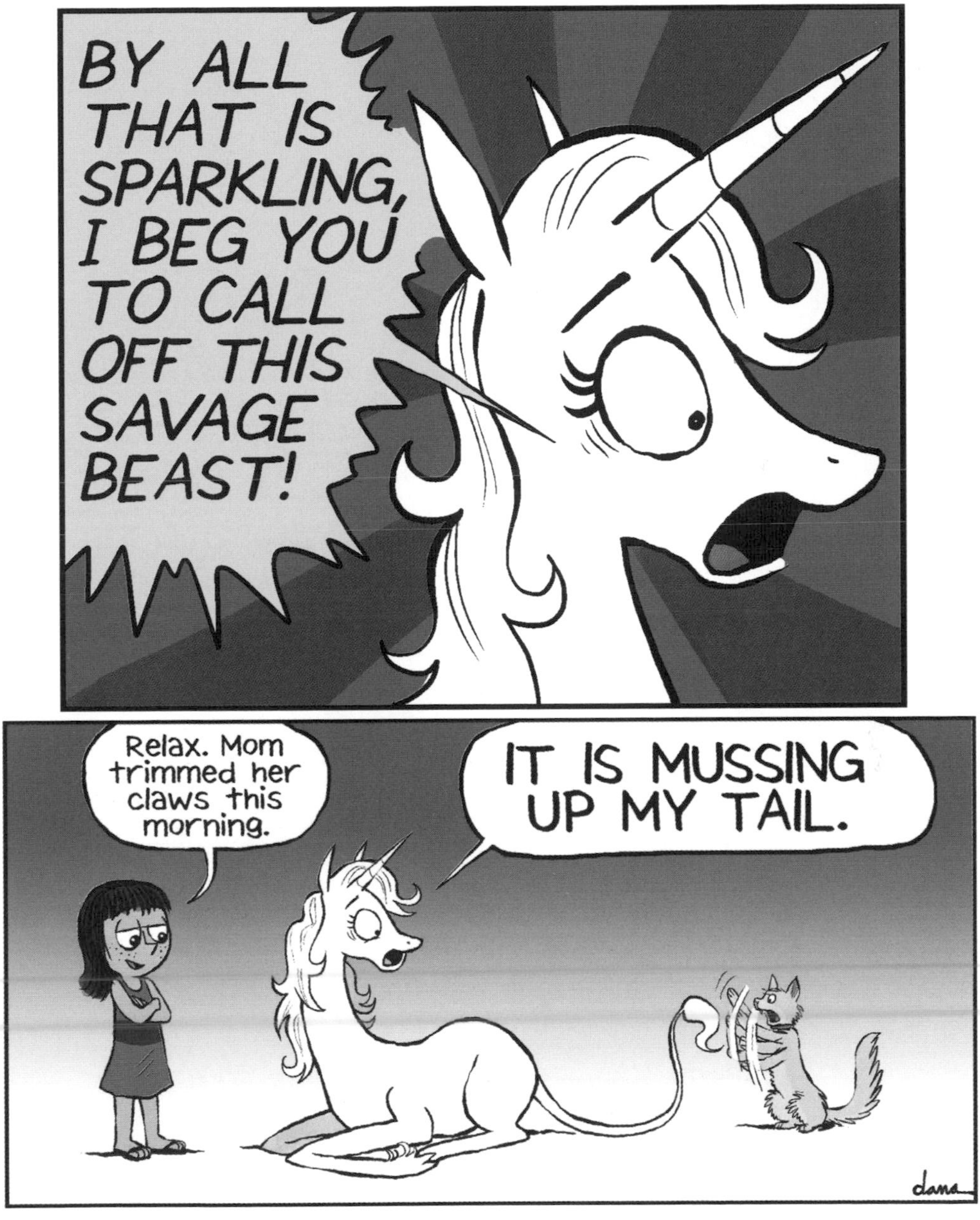
BY ALL THAT IS SPARKLING, I BEG YOU TO CALL OFF THIS SAVAGE BEAST!
Relax. Mom trimmed her claws this morning.
IT IS MUSSING UP MY TAIL.
dana

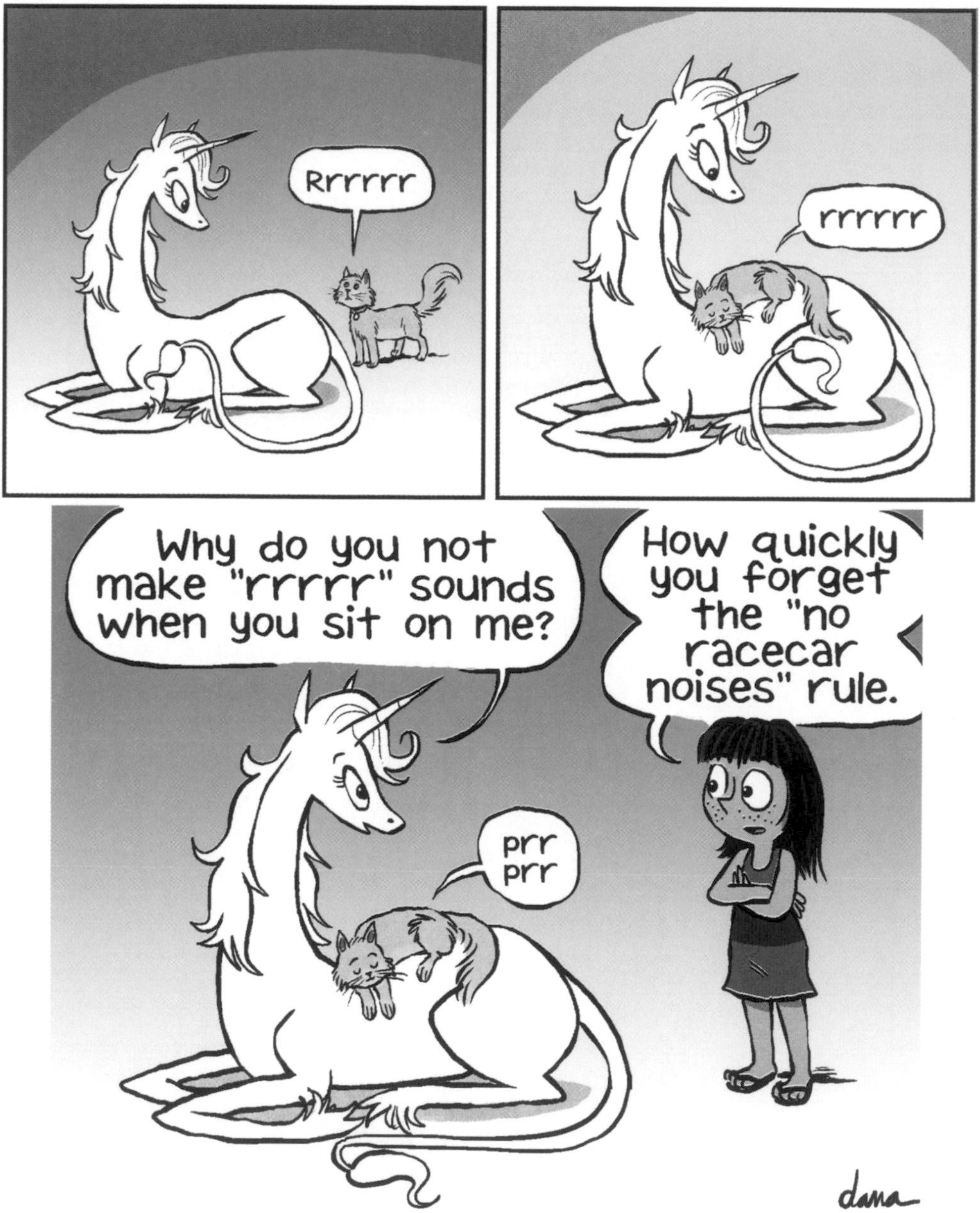
Rrrrrr
rrrrrr
Why do you not make "rrrrr" sounds when you sit on me?
How quickly you forget the "no racecar noises" rule.
prr prr
dana

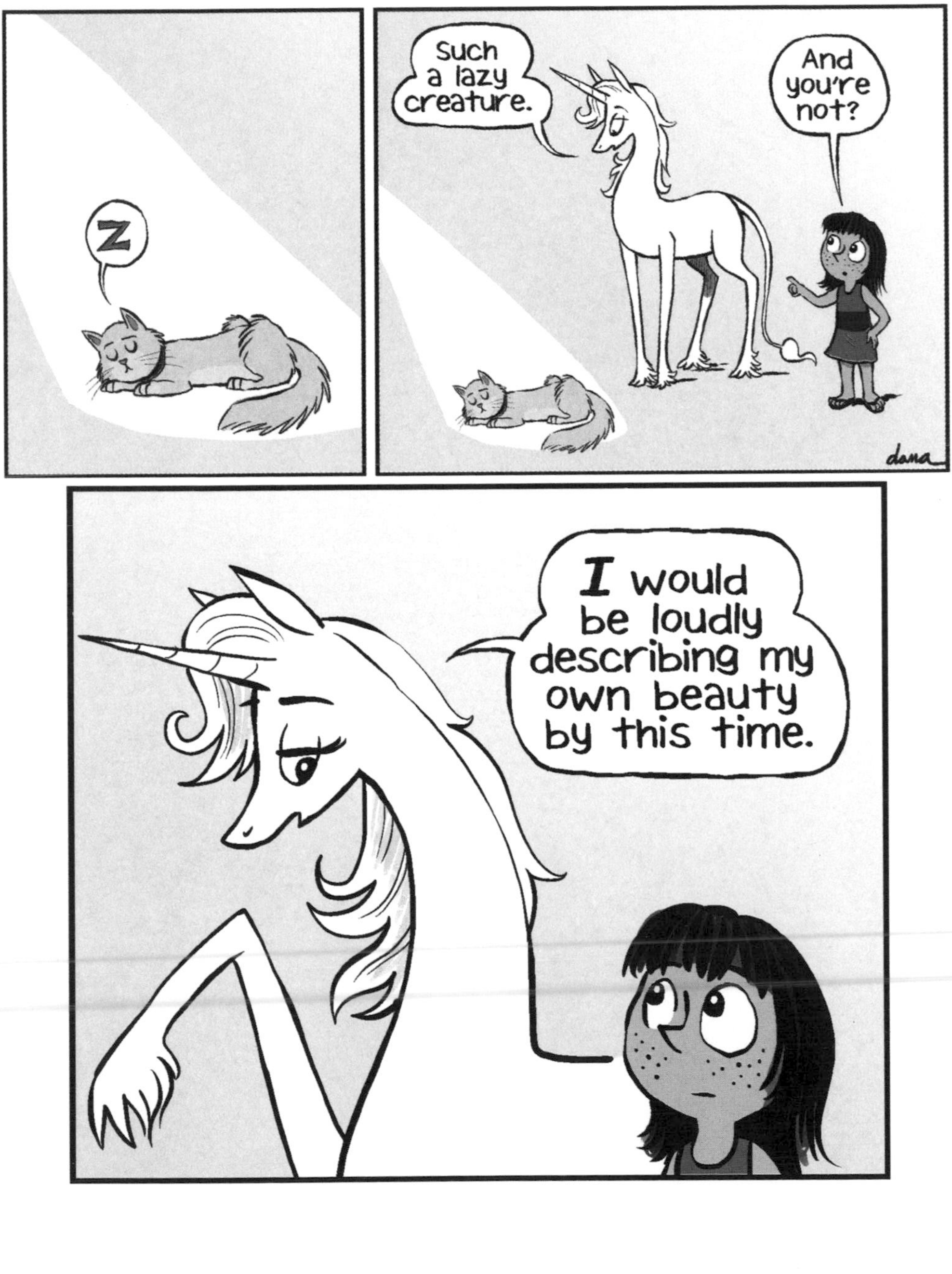
Z
Such a lazy creature.
And you're not?
dana
I would be loudly describing my own beauty by this time.

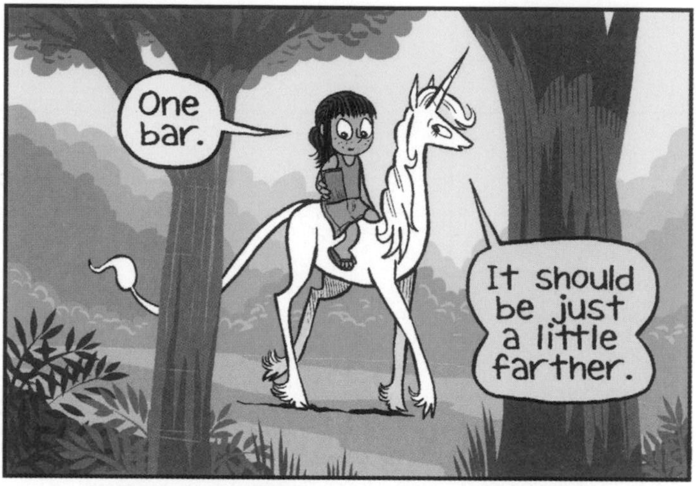
One bar.
It should be just a little farther.

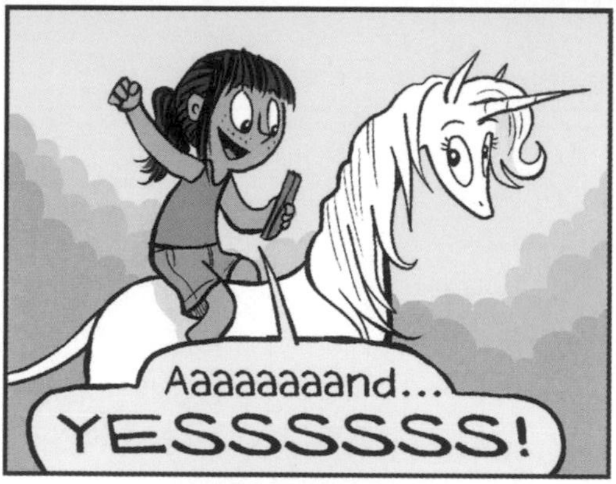
Aaaaaaaand...
YESSSSSS!

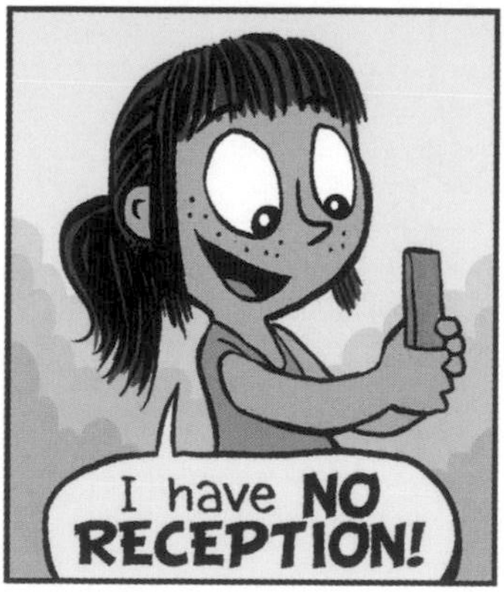
I have **NO RECEPTION!**

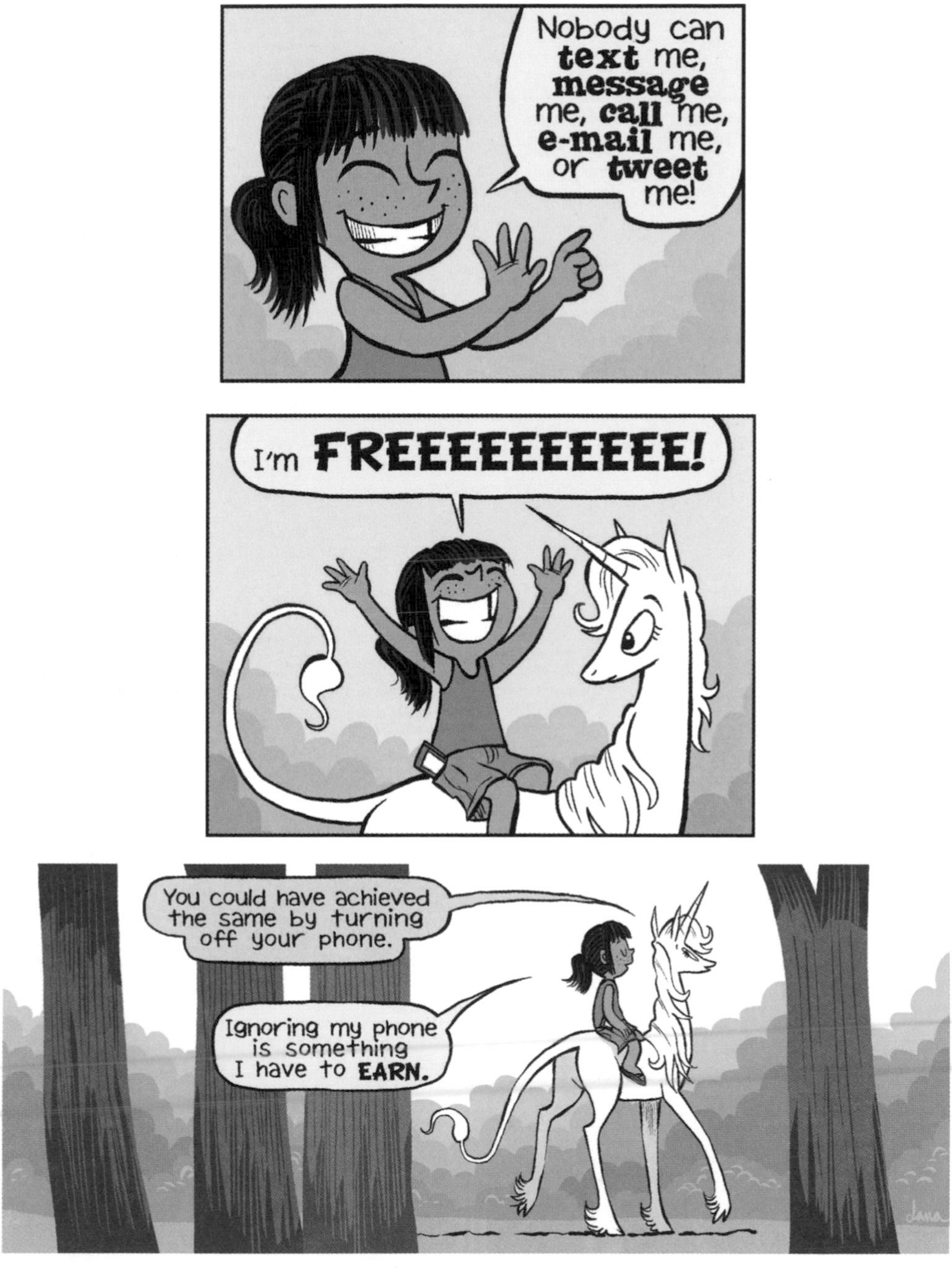
Nobody can **text** me, **message** me, **call** me, **e-mail** me, or **tweet** me!
I'm **FREEEEEEEEEE!**
You could have achieved the same by turning off your phone.
Ignoring my phone is something I have to **EARN.**
Dana

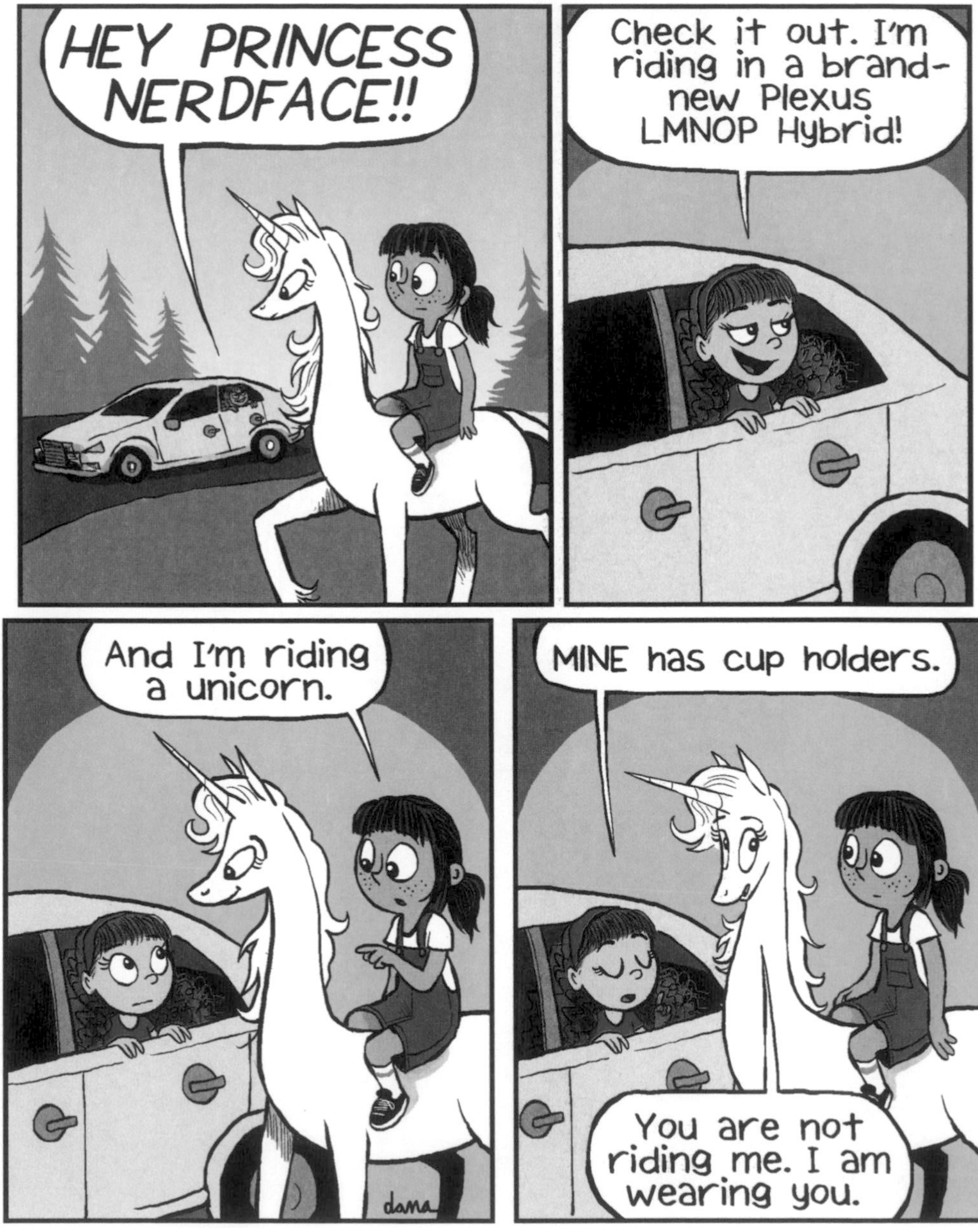
HEY PRINCESS NERDFACE!!
Check it out. I'm riding in a brand-new Plexus LMNOP Hybrid!
And I'm riding a unicorn.
MINE has cup holders.
You are not riding me. I am wearing you.
dana

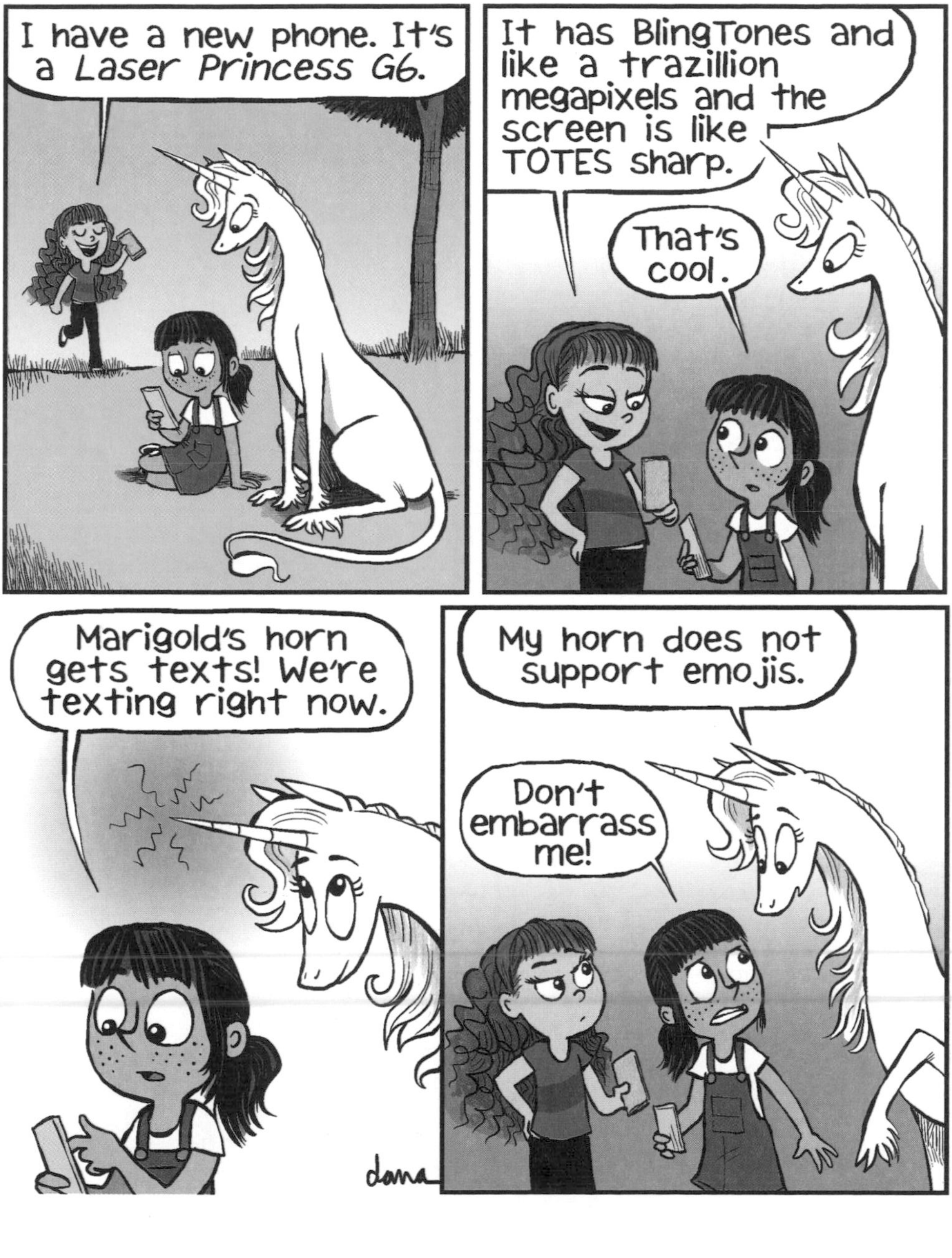
I have a new phone. It's a *Laser Princess G6.*
It has BlingTones and like a trazillion megapixels and the screen is like TOTES sharp.
That's cool.
Marigold's horn gets texts! We're texting right now.
My horn does not support emojis.
Don't embarrass me!
dana

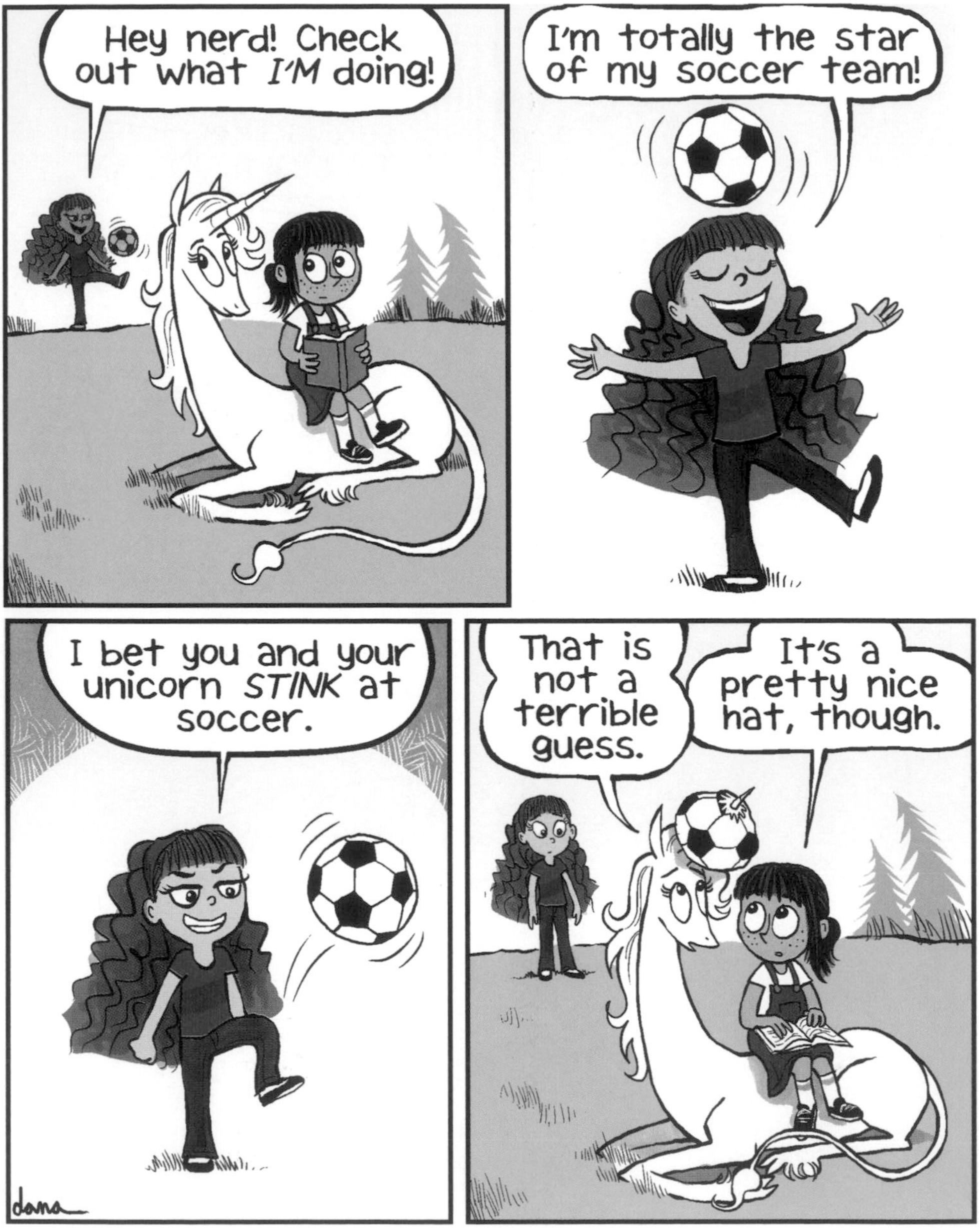
Hey nerd! Check out what I'M doing!
I'm totally the star of my soccer team!
I bet you and your unicorn STINK at soccer.
dana
That is not a terrible guess.
It's a pretty nice hat, though.

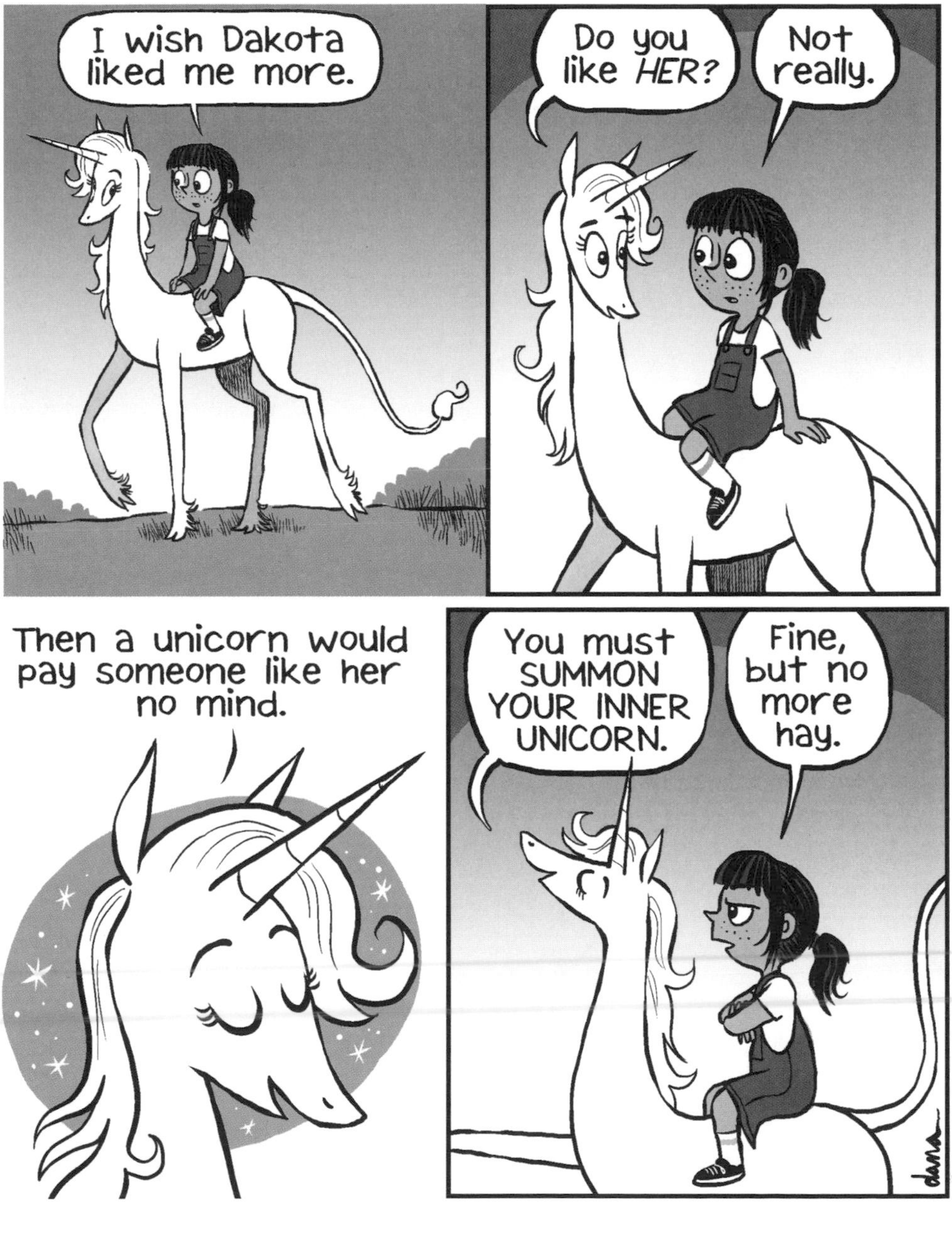
I wish Dakota liked me more.
Do you like *HER*?
Not really.
Then a unicorn would pay someone like her no mind.
You must SUMMON YOUR INNER UNICORN.
Fine, but no more hay.
dana

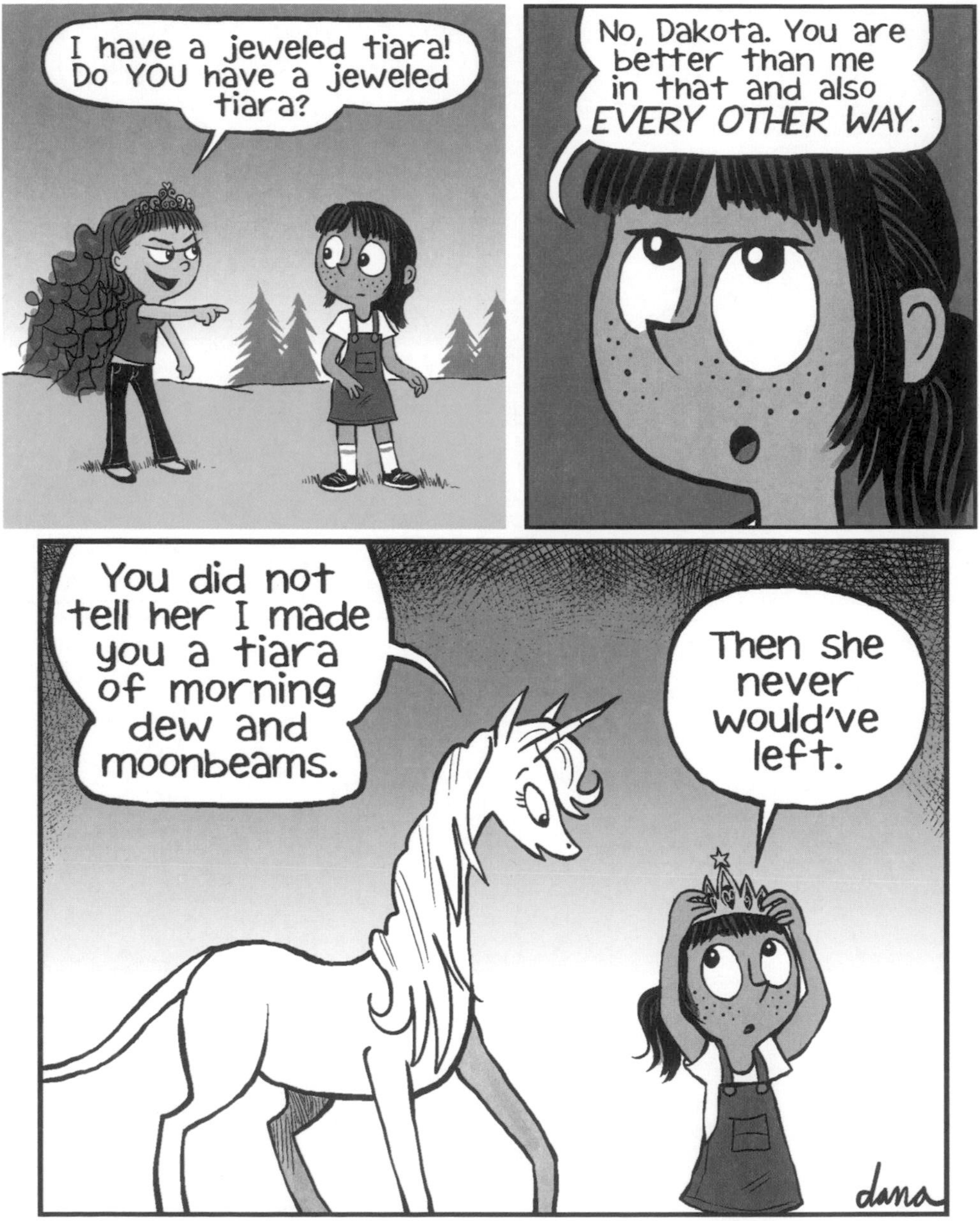
I have a jeweled tiara! Do YOU have a jeweled tiara?
No, Dakota. You are better than me in that and also EVERY OTHER WAY.
You did not tell her I made you a tiara of morning dew and moonbeams.
Then she never would've left.
dana

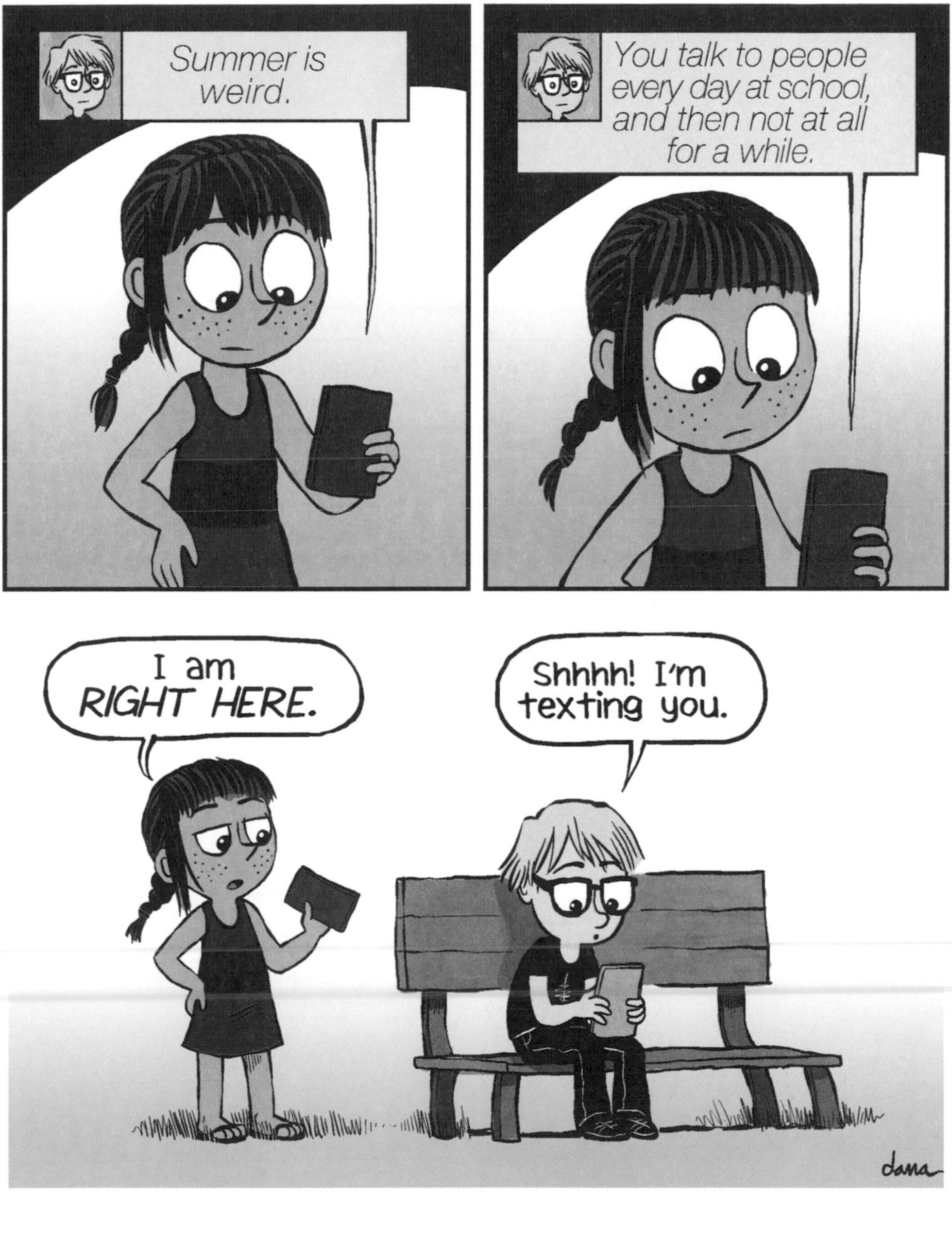
Summer is weird.
You talk to people every day at school, and then not at all for a while.
I am *RIGHT HERE.*
Shhhh! I'm texting you.
dana

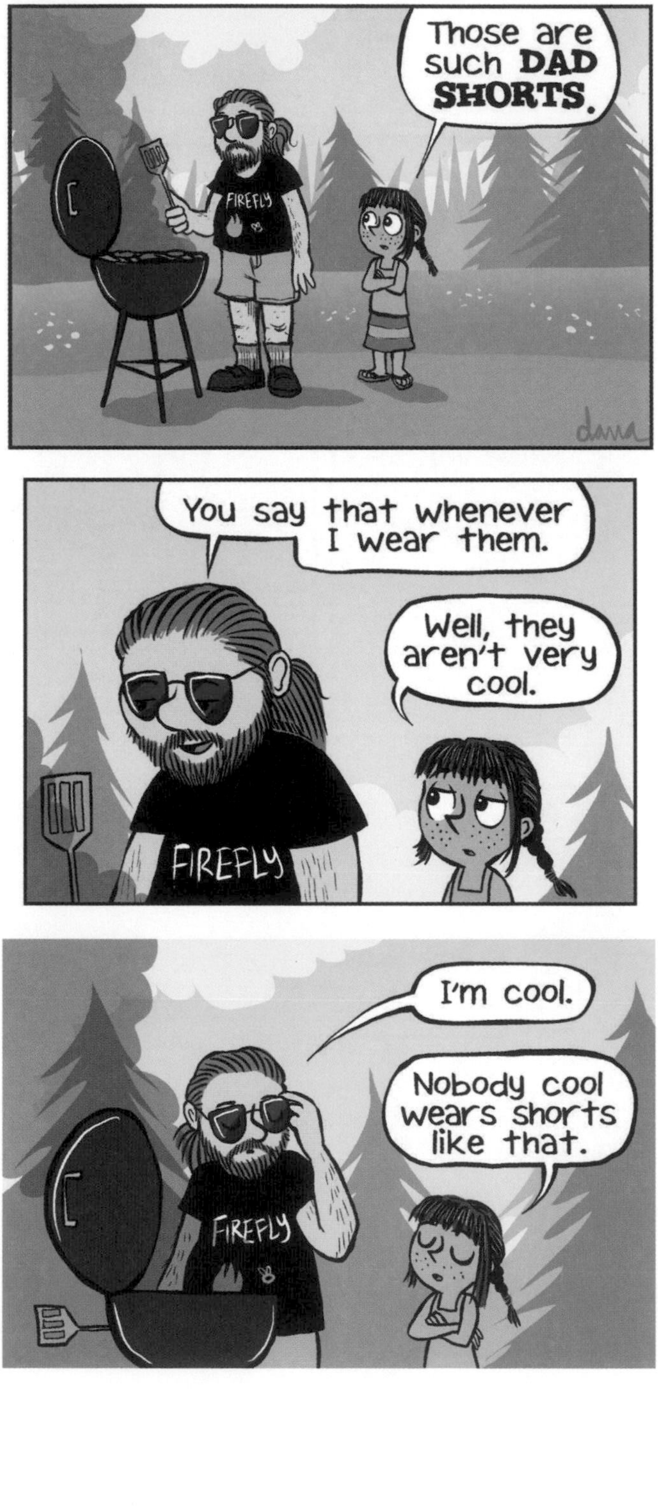
Those are such **DAD SHORTS**.
FIREFLY
dana
You say that whenever I wear them.
Well, they aren't very cool.
FIREFLY
I'm cool.
Nobody cool wears shorts like that.
FIREFLY

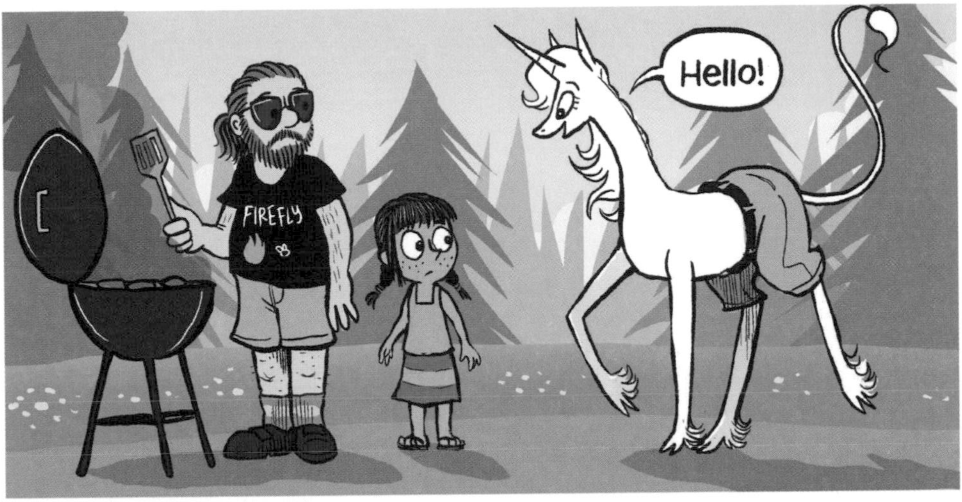
FIREFLY
Hello!

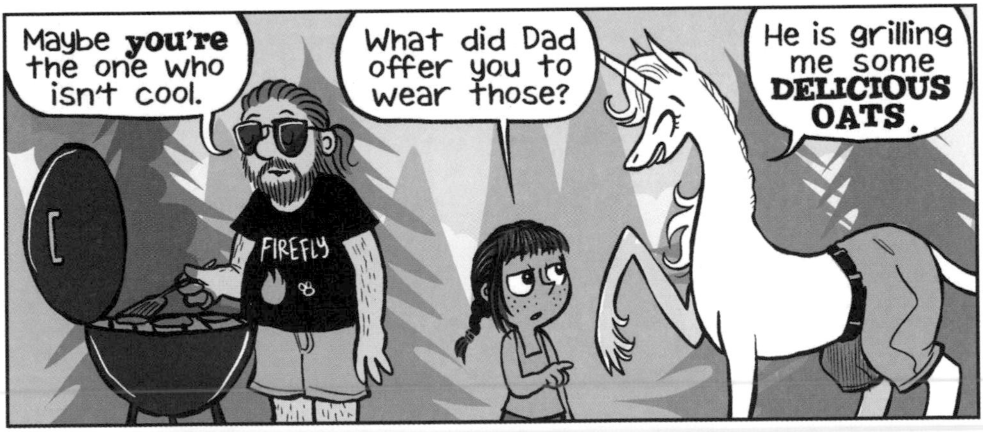
Maybe **you're** the one who isn't cool.
What did Dad offer you to wear those?
He is grilling me some **DELICIOUS OATS**.
FIREFLY

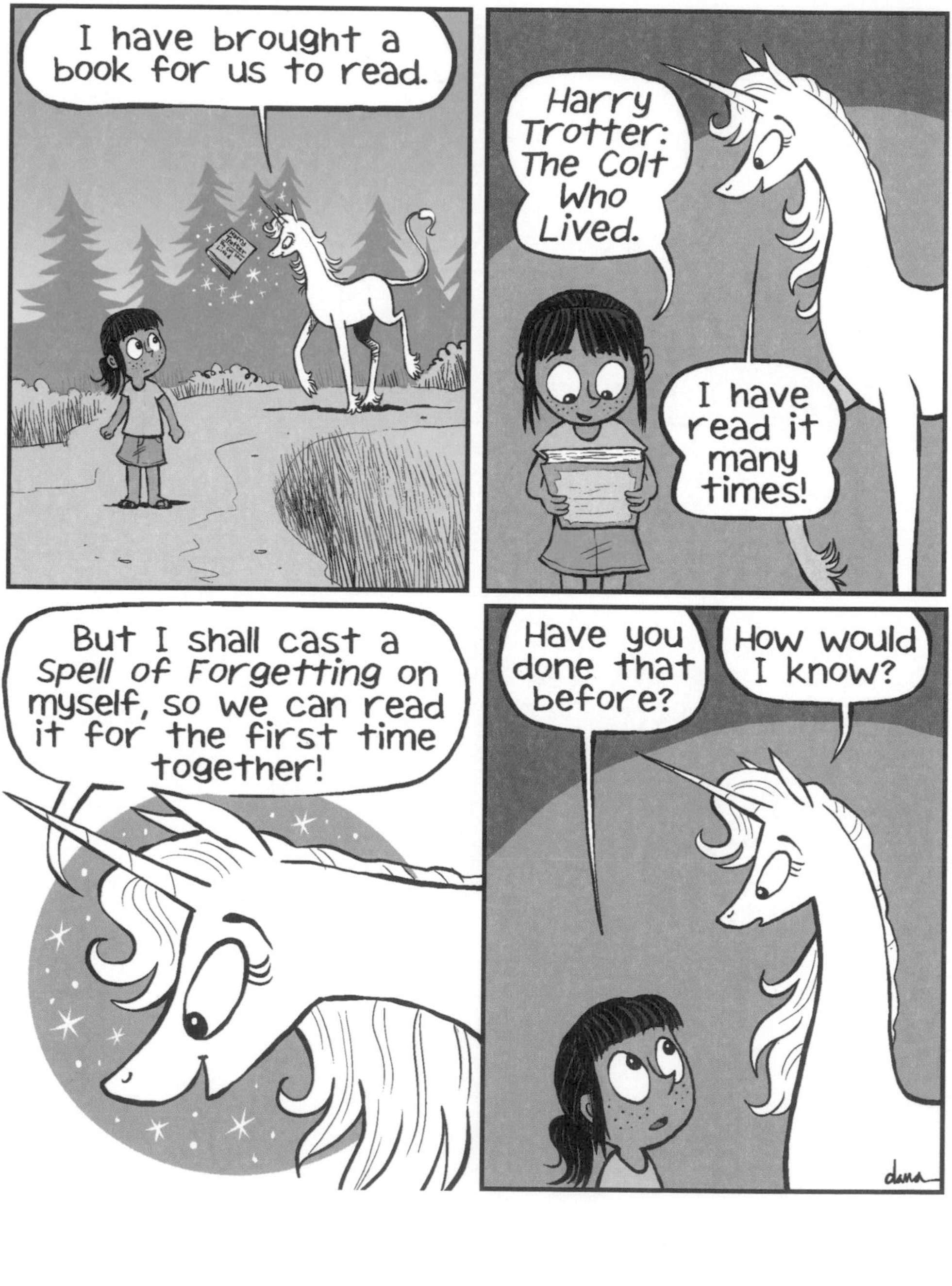
I have brought a book for us to read.
Harry Trotter
Harry Trotter: The Colt Who Lived.
I have read it many times!
But I shall cast a *Spell of Forgetting* on myself, so we can read it for the first time together!
Have you done that before?
How would I know?
dana

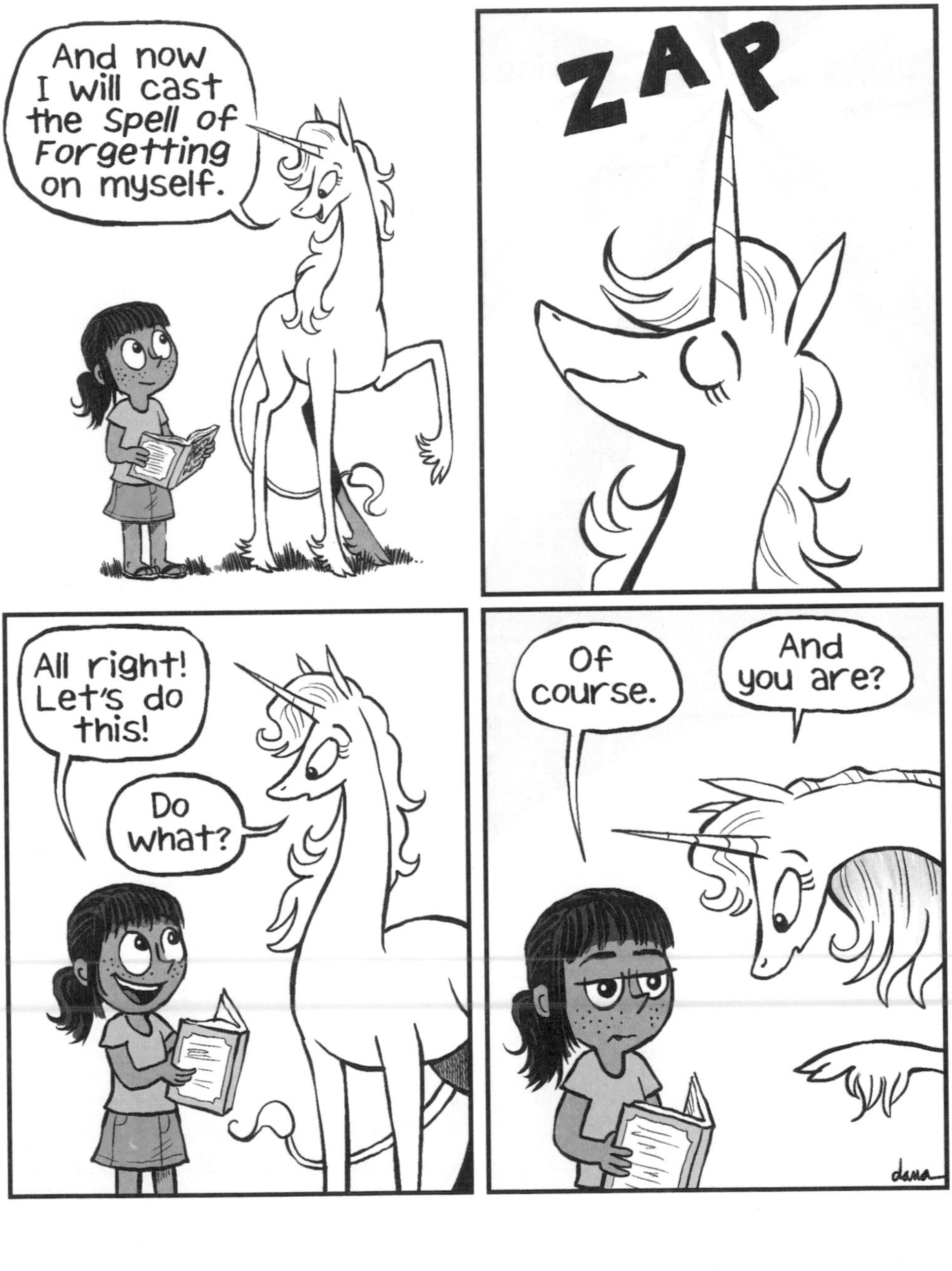
And now I will cast the *Spell of Forgetting* on myself.
ZAP
All right! Let's do this!
Do what?
Of course.
And you are?
dana

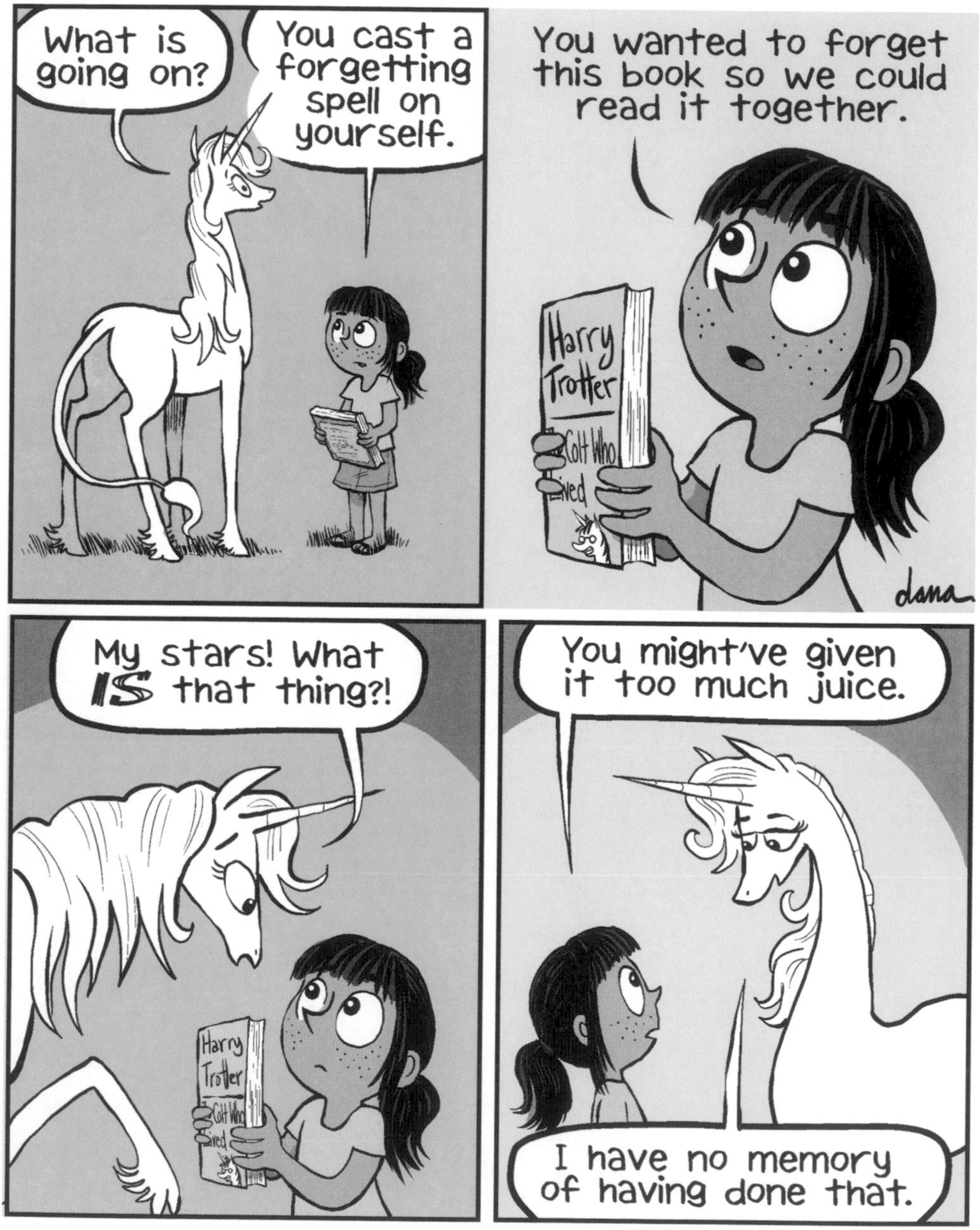
What is going on?
You cast a forgetting spell on yourself.
You wanted to forget this book so we could read it together.
Harry Trotter
Colt Who
ived
dana
My stars! What IS that thing?!
You might've given it too much juice.
I have no memory of having done that.

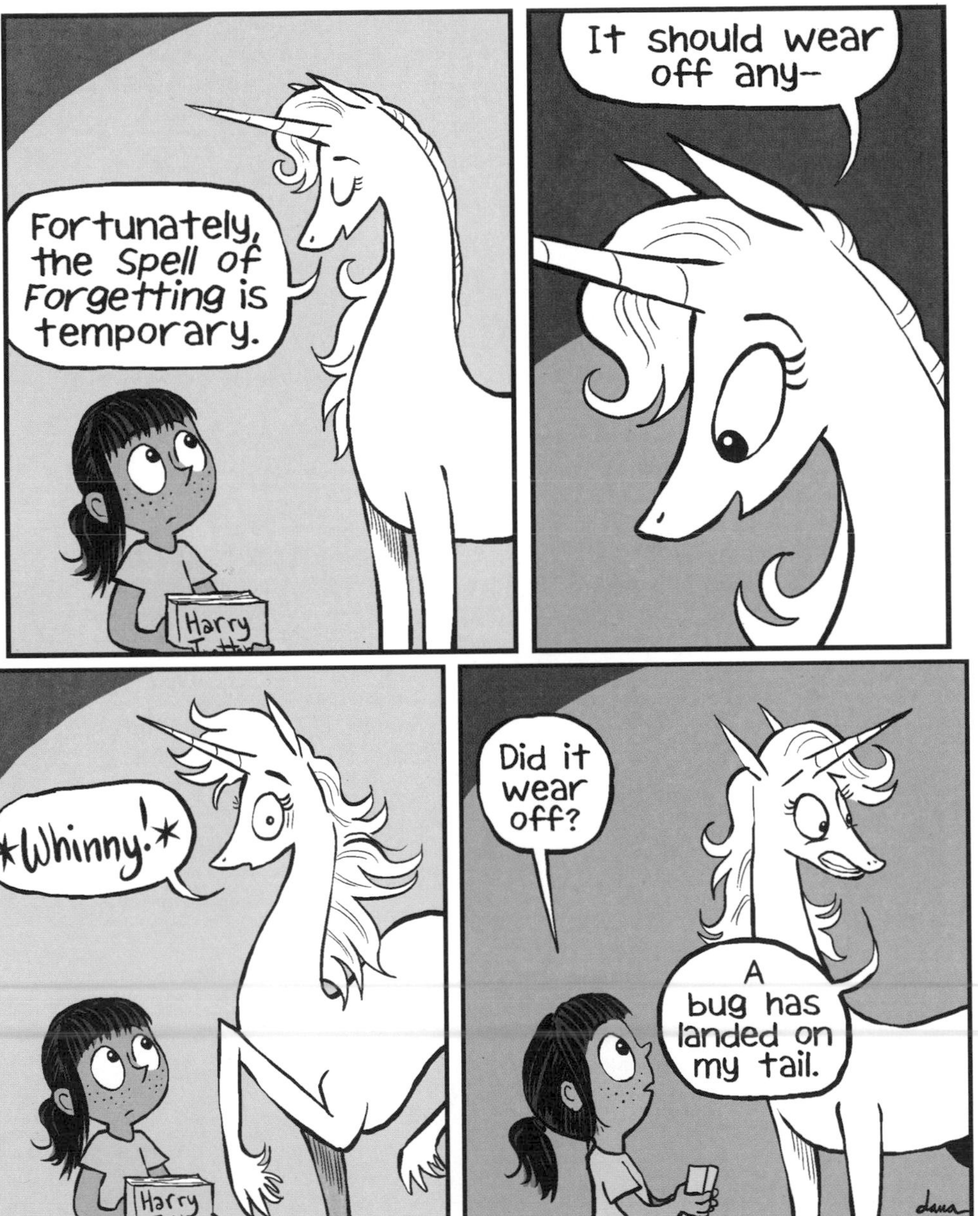
Fortunately, the *Spell of Forgetting* is temporary.
Harry
It should wear off any–
Whinny!
Harry
Did it wear off?
A bug has landed on my tail.
dana

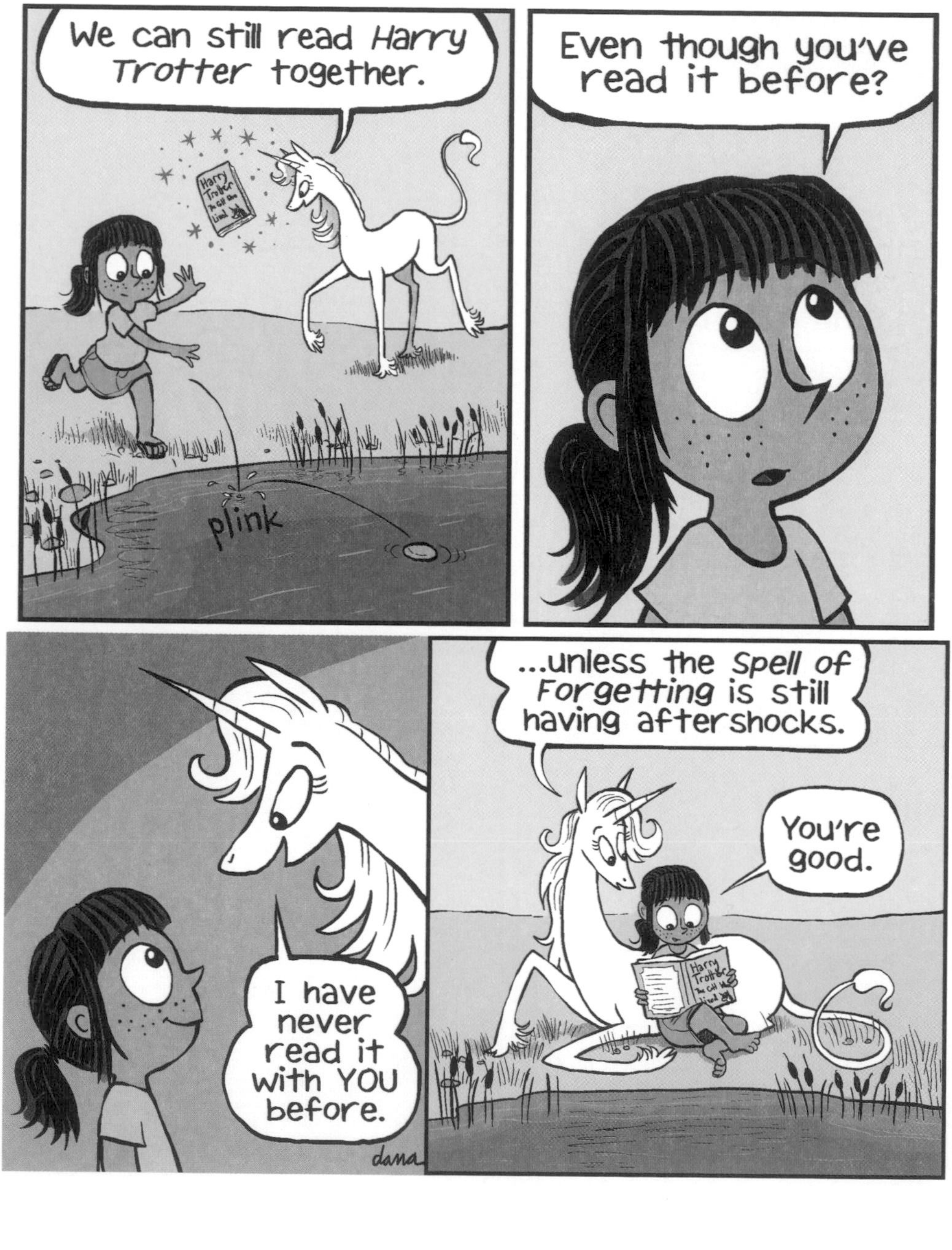
We can still read *Harry Trotter* together.
plink
Even though you've read it before?
I have never read it with YOU before.
...unless the *Spell of Forgetting* is still having aftershocks.
You're good.

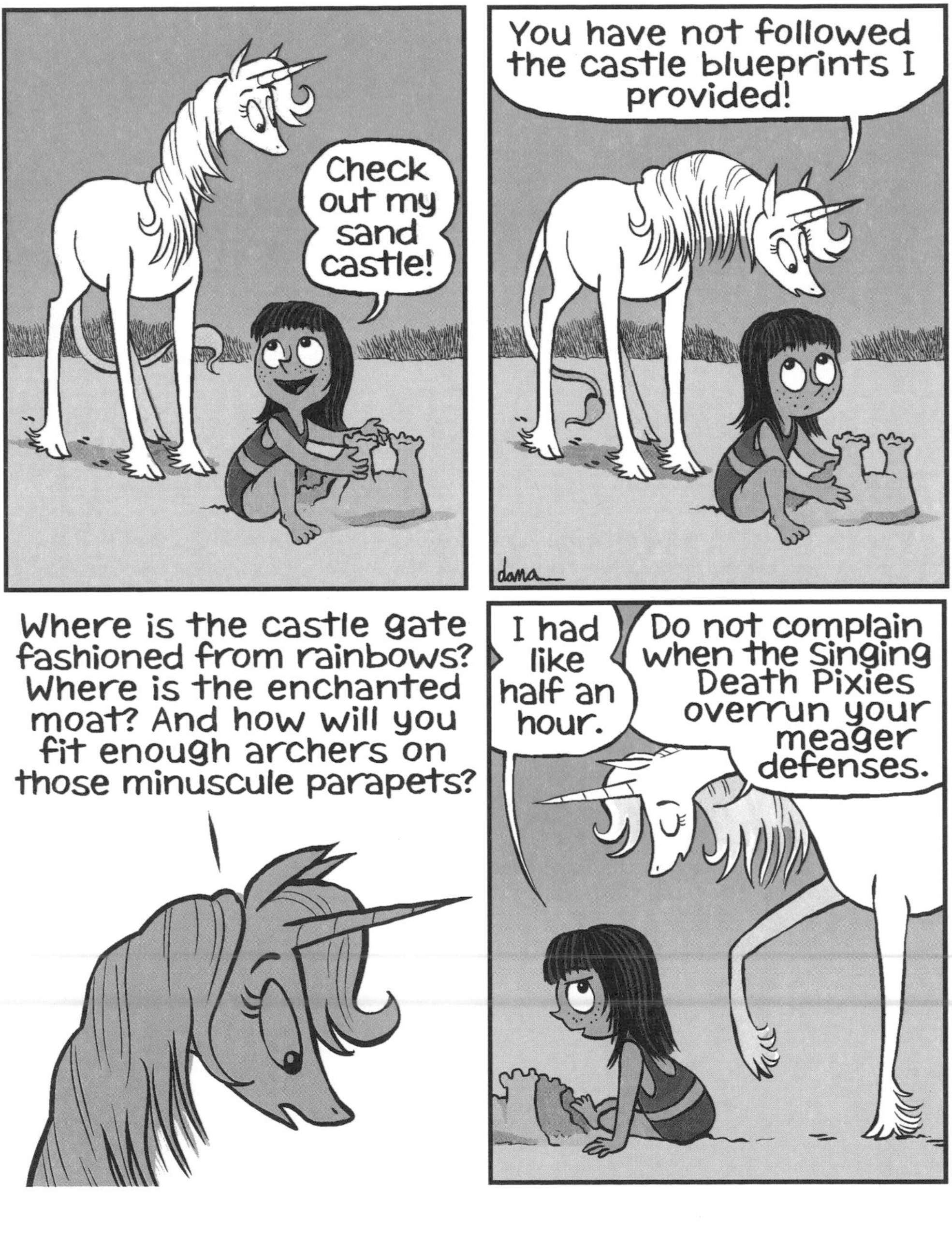
Check out my sand castle!
You have not followed the castle blueprints I provided!
Where is the castle gate fashioned from rainbows? Where is the enchanted moat? And how will you fit enough archers on those minuscule parapets?
I had like half an hour.
Do not complain when the Singing Death Pixies overrun your meager defenses.
dana

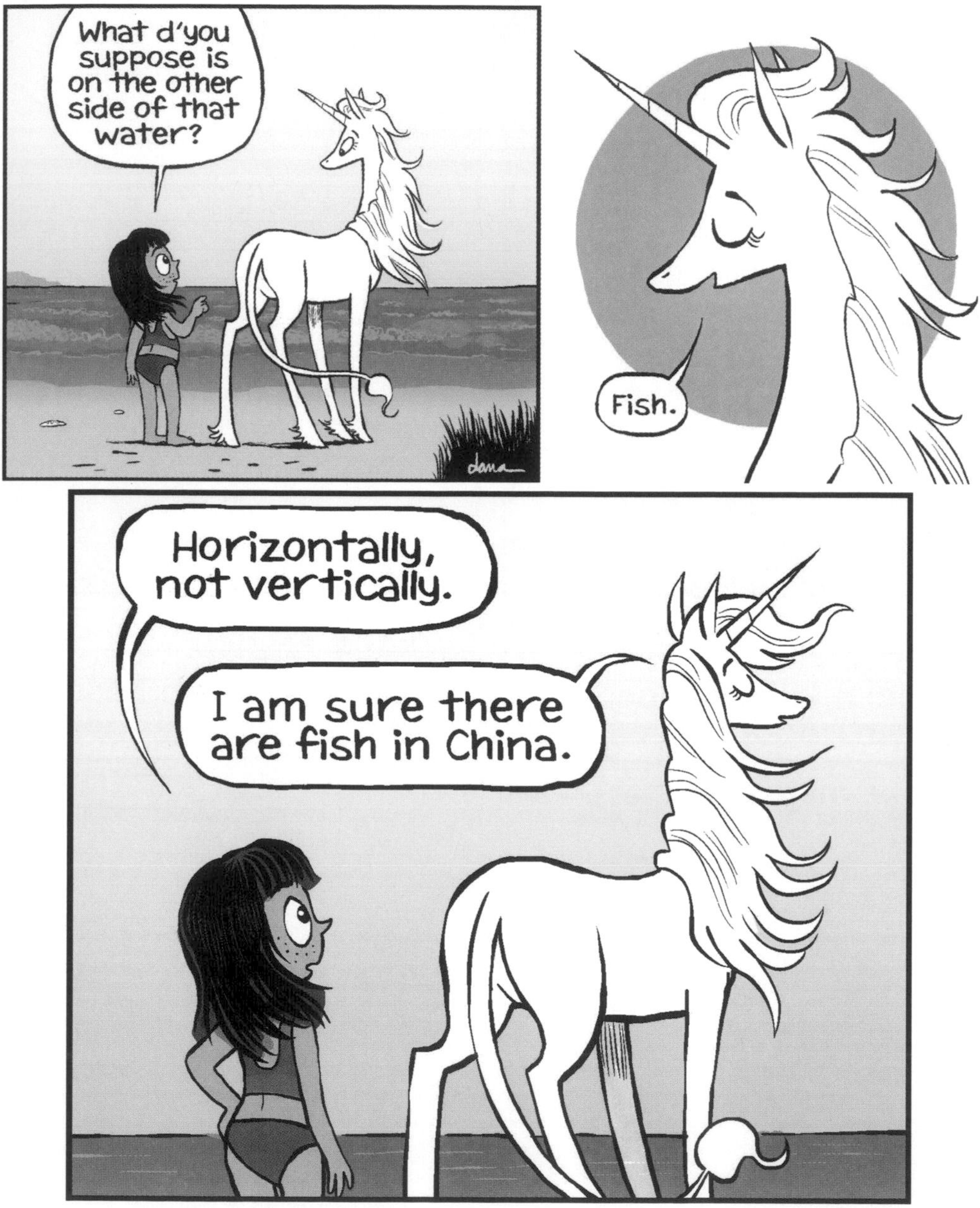
What d'you suppose is on the other side of that water?
Fish.
Horizontally, not vertically.
I am sure there are fish in China.

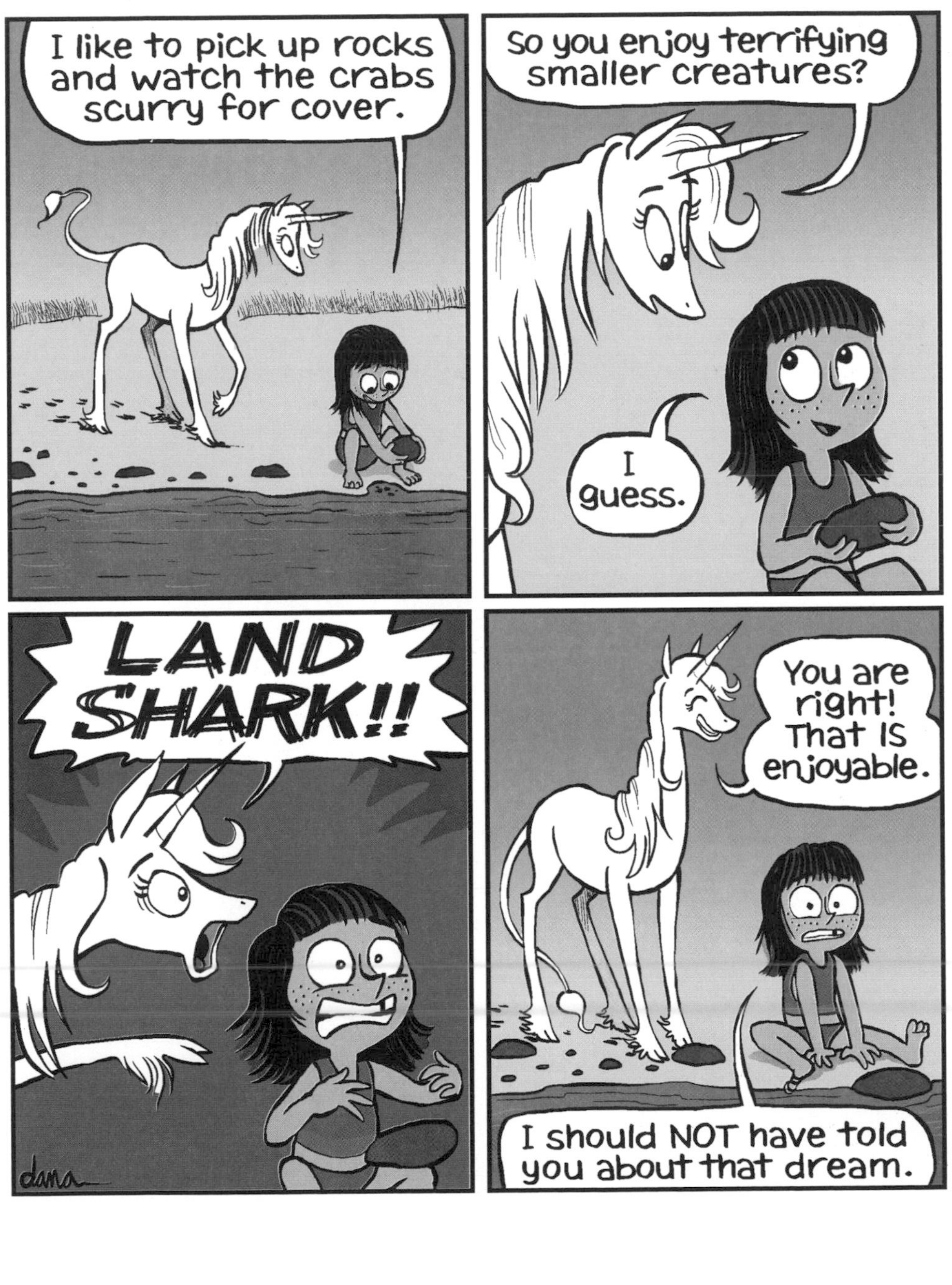
I like to pick up rocks and watch the crabs scurry for cover.
So you enjoy terrifying smaller creatures?
I guess.
LAND SHARK!!
You are right! That IS enjoyable.
I should NOT have told you about that dream.
dana

What are you reading?

My favorite book! Emily Zap, Witch Detective.

How do you know it is your favorite if you are still reading it?

This isn't the first time I've read it.

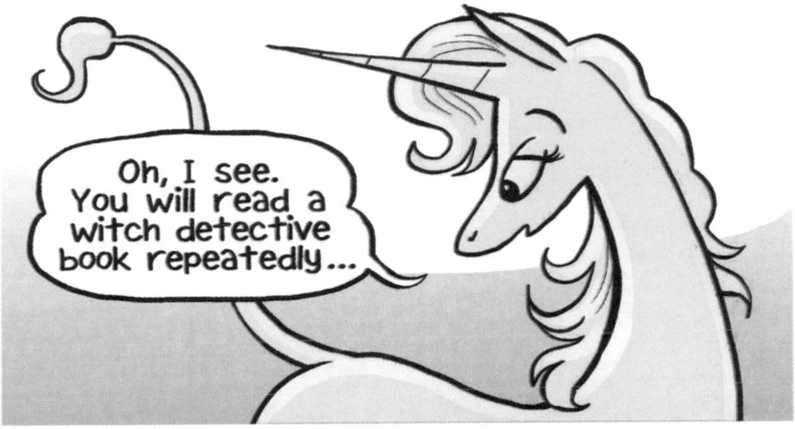
Oh, I see. You will read a witch detective book repeatedly...

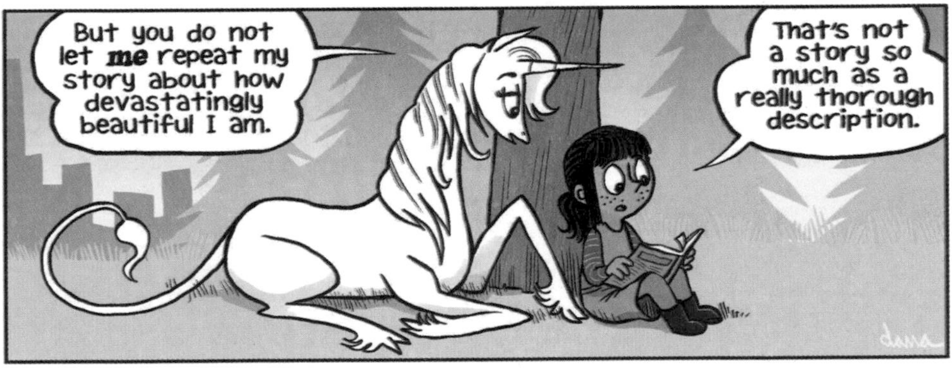
But you do not let **me** repeat my story about how devastatingly beautiful I am.
That's not a story so much as a really thorough description.

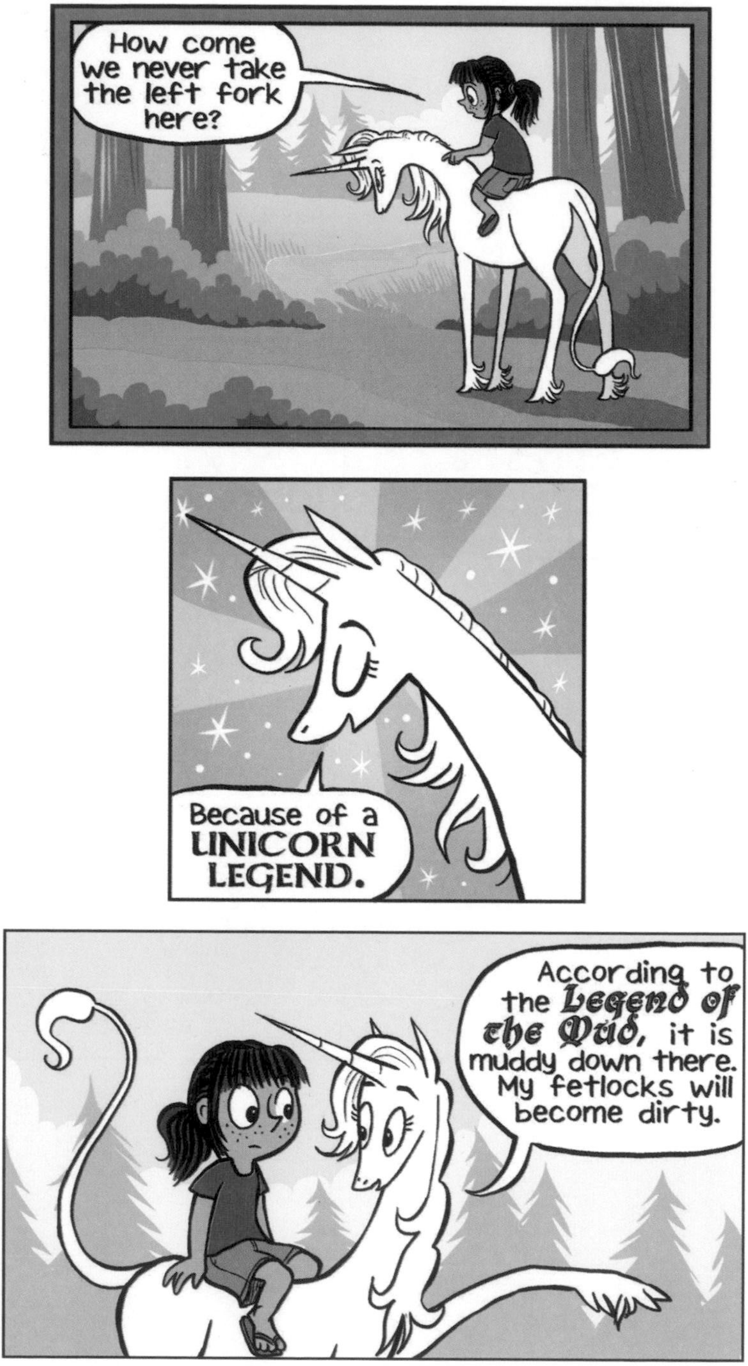
How come we never take the left fork here?
Because of a UNICORN LEGEND.
According to the Legend of the Mud, it is muddy down there. My fetlocks will become dirty.

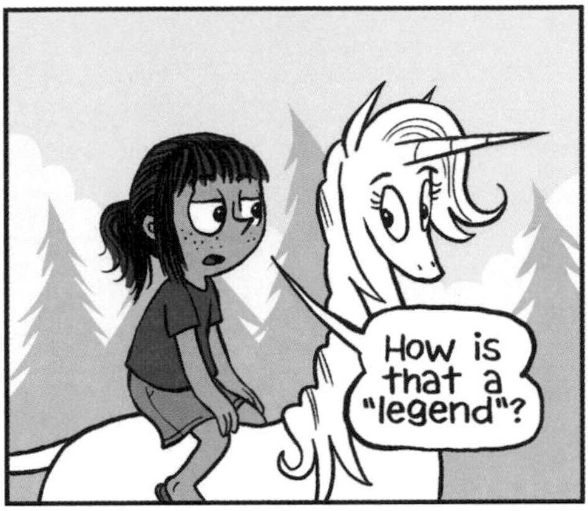
How is that a "legend"?

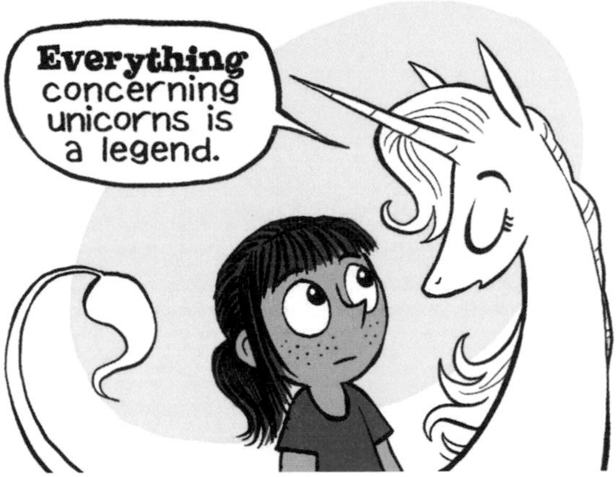
Everything concerning unicorns is a legend.

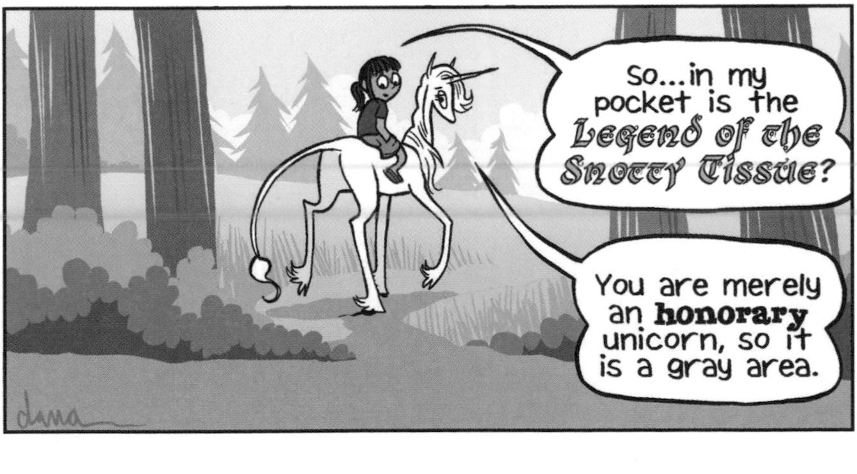
So...in my pocket is the Legend of the Snotty Tissue?
You are merely an **honorary** unicorn, so it is a gray area.
dana

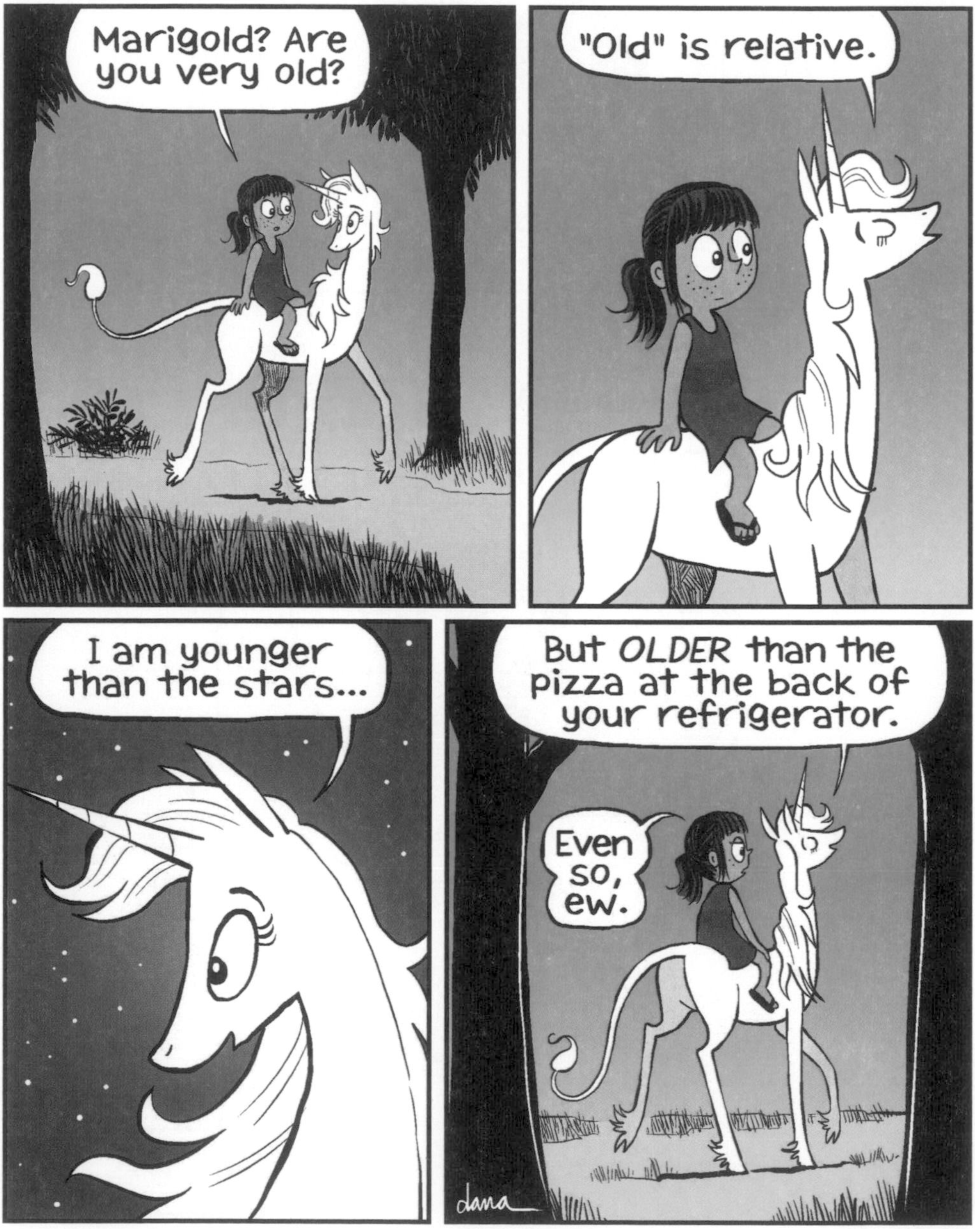
Marigold? Are you very old?
"Old" is relative.
I am younger than the stars...
But *OLDER* than the pizza at the back of your refrigerator.
Even so, ew.
dana

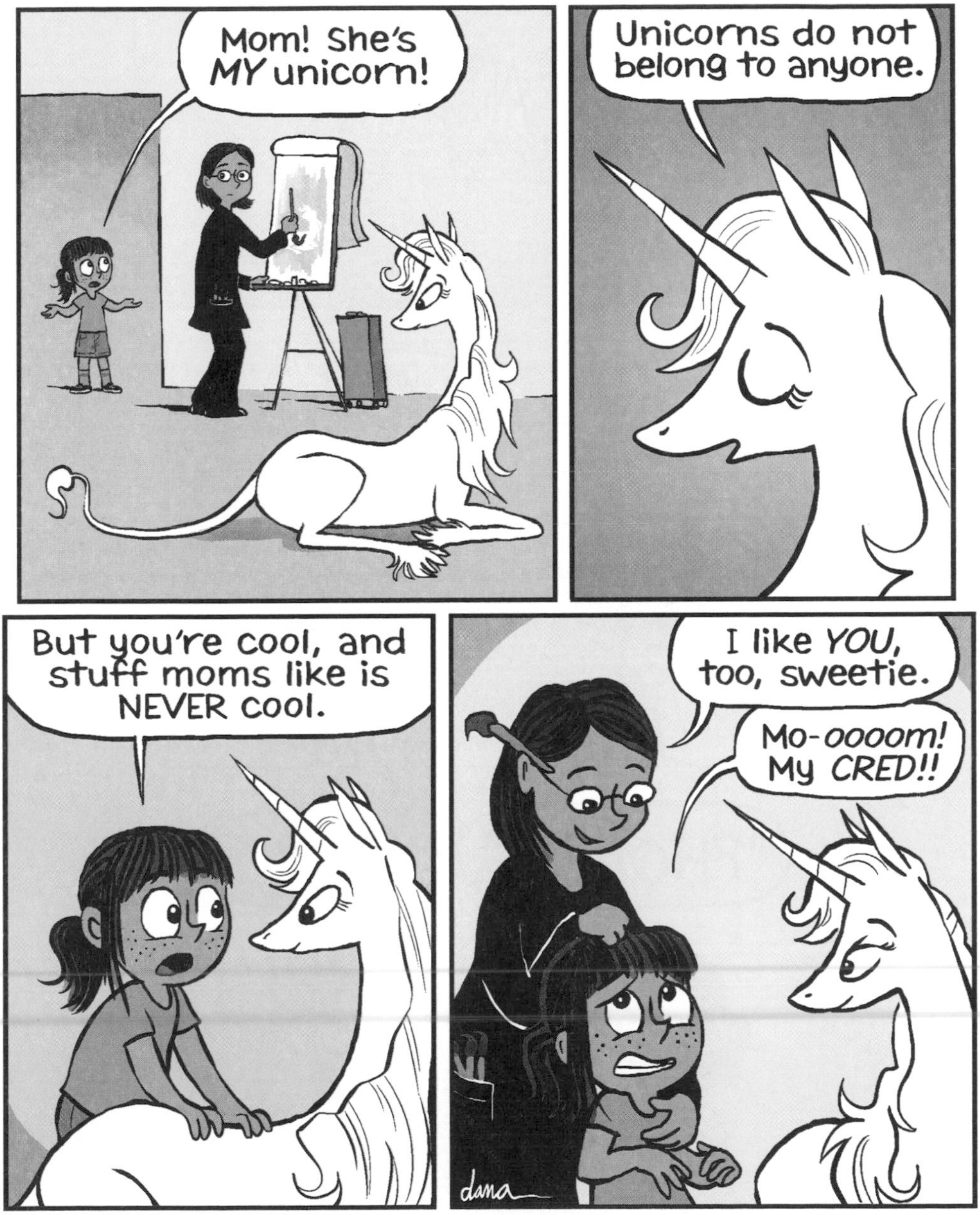
Mom! She's MY unicorn!
Unicorns do not belong to anyone.
But you're cool, and stuff moms like is NEVER cool.
I like YOU, too, sweetie.
Mo-oooom! My CRED!!
dana

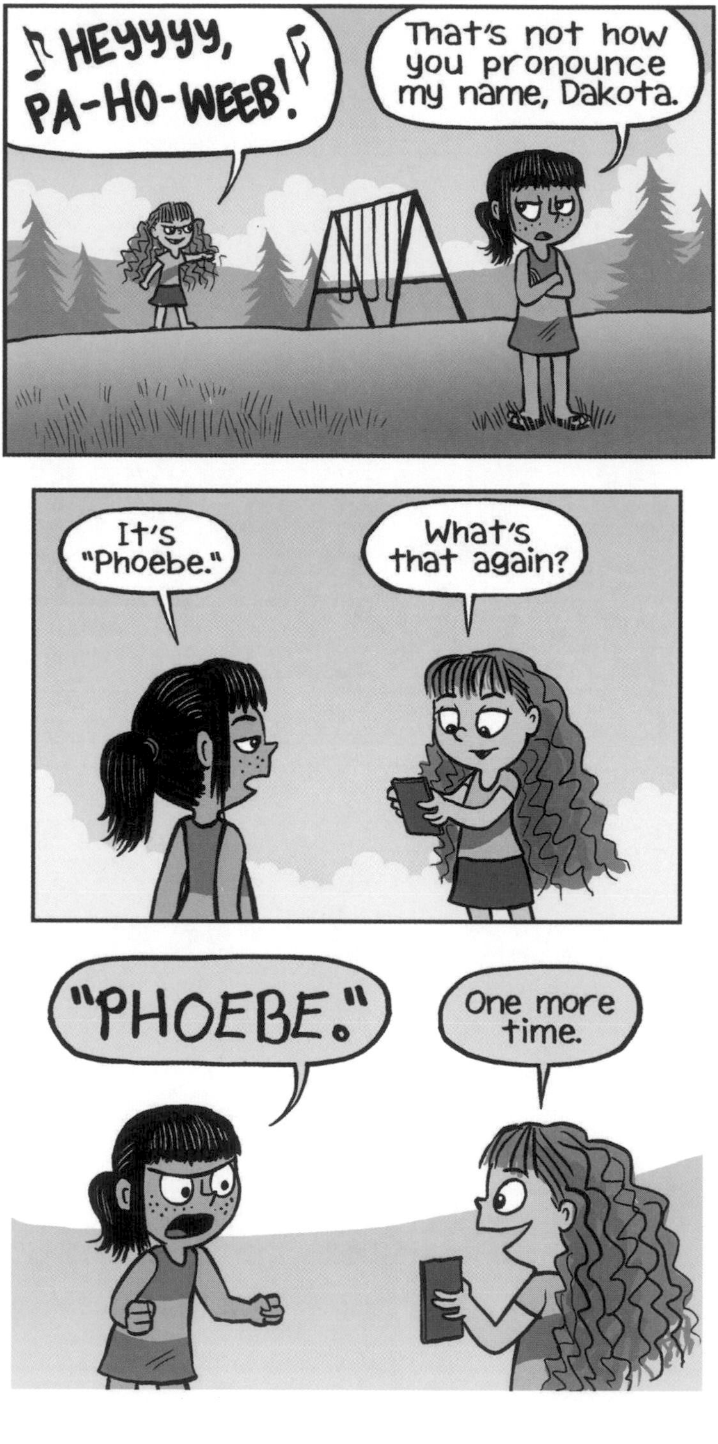
HEYYYY, PA-HO-WEEB!
That's not how you pronounce my name, Dakota.
It's "Phoebe."
What's that again?
"PHOEBE."
One more time.

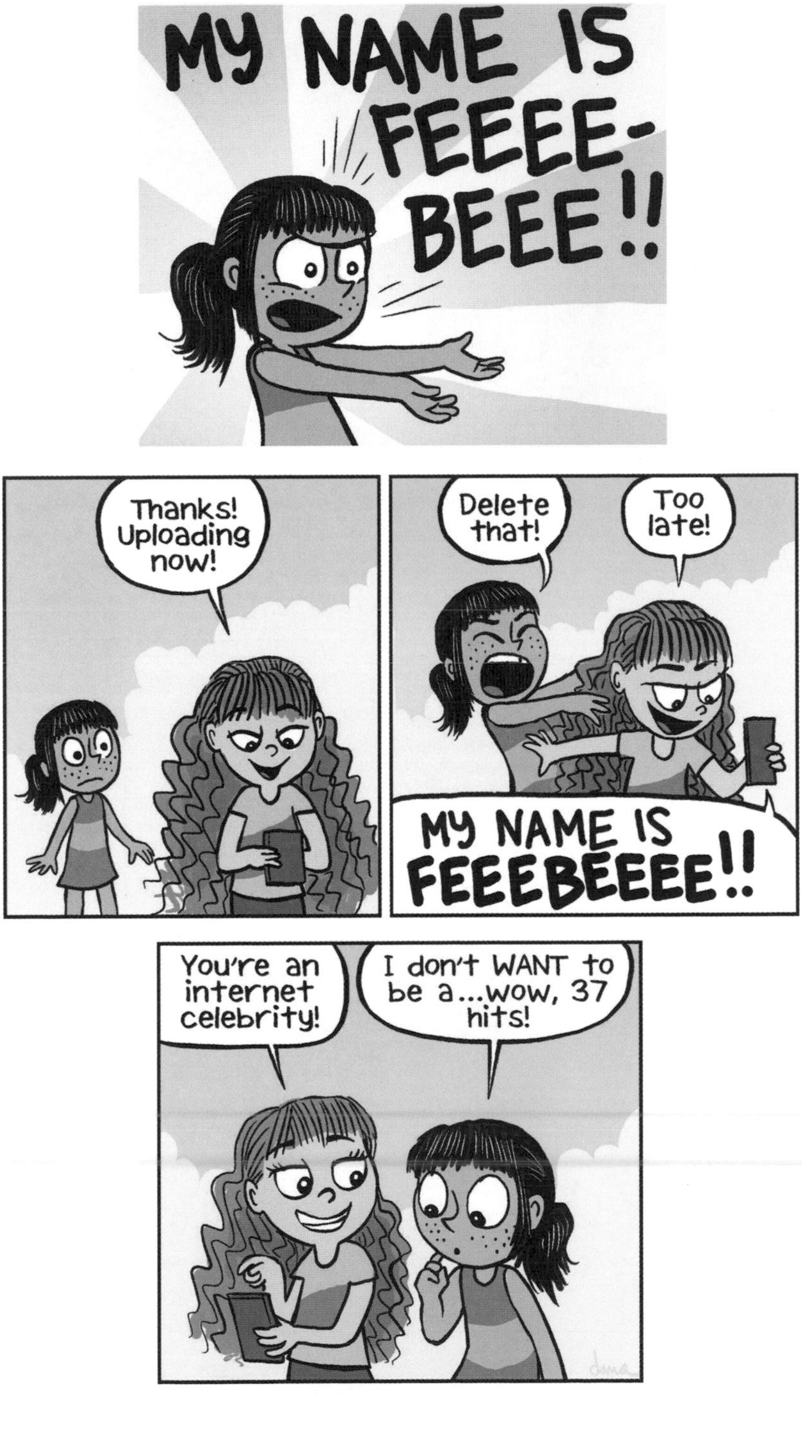
MY NAME IS FEEEE-BEEE!!
Thanks! Uploading now!
Delete that!
Too late!
MY NAME IS FEEEBEEEE!!
You're an internet celebrity!
I don't WANT to be a...wow, 37 hits!

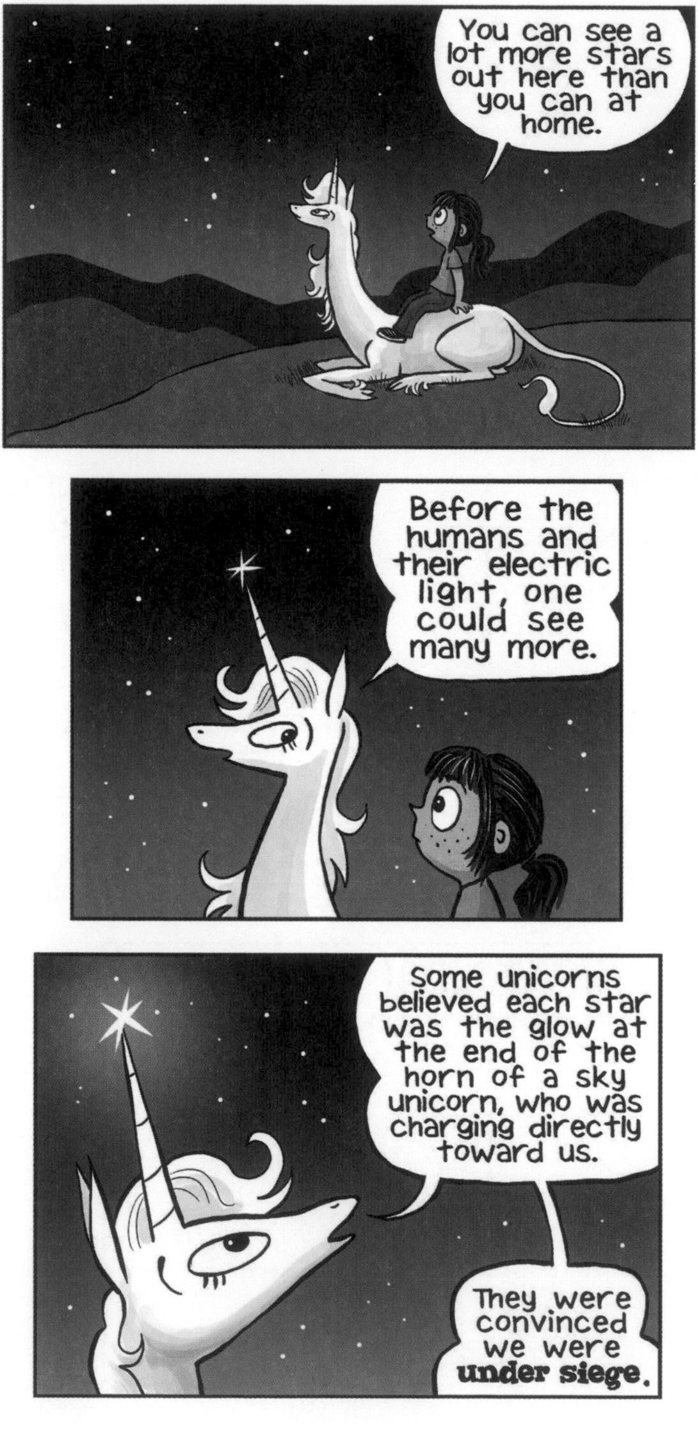

You can see a lot more stars out here than you can at home.
Before the humans and their electric light, one could see many more.
Some unicorns believed each star was the glow at the end of the horn of a sky unicorn, who was charging directly toward us.
They were convinced we were **under siege**.

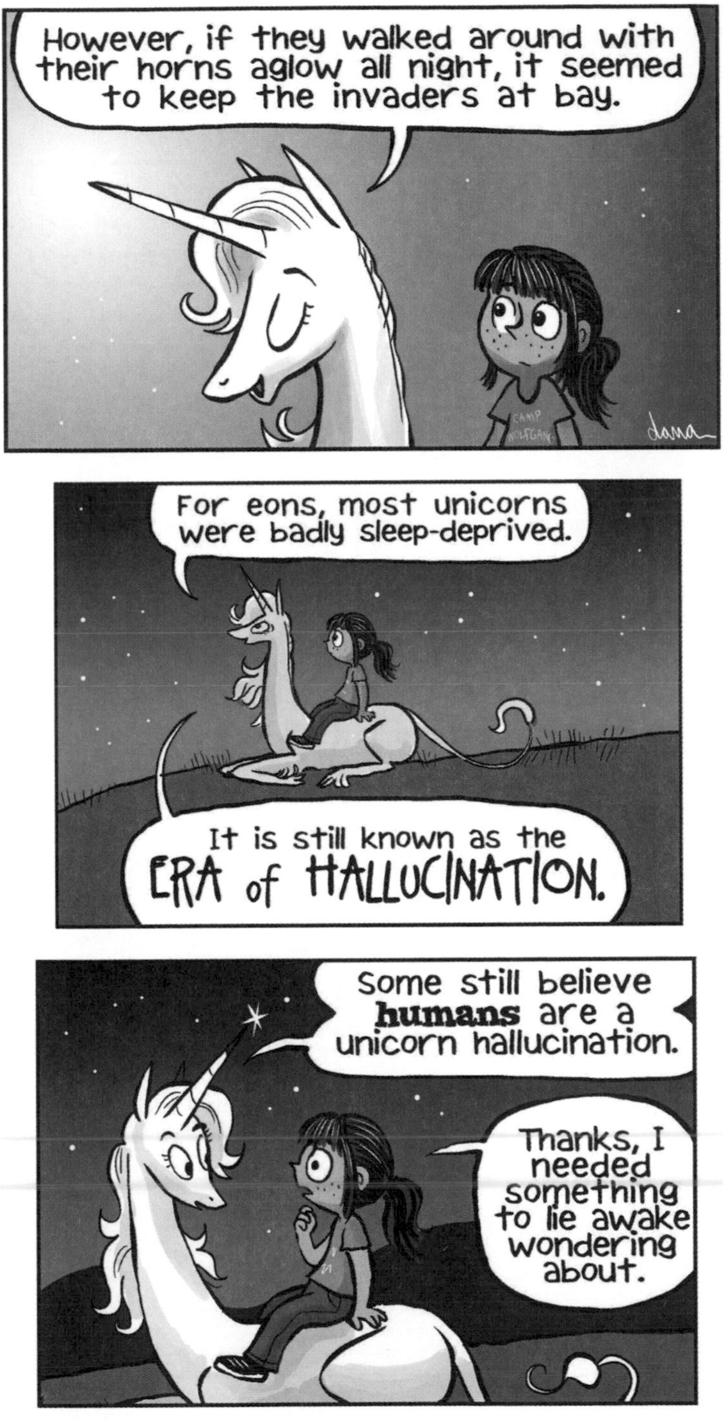
However, if they walked around with their horns aglow all night, it seemed to keep the invaders at bay.
For eons, most unicorns were badly sleep-deprived.
It is still known as the ERA of HALLUCINATION.
Some still believe **humans** are a unicorn hallucination.
Thanks, I needed something to lie awake wondering about.

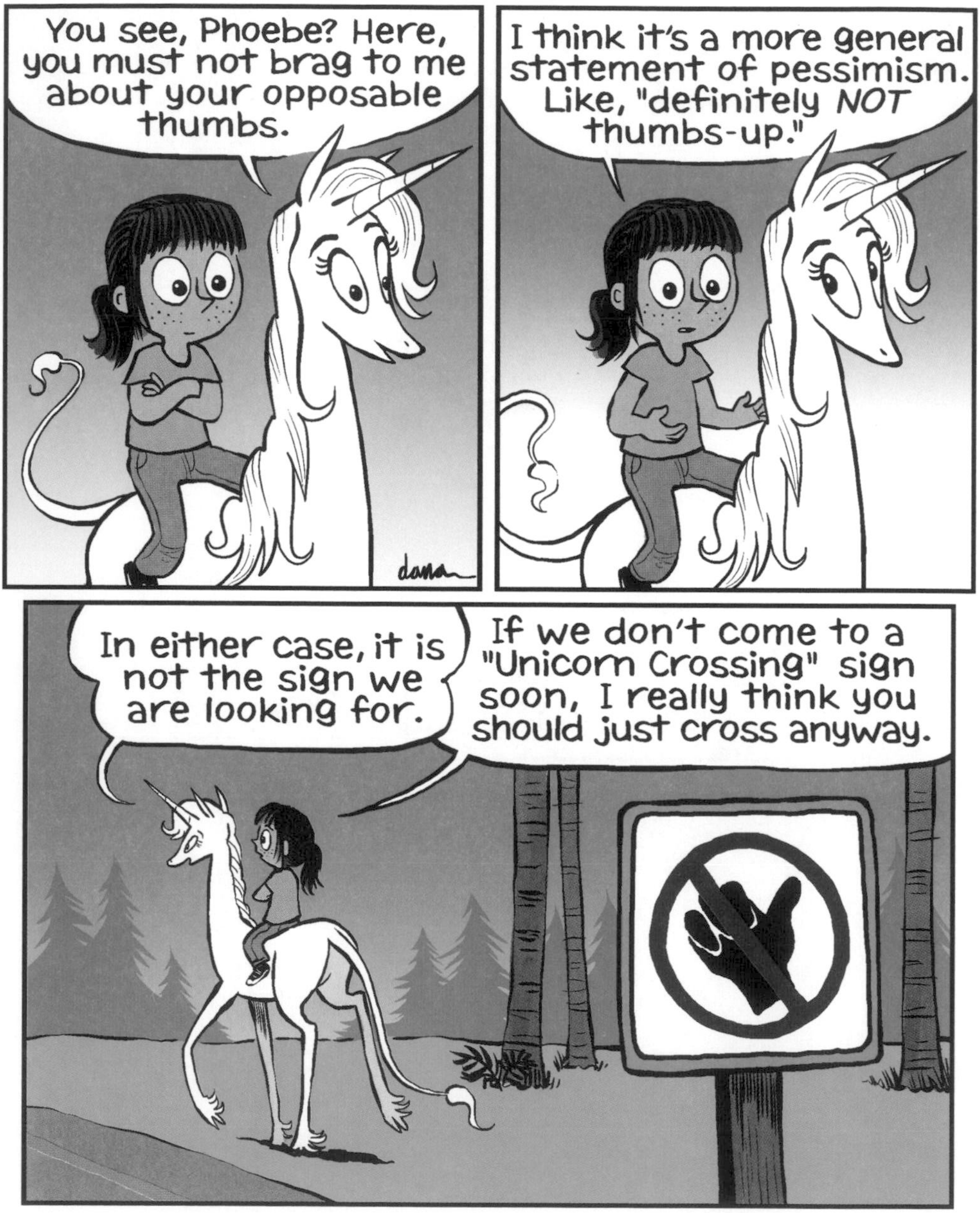
You see, Phoebe? Here, you must not brag to me about your opposable thumbs.
I think it's a more general statement of pessimism. Like, "definitely NOT thumbs-up."
dana
In either case, it is not the sign we are looking for.
If we don't come to a "Unicorn Crossing" sign soon, I really think you should just cross anyway.

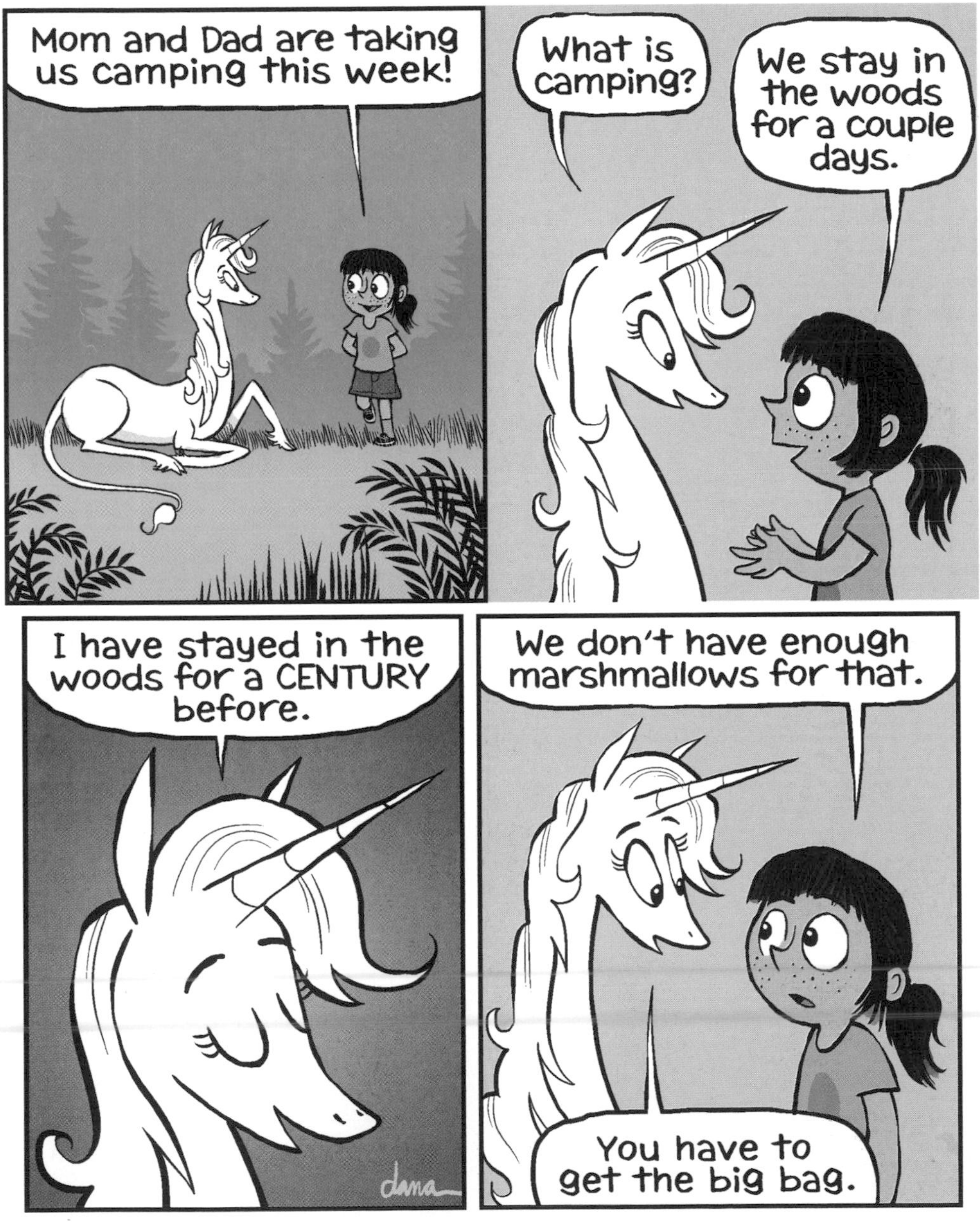
Mom and Dad are taking us camping this week!
What is camping?
We stay in the woods for a couple days.
I have stayed in the woods for a CENTURY before.
We don't have enough marshmallows for that.
You have to get the big bag.
dana

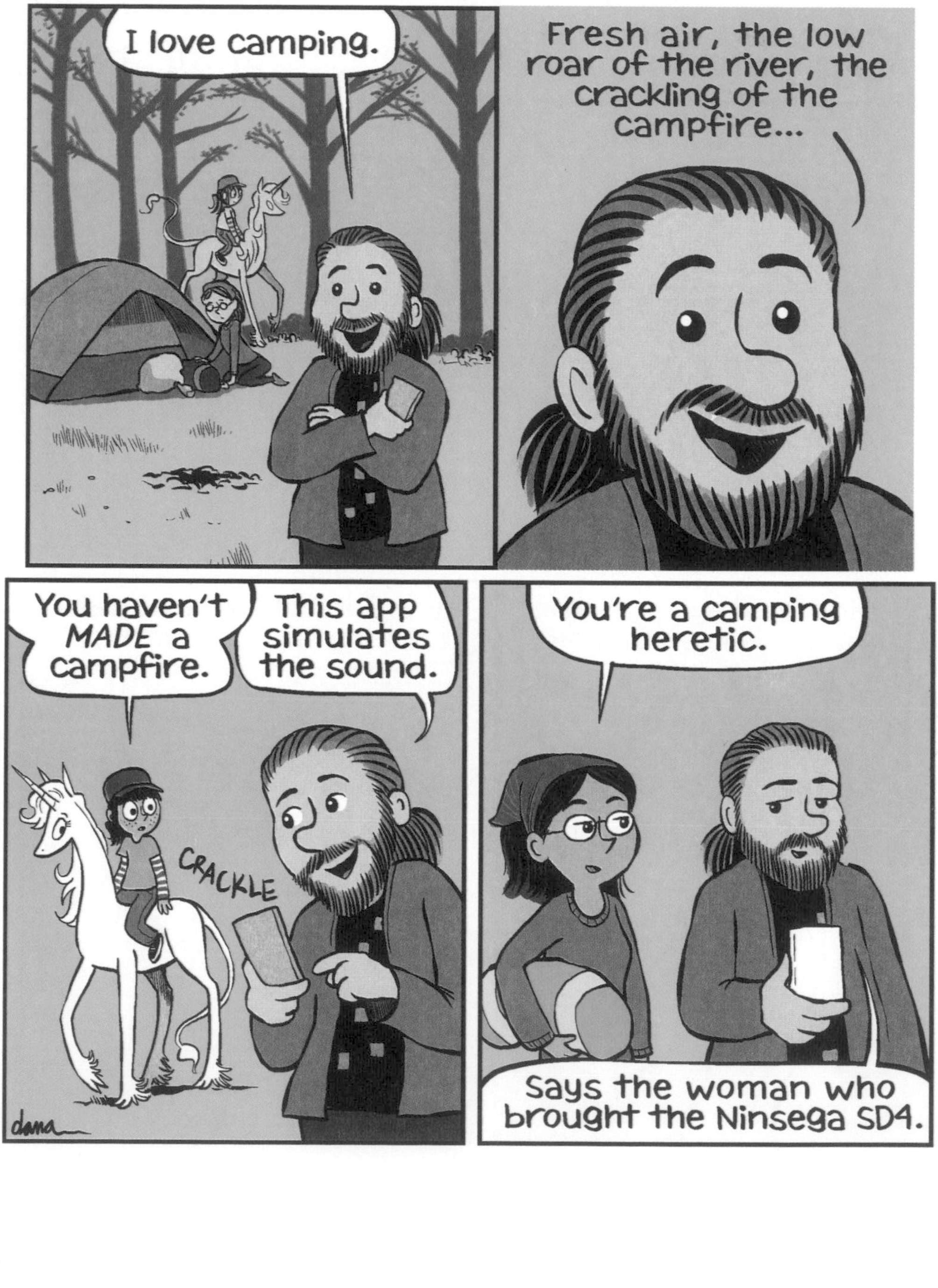
I love camping.
Fresh air, the low roar of the river, the crackling of the campfire...
You haven't *MADE* a campfire.
This app simulates the sound.
CRACKLE
dana
You're a camping heretic.
Says the woman who brought the Ninsega SD4.

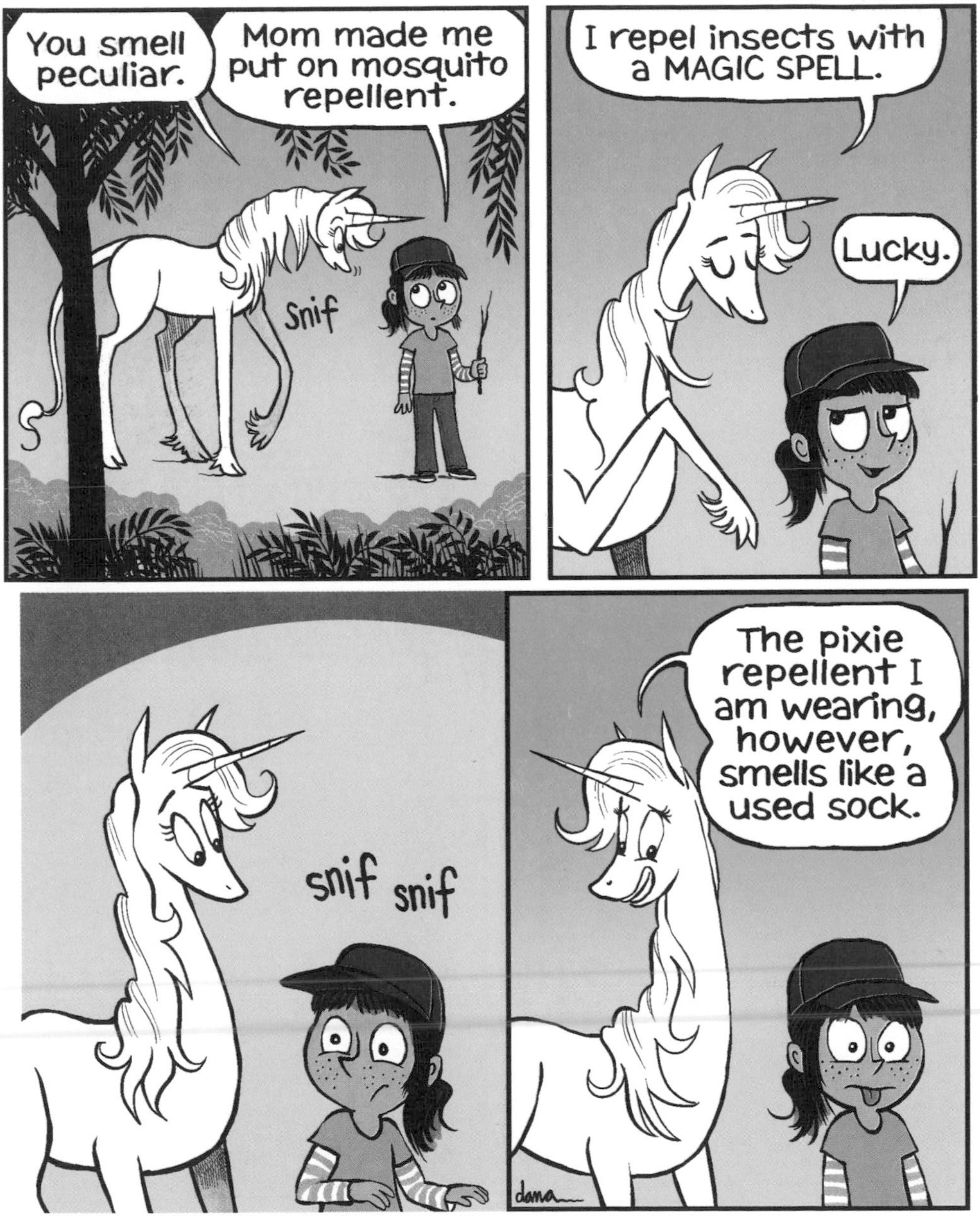
You smell peculiar.
Mom made me put on mosquito repellent.
Snif
I repel insects with a MAGIC SPELL.
Lucky.
snif snif
The pixie repellent I am wearing, however, smells like a used sock.
dana

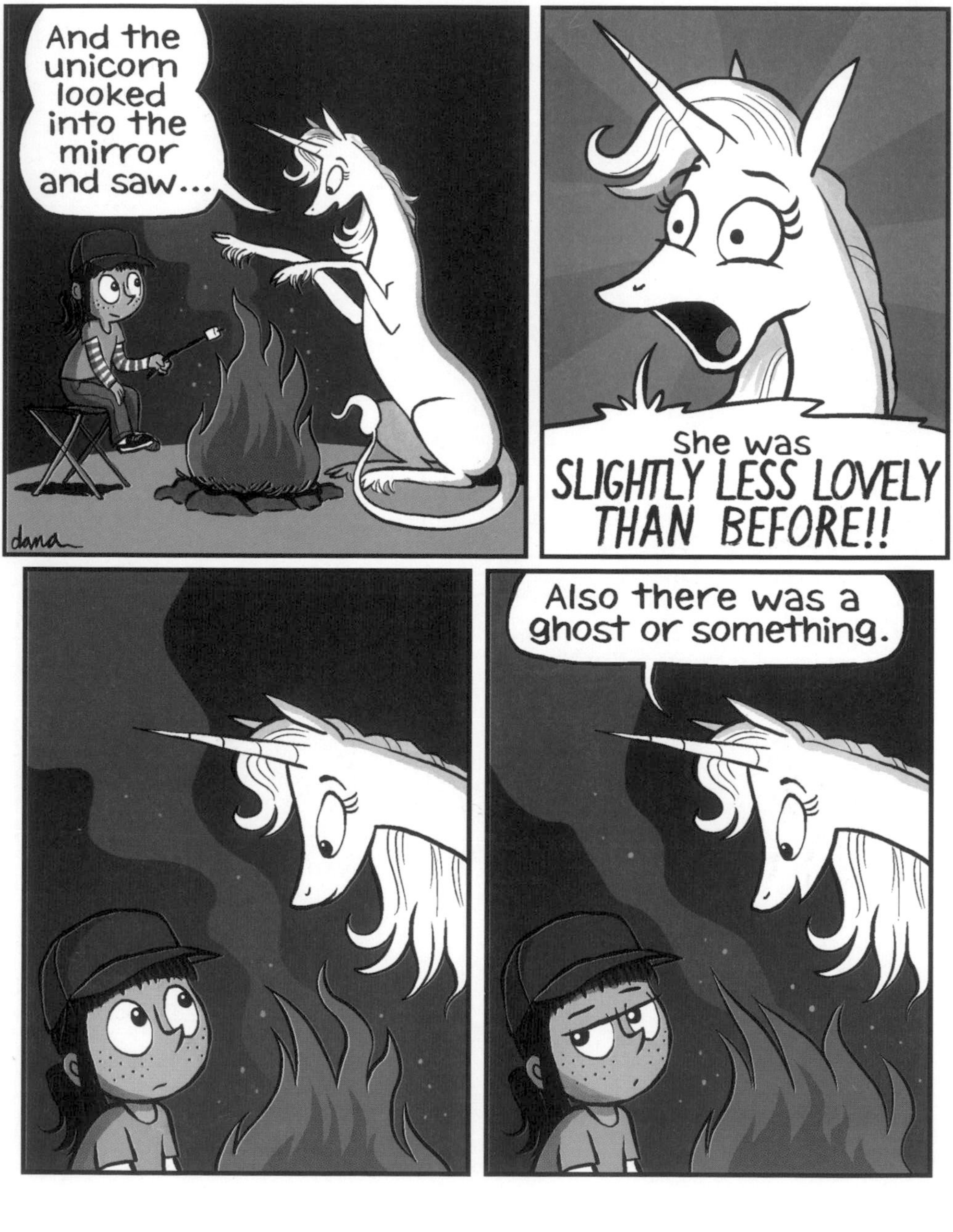
And the unicorn looked into the mirror and saw...
She was
SLIGHTLY LESS LOVELY THAN BEFORE!!
Also there was a ghost or something.

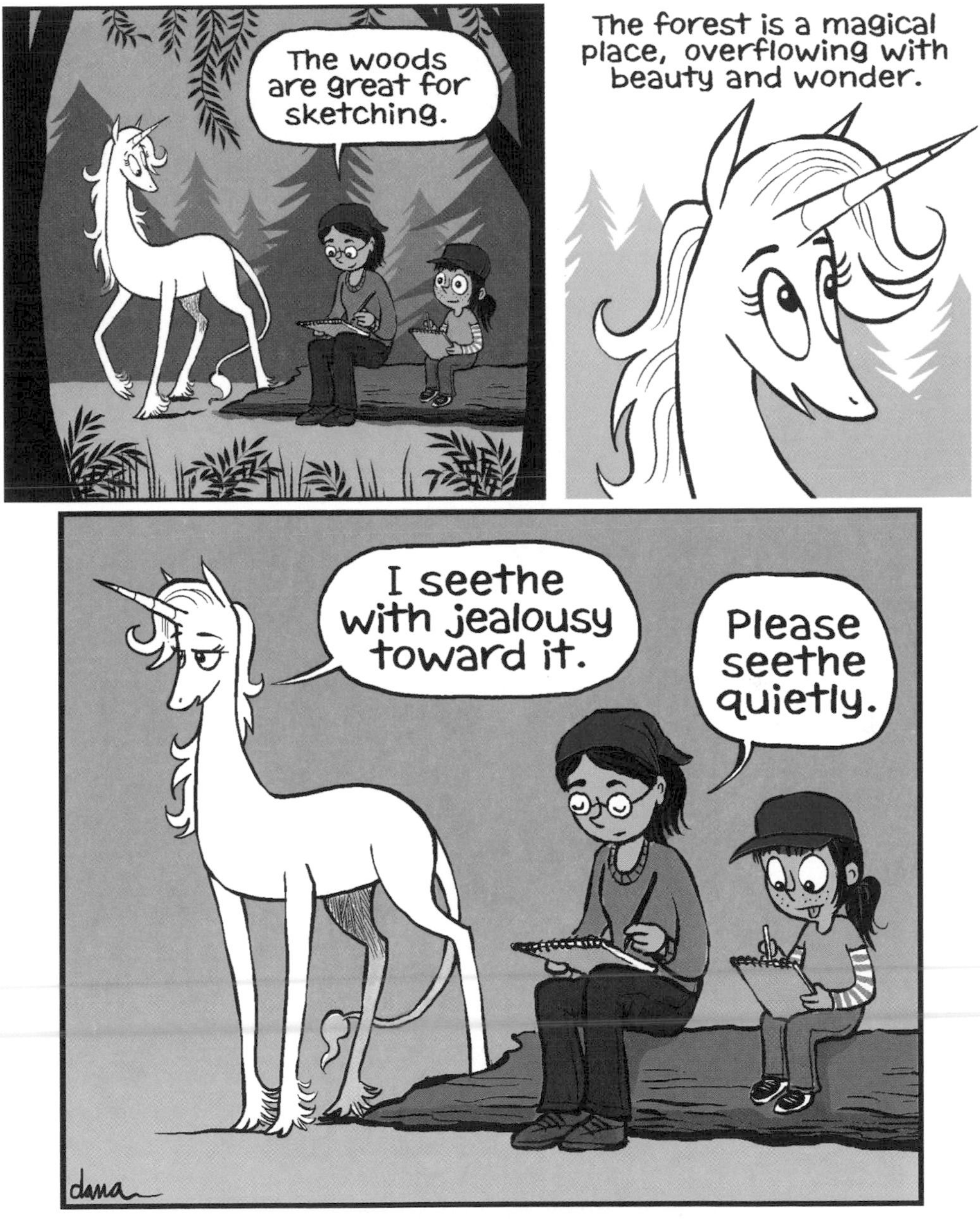
The woods are great for sketching.
The forest is a magical place, overflowing with beauty and wonder.
I seethe with jealousy toward it.
Please seethe quietly.
dana

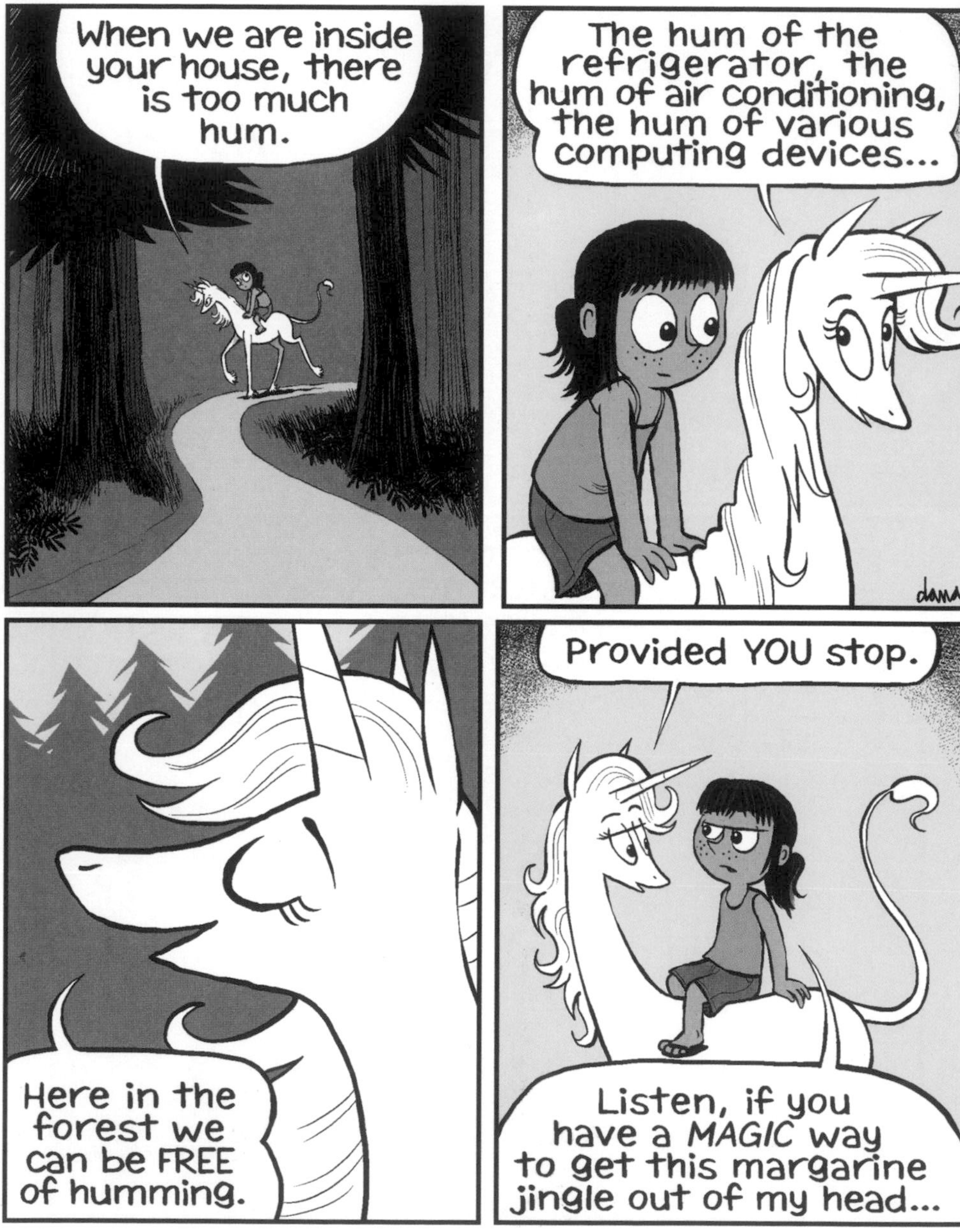
When we are inside your house, there is too much hum.
The hum of the refrigerator, the hum of air conditioning, the hum of various computing devices...
dana
Here in the forest we can be FREE of humming.
Provided YOU stop.
Listen, if you have a *MAGIC* way to get this margarine jingle out of my head...

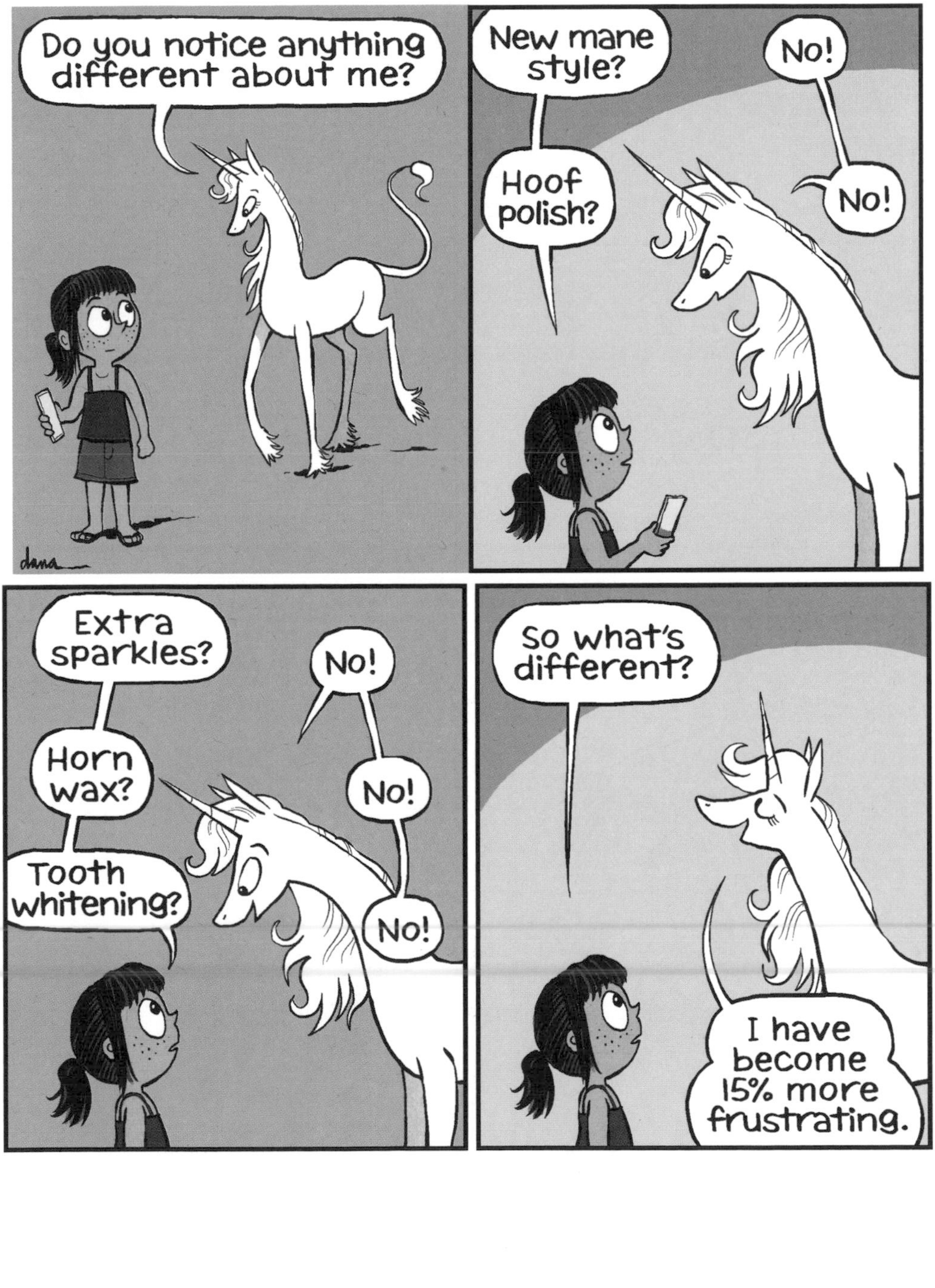
Do you notice anything different about me?
dana
New mane style?
No!
Hoof polish?
No!
Extra sparkles?
No!
Horn wax?
No!
Tooth whitening?
No!
So what's different?
I have become 15% more frustrating.

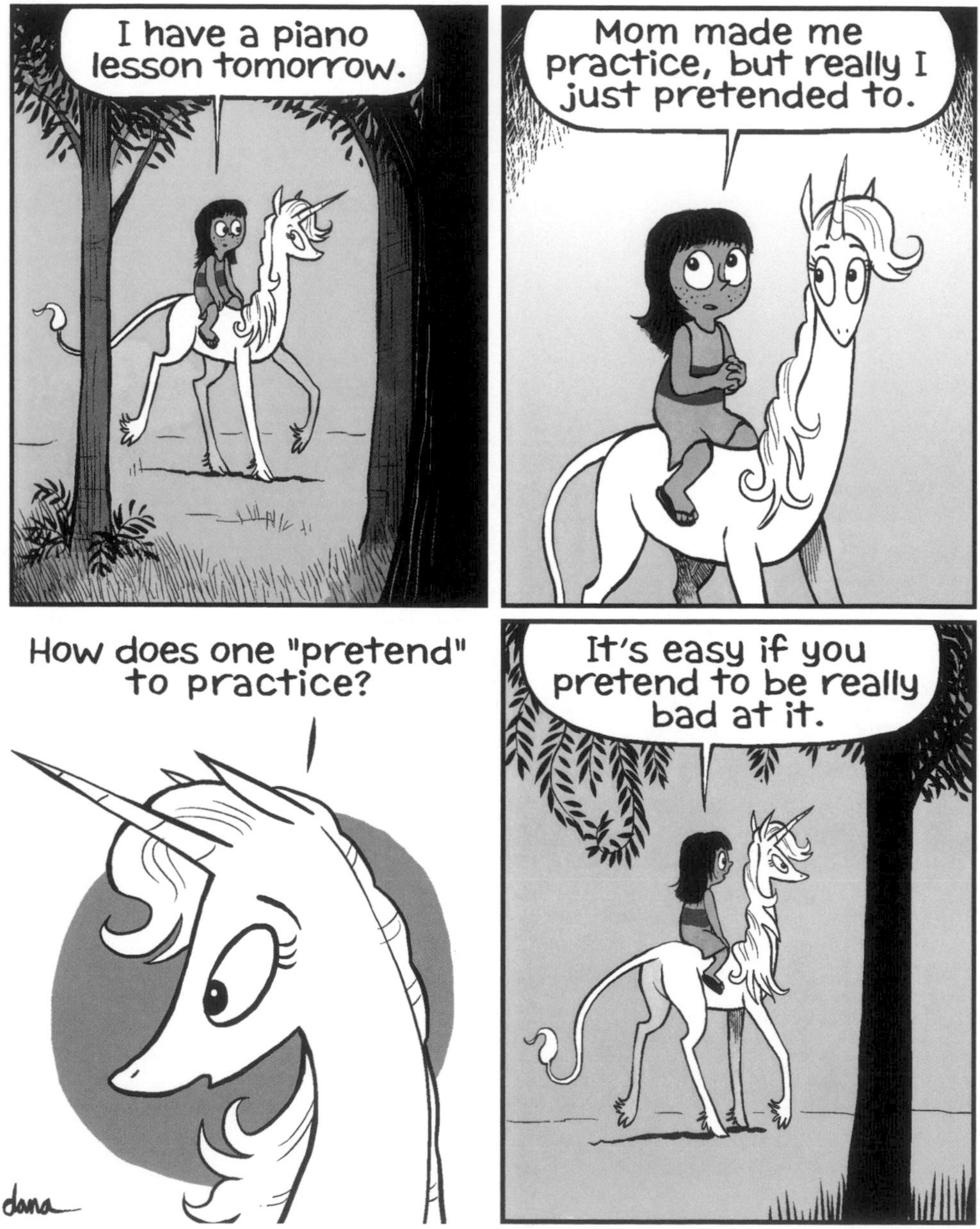
I have a piano lesson tomorrow.
Mom made me practice, but really I just pretended to.
How does one "pretend" to practice?
It's easy if you pretend to be really bad at it.
dana

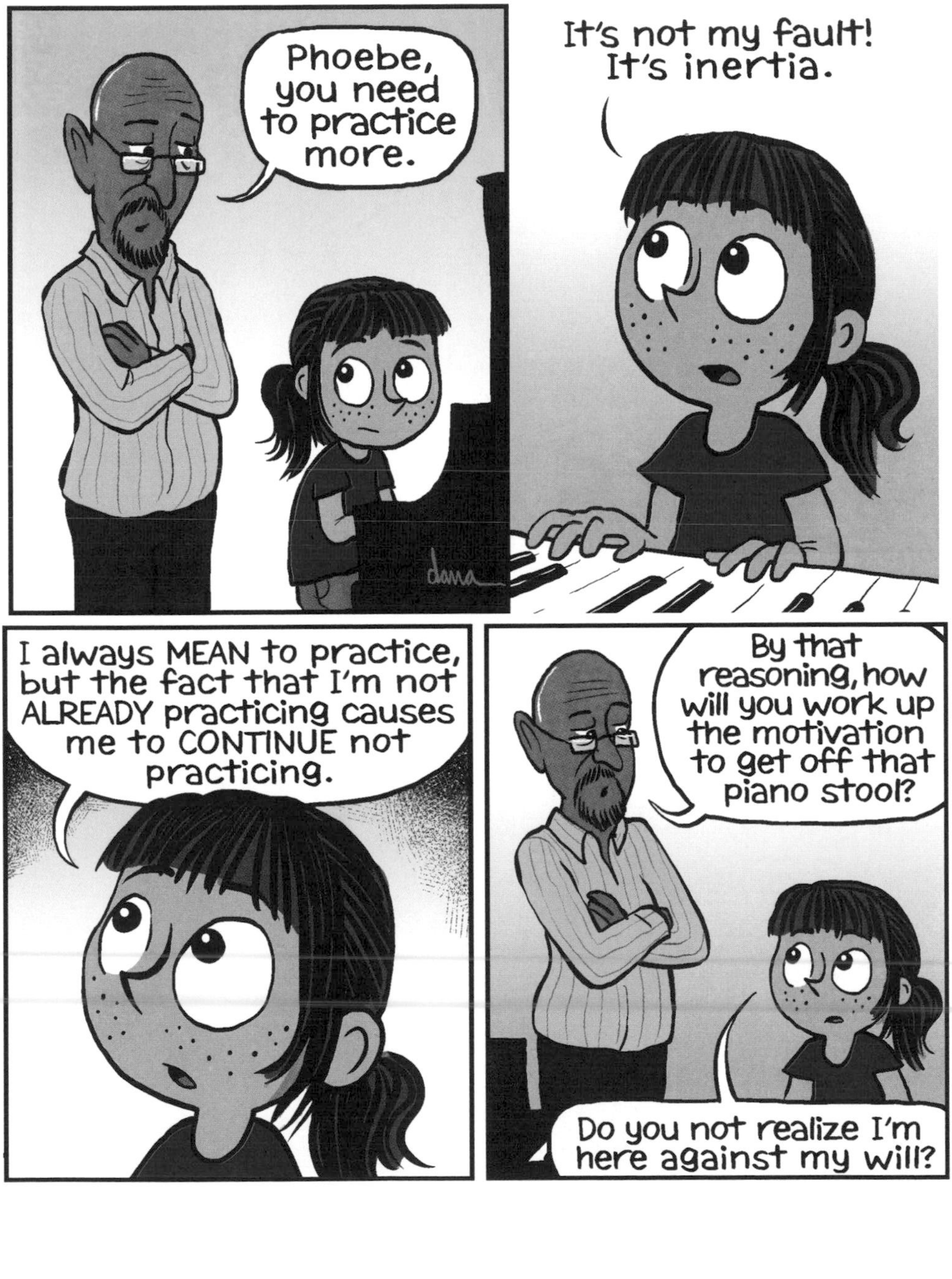
Phoebe, you need to practice more.
It's not my fault! It's inertia.
I always MEAN to practice, but the fact that I'm not ALREADY practicing causes me to CONTINUE not practicing.
By that reasoning, how will you work up the motivation to get off that piano stool?
Do you not realize I'm here against my will?

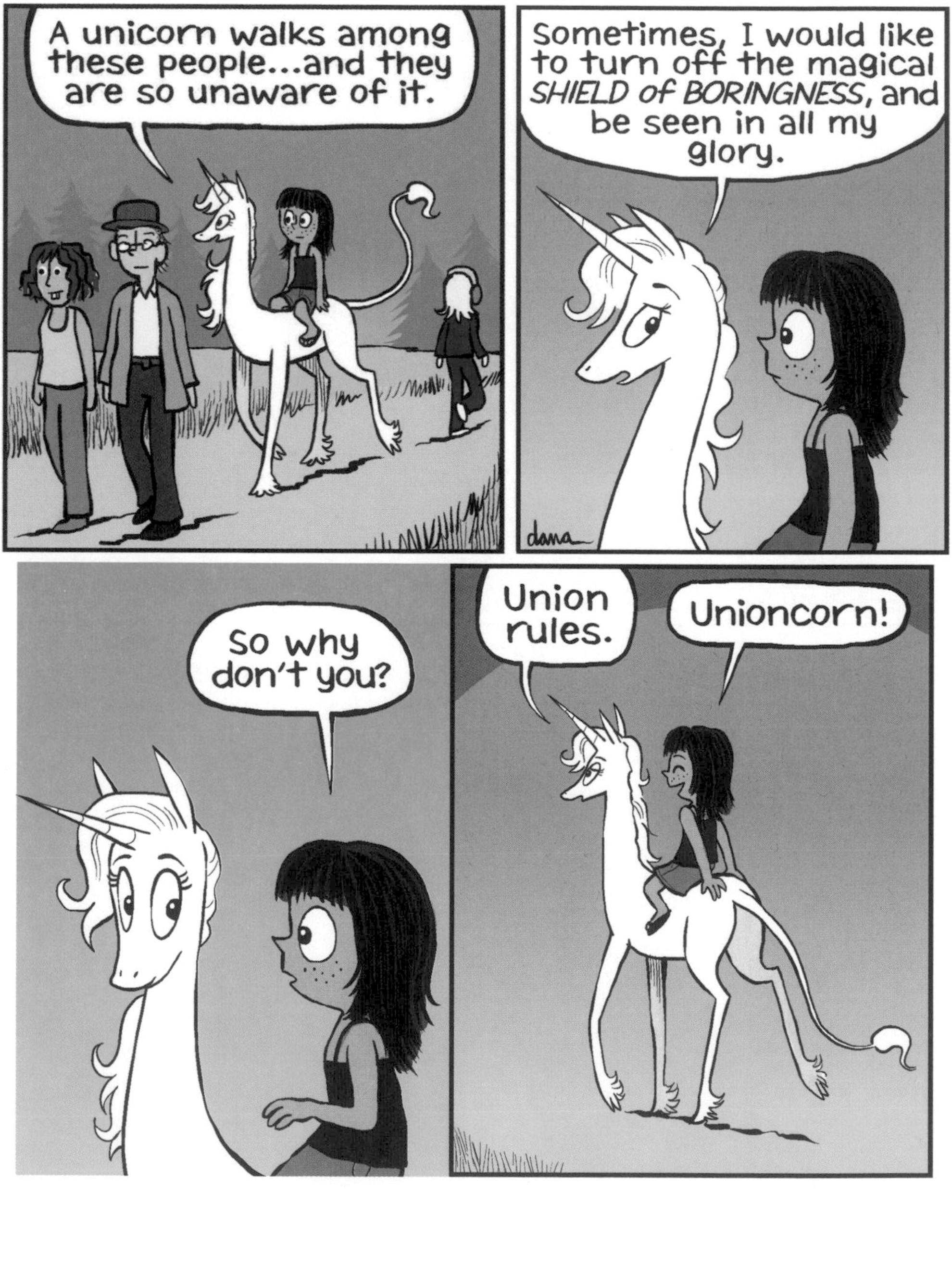
A unicorn walks among these people...and they are so unaware of it.
Sometimes, I would like to turn off the magical SHIELD of BORINGNESS, and be seen in all my glory.
dana
So why don't you?
Union rules.
Unioncorn!

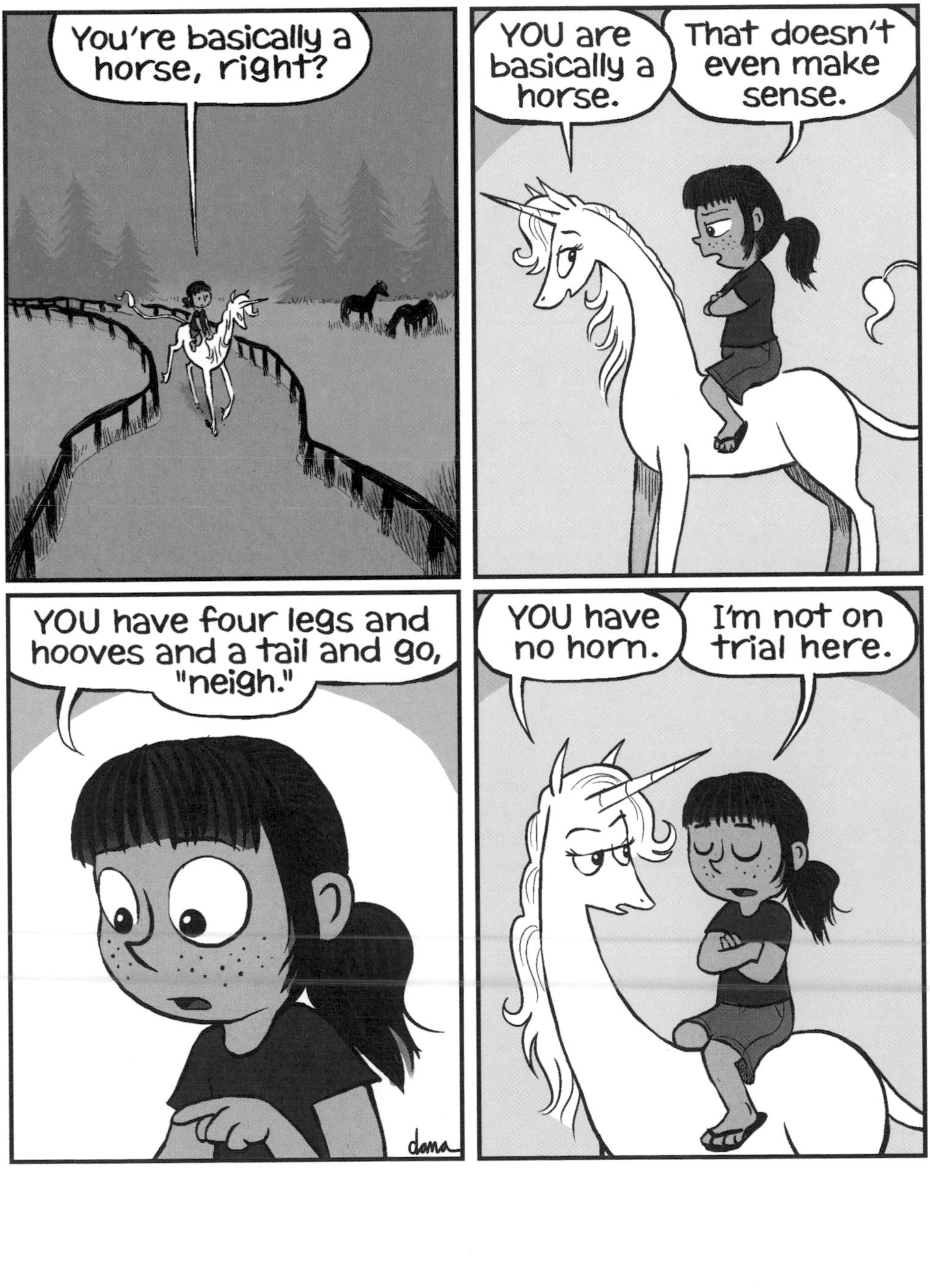
You're basically a horse, right?
YOU are basically a horse.
That doesn't even make sense.
YOU have four legs and hooves and a tail and go, "neigh."
YOU have no horn.
I'm not on trial here.
dana

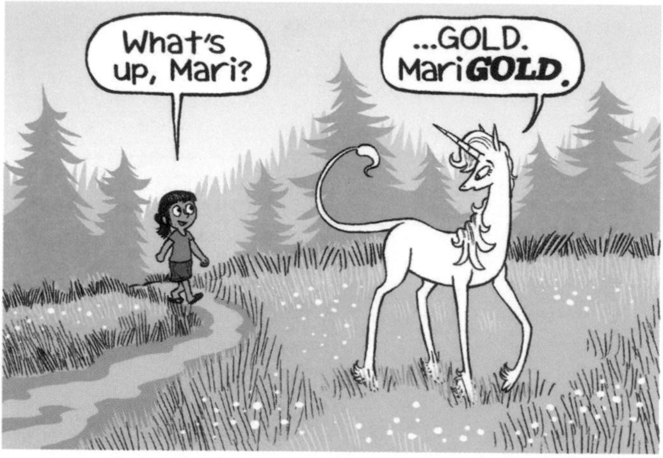
What's up, Mari?
...GOLD. Mari**GOLD**.

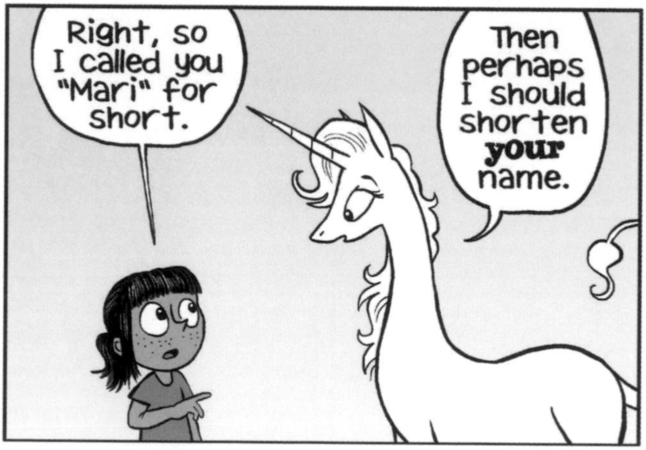
Right, so I called you "Mari" for short.
Then perhaps I should shorten **your** name.

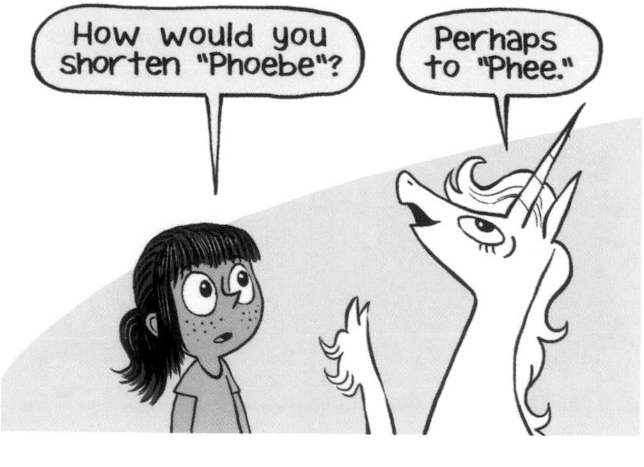
How would you shorten "Phoebe"?
Perhaps to "Phee."

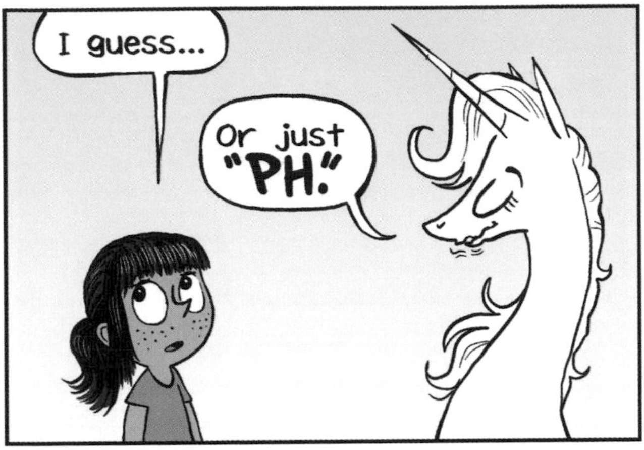
I guess...
Or just "PH."

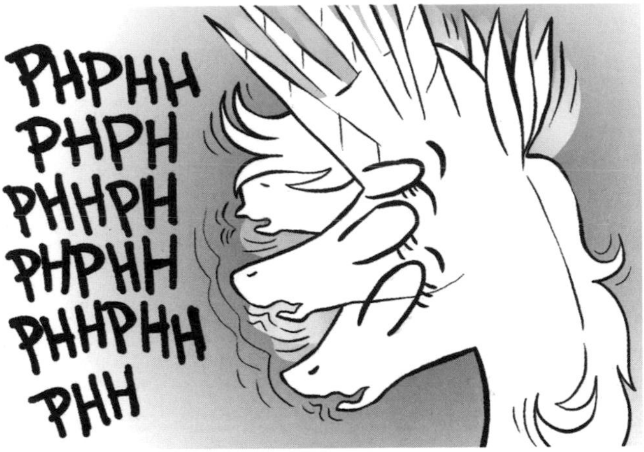
PHPHH
PHPH
PHHPH
PHPHH
PHHPHH
PHH

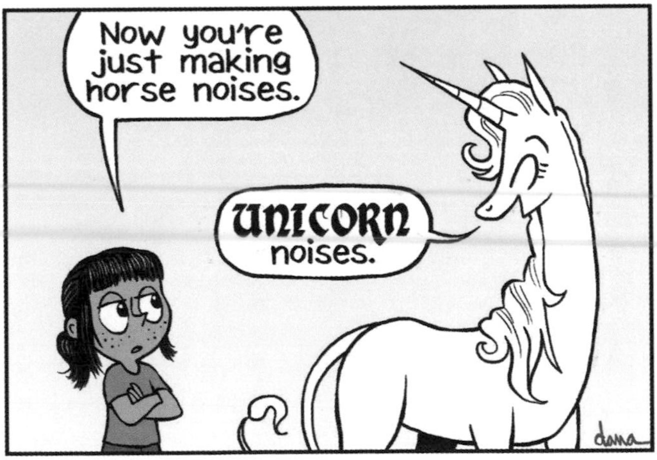
Now you're just making horse noises.
UNICORN noises.
dana

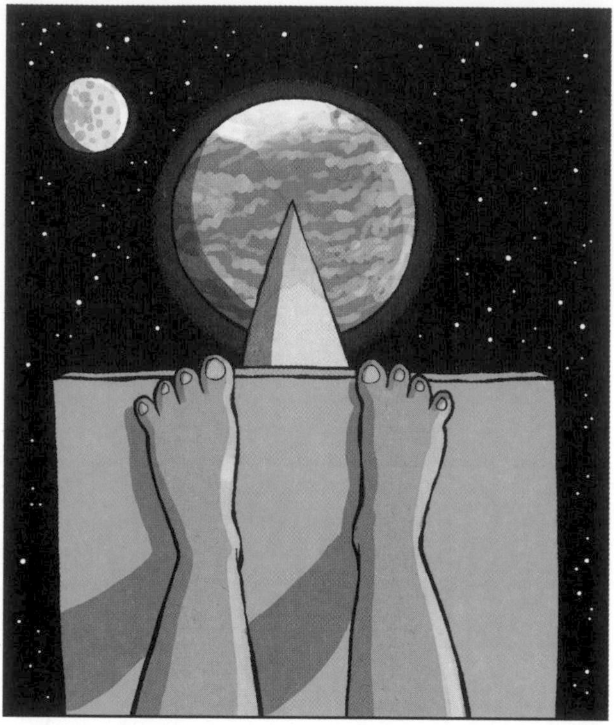

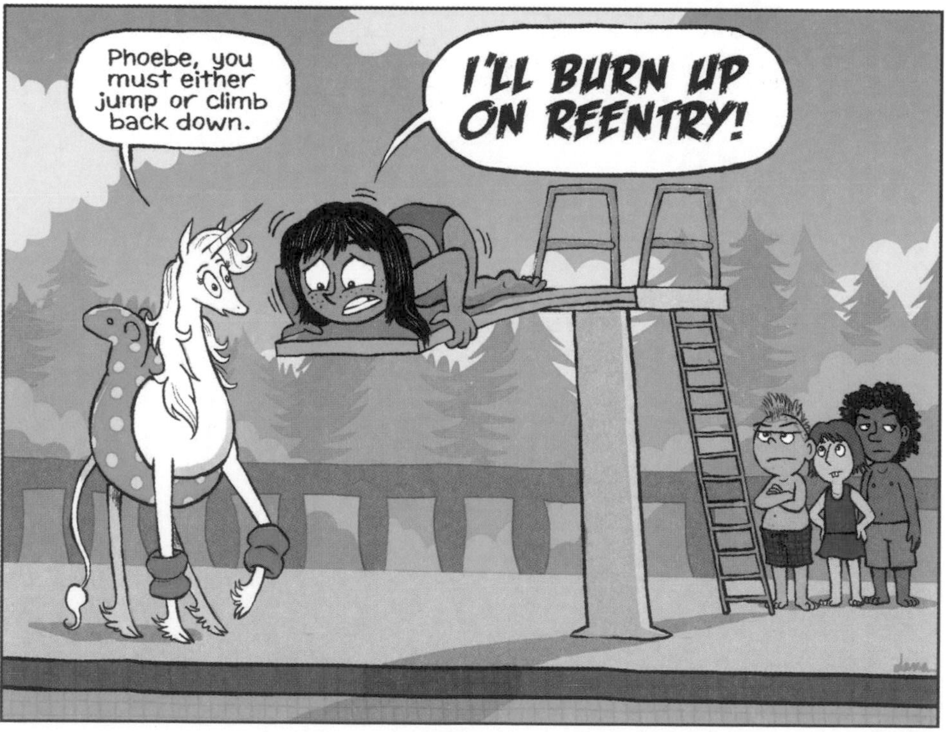
Phoebe, you must either jump or climb back down.
I'LL BURN UP ON REENTRY!

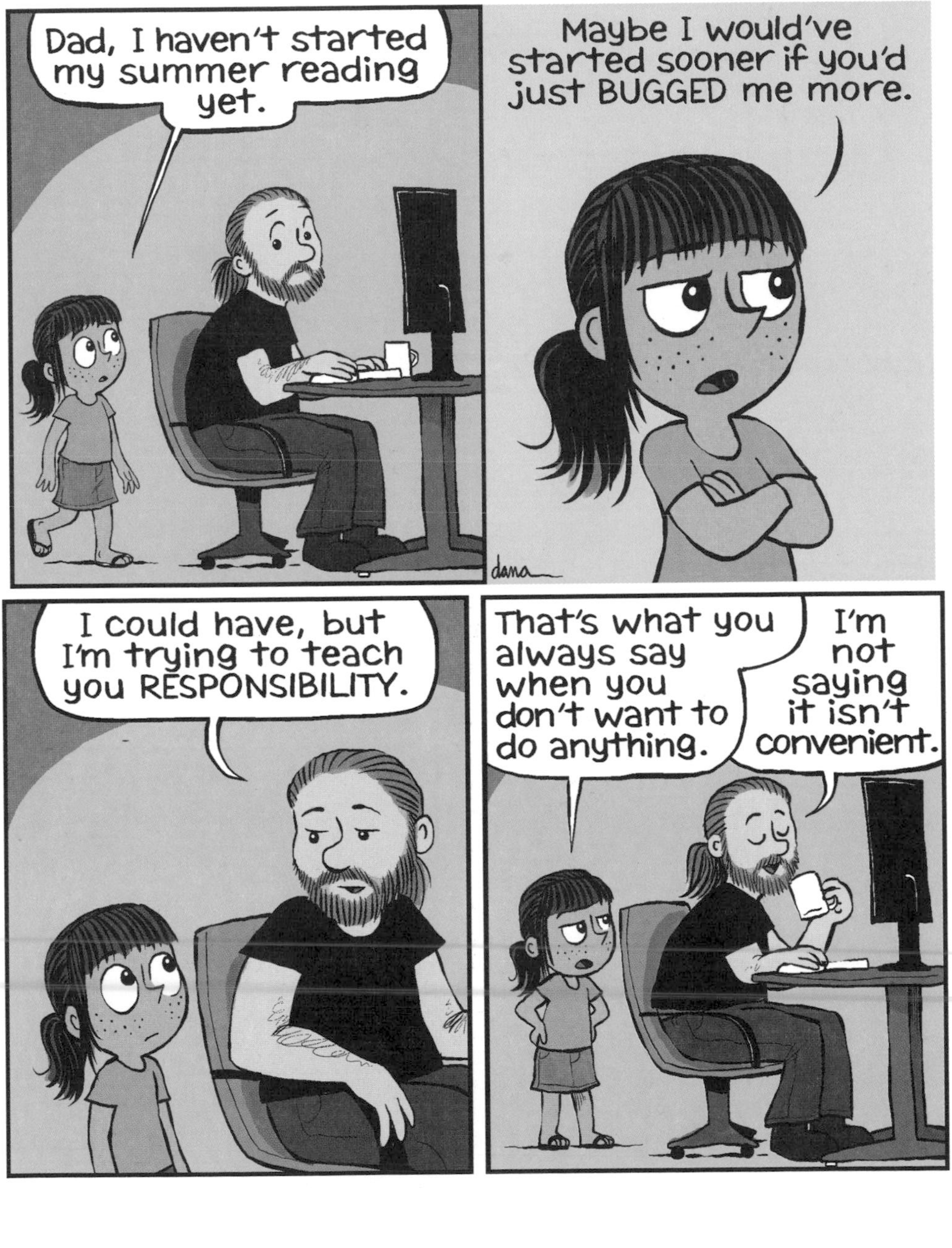

Dad, I haven't started my summer reading yet.
Maybe I would've started sooner if you'd just BUGGED me more.
dana
I could have, but I'm trying to teach you RESPONSIBILITY.
That's what you always say when you don't want to do anything.
I'm not saying it isn't convenient.

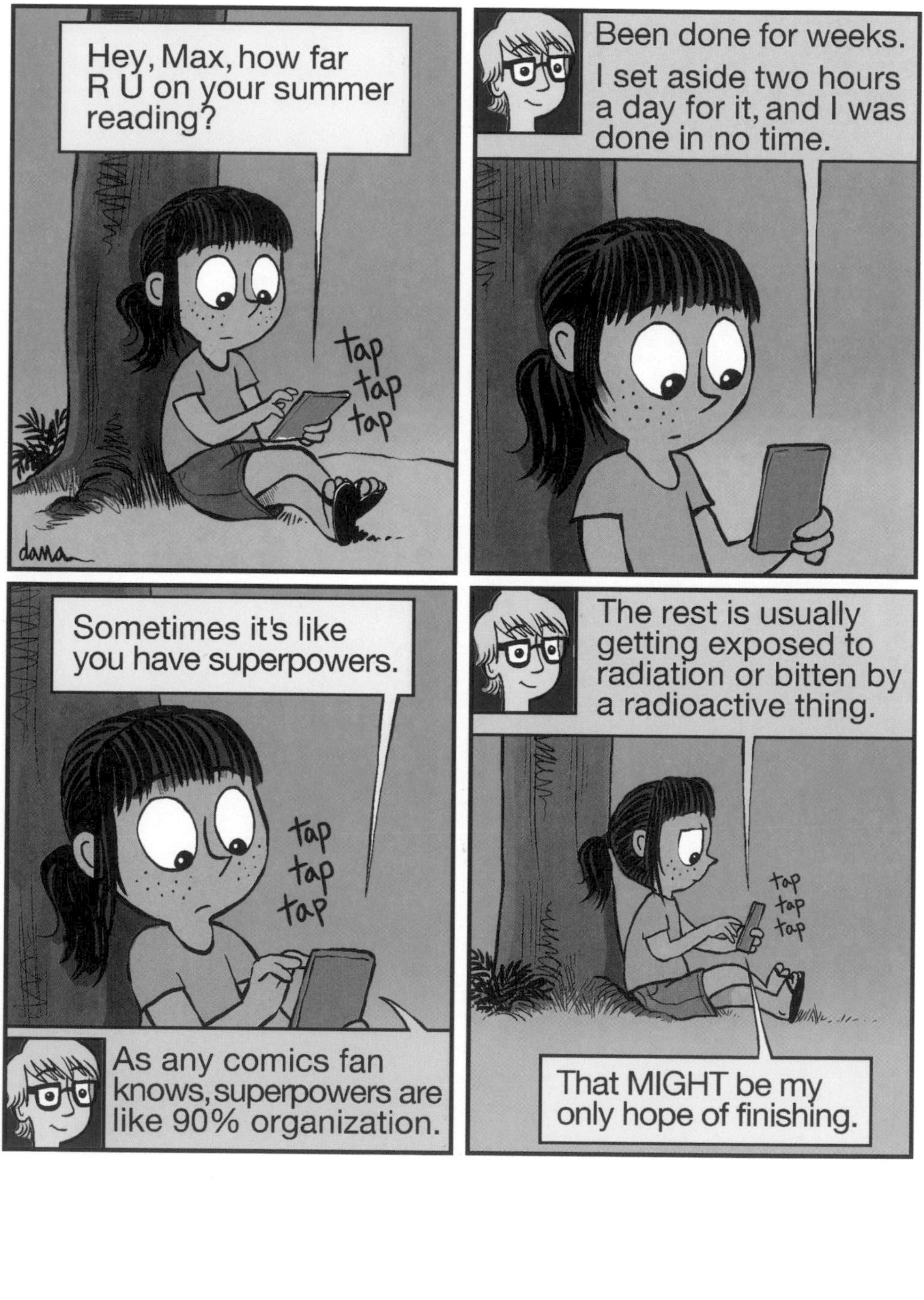
Hey, Max, how far R U on your summer reading?
tap tap tap
dana
Been done for weeks.
I set aside two hours a day for it, and I was done in no time.
Sometimes it's like you have superpowers.
tap tap tap
As any comics fan knows, superpowers are like 90% organization.
The rest is usually getting exposed to radiation or bitten by a radioactive thing.
tap tap tap
That MIGHT be my only hope of finishing.

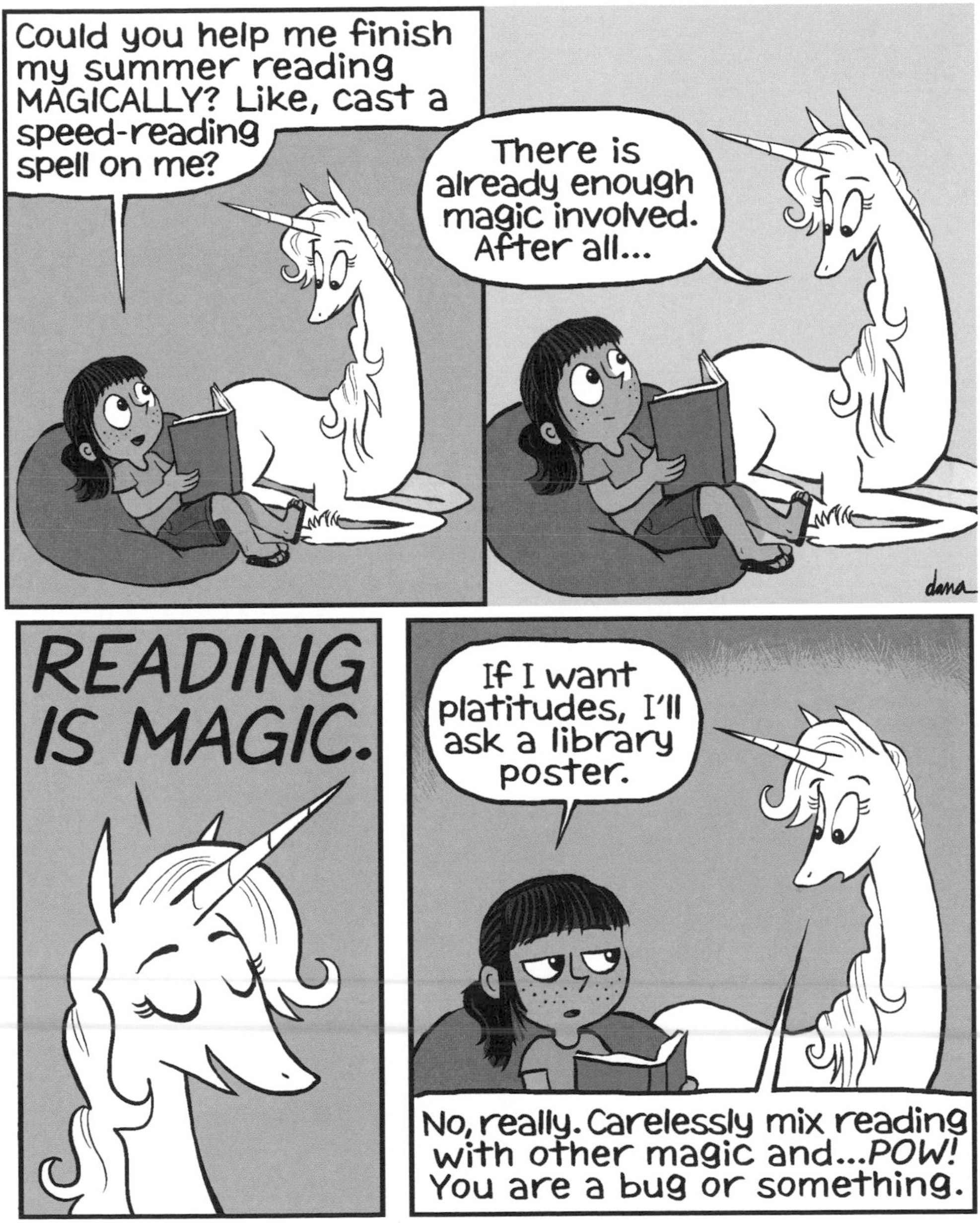
Could you help me finish my summer reading MAGICALLY? Like, cast a speed-reading spell on me?
There is already enough magic involved. After all...
dana
READING IS MAGIC.
If I want platitudes, I'll ask a library poster.
No, really. Carelessly mix reading with other magic and...*POW!* You are a bug or something.

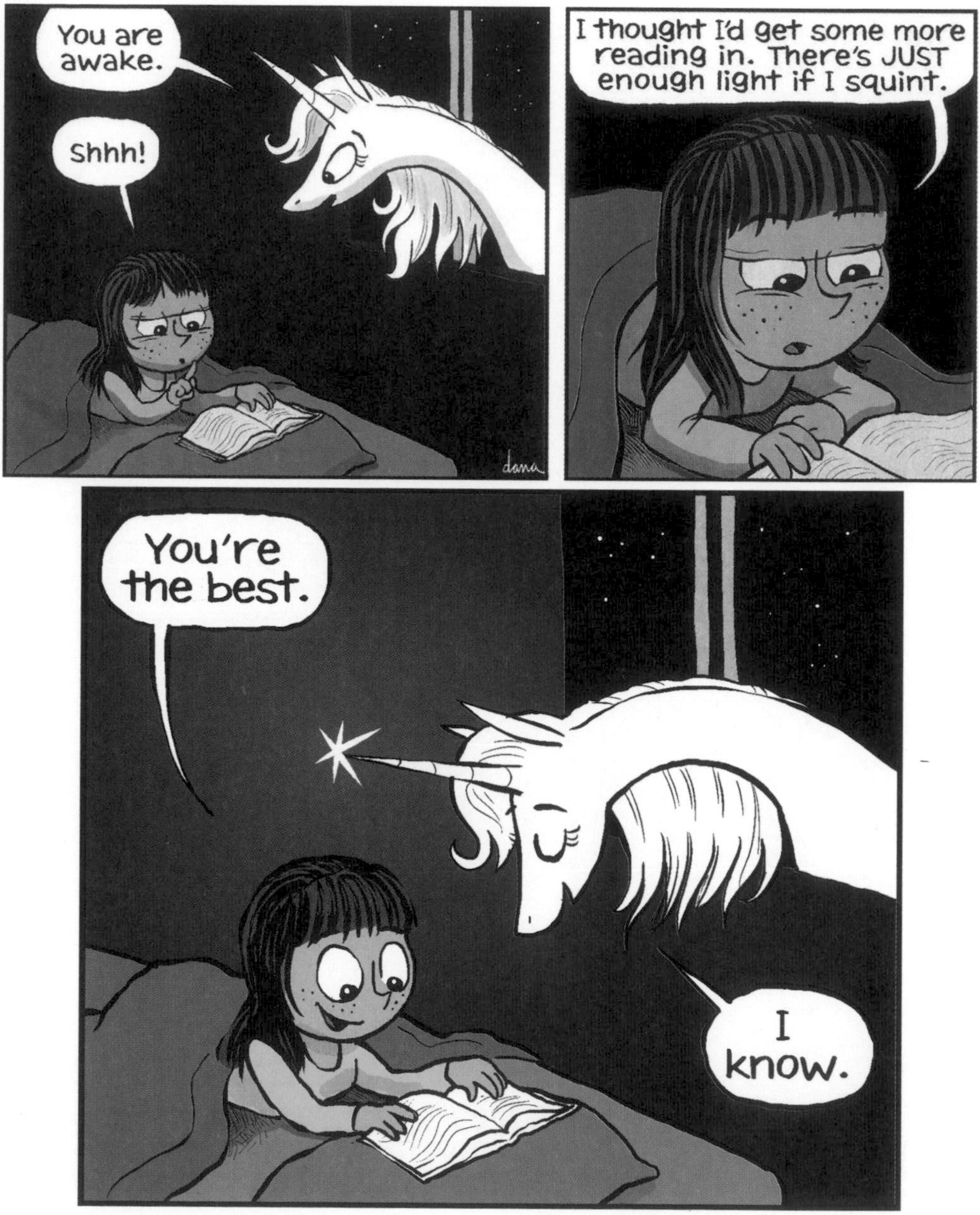
You are awake.
Shhh!
I thought I'd get some more reading in. There's JUST enough light if I squint.
You're the best.
I know.

MORE TO EXPLORE! A special section featuring words to learn!

Glossary

alfalfa (al-fal-fa): pg. 67 – noun / a type of grass grown for farm animals

amenities (a-men-it-ees): pg. 35 – noun / things that make life easier or more pleasant; comforts

antithesis (an-tith-e-sis): pg. 110 – noun / the exact opposite of something

artisanal (ar-tis-in-al): pg. 89 – adjective / traditionally made or grown with skill

asterisk (as-ter-isk): pg. 47 – noun / the symbol " * " that means something is not being said, or that there's more to an idea that's being left out

astounding (as-tound-ing): pg. 72 – adjective / surprising; amazing

benevolently (be-nev-o-lent-ly): pg. 44 – adverb / kindly; generously

brazen (bray-zen): pg. 76 – adjective / doing something shocking without any embarrassment; bold

contraption (con-trap-shun): pg. 59 – noun / machinery that is unusual or strange; gadget

cynical (sin-ick-al): pg. 113 – adjective / believing that people are typically selfish or dishonest; distrustful

deficient (de-fish-ent): pg. 81 – adjective / not having enough of something needed; lacking

denial (de-ni-al): pg. 63 – noun / a state of refusing to admit that something is sad, painful, true, or real

depression (de-pre-shun): pg. 66 – noun / a state of feeling sad, hopeless, or unimportant

discrimination (dis-crim-in-ay-shun): pg. 62 – noun / the practice of unfairly treating someone different from other people; prejudice

dodecahedron (do-dec-a-he-dron): pg. 93 – noun / a 3-D shape with twelve sides

ephemeral (ee-fem-er-al): pg. 80 – adjective / lasting a very short time; fleeting finesse (fin-ess): pg. 32 – noun / someone's skill when dealing with a tricky situation or problem; flair (see *panache*)

hallucination (ha-loo-sin-ay-shun): pg. 155 – noun / something that seems real but doesn't really exist (like a mirage)

heretic (hair-a-tick): pg. 158 – noun / someone who believes in an idea that goes against popular or accepted beliefs; a deviant rebel

horse d'oeuvres/horse doovers are really:

hors d'oeuvres (or dervs): pg. 71 – noun / a little food served before a meal; appetizers

impending (im-pen-ding): pg. 38 – adjective / about to occur; looming

inertia (in-er-sha): pg. 165 – noun / the idea that something that's not moving will stay still, and something in motion will keep going unless stopped; inaction

inopportune (in-op-por-tune): pg. 12 – adjective / happening at the wrong time; inconvenient

newfangled (new-fan-gled): pg. 58 – adjective / newly invented

organic co-op (or-gan-ick coh-op): pg. 27 – noun / a grocery store that is owned and operated by the people who work there or the people who buy from the store; sometimes called a "food cooperative"

ostentatious (os-ten-tay-shus): pg. 76 – adjective / showing off wealth or treasure to make people envious; flashy or showy

panache (pan-ash): pg. 79 – noun / lots of energy and style; flair (see *finesse*)

parapet (pair-a-pet): pg. 143 – noun / a low wall on a castle

passé (pass-ay): pg. 41 – adjective / no longer fashionable or cool; out-of-date

platitude (pla-ta-tude): pg. 173 – noun / something said that is dull, unoriginal, or cliché

pragmatic (prag-ma-tick): pg. 85 – adjective / dealing with problems in a reasonable way; wise or practical

rejuvenation (re-joo-ven-ay-shun): pg. 70 – noun / a state of feeling young or energetic again

repository (re-pos-it-or-ee): pg. 27 – noun / a place where a large amount of something is stored (like a warehouse, library, or store)

sadistic (sa-dis-tick): pg. 23 – adjective / cruel; enjoying someone else's pain

seethe (seethe): pg. 161 – verb / to show an uncontrollable emotion, like anger; to fume

siege (seeje): pg. 154 – noun / a long and intense attack on something (like a castle)

strobe (strobe): pg. 124 – noun / a device that flashes light at high speeds, over and over

subvert (sub-vert): pg. 13 – verb / to weaken something, or to make it less effective; sabotage (*see undermine*)

thwarted (thwart-ed): pg. 100 – noun / stopped someone from doing something; foiled

undermine (un-der-mine): pg. 13 – verb / to weaken something, or to make unstable (*see subvert*)

visage (vis-ij): pg. 86 – noun / a person's face; appearance

withdrawal (with-draw-al): pg. 63 – noun / the act of ending your involvement with something

Unicorn

of Many Hats

Another
Phoebe and Her Unicorn Adventure

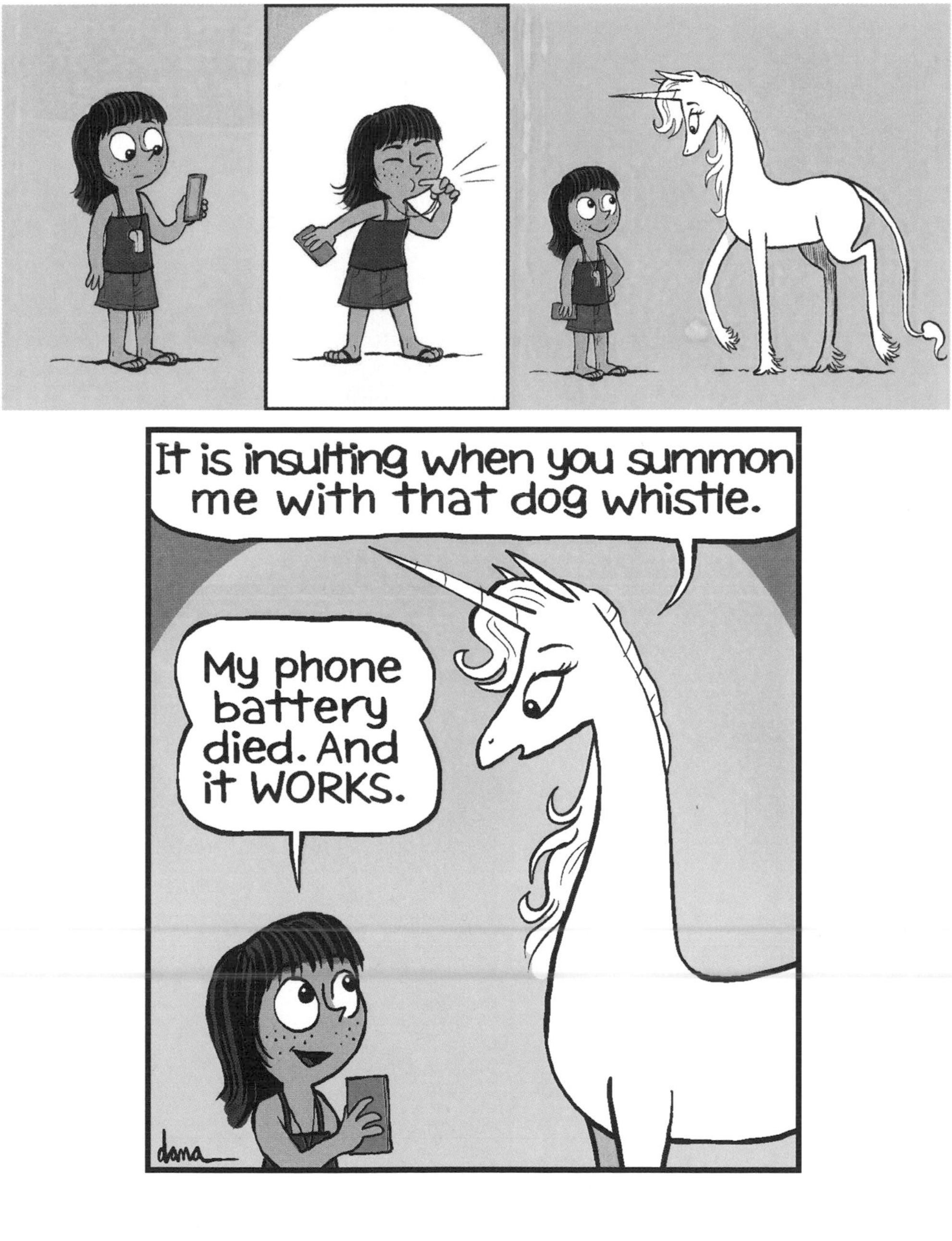
It is insulting when you summon me with that dog whistle.
My phone battery died. And it WORKS.
dana

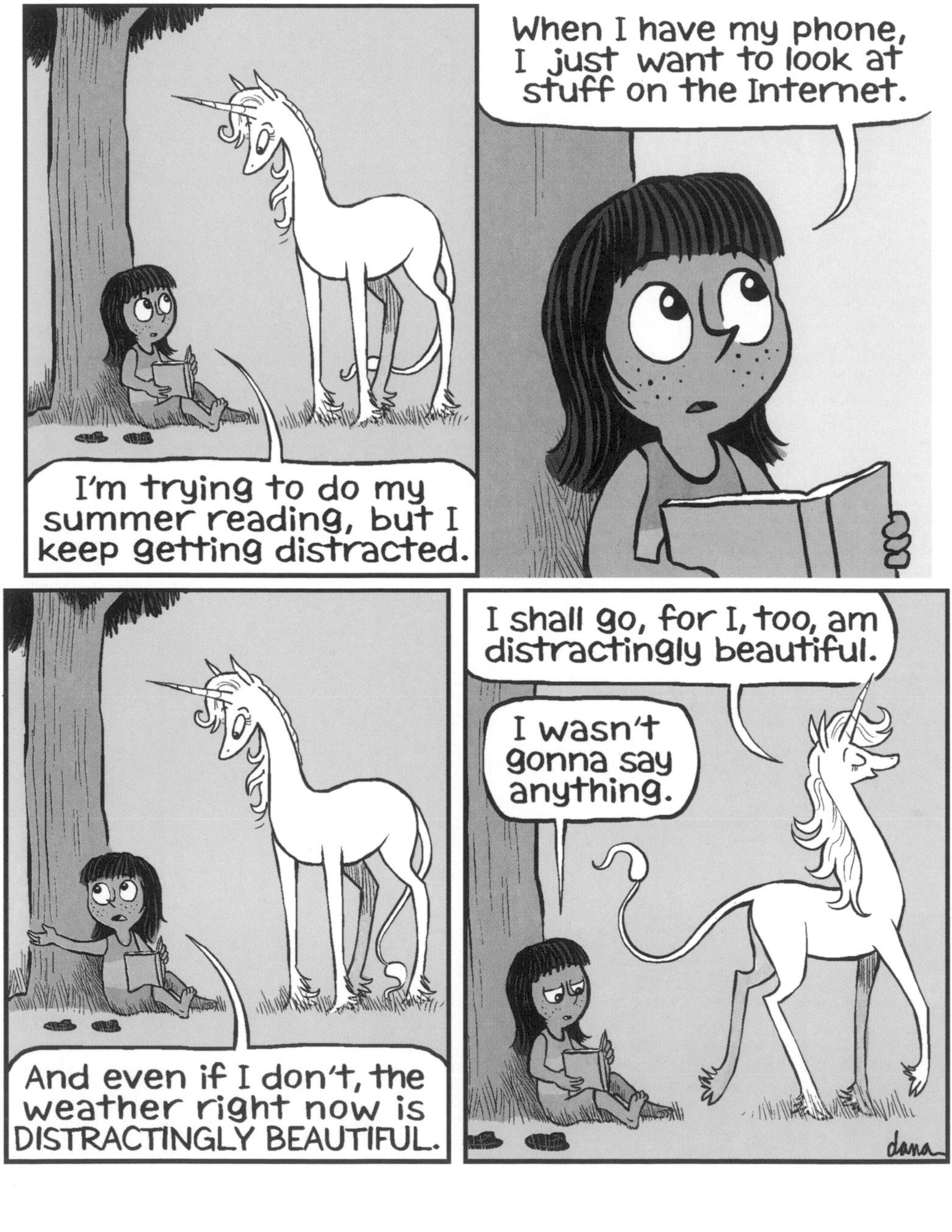
I'm trying to do my summer reading, but I keep getting distracted.
When I have my phone, I just want to look at stuff on the Internet.
And even if I don't, the weather right now is DISTRACTINGLY BEAUTIFUL.
I shall go, for I, too, am distractingly beautiful.
I wasn't gonna say anything.
dana

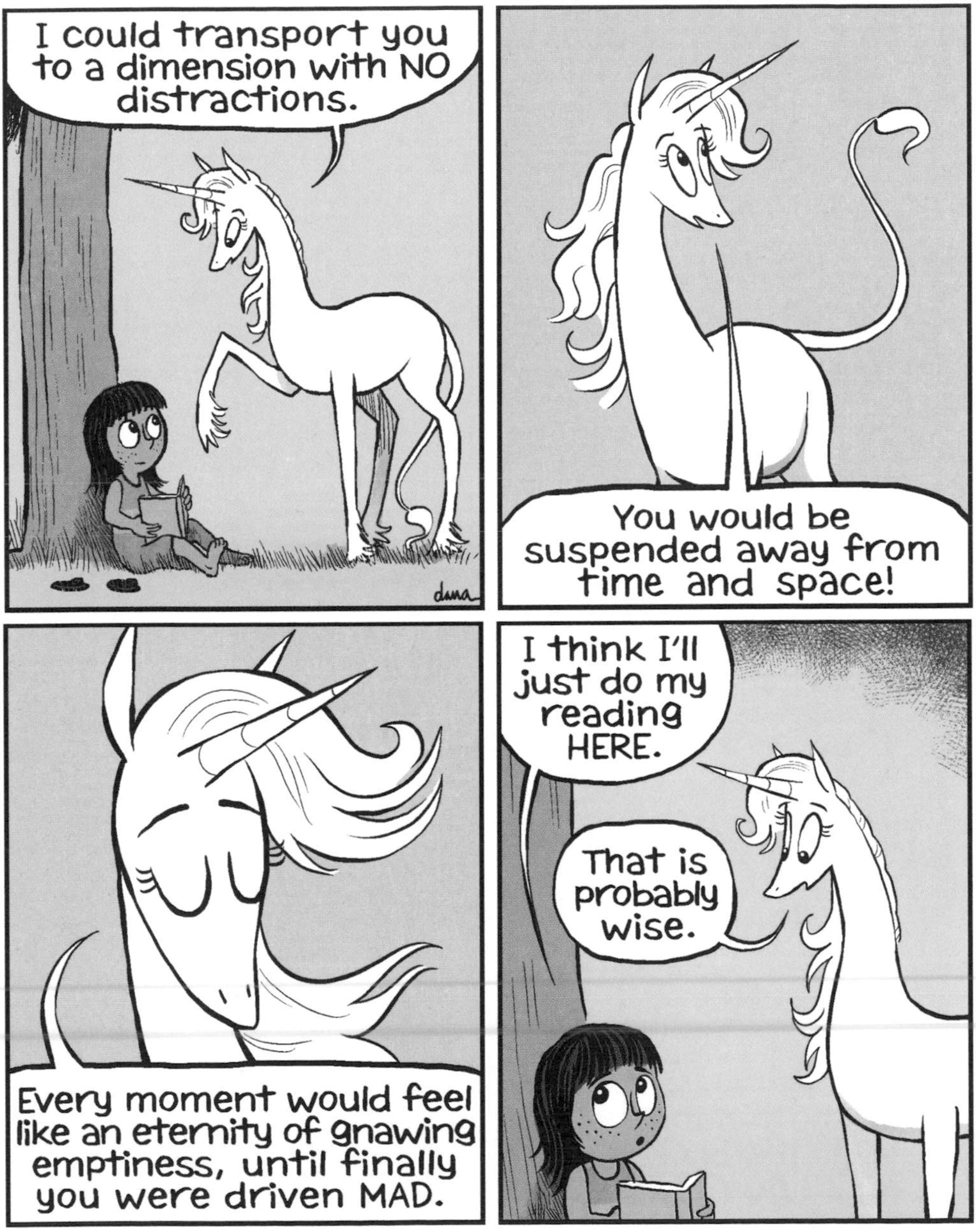
I could transport you to a dimension with NO distractions.
You would be suspended away from time and space!
Every moment would feel like an eternity of gnawing emptiness, until finally you were driven MAD.
I think I'll just do my reading HERE.
That is probably wise.
dana

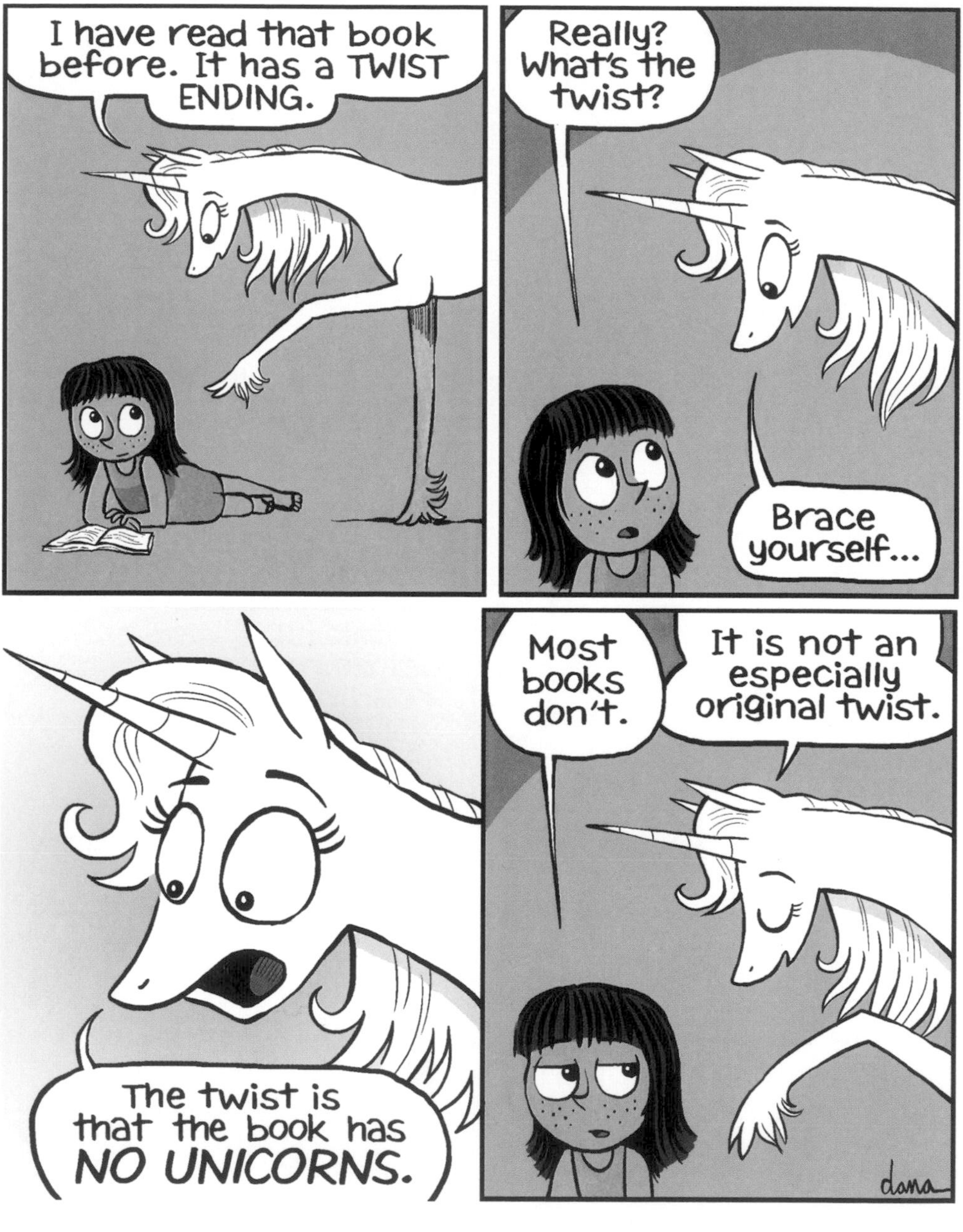
I have read that book before. It has a TWIST ENDING.
Really? What's the twist?
Brace yourself...
The twist is that the book has *NO UNICORNS.*
Most books don't.
It is not an especially original twist.
dana

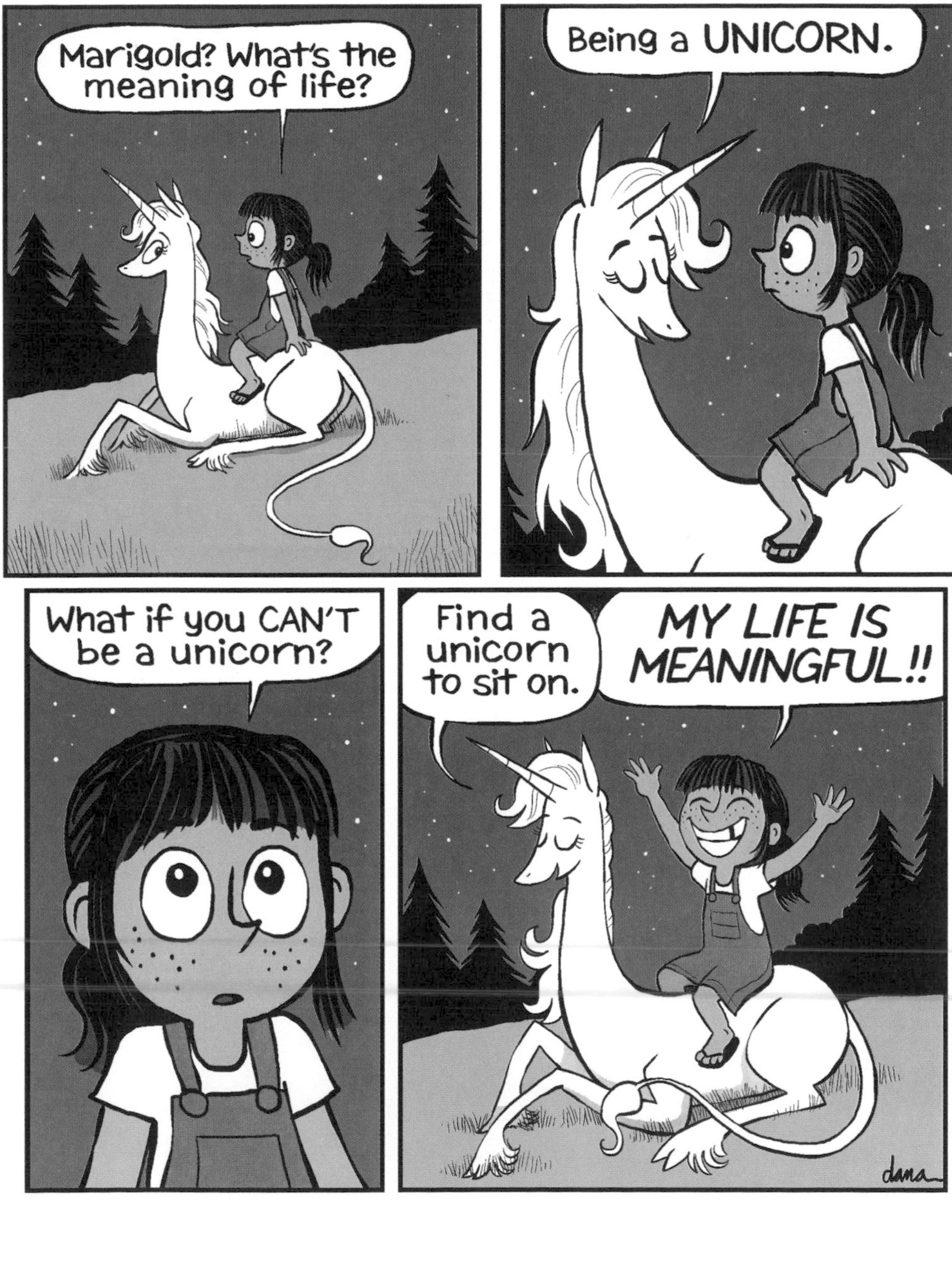
Marigold? What's the meaning of life?
Being a UNICORN.
What if you CAN'T be a unicorn?
Find a unicorn to sit on.
MY LIFE IS MEANINGFUL!!
dana

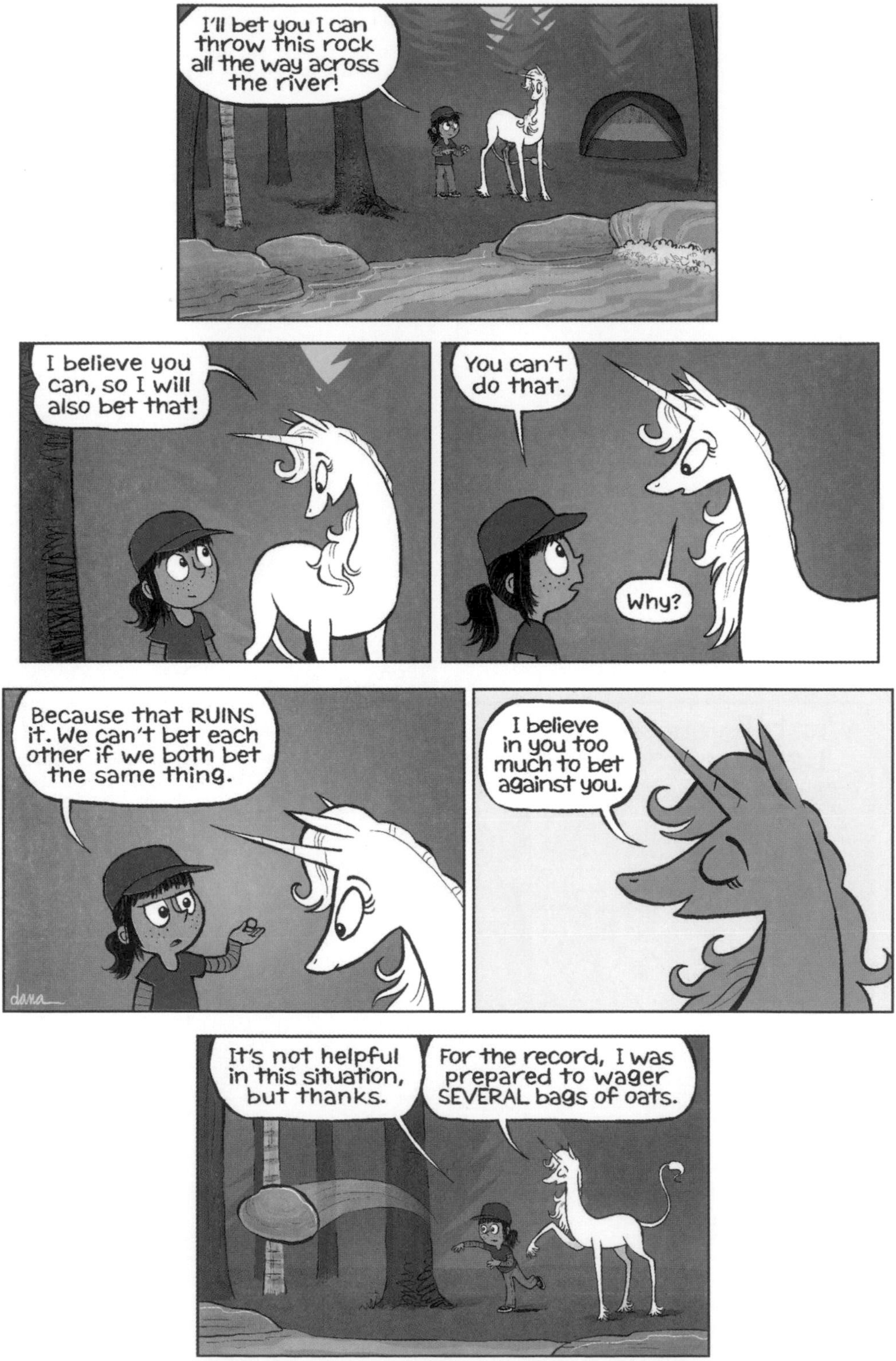
I'll bet you I can throw this rock all the way across the river!
I believe you can, so I will also bet that!
You can't do that.
Why?
Because that RUINS it. We can't bet each other if we both bet the same thing.
I believe in you too much to bet against you.
It's not helpful in this situation, but thanks.
For the record, I was prepared to wager SEVERAL bags of oats.
dana

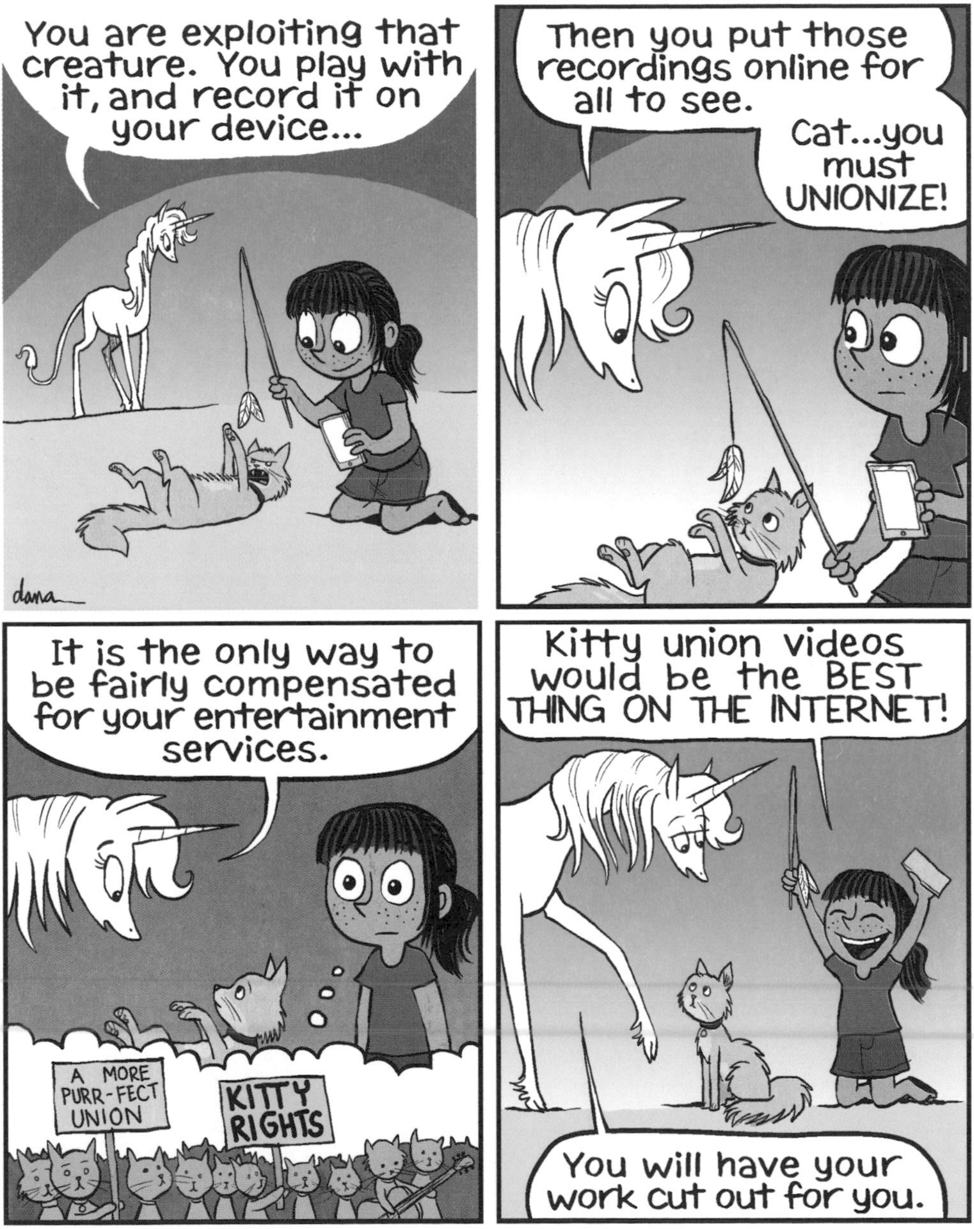
You are exploiting that creature. You play with it, and record it on your device...
dana
Then you put those recordings online for all to see.
Cat...you must UNIONIZE!
It is the only way to be fairly compensated for your entertainment services.
A MORE PURR-FECT UNION
KITTY RIGHTS
Kitty union videos would be the BEST THING ON THE INTERNET!
You will have your work cut out for you.

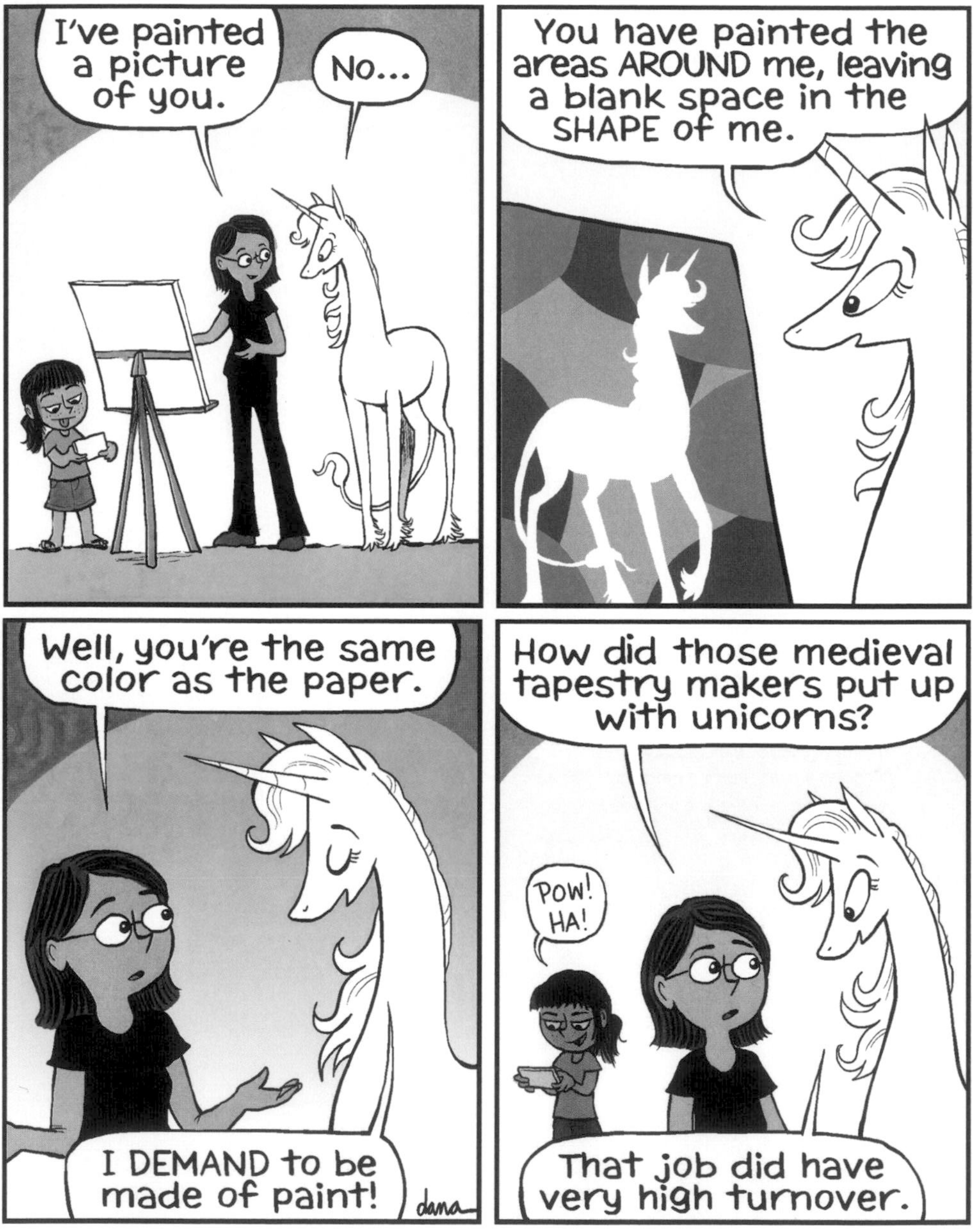
I've painted a picture of you.
No...
You have painted the areas AROUND me, leaving a blank space in the SHAPE of me.
Well, you're the same color as the paper.
I DEMAND to be made of paint!
dana
How did those medieval tapestry makers put up with unicorns?
POW! HA!
That job did have very high turnover.

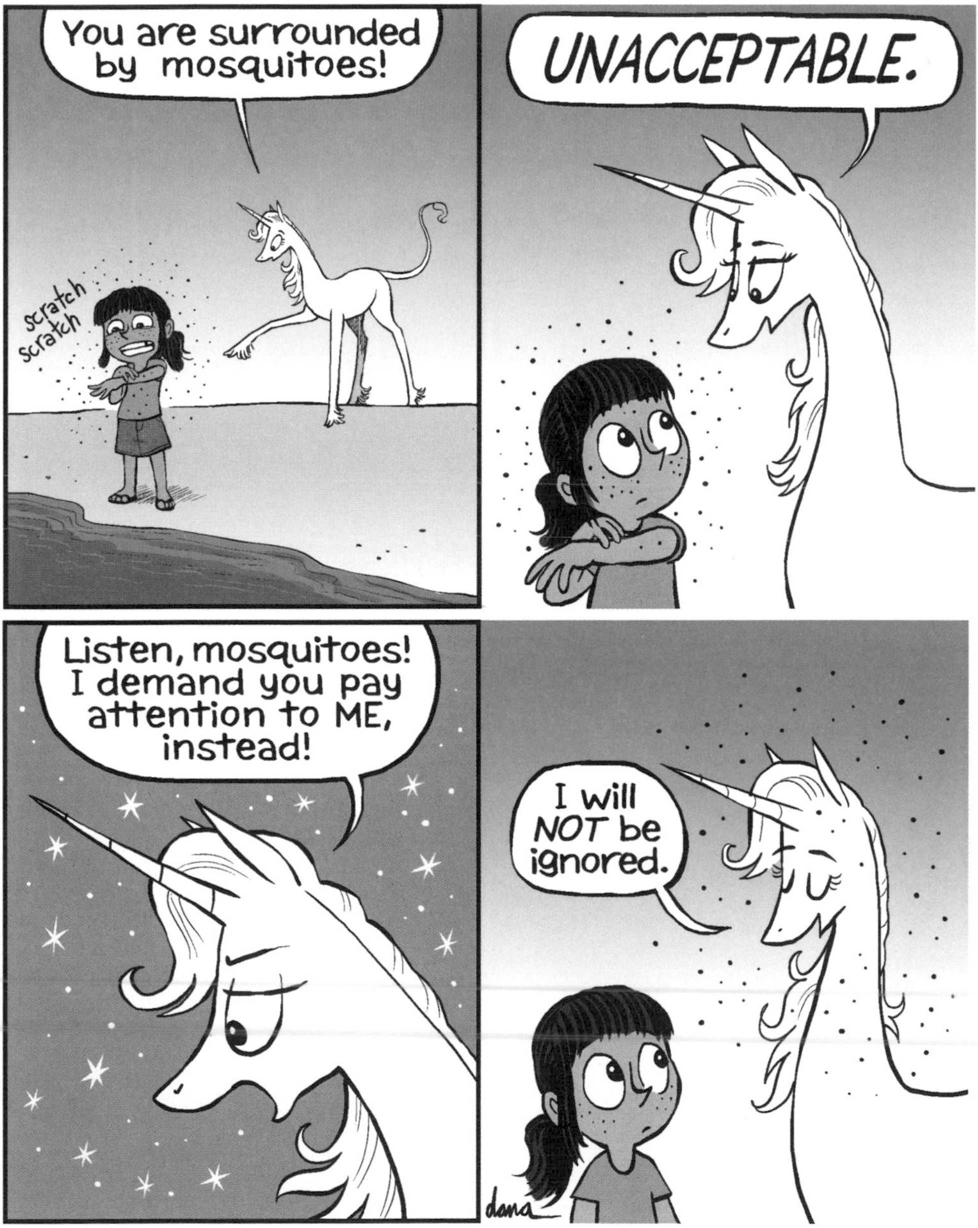
You are surrounded by mosquitoes!
scratch scratch
UNACCEPTABLE.
Listen, mosquitoes! I demand you pay attention to ME, instead!
I will NOT be ignored.
dana

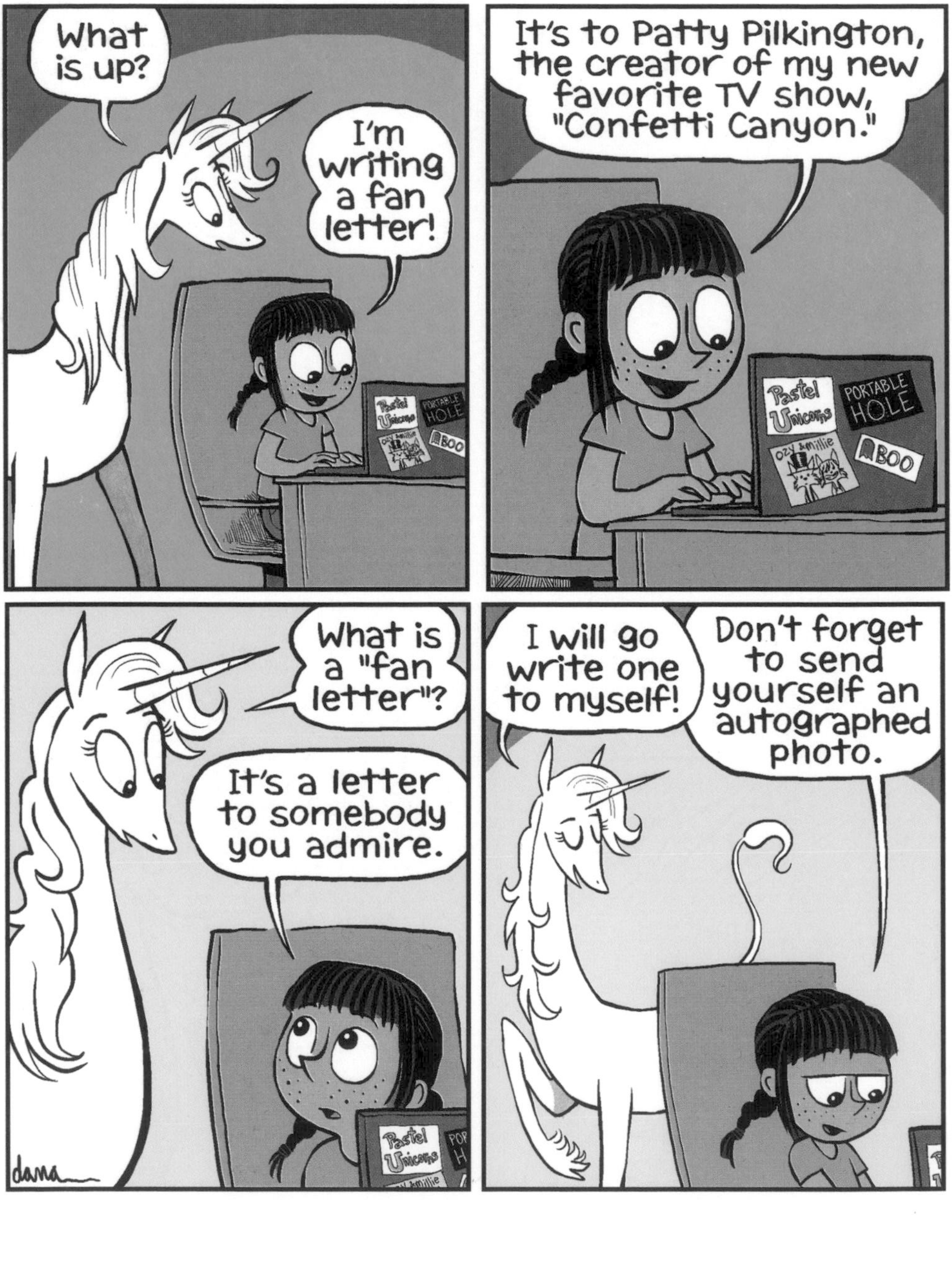
What is up?
I'm writing a fan letter!
It's to Patty Pilkington, the creator of my new favorite TV show, "Confetti Canyon."
Pastel Unicorns
PORTABLE HOLE
BOO
What is a "fan letter"?
It's a letter to somebody you admire.
I will go write one to myself!
Don't forget to send yourself an autographed photo.
dana

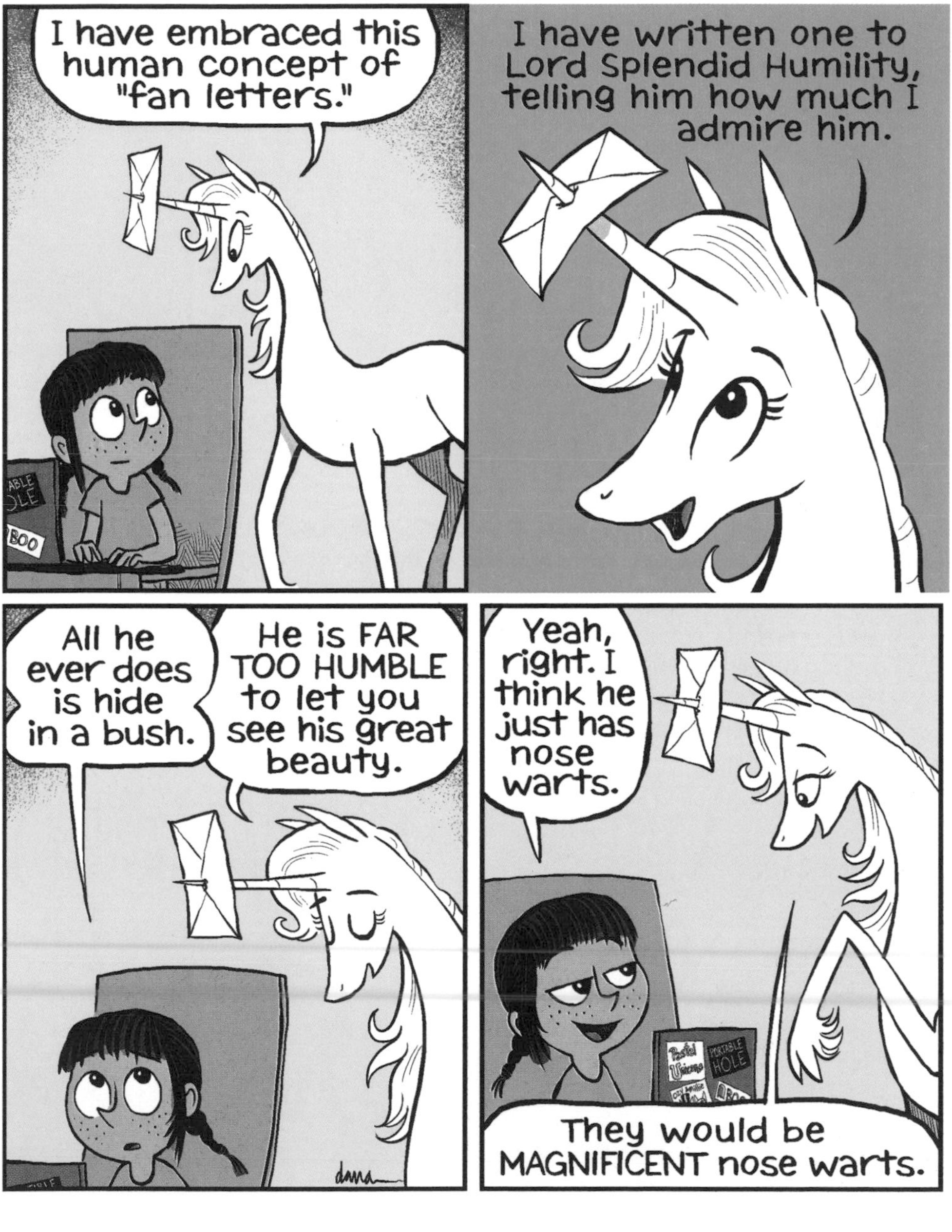
I have embraced this human concept of "fan letters."
I have written one to Lord Splendid Humility, telling him how much I admire him.
He is FAR TOO HUMBLE to let you see his great beauty.
All he ever does is hide in a bush.
Yeah, right. I think he just has nose warts.
They would be MAGNIFICENT nose warts.

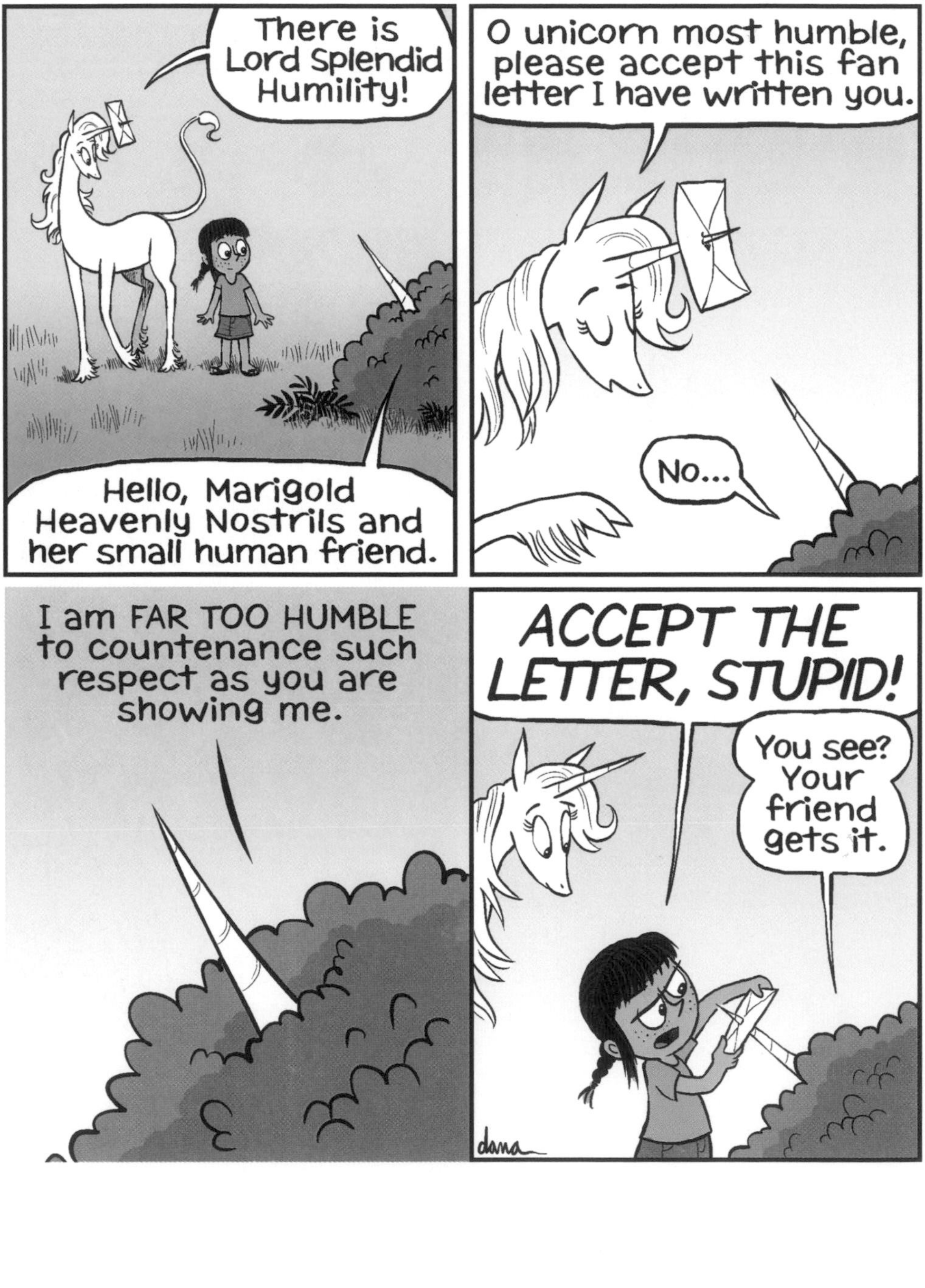
There is Lord Splendid Humility!
Hello, Marigold Heavenly Nostrils and her small human friend.
O unicorn most humble, please accept this fan letter I have written you.
No...
I am FAR TOO HUMBLE to countenance such respect as you are showing me.
ACCEPT THE LETTER, STUPID!
You see? Your friend gets it.
dana

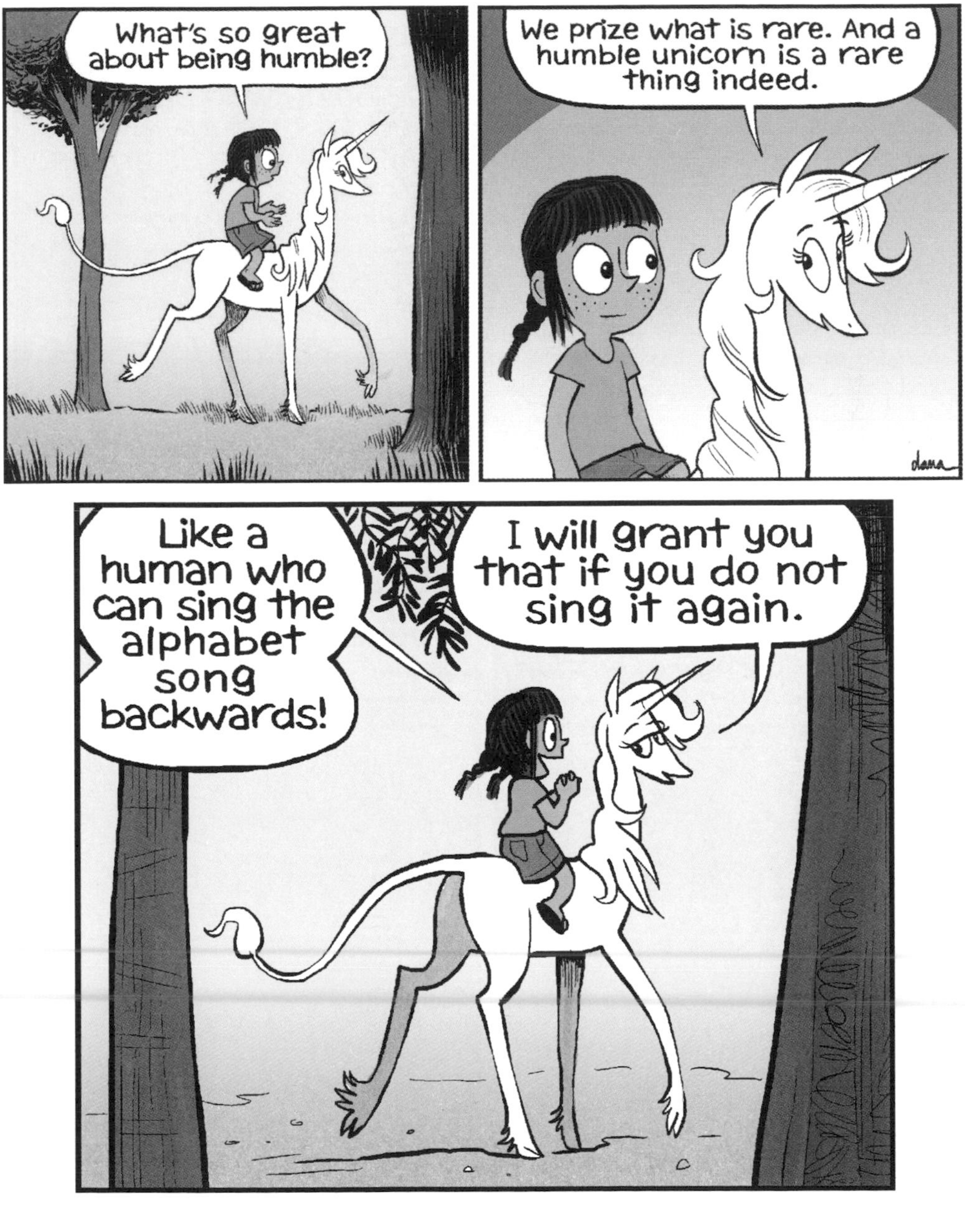
What's so great about being humble?
We prize what is rare. And a humble unicorn is a rare thing indeed.
dana
Like a human who can sing the alphabet song backwards!
I will grant you that if you do not sing it again.

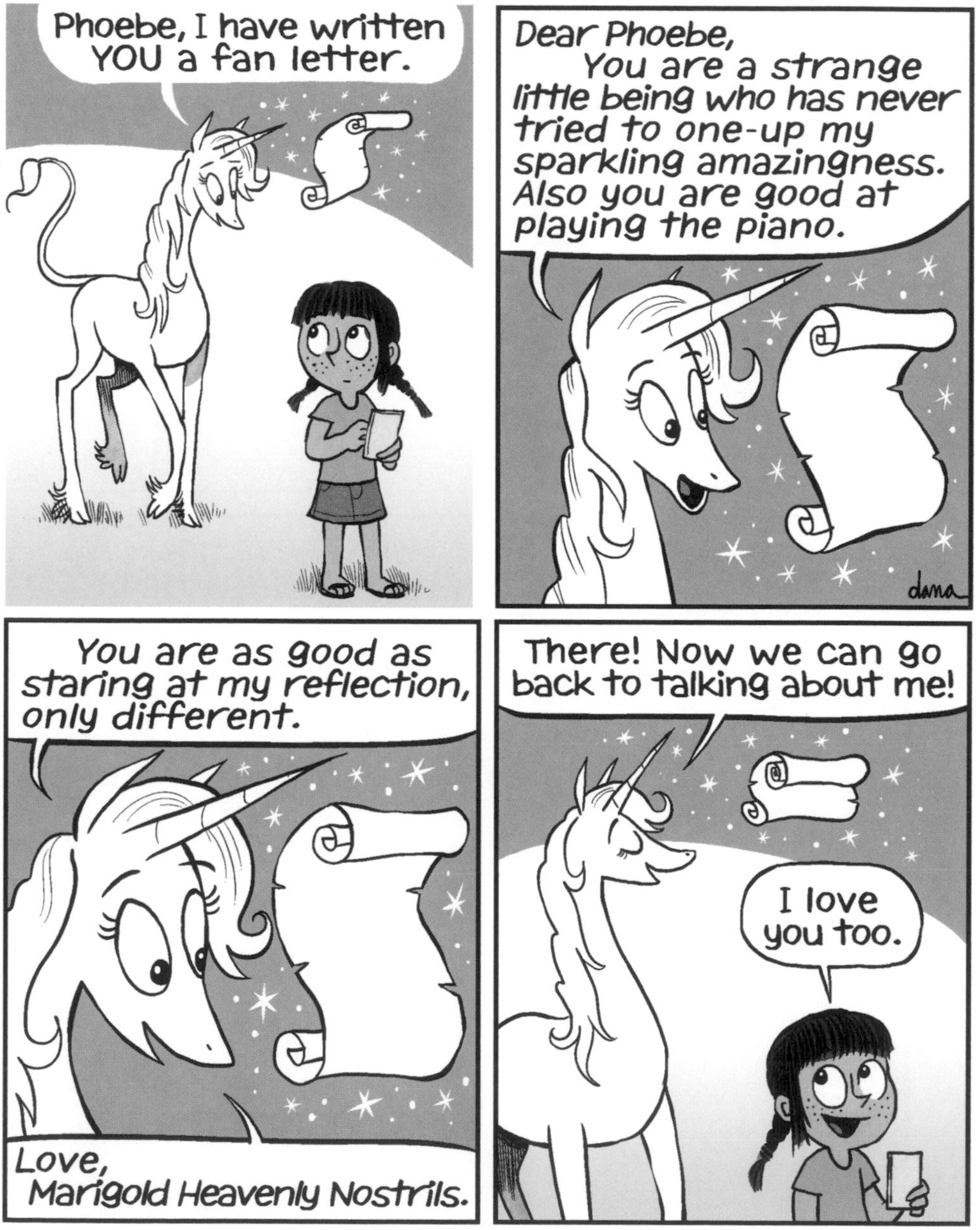
Phoebe, I have written YOU a fan letter.
Dear Phoebe, You are a strange little being who has never tried to one-up my sparkling amazingness. Also you are good at playing the piano.
dana
You are as good as staring at my reflection, only different.
Love, Marigold Heavenly Nostrils.
There! Now we can go back to talking about me!
I love you too.

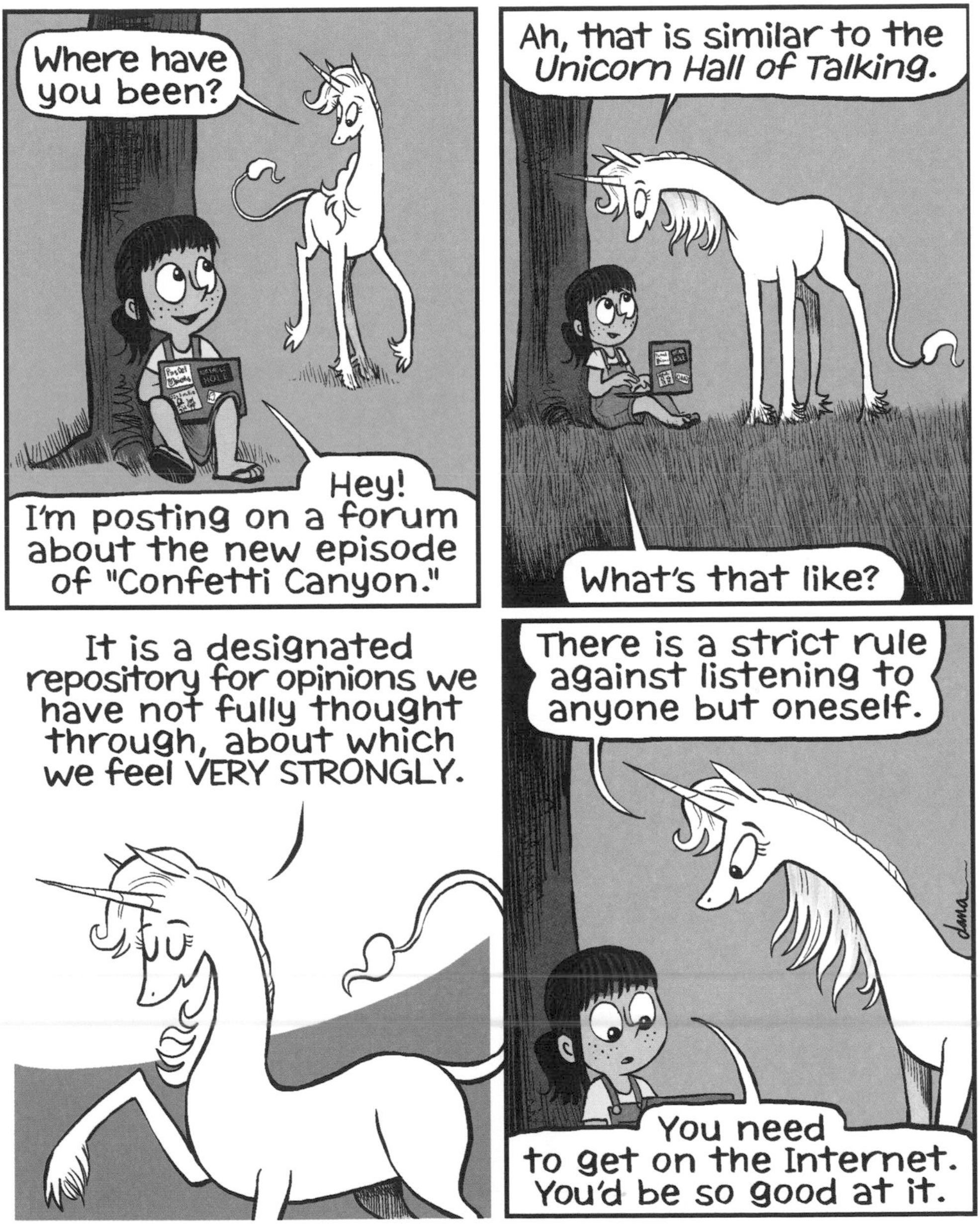
Where have you been?
Hey! I'm posting on a forum about the new episode of "Confetti Canyon."
Ah, that is similar to the *Unicorn Hall of Talking*.
What's that like?
It is a designated repository for opinions we have not fully thought through, about which we feel VERY STRONGLY.
There is a strict rule against listening to anyone but oneself.
You need to get on the Internet. You'd be so good at it.
dana

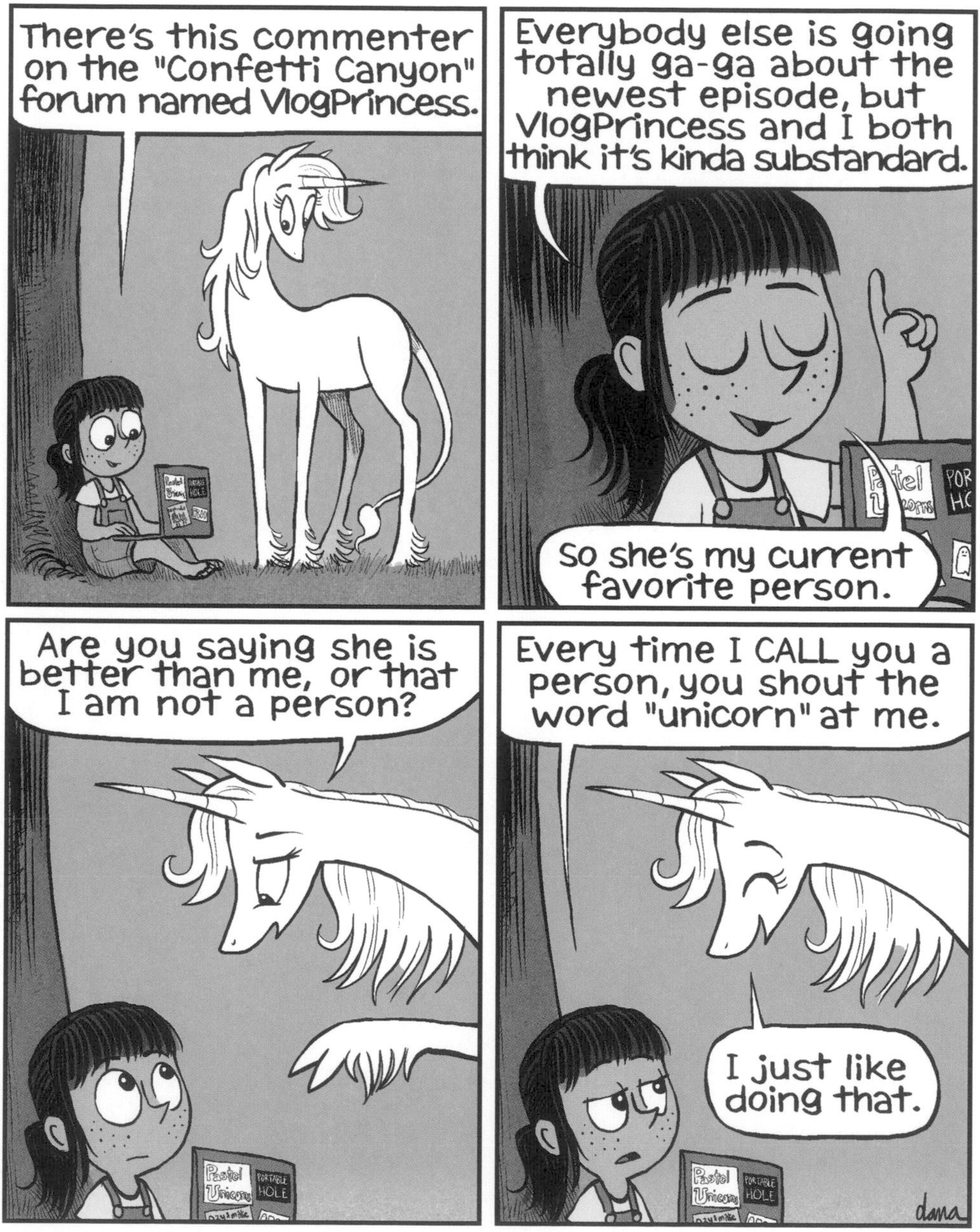
There's this commenter on the "Confetti Canyon" forum named VlogPrincess.
Everybody else is going totally ga-ga about the newest episode, but VlogPrincess and I both think it's kinda substandard.
So she's my current favorite person.
Are you saying she is better than me, or that I am not a person?
Every time I CALL you a person, you shout the word "unicorn" at me.
I just like doing that.
Pastel Unicorns
PORTABLE HOLE
dana

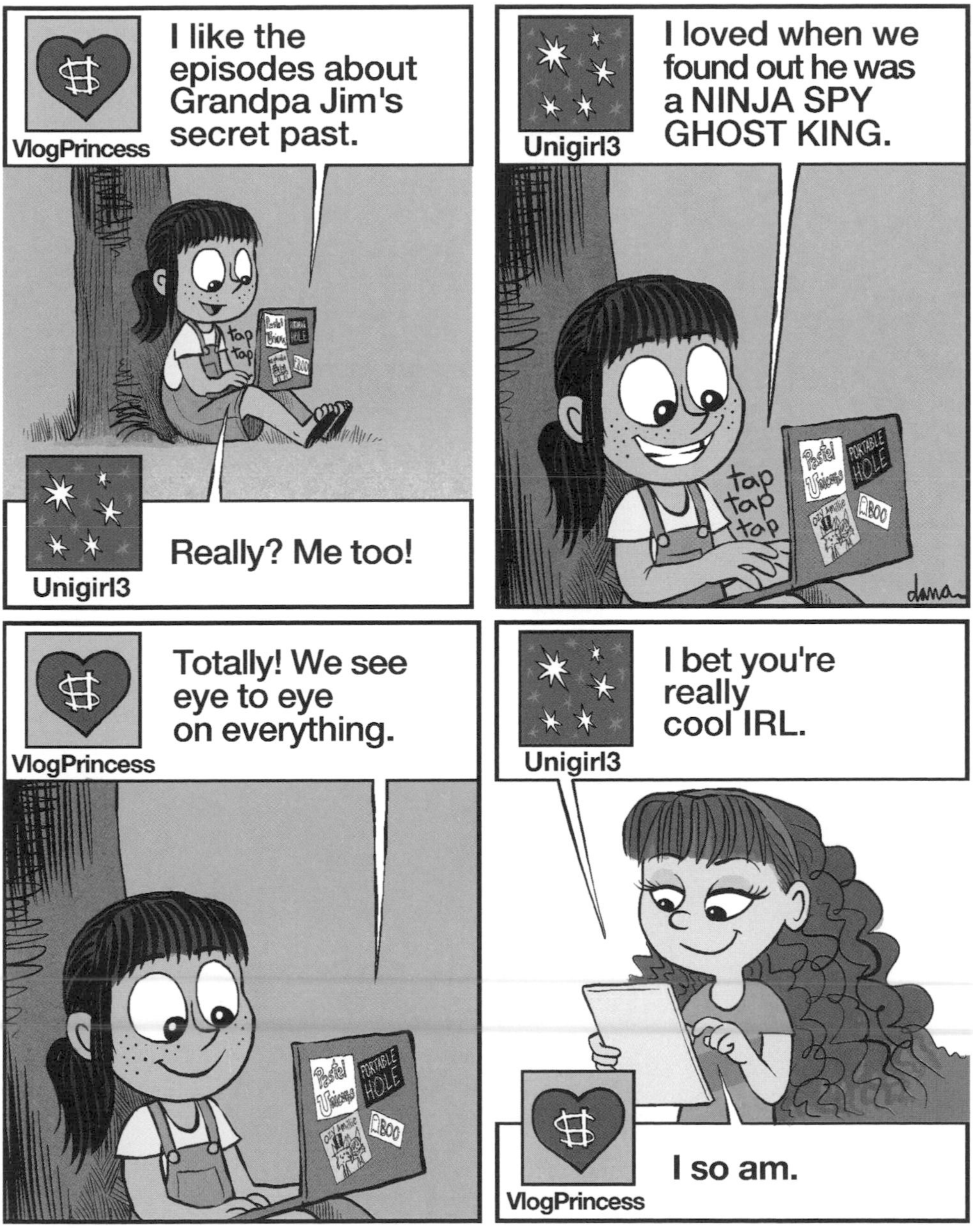
VlogPrincess
I like the episodes about Grandpa Jim's secret past.
Unigirl3
Really? Me too!
tap tap
Unigirl3
I loved when we found out he was a NINJA SPY GHOST KING.
tap tap tap
Pastel Unicorns
PORTABLE HOLE
BOO
dana
VlogPrincess
Totally! We see eye to eye on everything.
Unigirl3
I bet you're really cool IRL.
VlogPrincess
I so am.

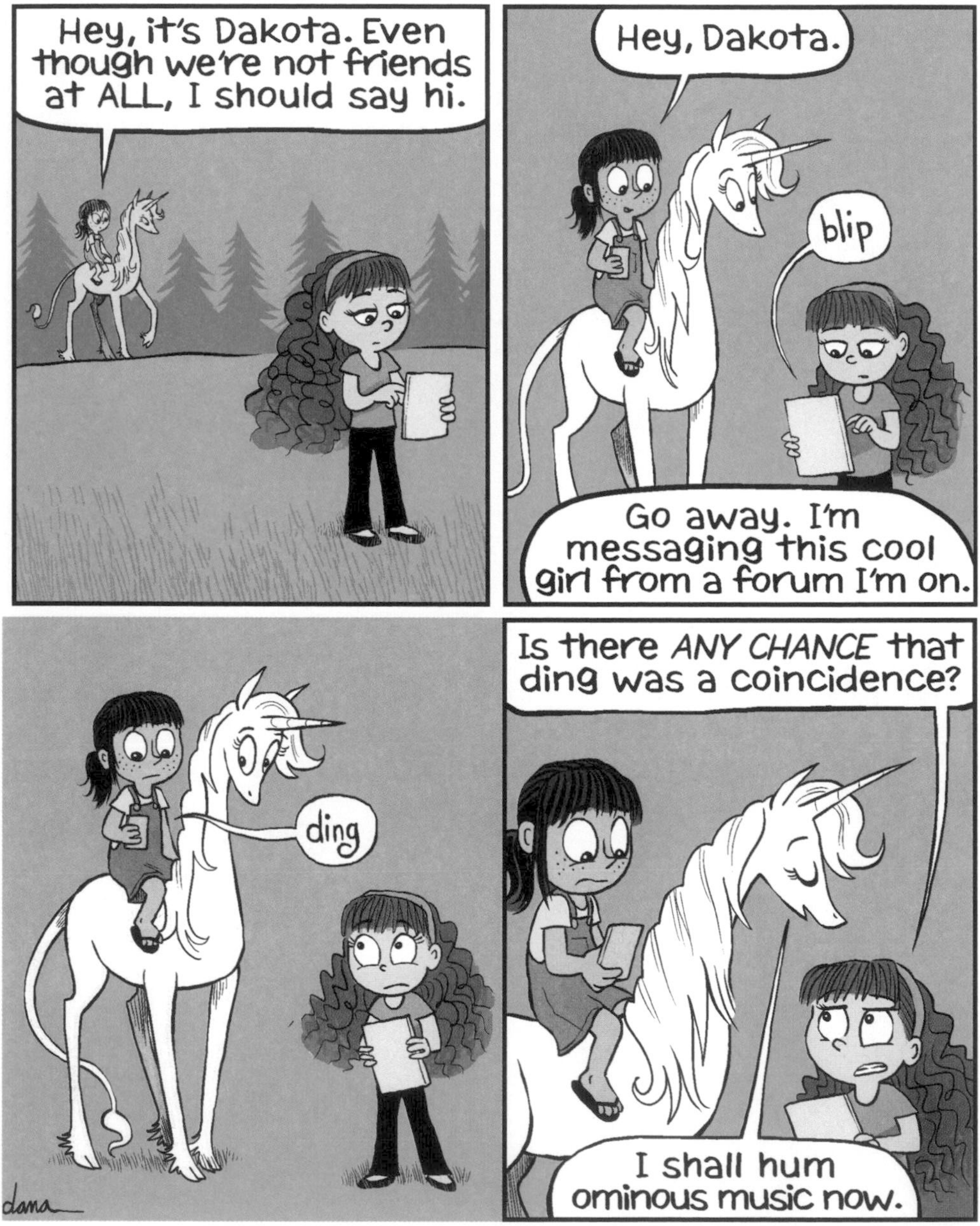
Hey, it's Dakota. Even though we're not friends at ALL, I should say hi.
Hey, Dakota.
blip
Go away. I'm messaging this cool girl from a forum I'm on.
ding
Is there *ANY CHANCE* that ding was a coincidence?
I shall hum ominous music now.
dana

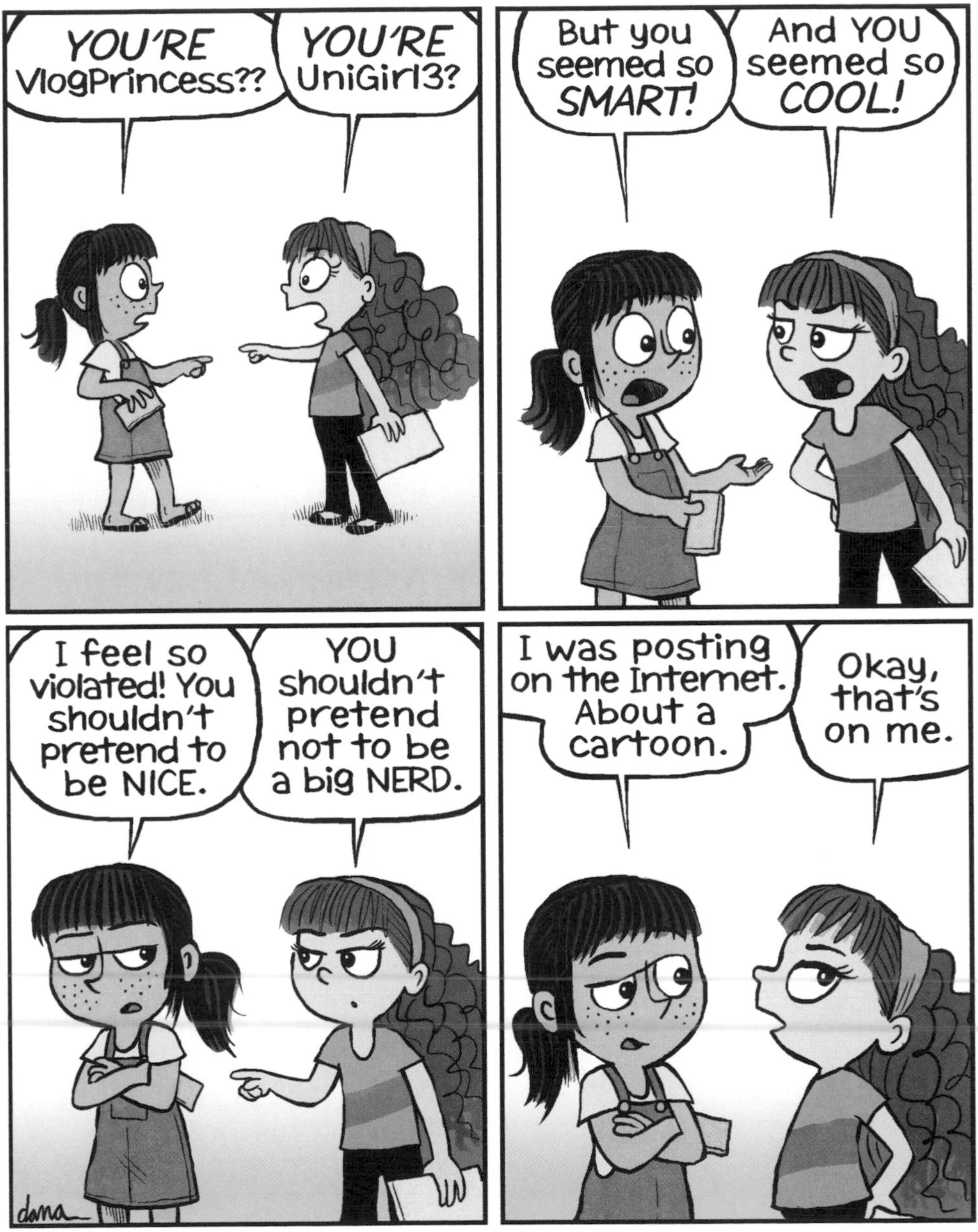
YOU'RE VlogPrincess??
YOU'RE UniGirl3?
But you seemed so SMART!
And YOU seemed so COOL!
I feel so violated! You shouldn't pretend to be NICE.
YOU shouldn't pretend not to be a big NERD.
I was posting on the Internet. About a cartoon.
Okay, that's on me.
dana

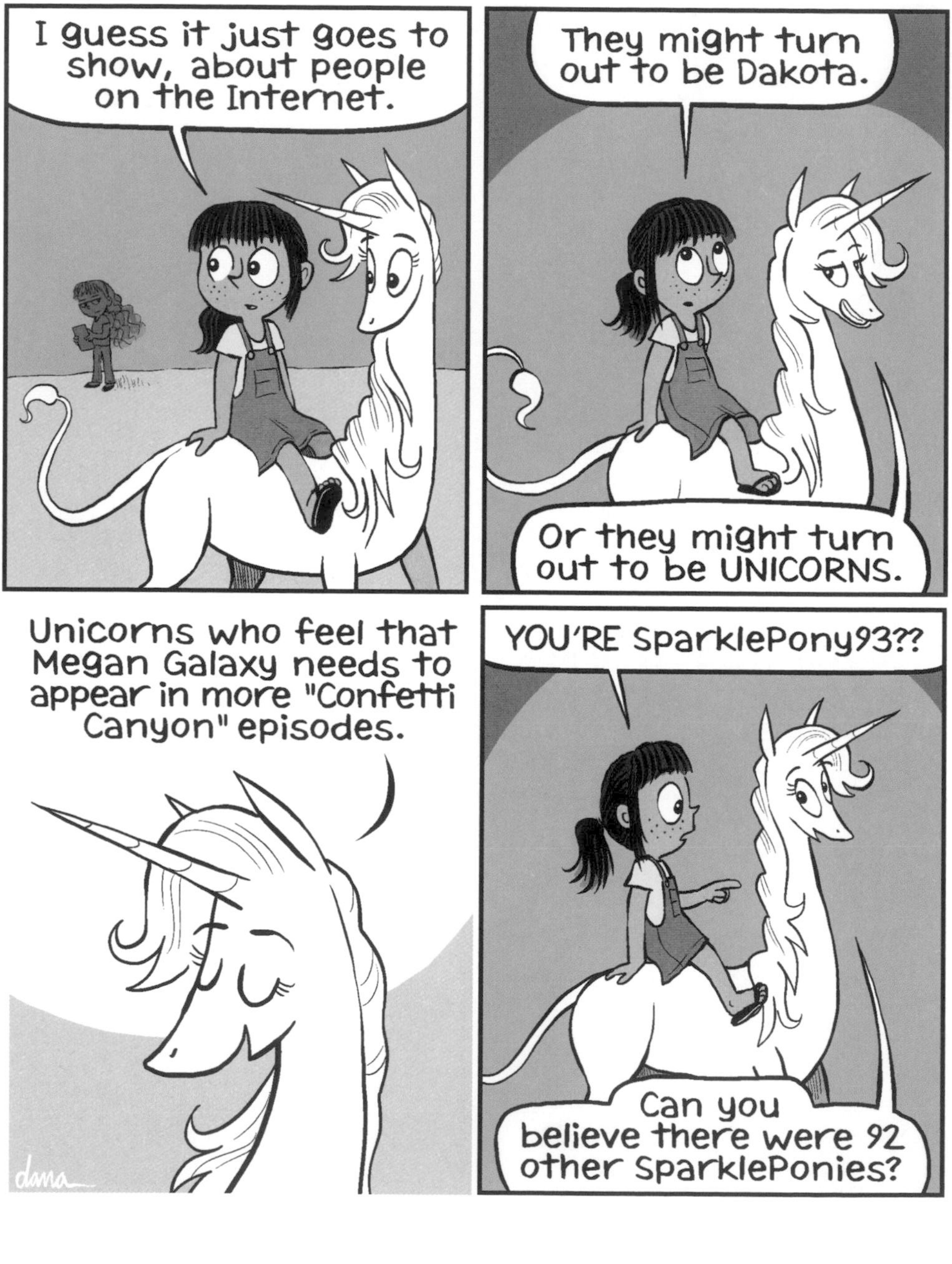
I guess it just goes to show, about people on the Internet.
They might turn out to be Dakota.
Or they might turn out to be UNICORNS.
Unicorns who feel that Megan Galaxy needs to appear in more "Confetti Canyon" episodes.
YOU'RE SparklePony93??
Can you believe there were 92 other SparklePonies?
dana

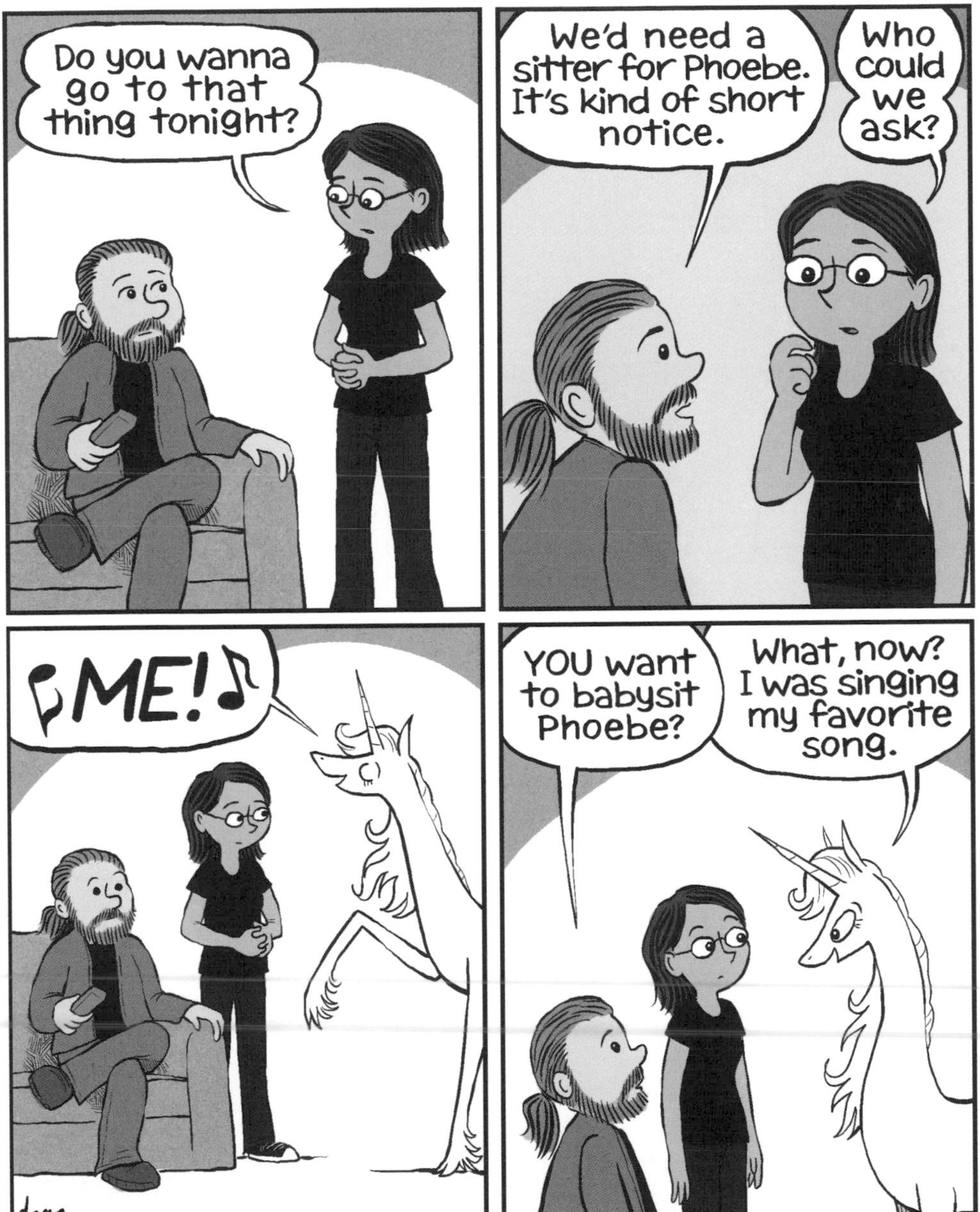
Do you wanna go to that thing tonight?
We'd need a sitter for Phoebe. It's kind of short notice.
Who could we ask?
ME!
YOU want to babysit Phoebe?
What, now? I was singing my favorite song.
dana

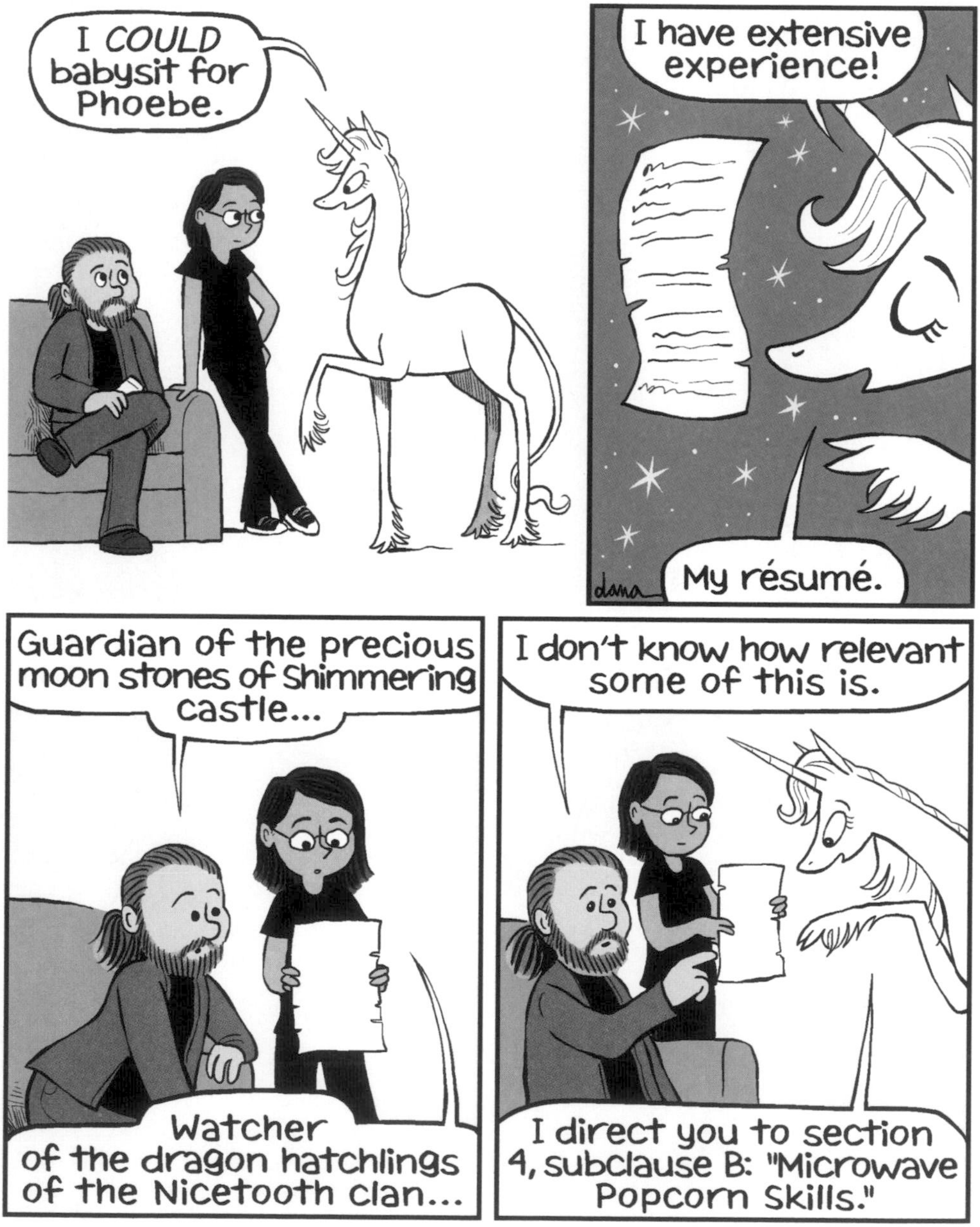
I COULD babysit for Phoebe.
I have extensive experience!
My résumé.
dana
Guardian of the precious moon stones of Shimmering castle...
Watcher of the dragon hatchlings of the Nicetooth clan...
I don't know how relevant some of this is.
I direct you to section 4, subclause B: "Microwave Popcorn Skills."

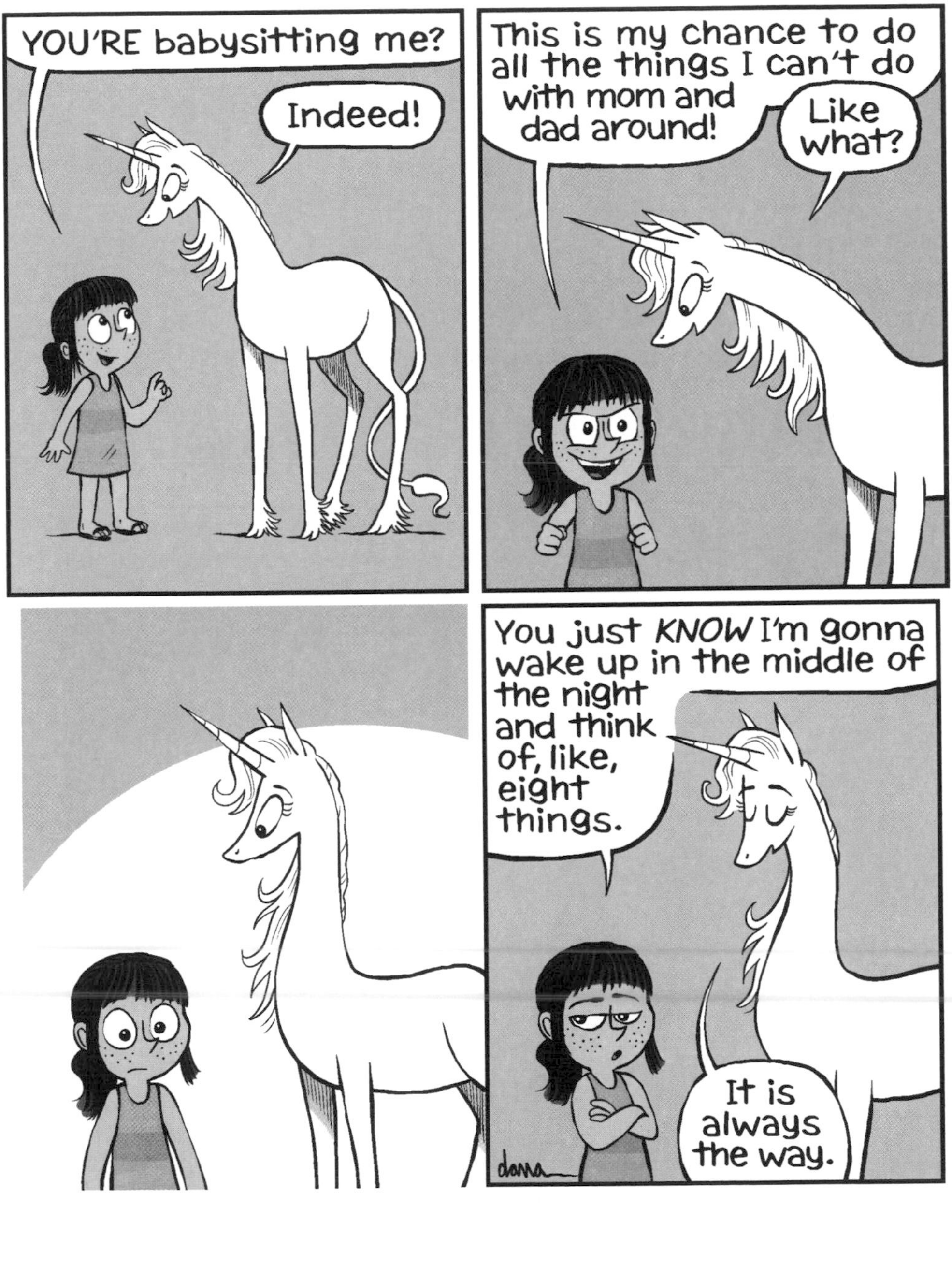
YOU'RE babysitting me?
Indeed!
This is my chance to do all the things I can't do with mom and dad around!
Like what?
You just KNOW I'm gonna wake up in the middle of the night and think of, like, eight things.
It is always the way.
dana

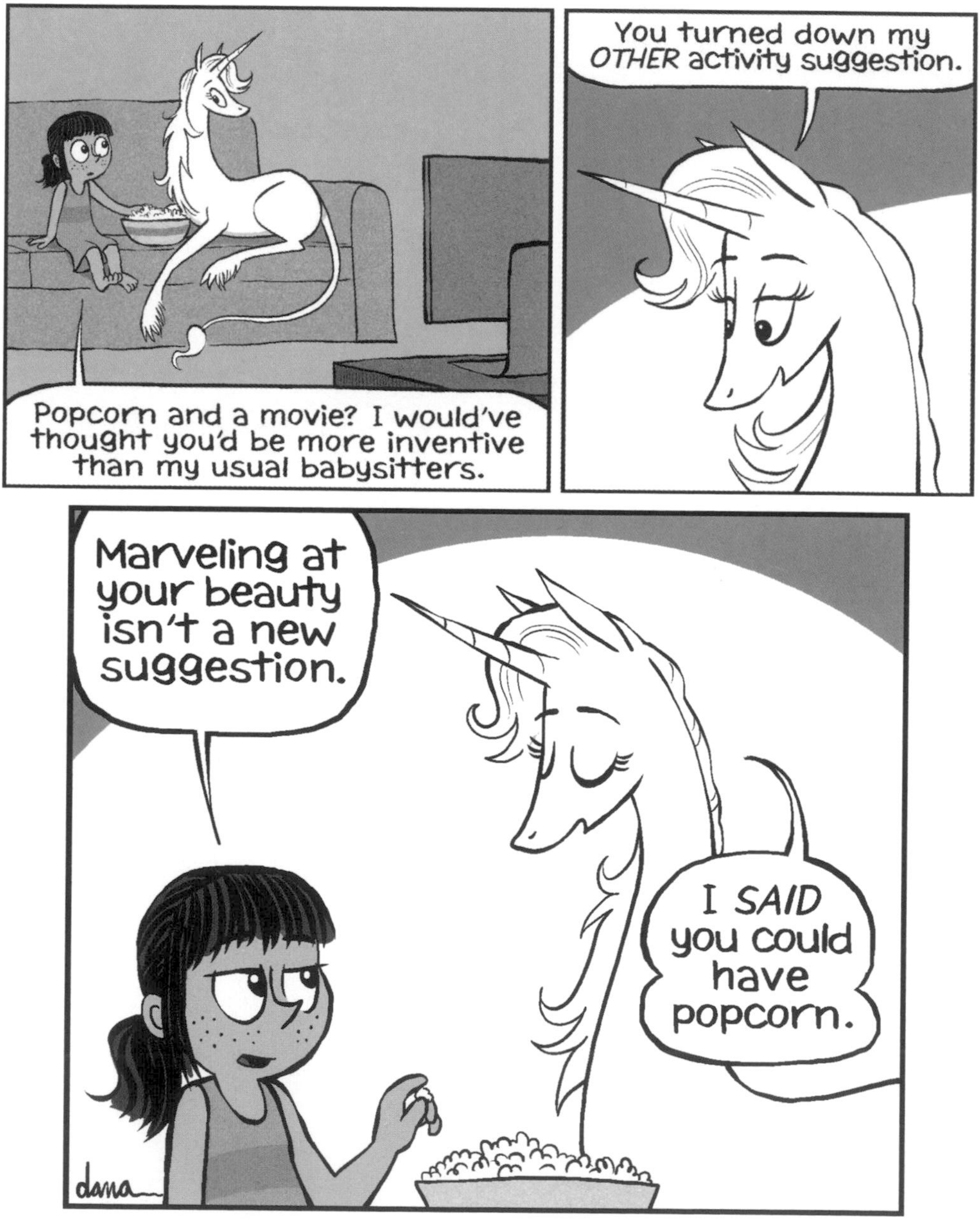
Popcorn and a movie? I would've thought you'd be more inventive than my usual babysitters.
You turned down my OTHER activity suggestion.
Marveling at your beauty isn't a new suggestion.
I SAID you could have popcorn.
dana

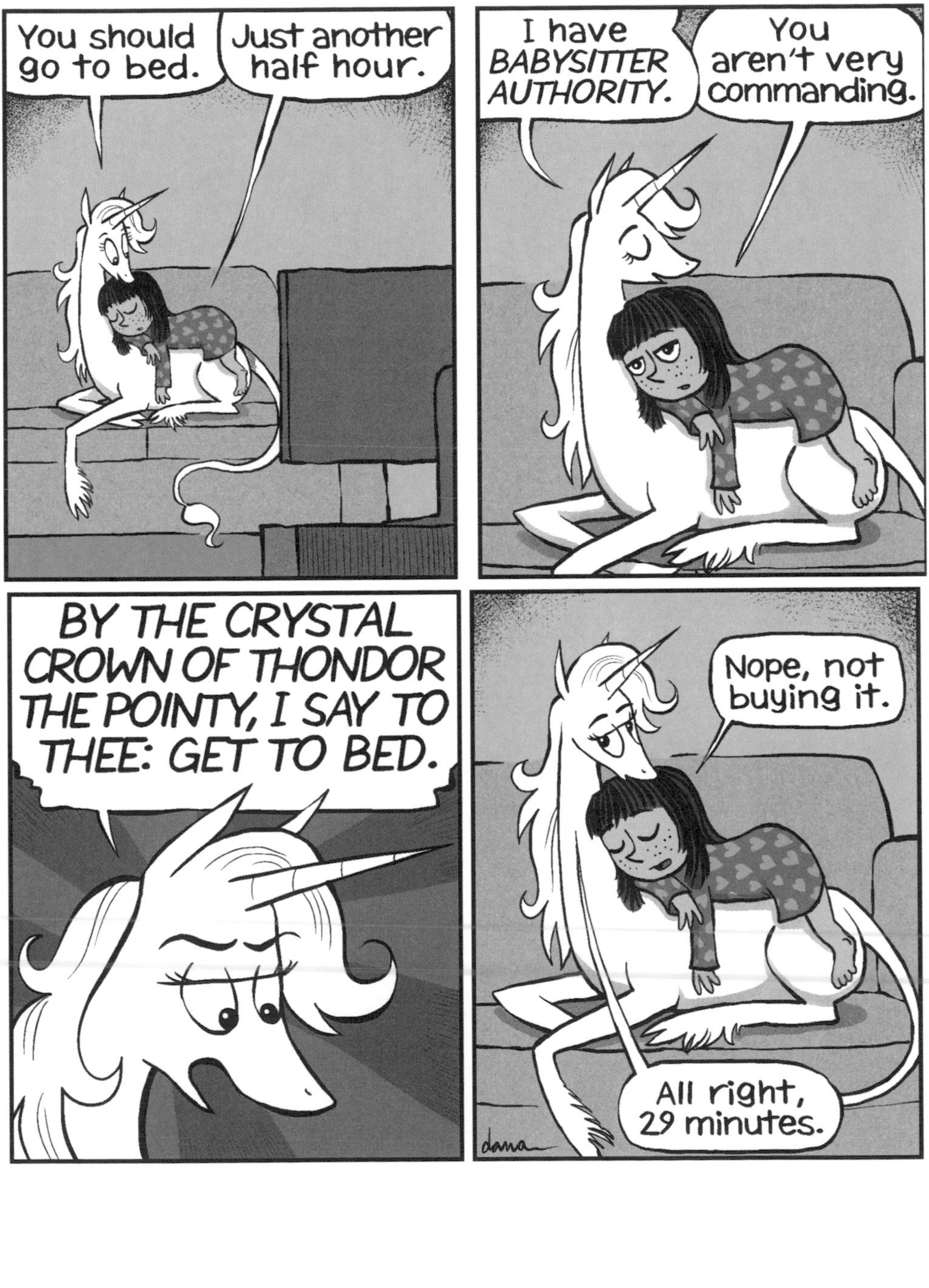
You should go to bed.
Just another half hour.
I have *BABYSITTER AUTHORITY.*
You aren't very commanding.
BY THE CRYSTAL CROWN OF THONDOR THE POINTY, I SAY TO THEE: GET TO BED.
Nope, not buying it.
All right, 29 minutes.
dana

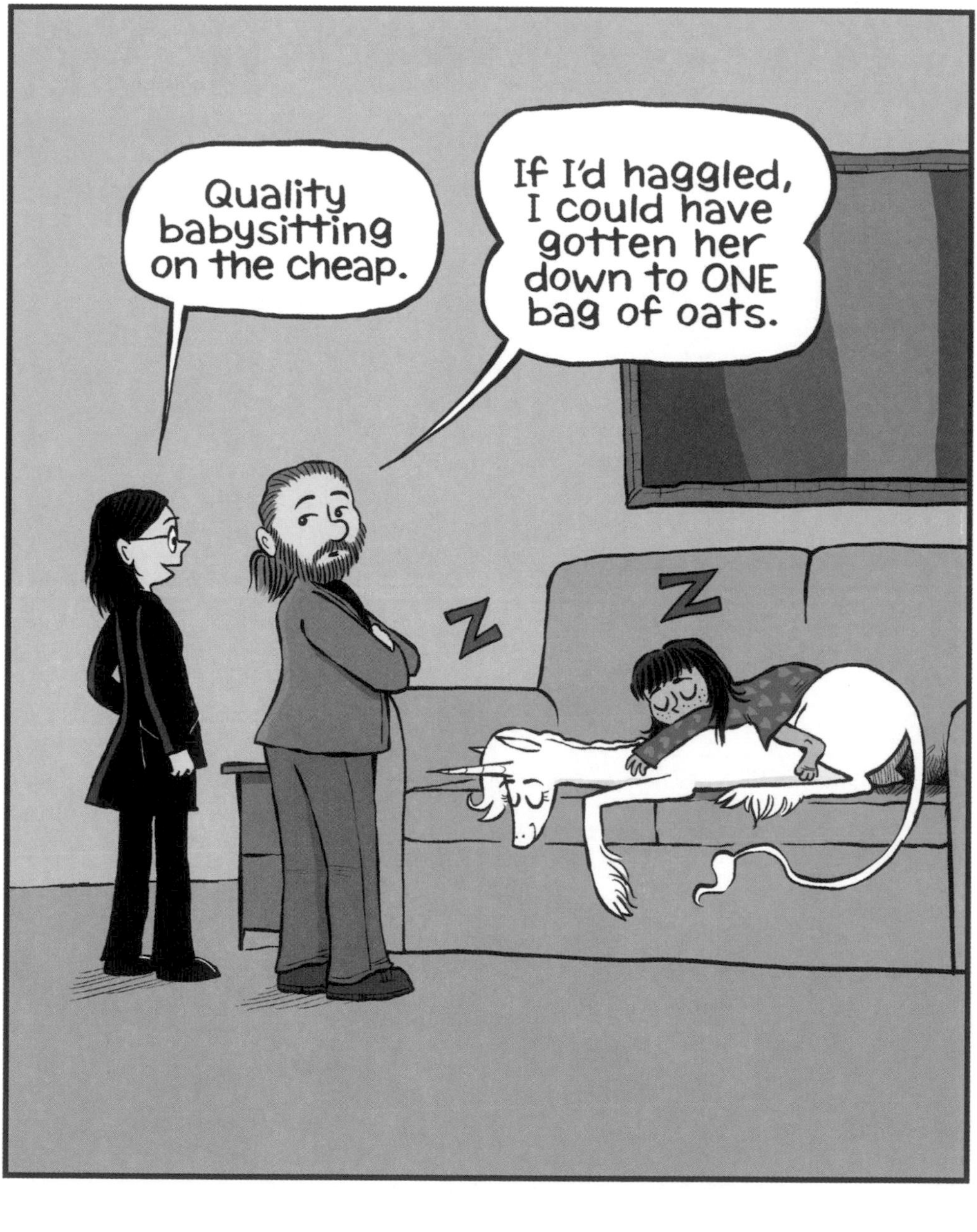
Quality babysitting on the cheap.
If I'd haggled, I could have gotten her down to ONE bag of oats.
Z
Z

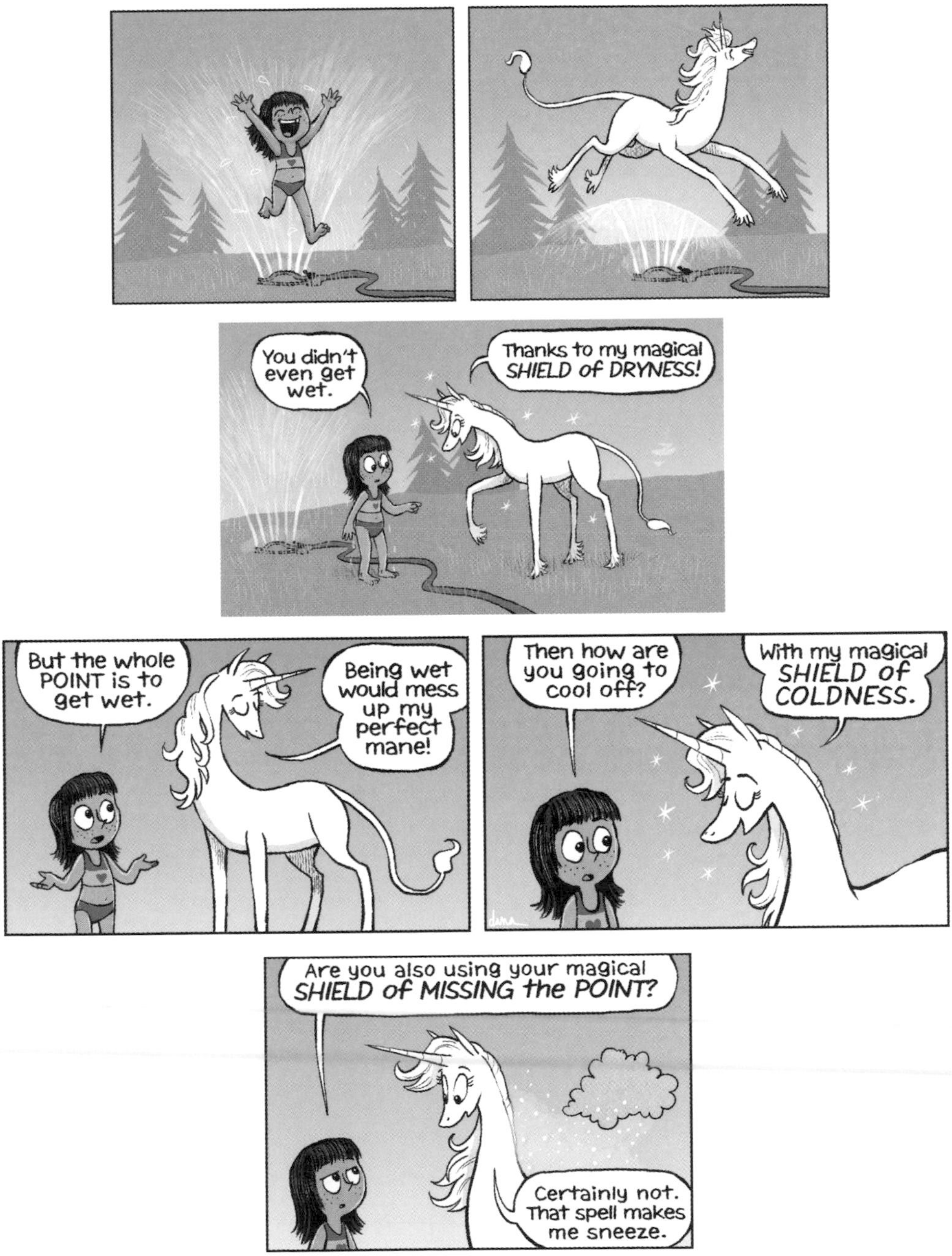
You didn't even get wet.
Thanks to my magical SHIELD of DRYNESS!
But the whole POINT is to get wet.
Being wet would mess up my perfect mane!
Then how are you going to cool off?
With my magical SHIELD of COLDNESS.
Are you also using your magical SHIELD of MISSING the POINT?
Certainly not. That spell makes me sneeze.

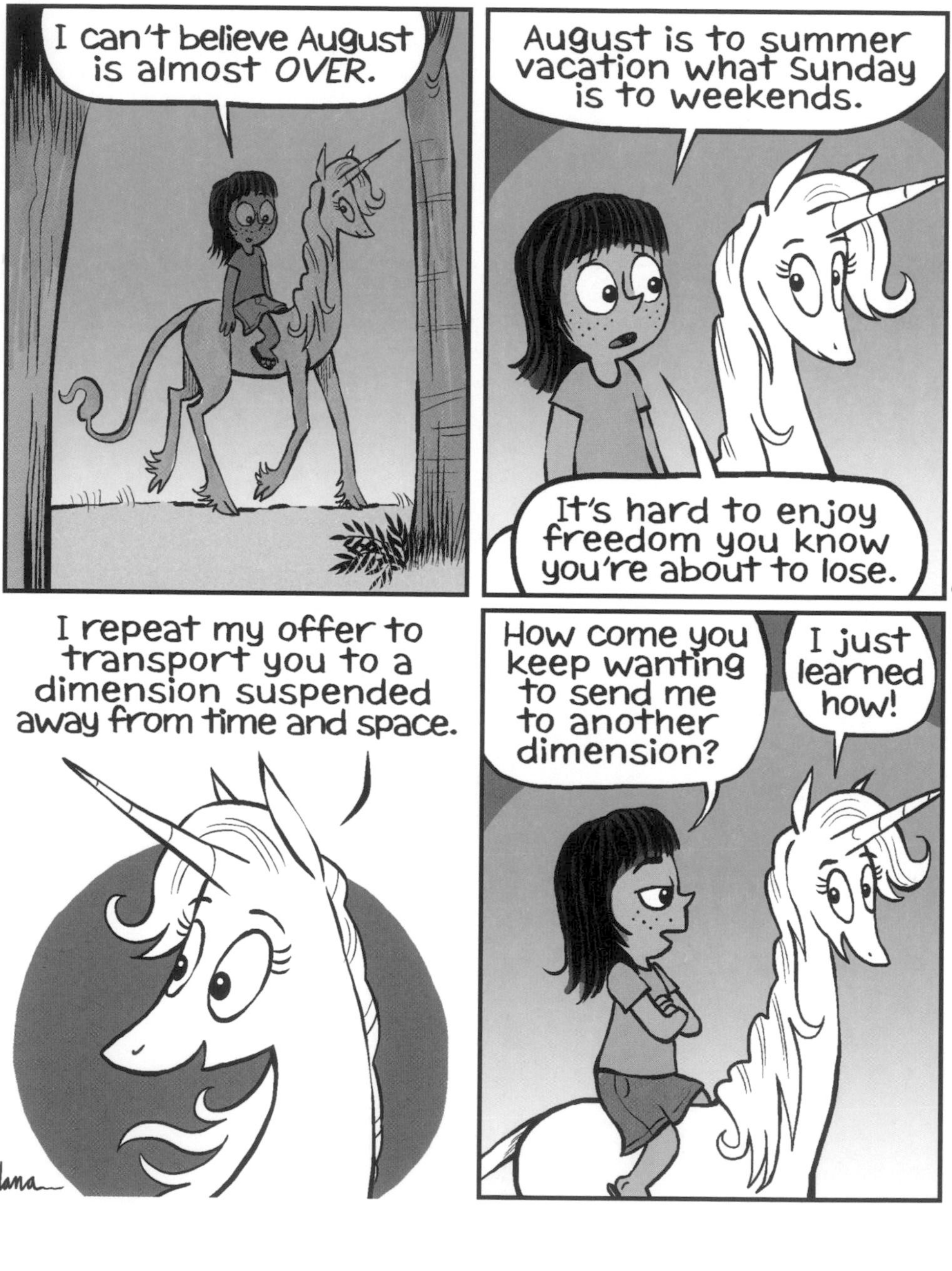

I can't believe August is almost OVER.
August is to summer vacation what Sunday is to weekends.
It's hard to enjoy freedom you know you're about to lose.
I repeat my offer to transport you to a dimension suspended away from time and space.
How come you keep wanting to send me to another dimension?
I just learned how!
dana

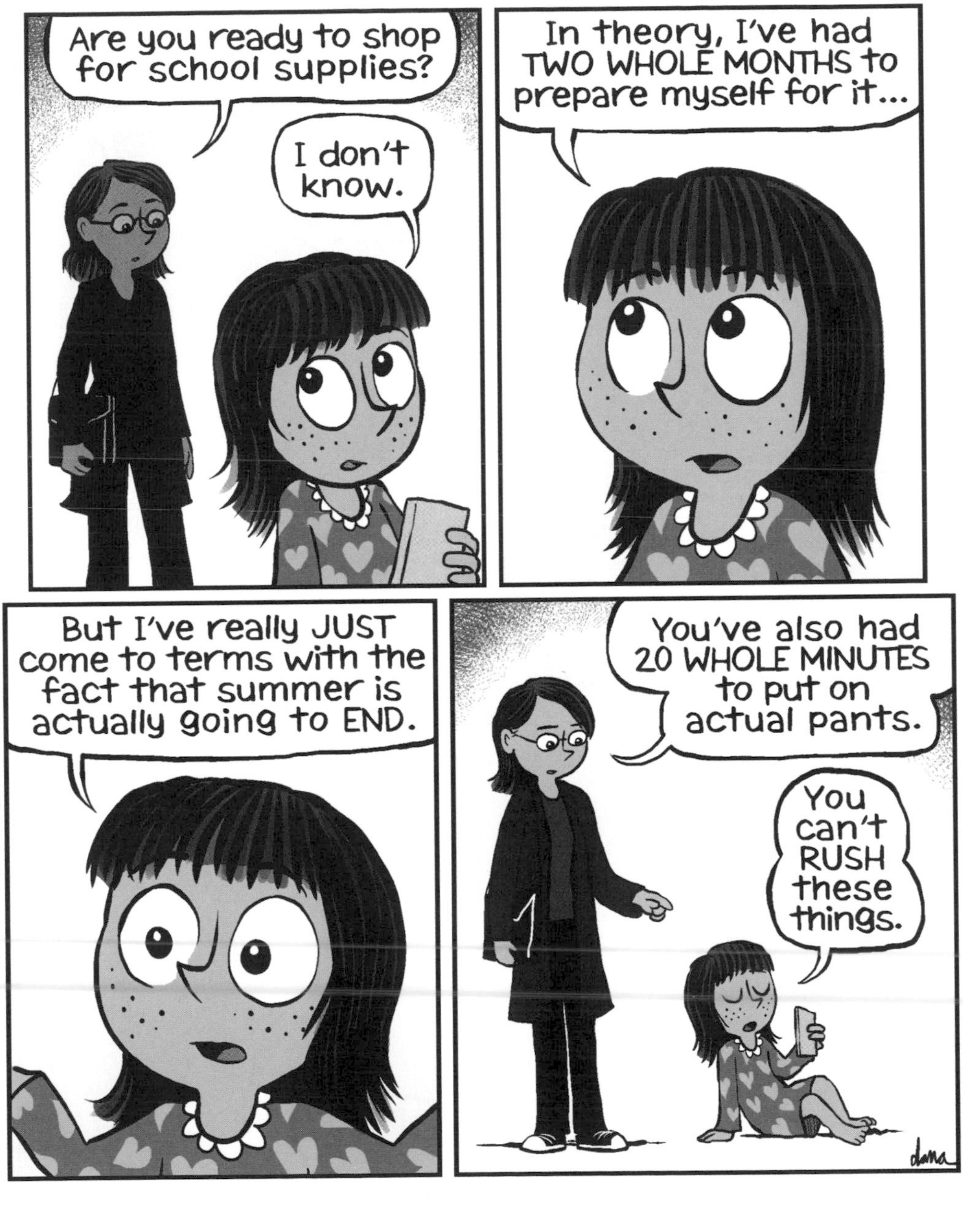

Are you ready to shop for school supplies?
I don't know.
In theory, I've had TWO WHOLE MONTHS to prepare myself for it...
But I've really JUST come to terms with the fact that summer is actually going to END.
You've also had 20 WHOLE MINUTES to put on actual pants.
You can't RUSH these things.
dana

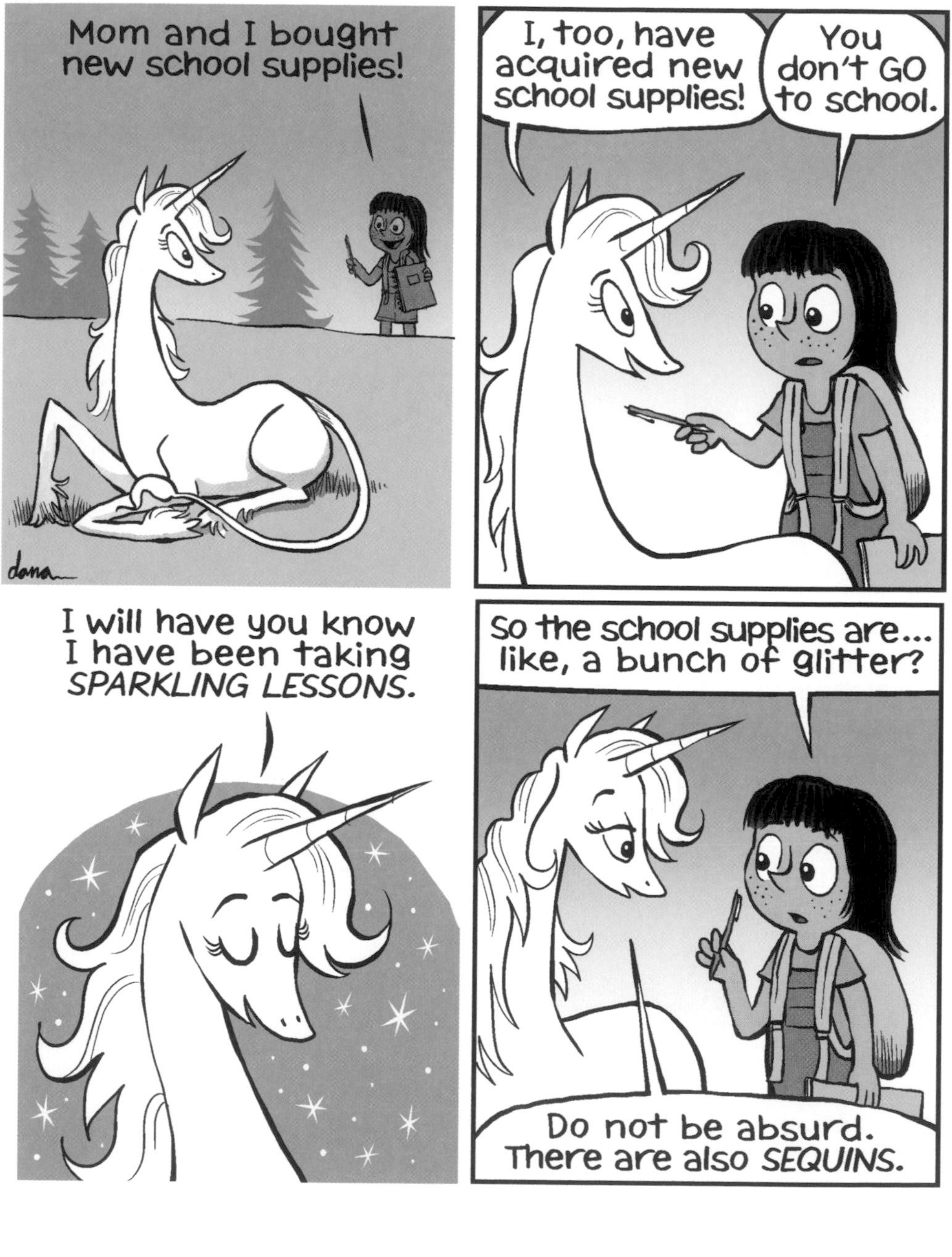

Mom and I bought new school supplies!
dana
I, too, have acquired new school supplies!
You don't GO to school.
I will have you know I have been taking *SPARKLING LESSONS*.
So the school supplies are... like, a bunch of glitter?
Do not be absurd. There are also *SEQUINS*.

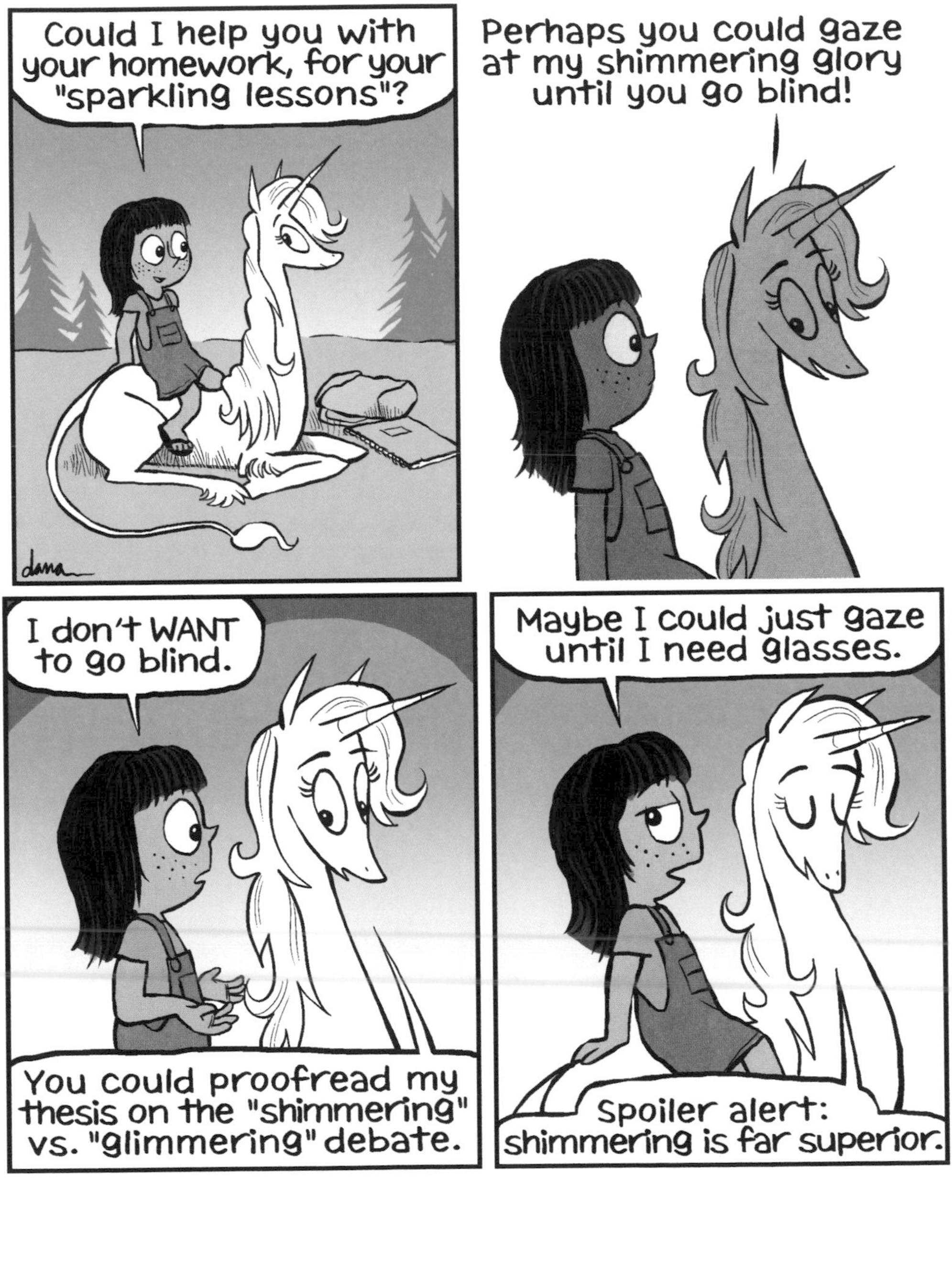
Could I help you with your homework, for your "sparkling lessons"?
dana
Perhaps you could gaze at my shimmering glory until you go blind!
I don't WANT to go blind.
You could proofread my thesis on the "shimmering" vs. "glimmering" debate.
Maybe I could just gaze until I need glasses.
Spoiler alert: shimmering is far superior.

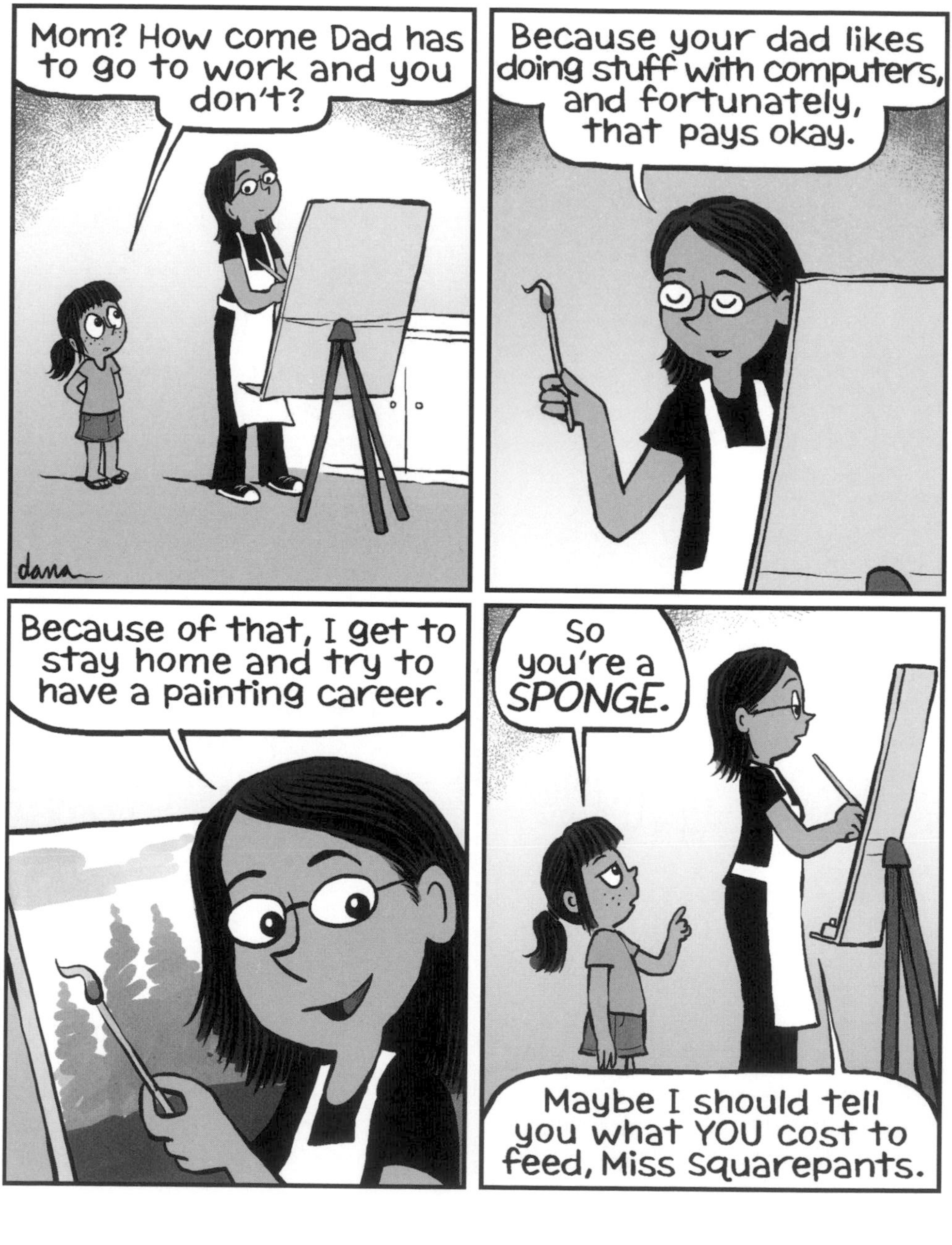
Mom? How come Dad has to go to work and you don't?
dana
Because your dad likes doing stuff with computers, and fortunately, that pays okay.
Because of that, I get to stay home and try to have a painting career.
So you're a *SPONGE*.
Maybe I should tell you what YOU cost to feed, Miss Squarepants.

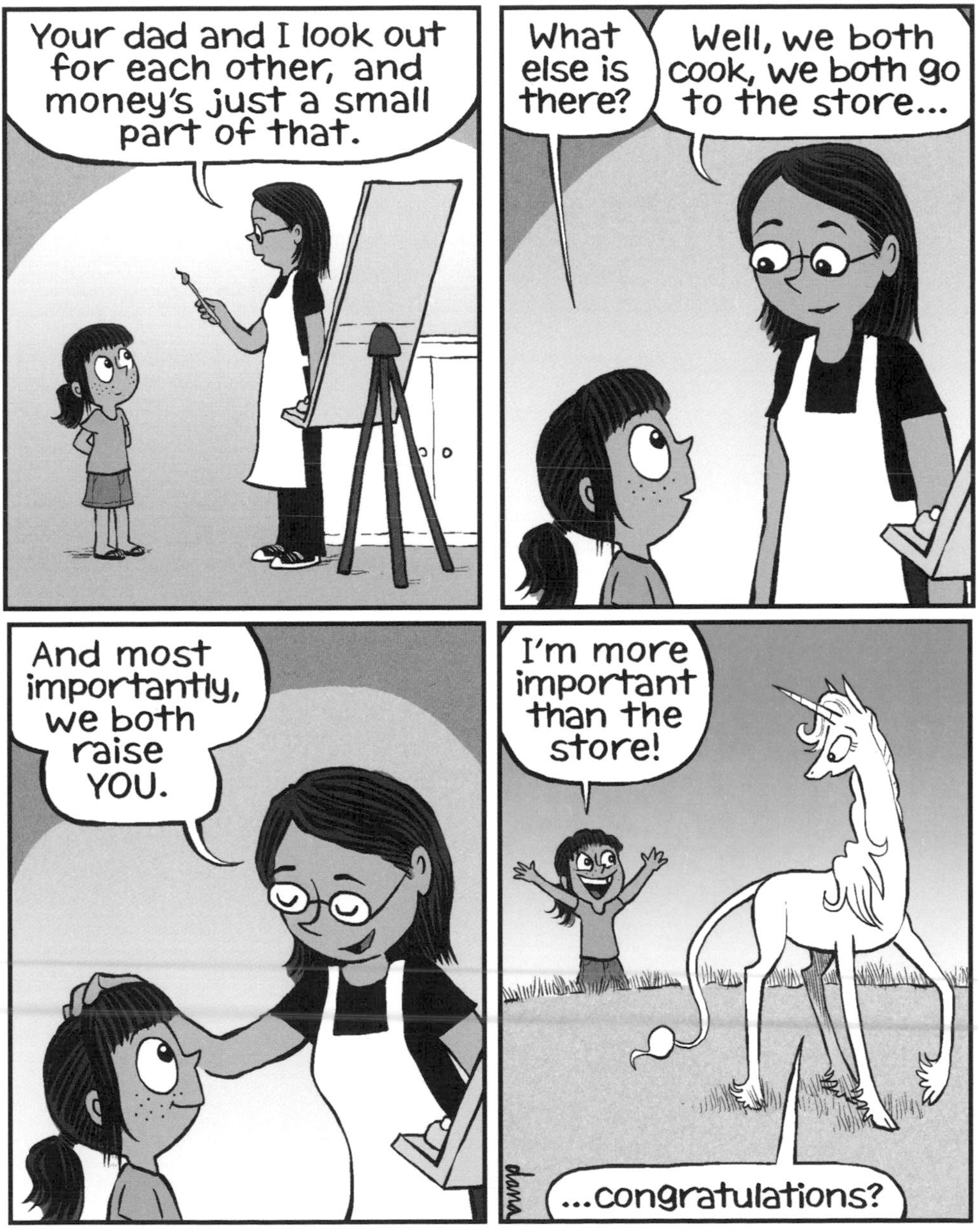
Your dad and I look out for each other, and money's just a small part of that.
What else is there?
Well, we both cook, we both go to the store...
And most importantly, we both raise YOU.
I'm more important than the store!
...congratulations?

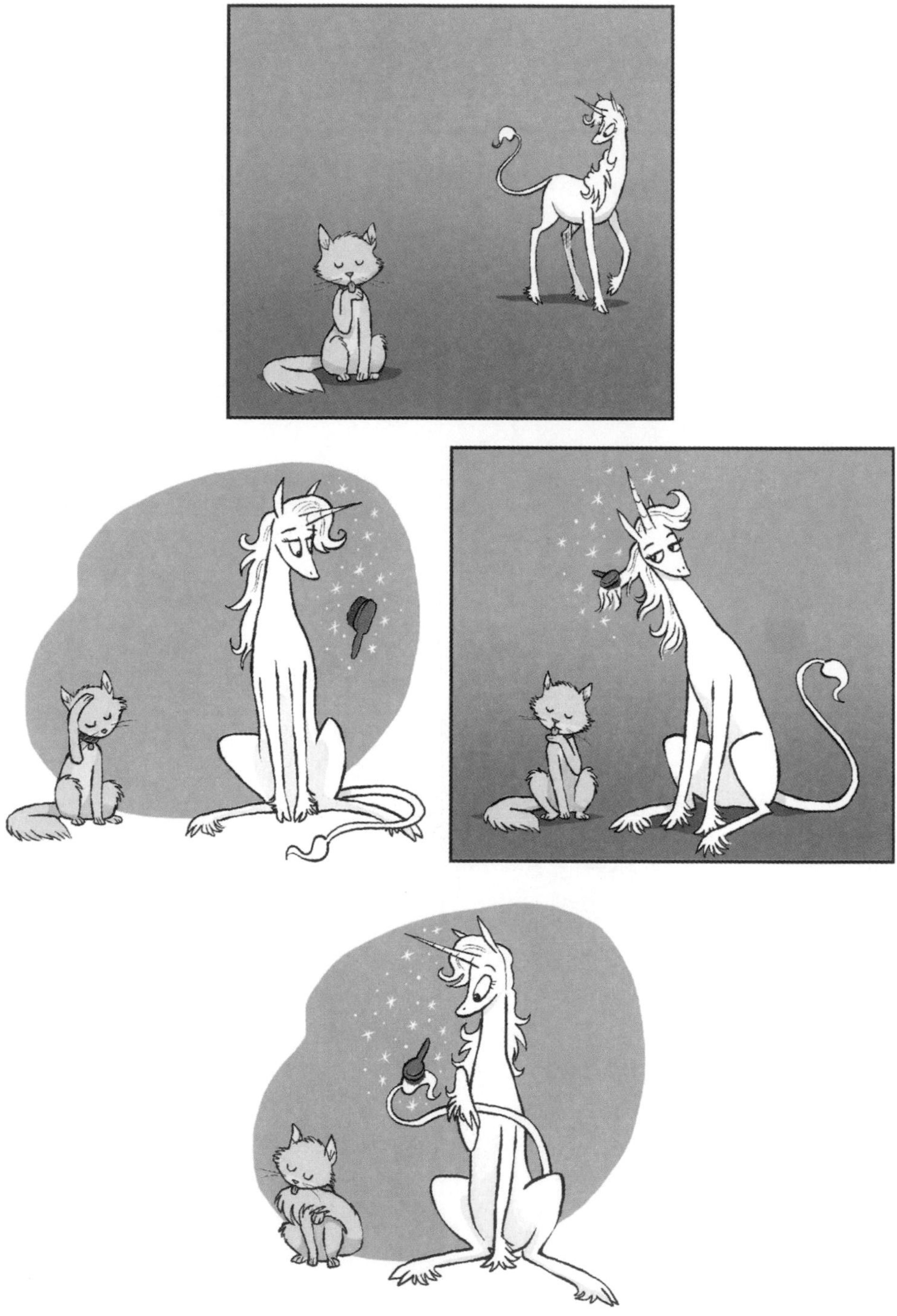

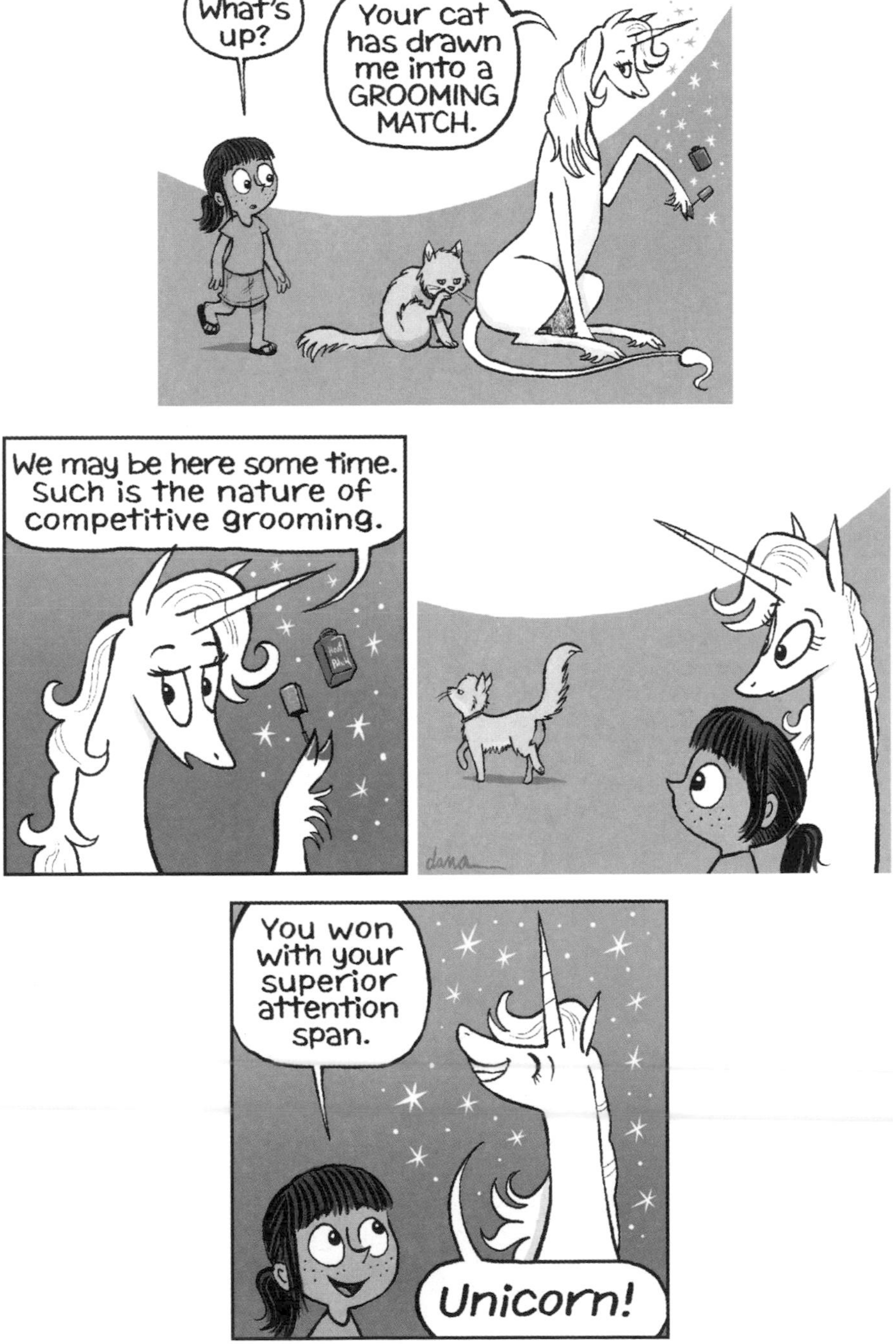
What's up?
Your cat has drawn me into a GROOMING MATCH.
We may be here some time. Such is the nature of competitive grooming.
You won with your superior attention span.
Unicorn!

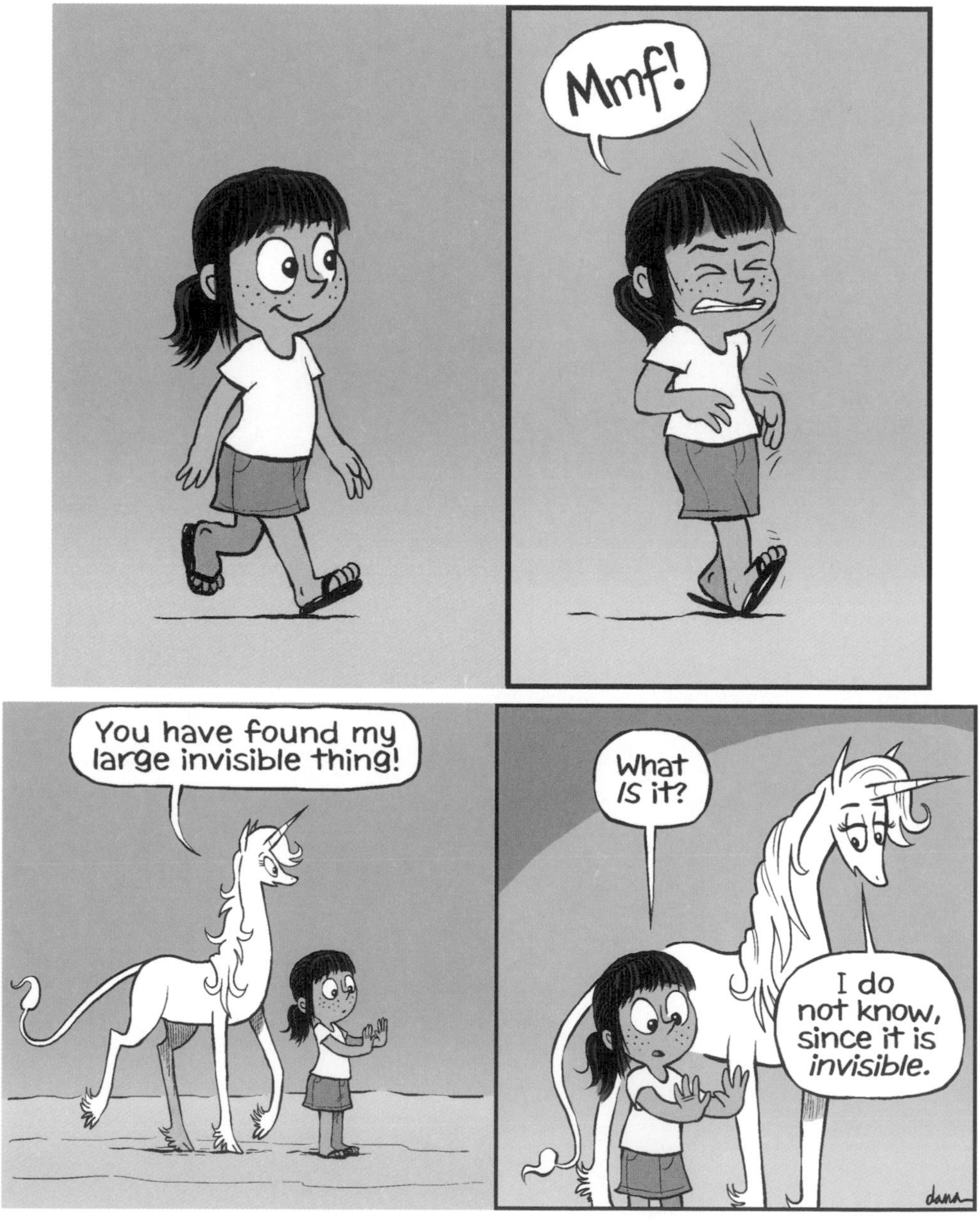
Mmf!
You have found my large invisible thing!
What *IS* it?
I do not know, since it is *invisible*.
dana

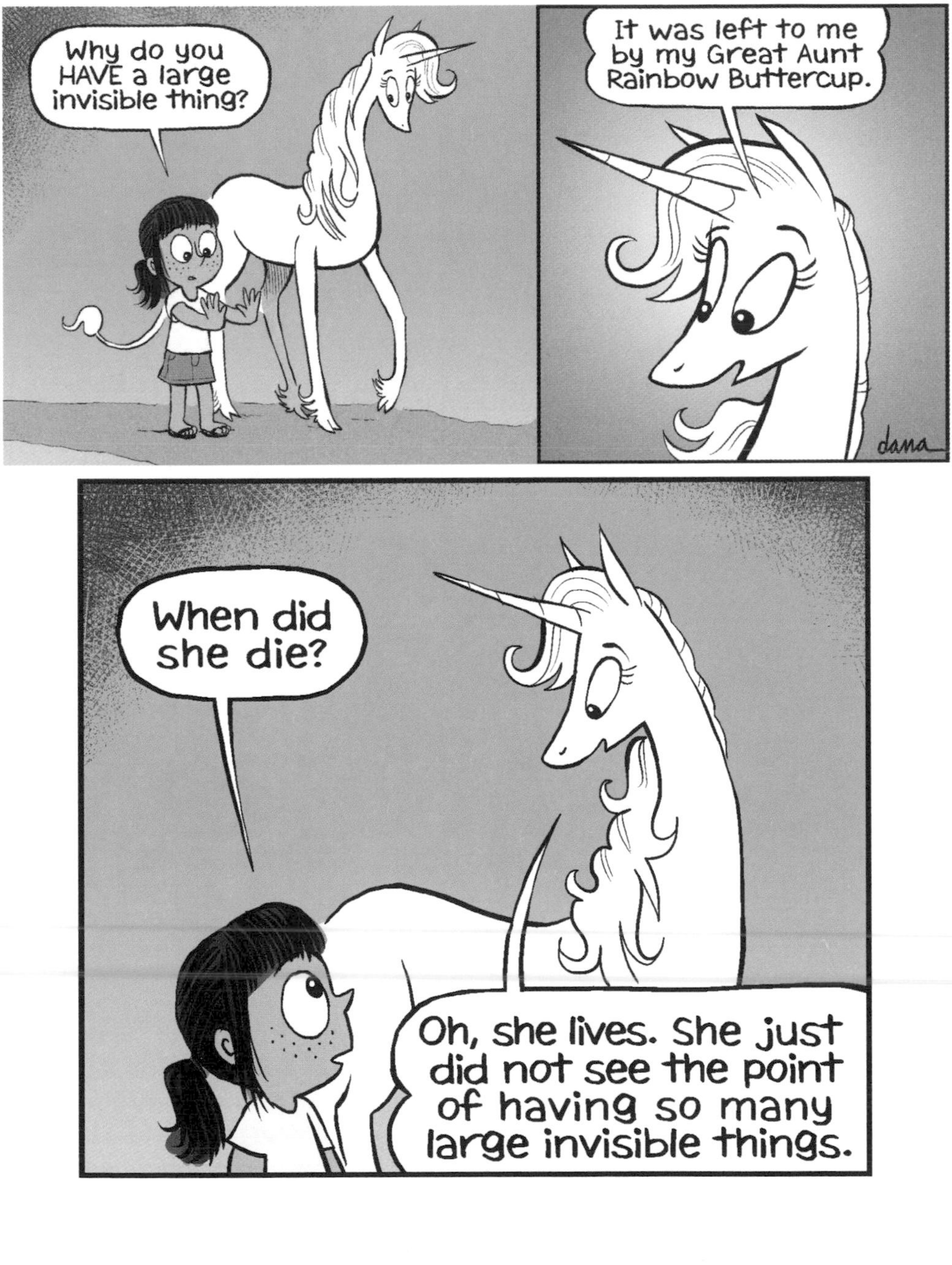
Why do you HAVE a large invisible thing?
It was left to me by my Great Aunt Rainbow Buttercup.
dana
When did she die?
Oh, she lives. She just did not see the point of having so many large invisible things.

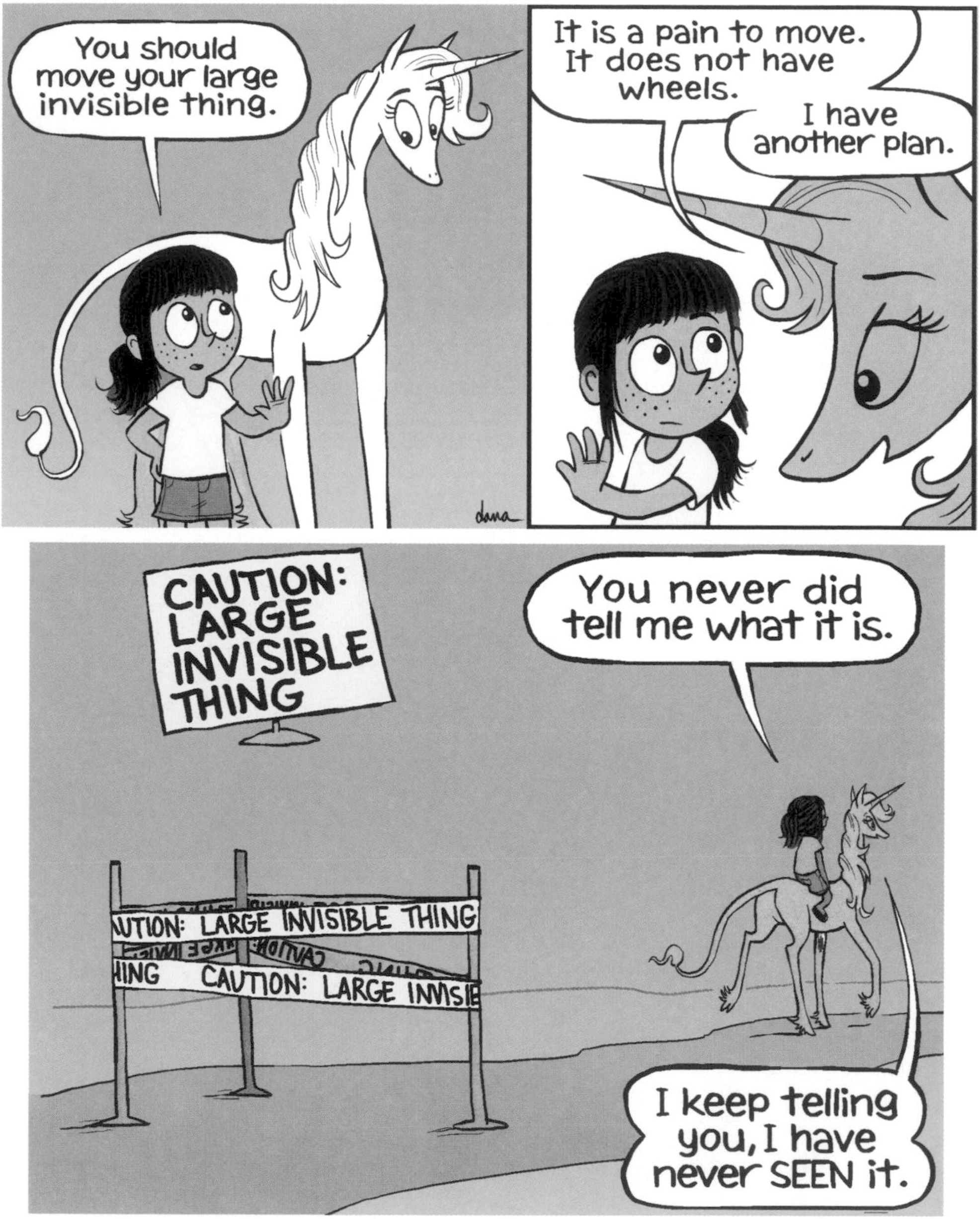
You should move your large invisible thing.
It is a pain to move. It does not have wheels.
I have another plan.
CAUTION: LARGE INVISIBLE THING
You never did tell me what it is.
UTION: LARGE INVISIBLE THING
HING CAUTION: LARGE INVISIE
I keep telling you, I have never SEEN it.

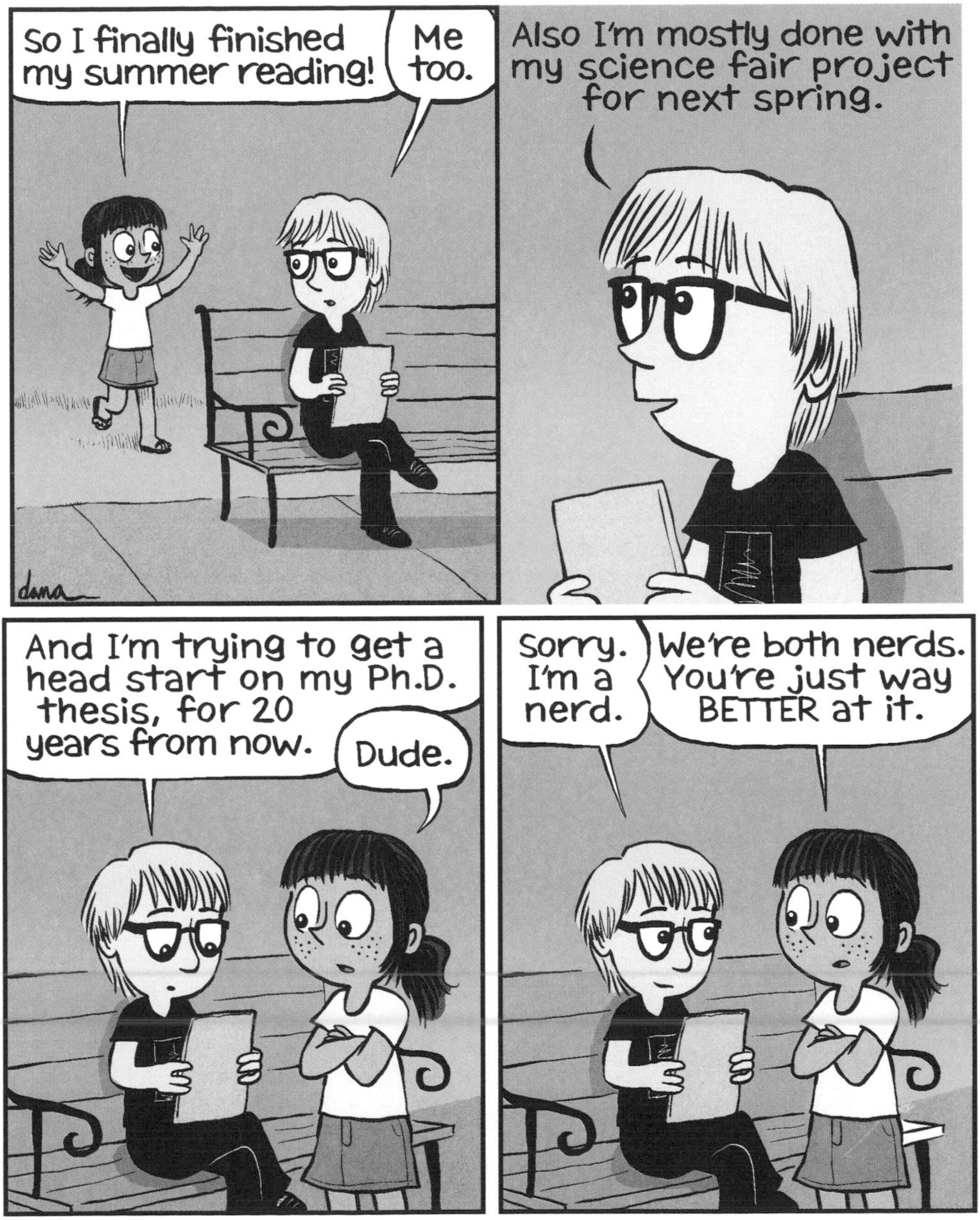
So I finally finished my summer reading!
Me too.
Also I'm mostly done with my science fair project for next spring.
And I'm trying to get a head start on my Ph.D. thesis, for 20 years from now.
Dude.
Sorry. I'm a nerd.
We're both nerds. You're just way BETTER at it.
dana

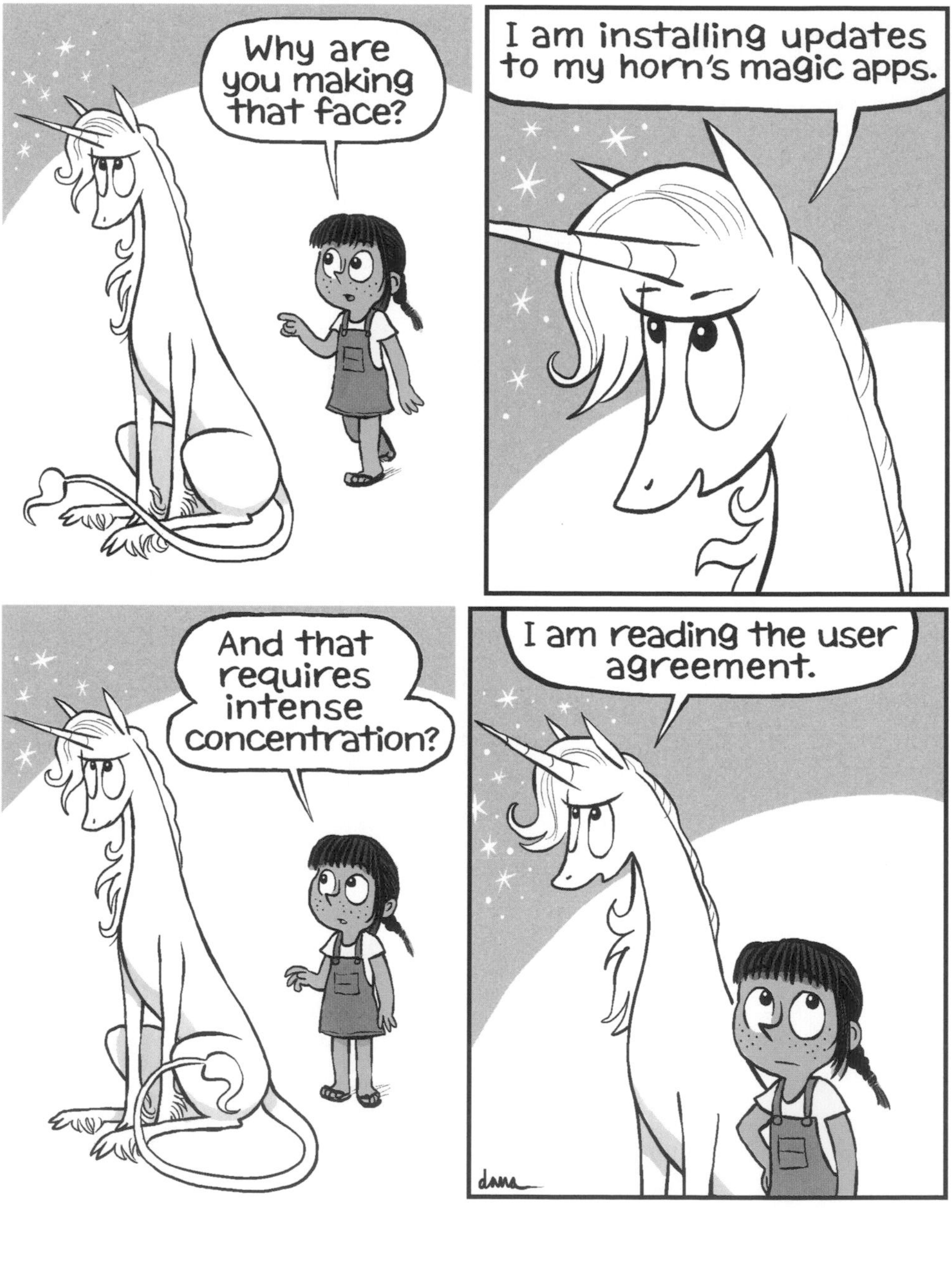
Why are you making that face?
I am installing updates to my horn's magic apps.
And that requires intense concentration?
I am reading the user agreement.
dana

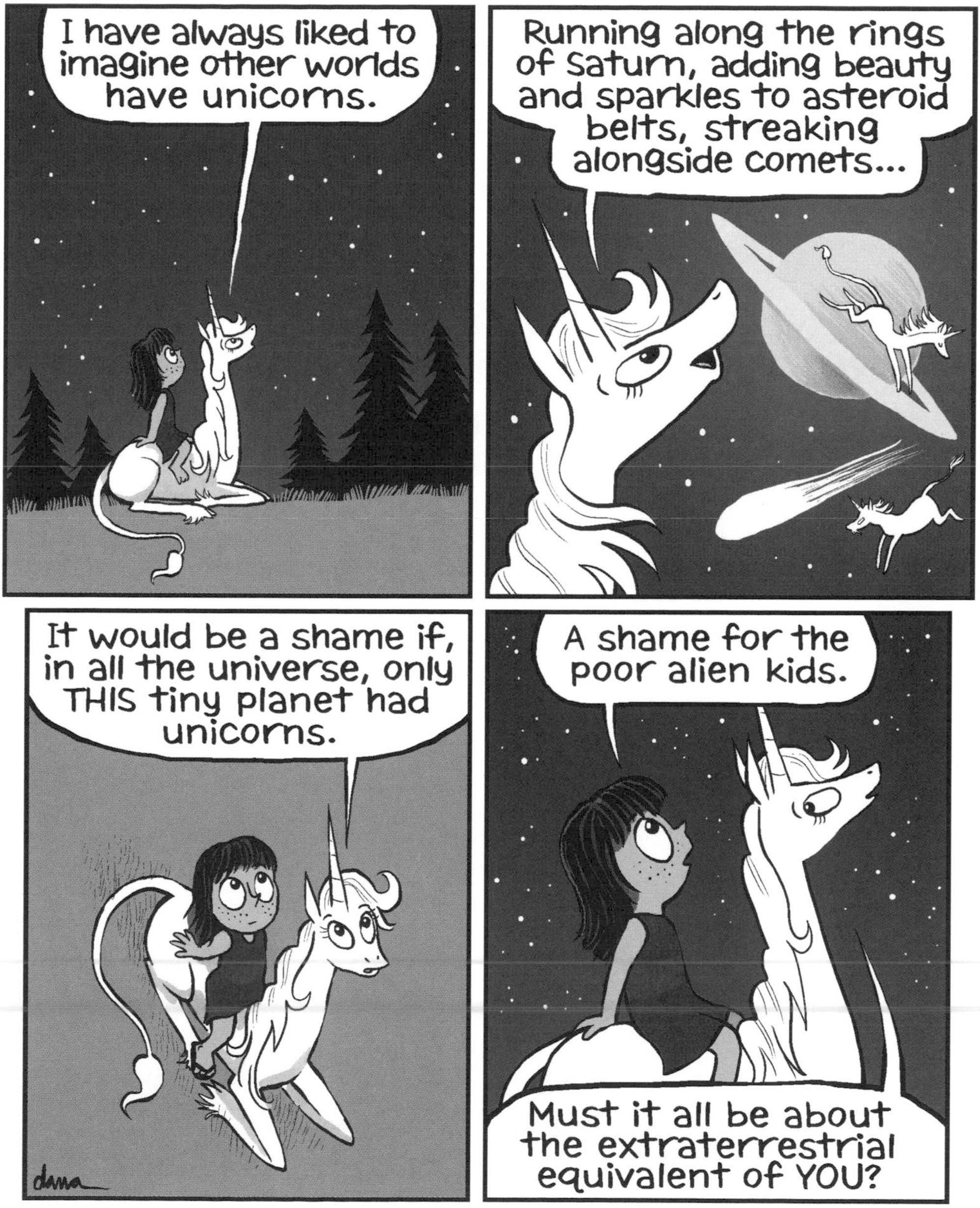
I have always liked to imagine other worlds have unicorns.
Running along the rings of Saturn, adding beauty and sparkles to asteroid belts, streaking alongside comets...
It would be a shame if, in all the universe, only THIS tiny planet had unicorns.
A shame for the poor alien kids.
Must it all be about the extraterrestrial equivalent of YOU?
dana

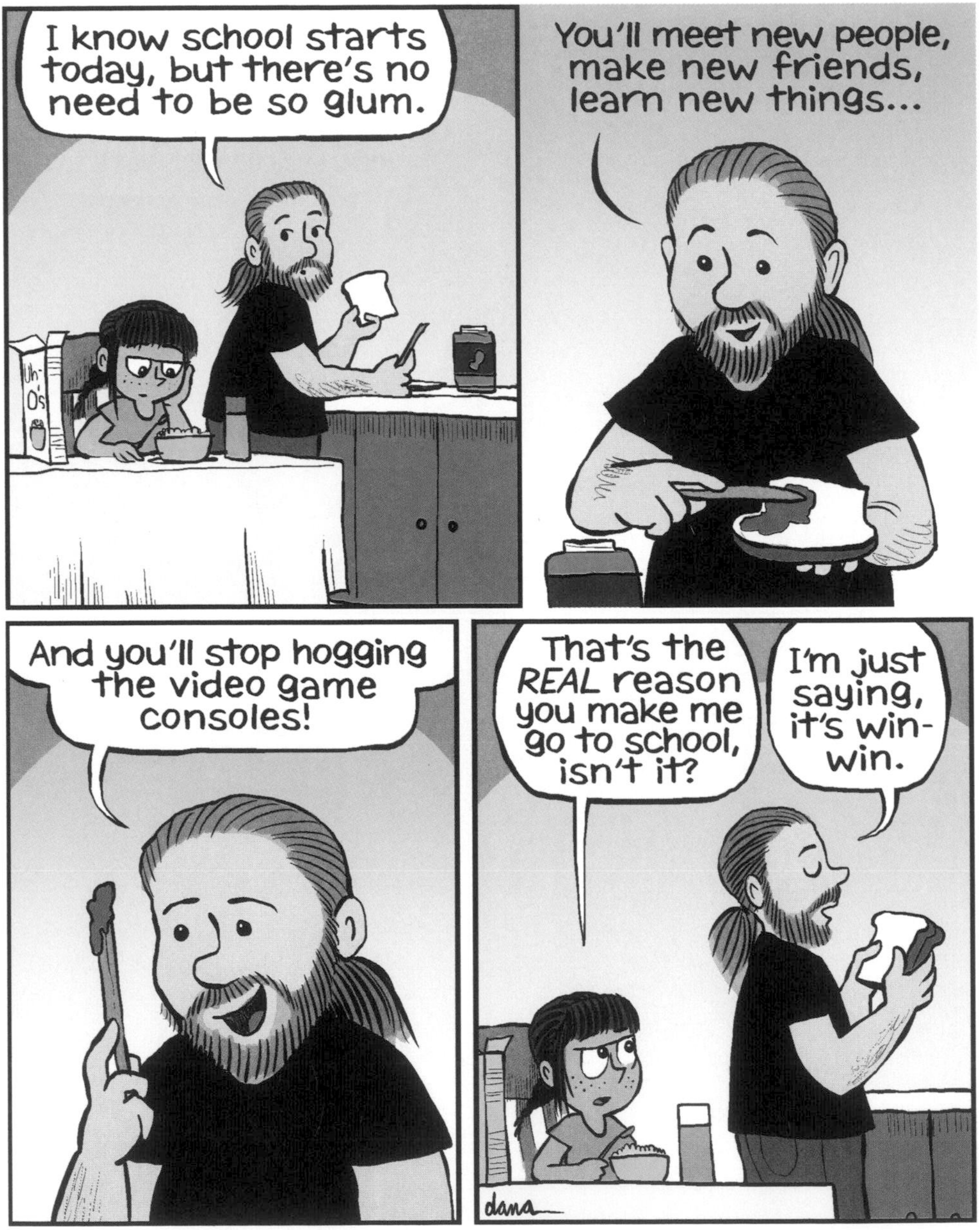
I know school starts today, but there's no need to be so glum.
Uh-O's
You'll meet new people, make new friends, learn new things...
And you'll stop hogging the video game consoles!
That's the *REAL* reason you make me go to school, isn't it?
I'm just saying, it's win-win.
dana

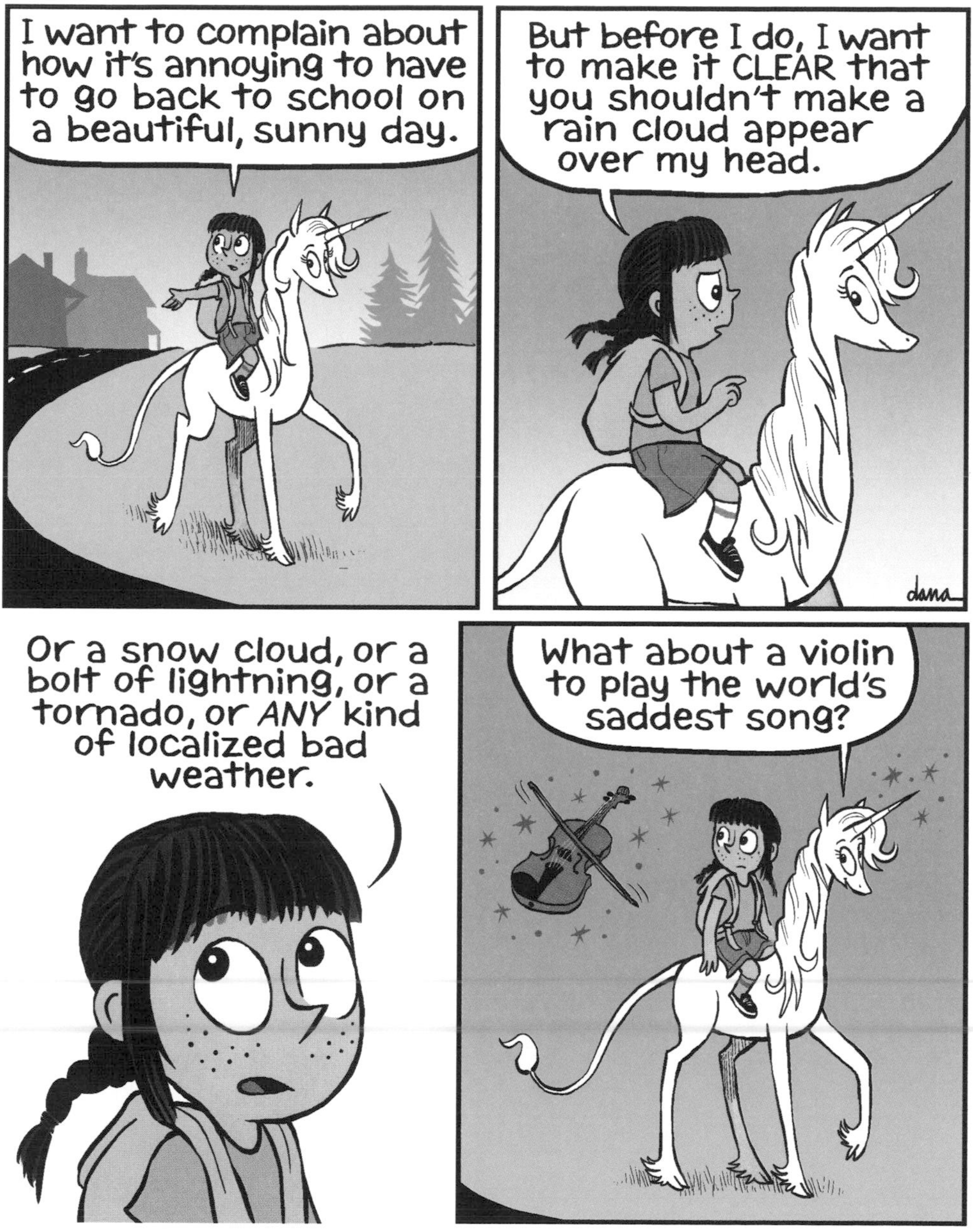
I want to complain about how it's annoying to have to go back to school on a beautiful, sunny day.
But before I do, I want to make it CLEAR that you shouldn't make a rain cloud appear over my head.
dana
Or a snow cloud, or a bolt of lightning, or a tornado, or ANY kind of localized bad weather.
What about a violin to play the world's saddest song?

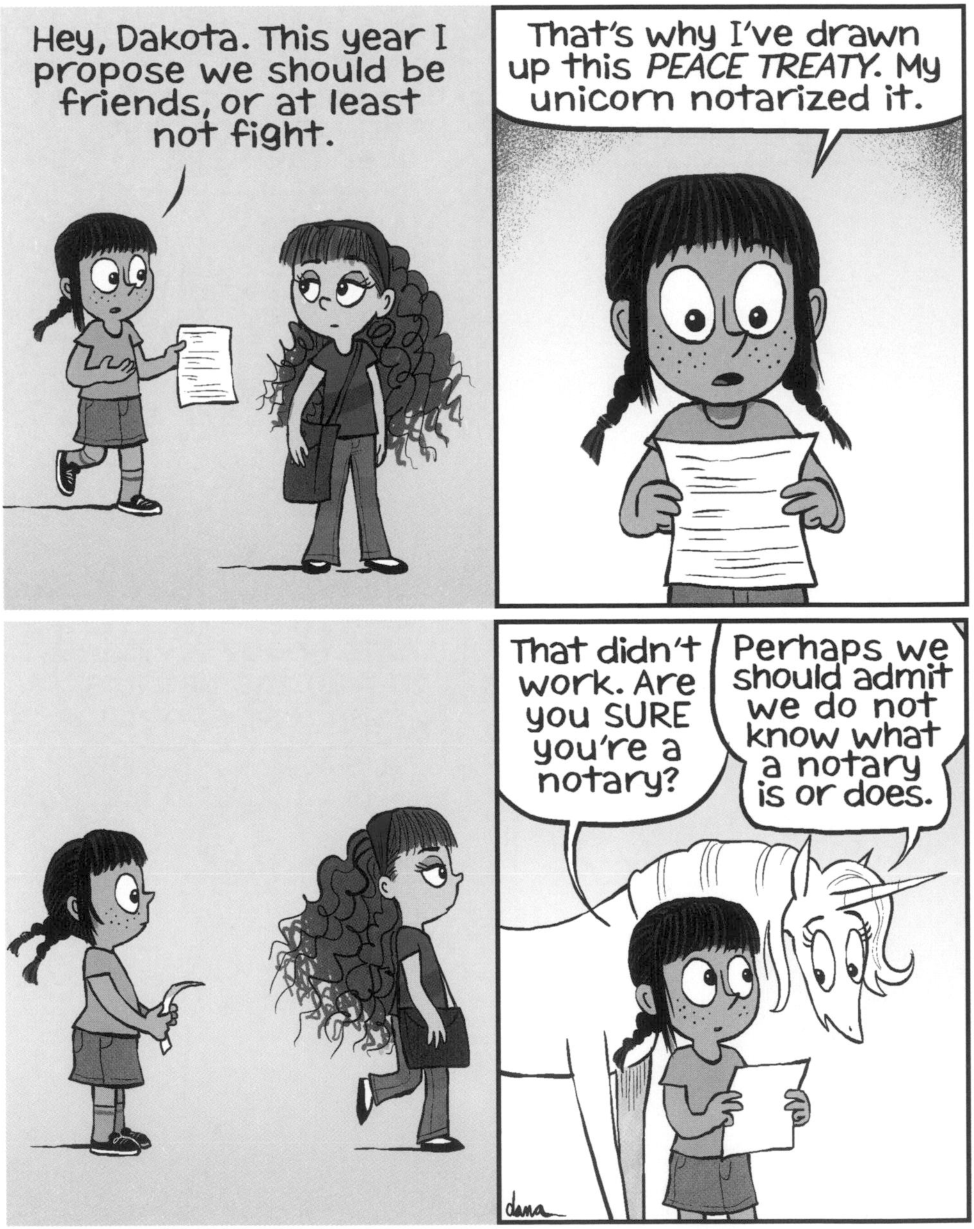
Hey, Dakota. This year I propose we should be friends, or at least not fight.
That's why I've drawn up this *PEACE TREATY*. My unicorn notarized it.
That didn't work. Are you SURE you're a notary?
Perhaps we should admit we do not know what a notary is or does.
dana

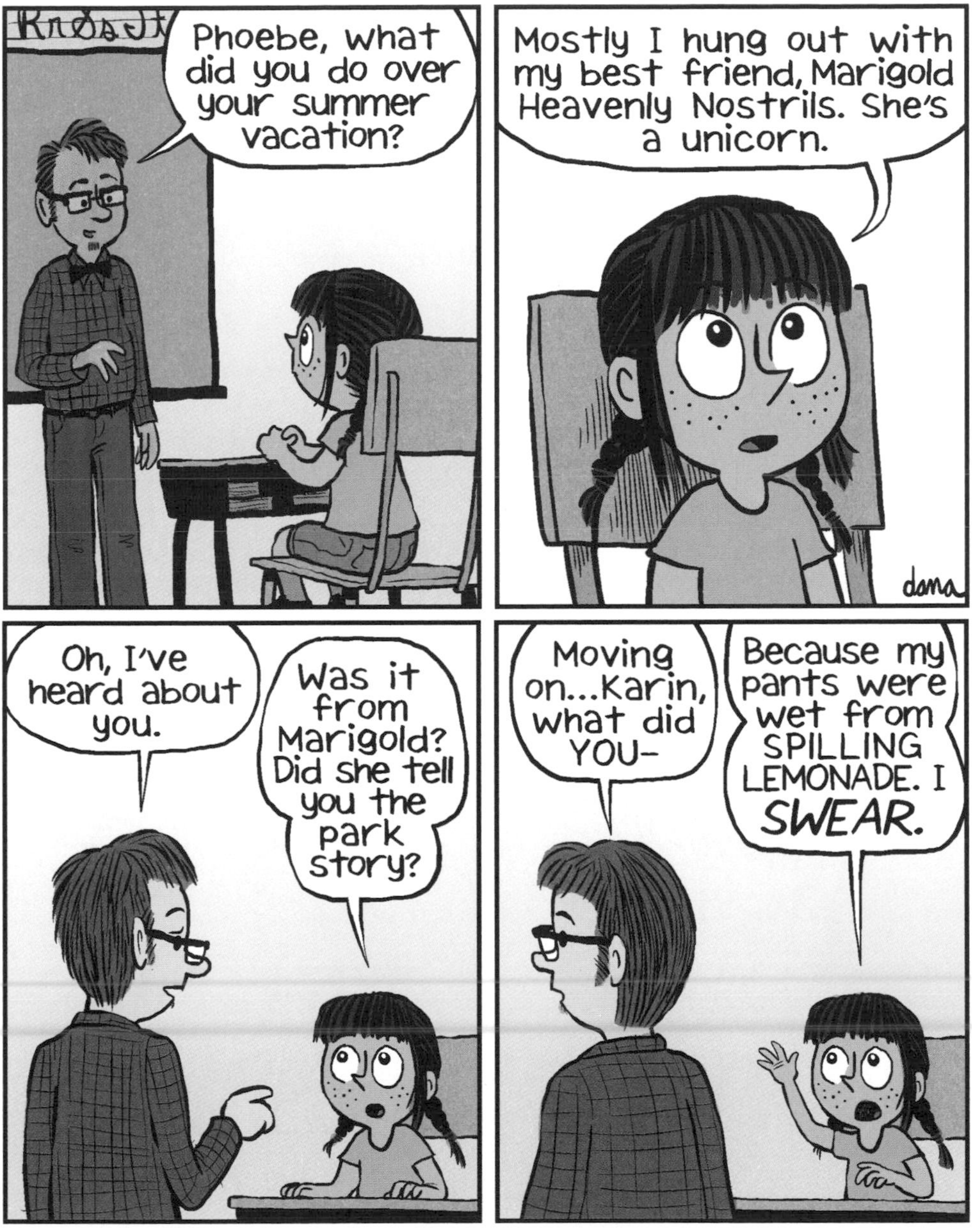
Phoebe, what did you do over your summer vacation?
Mostly I hung out with my best friend, Marigold Heavenly Nostrils. She's a unicorn.
dana
Oh, I've heard about you.
Was it from Marigold? Did she tell you the park story?
Moving on...Karin, what did YOU-
Because my pants were wet from SPILLING LEMONADE. I *SWEAR.*

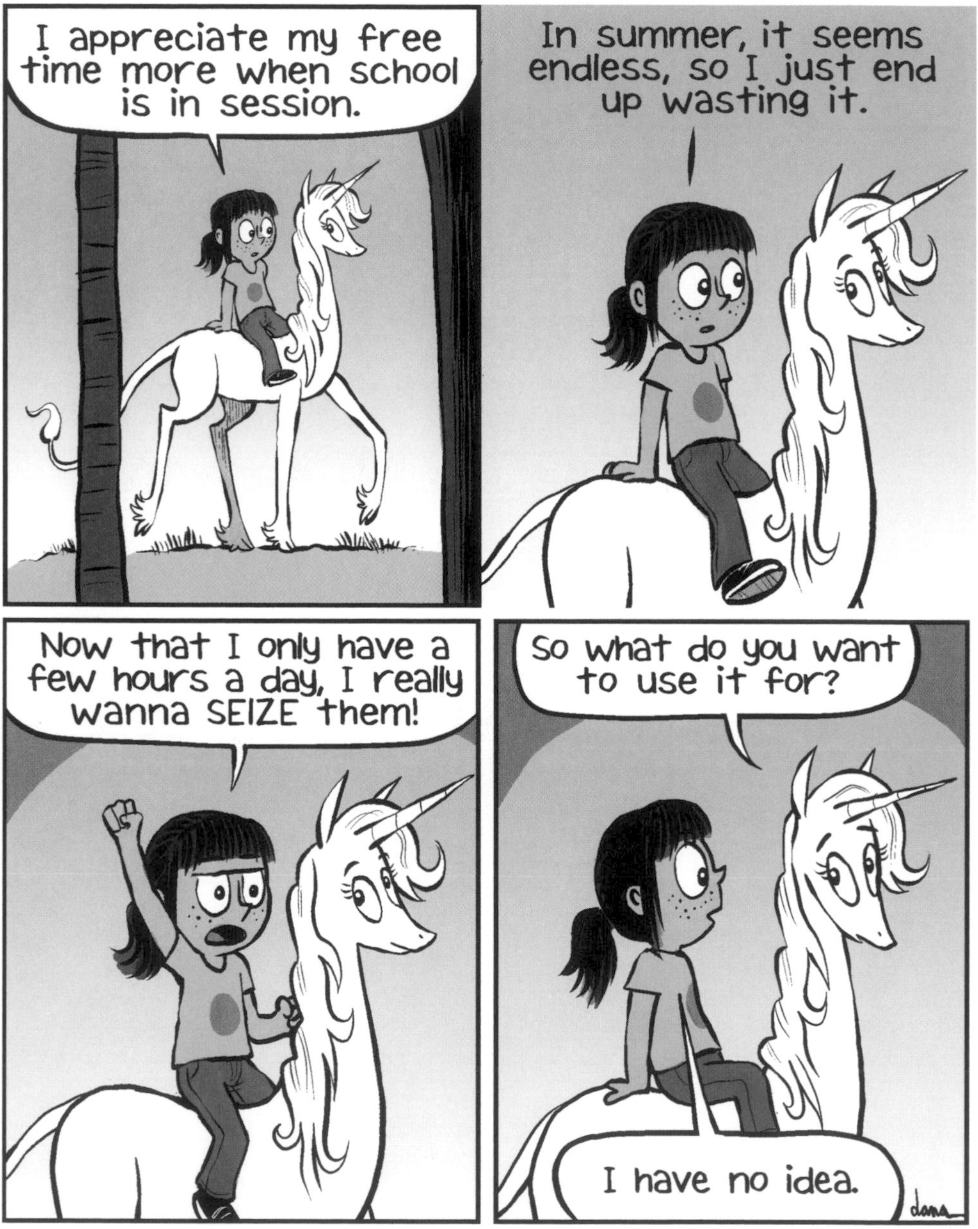
I appreciate my free time more when school is in session.
In summer, it seems endless, so I just end up wasting it.
Now that I only have a few hours a day, I really wanna SEIZE them!
So what do you want to use it for?
I have no idea.
dana

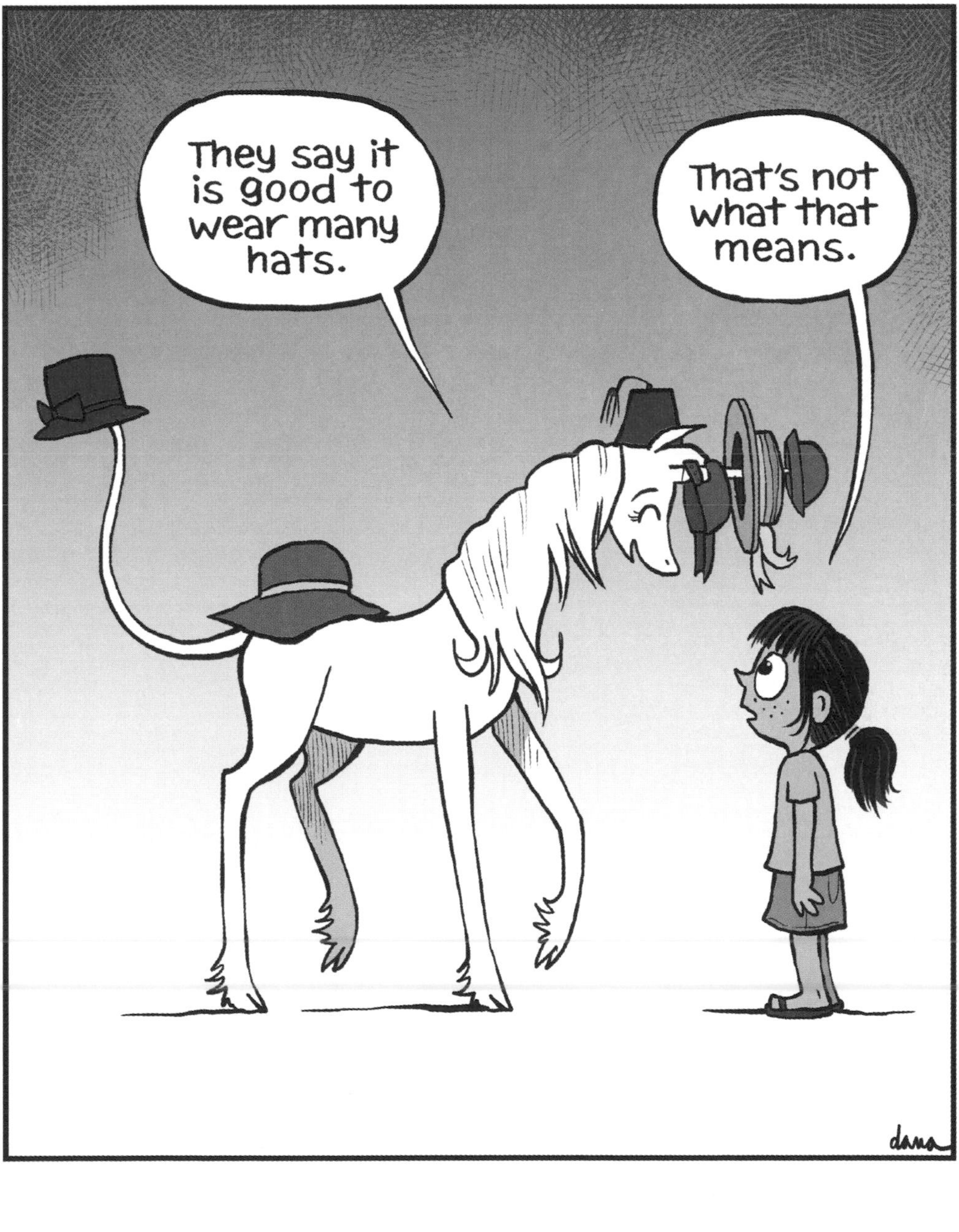
They say it is good to wear many hats.
That's not what that means.
dana

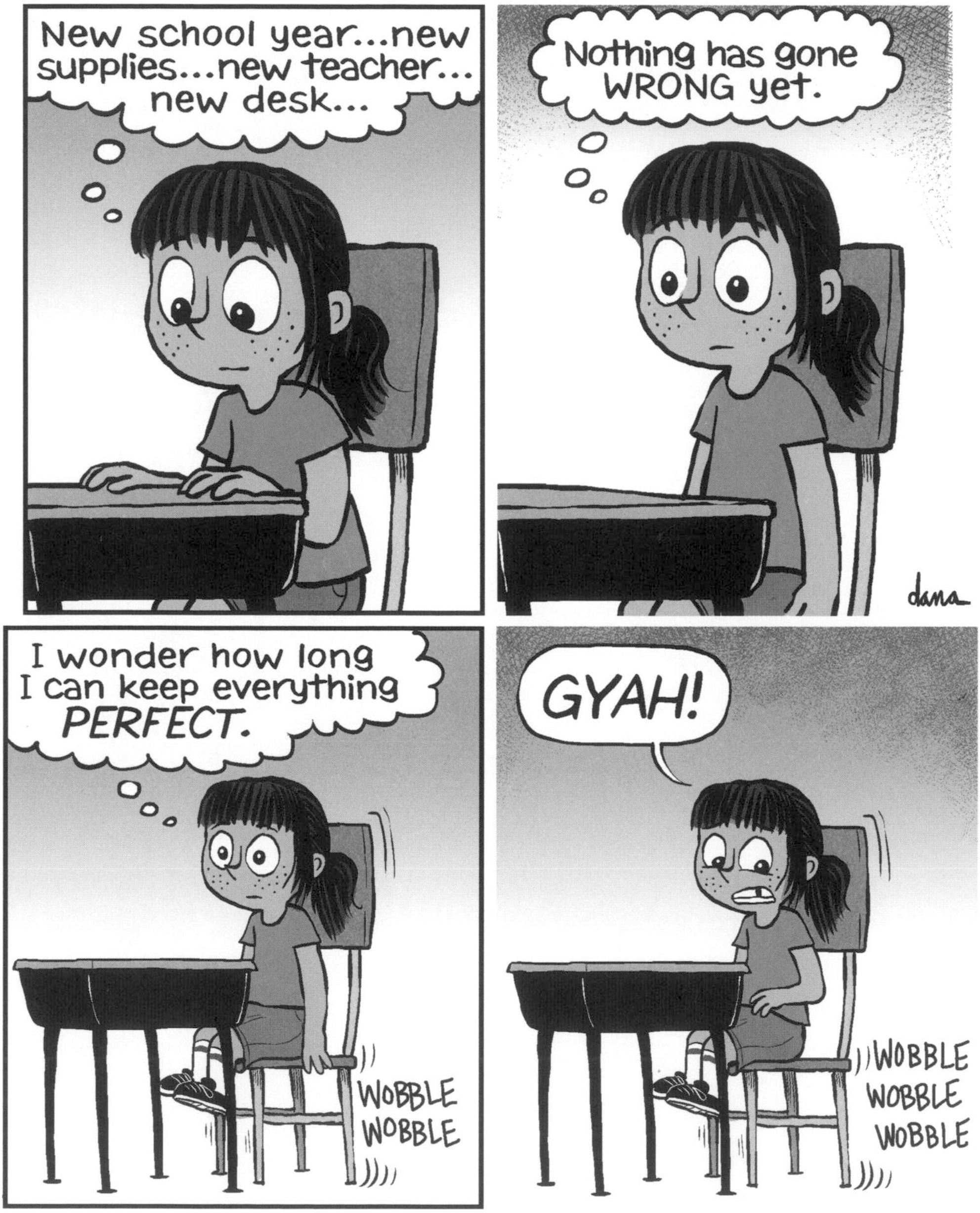
New school year...new supplies...new teacher... new desk...
Nothing has gone WRONG yet.
dana
I wonder how long I can keep everything *PERFECT*.
WOBBLE WOBBLE
GYAH!
WOBBLE WOBBLE WOBBLE

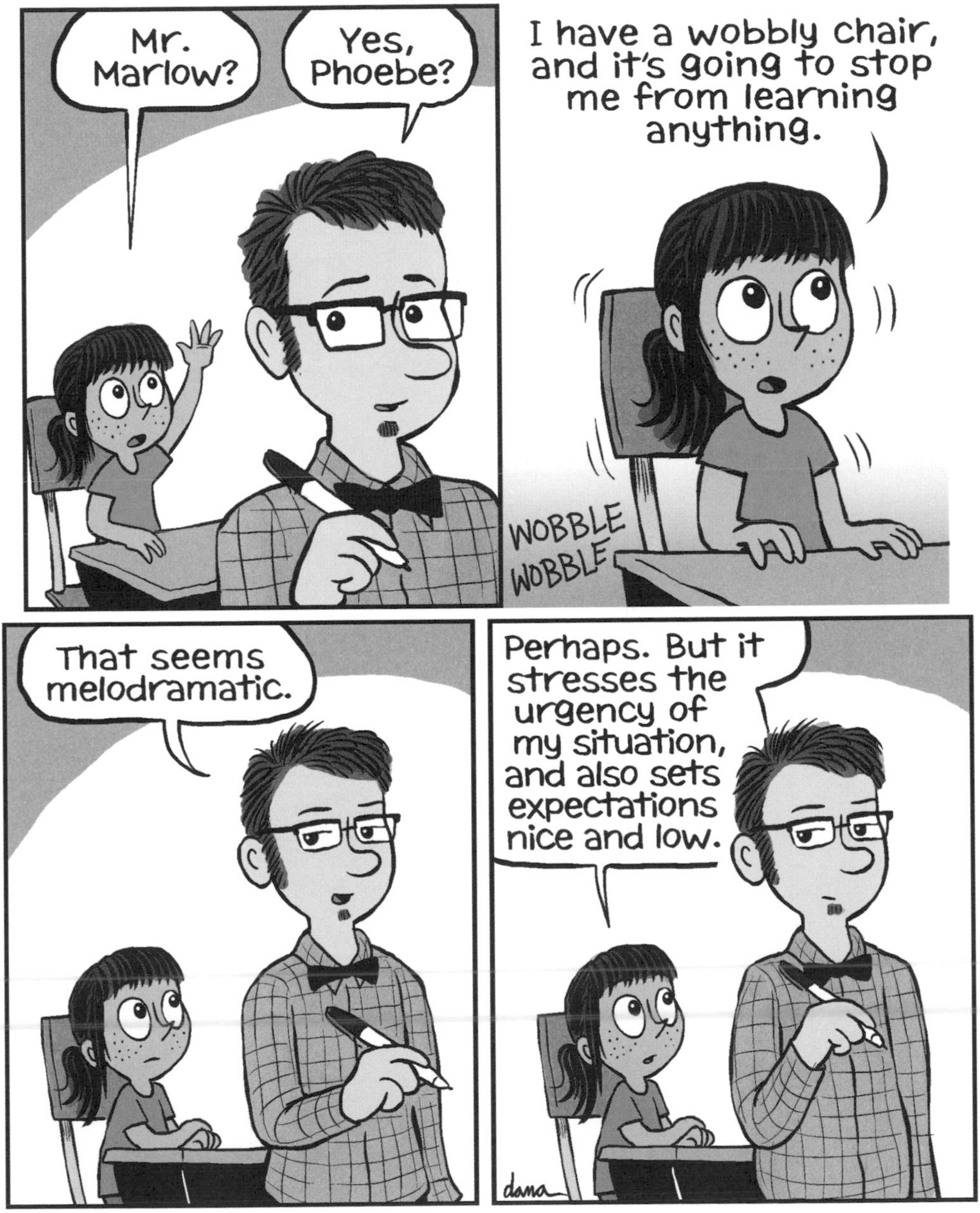
Mr. Marlow?
Yes, Phoebe?
I have a wobbly chair, and it's going to stop me from learning anything.
WOBBLE WOBBLE
That seems melodramatic.
Perhaps. But it stresses the urgency of my situation, and also sets expectations nice and low.
dana

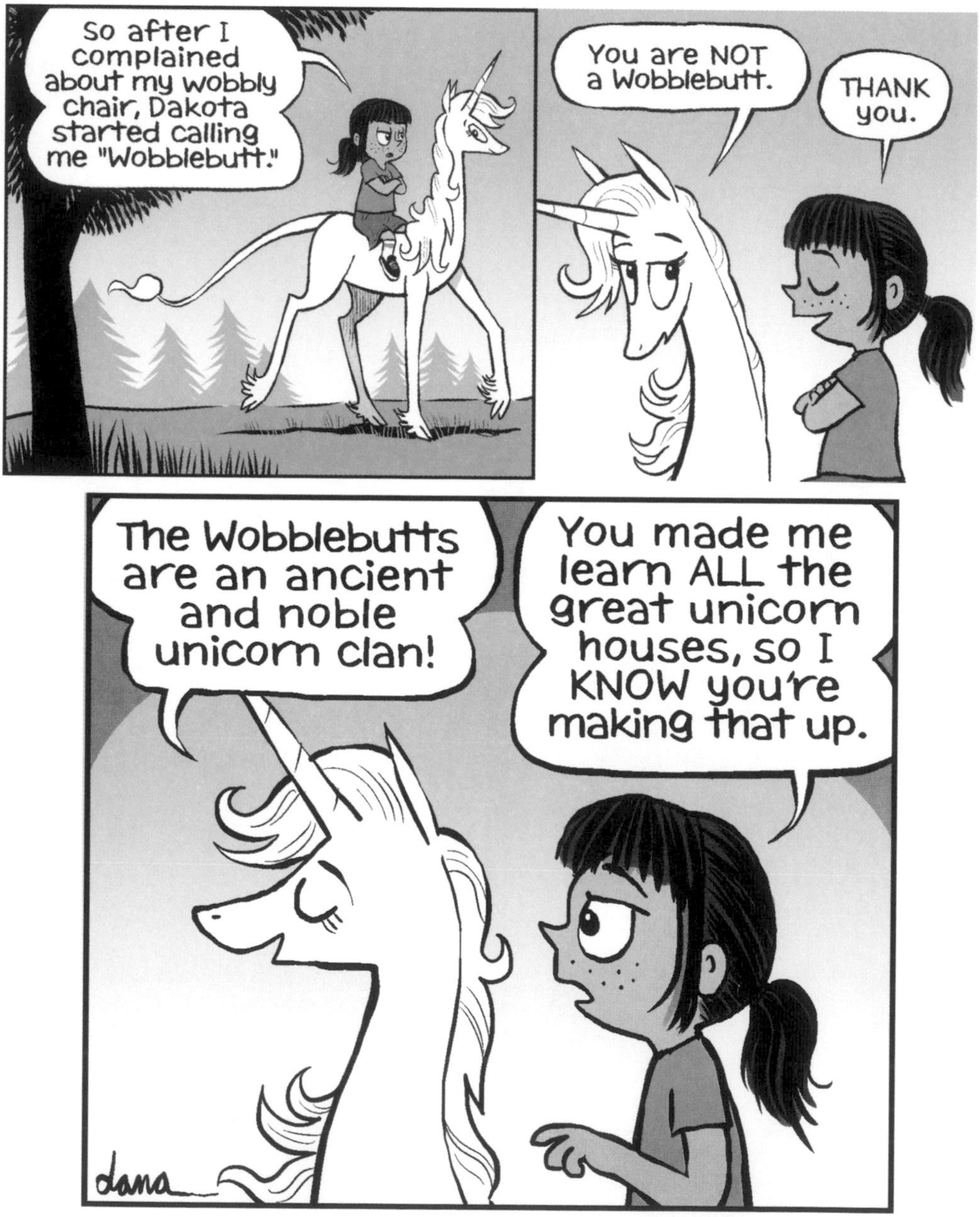
So after I complained about my wobbly chair, Dakota started calling me "Wobblebutt."
You are NOT a Wobblebutt.
THANK you.
The Wobblebutts are an ancient and noble unicorn clan!
You made me learn ALL the great unicorn houses, so I KNOW you're making that up.
dana

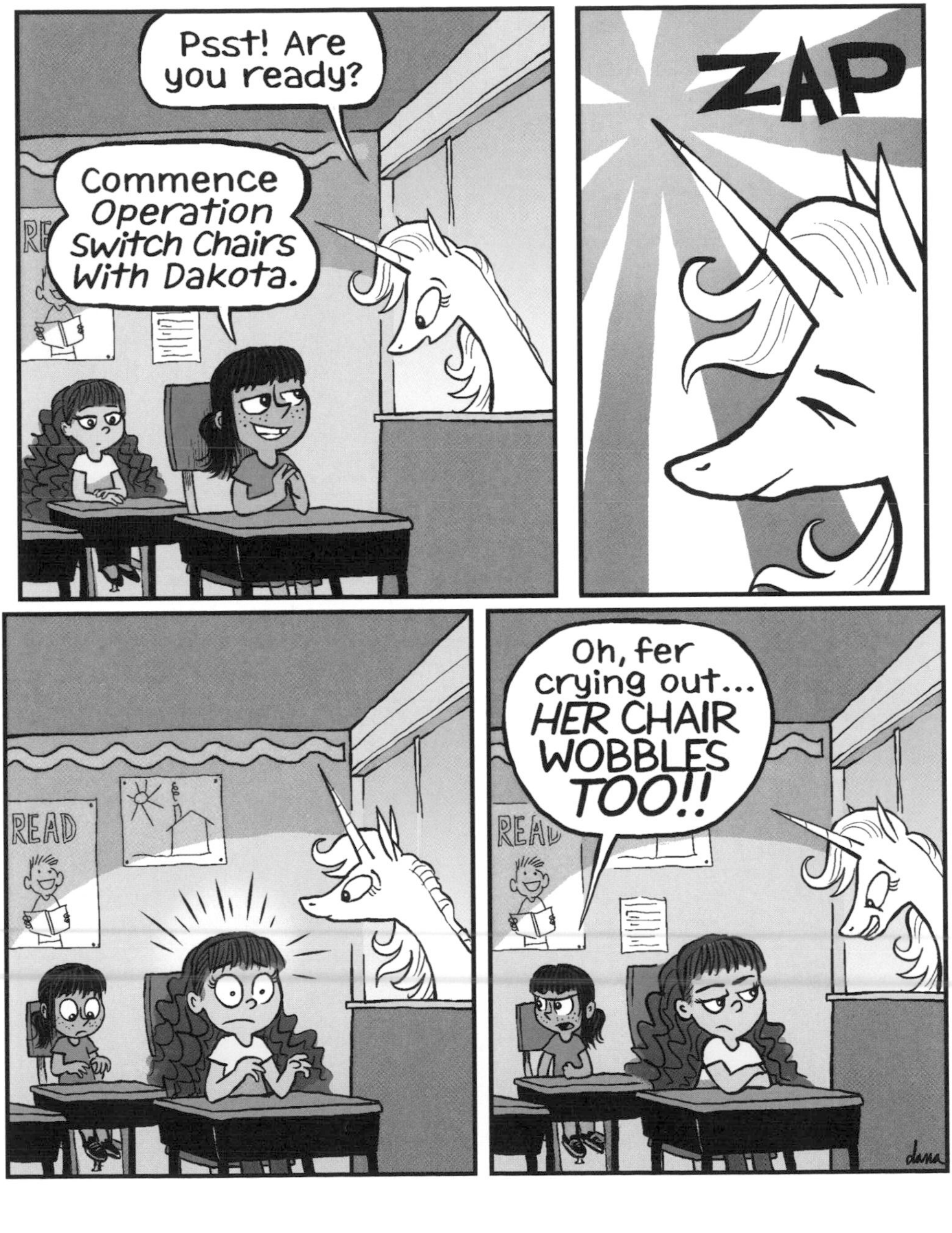
Psst! Are you ready?
Commence Operation Switch Chairs With Dakota.
ZAP
Oh, fer crying out... HER CHAIR WOBBLES TOO!!
dana

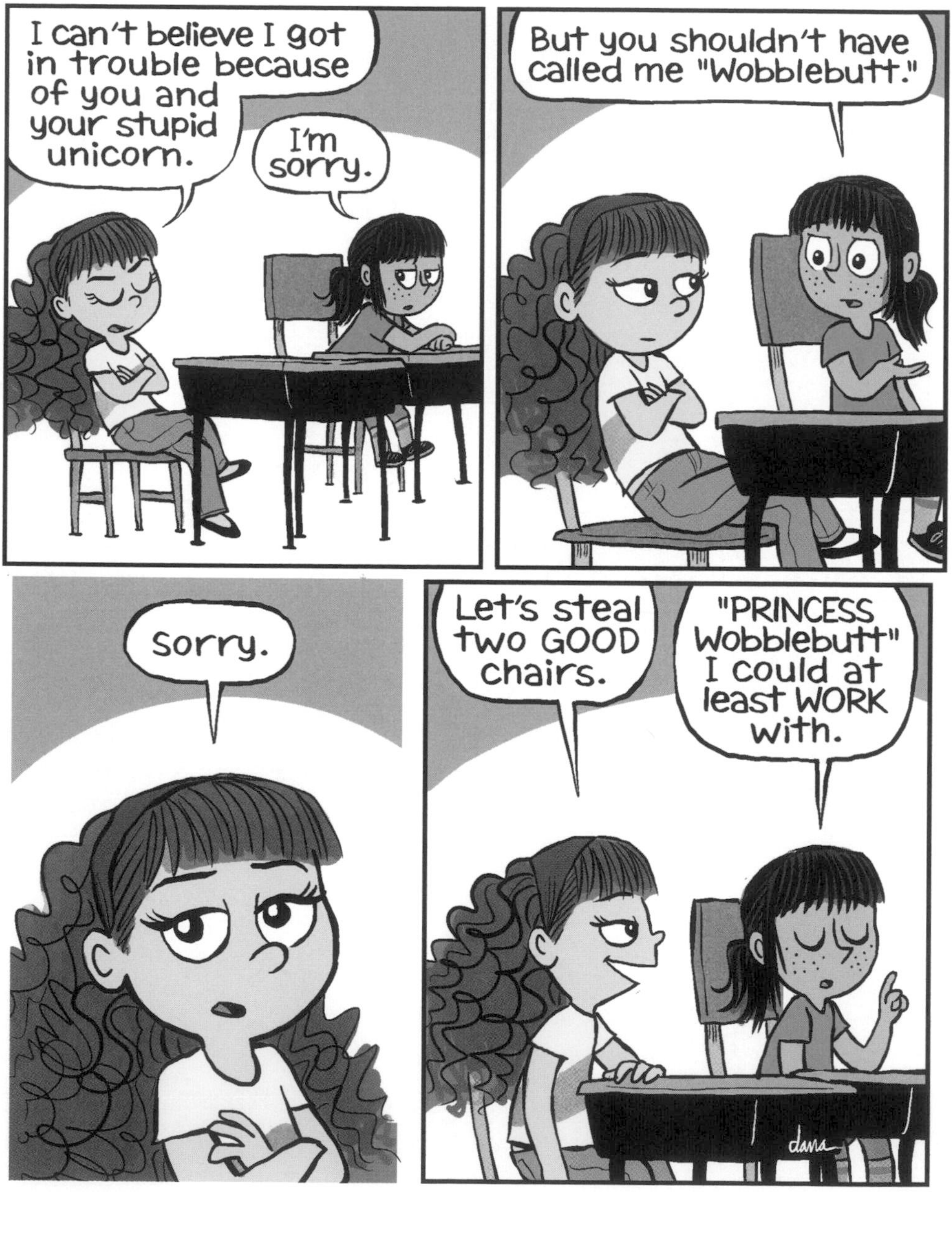
I can't believe I got in trouble because of you and your stupid unicorn.
I'm sorry.
But you shouldn't have called me "Wobblebutt."
Sorry.
Let's steal two GOOD chairs.
"PRINCESS Wobblebutt" I could at least WORK with.
dana

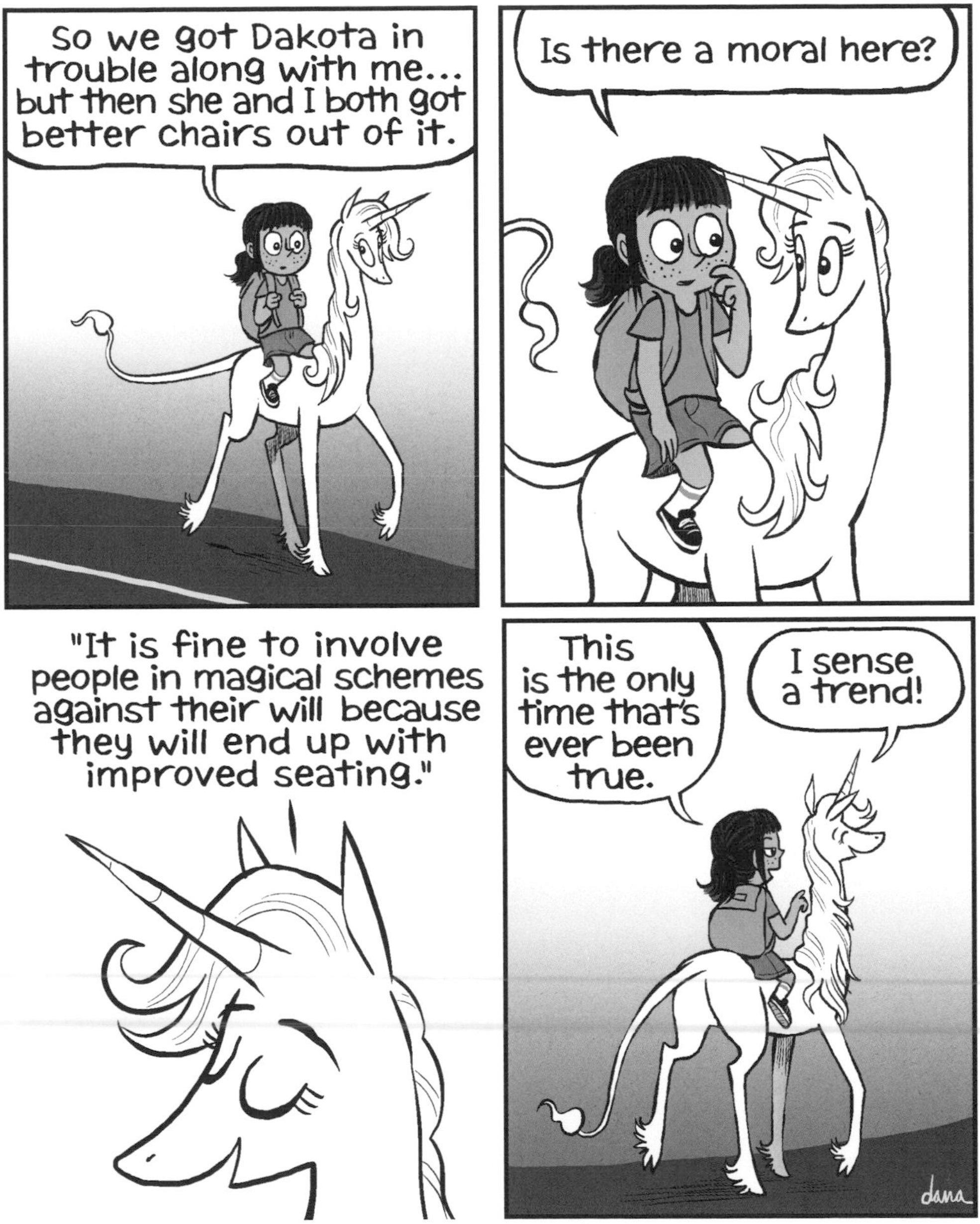
So we got Dakota in trouble along with me... but then she and I both got better chairs out of it.
Is there a moral here?
"It is fine to involve people in magical schemes against their will because they will end up with improved seating."
This is the only time that's ever been true.
I sense a trend!
dana

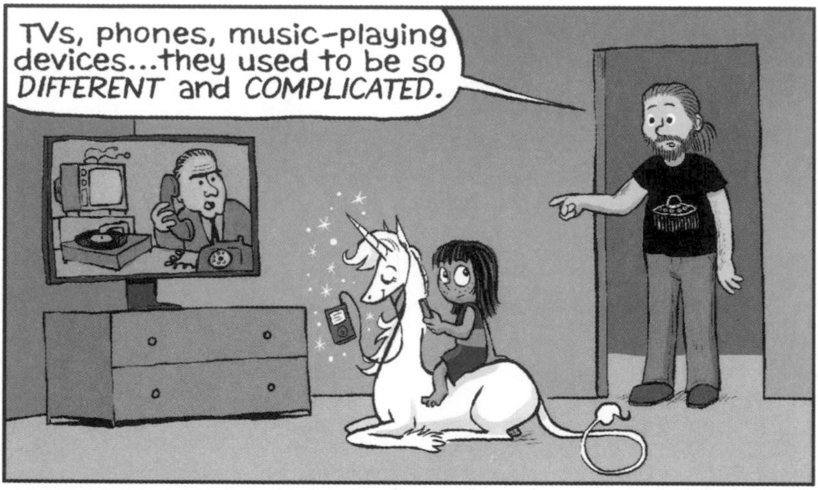
TVs, phones, music-playing devices...they used to be so DIFFERENT and COMPLICATED.

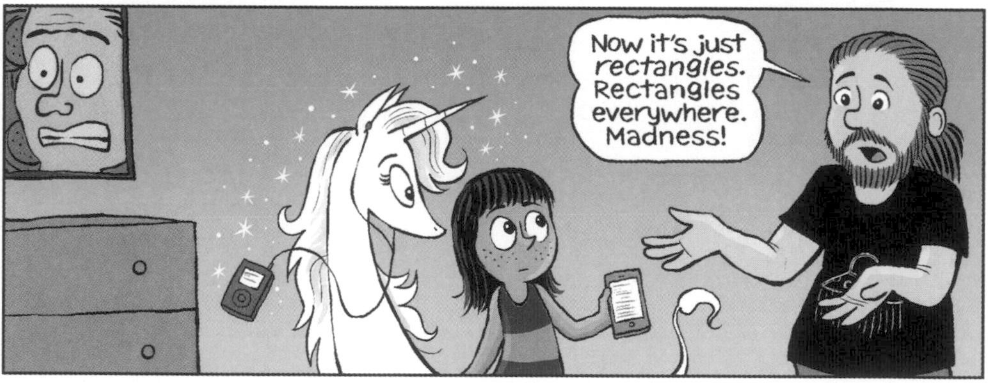
Now it's just rectangles. Rectangles everywhere. Madness!

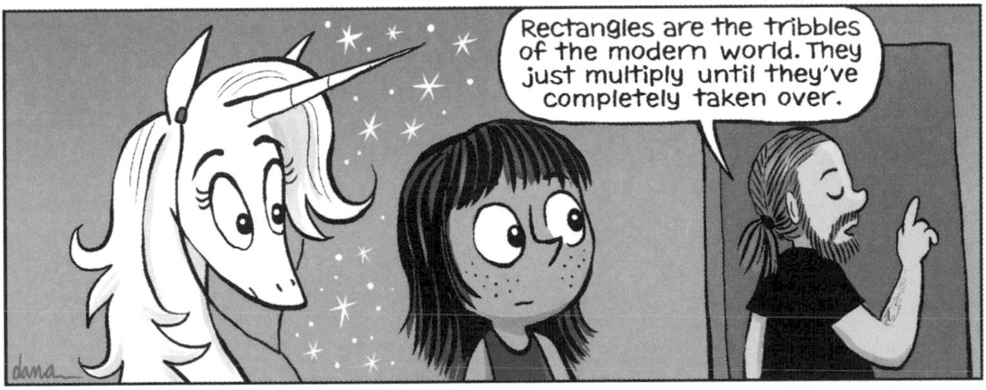
Rectangles are the tribbles of the modern world. They just multiply until they've completely taken over.
dana

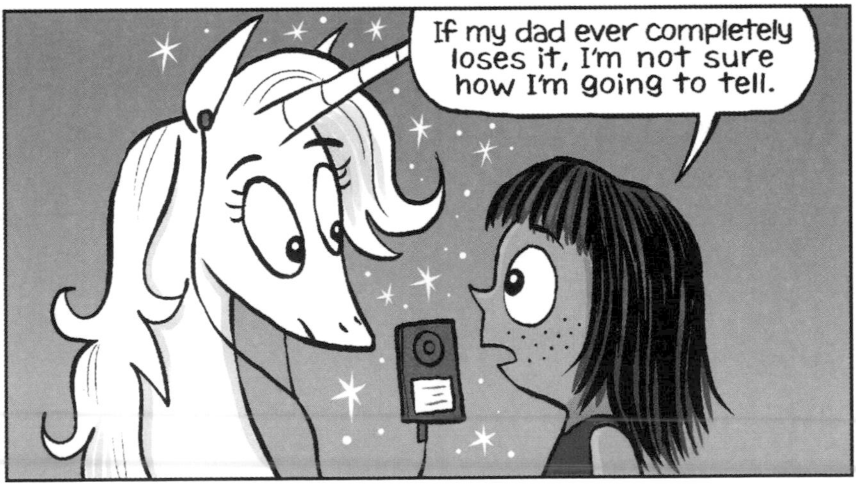
If my dad ever completely loses it, I'm not sure how I'm going to tell.

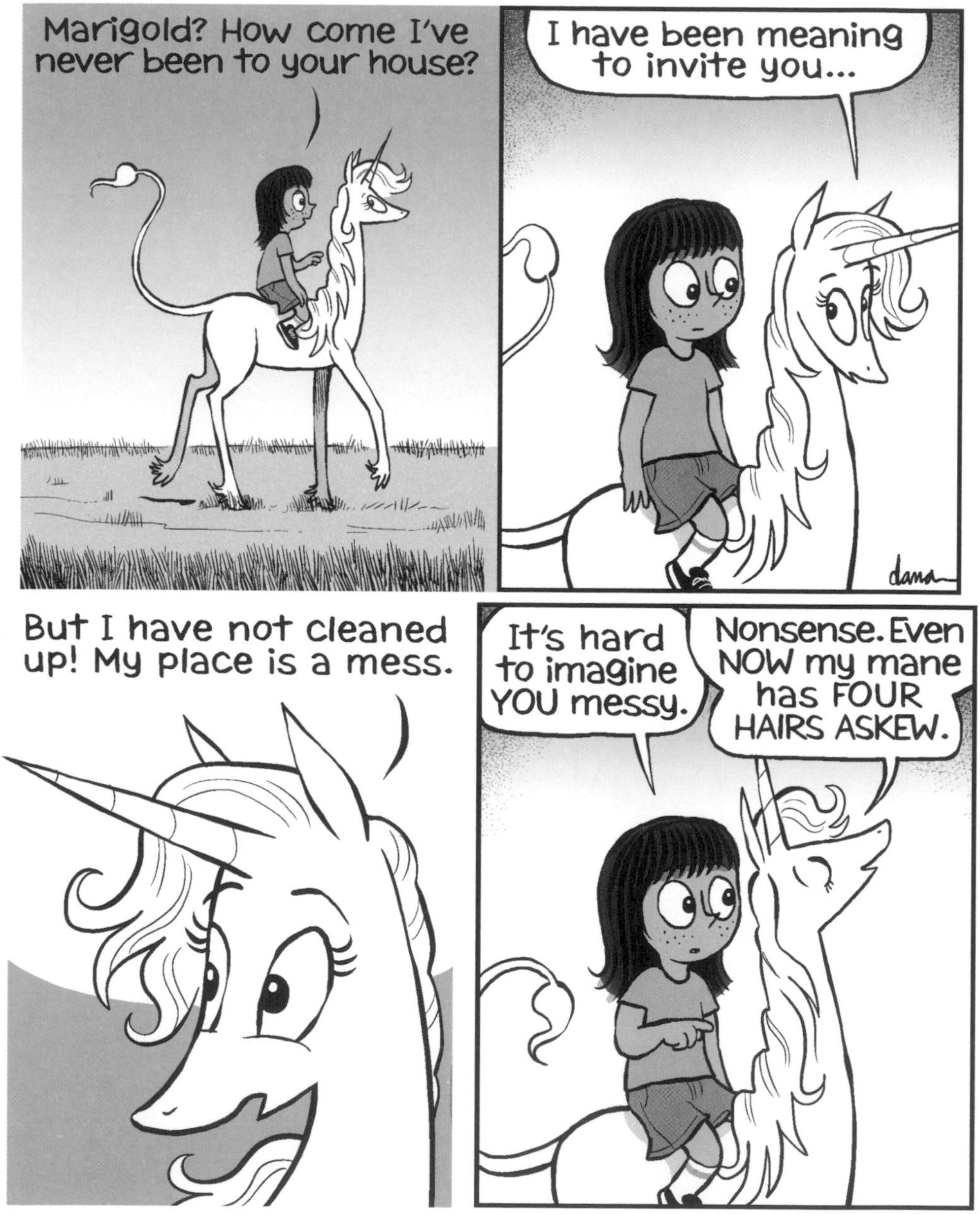
Marigold? How come I've never been to your house?
I have been meaning to invite you...
dana
But I have not cleaned up! My place is a mess.
It's hard to imagine YOU messy.
Nonsense. Even NOW my mane has FOUR HAIRS ASKEW.

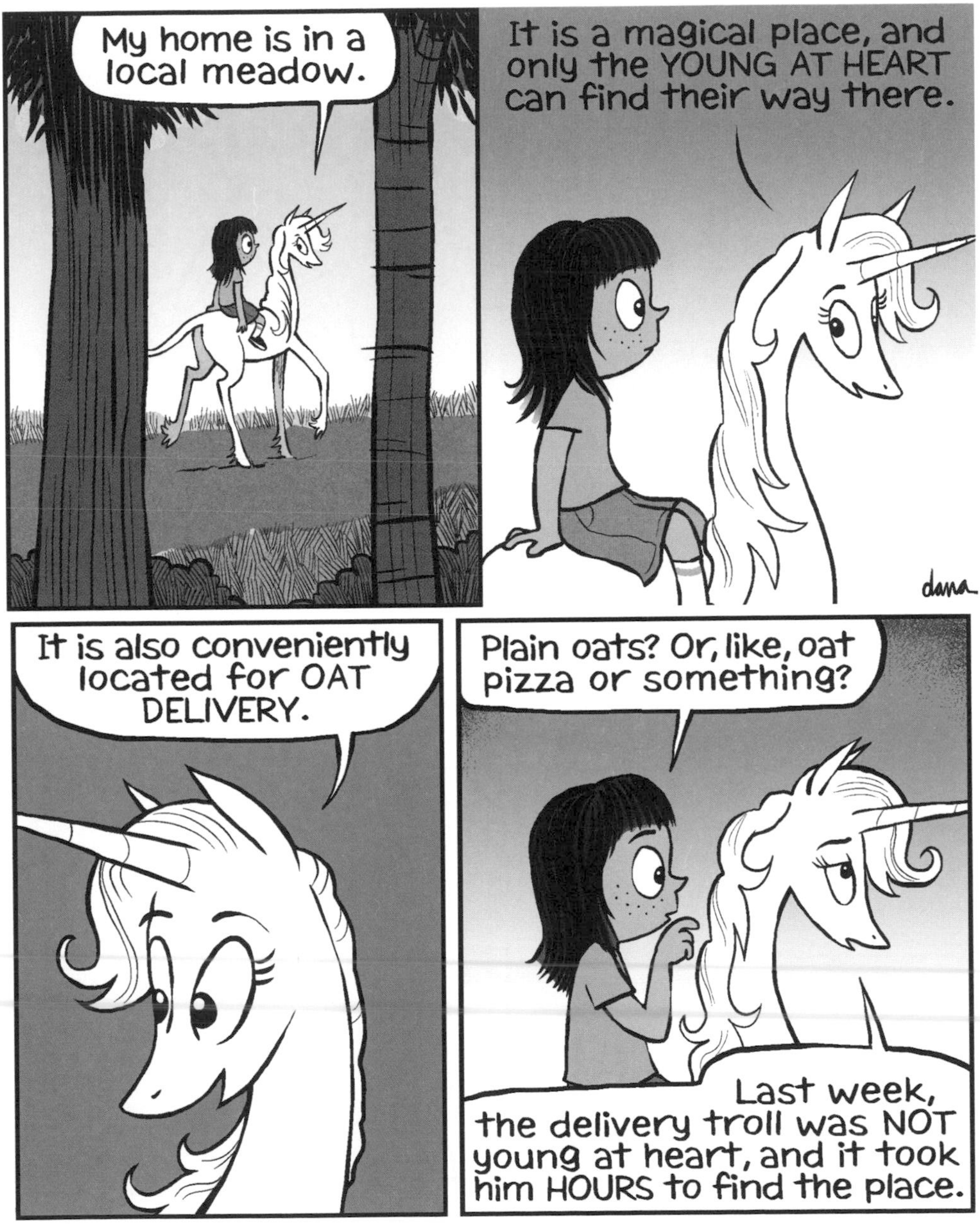
My home is in a local meadow.
It is a magical place, and only the YOUNG AT HEART can find their way there.
dana
It is also conveniently located for OAT DELIVERY.
Plain oats? Or, like, oat pizza or something?
Last week, the delivery troll was NOT young at heart, and it took him HOURS to find the place.

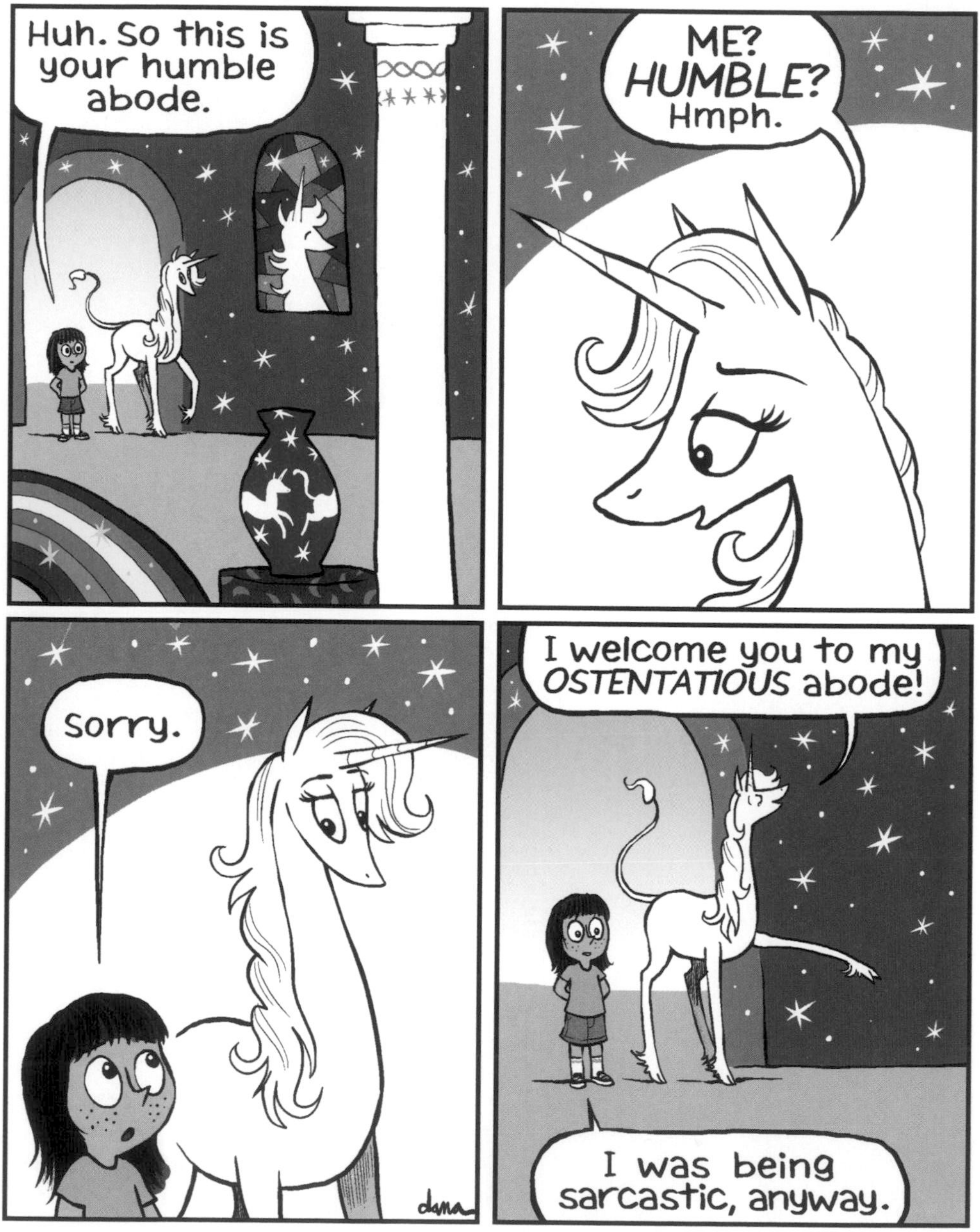
Huh. So this is your humble abode.
ME? HUMBLE? Hmph.
Sorry.
I welcome you to my OSTENTATIOUS abode!
I was being sarcastic, anyway.
dana

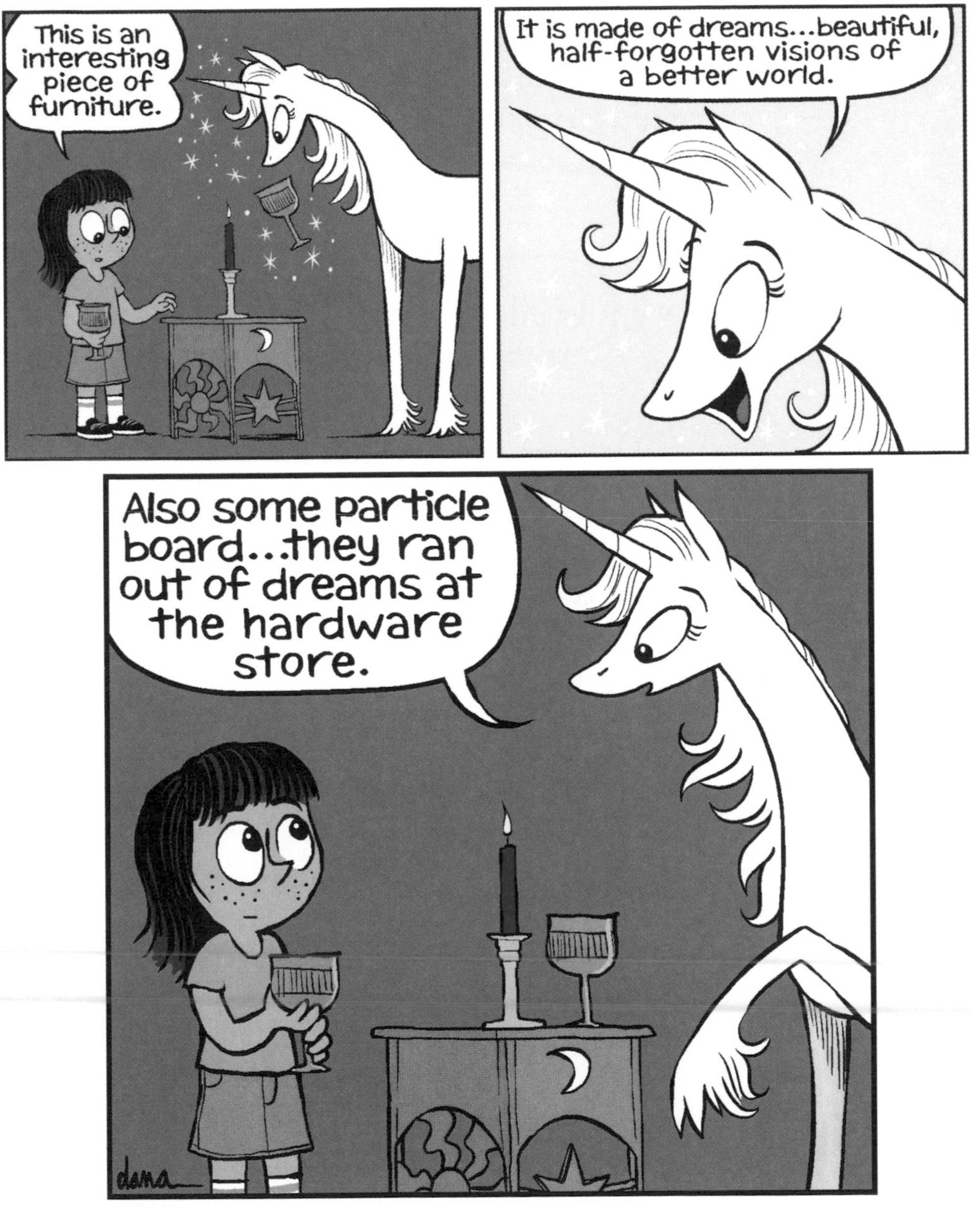
This is an interesting piece of furniture.
It is made of dreams...beautiful, half-forgotten visions of a better world.
Also some particle board...they ran out of dreams at the hardware store.
dana

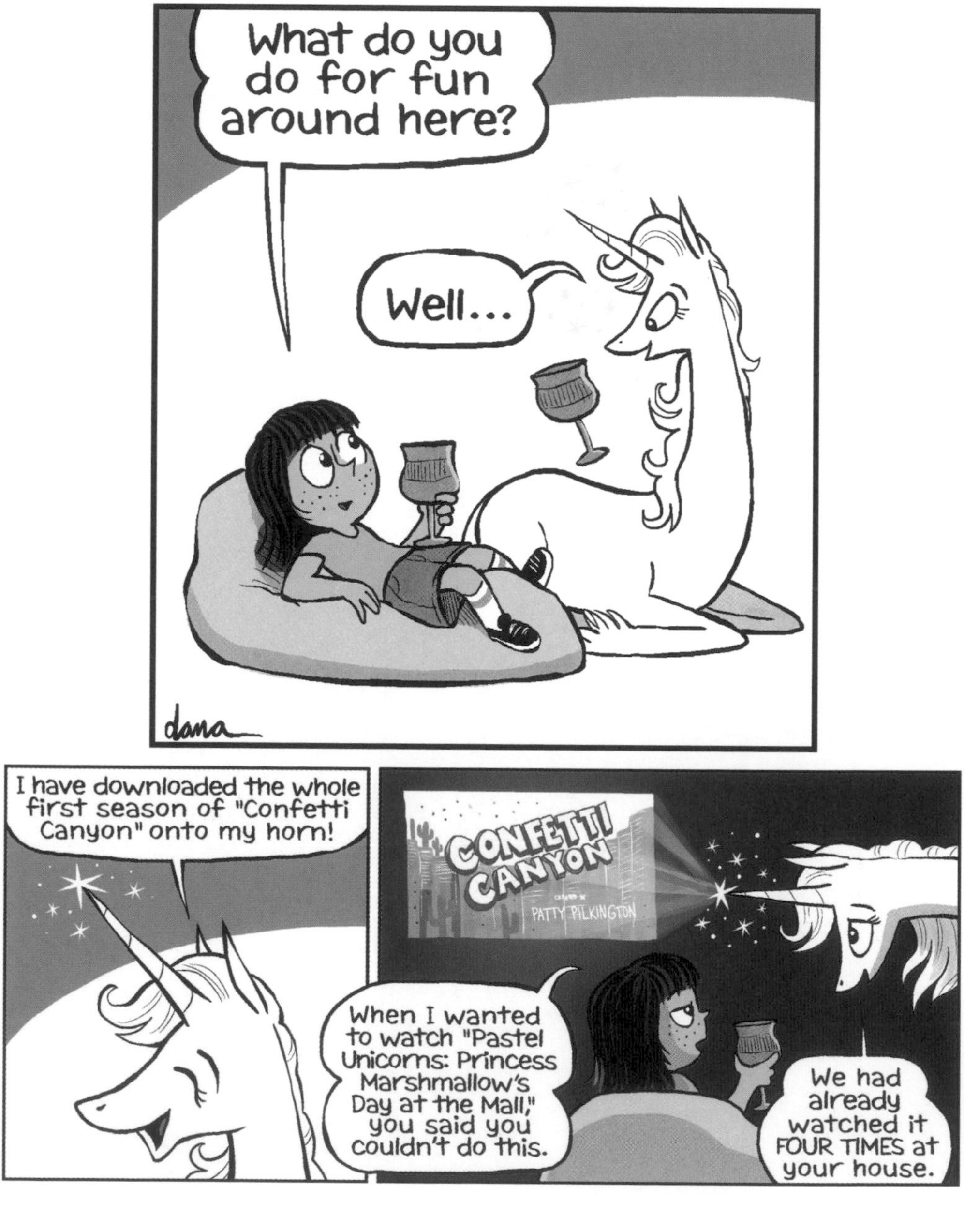
What do you do for fun around here?
Well...
dana
I have downloaded the whole first season of "Confetti Canyon" onto my horn!
CONFETTI CANYON
PATTY PILKINGTON
When I wanted to watch "Pastel Unicorns: Princess Marshmallow's Day at the Mall," you said you couldn't do this.
We had already watched it FOUR TIMES at your house.

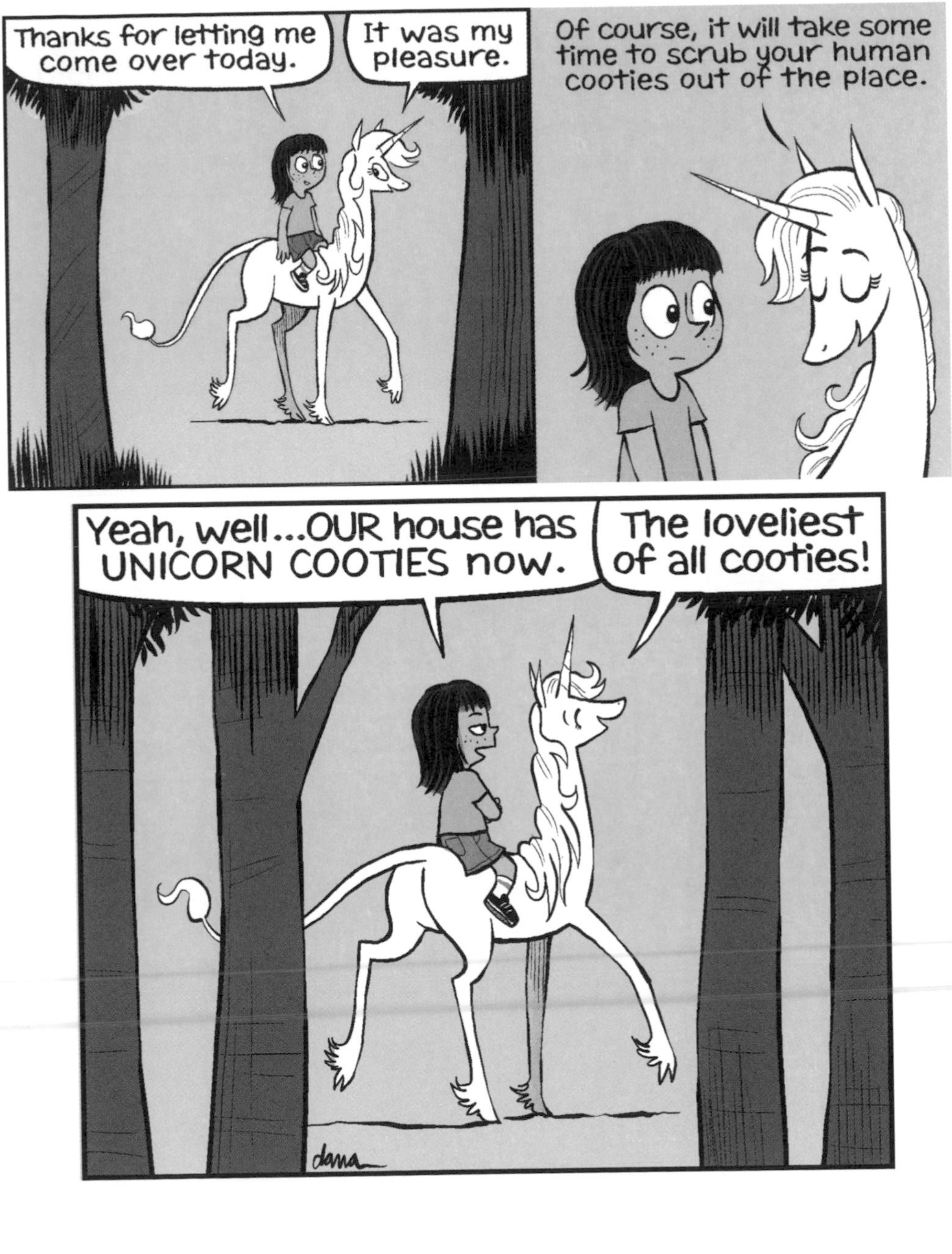
Thanks for letting me come over today.
It was my pleasure.
Of course, it will take some time to scrub your human cooties out of the place.
Yeah, well...OUR house has UNICORN COOTIES now.
The loveliest of all cooties!
dana

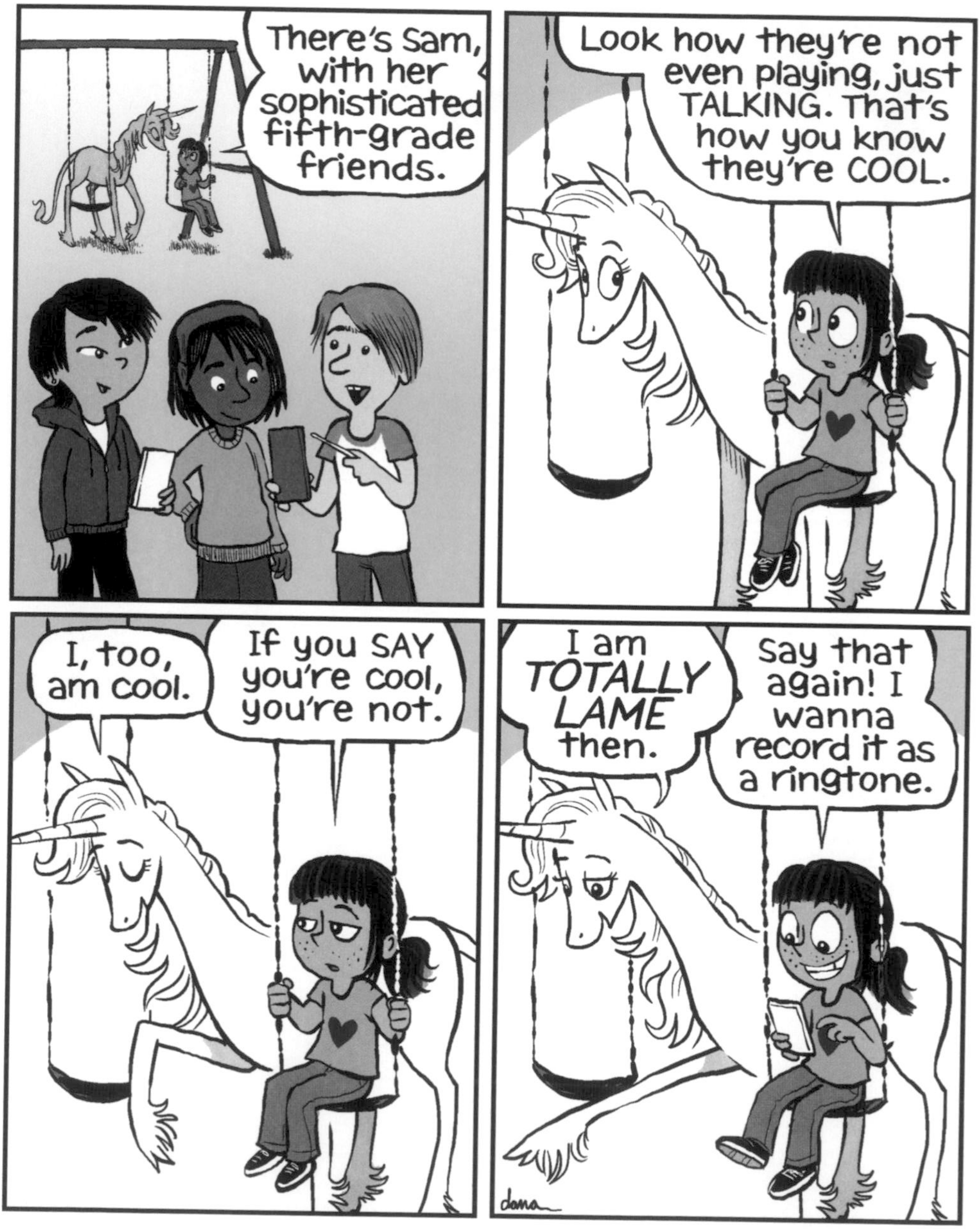
There's Sam, with her sophisticated fifth-grade friends.
Look how they're not even playing, just TALKING. That's how you know they're COOL.
I, too, am cool.
If you SAY you're cool, you're not.
I am *TOTALLY LAME* then.
Say that again! I wanna record it as a ringtone.
dana

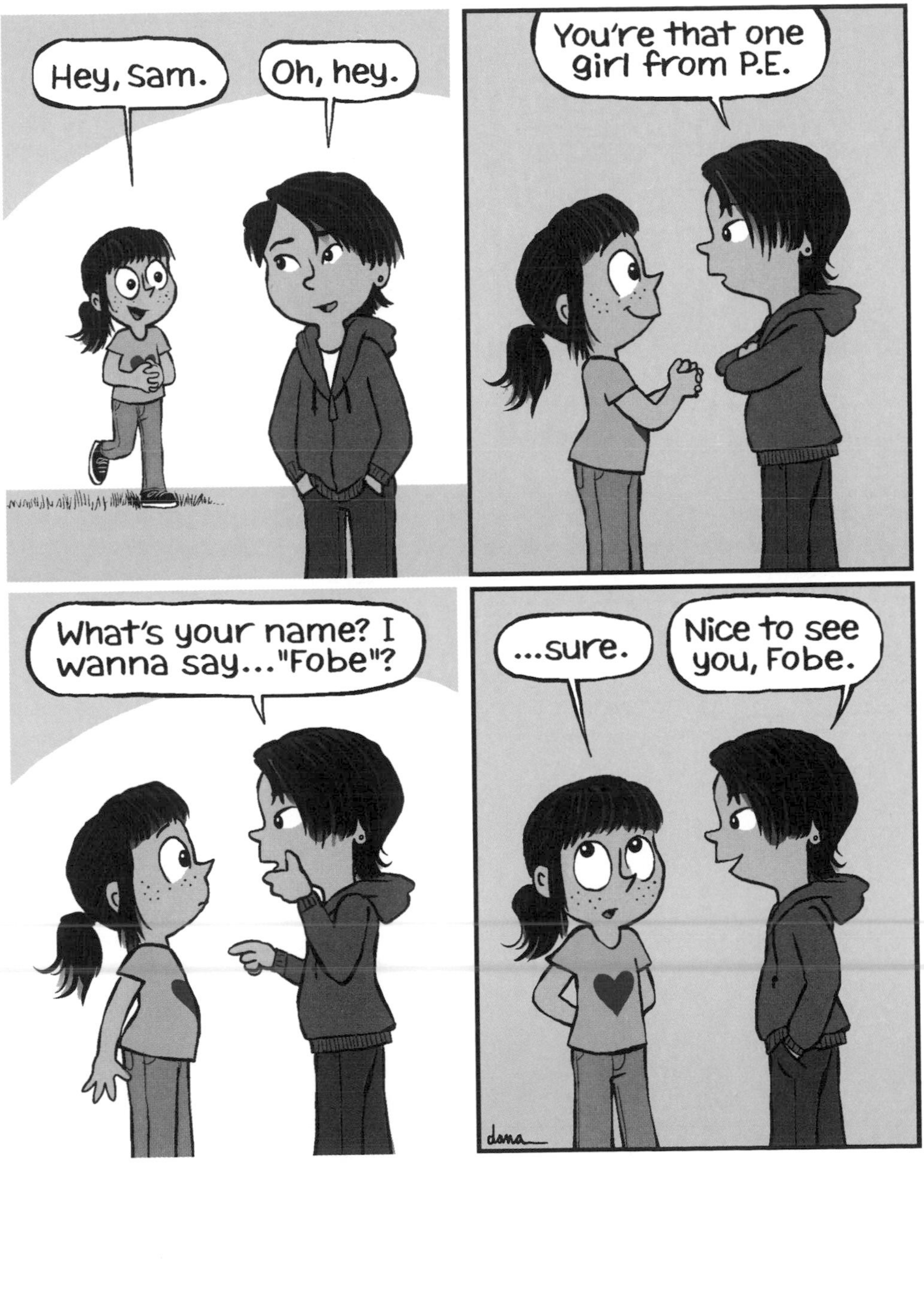
Hey, Sam.
Oh, hey.
You're that one girl from P.E.
What's your name? I wanna say..."Fobe"?
...sure.
Nice to see you, Fobe.
dana

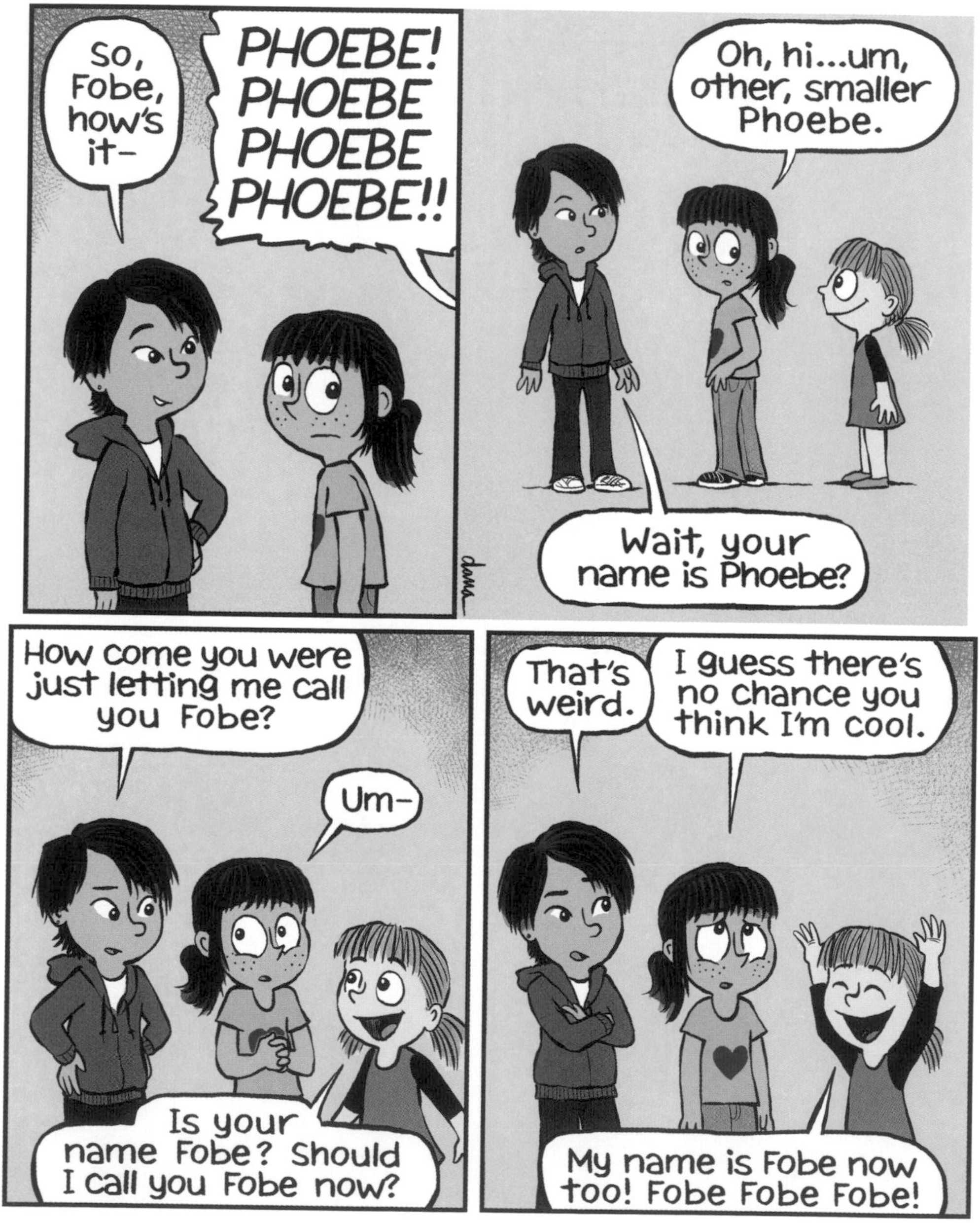
So, Fobe, how's it-
PHOEBE! PHOEBE PHOEBE PHOEBE!!
Oh, hi...um, other, smaller Phoebe.
Wait, your name is Phoebe?
How come you were just letting me call you Fobe?
Um-
Is your name Fobe? Should I call you Fobe now?
That's weird.
I guess there's no chance you think I'm cool.
My name is Fobe now too! Fobe Fobe Fobe!

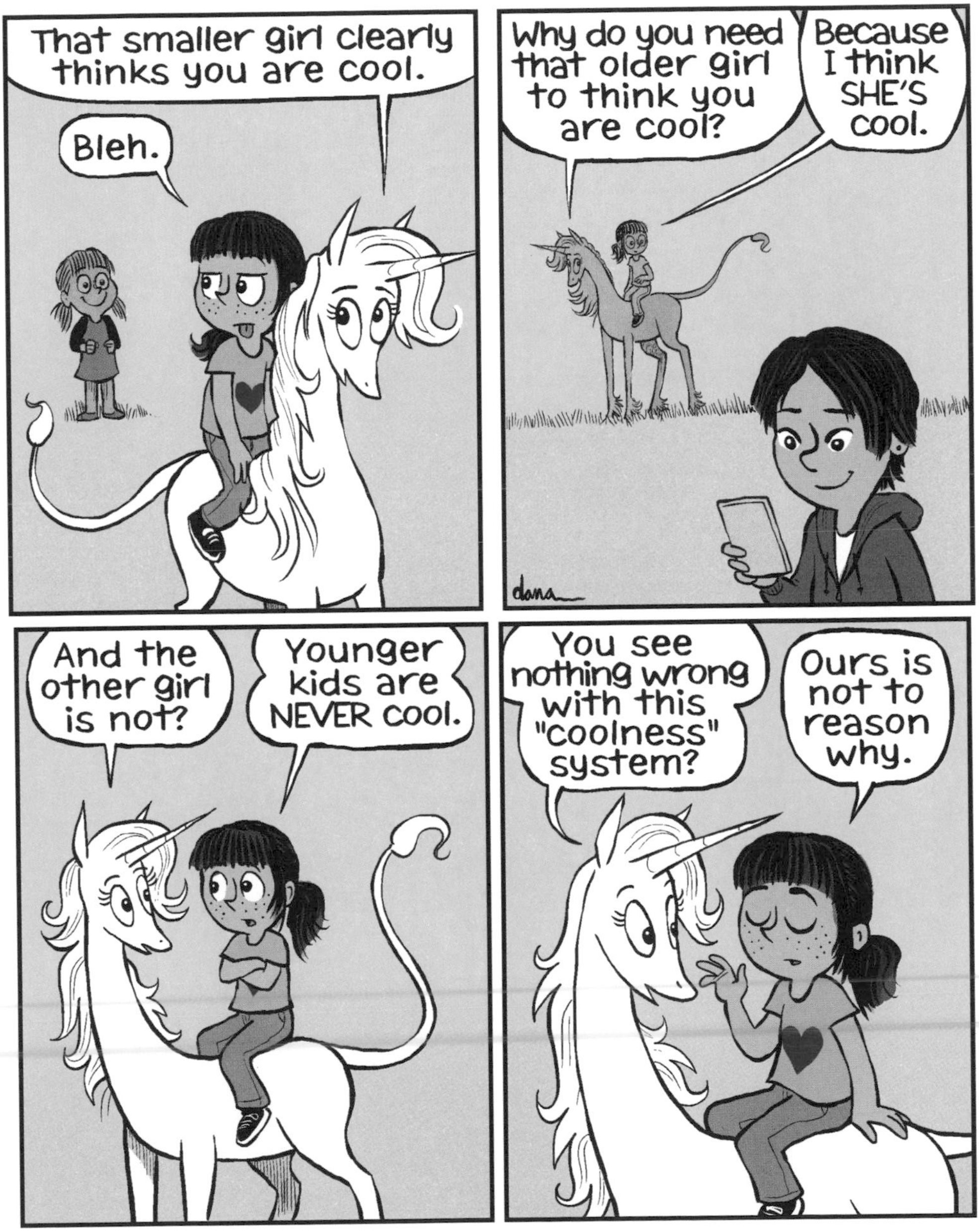
That smaller girl clearly thinks you are cool.
Bleh.
Why do you need that older girl to think you are cool?
Because I think SHE'S cool.
dana
And the other girl is not?
Younger kids are NEVER cool.
You see nothing wrong with this "coolness" system?
Ours is not to reason why.

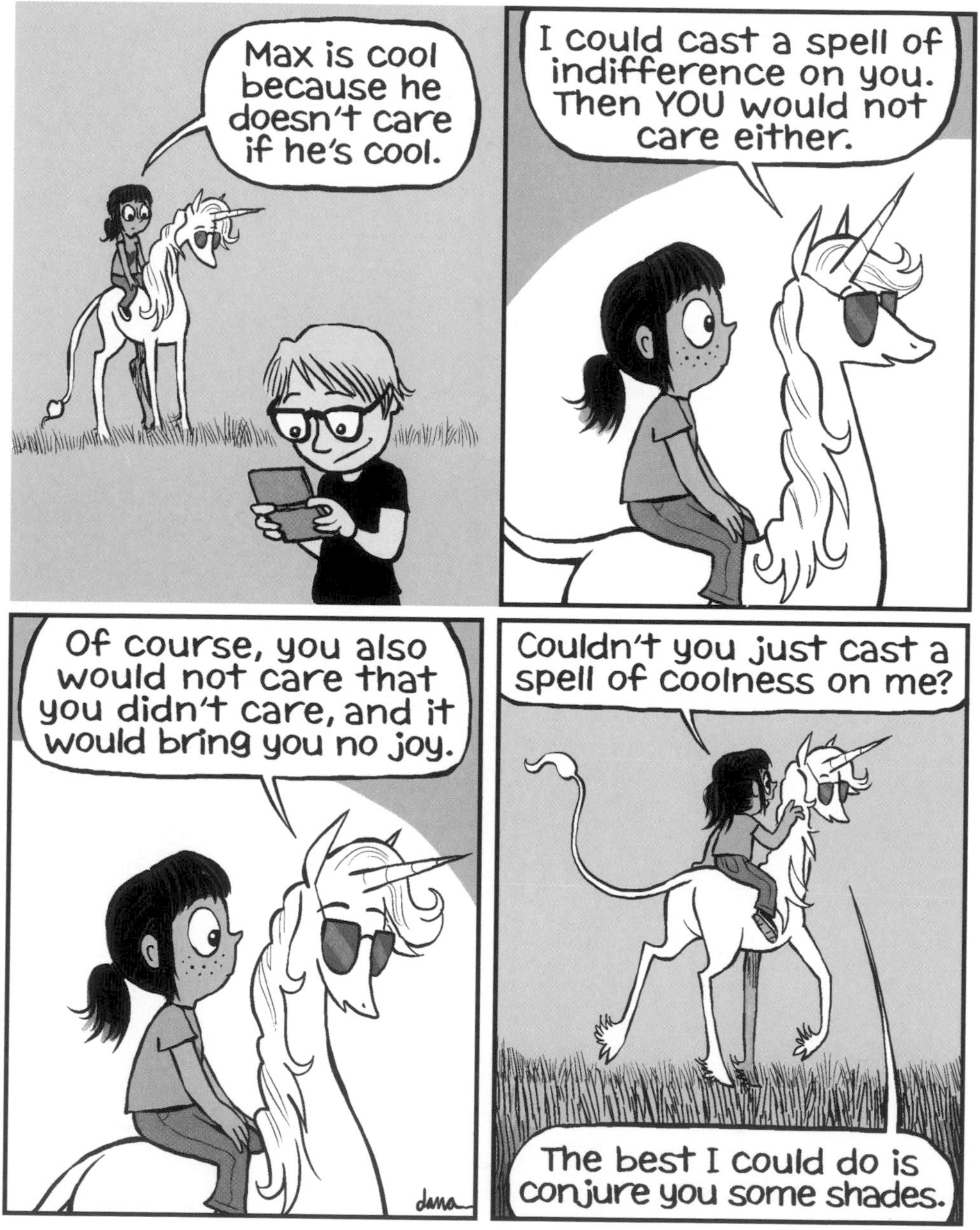
Max is cool because he doesn't care if he's cool.
I could cast a spell of indifference on you. Then YOU would not care either.
Of course, you also would not care that you didn't care, and it would bring you no joy.
dana
Couldn't you just cast a spell of coolness on me?
The best I could do is conjure you some shades.

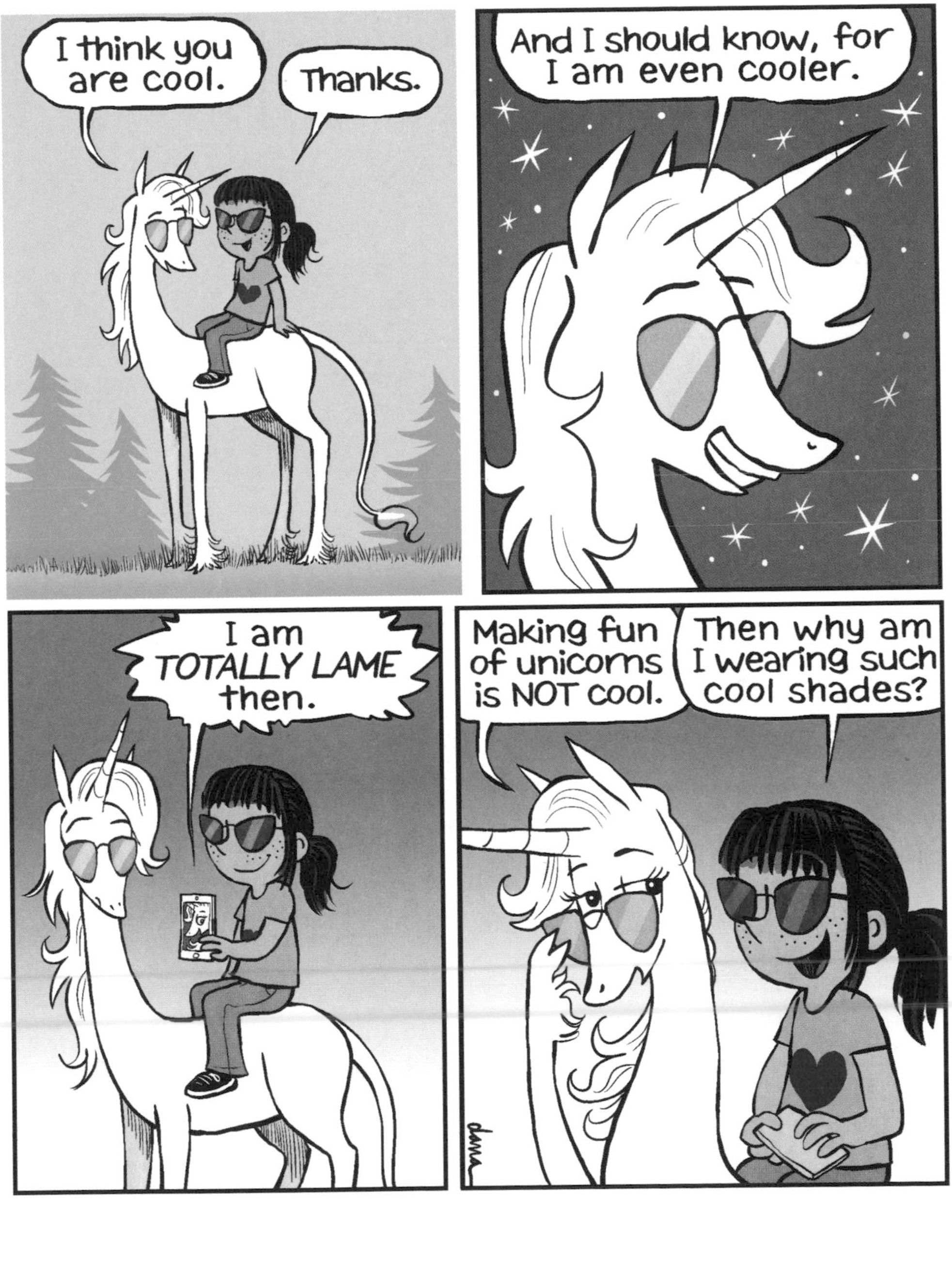
I think you are cool.
Thanks.
And I should know, for I am even cooler.
I am *TOTALLY LAME* then.
Making fun of unicorns is NOT cool.
Then why am I wearing such cool shades?

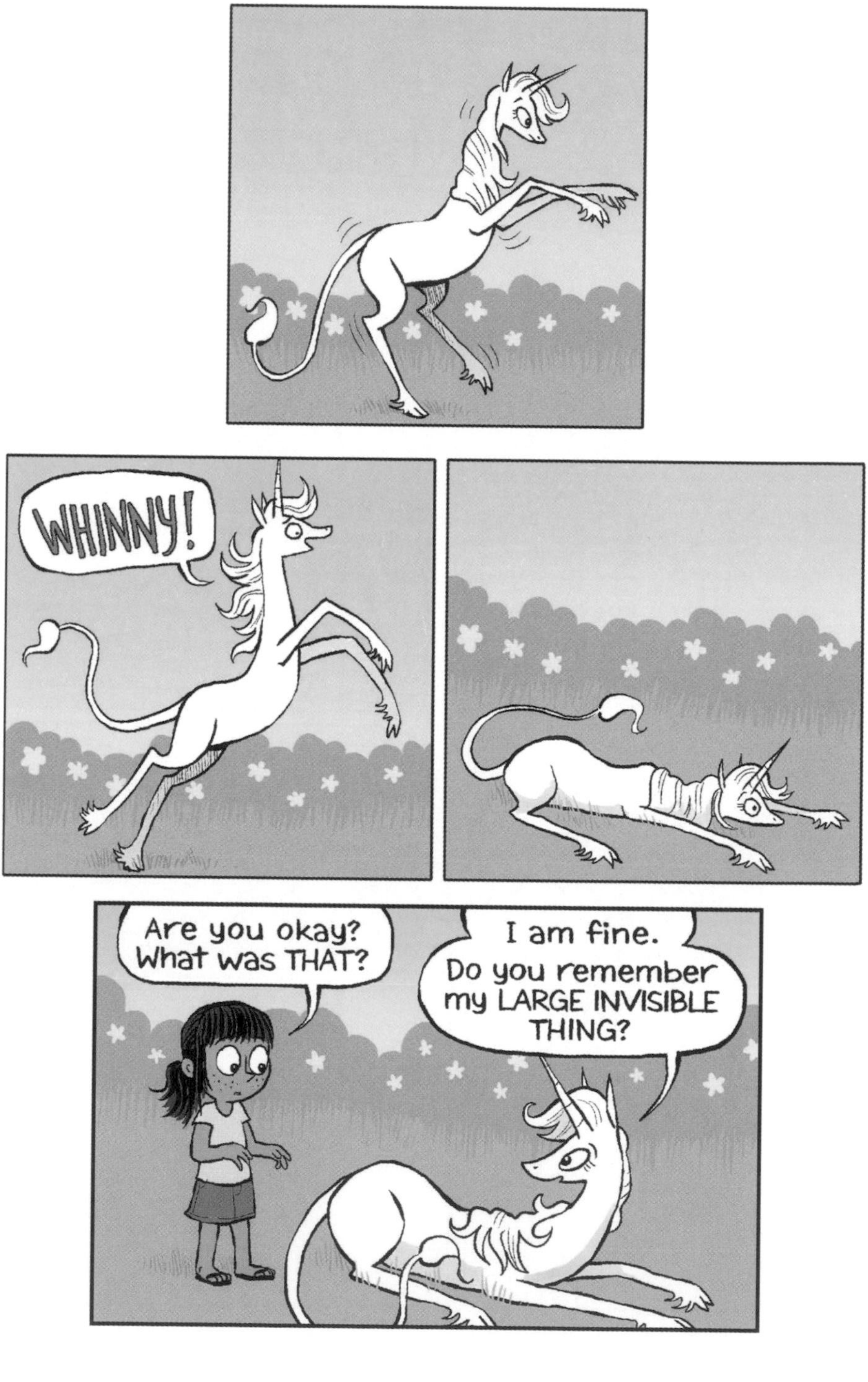
WHINNY!
Are you okay? What was THAT?
I am fine. Do you remember my LARGE INVISIBLE THING?

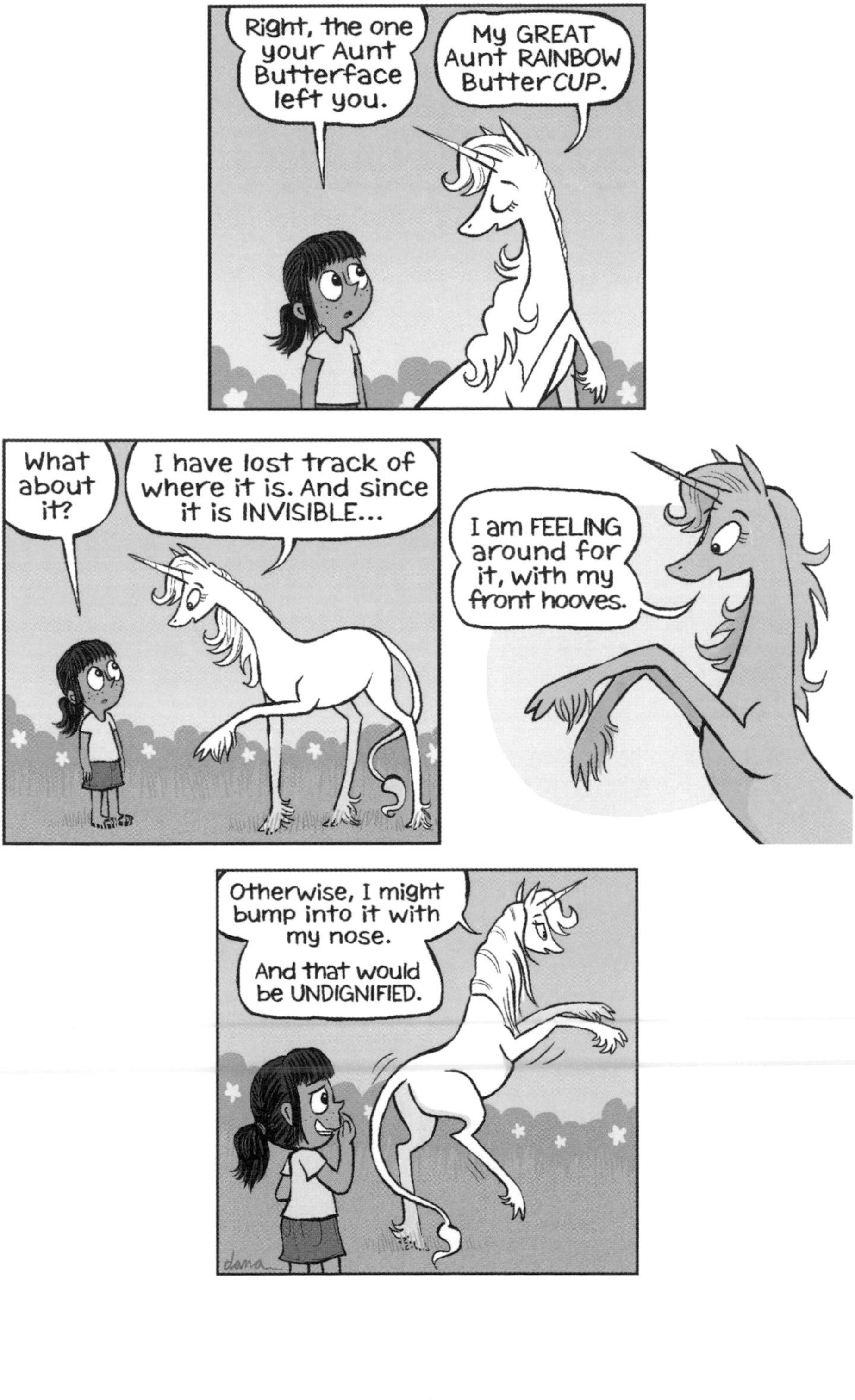
Right, the one your Aunt Butterface left you.
My GREAT Aunt RAINBOW ButterCUP.
What about it?
I have lost track of where it is. And since it is INVISIBLE...
I am FEELING around for it, with my front hooves.
Otherwise, I might bump into it with my nose.
And that would be UNDIGNIFIED.
dana

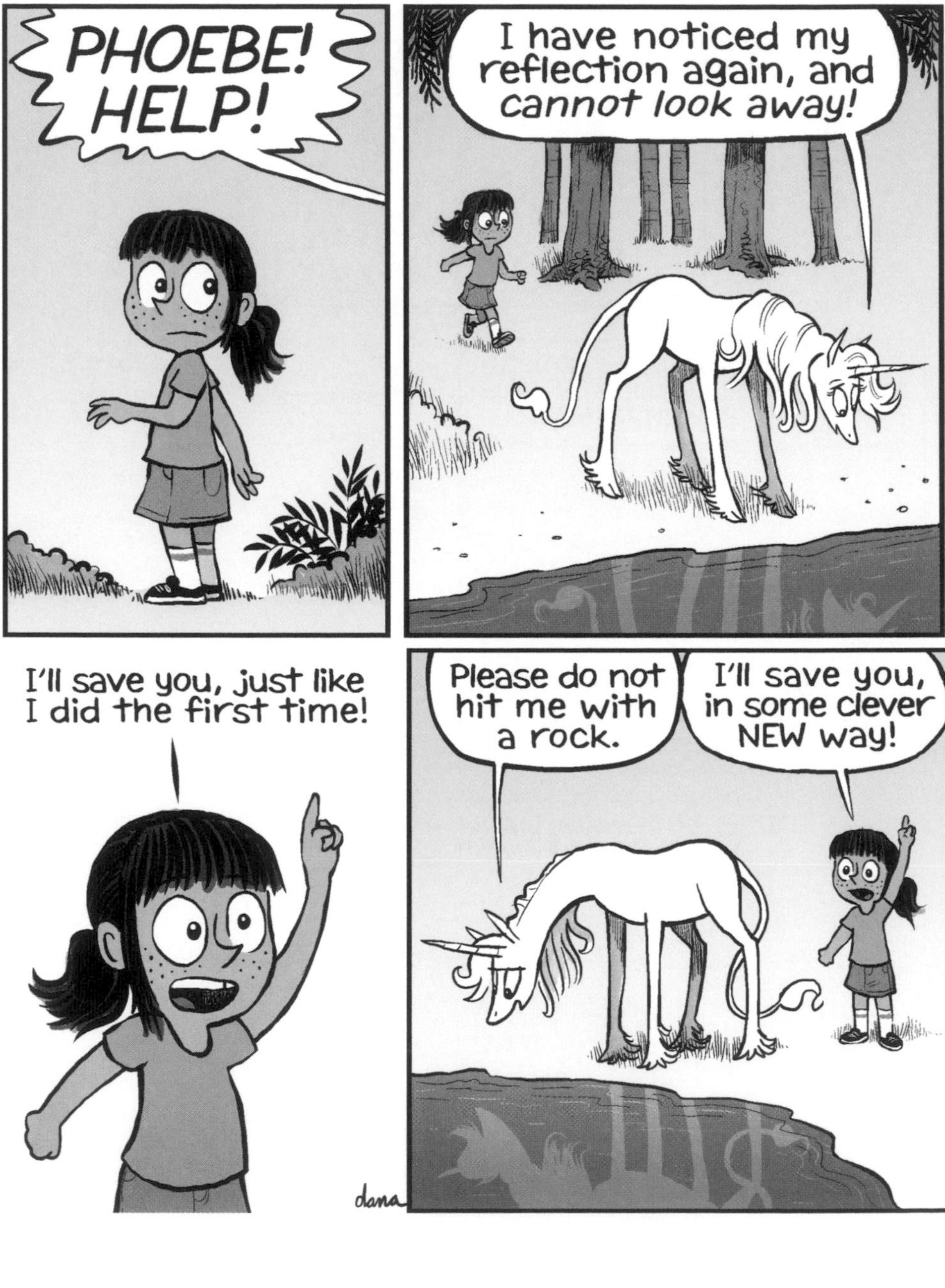
PHOEBE! HELP!
I have noticed my reflection again, and cannot look away!
I'll save you, just like I did the first time!
Please do not hit me with a rock.
I'll save you, in some clever NEW way!
dana

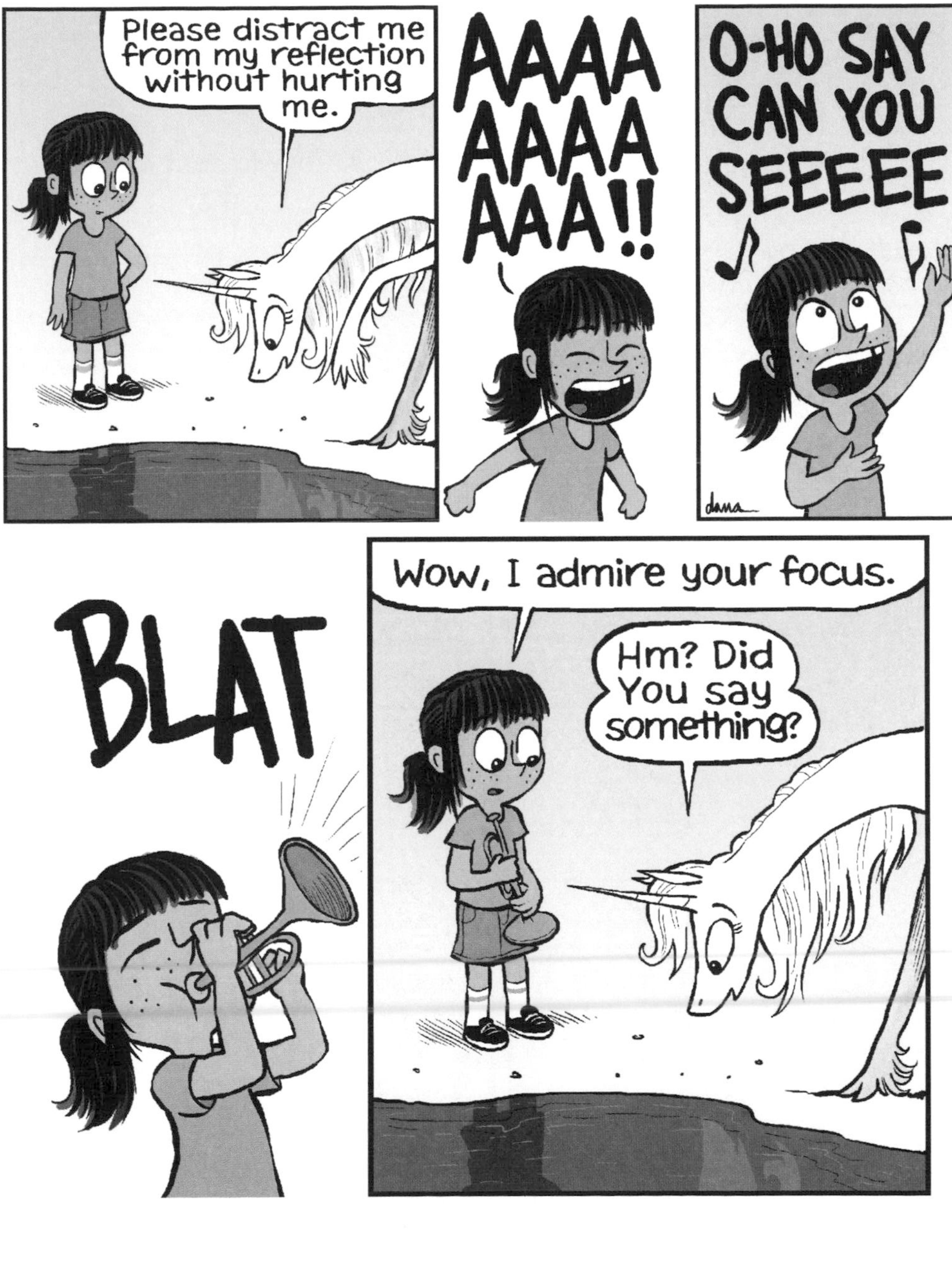
Please distract me from my reflection without hurting me.
AAAA AAAA AAA!!
O-HO SAY CAN YOU SEEEEE
BLAT
Wow, I admire your focus.
Hm? Did You say something?

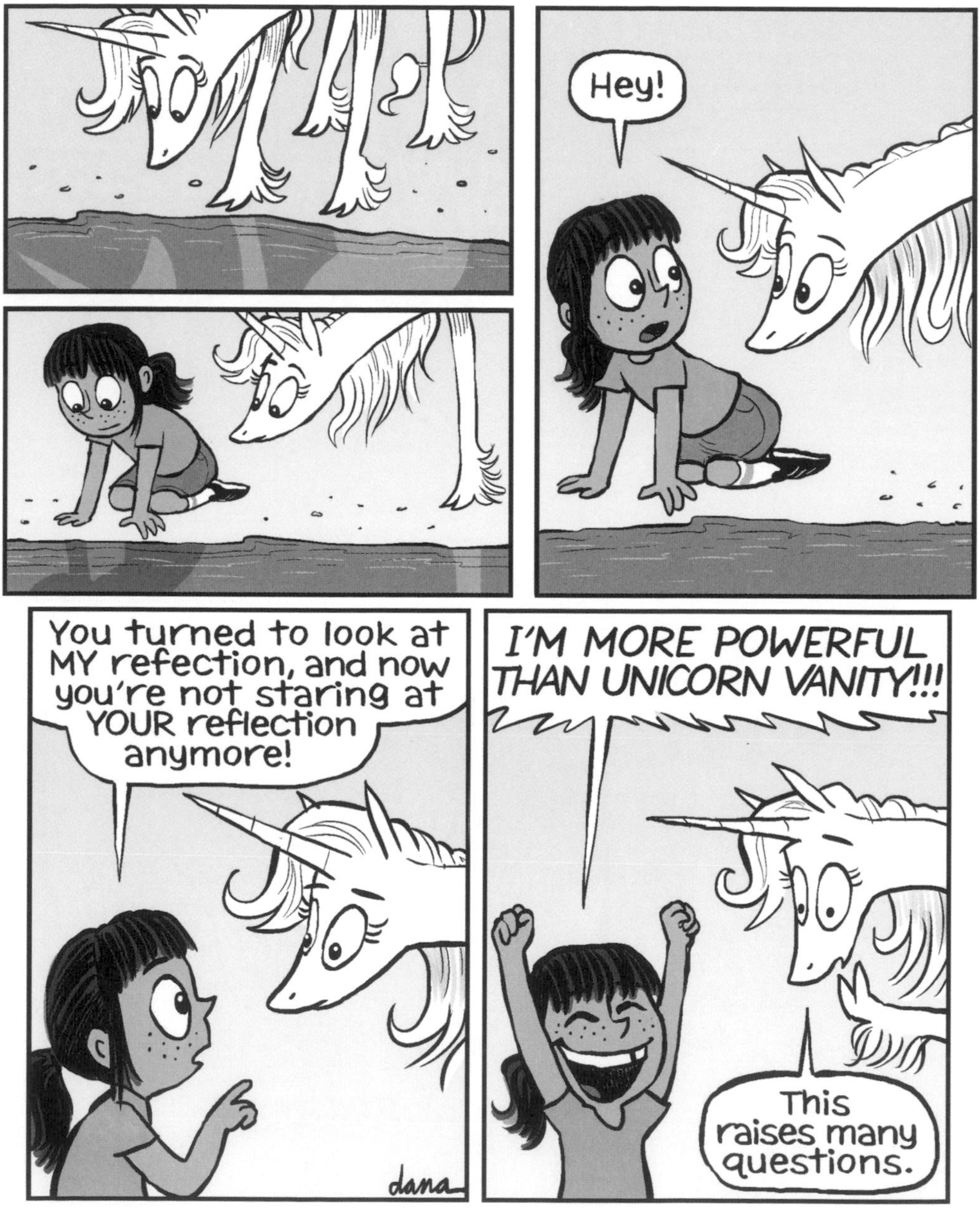
Hey!
You turned to look at MY refection, and now you're not staring at YOUR reflection anymore!
dana
I'M MORE POWERFUL THAN UNICORN VANITY!!!
This raises many questions.

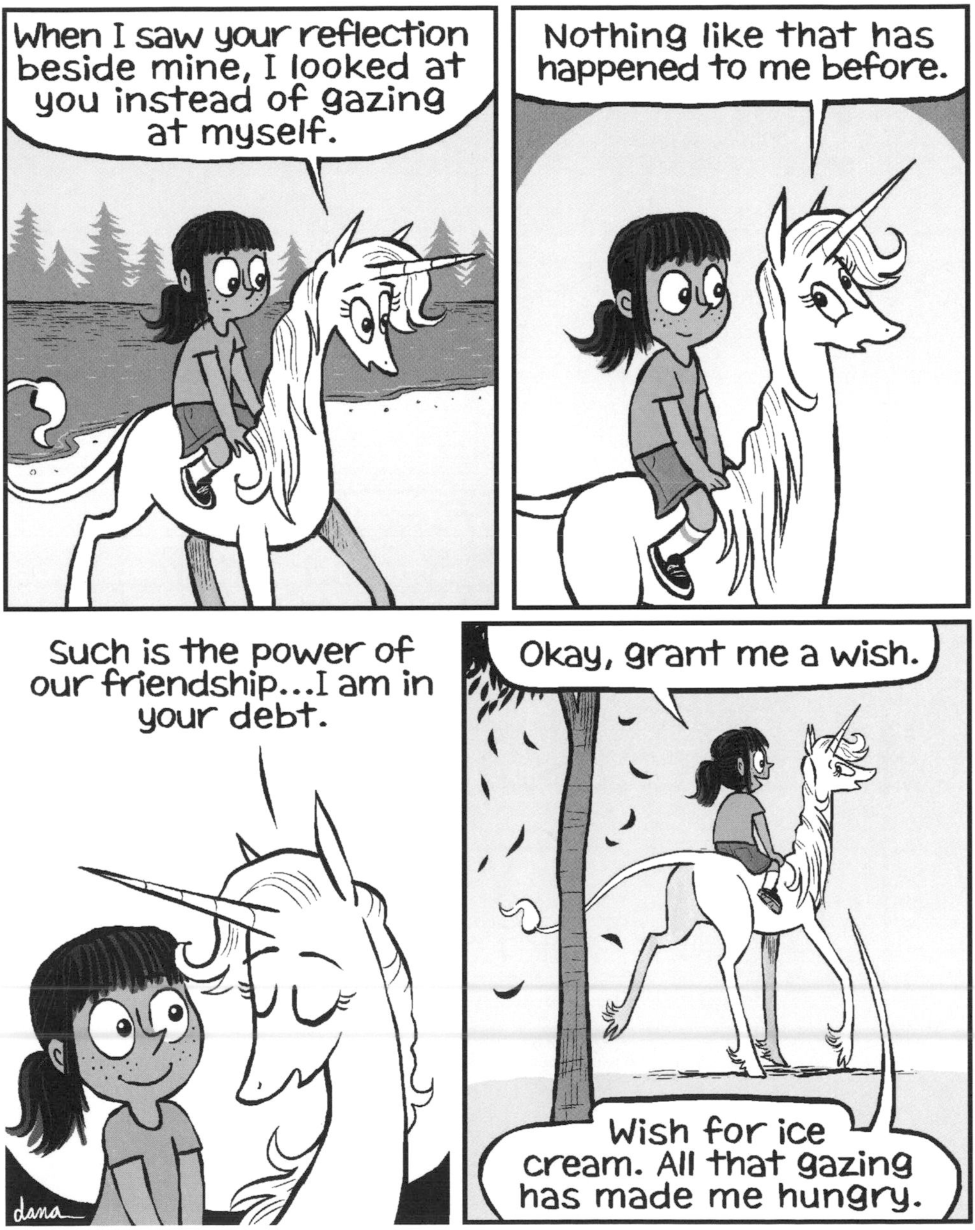
When I saw your reflection beside mine, I looked at you instead of gazing at myself.
Nothing like that has happened to me before.
Such is the power of our friendship...I am in your debt.
dana
Okay, grant me a wish.
Wish for ice cream. All that gazing has made me hungry.

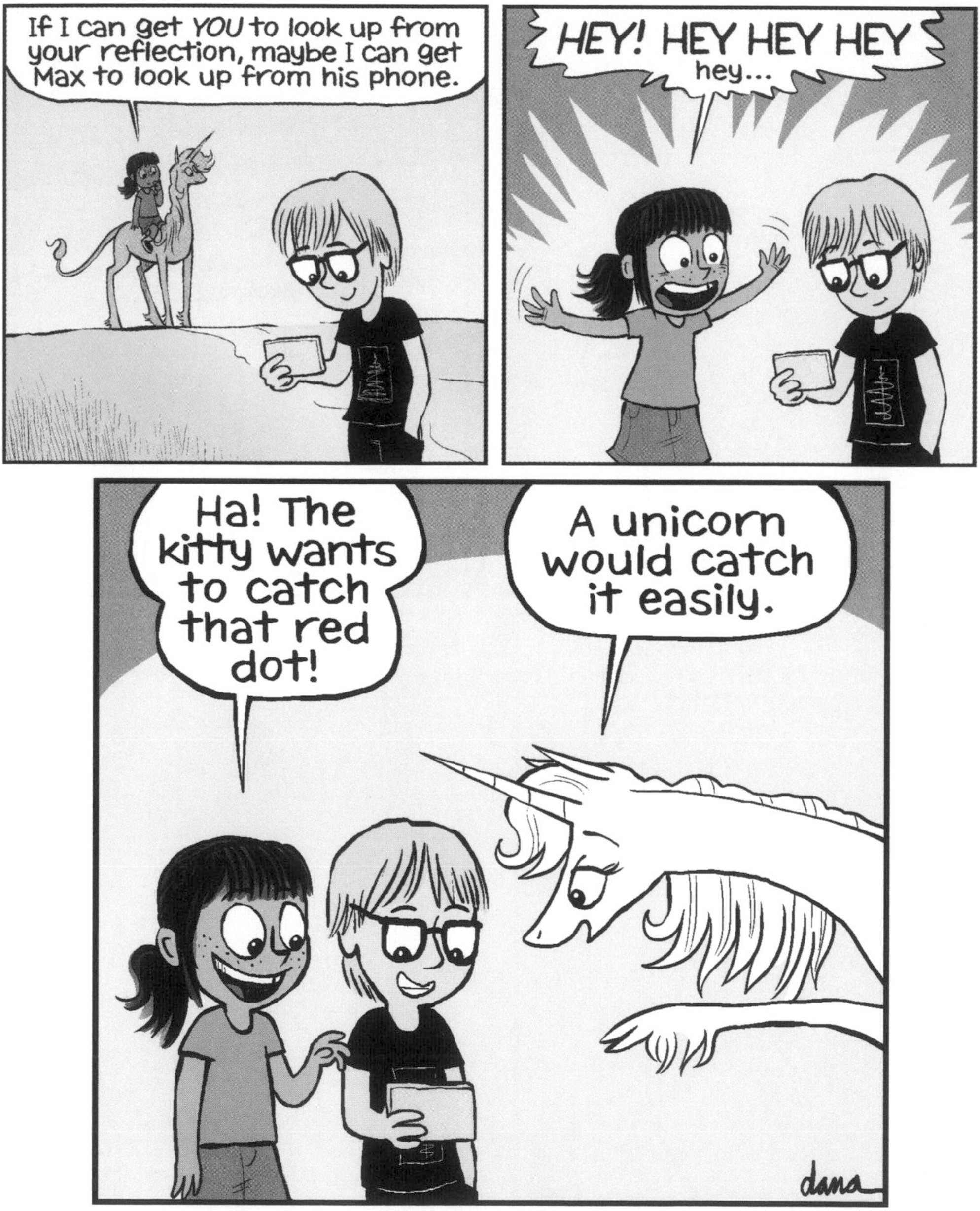
If I can get YOU to look up from your reflection, maybe I can get Max to look up from his phone.
HEY! HEY HEY HEY hey...
Ha! The kitty wants to catch that red dot!
A unicorn would catch it easily.
dana

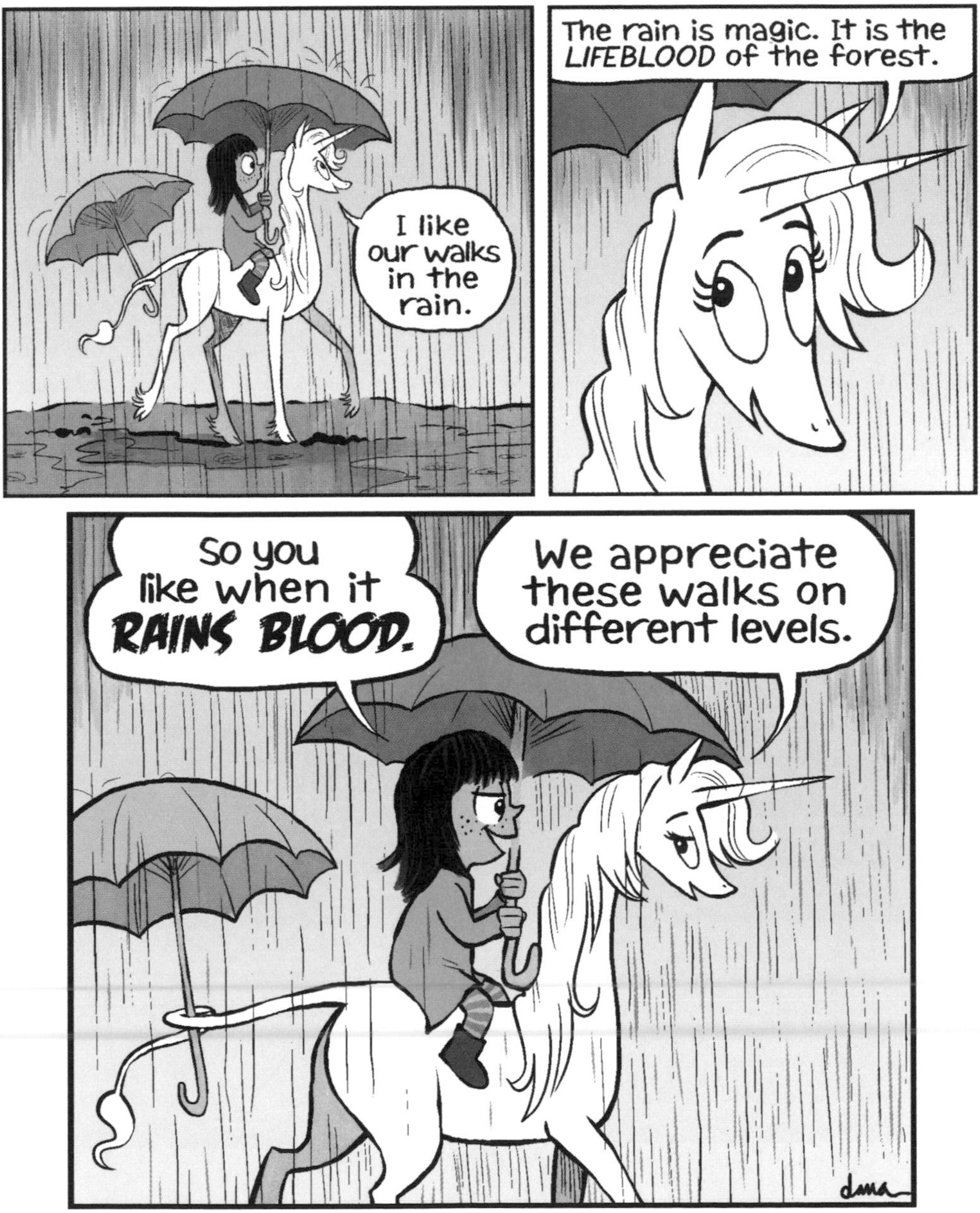
I like our walks in the rain.
The rain is magic. It is the LIFEBLOOD of the forest.
So you like when it RAINS BLOOD.
We appreciate these walks on different levels.
dana

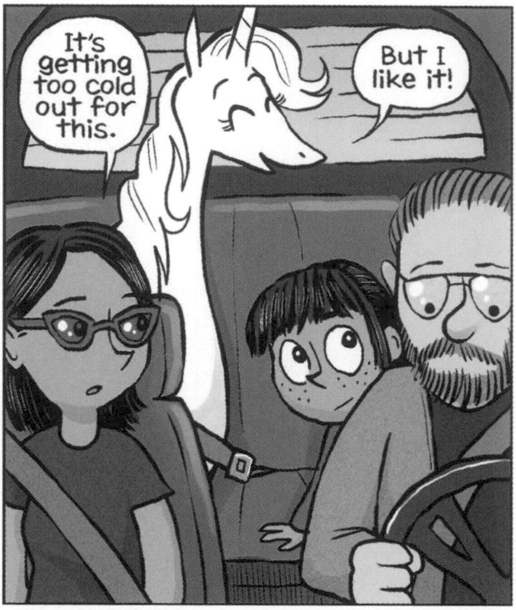
It's getting too cold out for this.
But I like it!

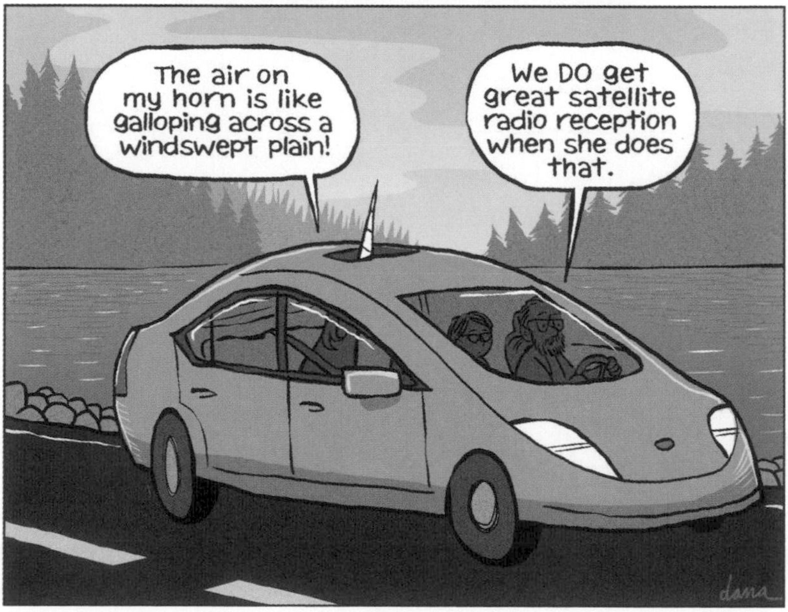
The air on my horn is like galloping across a windswept plain!
We DO get great satellite radio reception when she does that.
dana

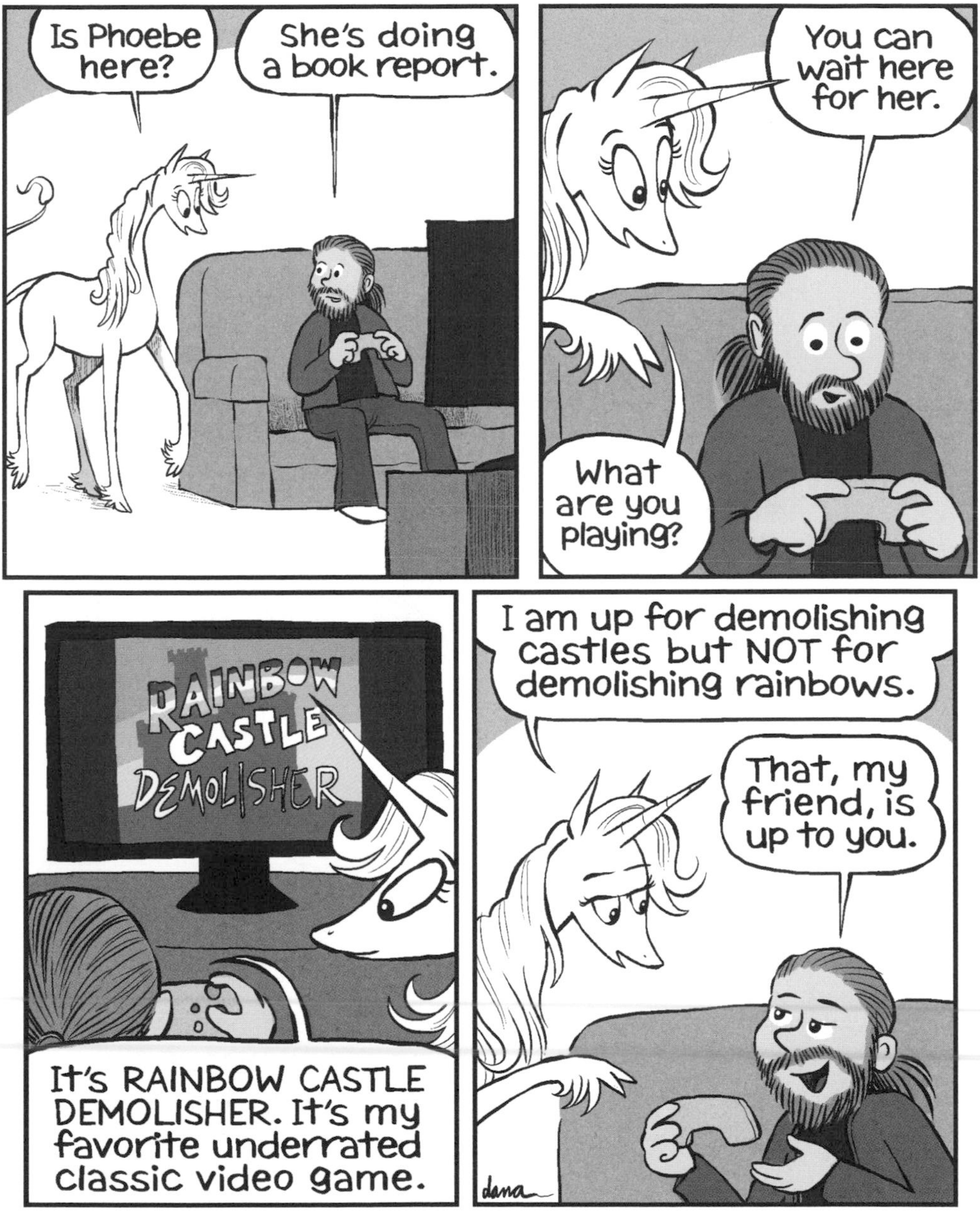
Is Phoebe here?
She's doing a book report.
You can wait here for her.
What are you playing?
RAINBOW CASTLE DEMOLISHER
It's RAINBOW CASTLE DEMOLISHER. It's my favorite underrated classic video game.
I am up for demolishing castles but NOT for demolishing rainbows.
That, my friend, is up to you.
dana

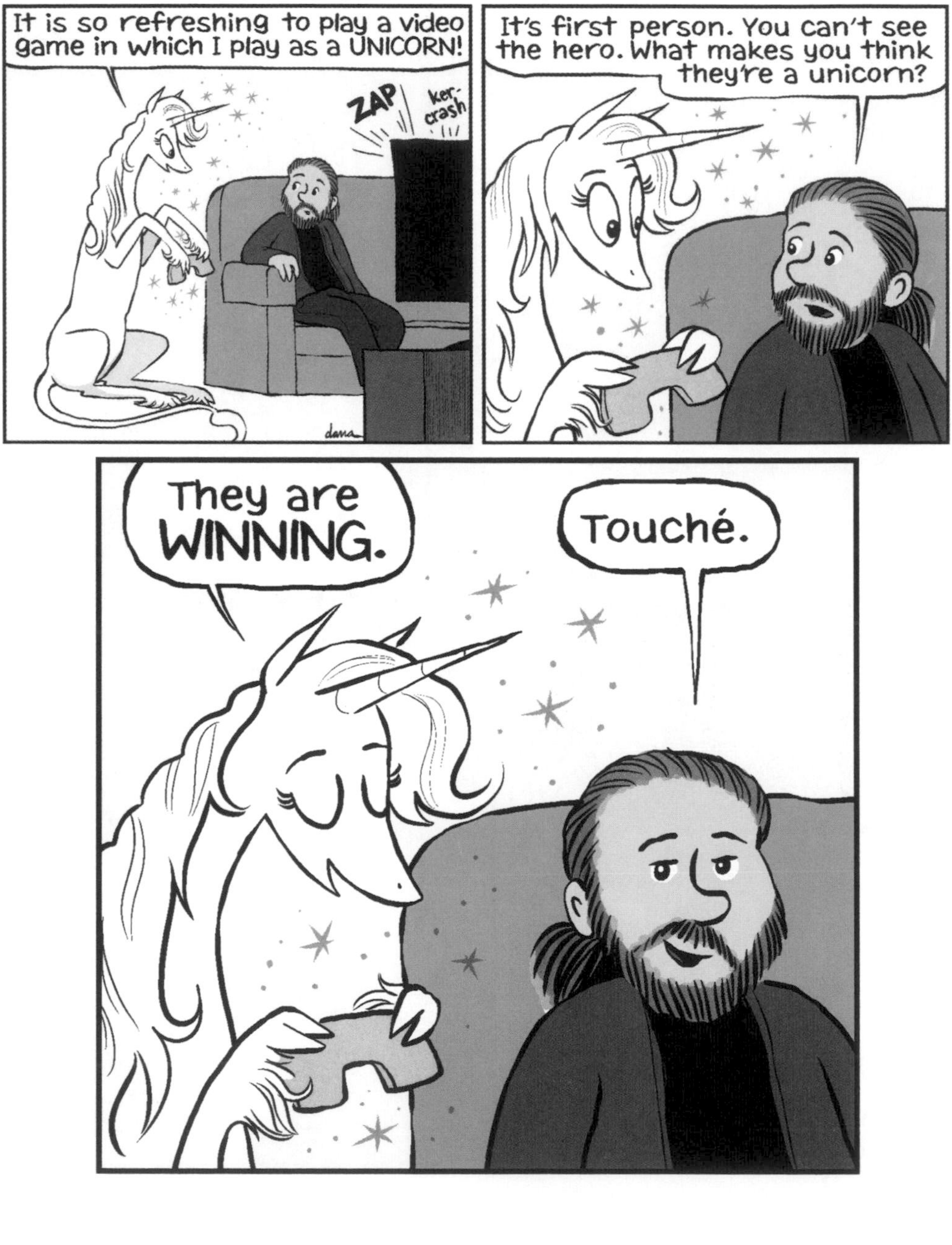
It is so refreshing to play a video game in which I play as a UNICORN!
ZAP
ker-crash
dana
It's first person. You can't see the hero. What makes you think they're a unicorn?
They are WINNING.
Touché.

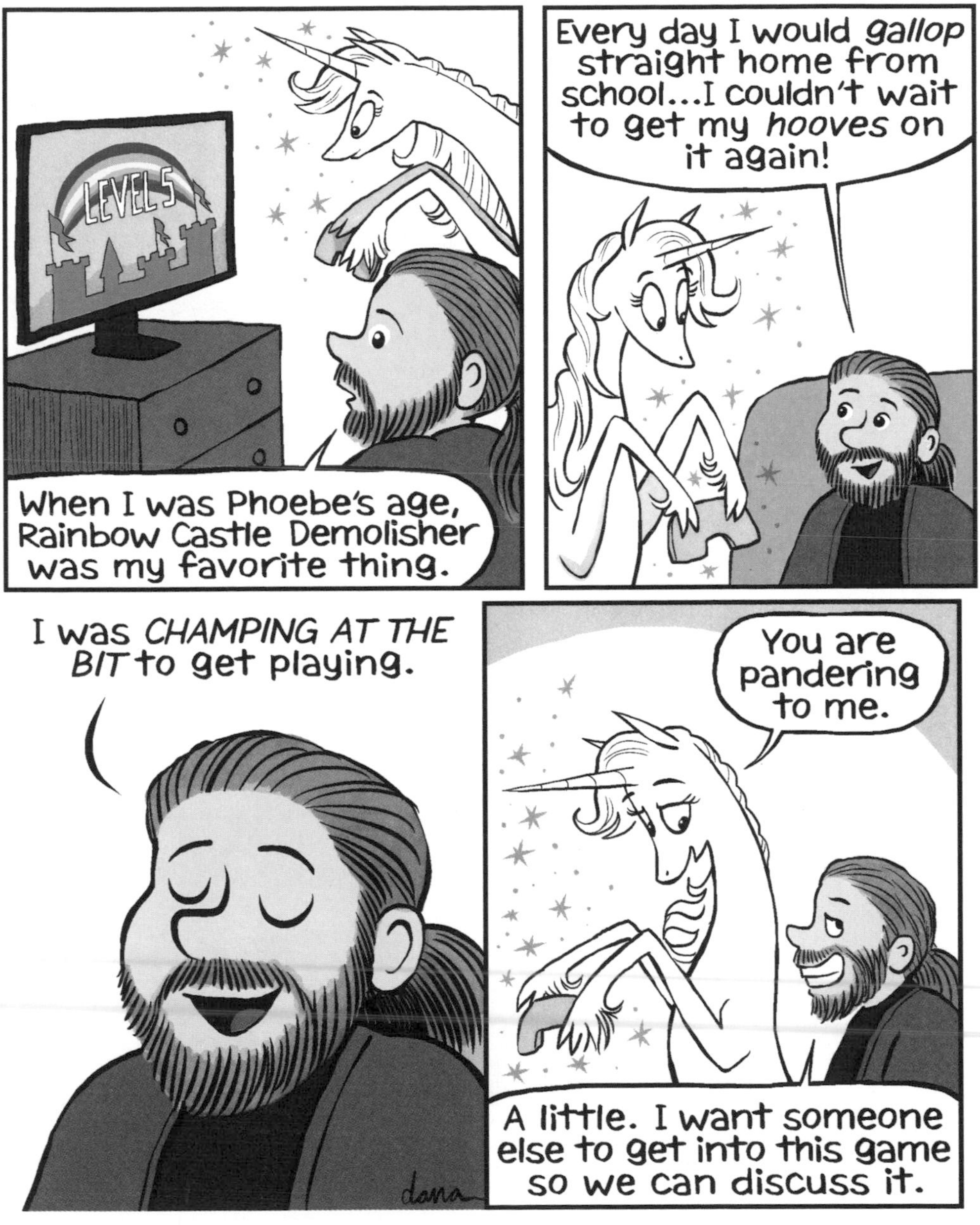
LEVEL 5
When I was Phoebe's age, Rainbow Castle Demolisher was my favorite thing.
Every day I would *gallop* straight home from school...I couldn't wait to get my *hooves* on it again!
I was *CHAMPING AT THE BIT* to get playing.
You are pandering to me.
A little. I want someone else to get into this game so we can discuss it.
dana

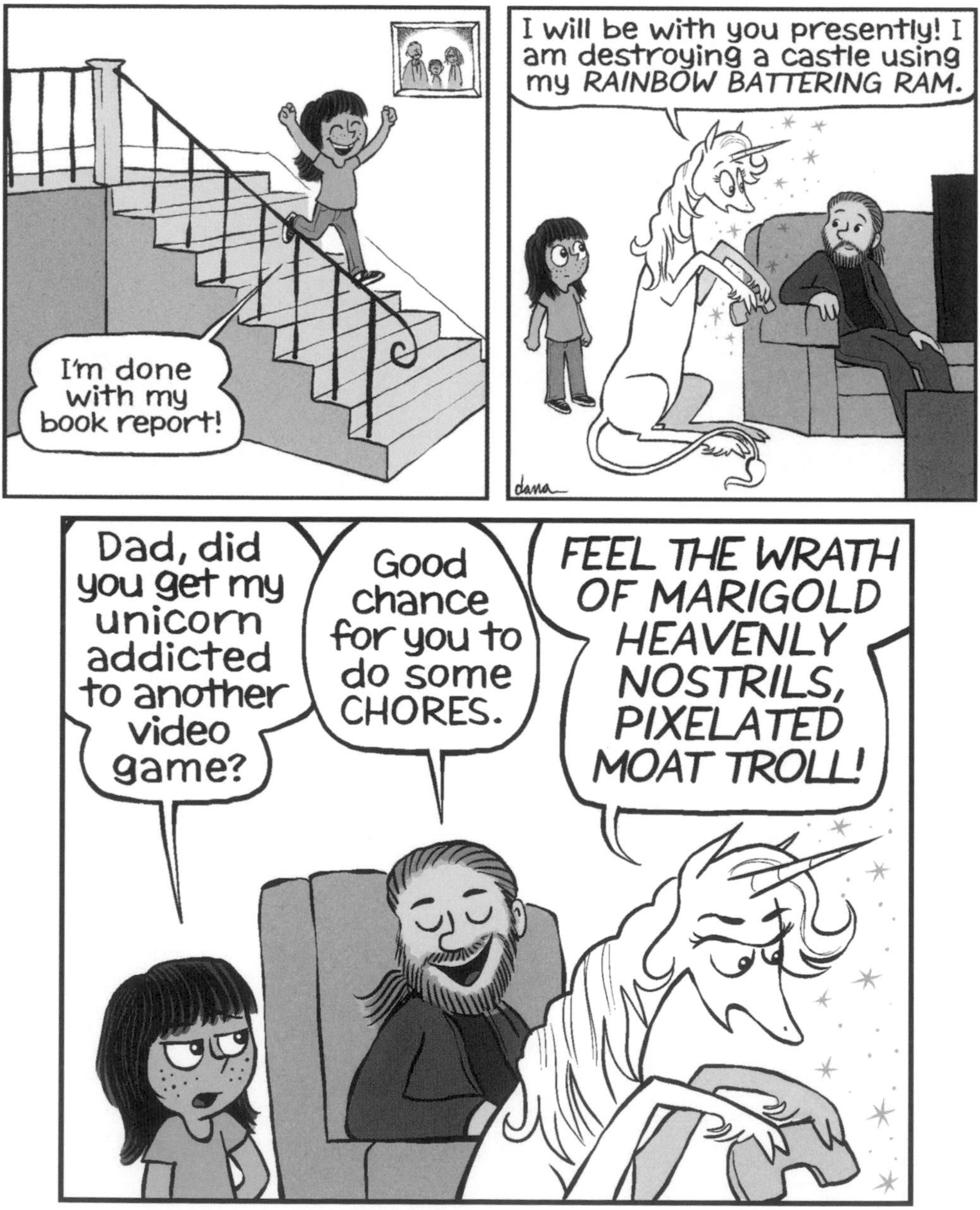
I'm done with my book report!
I will be with you presently! I am destroying a castle using my RAINBOW BATTERING RAM.
dana
Dad, did you get my unicorn addicted to another video game?
Good chance for you to do some CHORES.
FEEL THE WRATH OF MARIGOLD HEAVENLY NOSTRILS, PIXELATED MOAT TROLL!

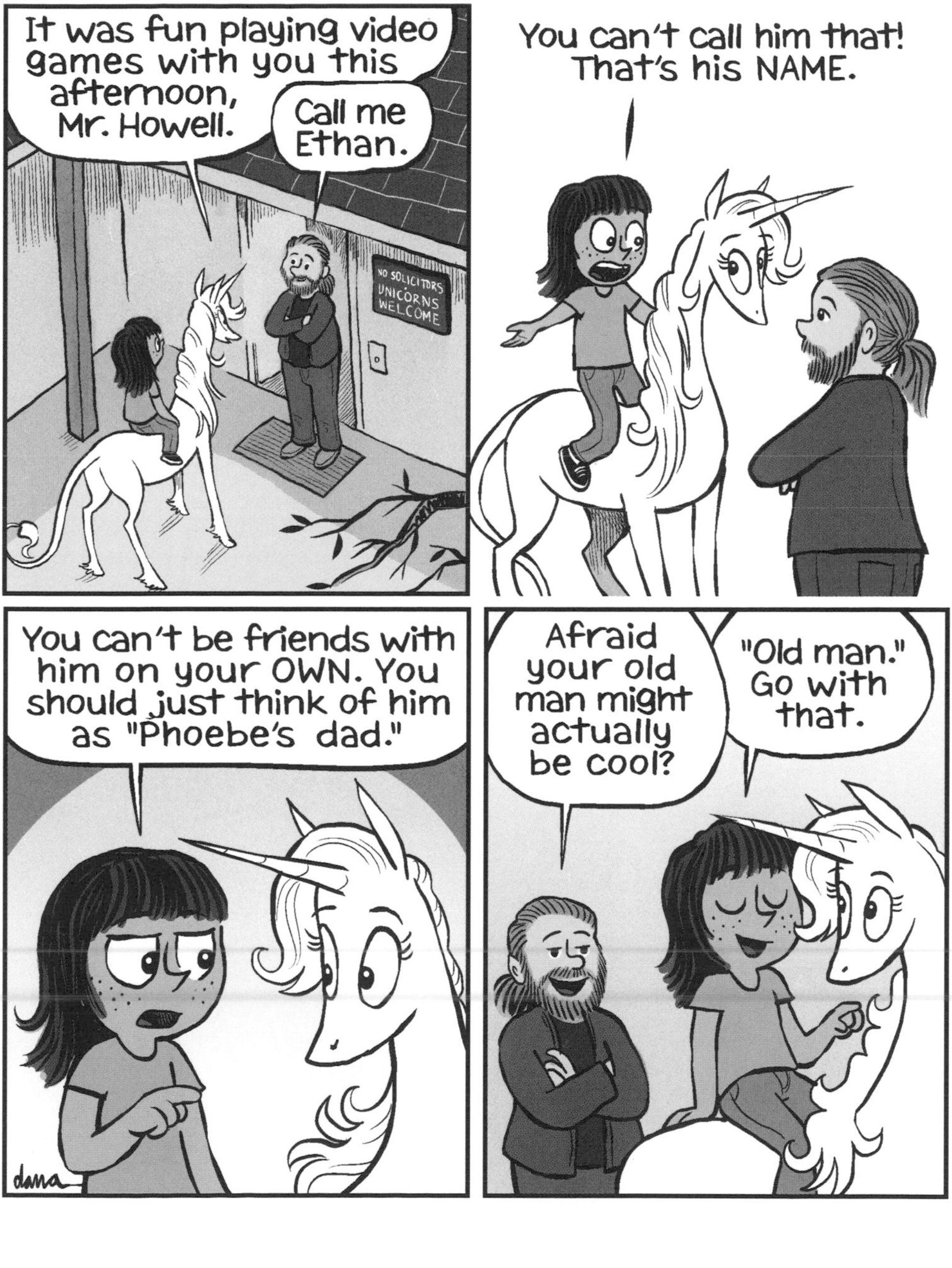
It was fun playing video games with you this afternoon, Mr. Howell.
Call me Ethan.
NO SOLICITORS
UNICORNS WELCOME
You can't call him that! That's his NAME.
You can't be friends with him on your OWN. You should just think of him as "Phoebe's dad."
dana
Afraid your old man might actually be cool?
"Old man." Go with that.

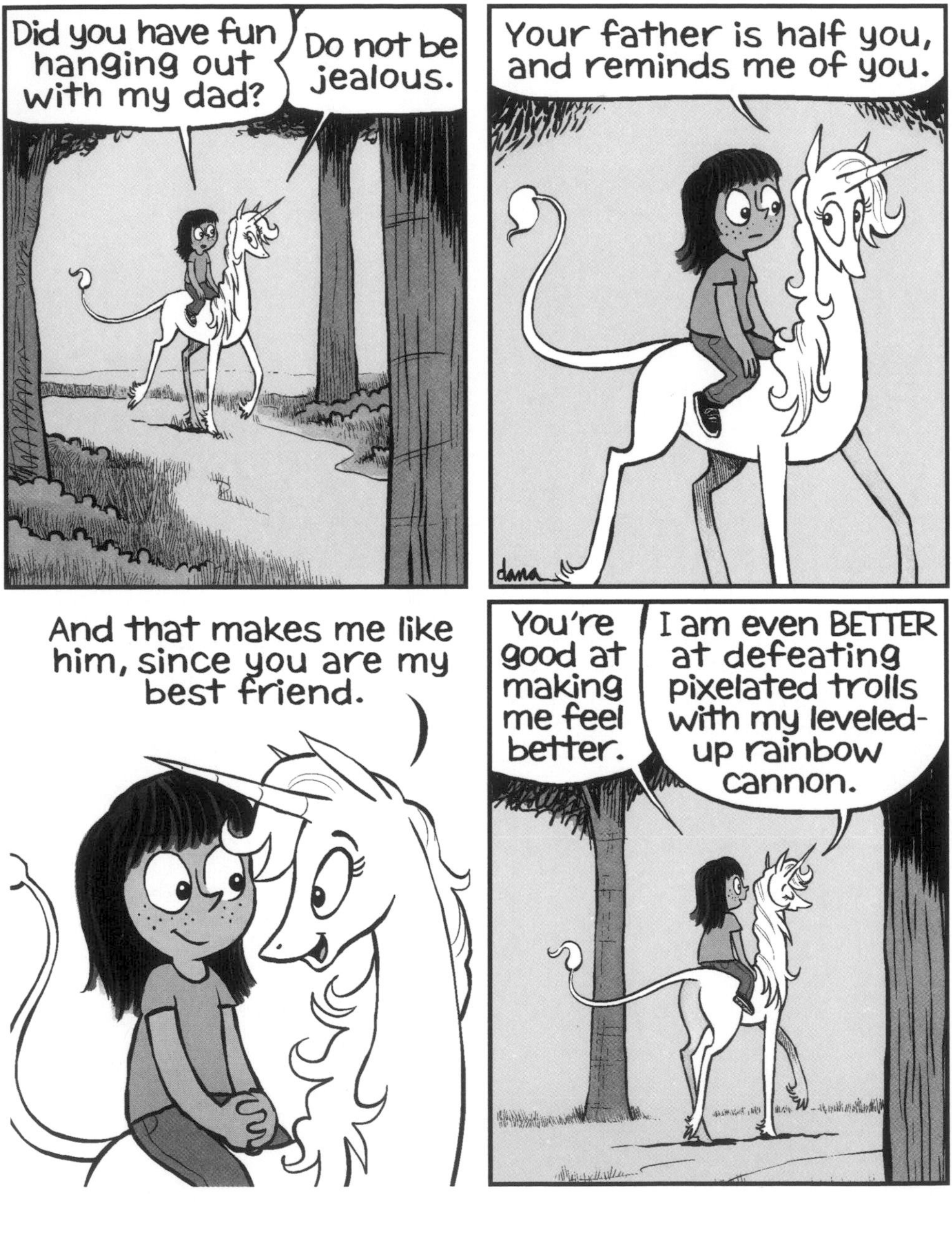
Did you have fun hanging out with my dad?
Do not be jealous.
Your father is half you, and reminds me of you.
dana
And that makes me like him, since you are my best friend.
You're good at making me feel better.
I am even BETTER at defeating pixelated trolls with my leveled-up rainbow cannon.

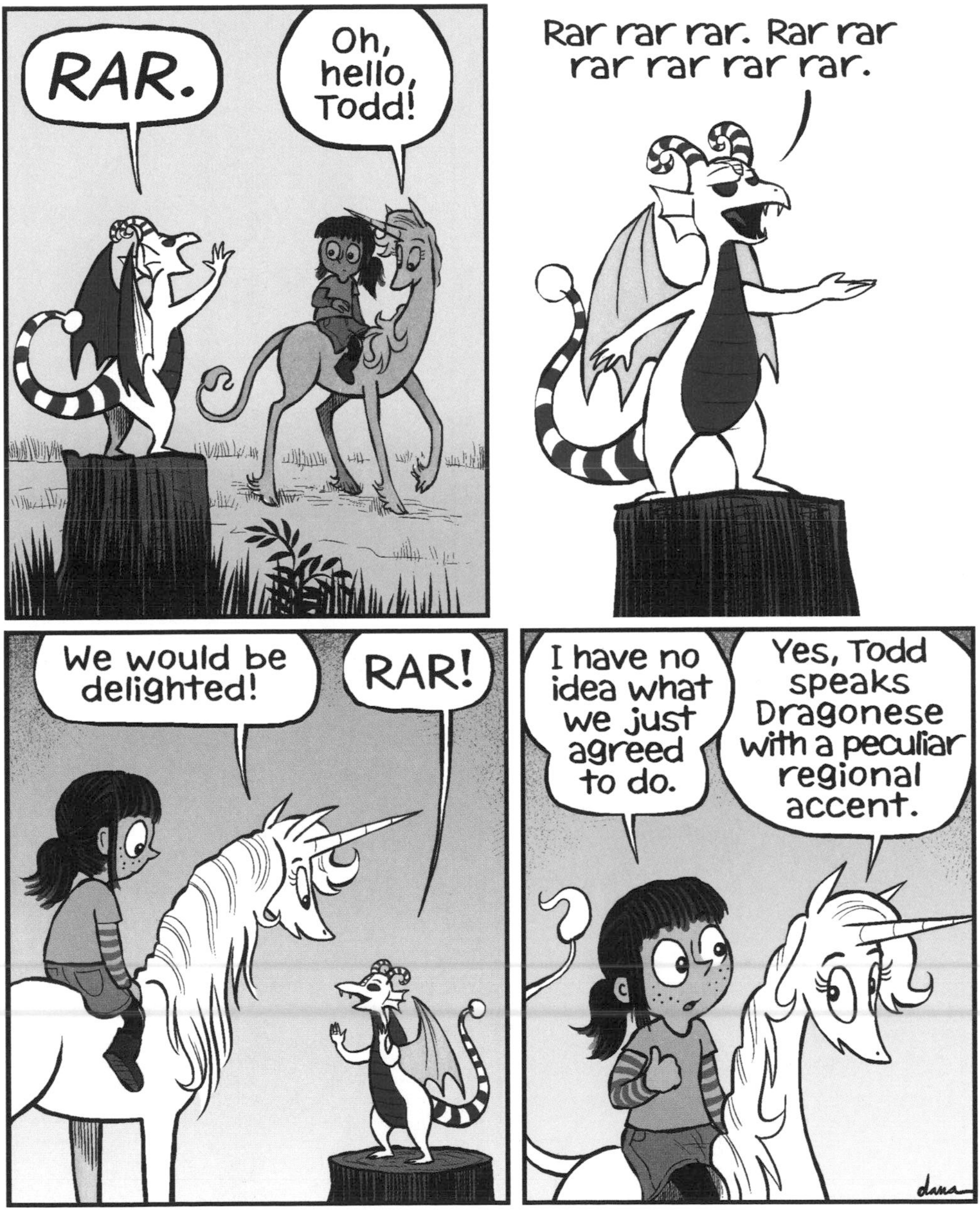
RAR.
Oh, hello, Todd!
Rar rar rar. Rar rar rar rar rar rar.
We would be delighted!
RAR!
I have no idea what we just agreed to do.
Yes, Todd speaks Dragonese with a peculiar regional accent.
dana

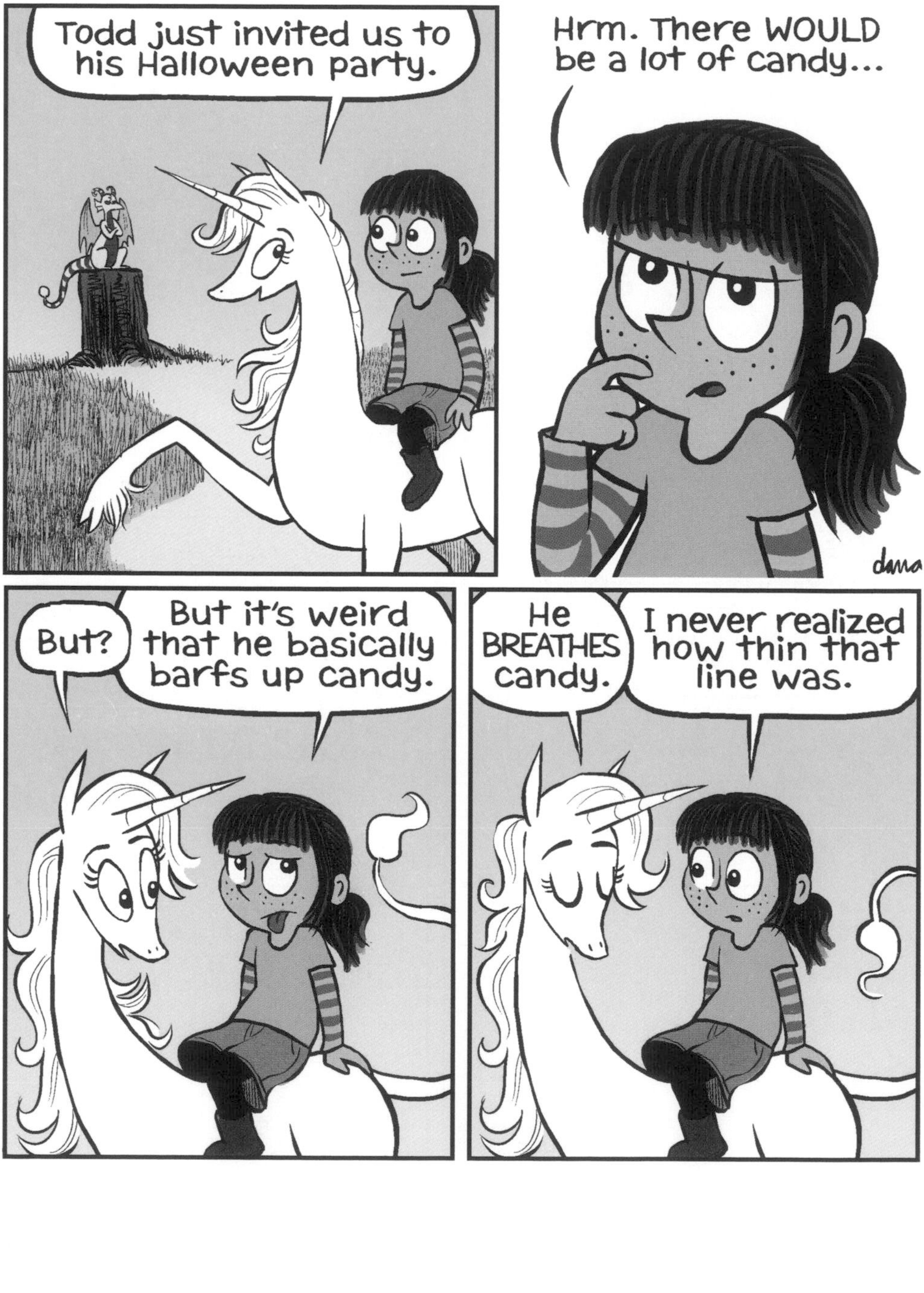
Todd just invited us to his Halloween party.
Hrm. There WOULD be a lot of candy...
dana
But?
But it's weird that he basically barfs up candy.
He BREATHES candy.
I never realized how thin that line was.

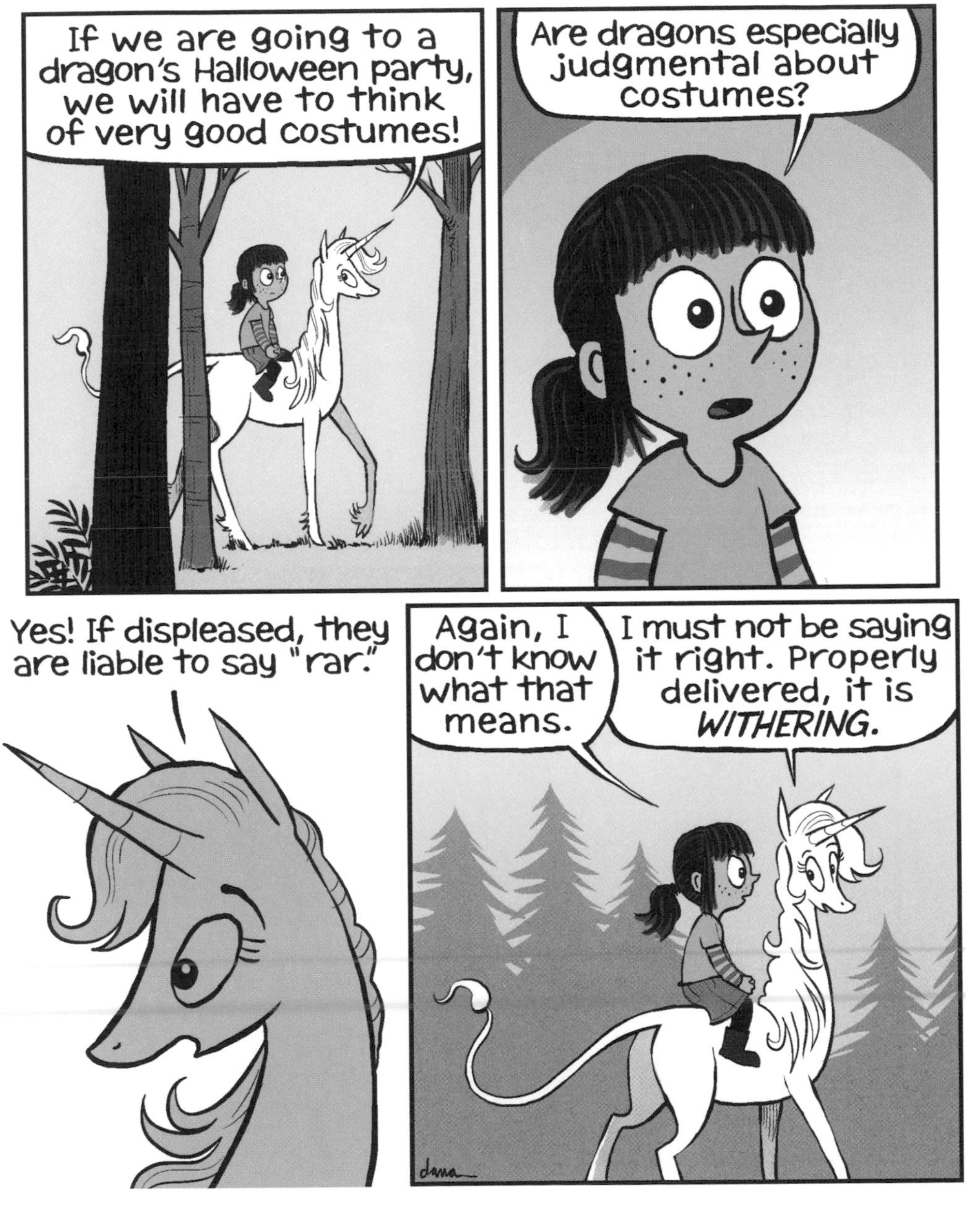
If we are going to a dragon's Halloween party, we will have to think of very good costumes!
Are dragons especially judgmental about costumes?
Yes! If displeased, they are liable to say "rar."
Again, I don't know what that means.
I must not be saying it right. Properly delivered, it is *WITHERING*.
dana

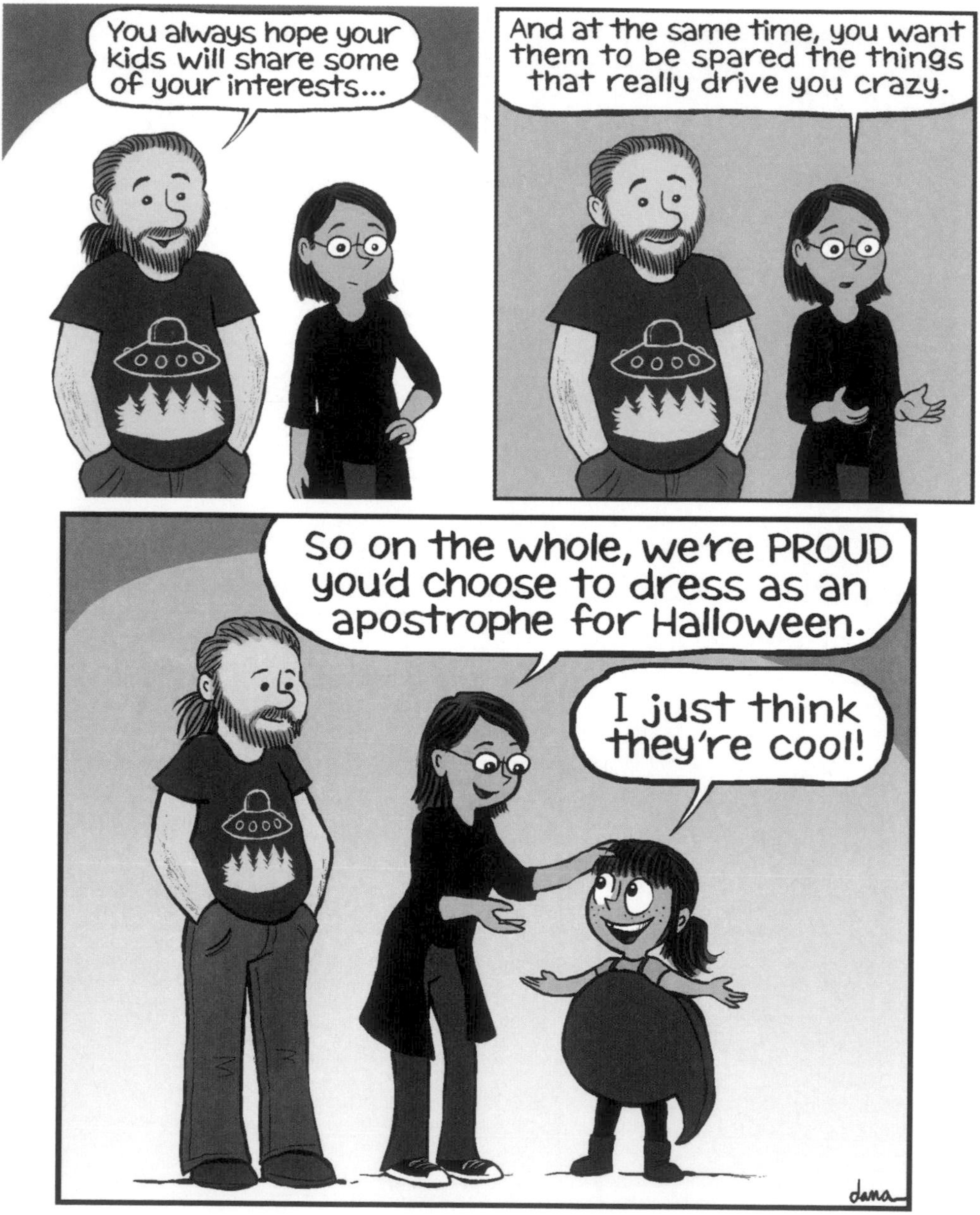
You always hope your kids will share some of your interests...
And at the same time, you want them to be spared the things that really drive you crazy.
So on the whole, we're PROUD you'd choose to dress as an apostrophe for Halloween.
I just think they're cool!
dana

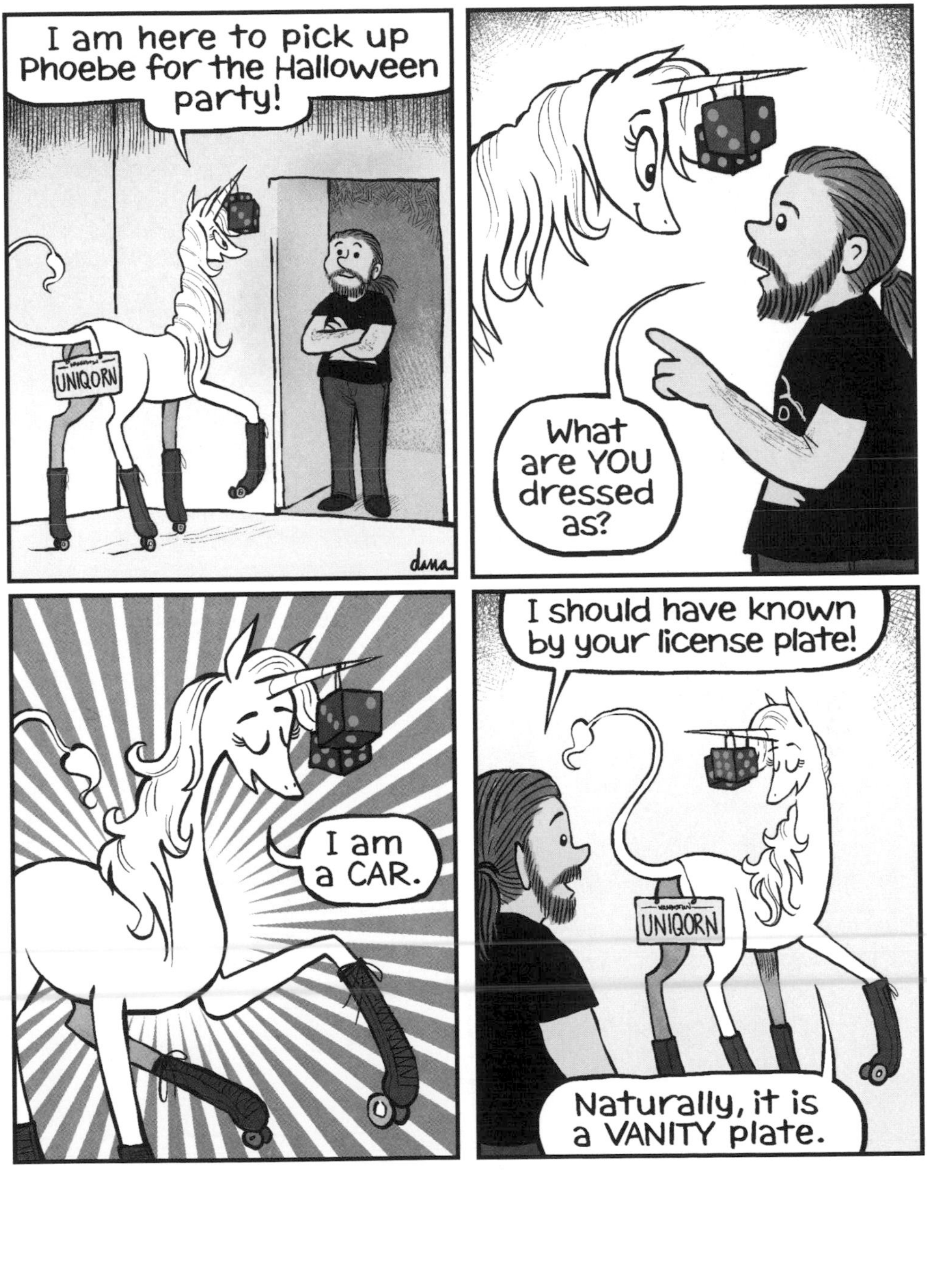
I am here to pick up Phoebe for the Halloween party!
UNIQORN
dana
What are YOU dressed as?
I am a CAR.
I should have known by your license plate!
UNIQORN
Naturally, it is a VANITY plate.

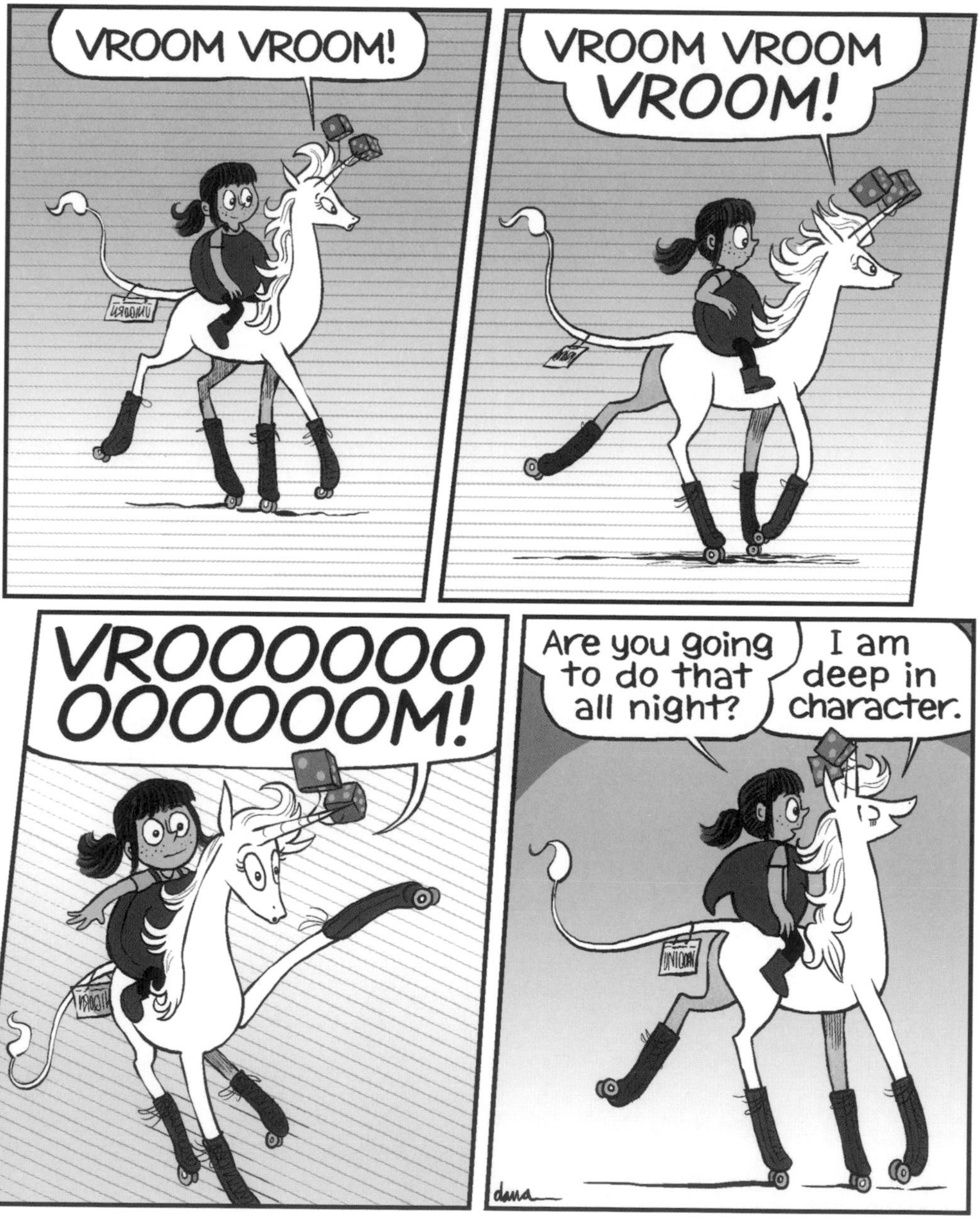
VROOM VROOM!
VROOM VROOM VROOM!
VROOOOOOOOOOOOOM!
Are you going to do that all night?
I am deep in character.
dana

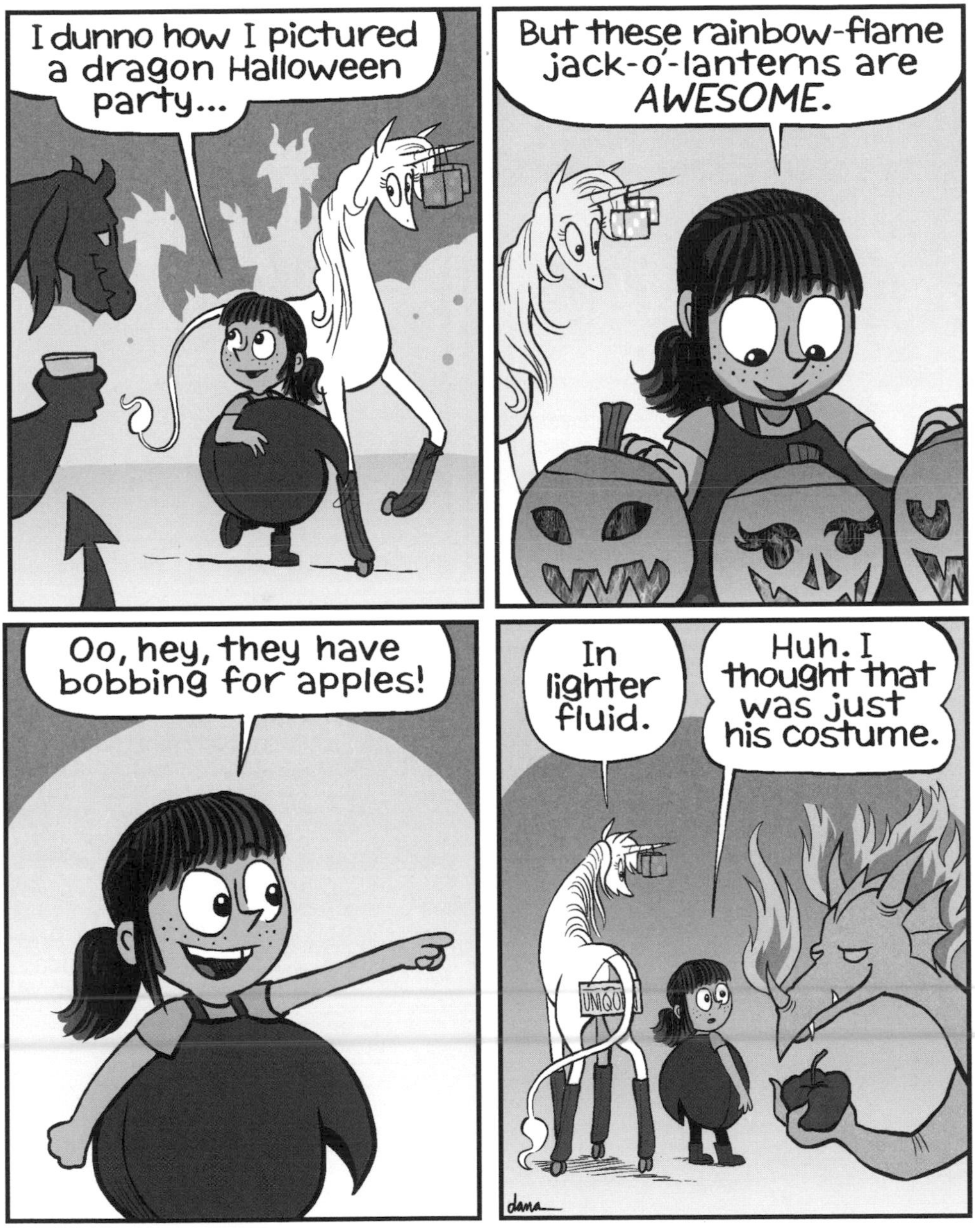
I dunno how I pictured a dragon Halloween party...
But these rainbow-flame jack-o'-lanterns are *AWESOME*.
Oo, hey, they have bobbing for apples!
Huh. I thought that was just his costume.
In lighter fluid.
dana

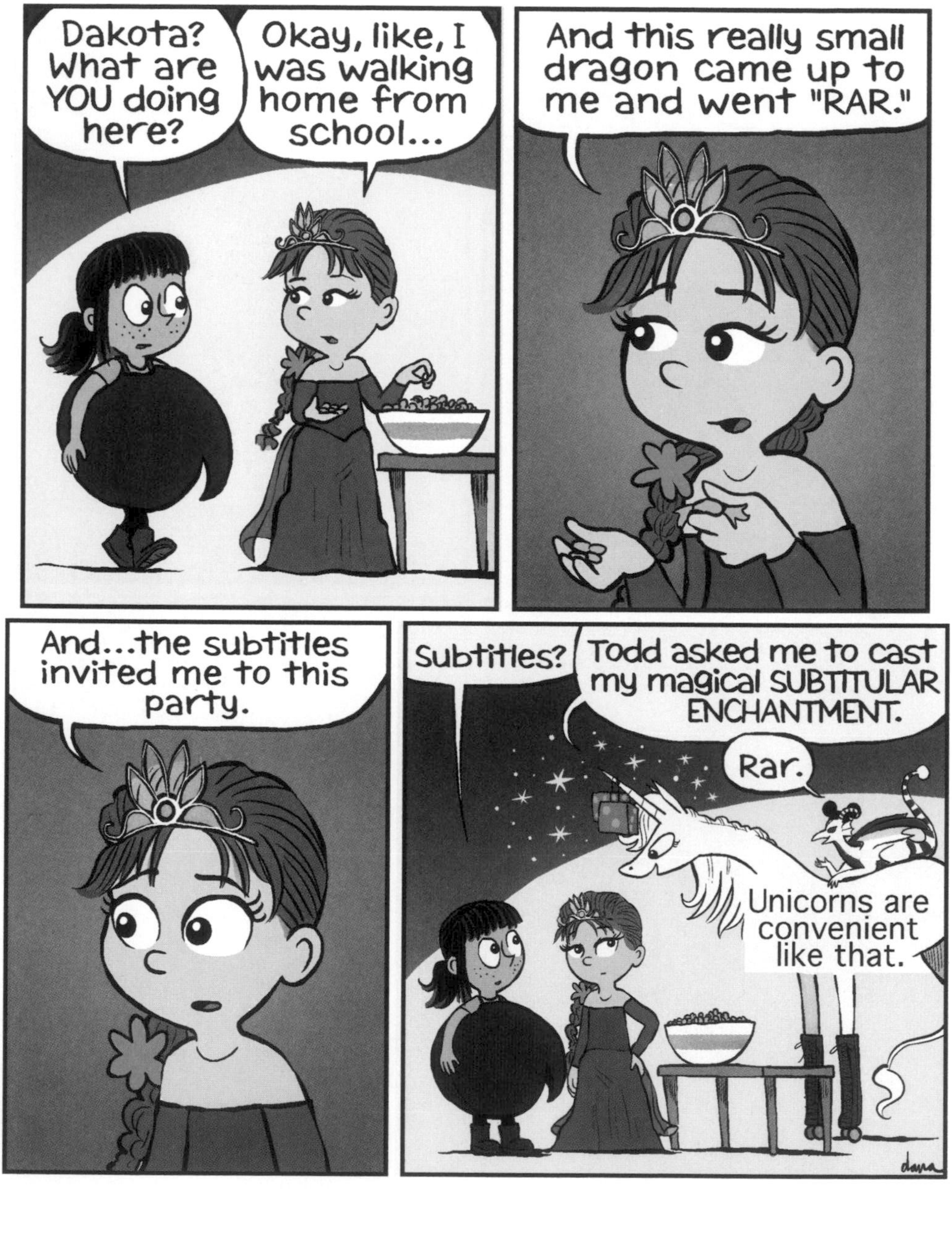

Dakota? What are YOU doing here?
Okay, like, I was walking home from school...
And this really small dragon came up to me and went "RAR."
And...the subtitles invited me to this party.
Subtitles?
Todd asked me to cast my magical SUBTITULAR ENCHANTMENT.
Rar.
Unicorns are convenient like that.

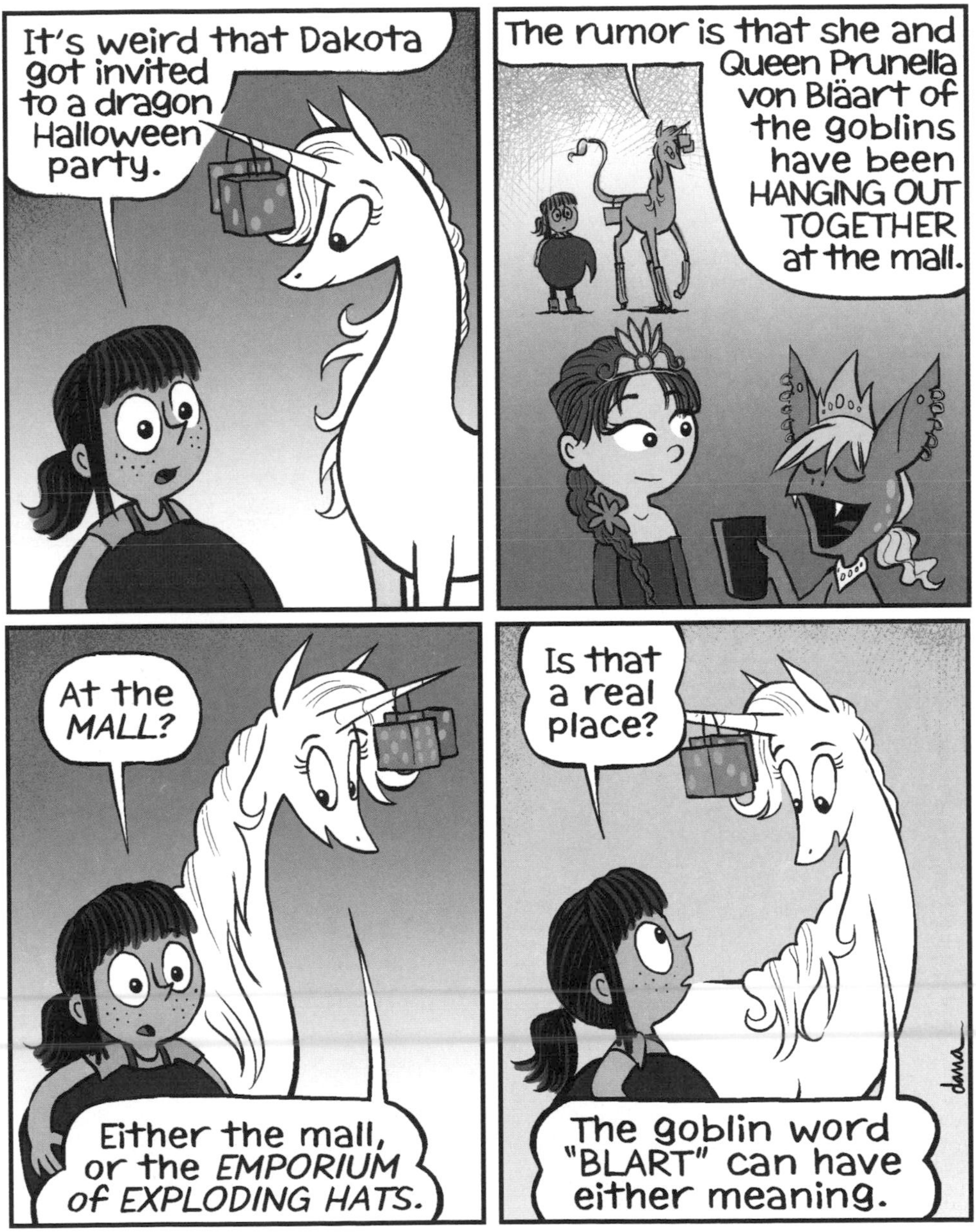

It's weird that Dakota got invited to a dragon Halloween party.
The rumor is that she and Queen Prunella von Bläart of the goblins have been HANGING OUT TOGETHER at the mall.
At the MALL?
Either the mall, or the EMPORIUM of EXPLODING HATS.
Is that a real place?
The goblin word "BLART" can have either meaning.
dana

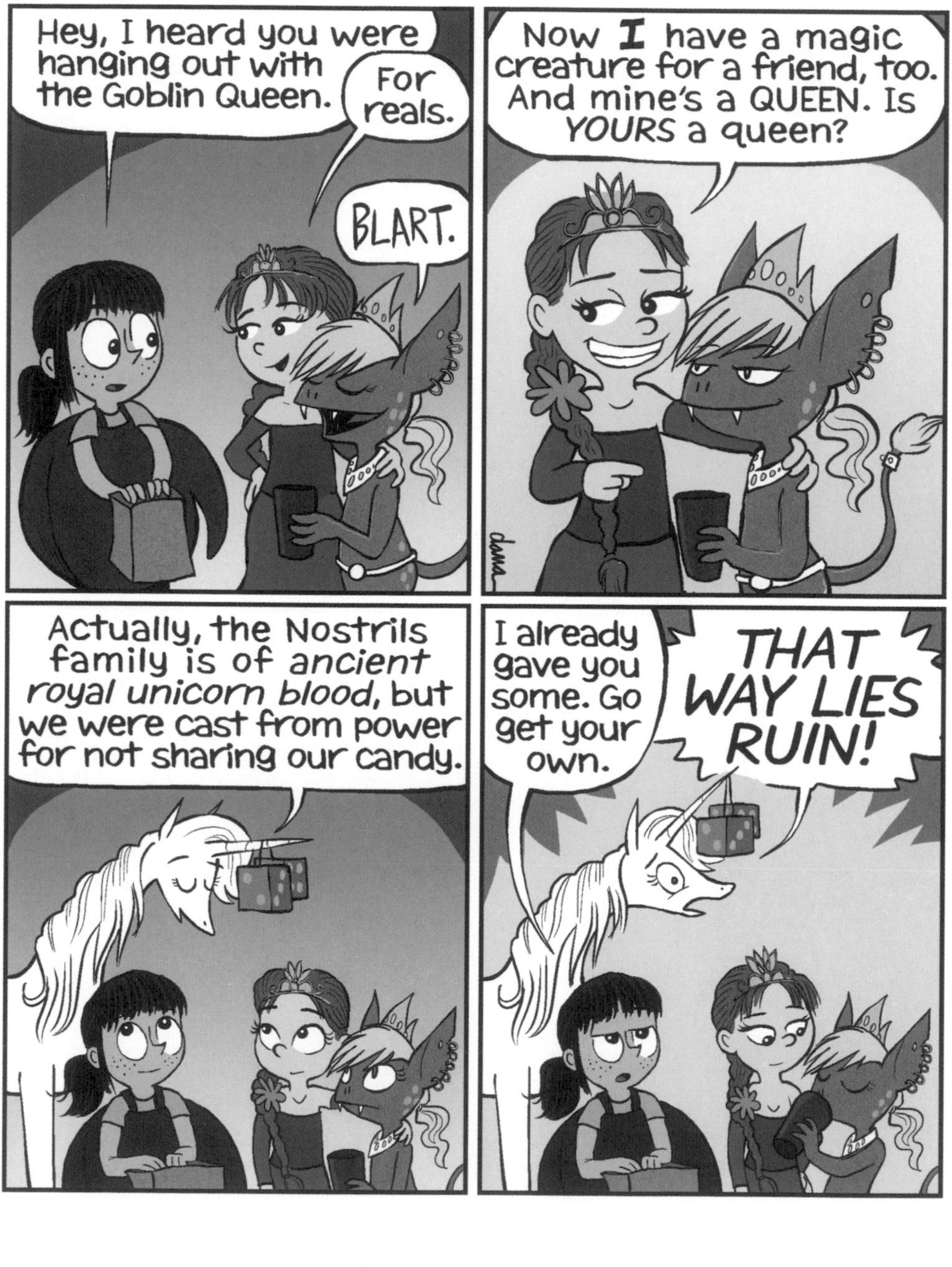
Hey, I heard you were hanging out with the Goblin Queen.
For reals.
BLART.
Now I have a magic creature for a friend, too. And mine's a QUEEN. Is YOURS a queen?
Actually, the Nostrils family is of ancient royal unicorn blood, but we were cast from power for not sharing our candy.
I already gave you some. Go get your own.
THAT WAY LIES RUIN!

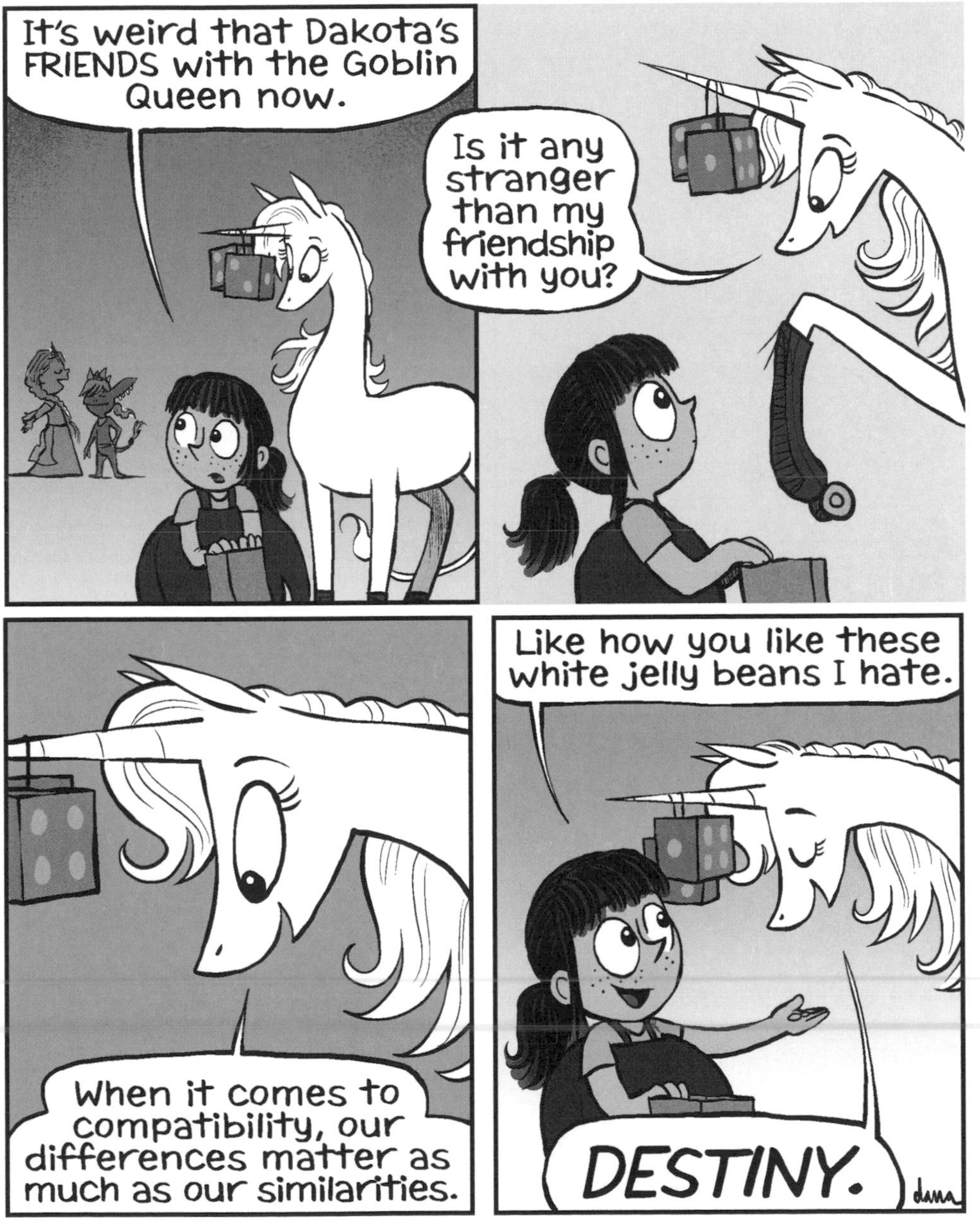
It's weird that Dakota's FRIENDS with the Goblin Queen now.
Is it any stranger than my friendship with you?
When it comes to compatibility, our differences matter as much as our similarities.
Like how you like these white jelly beans I hate.
DESTINY.
dana

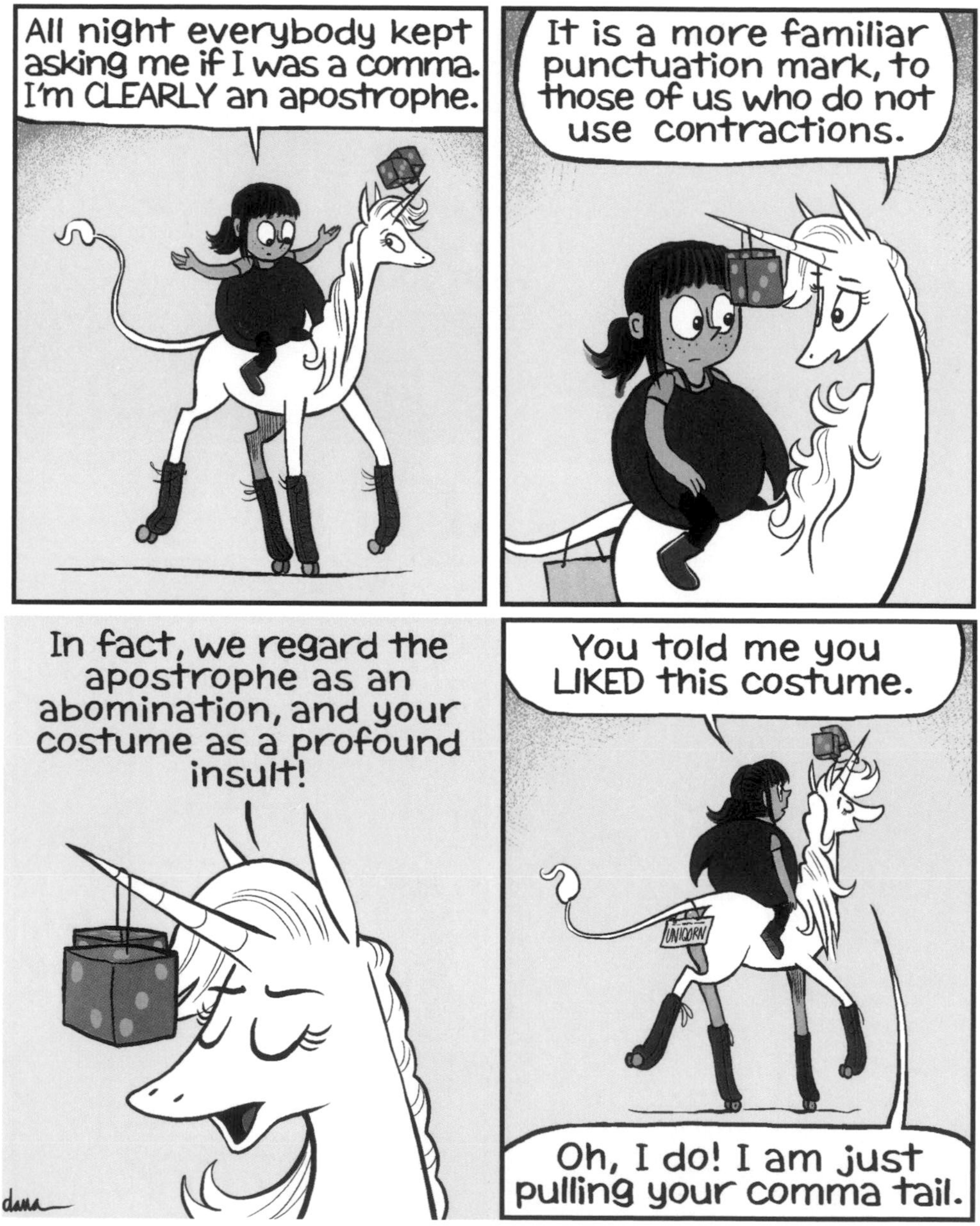
All night everybody kept asking me if I was a comma. I'm CLEARLY an apostrophe.
It is a more familiar punctuation mark, to those of us who do not use contractions.
In fact, we regard the apostrophe as an abomination, and your costume as a profound insult!
You told me you LIKED this costume.
UNICORN
Oh, I do! I am just pulling your comma tail.
dana

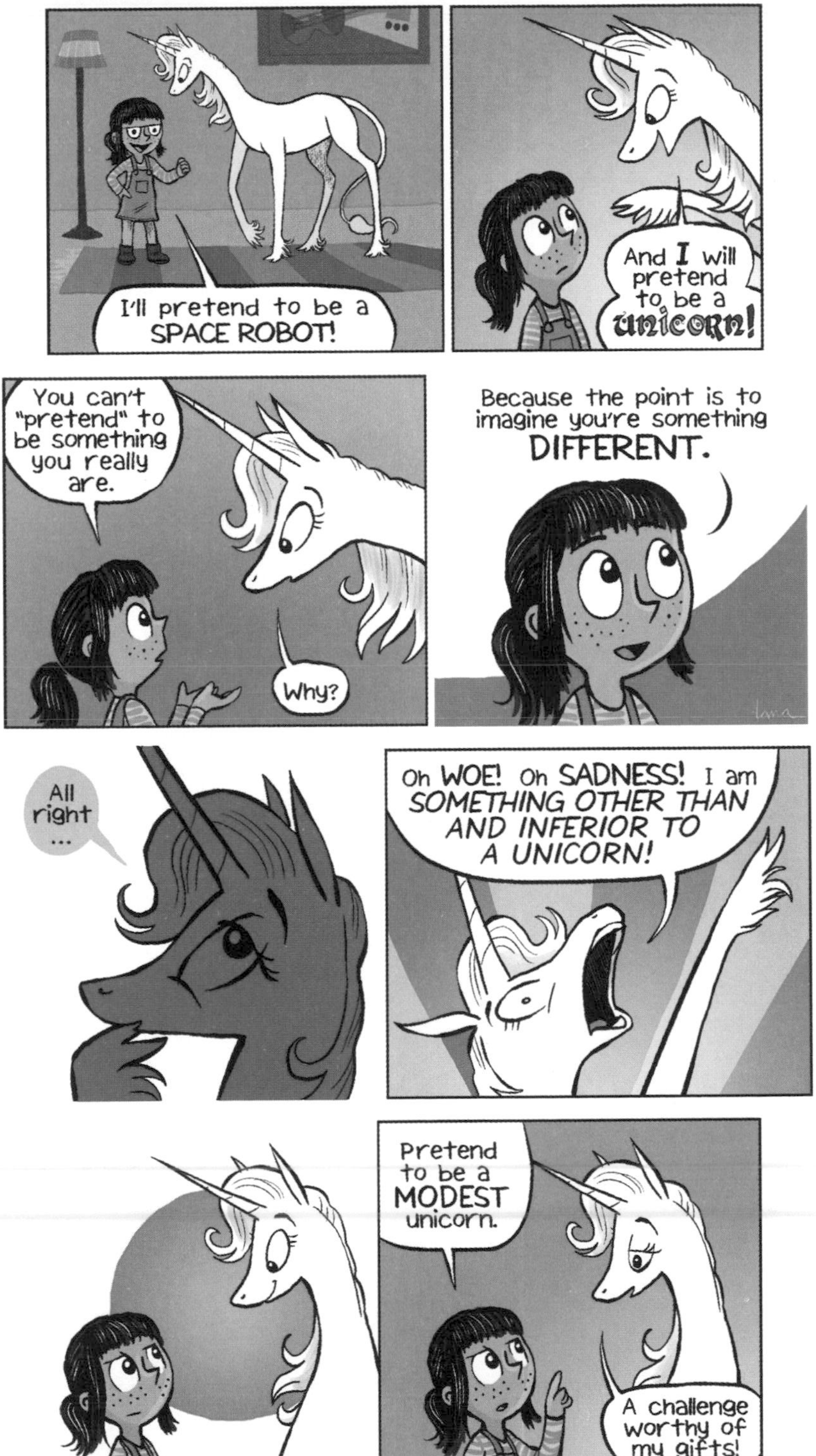

I'll pretend to be a SPACE ROBOT!
And I will pretend to be a UNICORN!
You can't "pretend" to be something you really are.
Why?
Because the point is to imagine you're something DIFFERENT.
All right ...
Oh WOE! Oh SADNESS! I am SOMETHING OTHER THAN AND INFERIOR TO A UNICORN!
Pretend to be a MODEST unicorn.
A challenge worthy of my gifts!

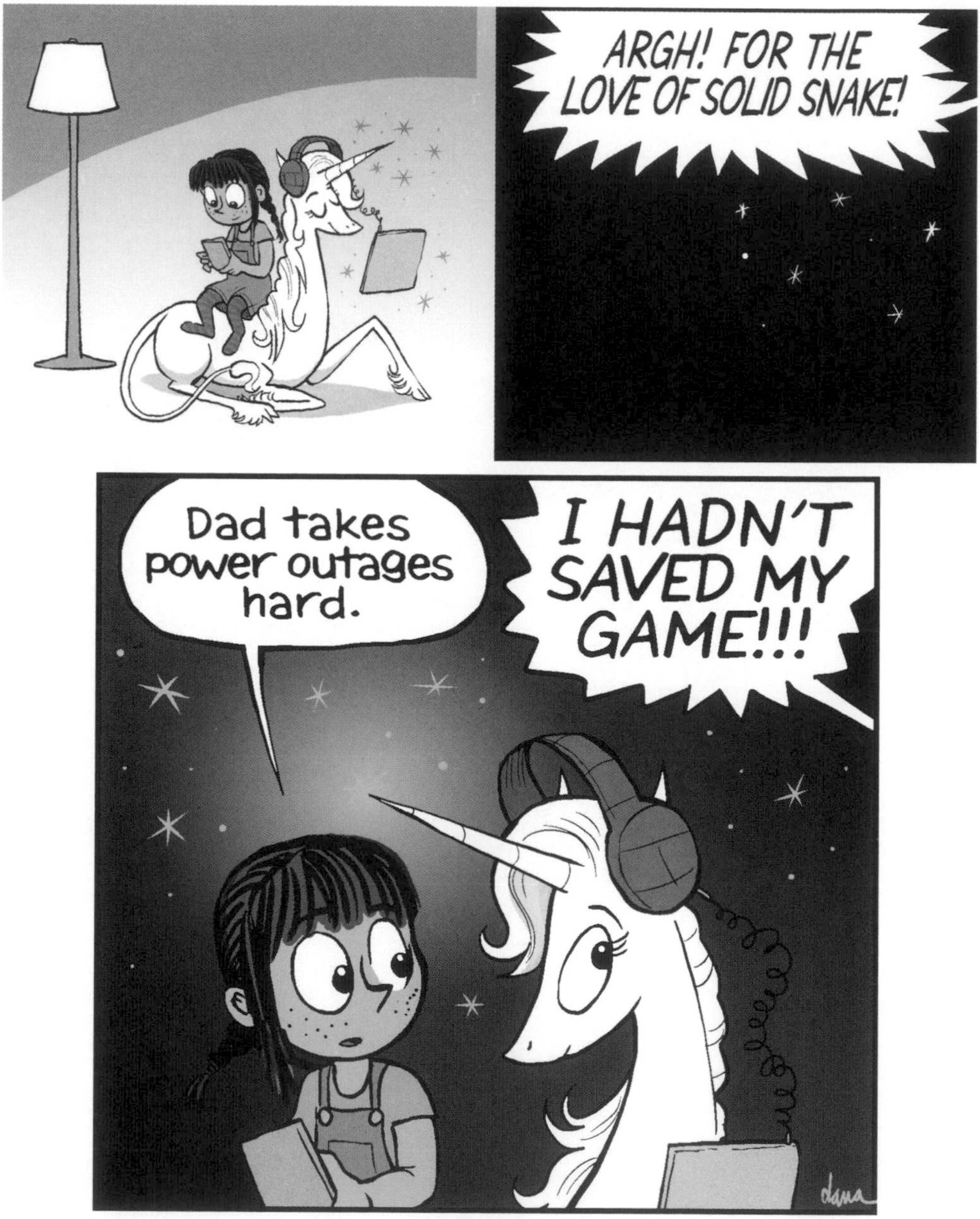
ARGH! FOR THE LOVE OF SOLID SNAKE!
Dad takes power outages hard.
I HADN'T SAVED MY GAME!!!
dana

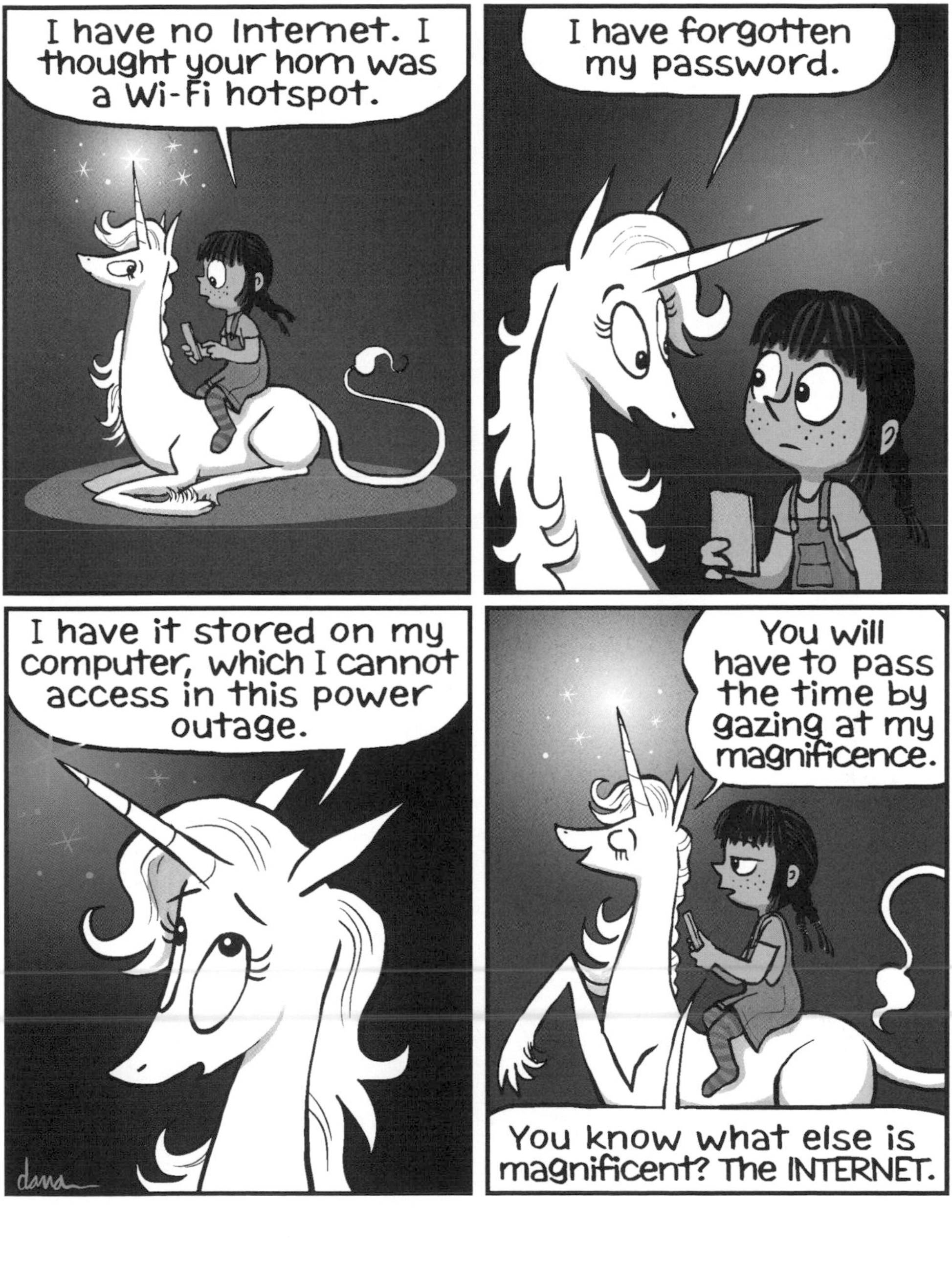
I have no Internet. I thought your horn was a Wi-Fi hotspot.
I have forgotten my password.
I have it stored on my computer, which I cannot access in this power outage.
You will have to pass the time by gazing at my magnificence.
You know what else is magnificent? The INTERNET.
dana

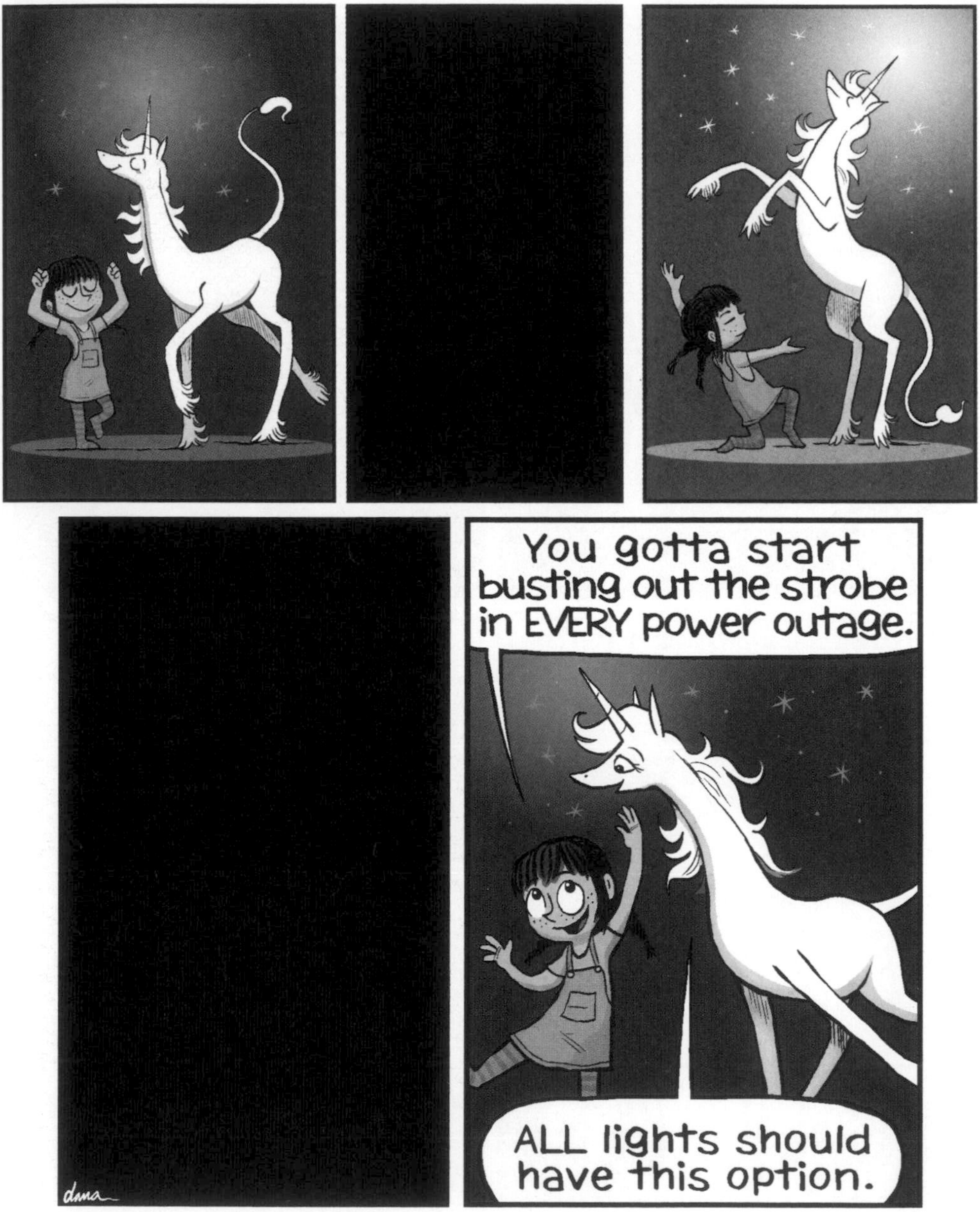
You gotta start busting out the strobe in EVERY power outage.
ALL lights should have this option.
dana

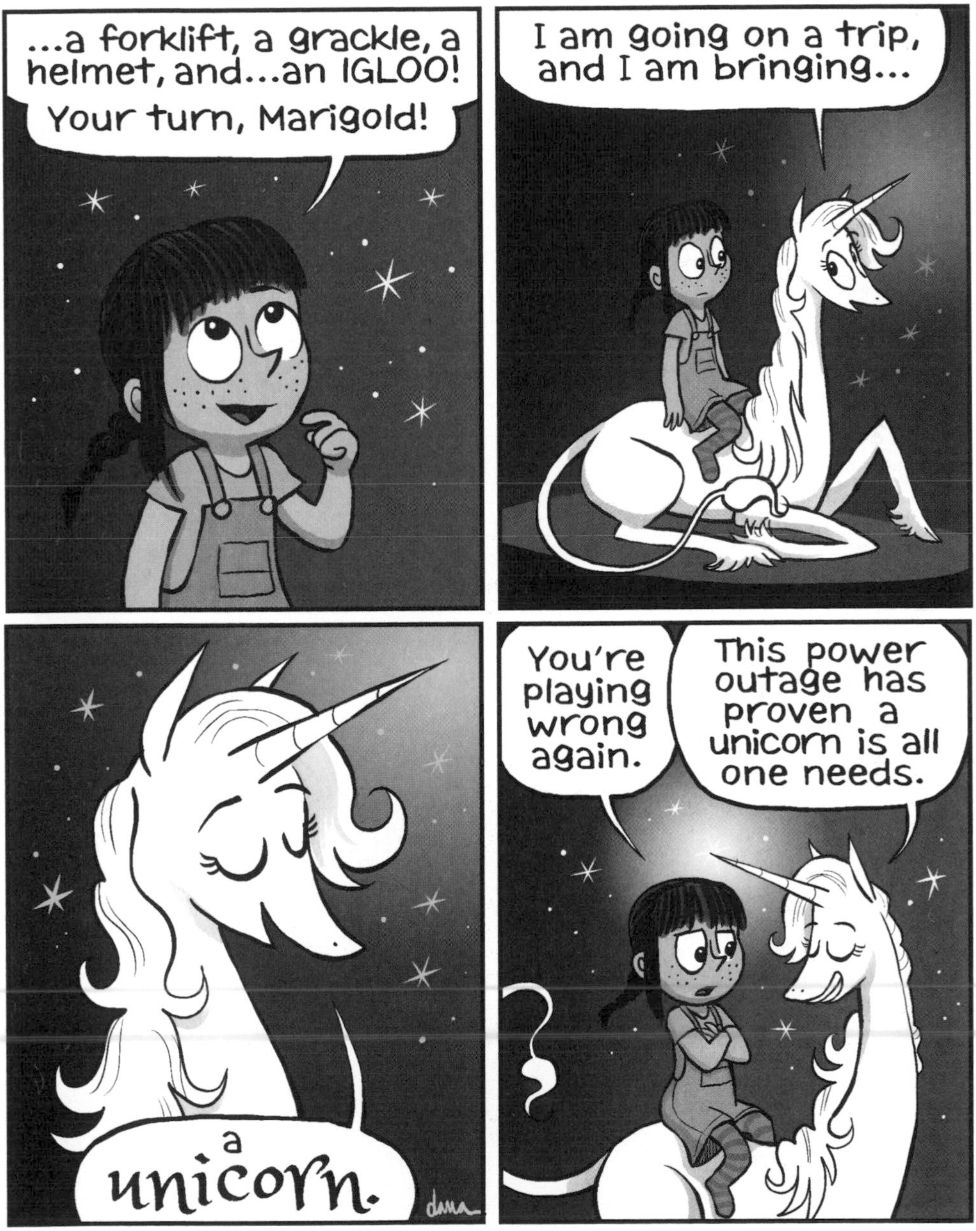
...a forklift, a grackle, a helmet, and...an IGLOO!
Your turn, Marigold!
I am going on a trip, and I am bringing...
a unicorn.
You're playing wrong again.
This power outage has proven a unicorn is all one needs.
dana

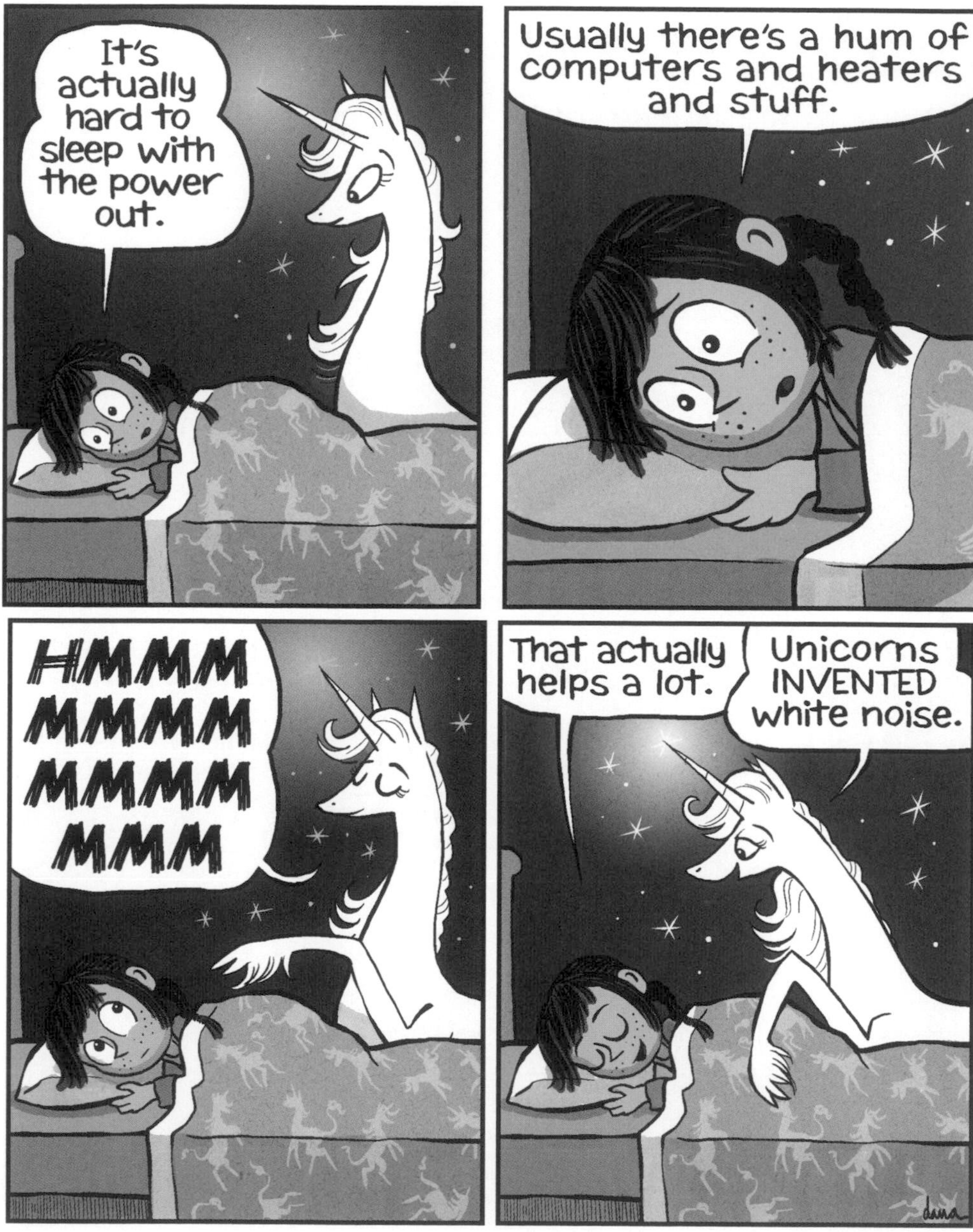
It's actually hard to sleep with the power out.
Usually there's a hum of computers and heaters and stuff.
HMMM MMMM MMMM MMM
That actually helps a lot.
Unicorns INVENTED white noise.
dana

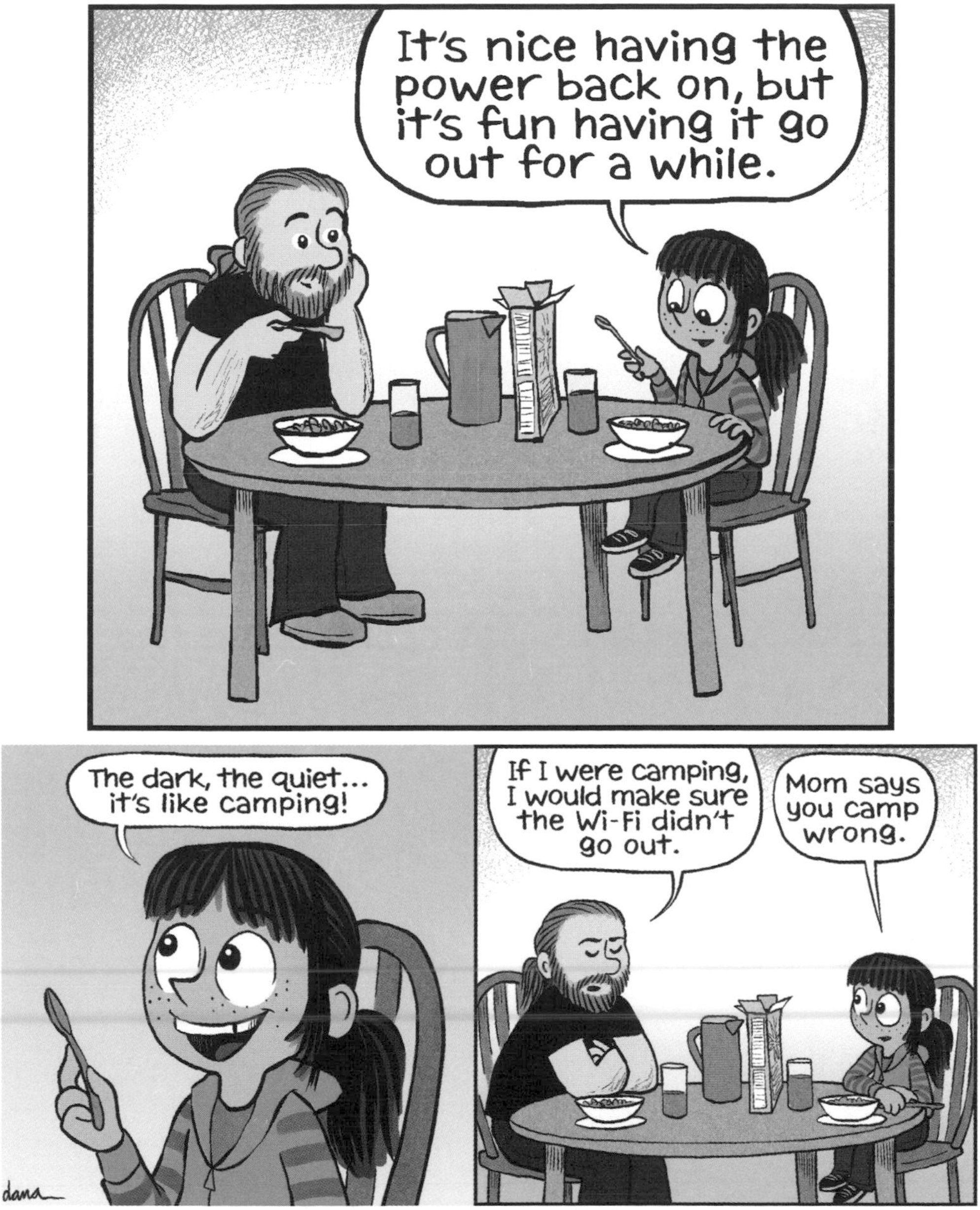
It's nice having the power back on, but it's fun having it go out for a while.
The dark, the quiet... it's like camping!
dana
If I were camping, I would make sure the Wi-Fi didn't go out.
Mom says you camp wrong.

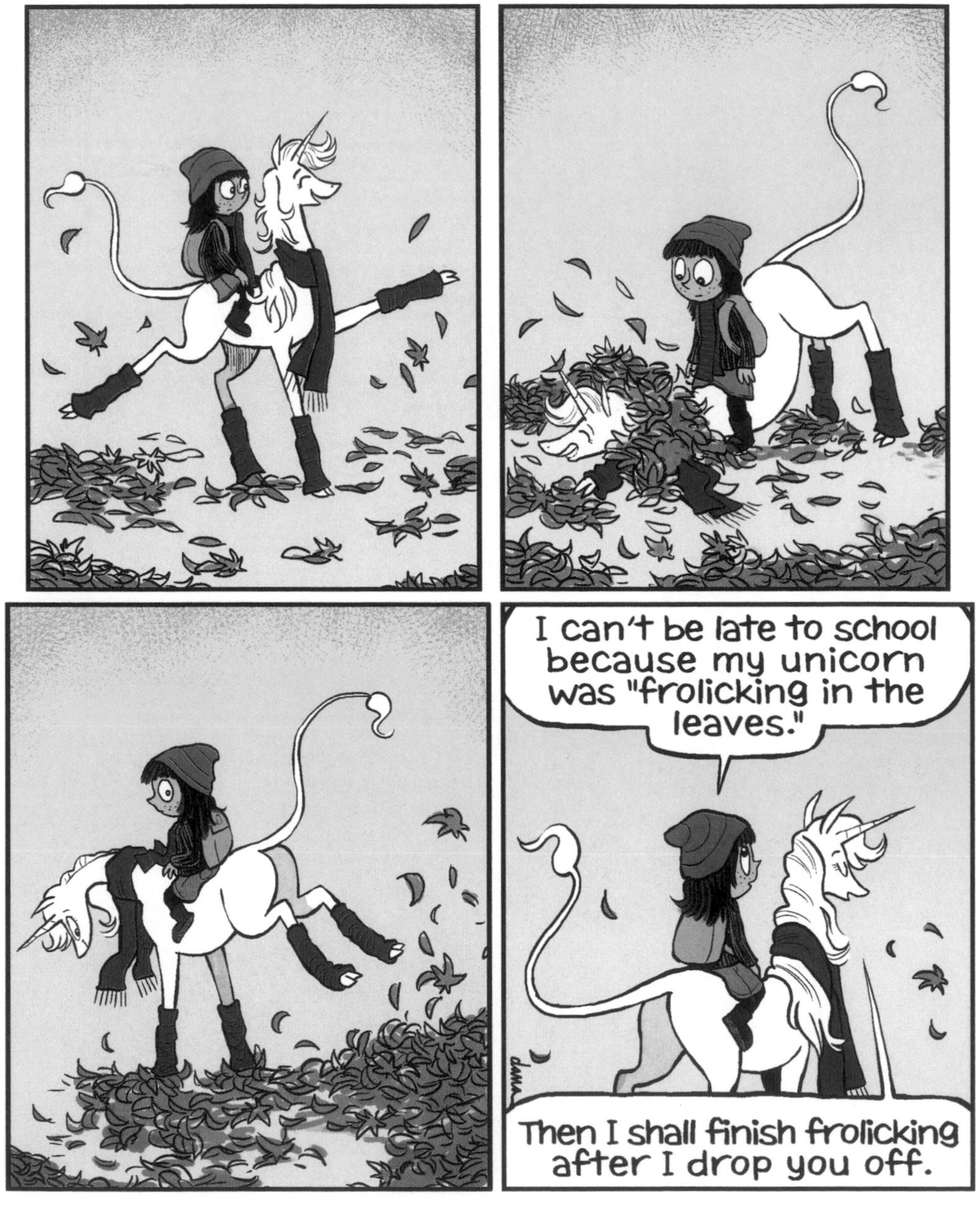
I can't be late to school because my unicorn was "frolicking in the leaves."
Then I shall finish frolicking after I drop you off.

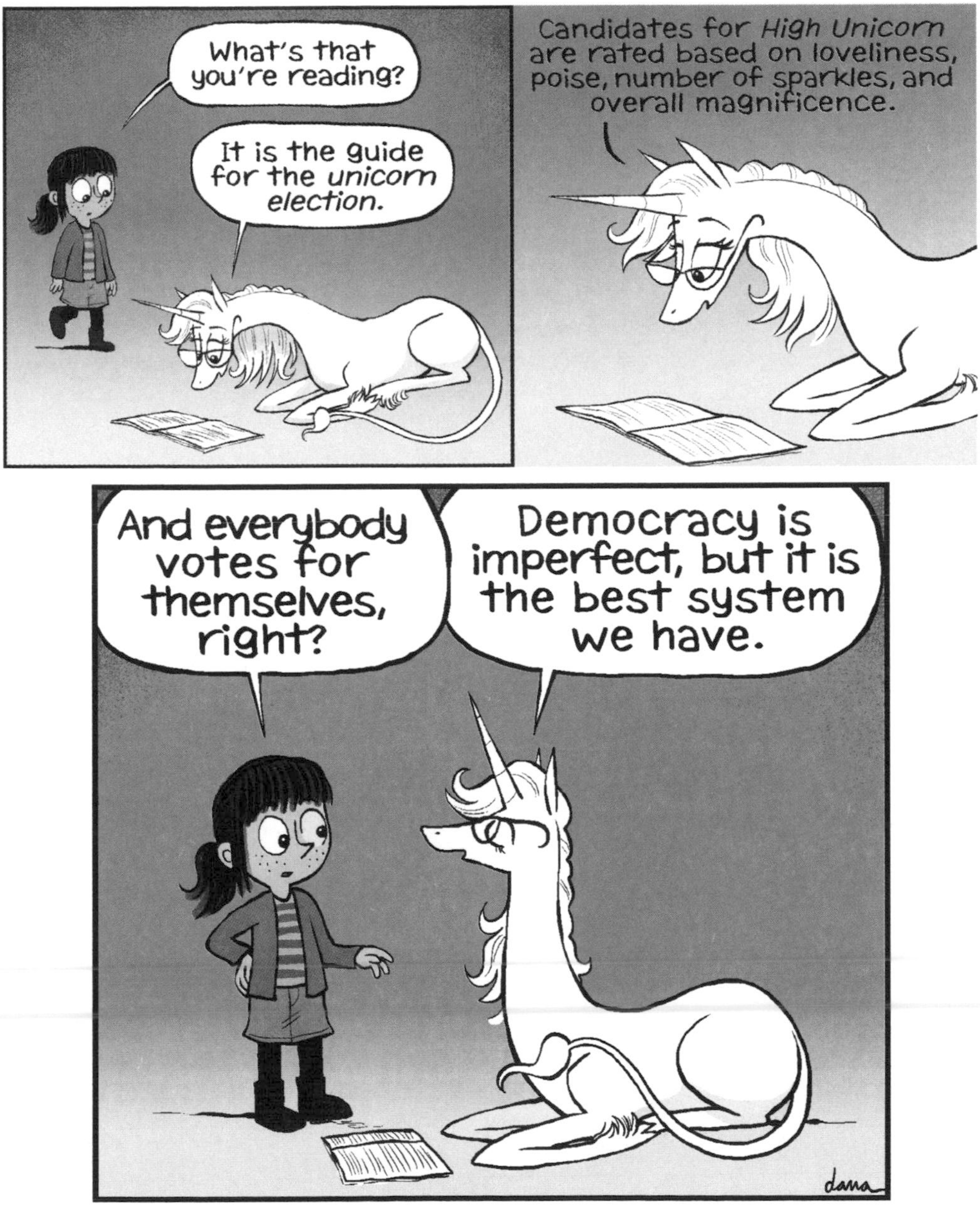
What's that you're reading?
It is the guide for the *unicorn election.*
Candidates for *High Unicorn* are rated based on loveliness, poise, number of sparkles, and overall magnificence.
And everybody votes for themselves, right?
Democracy is imperfect, but it is the best system we have.
dana

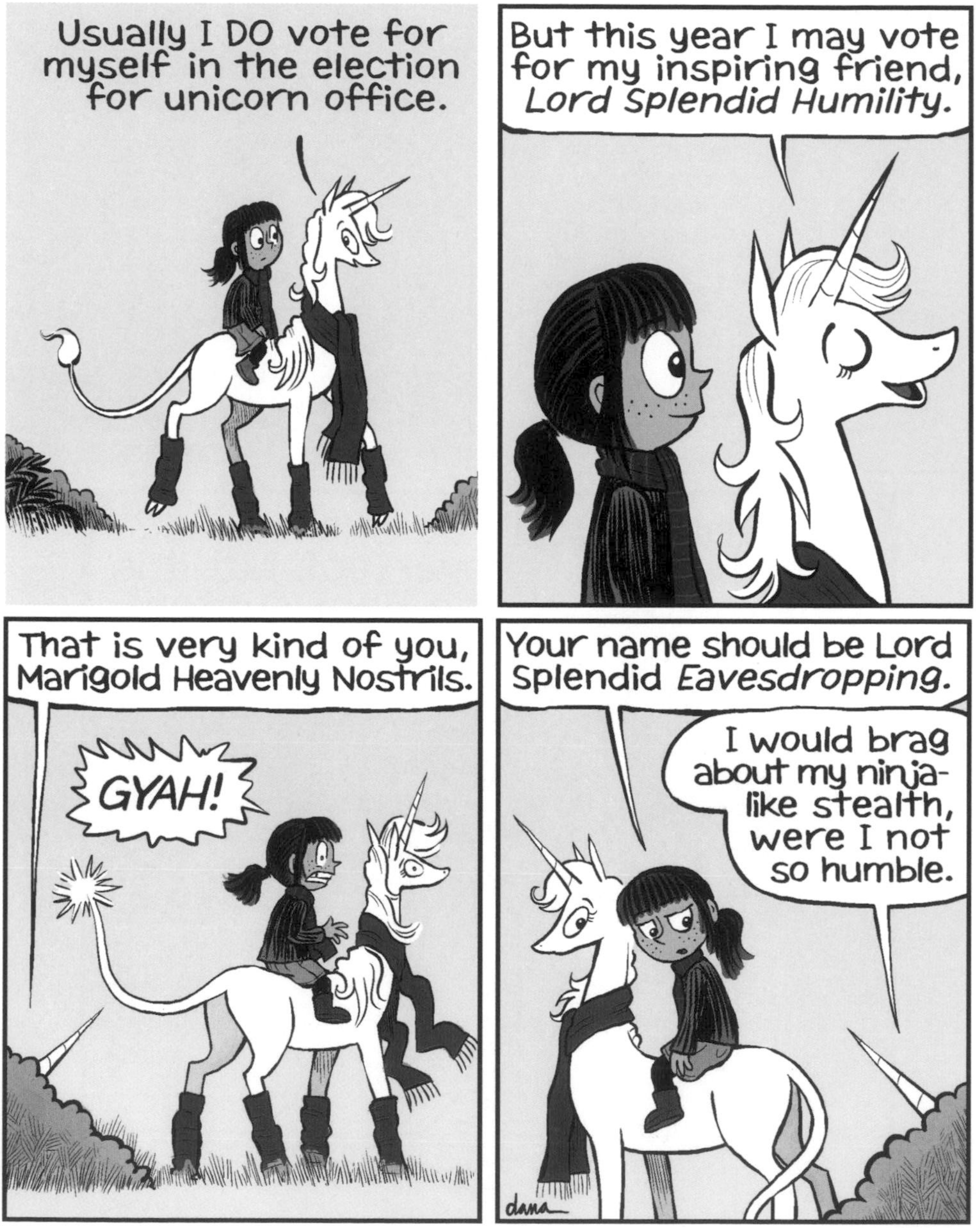
Usually I DO vote for myself in the election for unicorn office.
But this year I may vote for my inspiring friend, *Lord Splendid Humility*.
That is very kind of you, Marigold Heavenly Nostrils.
GYAH!
Your name should be Lord Splendid *Eavesdropping*.
I would brag about my ninja-like stealth, were I not so humble.
dana

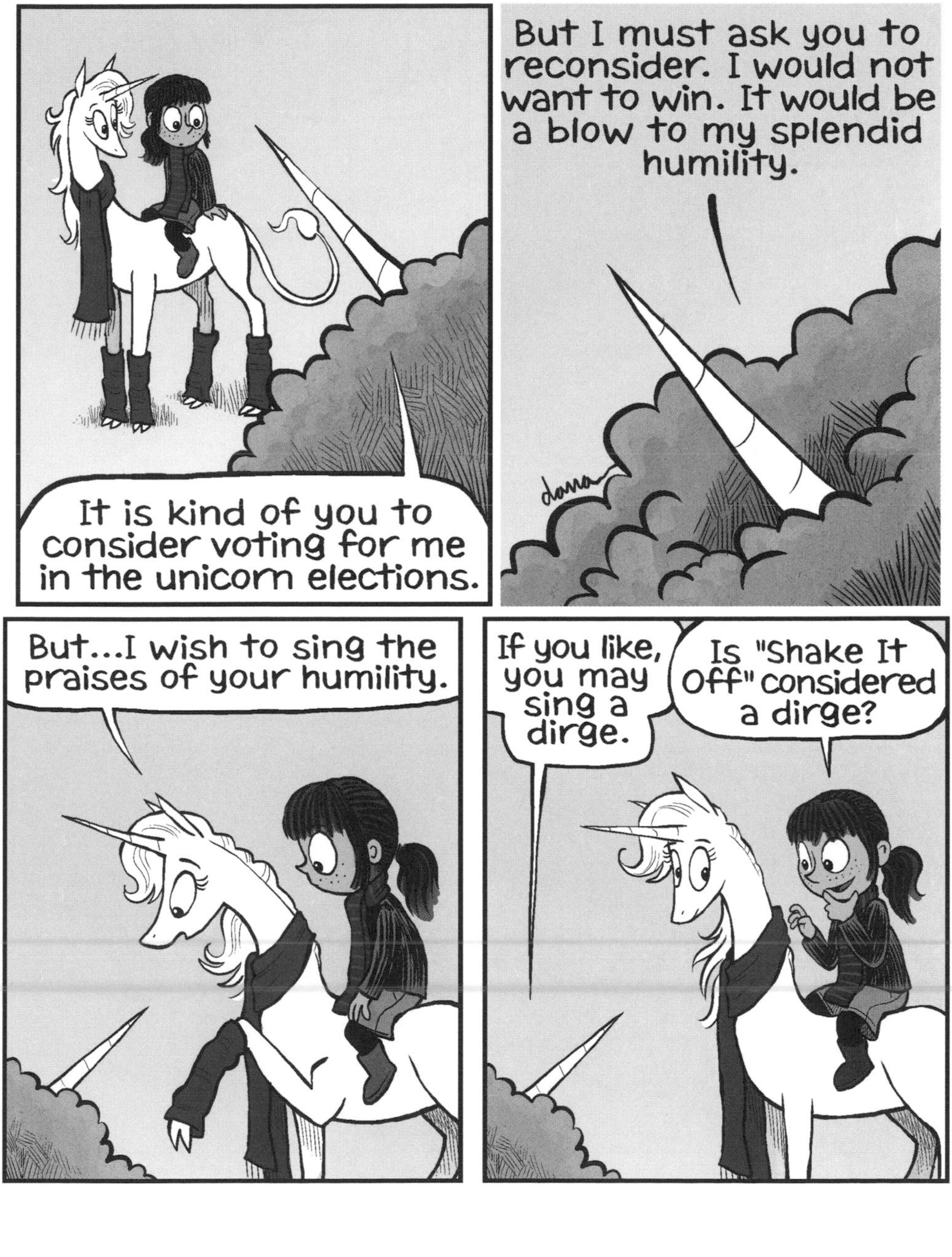
It is kind of you to consider voting for me in the unicorn elections.
But I must ask you to reconsider. I would not want to win. It would be a blow to my splendid humility.
dana
But...I wish to sing the praises of your humility.
If you like, you may sing a dirge.
Is "Shake It Off" considered a dirge?

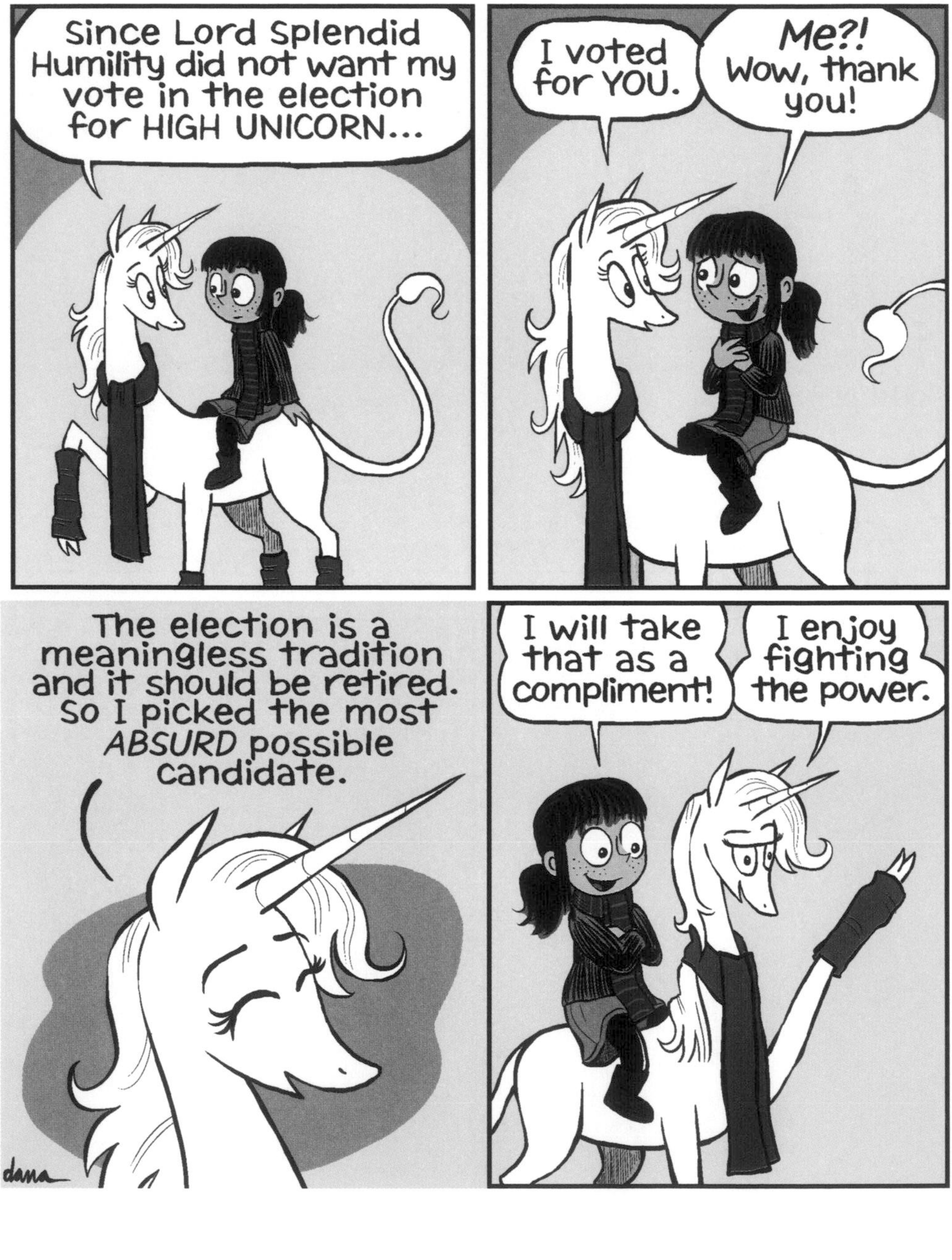
Since Lord Splendid Humility did not want my vote in the election for HIGH UNICORN...
I voted for YOU.
Me?! Wow, thank you!
The election is a meaningless tradition and it should be retired. So I picked the most *ABSURD* possible candidate.
I will take that as a compliment!
I enjoy fighting the power.
dana

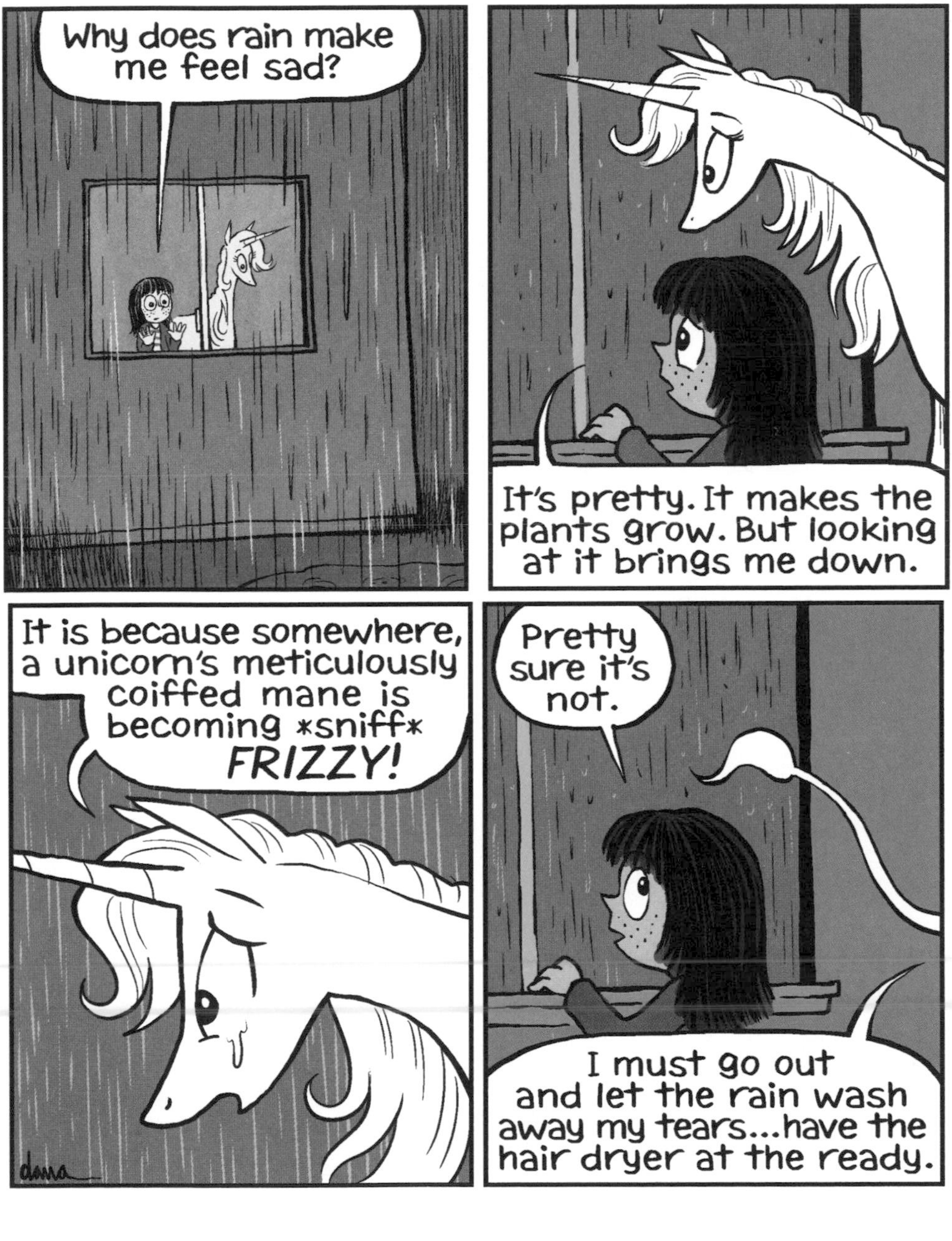
Why does rain make me feel sad?
It's pretty. It makes the plants grow. But looking at it brings me down.
It is because somewhere, a unicorn's meticulously coiffed mane is becoming *sniff* FRIZZY!
Pretty sure it's not.
I must go out and let the rain wash away my tears...have the hair dryer at the ready.

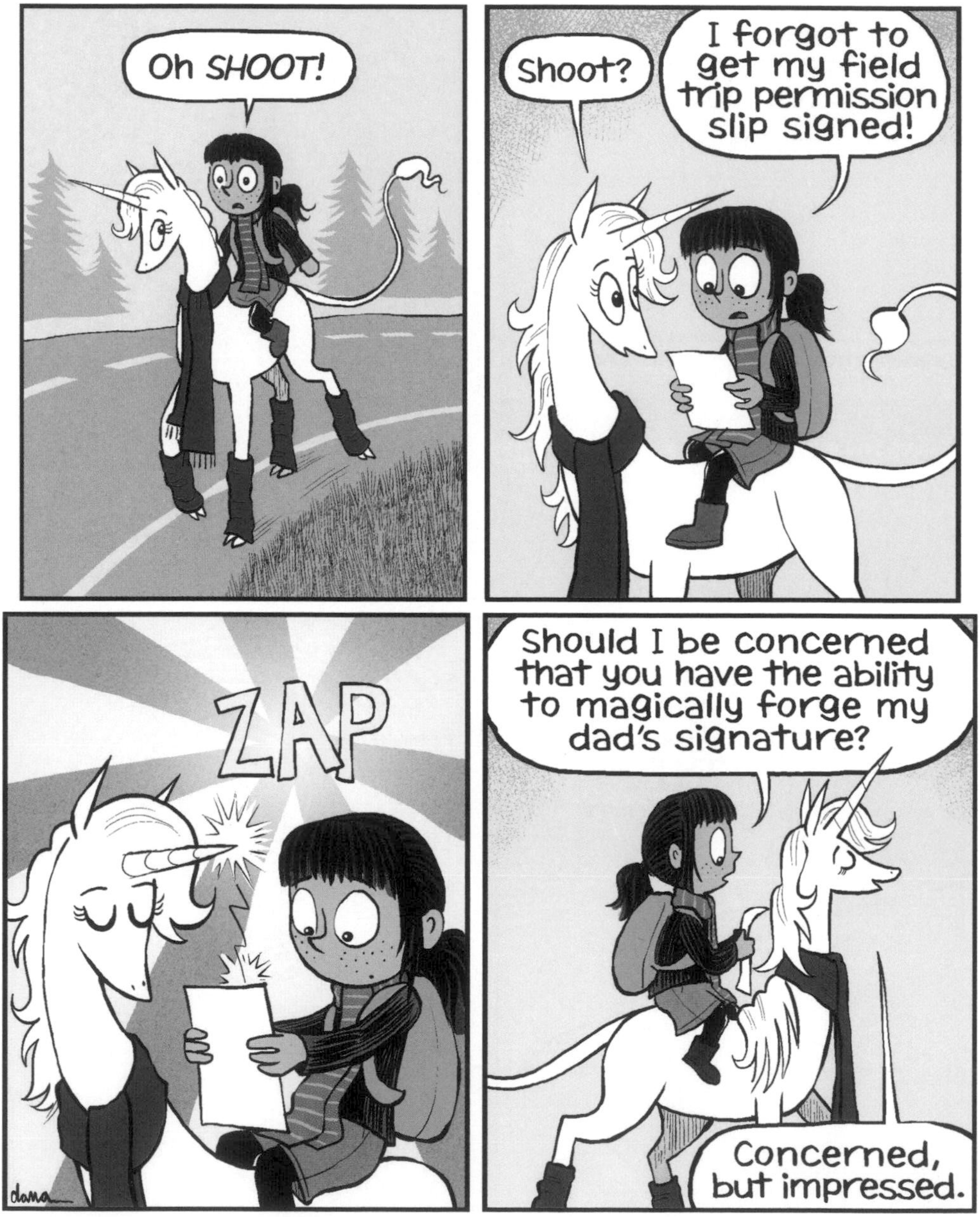
Oh SHOOT!
Shoot?
I forgot to get my field trip permission slip signed!
ZAP
Should I be concerned that you have the ability to magically forge my dad's signature?
Concerned, but impressed.
dana

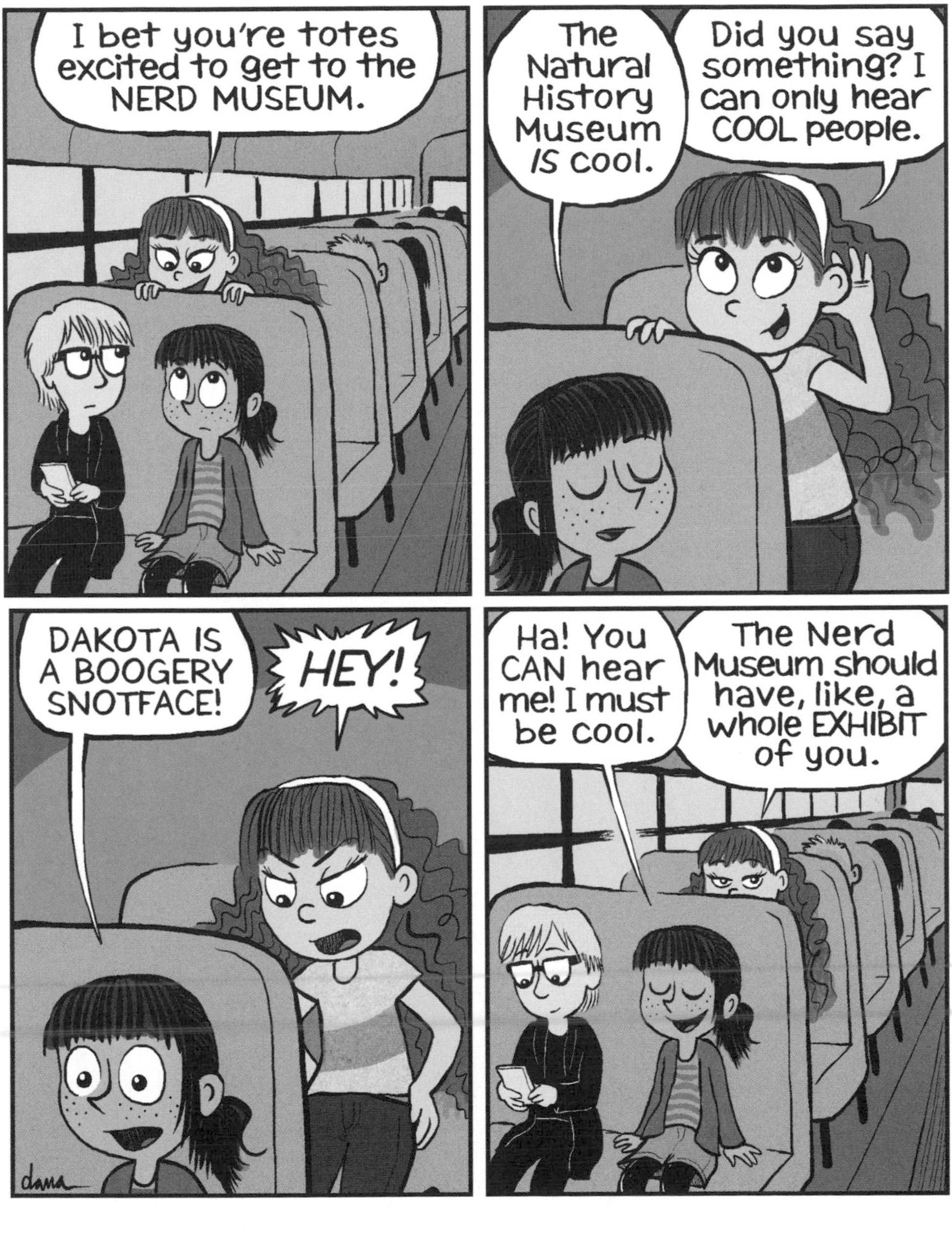
I bet you're totes excited to get to the NERD MUSEUM.
The Natural History Museum *IS* cool.
Did you say something? I can only hear COOL people.
DAKOTA IS A BOOGERY SNOTFACE!
HEY!
Ha! You CAN hear me! I must be cool.
The Nerd Museum should have, like, a whole EXHIBIT of you.
dana

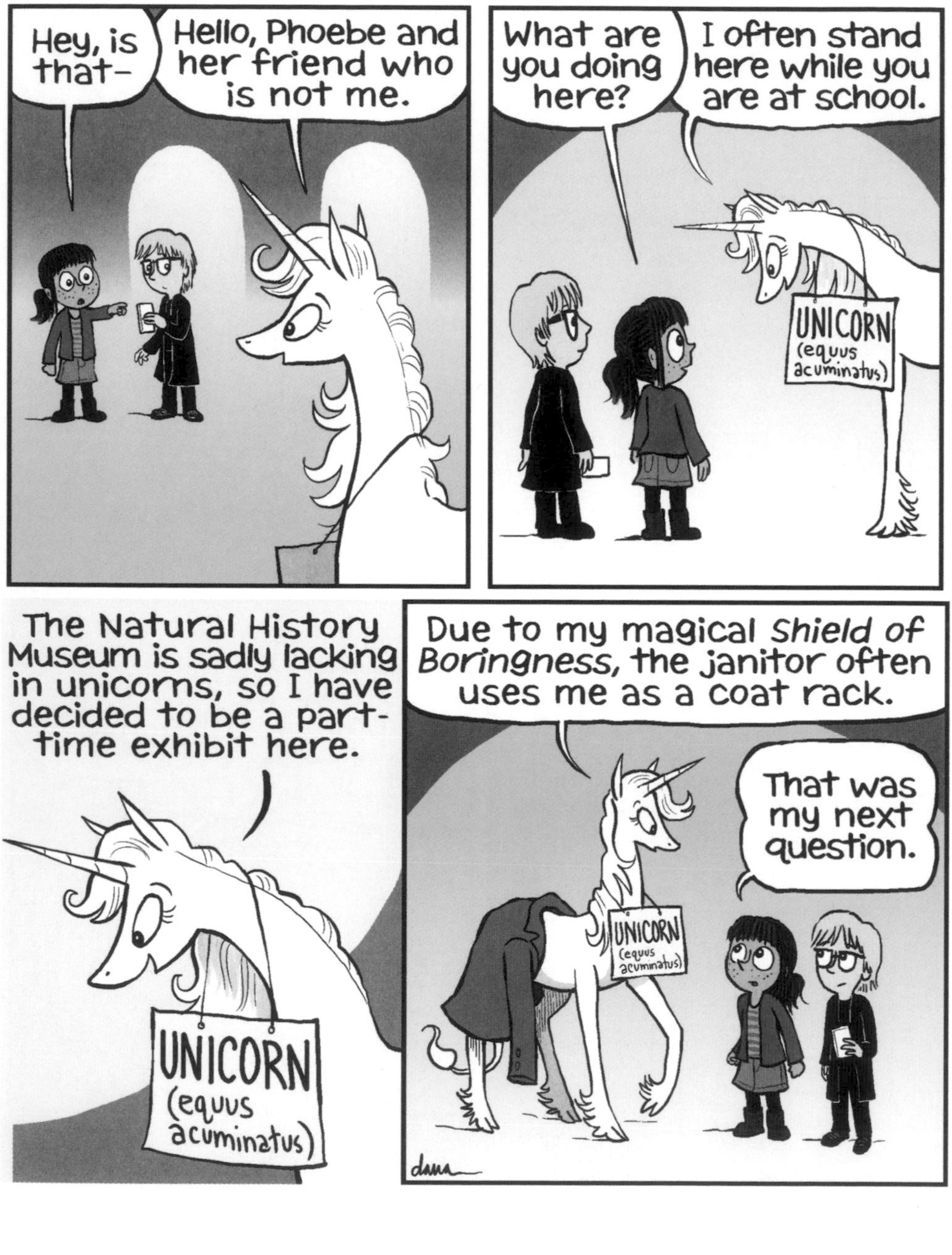
Hey, is that-
Hello, Phoebe and her friend who is not me.
What are you doing here?
I often stand here while you are at school.
UNICORN (equus acuminatus)
The Natural History Museum is sadly lacking in unicorns, so I have decided to be a part-time exhibit here.
UNICORN (equus acuminatus)
Due to my magical *Shield of Boringness,* the janitor often uses me as a coat rack.
UNICORN (equus acuminatus)
That was my next question.
dana

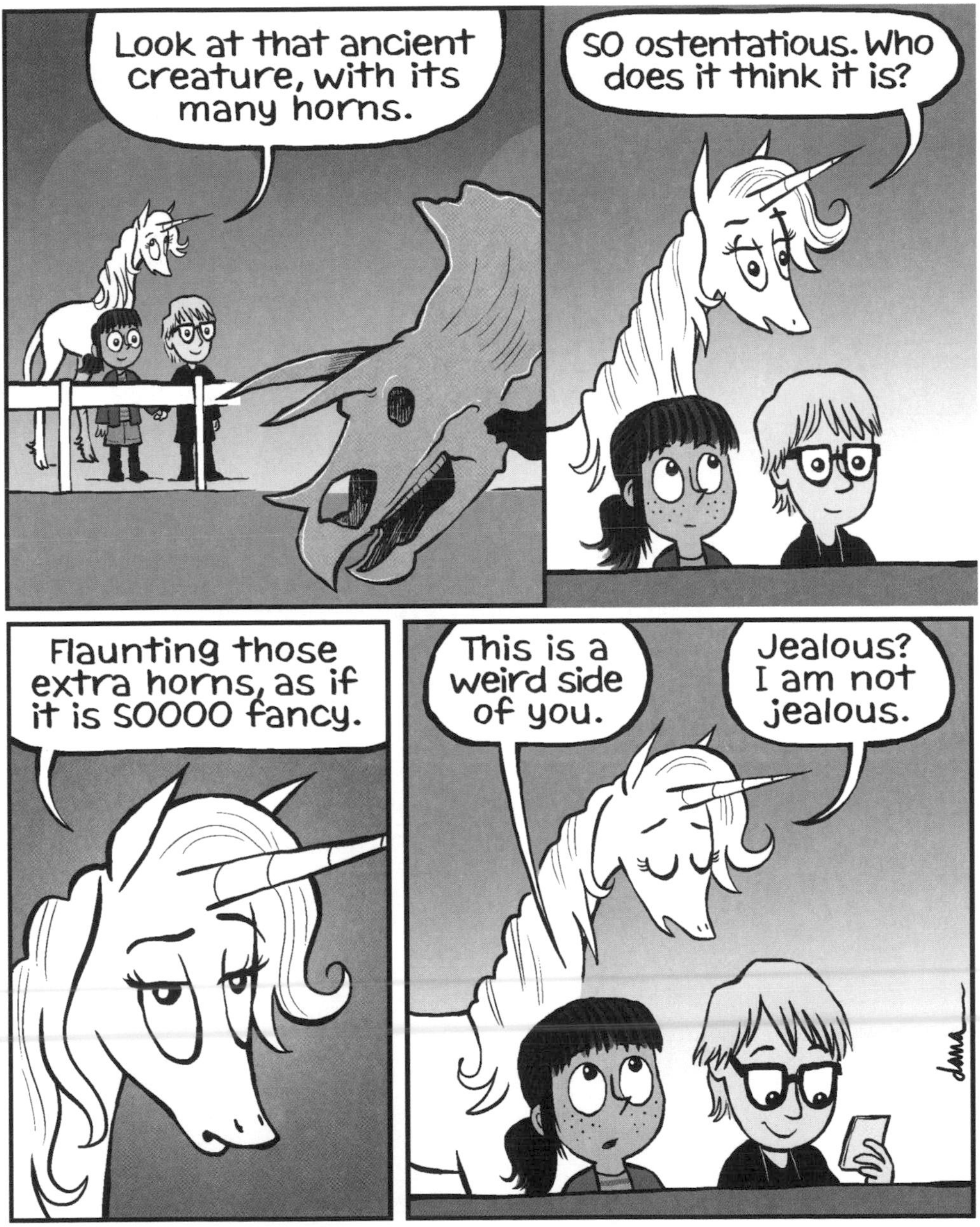
Look at that ancient creature, with its many horns.
SO ostentatious. Who does it think it is?
Flaunting those extra horns, as if it is SOOOO fancy.
This is a weird side of you.
Jealous? I am not jealous.
dana

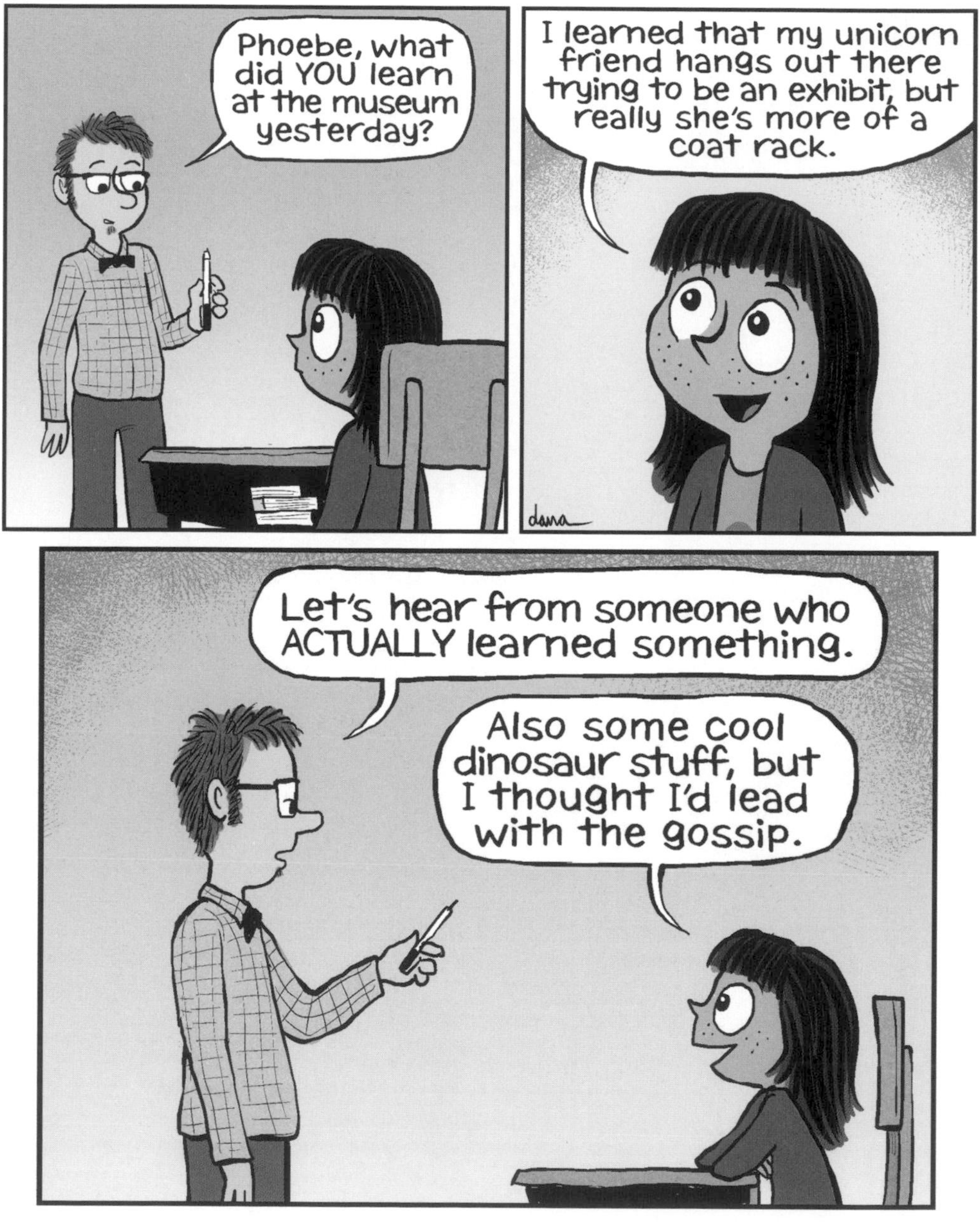
Phoebe, what did YOU learn at the museum yesterday?
I learned that my unicorn friend hangs out there trying to be an exhibit, but really she's more of a coat rack.
dana
Let's hear from someone who ACTUALLY learned something.
Also some cool dinosaur stuff, but I thought I'd lead with the gossip.

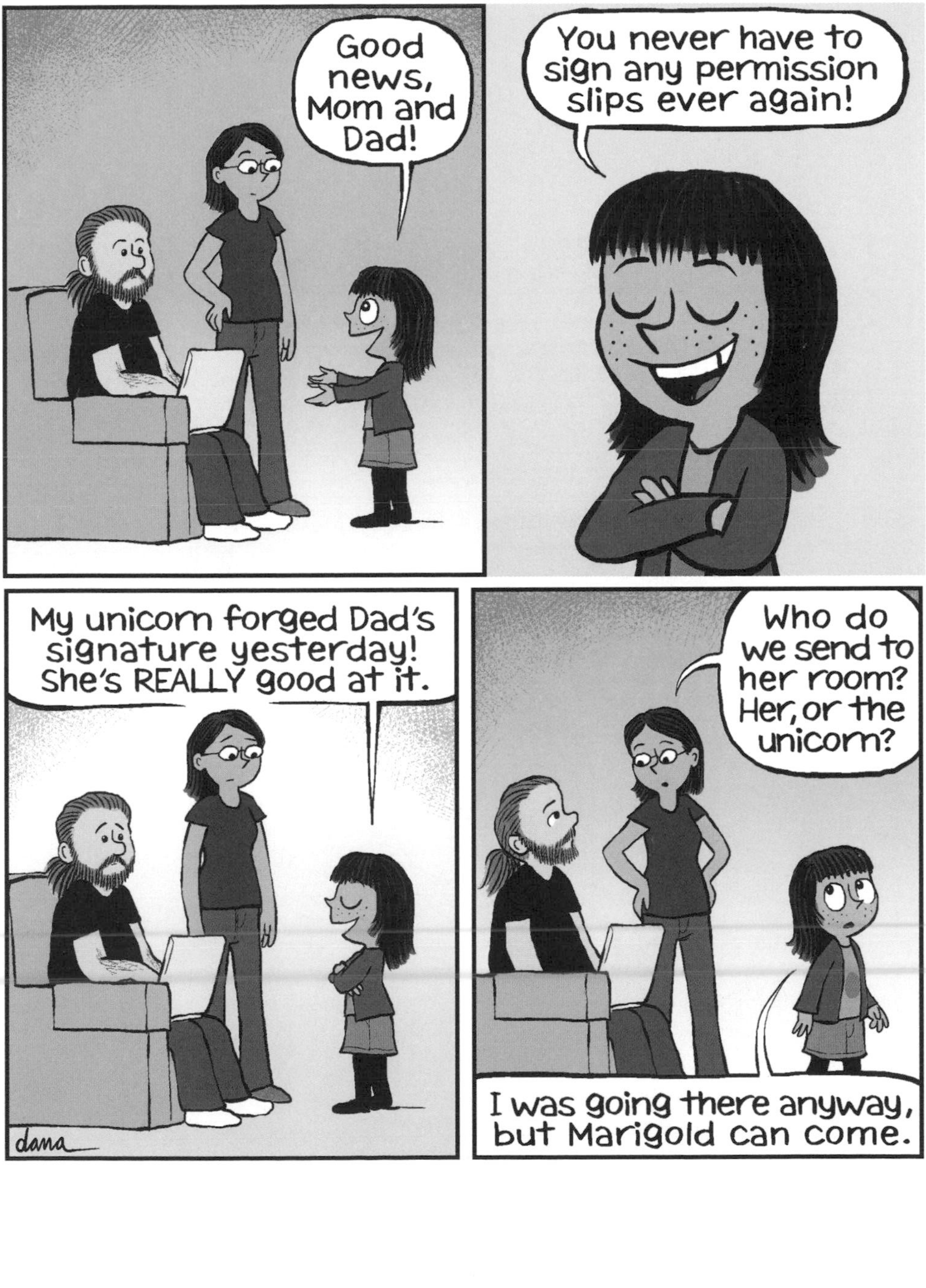
Good news, Mom and Dad!
You never have to sign any permission slips ever again!
My unicorn forged Dad's signature yesterday! She's REALLY good at it.
dana
Who do we send to her room? Her, or the unicorn?
I was going there anyway, but Marigold can come.

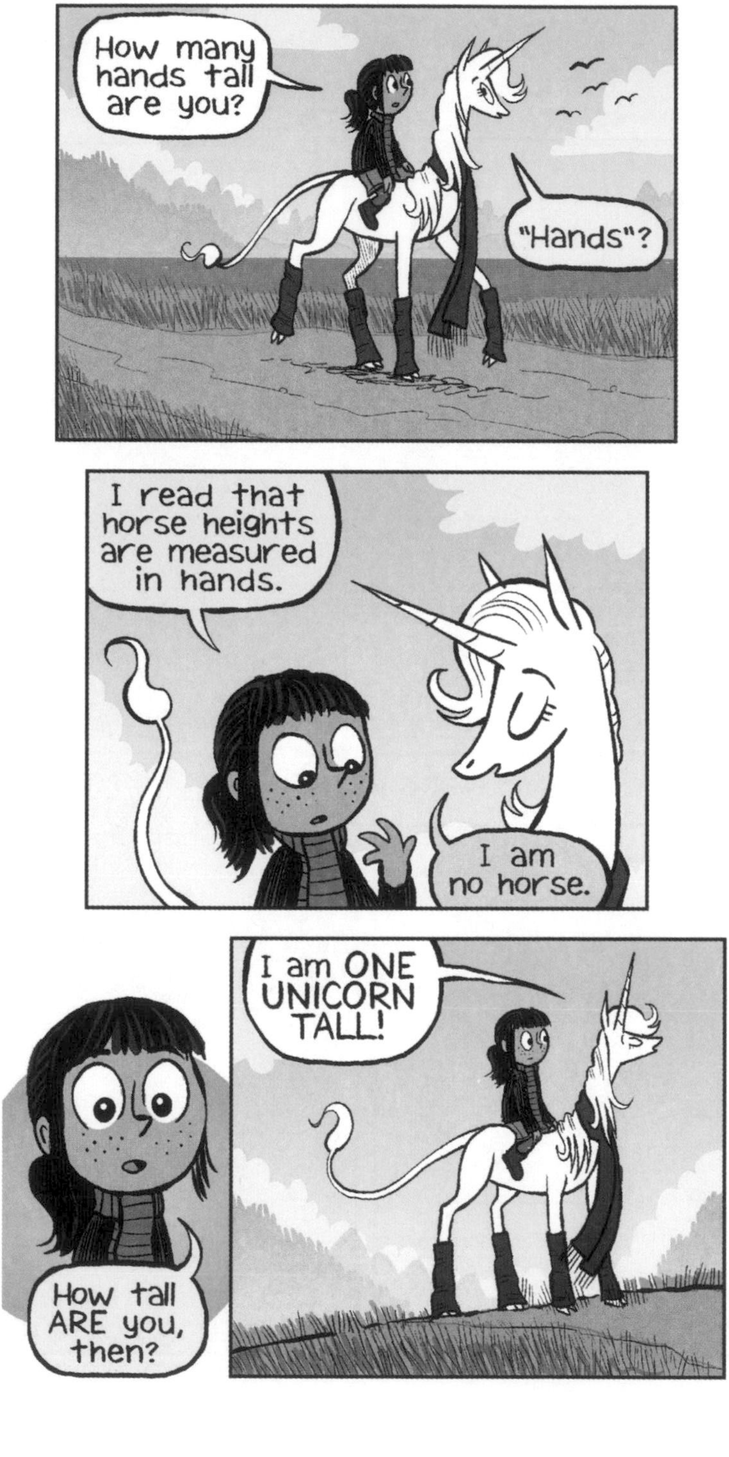
How many hands tall are you?
"Hands"?
I read that horse heights are measured in hands.
I am no horse.
How tall ARE you, then?
I am ONE UNICORN TALL!

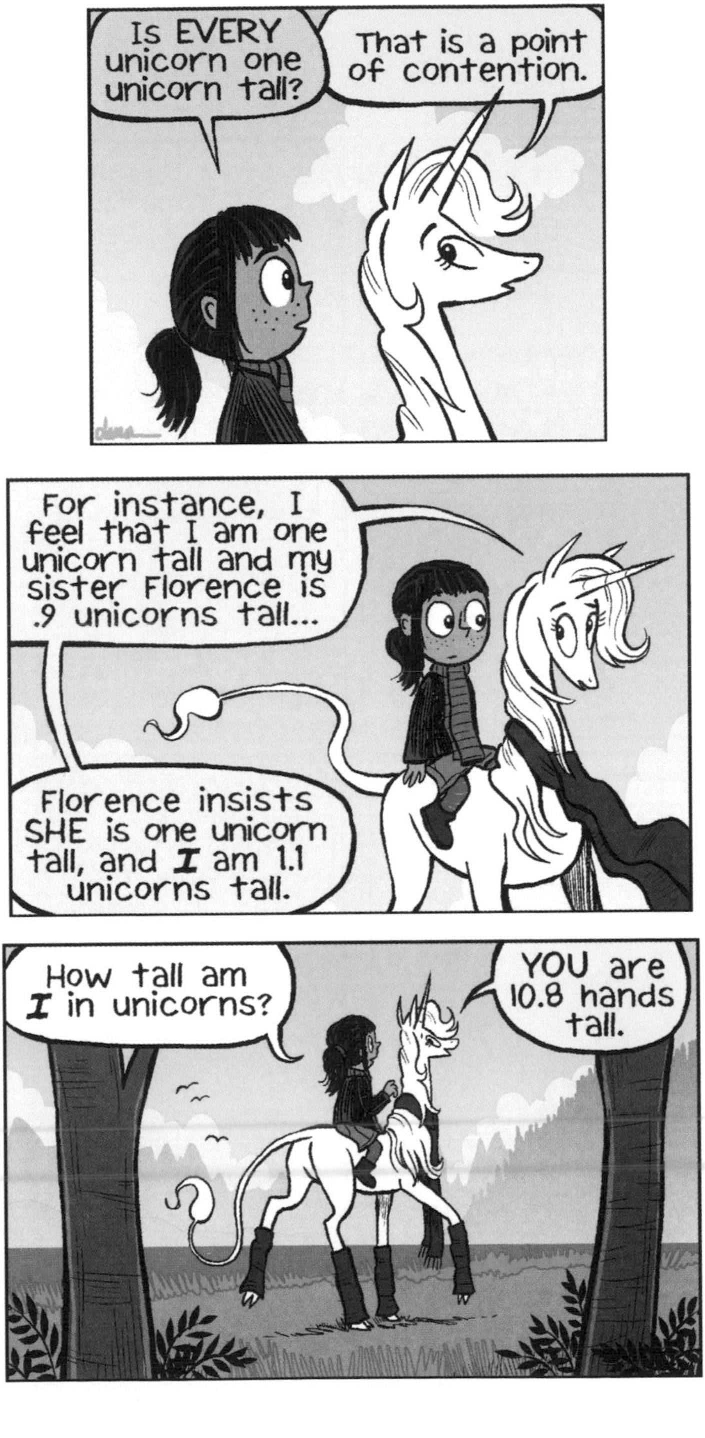

Is EVERY unicorn one unicorn tall?
That is a point of contention.
For instance, I feel that I am one unicorn tall and my sister Florence is .9 unicorns tall...
Florence insists SHE is one unicorn tall, and I am 1.1 unicorns tall.
How tall am I in unicorns?
YOU are 10.8 hands tall.

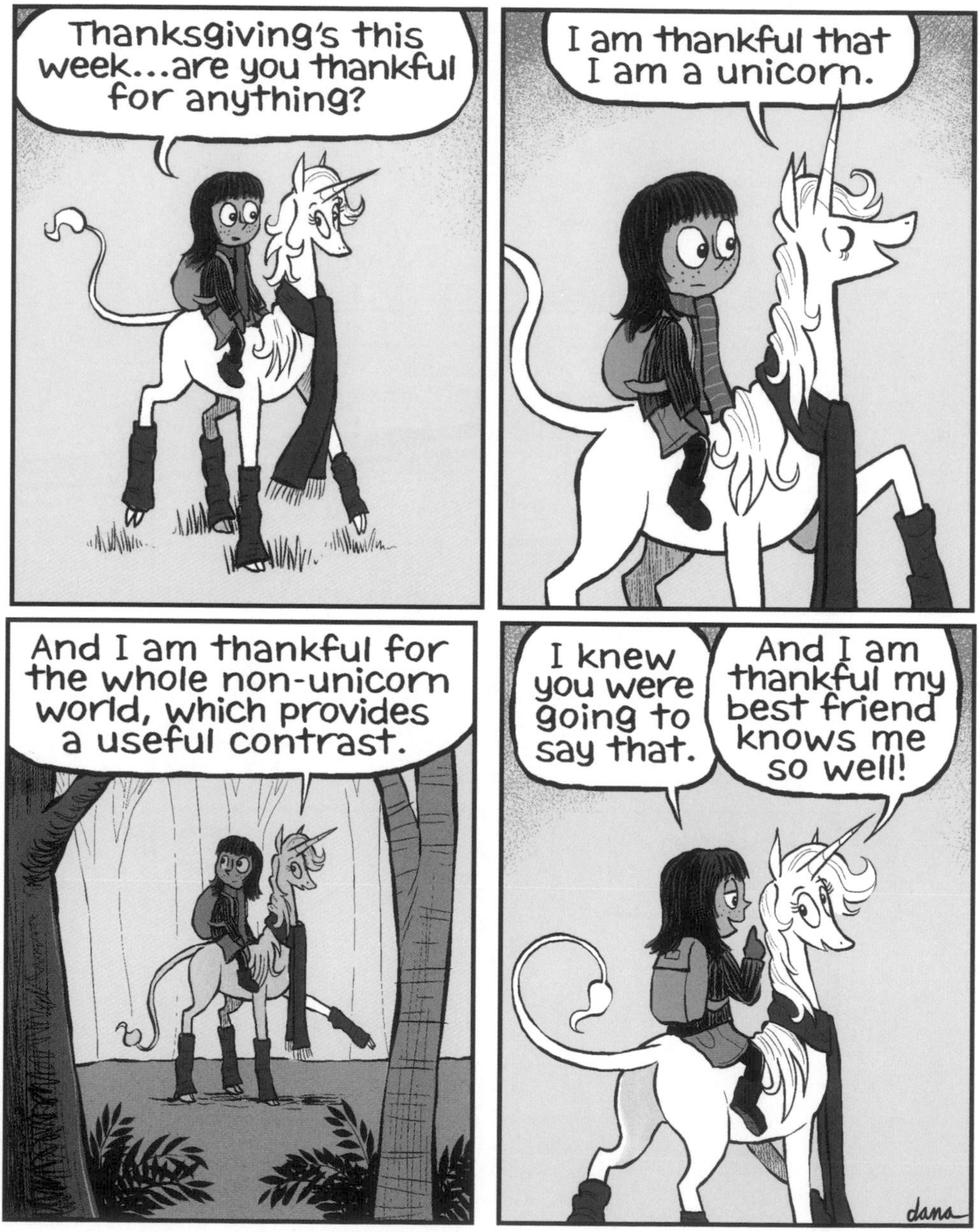
Thanksgiving's this week...are you thankful for anything?
I am thankful that I am a unicorn.
And I am thankful for the whole non-unicorn world, which provides a useful contrast.
I knew you were going to say that.
And I am thankful my best friend knows me so well!
dana

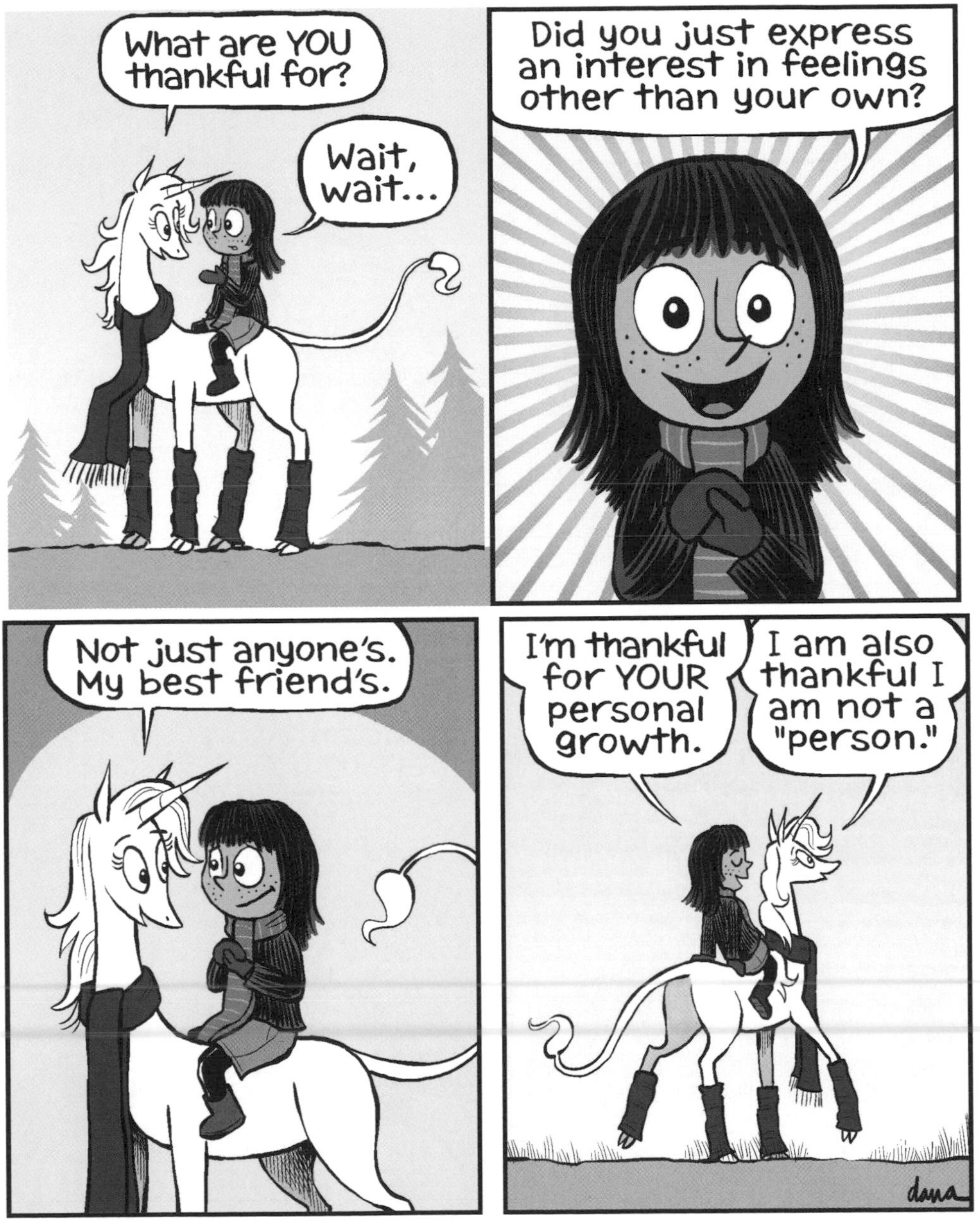
What are YOU thankful for?
Wait, wait...
Did you just express an interest in feelings other than your own?
Not just anyone's. My best friend's.
I'm thankful for YOUR personal growth.
I am also thankful I am not a "person."
dana

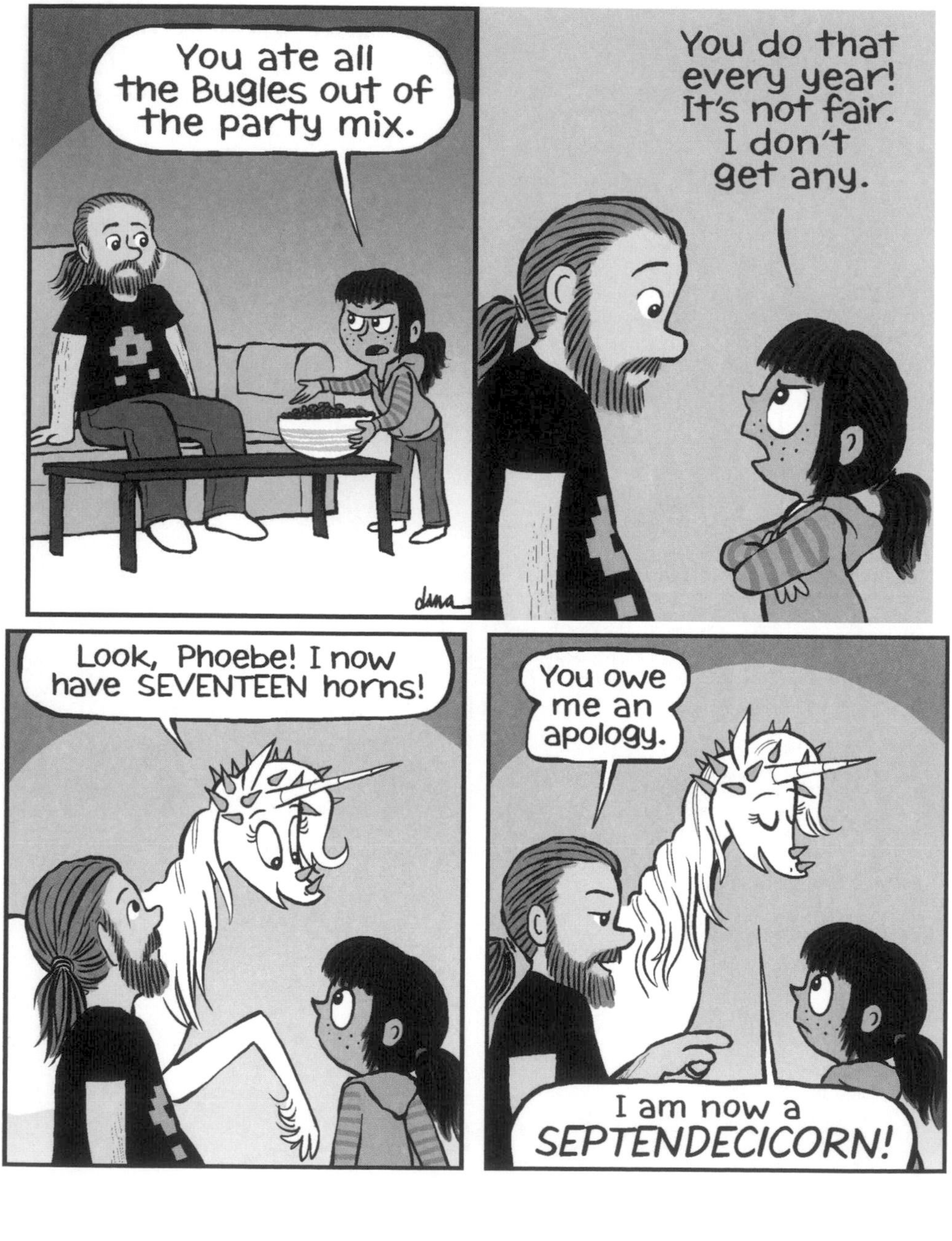
You ate all the Bugles out of the party mix.
You do that every year! It's not fair. I don't get any.
dana
Look, Phoebe! I now have SEVENTEEN horns!
You owe me an apology.
I am now a *SEPTENDECICORN!*

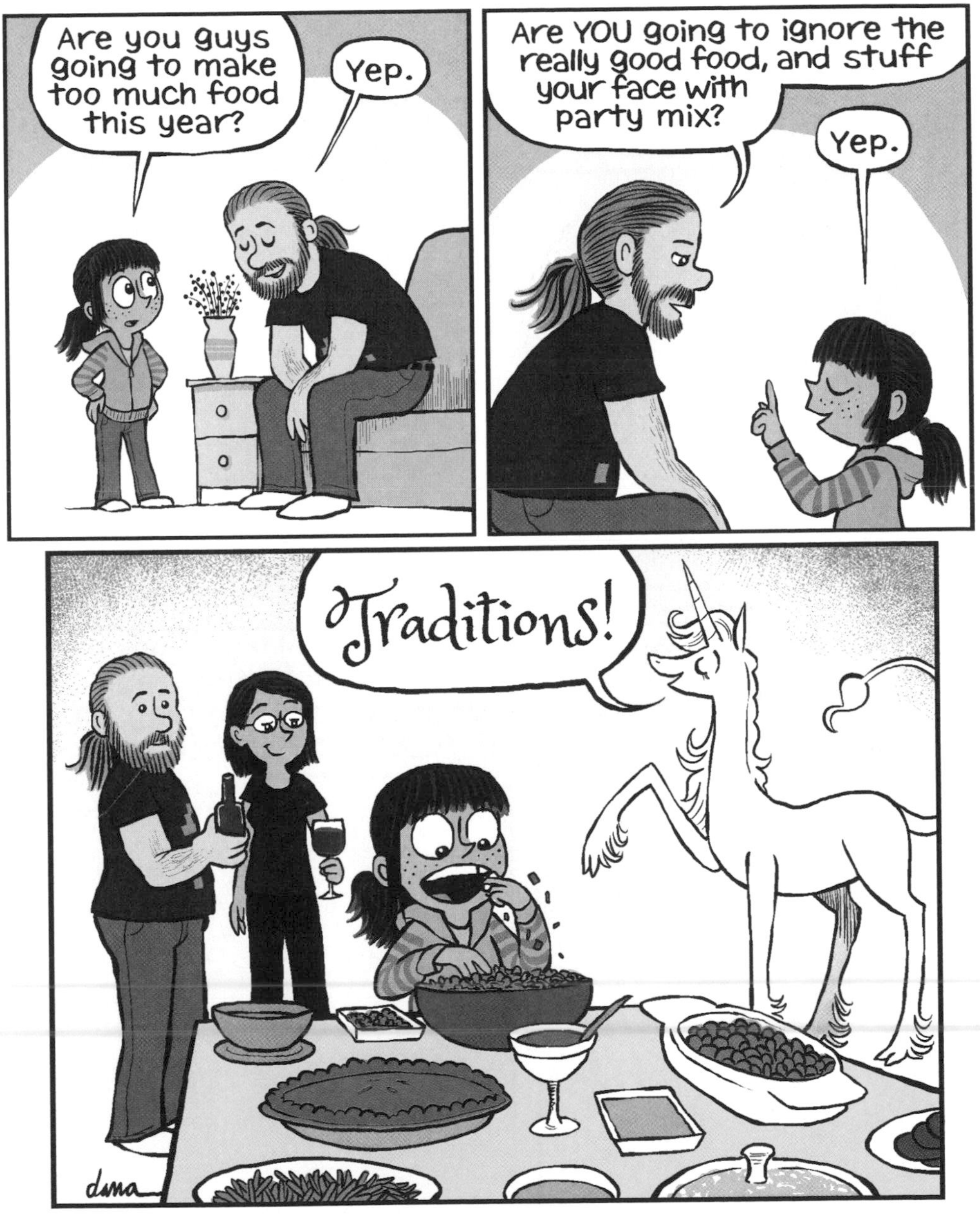
Are you guys going to make too much food this year?
Yep.
Are YOU going to ignore the really good food, and stuff your face with party mix?
Yep.
Traditions!
dana

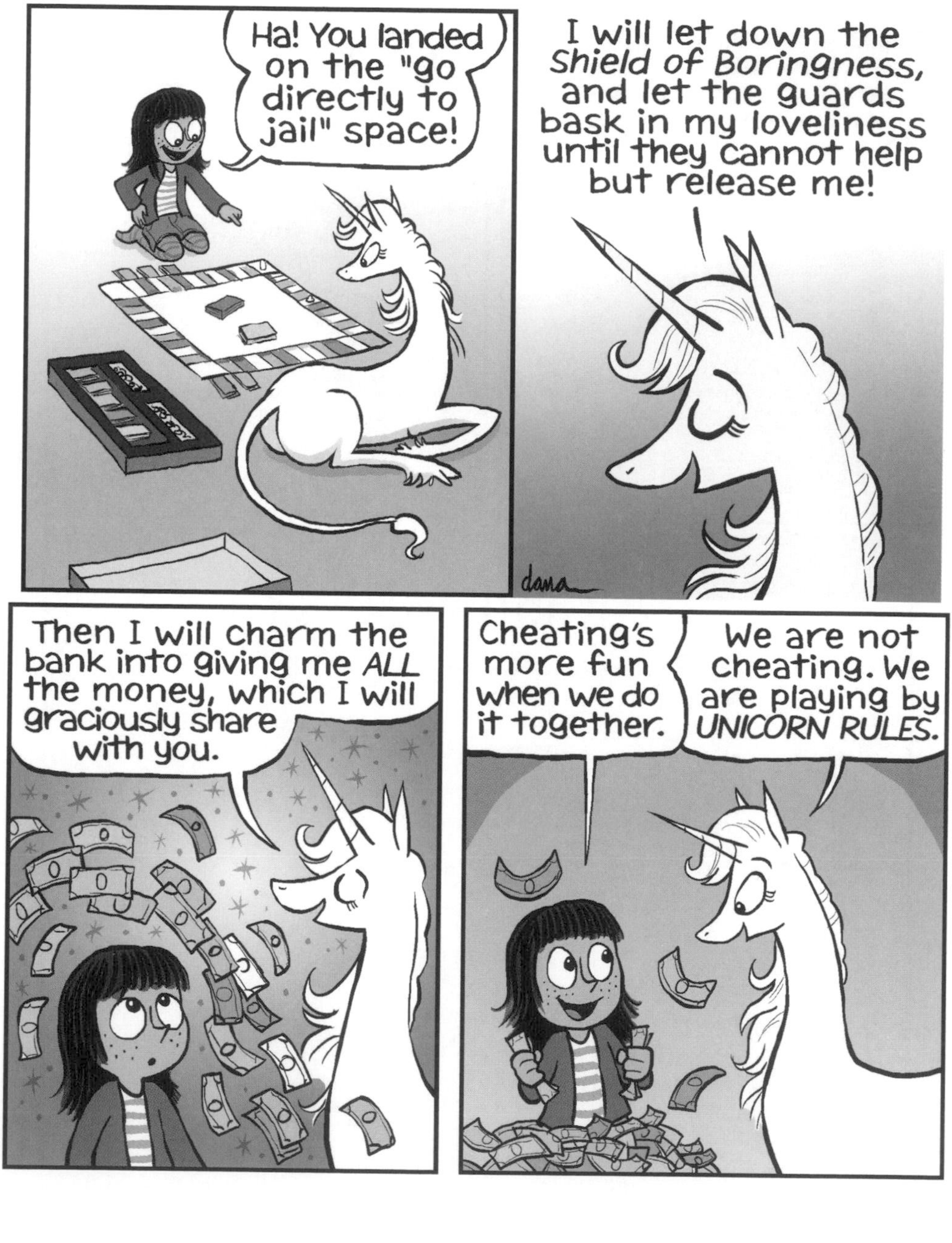
Ha! You landed on the "go directly to jail" space!
I will let down the *Shield of Boringness*, and let the guards bask in my loveliness until they cannot help but release me!
dana
Then I will charm the bank into giving me *ALL* the money, which I will graciously share with you.
Cheating's more fun when we do it together.
We are not cheating. We are playing by *UNICORN RULES*.

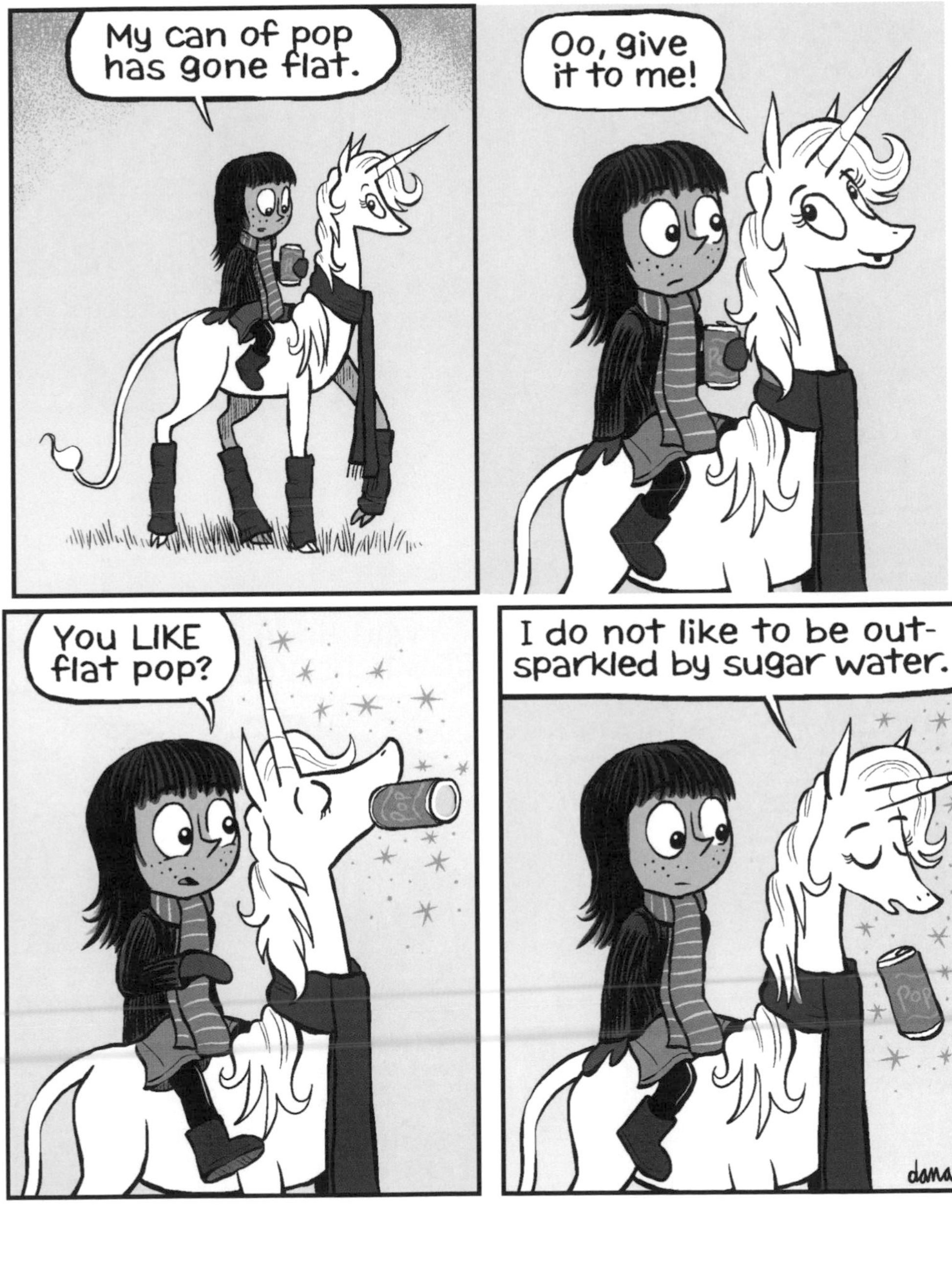
My can of pop has gone flat.
Oo, give it to me!
You LIKE flat pop?
POP
I do not like to be out-sparkled by sugar water.
POP
dana

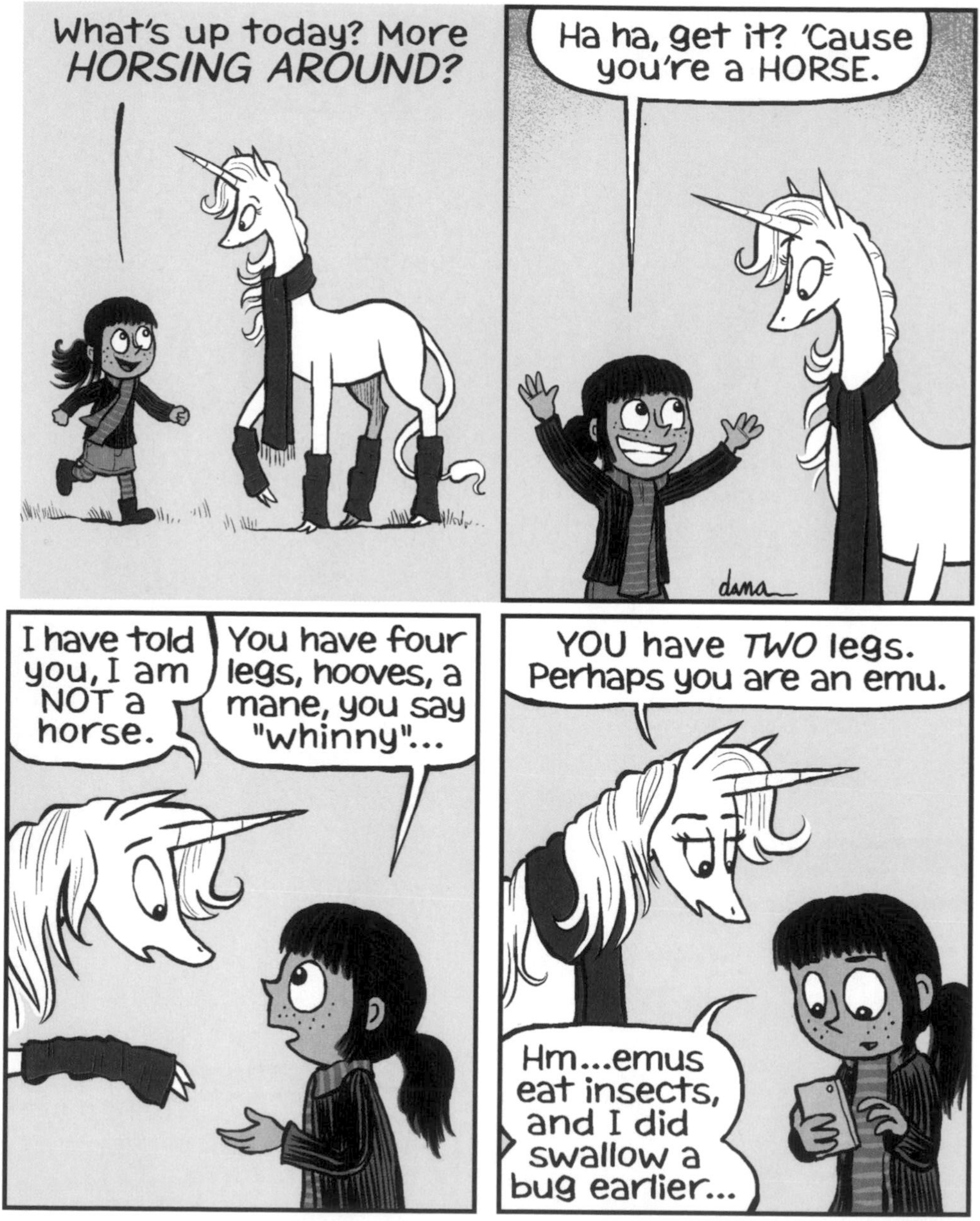
What's up today? More *HORSING AROUND?*
Ha ha, get it? 'Cause you're a HORSE.
dana
I have told you, I am NOT a horse.
You have four legs, hooves, a mane, you say "whinny"...
YOU have *TWO* legs. Perhaps you are an emu.
Hm...emus eat insects, and I did swallow a bug earlier...

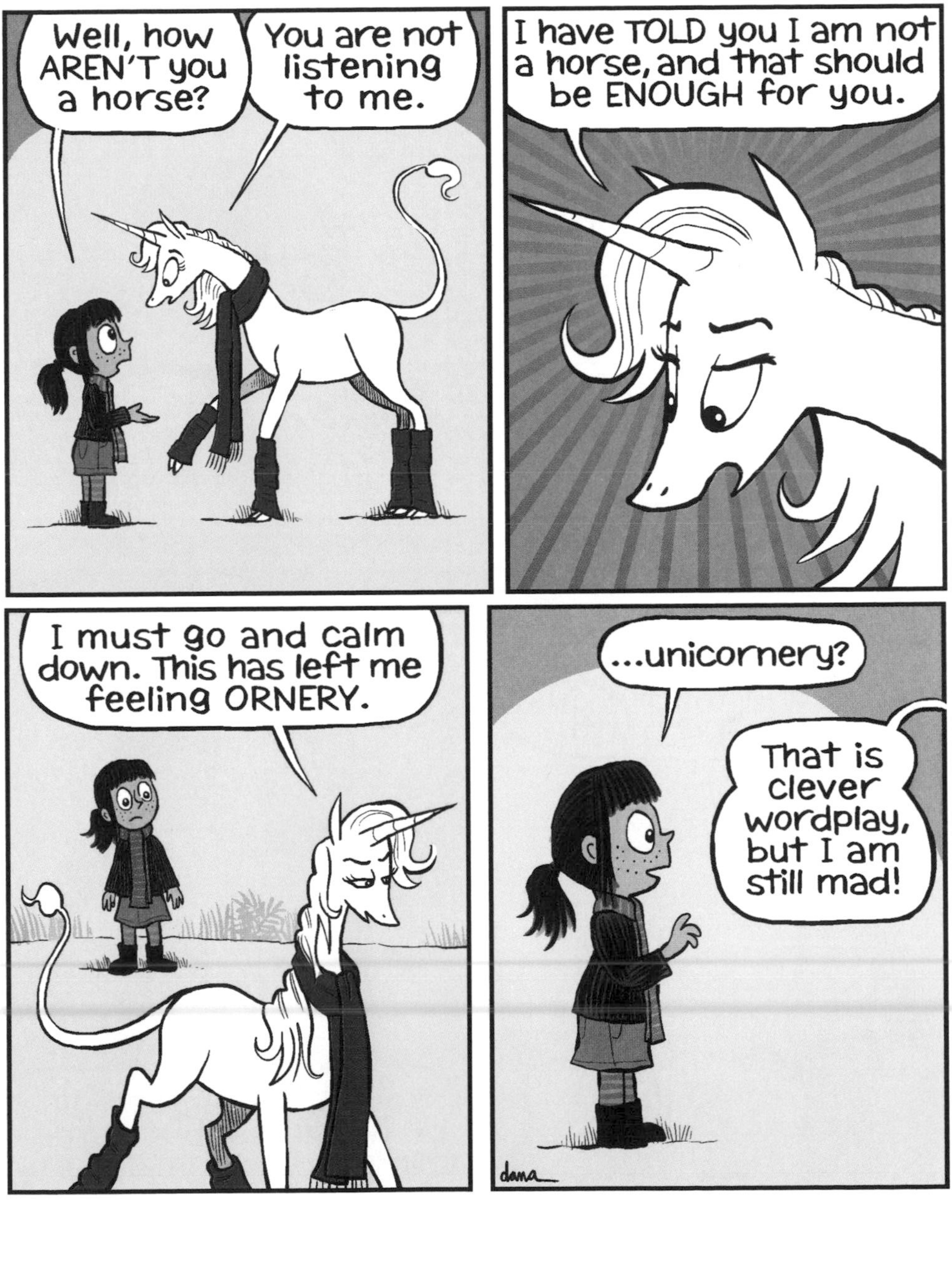
Well, how AREN'T you a horse?
You are not listening to me.
I have TOLD you I am not a horse, and that should be ENOUGH for you.
I must go and calm down. This has left me feeling ORNERY.
...unicornery?
That is clever wordplay, but I am still mad!
dana

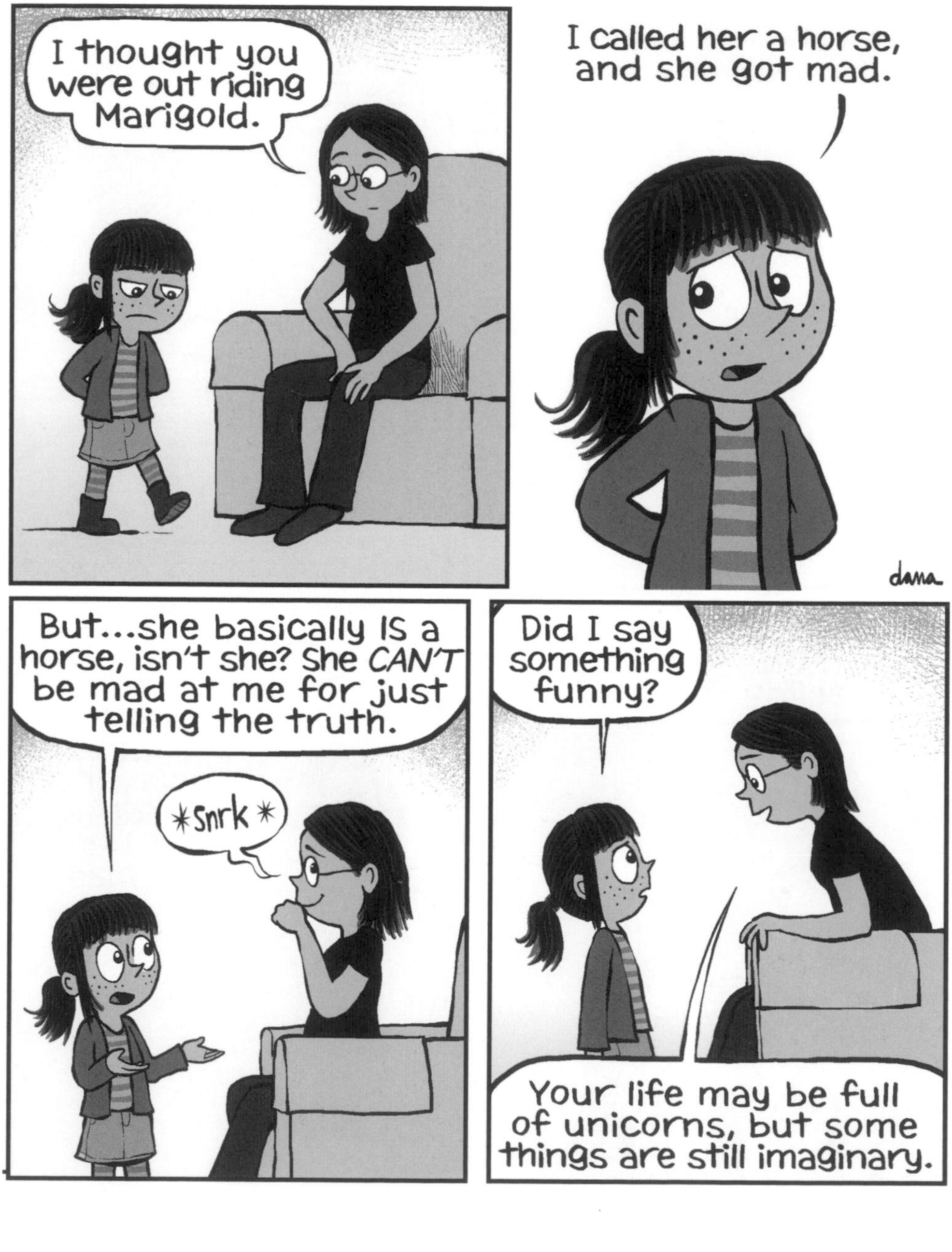
I thought you were out riding Marigold.
I called her a horse, and she got mad.
dana
But...she basically IS a horse, isn't she? She *CAN'T* be mad at me for just telling the truth.
snrk
Did I say something funny?
Your life may be full of unicorns, but some things are still imaginary.

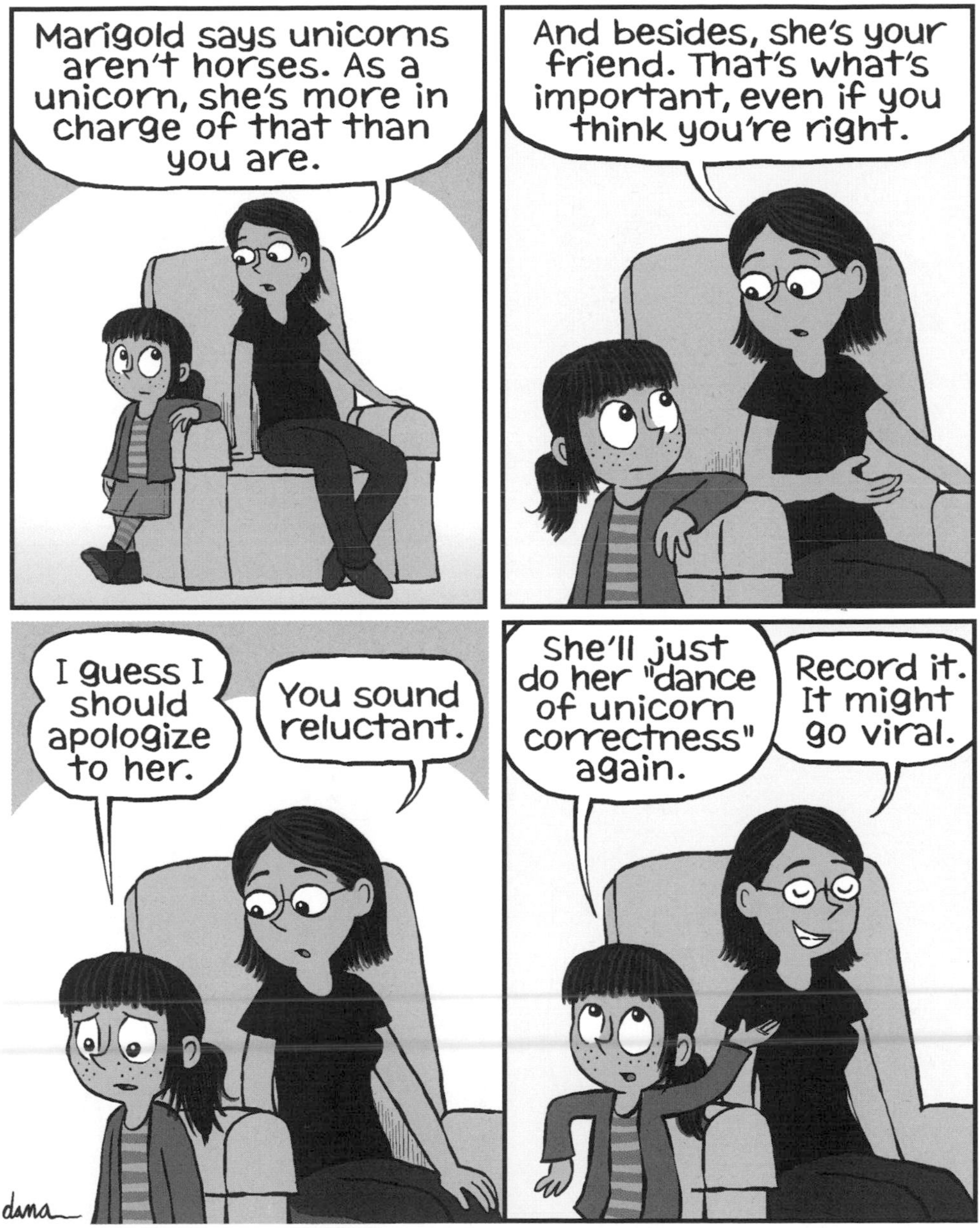
Marigold says unicorns aren't horses. As a unicorn, she's more in charge of that than you are.
And besides, she's your friend. That's what's important, even if you think you're right.
I guess I should apologize to her.
You sound reluctant.
She'll just do her "dance of unicorn correctness" again.
Record it. It might go viral.
dana

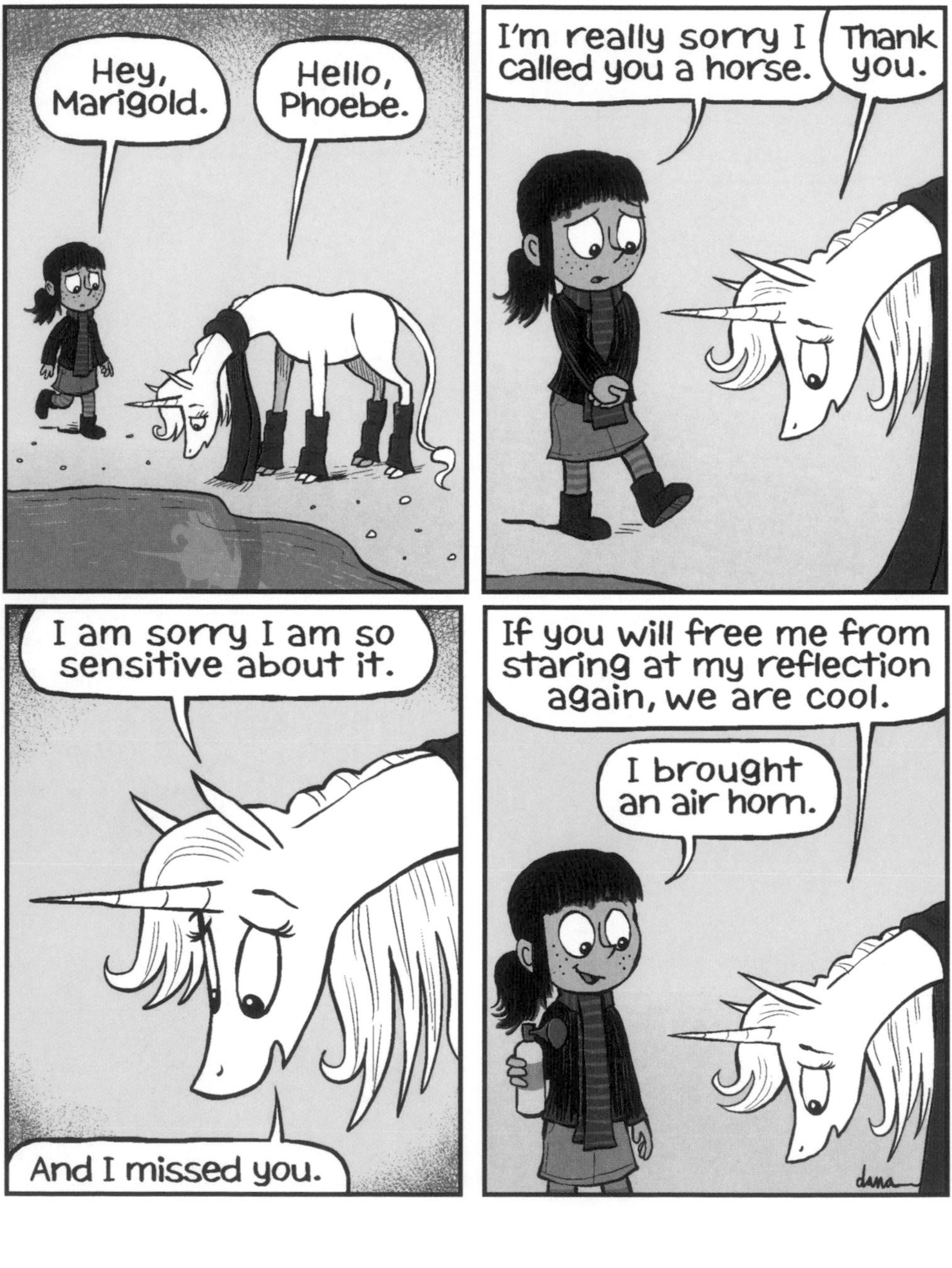
Hey, Marigold.
Hello, Phoebe.
I'm really sorry I called you a horse.
Thank you.
I am sorry I am so sensitive about it.
And I missed you.
If you will free me from staring at my reflection again, we are cool.
I brought an air horn.
dana

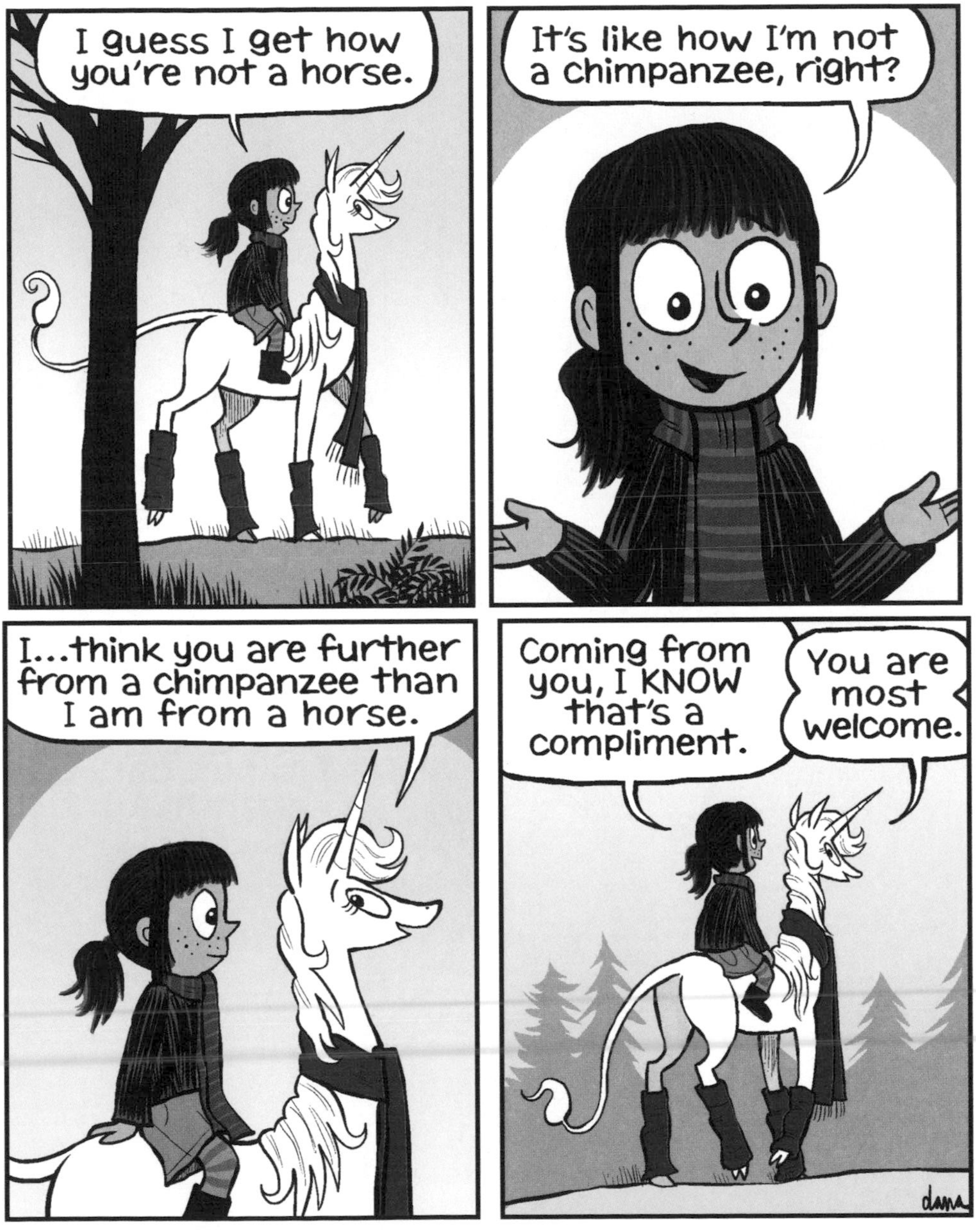
I guess I get how you're not a horse.
It's like how I'm not a chimpanzee, right?
I...think you are further from a chimpanzee than I am from a horse.
Coming from you, I KNOW that's a compliment.
You are most welcome.
dana

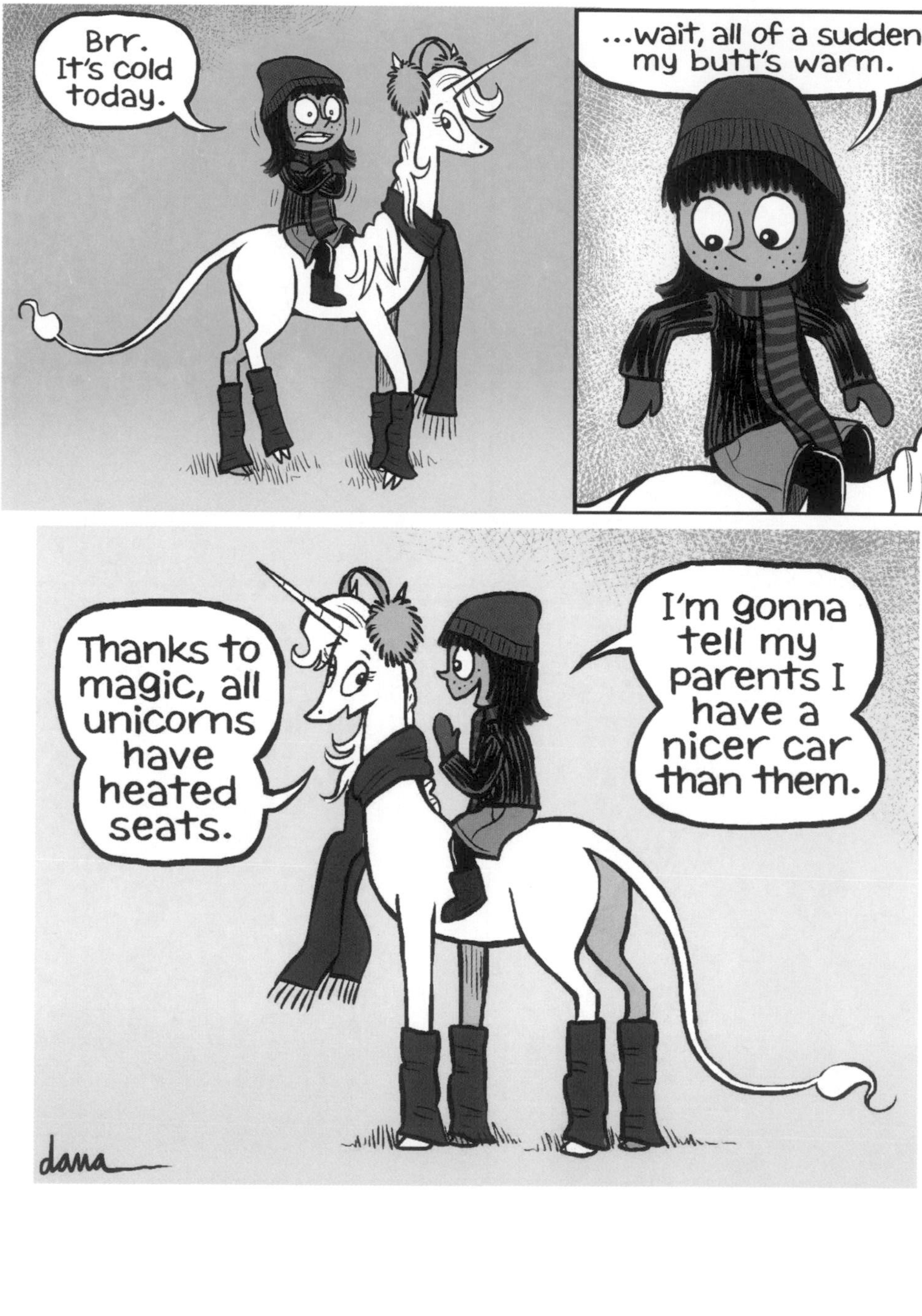
Brr. It's cold today.
...wait, all of a sudden my butt's warm.
Thanks to magic, all unicorns have heated seats.
I'm gonna tell my parents I have a nicer car than them.
dana

Marigold? Strictly hypothetically, say you had a friend exactly like you, but NOT you.

What would you get them for Christmas?

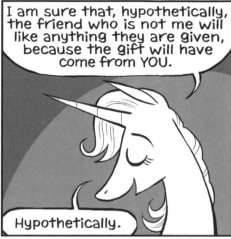

I am sure that, hypothetically, the friend who is not me will like anything they are given, because the gift will have come from YOU.

Hypothetically.

That's, like, the least helpful possible answer.

Well, disguise your hypotheticals more effectively.

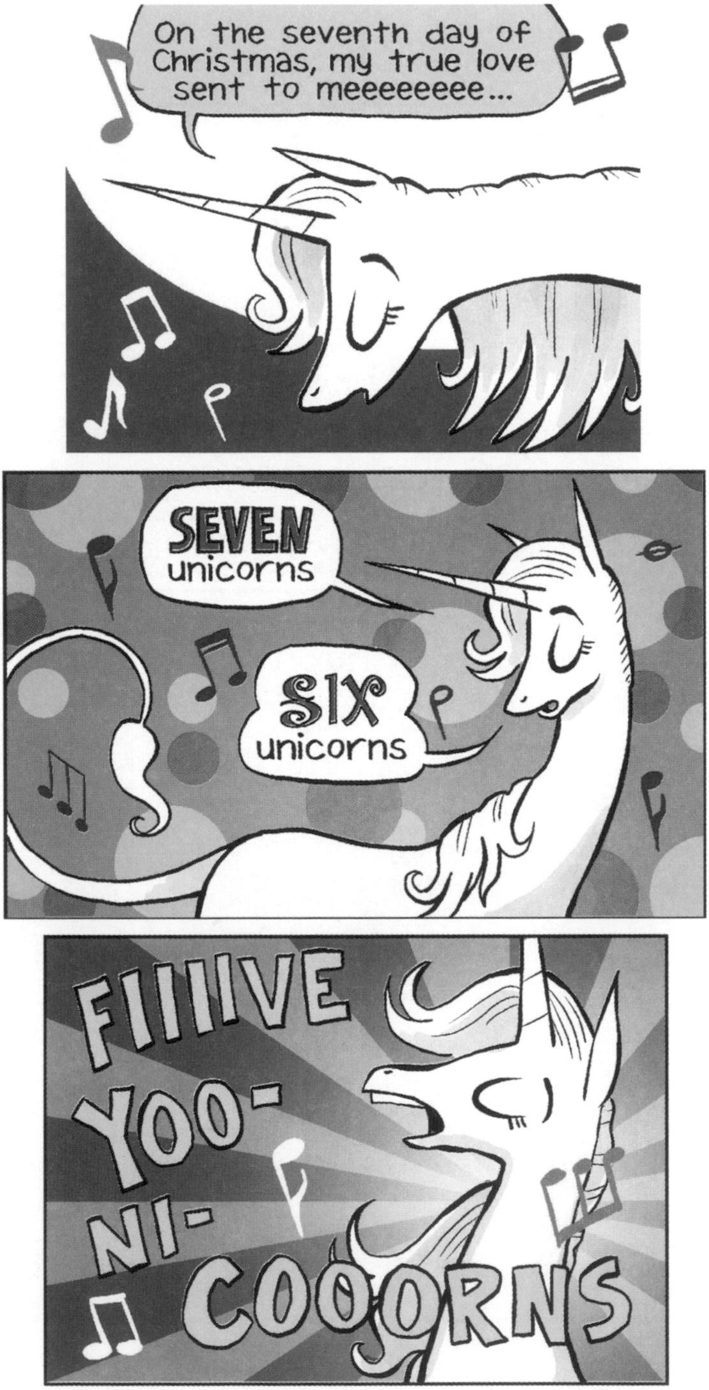
On the seventh day of Christmas, my true love sent to meeeeeeee...
SEVEN unicorns
SIX unicorns
FIIIVE YOO-NI-COOORNS

FOUR unicorns
THREE unicorns
TWO-OO unicorns
And a YOO-OO-OO OO-NI-COOORN!
Now you have a UNICORNAMENT!
dana

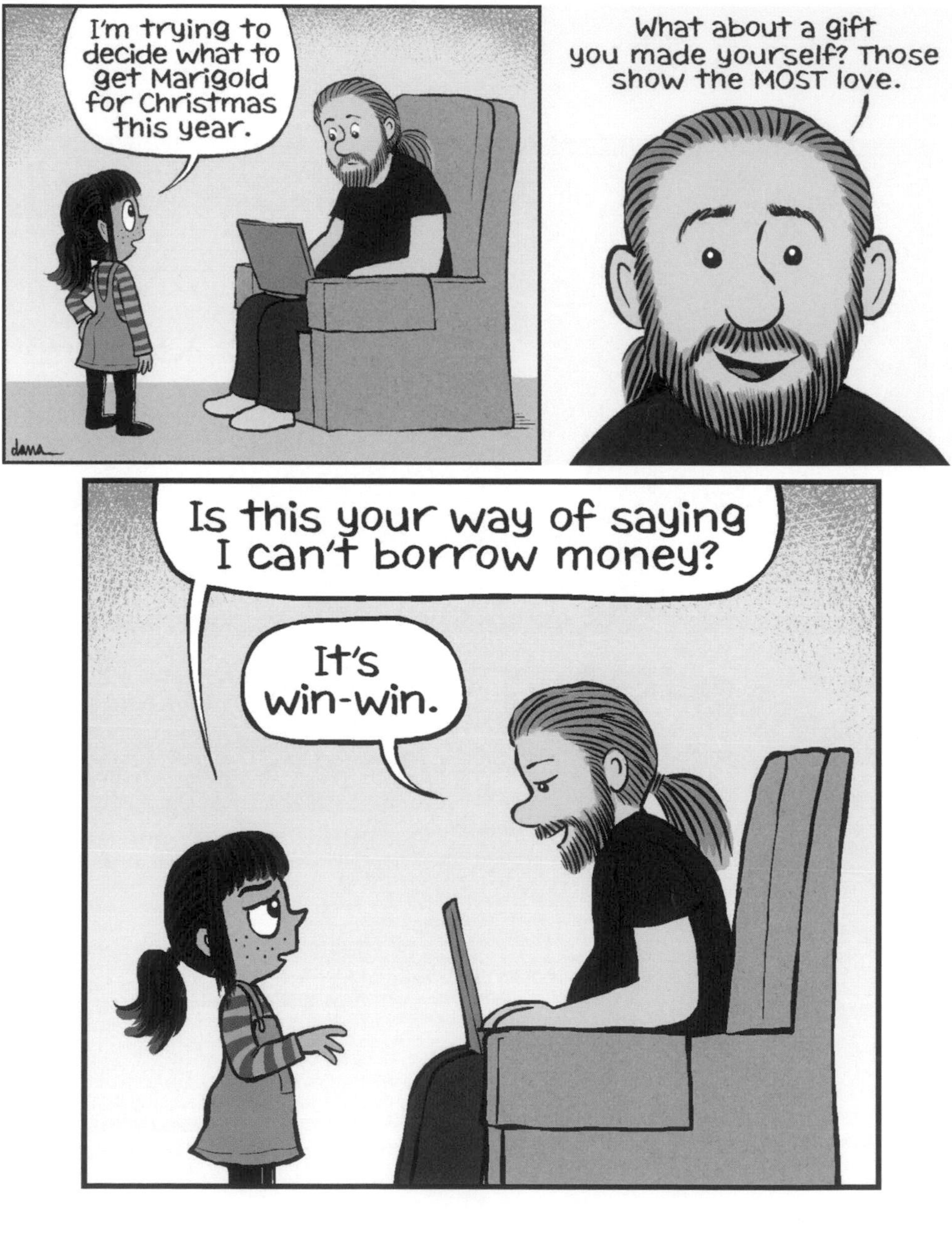
I'm trying to decide what to get Marigold for Christmas this year.
dana
What about a gift you made yourself? Those show the MOST love.
Is this your way of saying I can't borrow money?
It's win-win.

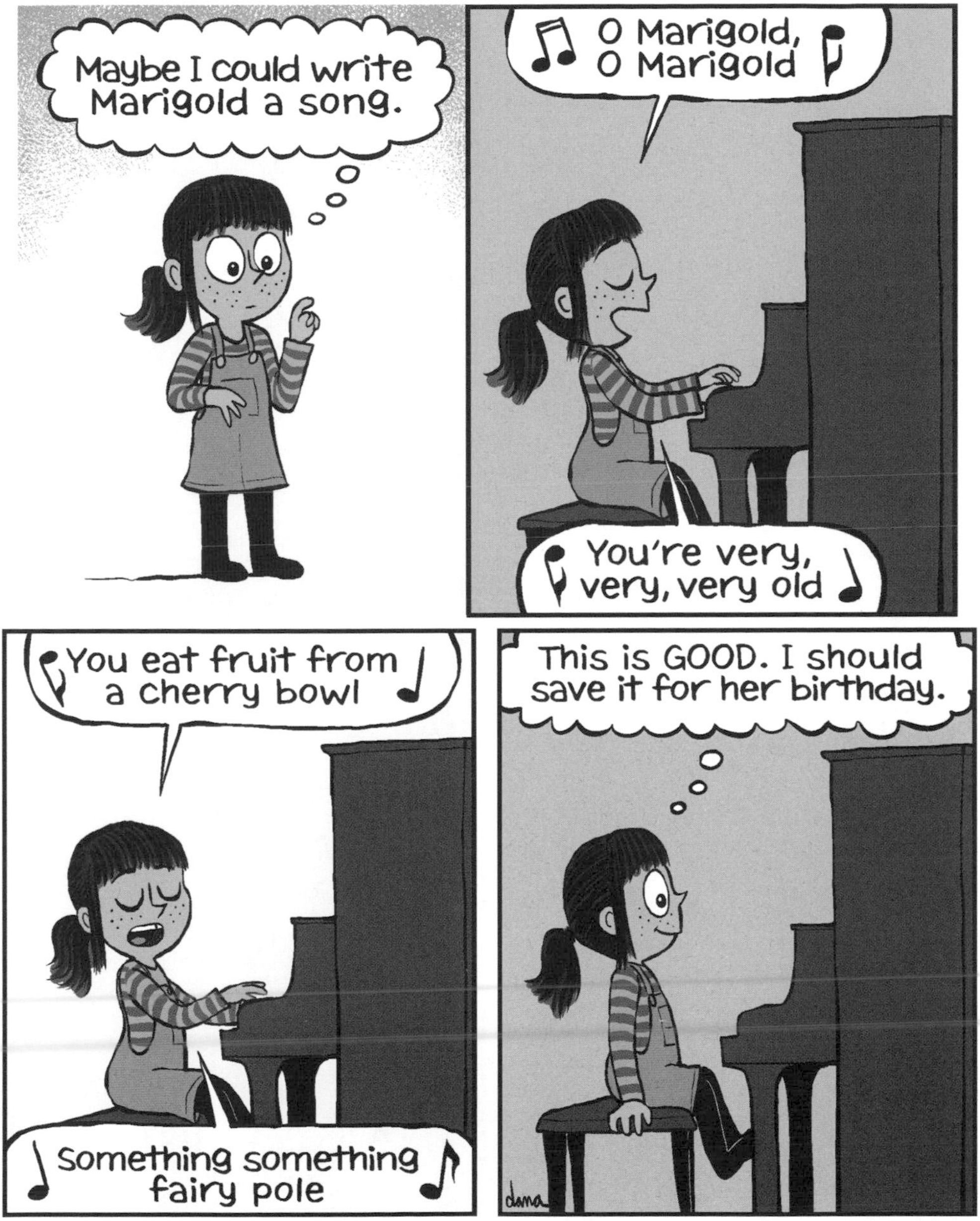
Maybe I could write Marigold a song.
O Marigold, O Marigold
You're very, very, very old
You eat fruit from a cherry bowl
Something something fairy pole
This is GOOD. I should save it for her birthday.
dana

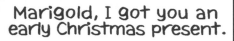

Marigold, I got you an early Christmas present.

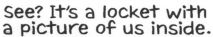

See? It's a locket with a picture of us inside.

Hooray! I look lovely in it!

I'm ALSO in it.

And YOU are my most flattering accessory!

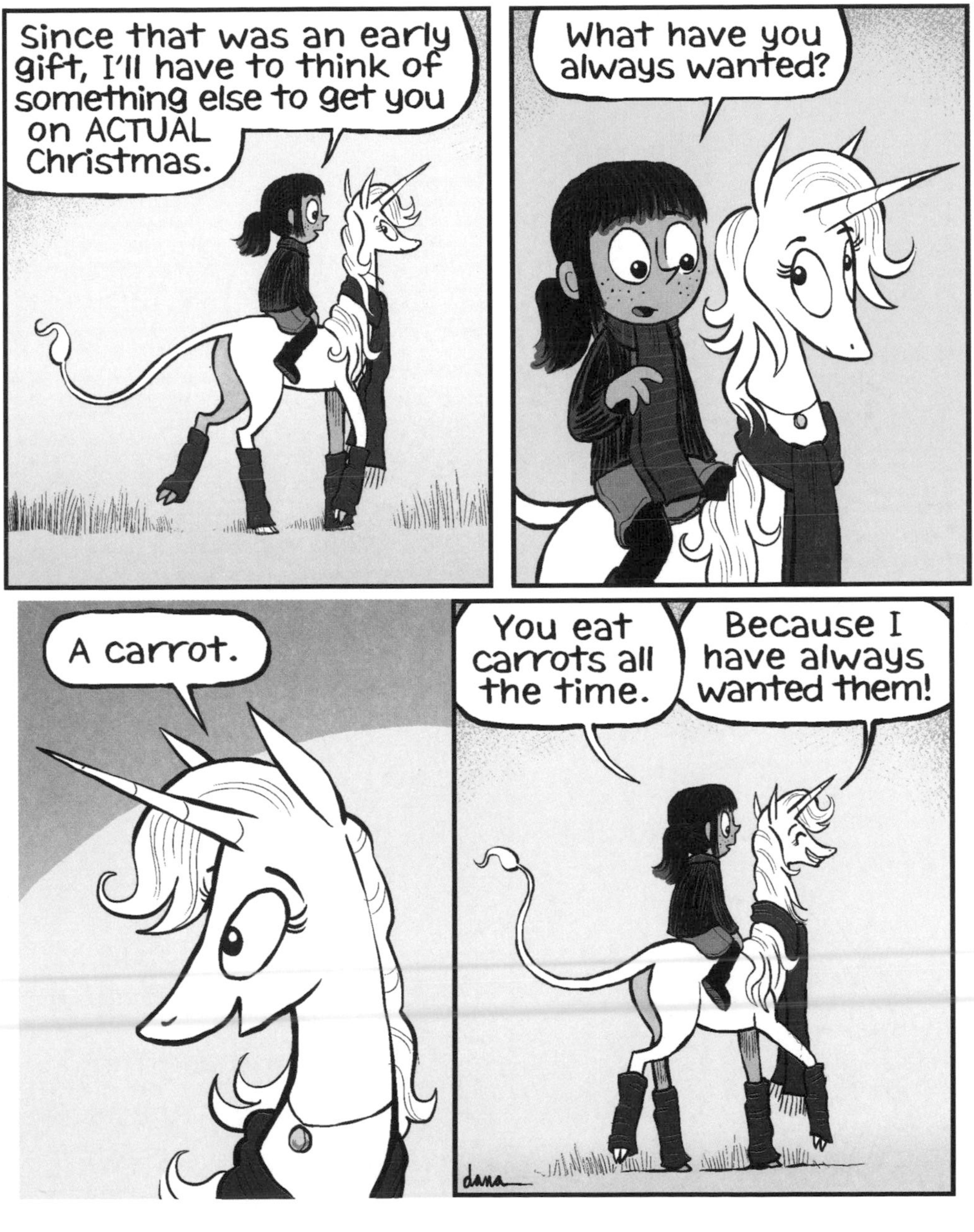
Since that was an early gift, I'll have to think of something else to get you on ACTUAL Christmas.
What have you always wanted?
A carrot.
You eat carrots all the time.
Because I have always wanted them!
dana

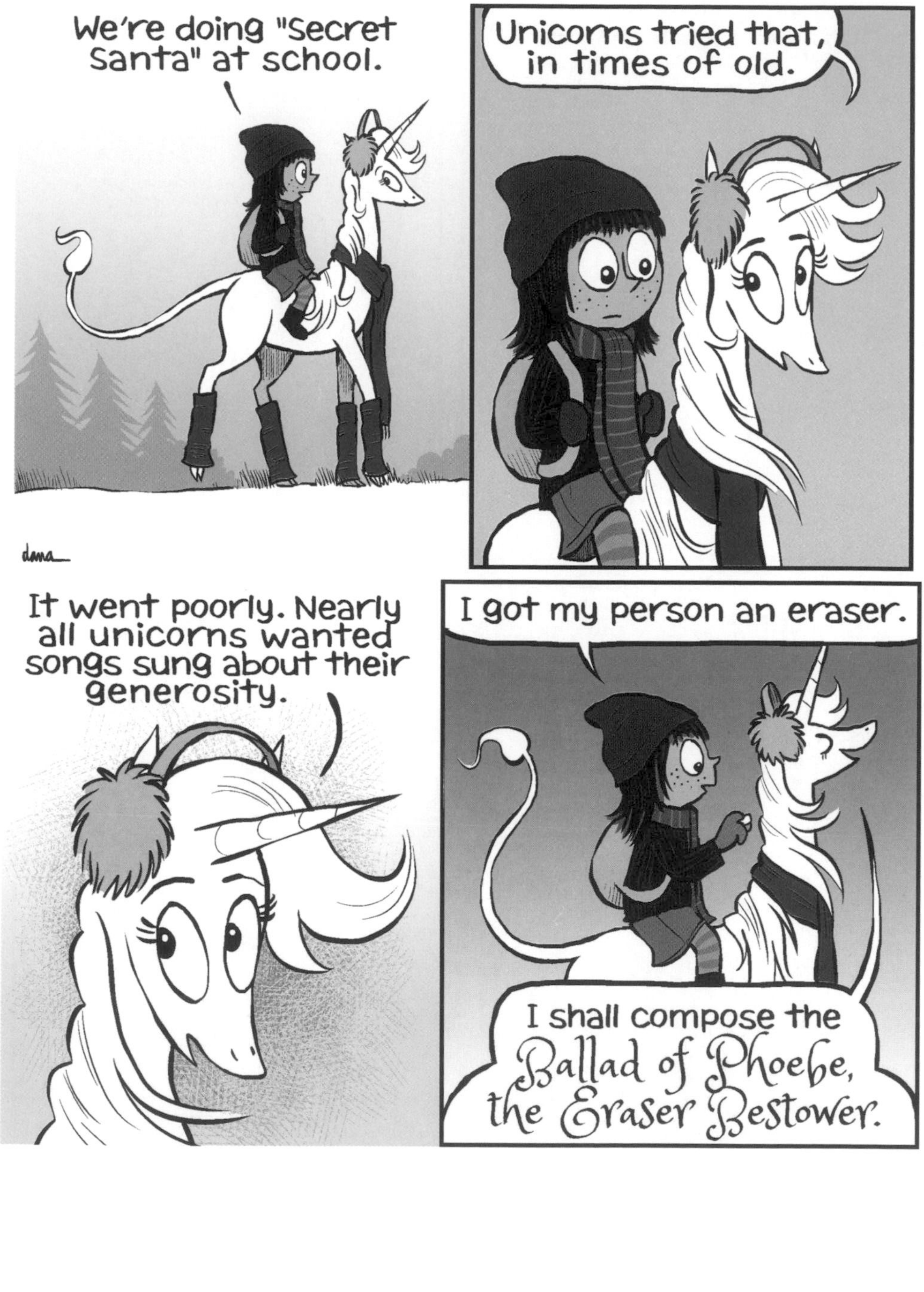
We're doing "Secret Santa" at school.
dana
Unicorns tried that, in times of old.
It went poorly. Nearly all unicorns wanted songs sung about their generosity.
I got my person an eraser.
I shall compose the Ballad of Phoebe, the Eraser Bestower.

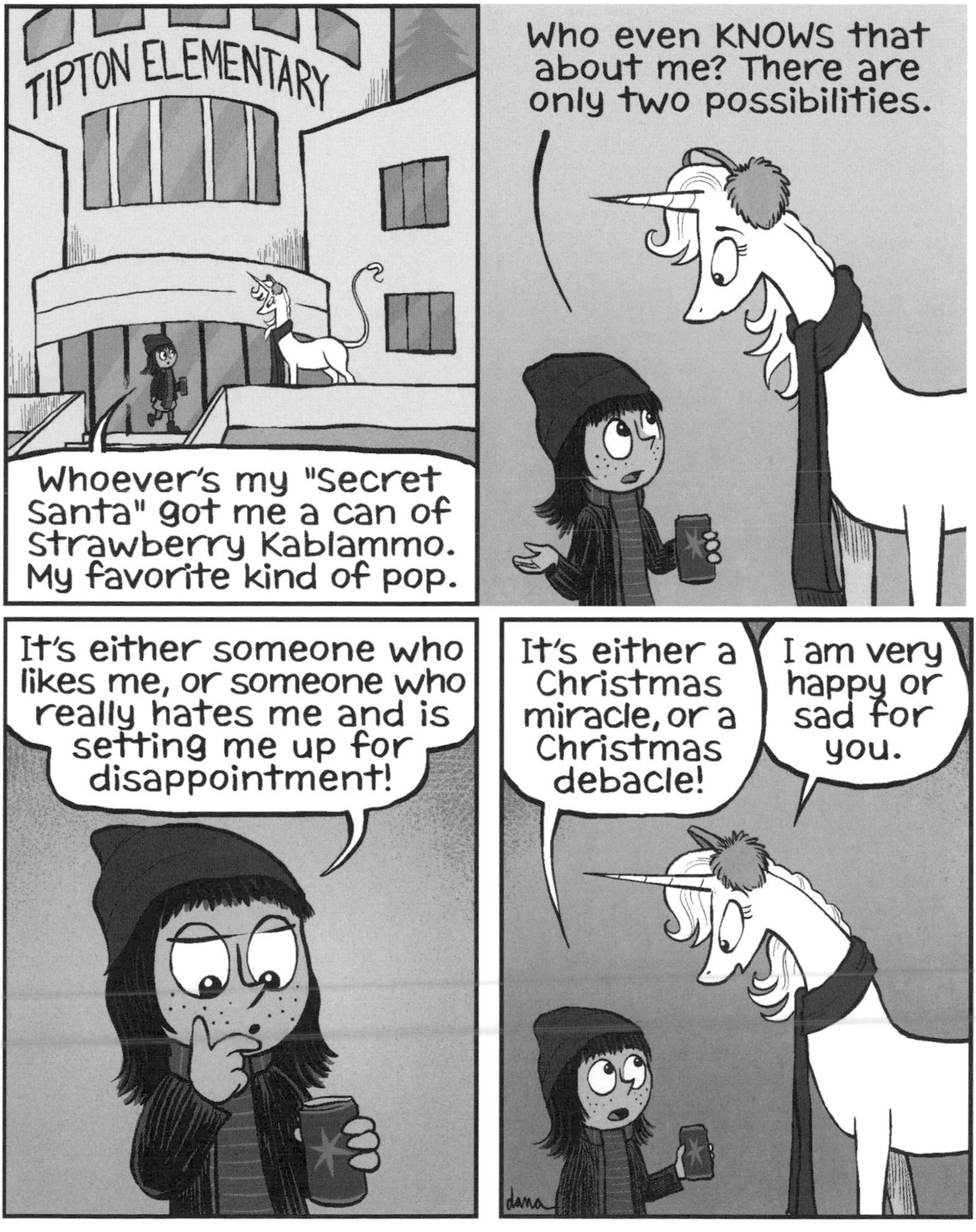
TIPTON ELEMENTARY
Whoever's my "Secret Santa" got me a can of Strawberry Kablammo. My favorite kind of pop.
Who even KNOWS that about me? There are only two possibilities.
It's either someone who likes me, or someone who really hates me and is setting me up for disappointment!
It's either a Christmas miracle, or a Christmas debacle!
I am very happy or sad for you.
dana

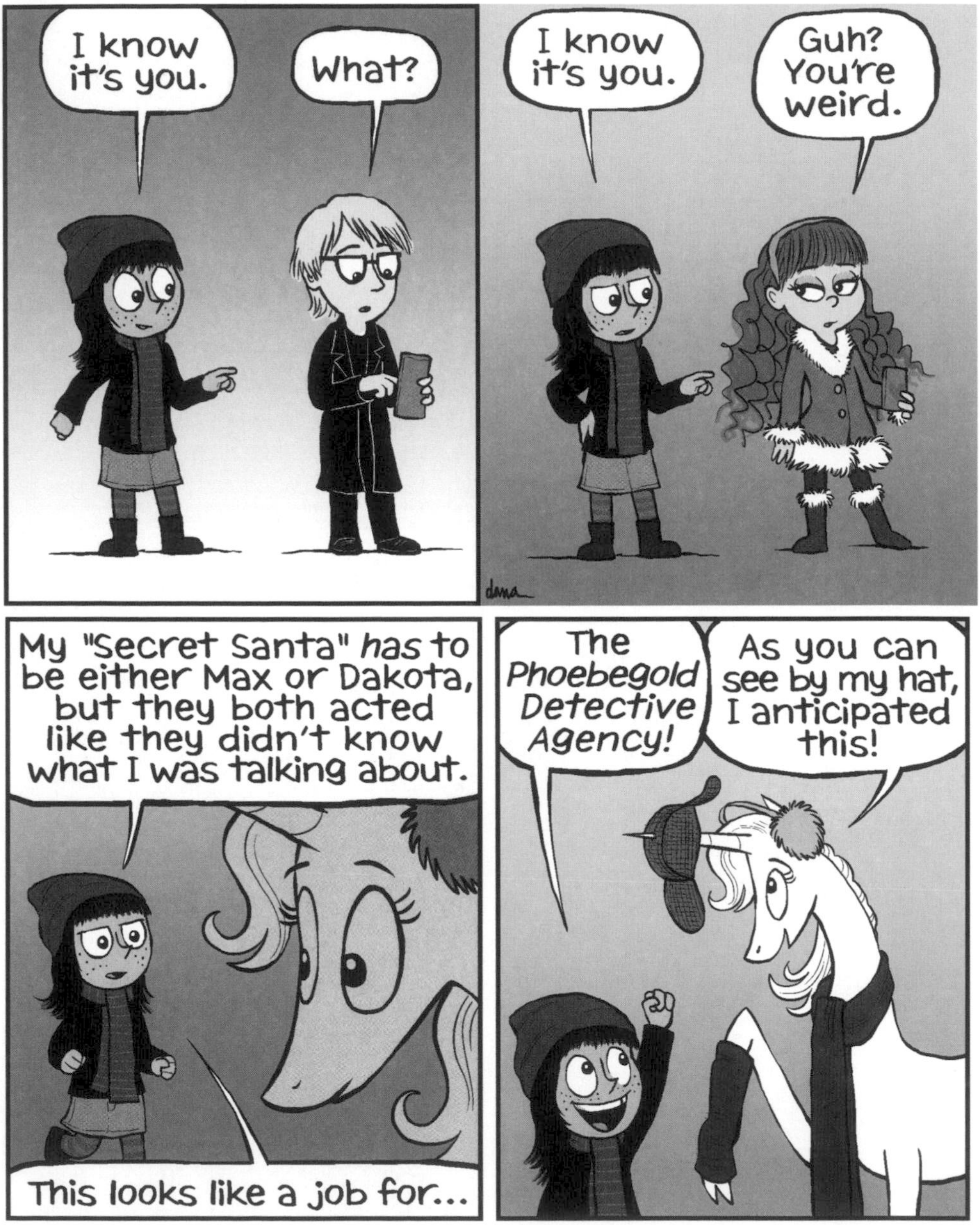
I know it's you.
What?
I know it's you.
Guh? You're weird.
My "Secret Santa" *has* to be either Max or Dakota, but they both acted like they didn't know what I was talking about.
This looks like a job for...
The *Phoebegold Detective Agency!*
As you can see by my hat, I anticipated this!

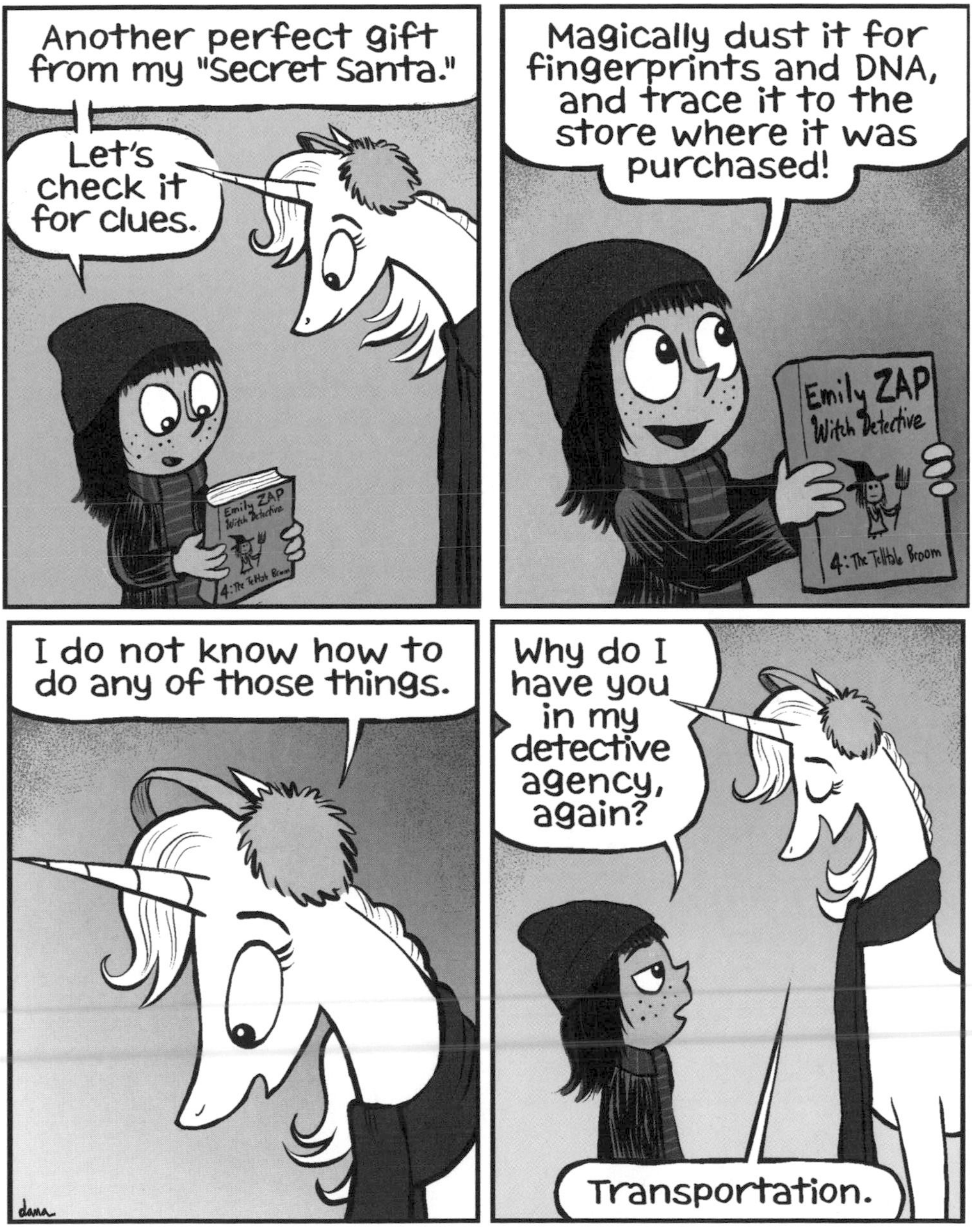
Another perfect gift from my "Secret Santa."
Let's check it for clues.
Emily ZAP Witch Detective 4: The Telltale Broom
Magically dust it for fingerprints and DNA, and trace it to the store where it was purchased!
Emily ZAP Witch Detective 4: The Telltale Broom
I do not know how to do any of those things.
Why do I have you in my detective agency, again?
Transportation.
dana

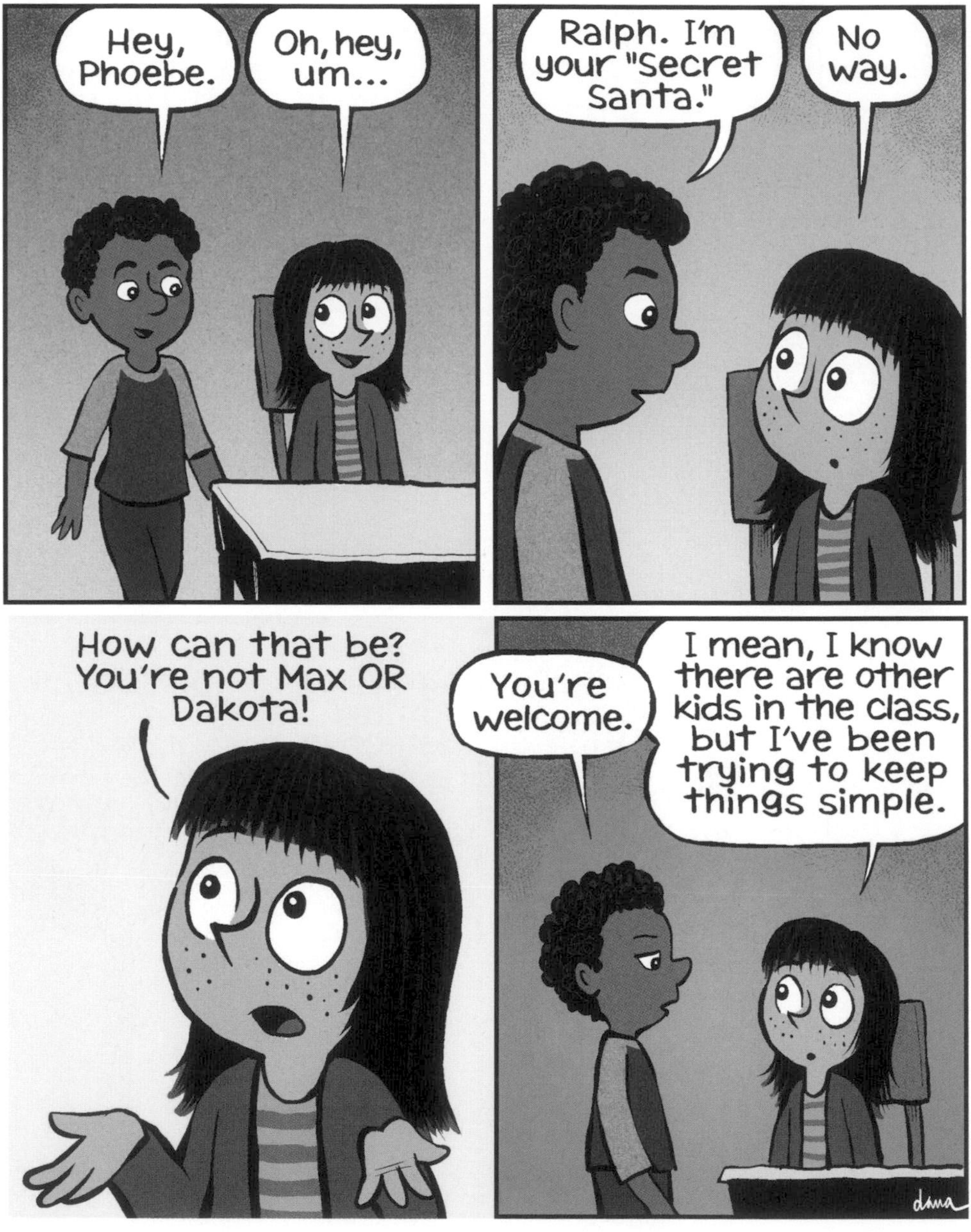
Hey, Phoebe.
Oh, hey, um...
Ralph. I'm your "Secret Santa."
No way.
How can that be? You're not Max OR Dakota!
You're welcome.
I mean, I know there are other kids in the class, but I've been trying to keep things simple.
dana

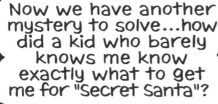

Now we have another mystery to solve...how did a kid who barely knows me know exactly what to get me for "Secret Santa"?

Unless...

Hee hee hee!

Yes, I cast a spell of my own creation, using my detailed knowledge of my best friend.

I call it...

The *Spell of Knowing What Sorts of Things Make Phoebe Happy.*

It's not your punchiest name ever, but it's sweet.

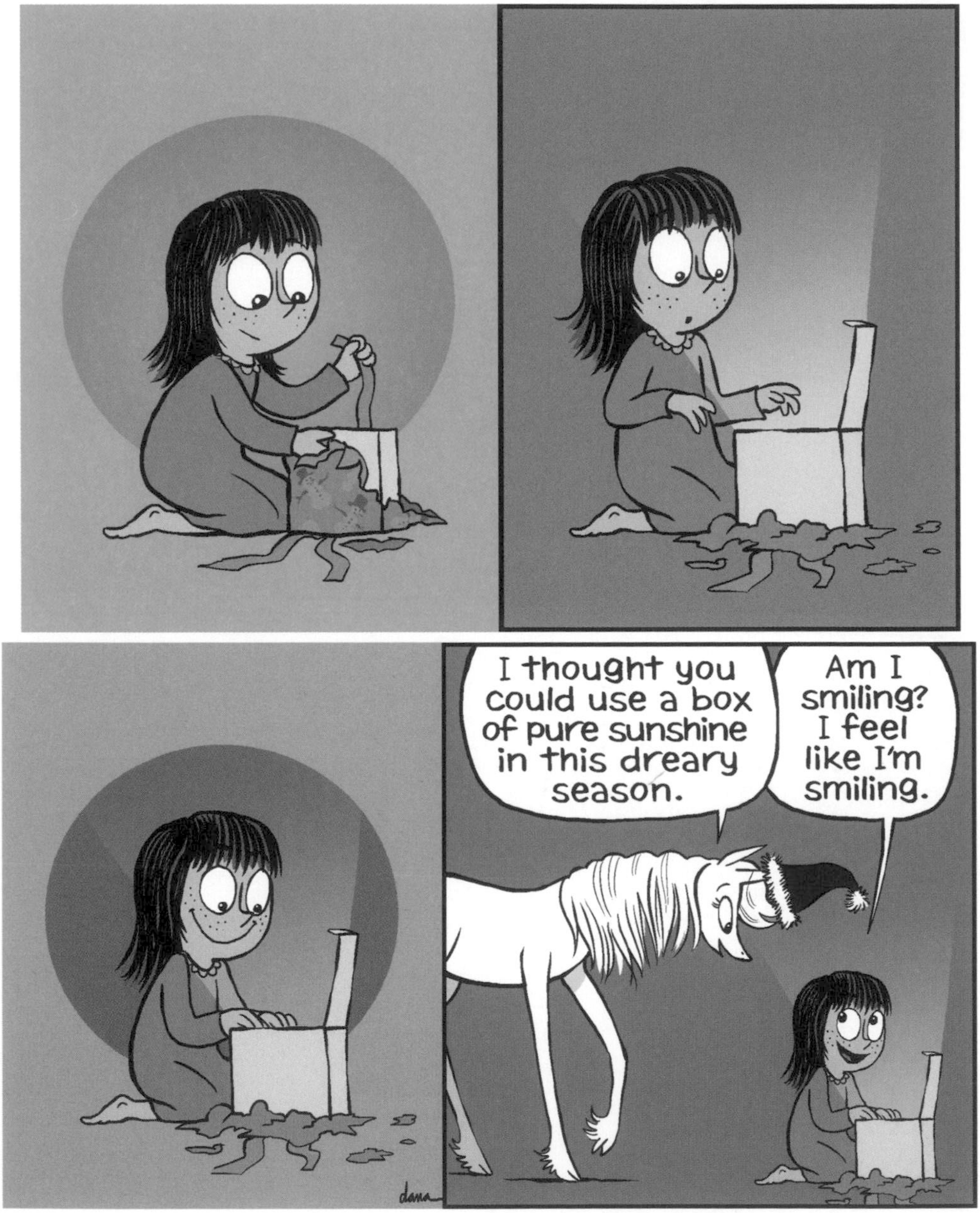
I thought you could use a box of pure sunshine in this dreary season.
Am I smiling? I feel like I'm smiling.
dana

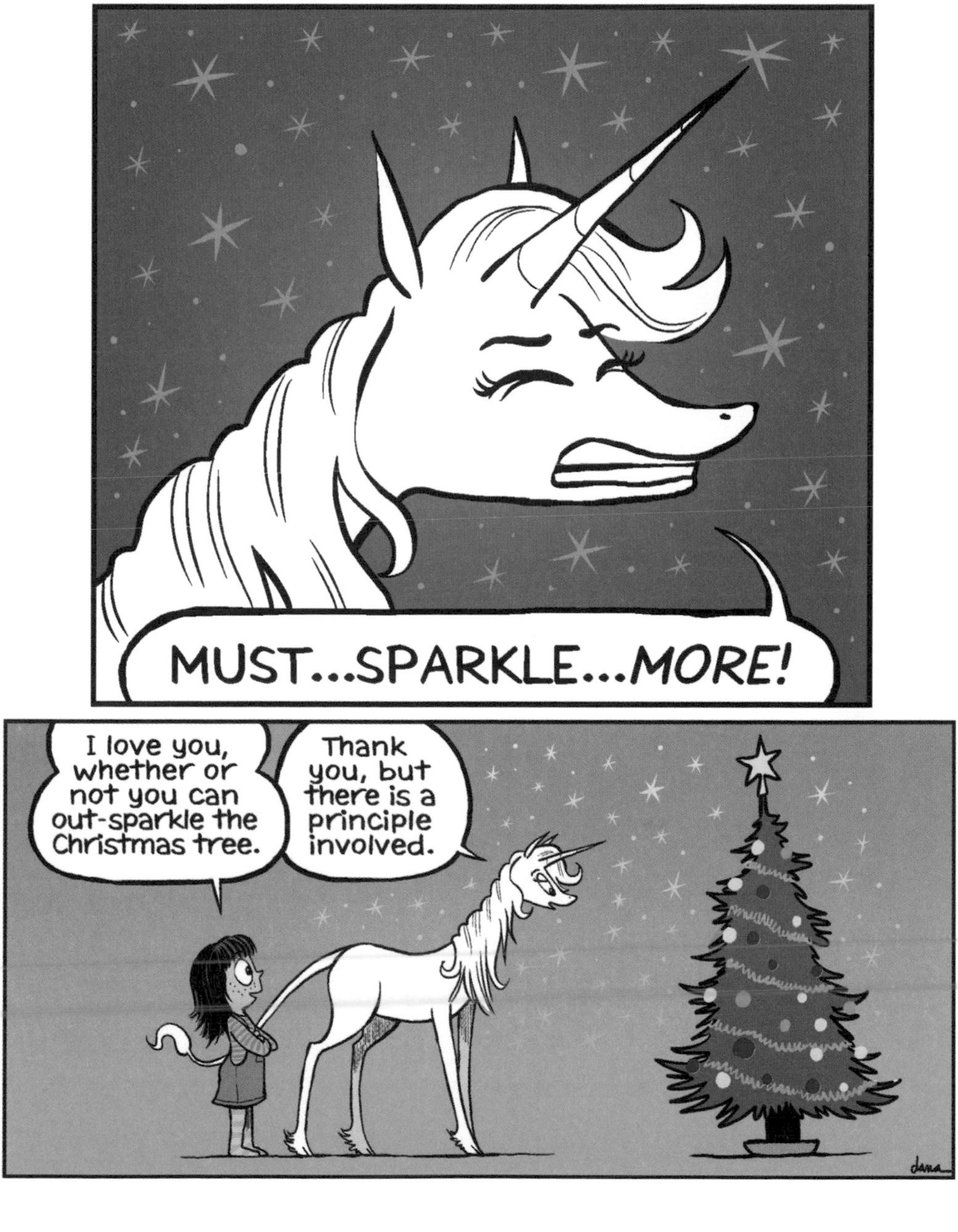
MUST...SPARKLE...MORE!
I love you, whether or not you can out-sparkle the Christmas tree.
Thank you, but there is a principle involved.
dana

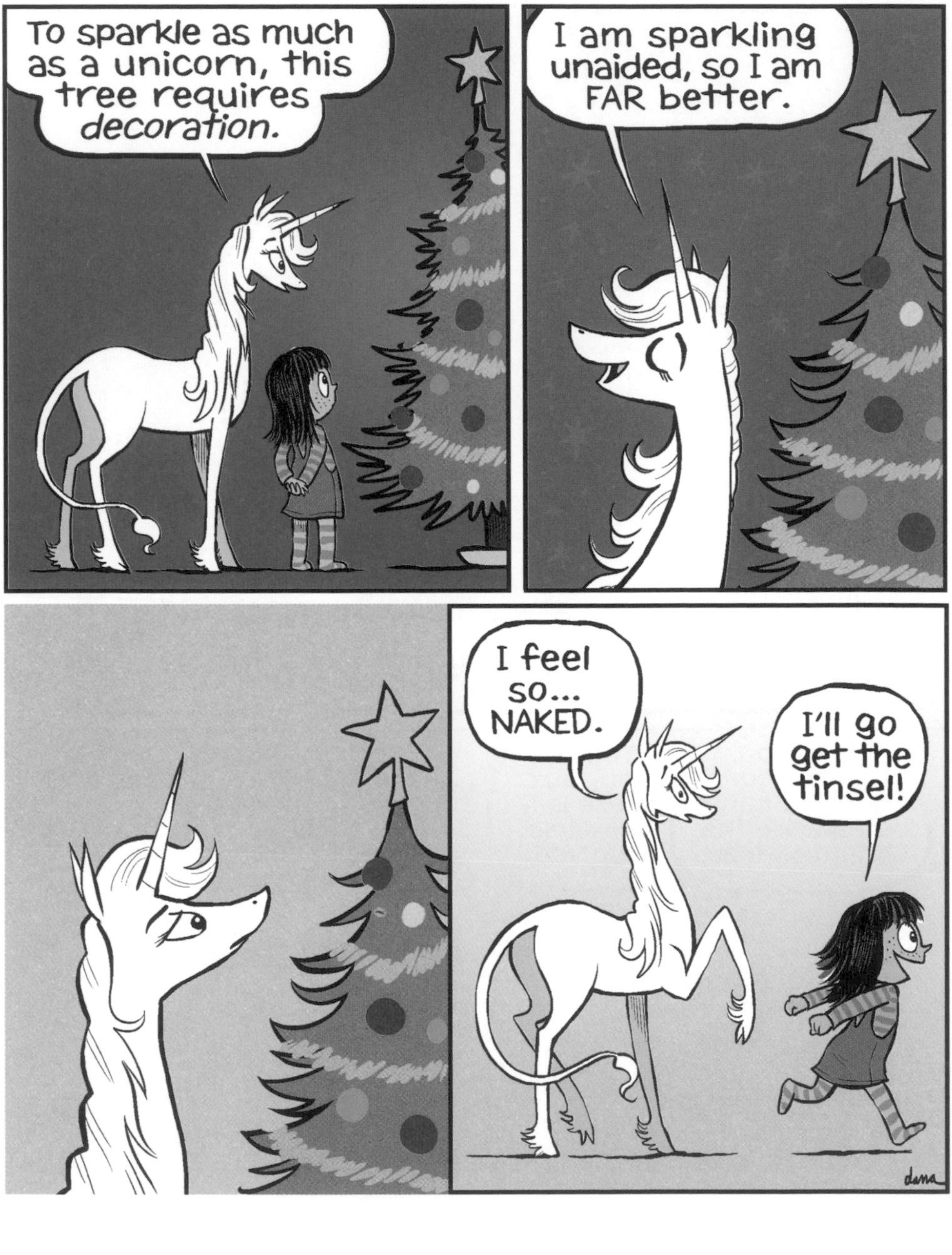
To sparkle as much as a unicorn, this tree requires *decoration.*
I am sparkling unaided, so I am FAR better.
I feel so... NAKED.
I'll go get the tinsel!
dana

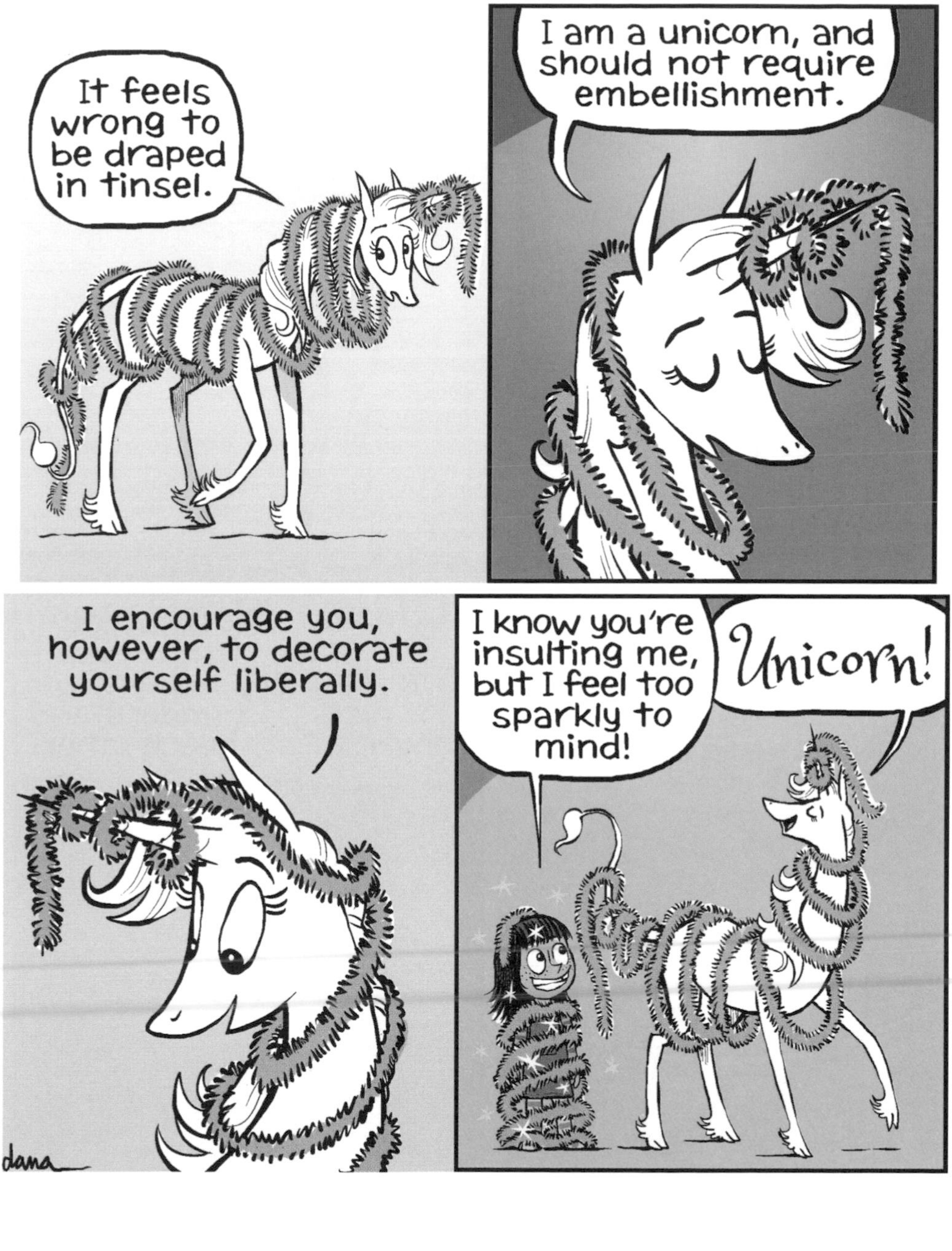
It feels wrong to be draped in tinsel.
I am a unicorn, and should not require embellishment.
I encourage you, however, to decorate yourself liberally.
I know you're insulting me, but I feel too sparkly to mind!
Unicorn!
dana

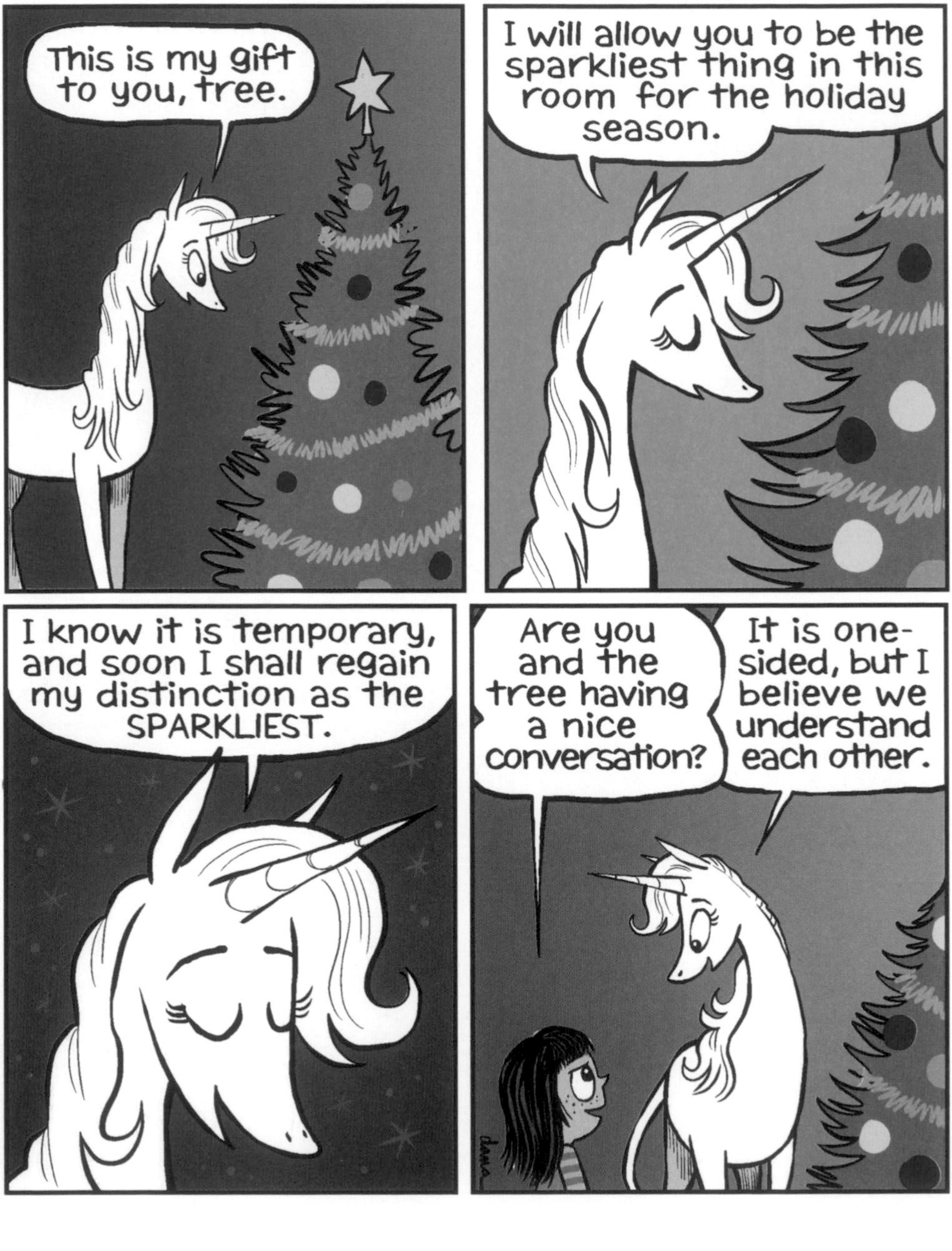
This is my gift to you, tree.
I will allow you to be the sparkliest thing in this room for the holiday season.
I know it is temporary, and soon I shall regain my distinction as the SPARKLIEST.
Are you and the tree having a nice conversation?
It is one-sided, but I believe we understand each other.

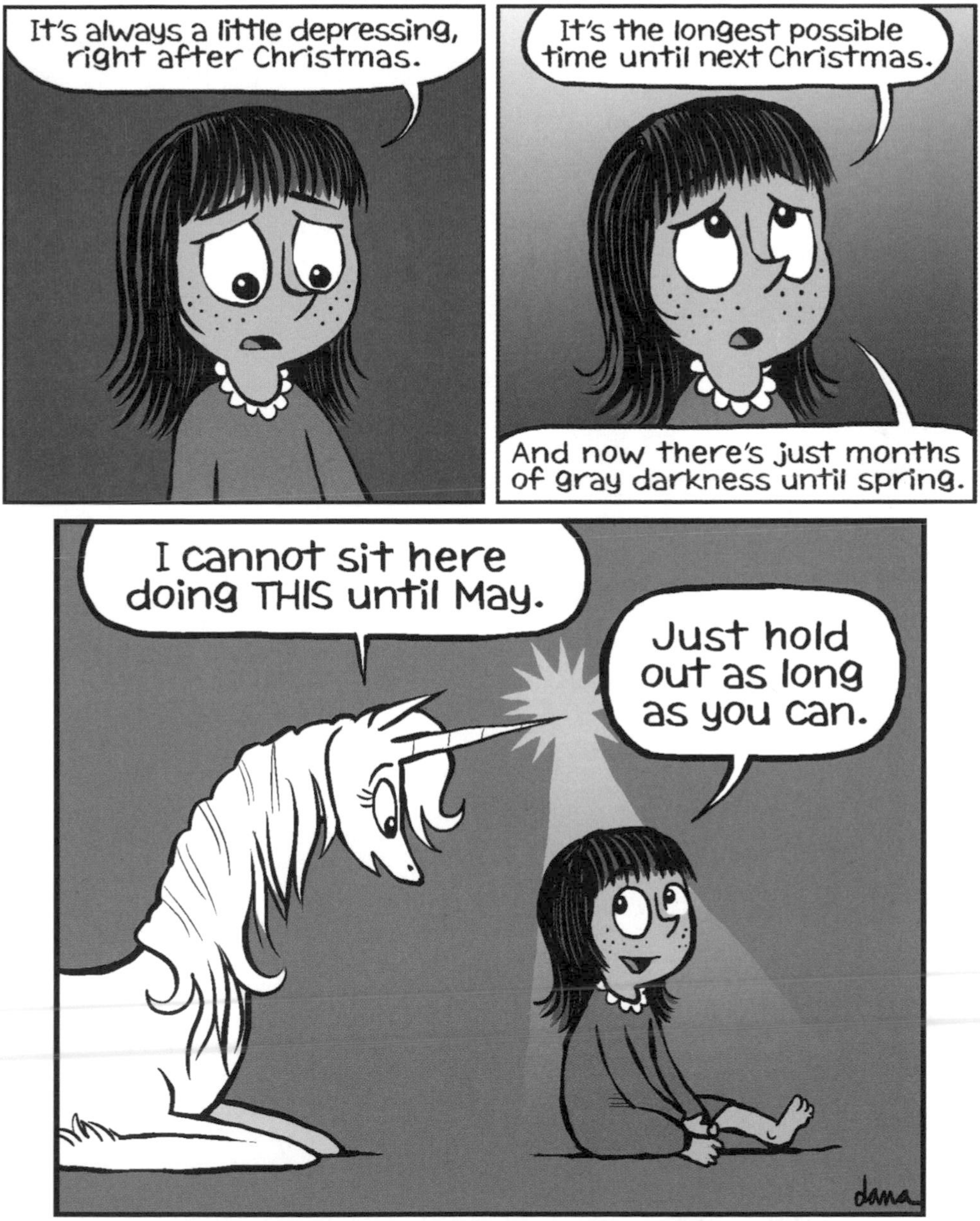
It's always a little depressing, right after Christmas.
It's the longest possible time until next Christmas.
And now there's just months of gray darkness until spring.
I cannot sit here doing THIS until May.
Just hold out as long as you can.
dana

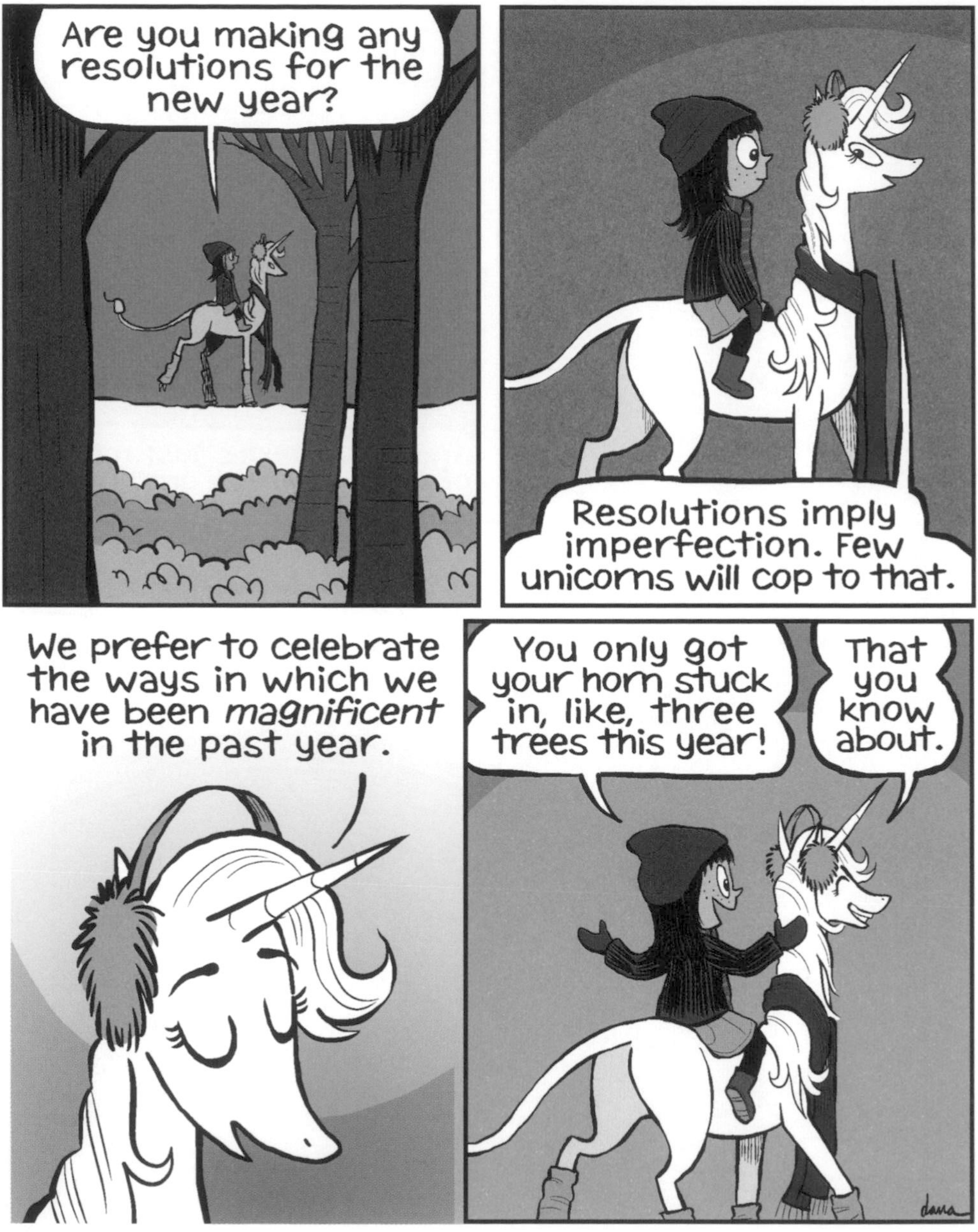
Are you making any resolutions for the new year?
Resolutions imply imperfection. Few unicorns will cop to that.
We prefer to celebrate the ways in which we have been *magnificent* in the past year.
You only got your horn stuck in, like, three trees this year!
That you know about.
dana

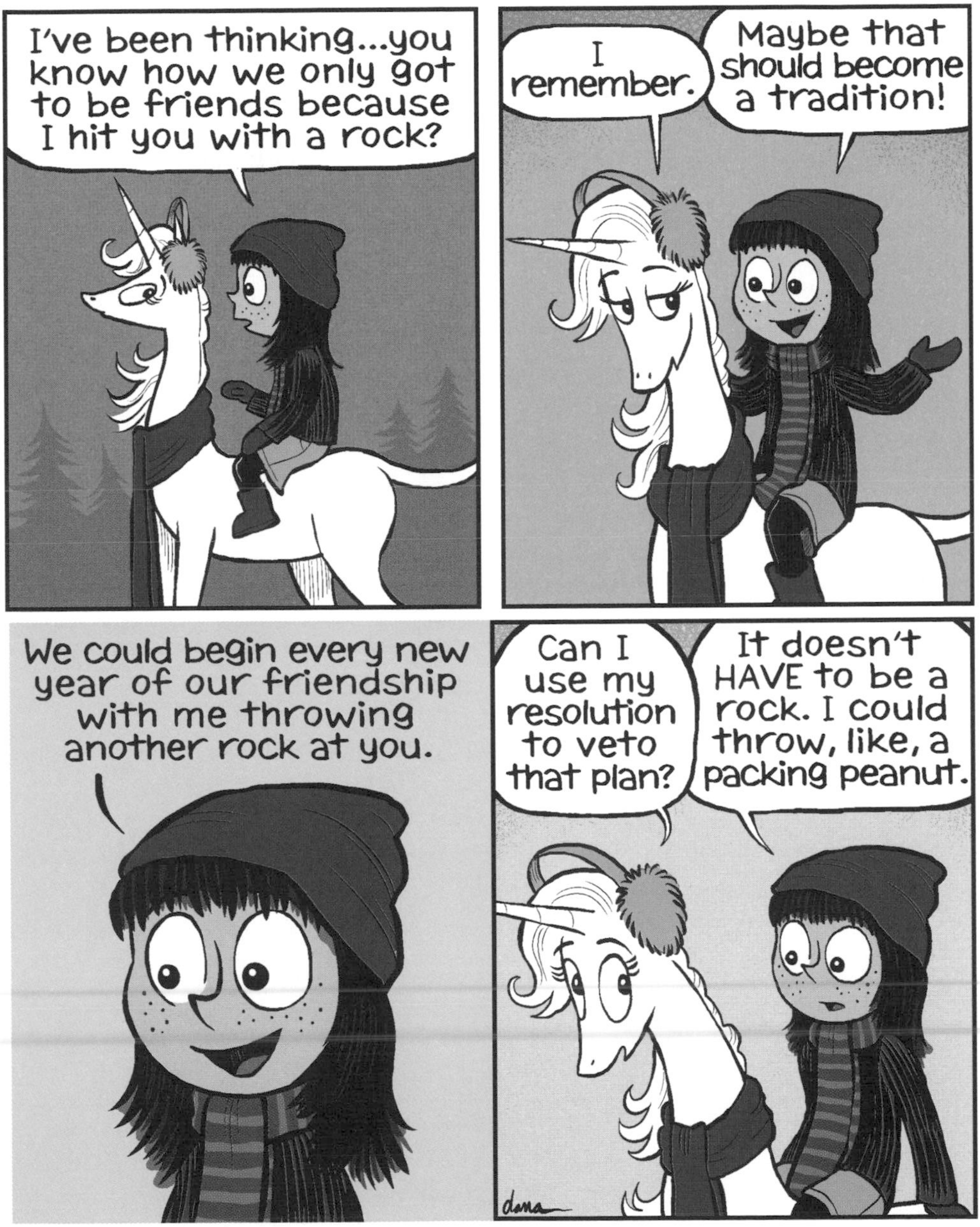
I've been thinking...you know how we only got to be friends because I hit you with a rock?
I remember.
Maybe that should become a tradition!
We could begin every new year of our friendship with me throwing another rock at you.
Can I use my resolution to veto that plan?
It doesn't HAVE to be a rock. I could throw, like, a packing peanut.
dana

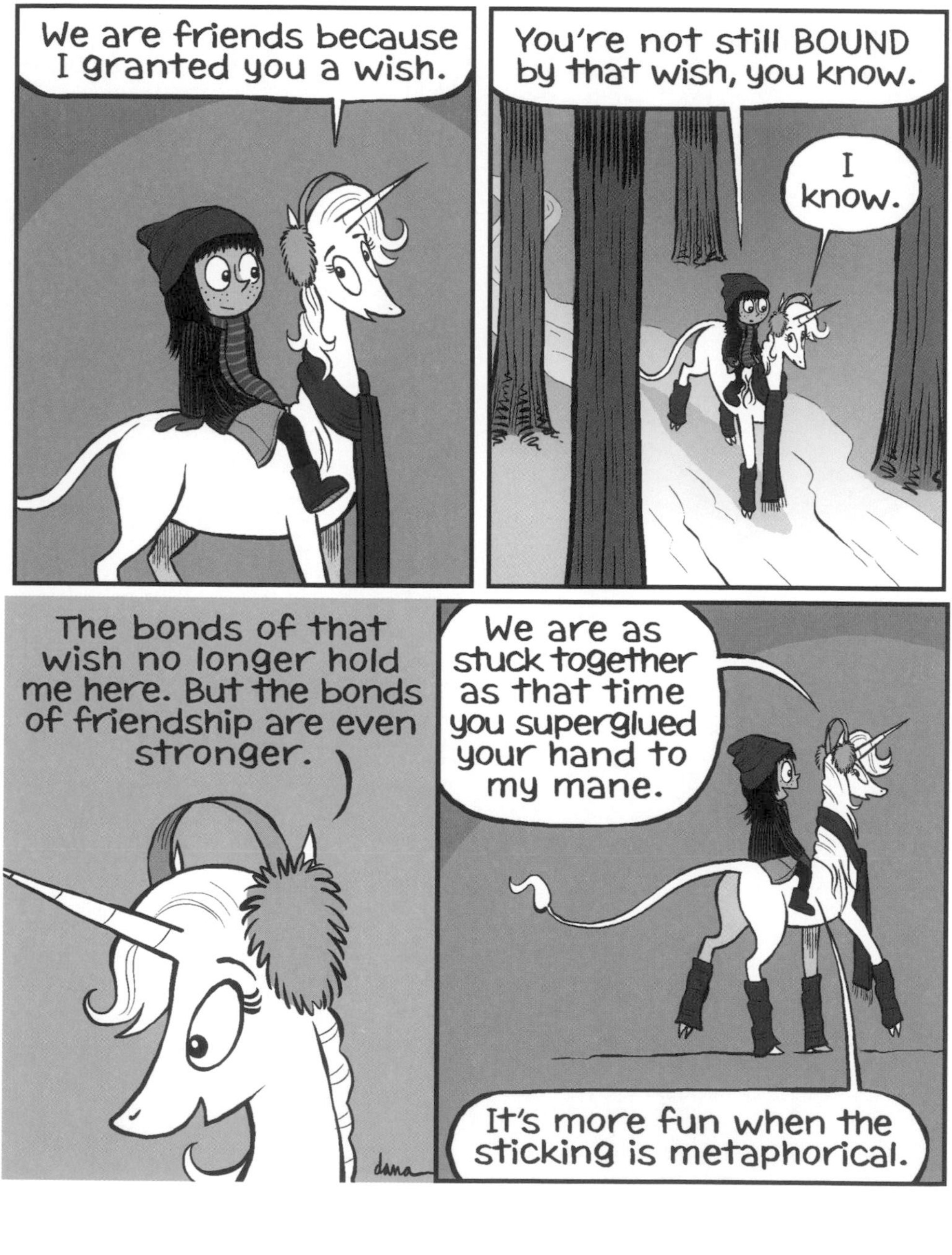
We are friends because I granted you a wish.
You're not still BOUND by that wish, you know.
I know.
The bonds of that wish no longer hold me here. But the bonds of friendship are even stronger.
We are as stuck together as that time you superglued your hand to my mane.
It's more fun when the sticking is metaphorical.
dana

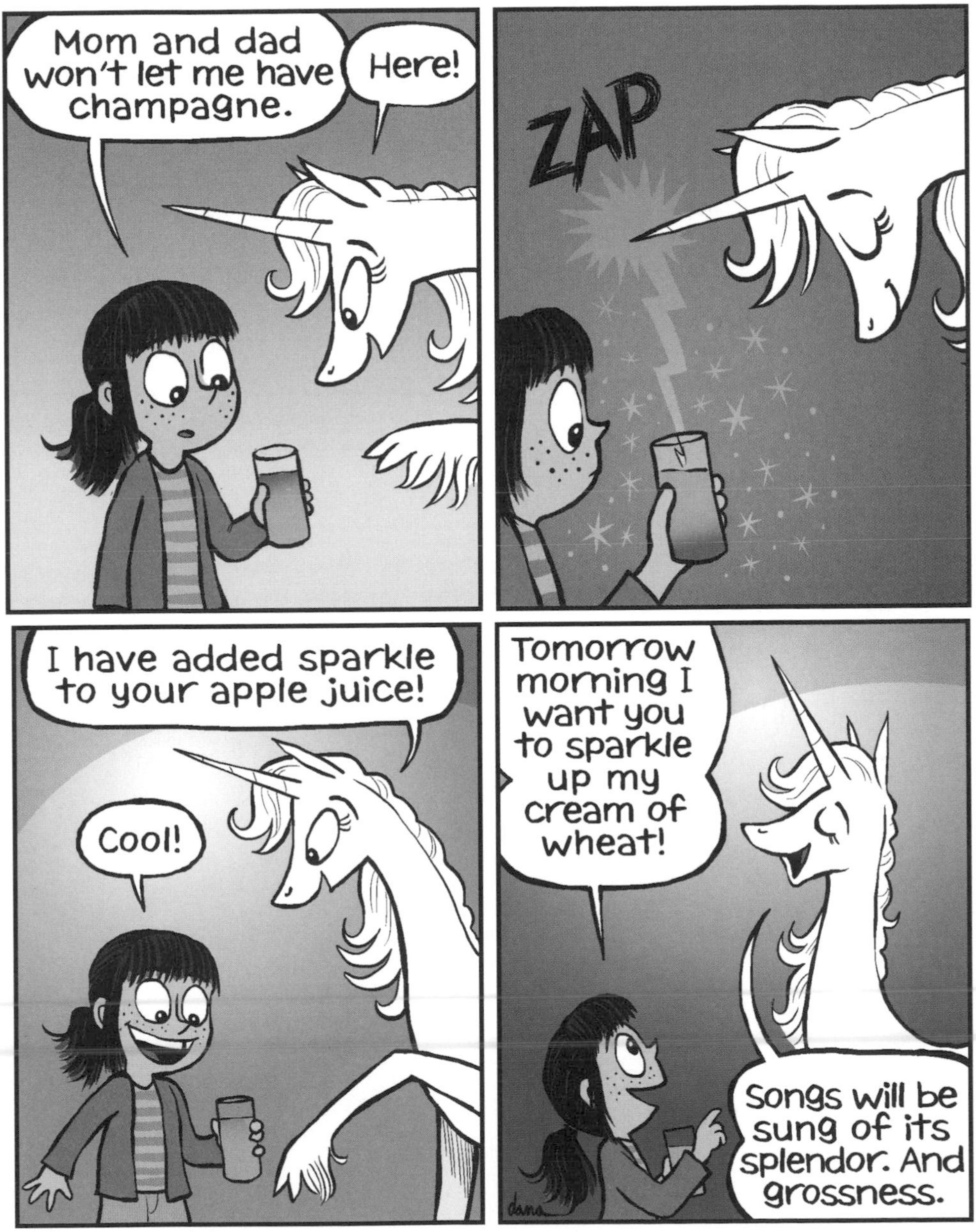
Mom and dad won't let me have champagne.
Here!
ZAP
I have added sparkle to your apple juice!
Cool!
Tomorrow morning I want you to sparkle up my cream of wheat!
Songs will be sung of its splendor. And grossness.

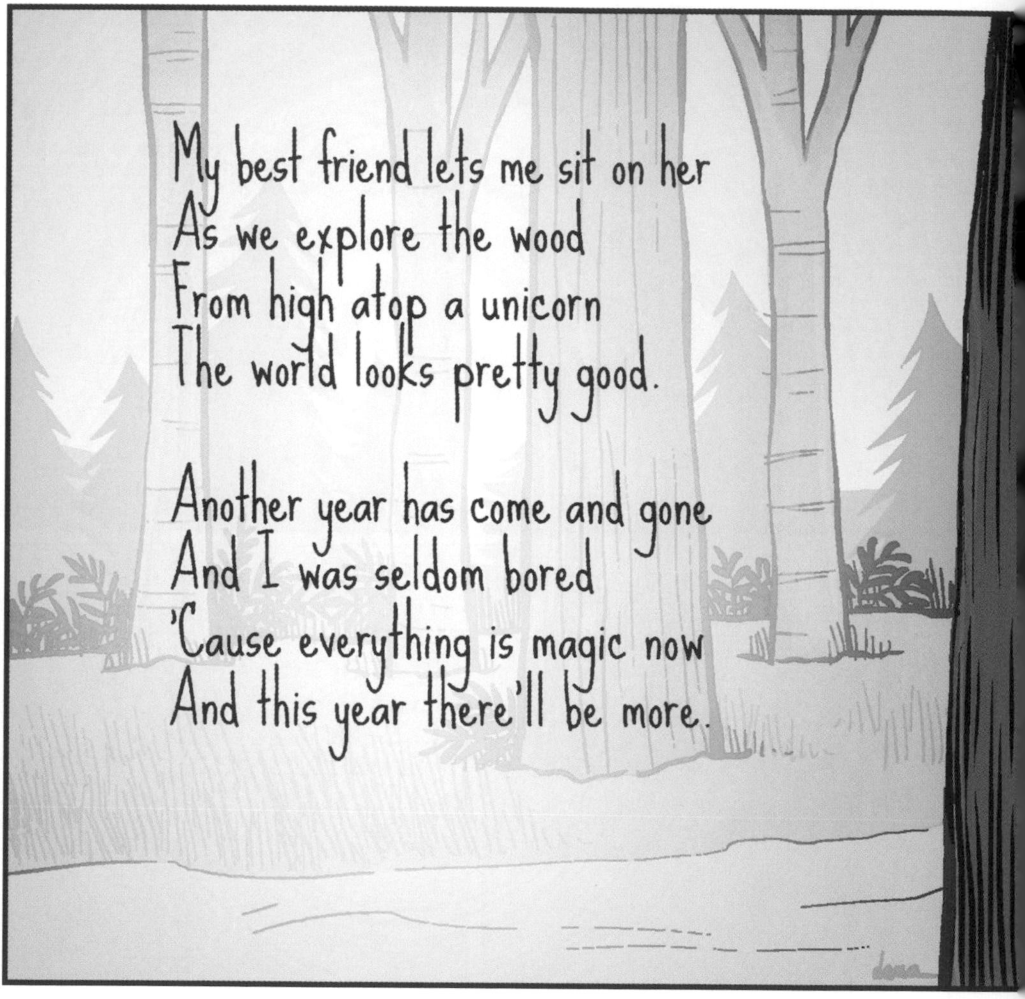
My best friend lets me sit on her
As we explore the wood
From high atop a unicorn
The world looks pretty good.

Another year has come and gone
And I was seldom bored
'Cause everything is magic now
And this year there'll be more.

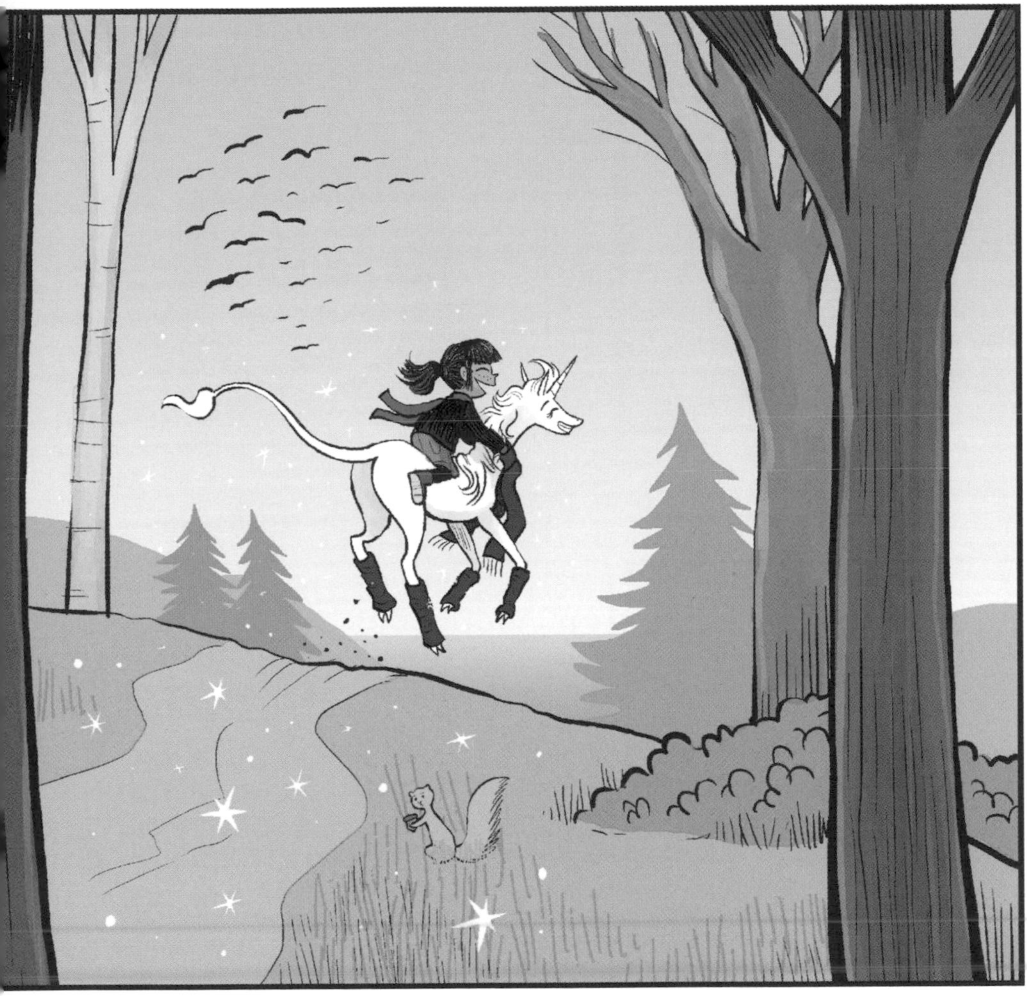

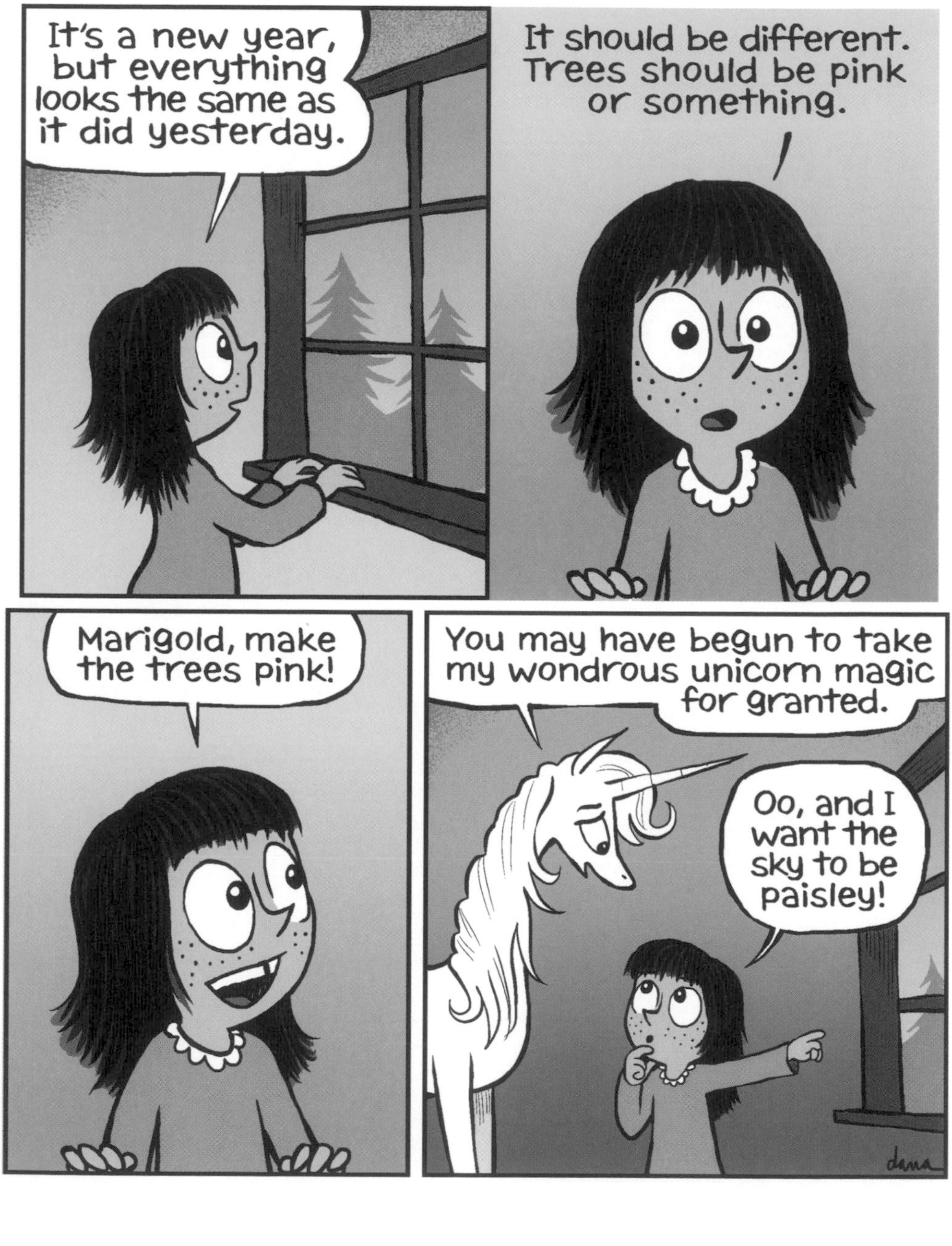
It's a new year, but everything looks the same as it did yesterday.
It should be different. Trees should be pink or something.
Marigold, make the trees pink!
You may have begun to take my wondrous unicorn magic for granted.
Oo, and I want the sky to be paisley!
dana

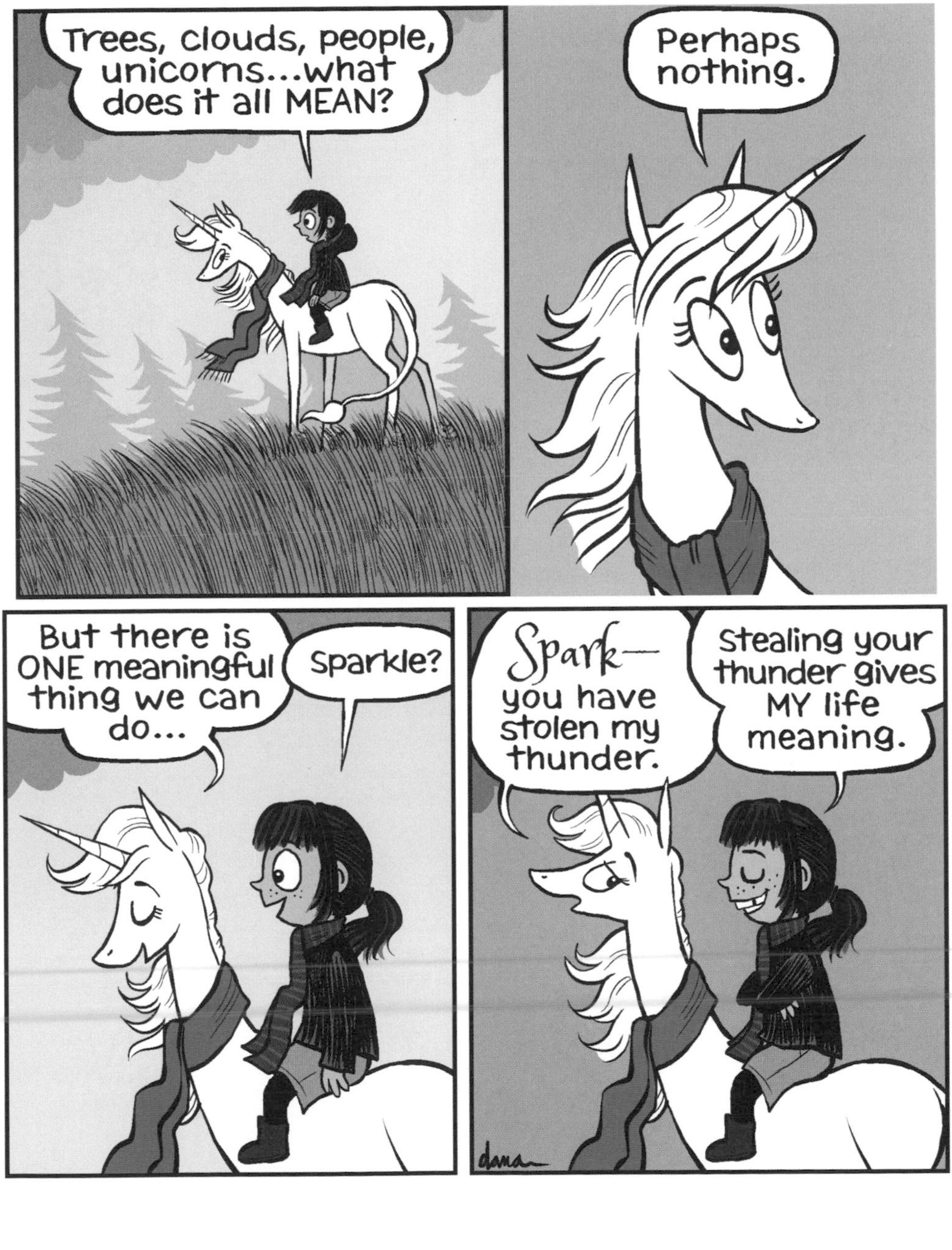
Trees, clouds, people, unicorns...what does it all MEAN?
Perhaps nothing.
But there is ONE meaningful thing we can do...
Sparkle?
Spark— you have stolen my thunder.
Stealing your thunder gives MY life meaning.
dana

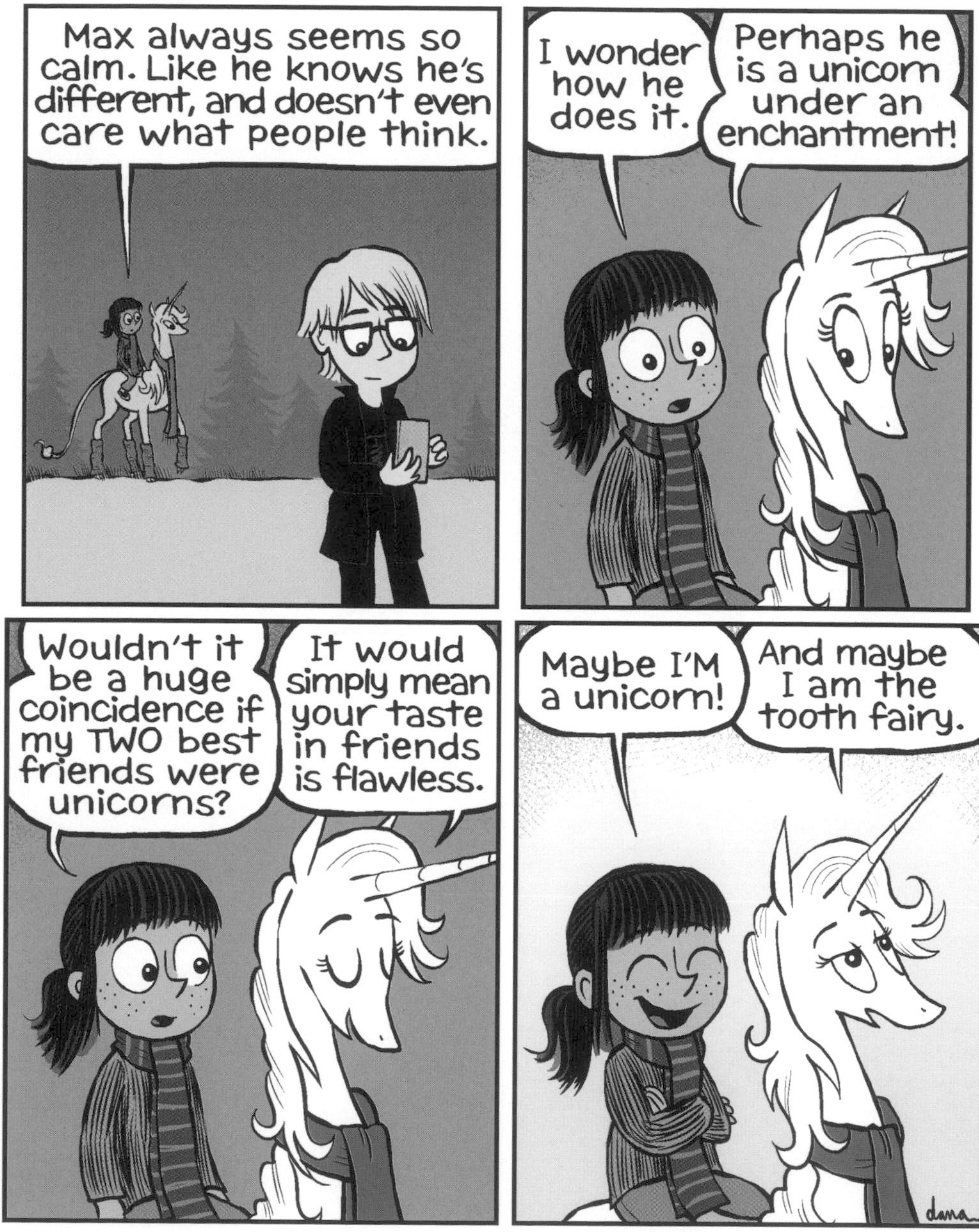
Max always seems so calm. Like he knows he's different, and doesn't even care what people think.
I wonder how he does it.
Perhaps he is a unicorn under an enchantment!
Wouldn't it be a huge coincidence if my TWO best friends were unicorns?
It would simply mean your taste in friends is flawless.
Maybe I'M a unicorn!
And maybe I am the tooth fairy.
dana

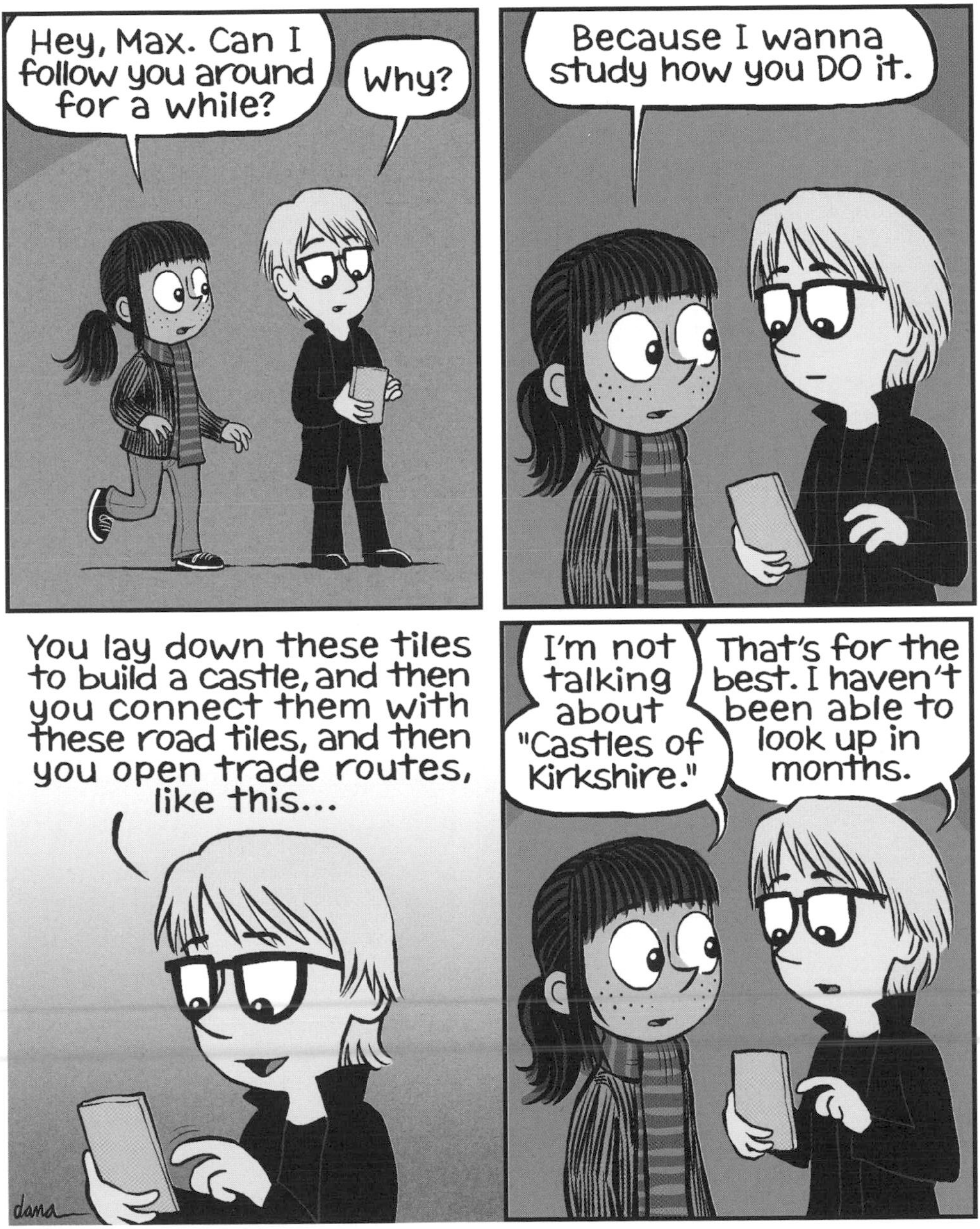
Hey, Max. Can I follow you around for a while?
Why?
Because I wanna study how you DO it.
You lay down these tiles to build a castle, and then you connect them with these road tiles, and then you open trade routes, like this...
I'm not talking about "Castles of Kirkshire."
That's for the best. I haven't been able to look up in months.
dana

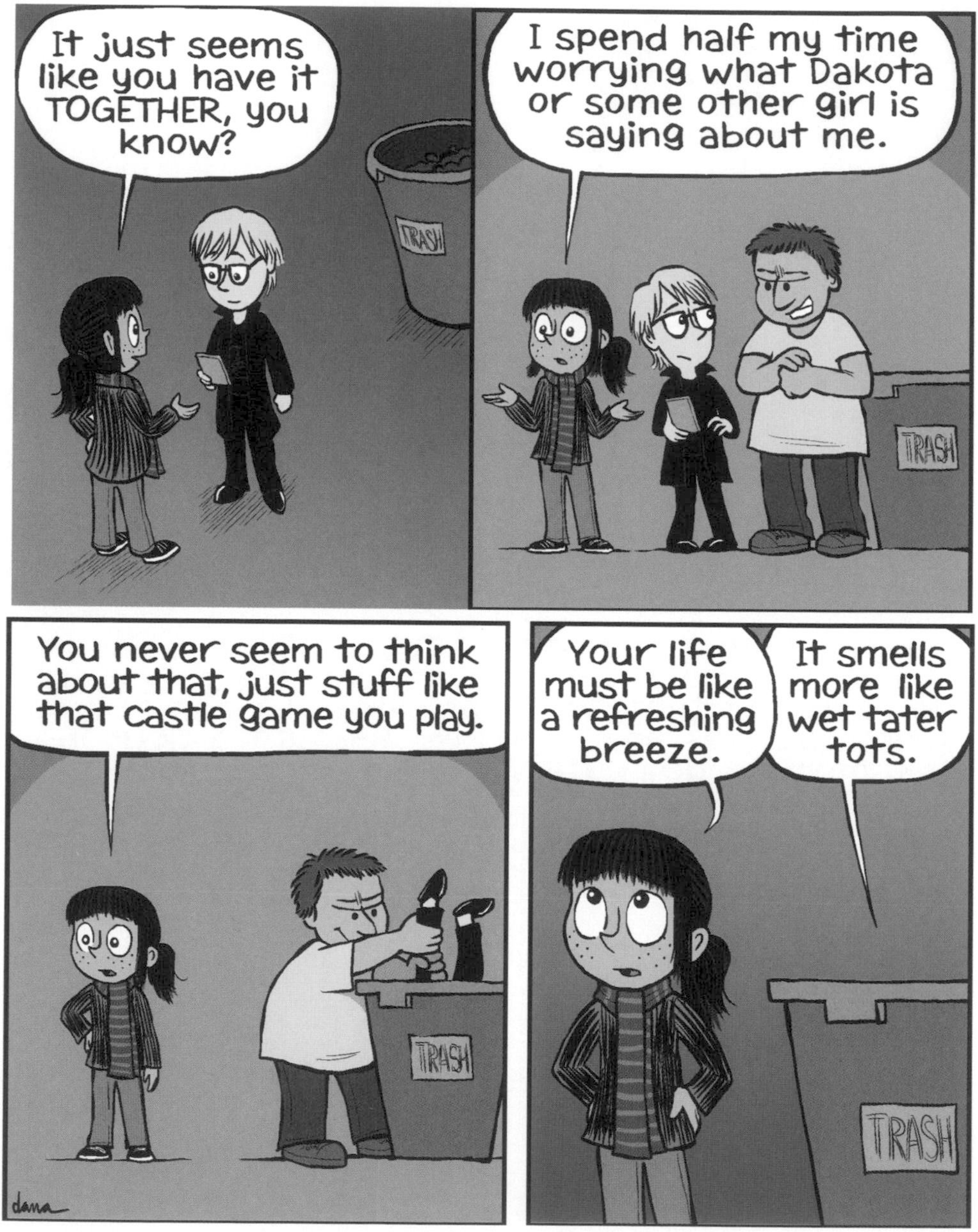
It just seems like you have it TOGETHER, you know?
TRASH
I spend half my time worrying what Dakota or some other girl is saying about me.
TRASH
You never seem to think about that, just stuff like that castle game you play.
TRASH
dana
Your life must be like a refreshing breeze.
It smells more like wet tater tots.
TRASH

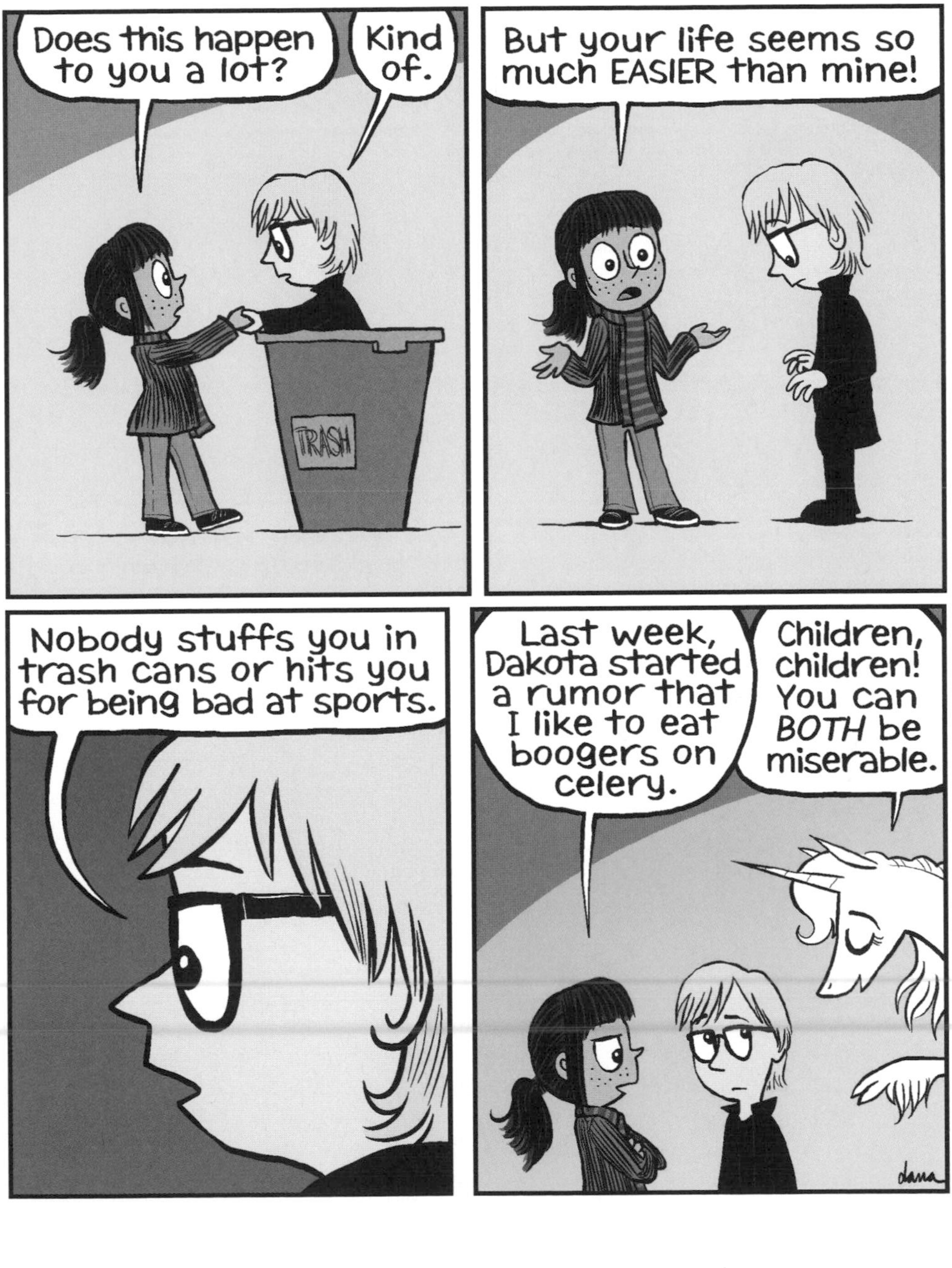
Does this happen to you a lot?
Kind of.
TRASH
But your life seems so much EASIER than mine!
Nobody stuffs you in trash cans or hits you for being bad at sports.
Last week, Dakota started a rumor that I like to eat boogers on celery.
Children, children! You can *BOTH* be miserable.
dana

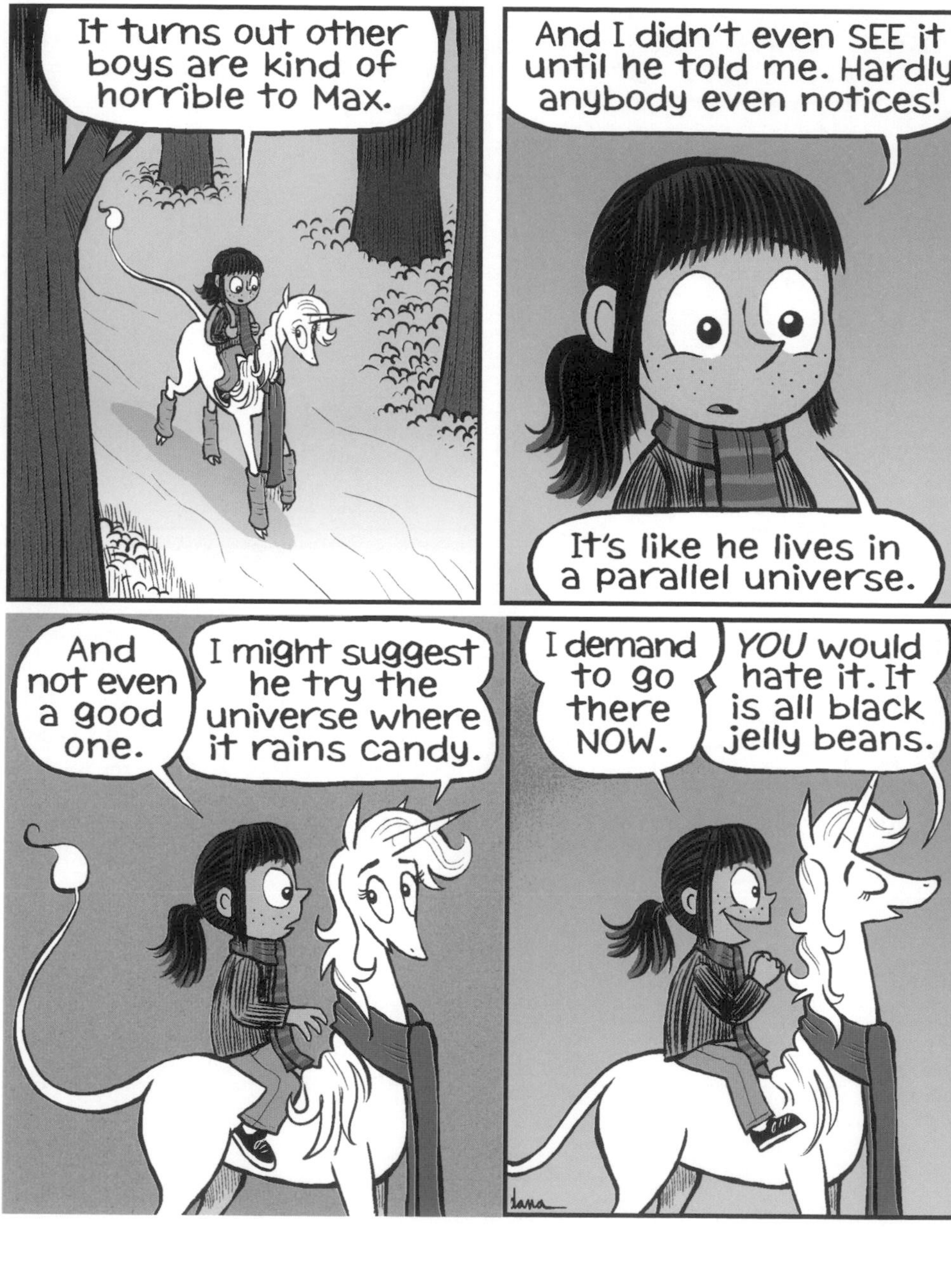
It turns out other boys are kind of horrible to Max.
And I didn't even SEE it until he told me. Hardly anybody even notices!
It's like he lives in a parallel universe.
And not even a good one.
I might suggest he try the universe where it rains candy.
I demand to go there NOW.
YOU would hate it. It is all black jelly beans.
lana

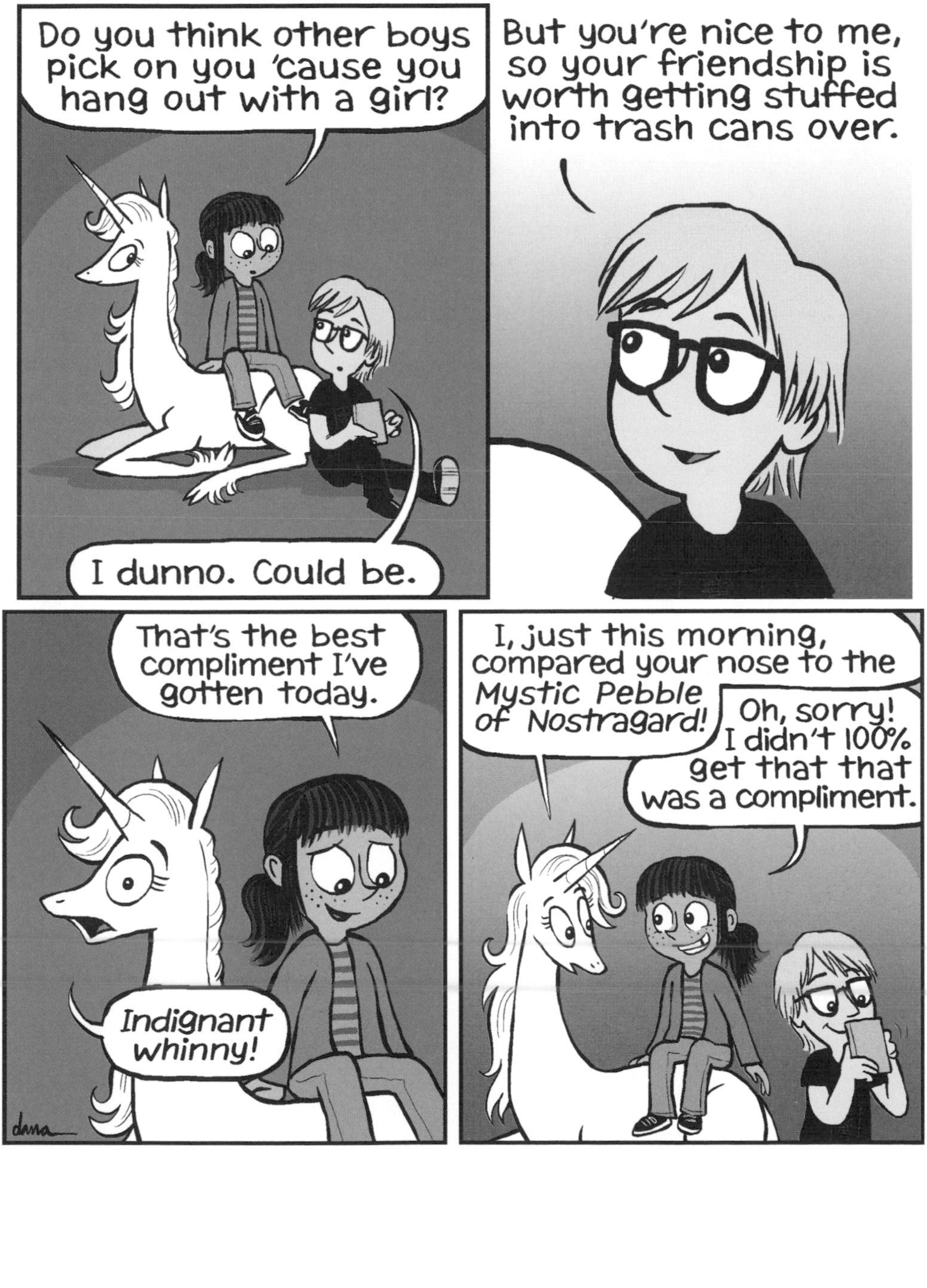
Do you think other boys pick on you 'cause you hang out with a girl?
I dunno. Could be.
But you're nice to me, so your friendship is worth getting stuffed into trash cans over.
That's the best compliment I've gotten today.
Indignant whinny!
I, just this morning, compared your nose to the *Mystic Pebble of Nostragard!*
Oh, sorry! I didn't 100% get that that was a compliment.
dana

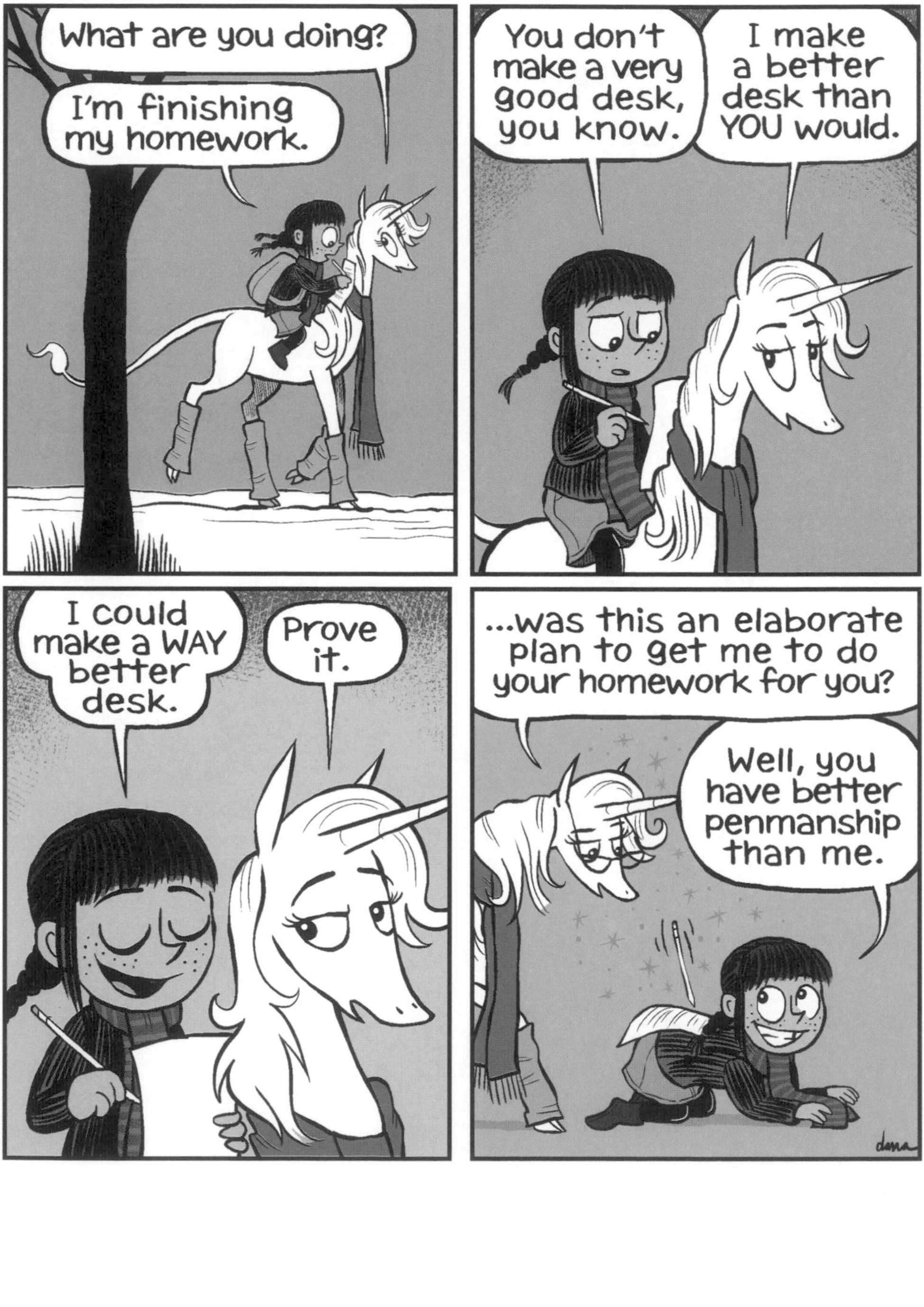
What are you doing?
I'm finishing my homework.
You don't make a very good desk, you know.
I make a better desk than YOU would.
I could make a WAY better desk.
Prove it.
...was this an elaborate plan to get me to do your homework for you?
Well, you have better penmanship than me.
dana

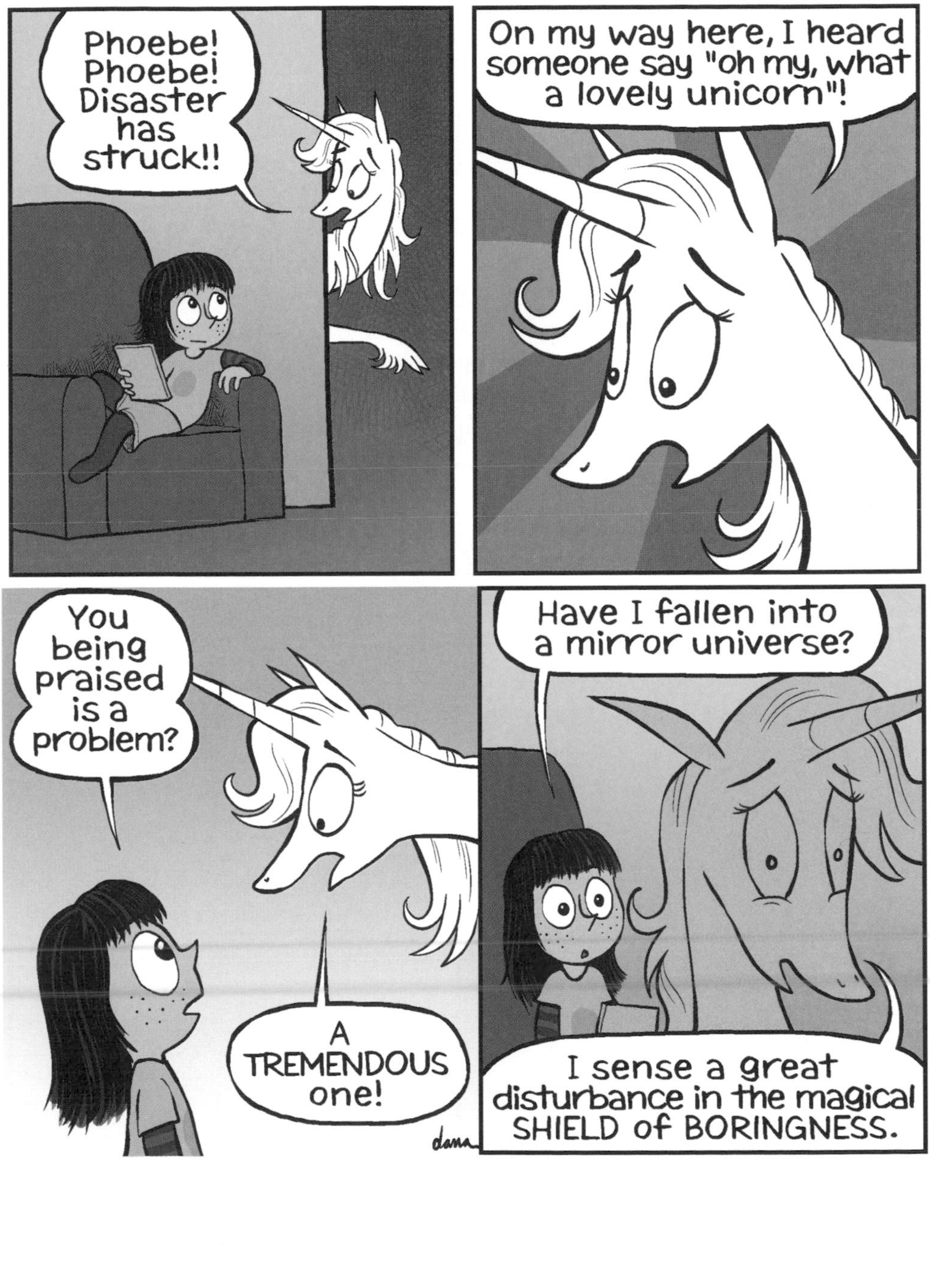
Phoebe! Phoebe! Disaster has struck!!
On my way here, I heard someone say "oh my, what a lovely unicorn"!
You being praised is a problem?
A TREMENDOUS one!
Have I fallen into a mirror universe?
I sense a great disturbance in the magical SHIELD of BORINGNESS.
dana

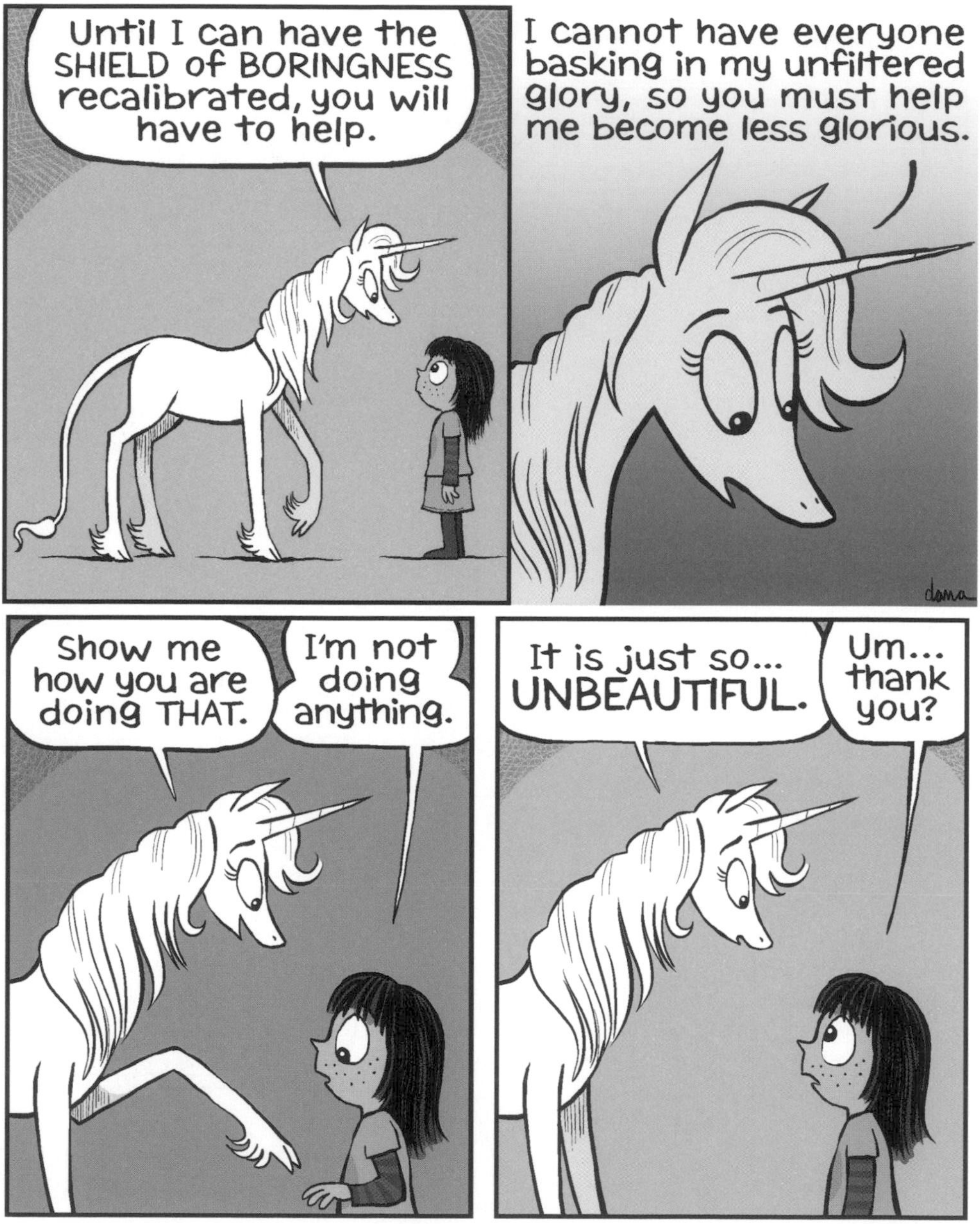
Until I can have the SHIELD of BORINGNESS recalibrated, you will have to help.
I cannot have everyone basking in my unfiltered glory, so you must help me become less glorious.
dana
Show me how you are doing THAT.
I'm not doing anything.
It is just so... UNBEAUTIFUL.
Um... thank you?

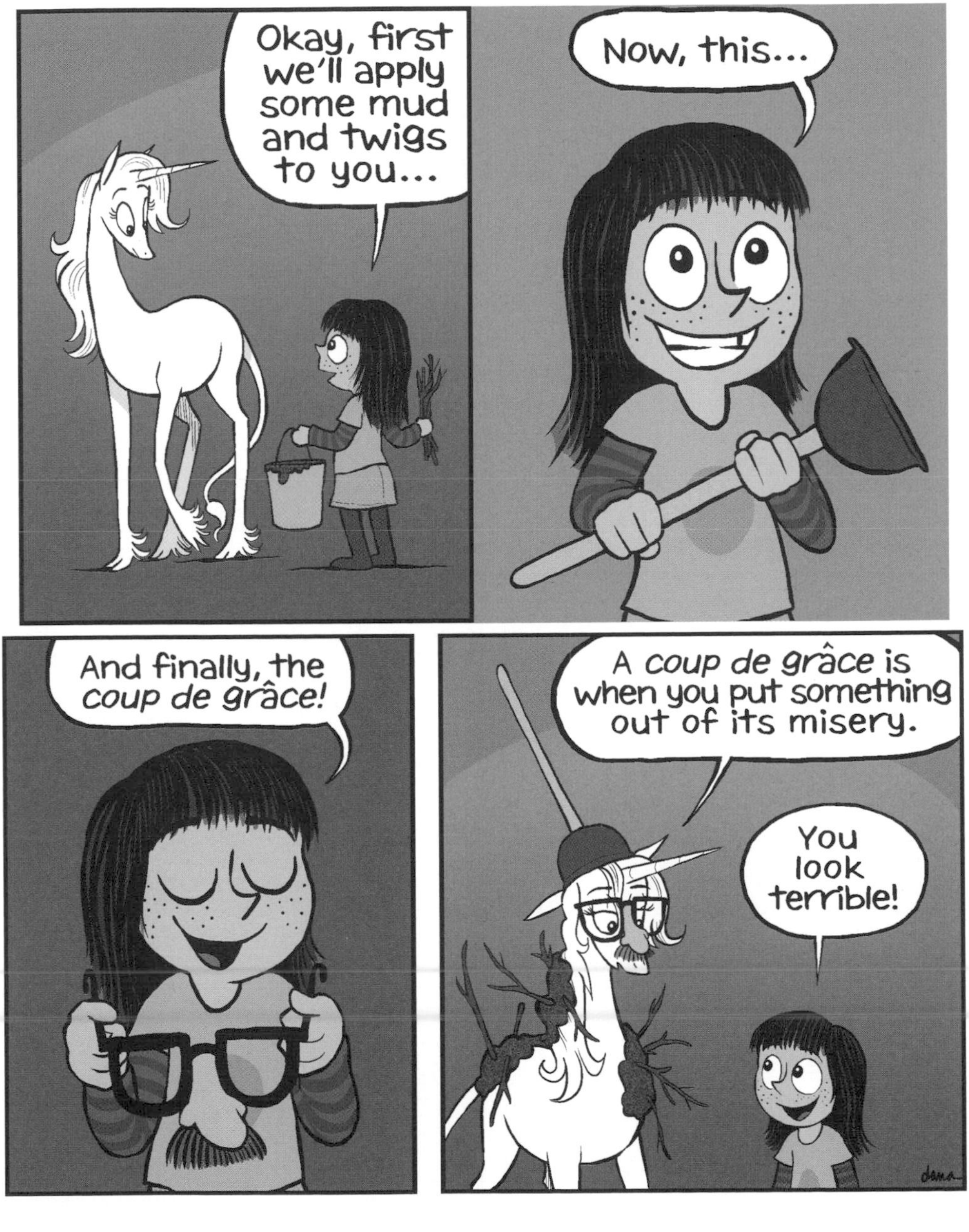
Okay, first we'll apply some mud and twigs to you...
Now, this...
And finally, the *coup de grâce!*
A *coup de grâce* is when you put something out of its misery.
You look terrible!
dana

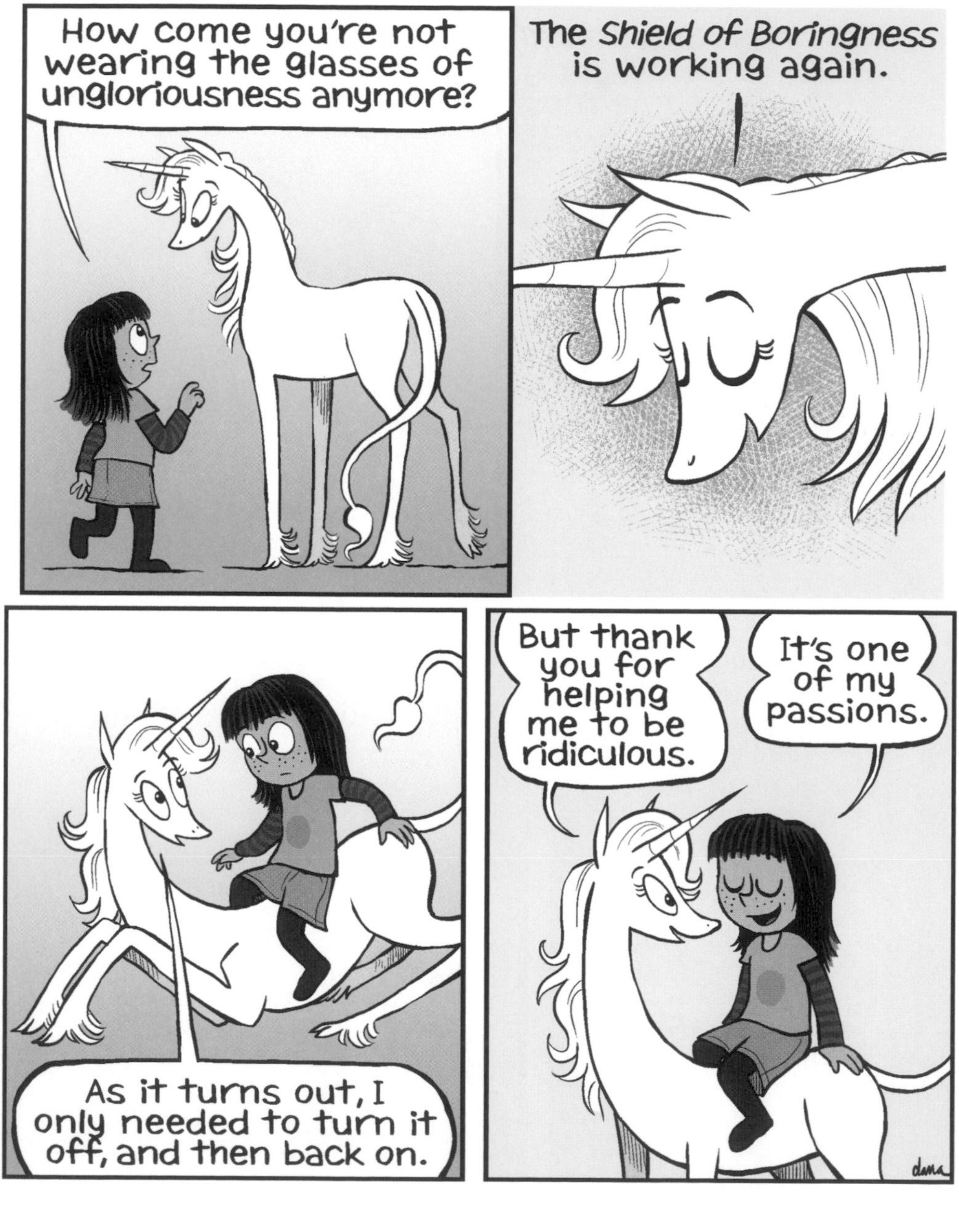
How come you're not wearing the glasses of ungloriousness anymore?
The *Shield of Boringness* is working again.
As it turns out, I only needed to turn it off, and then back on.
But thank you for helping me to be ridiculous.
It's one of my passions.
dana

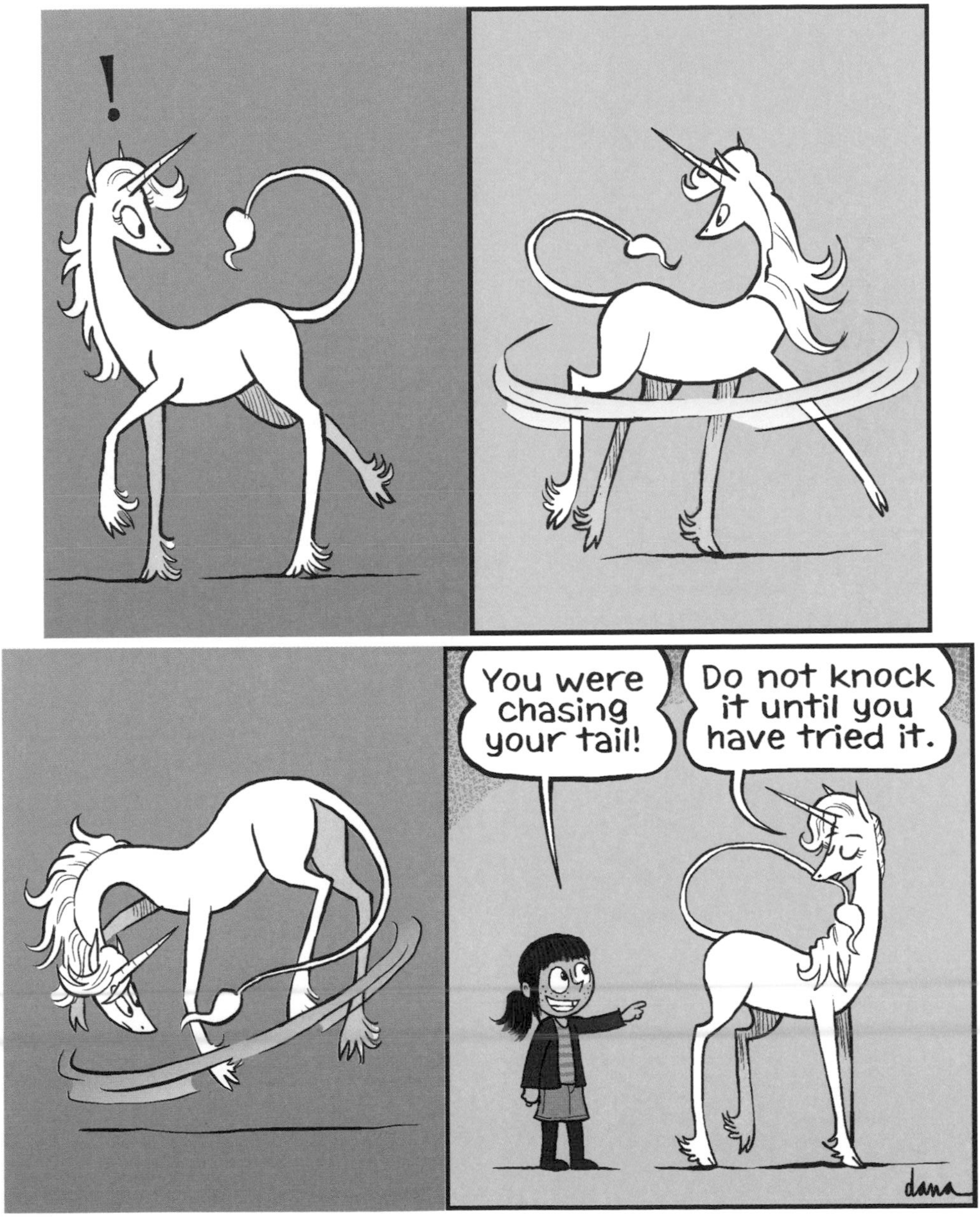
!
You were chasing your tail!
Do not knock it until you have tried it.
dana

GLOSSARY

abode (uh-bode): pg. 238 — noun / a place where a person lives; home

abomination (uh-bom-uh-nay-shun): pg. 274 — noun / something that is greatly disliked or loathed

askew (uh-skyoo): pg. 236 — adverb / out of position

battering ram (ba-ter-ing ram): pg. 260 — noun / an ancient military machine with a horizontal beam used to beat down walls, gates, etc.

bestower (bee-stoe-ur): pg. 316 — noun / gift giver

compensated (kom-pun-sayt-ud): pg. 187 — verb / made a payment in order to make up for something

conjure (kon-jer): pg. 246 — verb / to produce or bring into being by magic

contention (kun-ten-shun): pg. 295 — noun / a point used in a debate or an argument

countenance (koun-tun-unce): pg. 192 — verb / to approve or support

debacle (duh-bah-kul): pg. 317 — noun / total failure

dirge (durj): pg. 285 — noun / a mournful sound like a funeral song

embellishment (em-bel-ish-munt): pg. 325 — noun / ornament or decoration

extraterrestrial (ek-struh-tuh-res-tree-ul): pg. 221 — adjective / outside the limits of the earth

flaunting (flont-ing): pg. 291 — verb / conspicuously displaying; attracting attention

frolicking (frol-ik-ing): pg. 282 — verb / playing merrily

grackle (grak-uhl): pg. 279 — noun / any of a type of blackbirds with shiny black plumage (feathers)

haggled (hag-uhld): pg. 206 — verb / bargained; wrangled, especially over a price

hypothetically (hi-puh-thet-i-kuh-lee): pg. 309 – adverb / supposedly

liberally (lib-er-uhl-ee): pg. 325 – adverb / freely; abundantly

metaphorical (met-uh-fore-i-kuhl): pg. 330 – adjective / something used in a way to represent something else

notarized (noe-tih-rized): pg. 224 – verb / certified a document through a notary public

notary (noe-tih-ree): pg. 224 – noun / a person authorized to authenticate contracts and other legal documents

ornery (ore-nuh-ree): pg. 303 – adjective / unpleasant; cranky

ostentatious (os-ten-tay-shus): pg. 238, 291 – adjective / showing off wealth or treasure to make people envious; flashy or showy

paisley (payz-lee): pg. 334 – adjective / covered in a pattern of colorful, curvy designs

pandering (pan-der-ing): pg. 259 – verb / doing or saying what someone wants in order to please them

Ph.D. (pee-aich-dee): pg. 219 – abbreviation / Doctor of Philosophy; the highest academic degree awarded by universities

pixelated (pik-suh-layt-ed): pg. 260 – adjective / displayed in a way that individual pixels of a computer graphic are visible

poise (poiz): pg. 283 – noun / a dignified manner

recalibrated (ree-kal-uh-bray-ted): pg. 344 – verb / readjusted something for a particular function

reluctant (ree-luck-tunt): pg. 305 – adjective / unwilling; disinclined

repository (re-pos-it-or-ee): pg. 195 – noun / a place where a large amount of something is stored (like a warehouse, library, or store)

résumé (rez-oo-may): pg. 202 – noun / a brief written account of personal qualifications and experience, prepared by someone applying for a job

sophisticated (suh-fiss-tuh-kay-ted): pg. 242 – adjective / refined; worldly

thesis (thee-sis): pg. 219 – noun / a scholarly paper prepared with original research to prove a specific view

touché (too-shay): pg. 258 – interjection / an expression used to acknowledge something true, funny, or clever

tribbles (trib-ulz): pg. 235 – noun / fictional alien species in the *Star Trek* universe

unionize (yoon-yuh-nize): pg. 187 – verb / to organize into a labor union to protect workers' rights

Look for these books!

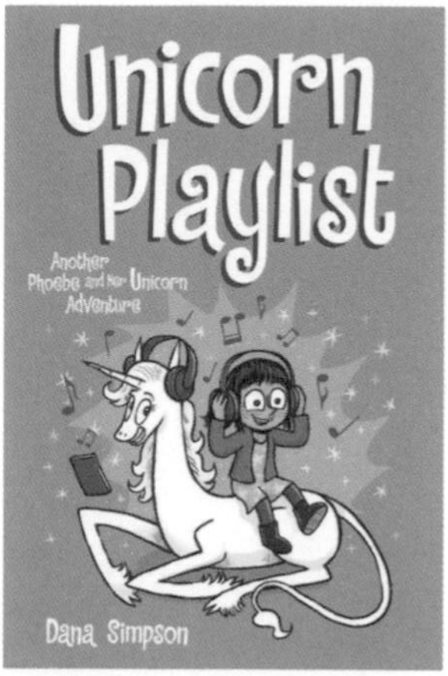
Unicorn Playlist
Another Phoebe and Her Unicorn Adventure
Dana Simpson

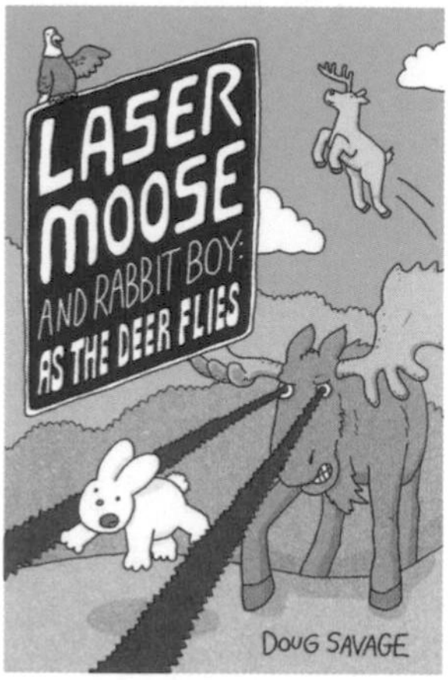
LASER MOOSE AND RABBIT BOY: AS THE DEER FLIES
DOUG SAVAGE

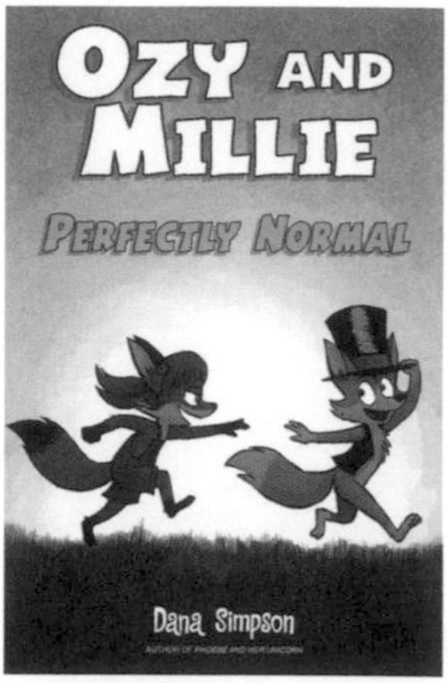
OZY AND MILLIE
PERFECTLY NORMAL
Dana Simpson

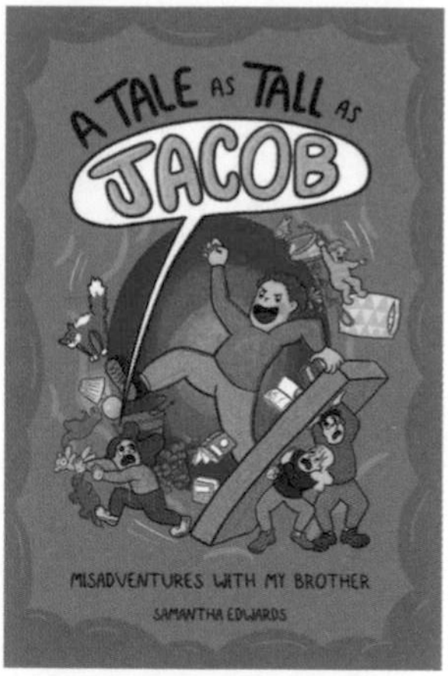
A TALE AS TALL AS JACOB
MISADVENTURES WITH MY BROTHER
SAMANTHA EDWARDS

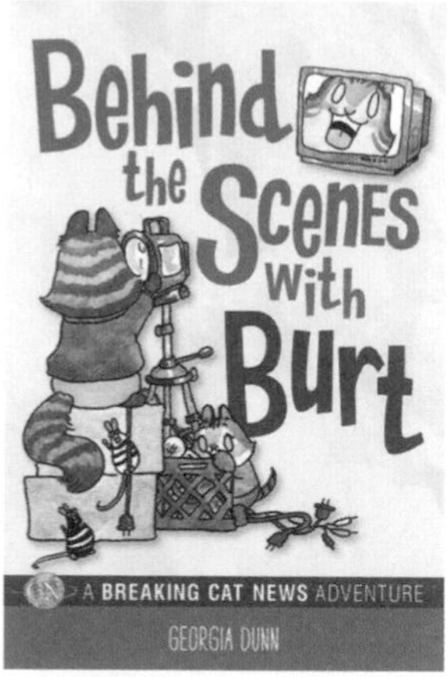
Behind the Scenes with Burt
A BREAKING CAT NEWS ADVENTURE
GEORGIA DUNN

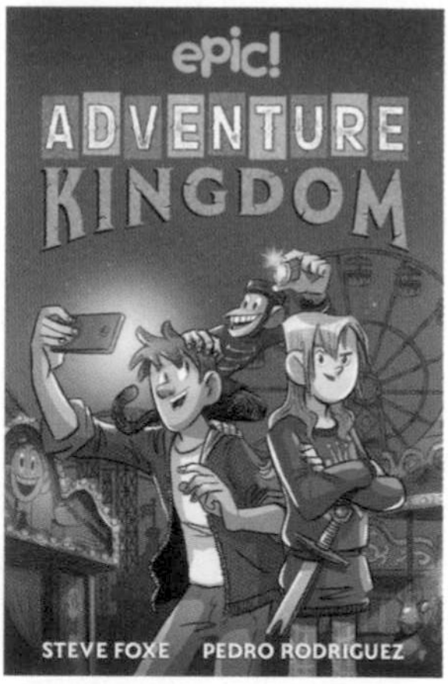
epic!
ADVENTURE KINGDOM
STEVE FOXE
PEDRO RODRIGUEZ

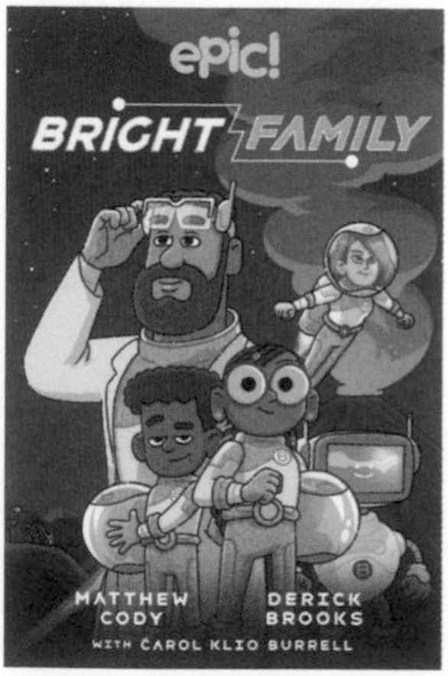
epic!
BRIGHT FAMILY
MATTHEW CODY
DERICK BROOKS
WITH CAROL KLIO BURRELL

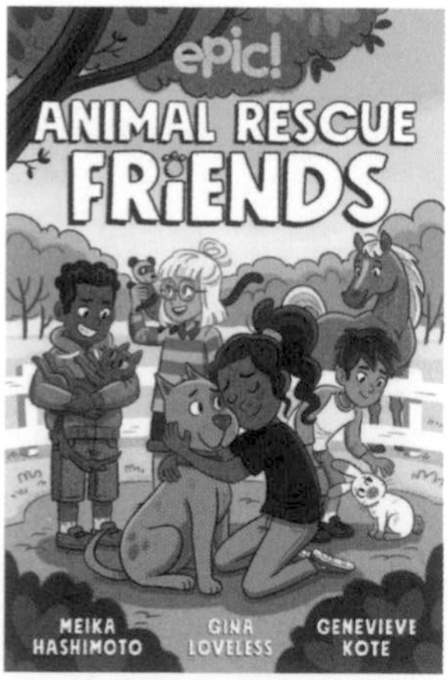
epic!
ANIMAL RESCUE FRIENDS
MEIKA HASHIMOTO
GINA LOVELESS
GENEVIEVE KOTE

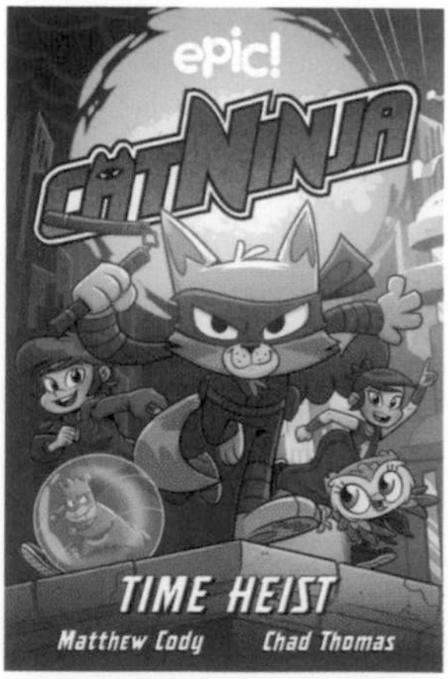
epic!
CAT NINJA
TIME HEIST
Matthew Cody
Chad Thomas